THE FIRE COURT

THE FIRE COURT

ANDREW TAYLOR

THORNDIKE PRESS
A part of Gale, a Cengage Company

Copyright © 2018 by Andrew Taylor.
James Marwood and Cat Lovett.
Andrew Taylor asserts the moral right to be identified as the author of the work.
Thorndike Press, a part of Gale, a Cengage Company.

Thorndike Press® Large Print Mystery.
The text of this Large Print edition is unabridged.
Other aspects of the book may vary from the original edition.
Set in 16 pt. Plantin.

LIBRARY OF CONGRESS CIP DATA ON FILE.
CATALOGUING IN PUBLICATION FOR THIS BOOK
IS AVAILABLE FROM THE LIBRARY OF CONGRESS

ISBN-13: 978-1-4328-7995-2 (hardcover alk. paper)

Published in 2020 by arrangement with HarperCollins Publishers Ltd

Printed in Mexico
Print Number: 01   Print Year: 2020

For Caroline

THE PEOPLE

Infirmary Close, The Savoy

James Marwood, clerk to Joseph Williamson, and to the Board of Red Cloth

Nathaniel Marwood, his father, widowed husband of Rachel; formerly a printer

Margaret and Sam Witherdine, their servants

The Drawing Office, Henrietta Street

Simon Hakesby, surveyor and architect

'Jane Hakesby', his maid, formerly known as Catherine Lovett

Brennan, his draughtsman

Clifford's Inn and the Fire Court

Lucius Gromwell, antiquary

Theophilus Chelling, clerk to the Fire Court

Sir Thomas Twisden, a judge at the Fire Court

Miriam, a servant at Clifford's Inn

7

Pall Mall

Sir Philip Limbury

Jemima, Lady Limbury, daughter of Sir George Syre

Mary, her maid

Richard, Sir Philip's manservant; also known as Sourface

Hester, a maid

Whitehall

Joseph Williamson, Under-Secretary of State to Lord Arlington

William Chiffinch, Keeper of the King's Private Closet

Others

Roger Poulton, retired cloth merchant; late of Dragon Yard

Elizabeth Lee, his housekeeper

Celia Hampney, his widowed niece

Tabitha, Mistress Hampney's maid

Mistress Grove, of Lincoln's Inn Fields; who lets lodgings to Mistress Hampney

Barty, a crossing-sweeper in Fleet Street, by Temple Bar

8

CHAPTER ONE

Rachel. There you are.

She hesitated in the doorway that led from the Savoy Stairs and the river. She wore a long blue cloak over a grey dress he did not recognize. In her hand was a covered basket. She walked across the garden to the archway in the opposite corner. Her pattens clacked on the flagged path.

That's my Rachel, he thought. Always busy. But why did she not greet him?

You are like the river, my love, he had told her once, always moving and always the same.

They had been sitting by the Thames in Barnes Wood. She had let down her hair, which was brown but shot through with golden threads that glowed in the sunlight.

She had looked like a whore, with her loose, glorious hair.

He felt a pang of repulsion. Then he rallied. A woman's hair encouraged lustful

9

thoughts, he argued with himself, but it could not be sinful when the woman was your wife, joined to you in the sight of God, flesh of your flesh, bone of your bone.

Now the garden was empty. There was no reason why he should not go after her. Indeed, it was his duty. Was not woman the weaker vessel?

He used his stick as a prop to help him rise. He was still hale and hearty, thank God, but his limbs grew stiff if he did not move them for a while.

He walked towards the archway. The path beyond made a turn to the right, rounding the corner of one of the old hospital buildings of the Savoy. He glimpsed Rachel ahead, passing through the gate that led up to the Strand. She paused to look at something — a piece of paper? — in her hand. Then she was gone.

She must be going shopping. A harmless pleasure, but only as long as it did not encourage vanity, a woman's besetting sin. Women were weak, women were sinful, which was why God had placed men to watch over them and to correct them when they erred.

The porter in his lodge took no notice of him. A cobbled path led up to the south side of the Strand. The traffic roared and clattered along the roadway.

He looked towards Charing Cross, thinking that the shops of the New Exchange would have drawn her like a moth to a blaze of candles. No sign of her. Could he have lost her already? He looked the other way, and there she was, walking towards the ruins of the City.

He waved his stick. 'Rachel,' he cried. 'Come here.'

The racket and clatter of the Strand drowned his words.

He followed her, the stiffness dropping from his limbs, his legs gathering strength and momentum with the exercise. On and on she walked, past Somerset House and Arundel House, past St Clement's and under Temple Bar into Fleet Street and the Liberties of the City.

He kept his eyes fixed on the cloak, and the rhythm of his walking lulled his mind until he almost forgot why he was here. By the Temple, Rachel hesitated, turning towards the roadway with its sluggish currents of vehicles and animals. She looked down at the paper in her hand. A painted coach lumbered to a halt on the opposite side of the road. At that moment, a brewer's dray, coming from the other direction and laden with barrels, drew up beside it. Between them, they blocked the street.

Rachel slipped among the traffic and threaded her way across the street.

The brewer's men were unloading the dray outside the Devil Tavern. A barrel broke free and crashed into the roadway. The impact shattered the staves on one side. Beer spurted into the street. Two beggars ran whooping towards the growing puddle. They crouched and lapped like dogs. The traffic came to a complete halt, jammed solid by its own weight pressing from either side.

A sign, he thought, a sign from God. He has parted this river of traffic for me just as it had pleased Him to part the Red Sea before Moses and the Chosen People.

He walked across the street, his eyes fixed on Rachel's cloak. She turned to the left in the shadow of the square tower of St Dunstan-in-the-West.

Why was she leading him such a merry dance? Suspicion writhed within him. Had the serpent tempted her? Had she succumbed to the devil's wiles?

An alley ran past the west side of the church to a line of iron railings with a gateway in the middle. Beside it, a porter's lodge guarded the entrance to a cramped court. Men were milling around the doorway of a stone-faced building with high, pointed windows.

Rachel was there too, looking once again at the paper in her hand. She passed through the doorway. He followed, but the crowd held him back.

'By your leave, sirs, by your leave,' he cried. 'Pray, sirs, by your leave.'

'Hush, moderate your voice,' hissed a plump clerk dressed in black. 'Stand back, the judges are coming through.'

He stared stupidly at the clerk. 'The judges?'

'The Fire Court, of course. The judges are sitting this afternoon.'

Three gentlemen came in procession, attended by their clerks and servants. They were conducted through the archway.

He pressed after them. The doorway led to a passage. At the other end of it a second doorway gave on to a larger courtyard, irregular in shape. Beyond it was a garden, a green square among the soot-stained buildings.

Was that Rachel over there by the garden?

He called her name. His voice was thin and reedy, as it was in dreams. She did not hear him, though two men in black gowns stared curiously at him.

How dared she ignore him? What was this place full of men? Why had she not told him

13

she was coming here? Surely, please God, she did not intend to betray him?

On the first floor of the building to the right of the garden, a tall man stood at one of the nearer windows, looking down on the court below. The panes of glass reduced him to little more than a shadow. Rachel turned into a doorway at the nearer end of a building to the right of the garden, next to a fire-damaged ruin.

His breath heaved in his chest. He had the strangest feeling that the man had seen Rachel, and perhaps himself as well.

The man had gone. This was Rachel's lover. He had been watching for her, and now she was come.

His own duty was plain. He crossed the court to the doorway. The door was ajar. On the wall to one side, sheltered by the overhang of the porch, was a painted board. White letters marched, or rather staggered, across a black background:

<u>XIV</u>
6 Mr Harrison
5 Mr Moran
4 Mr Gorvin
3 Mr Gromwell
2 Mr Drury
1 Mr Bews

Distracted, he frowned. Taken as a whole, the board was an offence to a man's finer feelings and displeasing to God. The letters varied in size, and their spacing was irregular. In particular, the lettering of Mr Gromwell's name had been quite barbarously executed. It was clearly a later addition, obliterating the original name that had been there. A trickle of paint trailed from the final 'l' of Gromwell. The sign-painter had tried ineffectually to brush it away, probably with his finger, and had succeeded only in leaving the corpse of a small insect attached to it.

Perhaps, he thought, fumbling in his pocket, temporarily diverted from Rachel, a man might scrape away the worst of the drip with the blade of a pocket knife. If only —

He heard sounds within. And a man's voice. Then a second voice — a woman's.

Oh, Rachel, how could you?

He pushed the door wide and crossed the threshold. Two doors faced each other across a small lobby. At the back, a staircase rose into the shadows.

He listened, but heard only silence. He caught sight of something gleaming on the second step of the stairs. He stepped closer and peered at it.

A speck of damp mud. The moisture

caught the light from the open door behind him.

'Rachel?' he called.

There was no reply. His mind conjured up a vision of her in a man's chamber, her skirts thrown up, making the two-backed beast with him. He shook his head violently, trying to shake the foul images out of it.

He climbed the stairs. On the next landing, two more doors faced each other, number three on the right and number four on the left. Another, smaller door had been squeezed into the space between the staircase and the back of the landing.

Number three. Three was a number of great importance. There were three doors and three Christian virtues, Faith, Hope and Charity. Man has three enemies, the world, the flesh and the devil. Mr Gromwell's number was three, whoever Gromwell was.

In God's creation, everything had meaning, nothing was by chance, all was pre-ordained, even the insect trapped in the paint, placed there to show him the way.

He raised the latch. The door swung slowly backwards, revealing a square sitting room. Late afternoon sunshine filled the chamber, and for a moment he was transfixed by the loveliness of the light.

A window to God . . .

16

He blinked, and loveliness became mere sunshine. The light caught on a picture in a carved gilt frame, which hung over the mantelpiece. He stared at it, at the women it portrayed, who were engaged in a scene of such wickedness that it took his breath away. He forced himself to look away and the rest of the room came slowly to his attention: a press of blackened oak; chair and stools; a richly coloured carpet; a table on which were papers, wine, sweetmeats and two glasses; and a couch strewn with velvet cushions the colour of leaves in spring.

And on the couch —

Inside his belly, the serpent twisted and sunk its teeth.

Something did not fit, something was wrong —

The woman lay sleeping on the couch, her head turned away from him. Her hair was loose — dark ringlets draped over white skin. Her silk gown was designed to reveal her breasts rather than conceal them. The gown was yellow, and also red in places.

She had kicked off her shoes before falling asleep, and they lay beside the couch. They were silly, feminine things with high heels and silver buckles. The hem of the gown had risen almost to the knees, revealing a

17

froth of lace beneath. One hand lay carelessly on her bosom. She wore a ring with a sapphire.

But she wasn't Rachel. She didn't resemble Rachel in the slightest. She was older, for a start, thinner, smaller, and less well-favoured.

His mind whirred, useless as a child's spinning top. He had a sudden, shameful urge to touch the woman's breast.

'Mistress,' he said. 'Mistress? Are you unwell?'

She did not reply.

'Mistress,' he said sharply, angry with himself as well as with her for leading him into temptation. 'Are you drunk? Wake up.'

He drew closer, and stooped over her. Such a wanton, sinful display of flesh. The devil's work to lead mankind astray. He stared at the breasts, unable to look away. They were quite still. The woman might have been a painted statue in a Popish church.

She had a foolish face, of course. Her mouth was open, which showed her teeth; some were missing, and the rest were stained. Dull, sad eyes stared at him.

Oh God, he thought, and for a moment the fog in his mind cleared and he saw the wretch for what she truly was.

Merciful father, here are the wages of sin, for me as well as for her. God had punished his lust, and this poor woman's. God be blessed in his infinite wisdom.

And yet — what if there were still life in this fallen woman? Would not God wish him to urge her to repent?

Her complexion was unnaturally white. There was a velvet beauty patch at the corner of her left eye in the shape of a coach and horses, and another on her cheek in the form of a heart. The poor vain woman, tricking herself out with her powders and patches, and for what? To entice men into her sinful embrace.

He knelt beside her and rested his ear against the left side of her breast, hoping to hear or feel through the thickness of the gown and the shift beneath the beating of a heart. Nothing. He shifted his fingers to one side. He could not find a heartbeat.

His fingertips touched something damp, a stickiness. He smelled iron. He was reminded of the butcher's shop beside his old premises in Pater Noster Row.

Was that another sound? On the landing? On the stairs.

He withdrew his hand. The fingers were red with blood. Like the butcher's fingers when he had killed a pig on the step, and

19

the blood drained down to the gutter, a feast for flies. Why was there so much blood? It was blood on the yellow gown: that was why some of it was red.

Thank God it was not Rachel. He sighed and drew down the lids over the sightless eyes. He knew what was due to death. When Rachel had drawn her last labouring breath —

The cuff of his shirt had trailed across the blood. He blinked, his train of thought broken. There was blood on his sleeve. They would be angry with him for fouling his linen.

He took a paper from the table and wiped his hand and the cuff as best he could. He stuffed the paper in his pocket to tidy it away and rose slowly to his feet.

Rachel — how in God's name could he have forgotten her? Perhaps she had gone outside while he was distracted.

In his haste, he collided with a chair and knocked it over. On the landing, he closed the door behind him. He went downstairs. As he came out into the sunshine, something shifted in his memory and suddenly he knew this place for what it was: one of those nests of lawyers that had grown up outside the old city walls, as nests of rooks cluster in garden trees about a house.

Lawyers. The devil's spawn. They argued white into black with their lies and their Latin, and they sent innocent, God-fearing men to prison, as he knew to his cost.

Birds sang in the garden. The courtyard was full of people, mainly men, mainly dressed in lawyers' black which reminded him again of rooks, talking among themselves. Caw, caw, he murmured to himself, caw, caw.

He walked stiffly towards the hall with its high, pointed windows. At the door, he paused, and looked back. His eyes travelled up the building he had just left. The shadowy man was back at the first-floor window. He raised his arm at the shadow, partly in accusation and partly in triumph: there, see the rewards of sin. Fall on your knees and repent.

Suddenly, there was Rachel herself. She was coming out of the doorway of the blackened ruin next to Staircase XIV. She had pulled her cloak over her face to cover her shame. She was trying to hide from him. She was trying to hide from God.

Caw, caw, said the rooks.

'Rachel,' he said, or perhaps he only thought it. 'Rachel.'

A lawyer passed her, jostling her shoulder, and for a moment the cloak slipped. To his astonishment, he saw that the woman was not Rachel, after all. This woman wore the mark of Cain on her face. Cain was jealous of his brother Abel, so he slew him.

Not Rachel. His wife was dead, rotting in her grave, waiting among the worms for the Second Coming of the Lord and the ever-lasting reign of King Jesus. Nor had Rachel borne the mark of Cain.

'Sinner!' he cried, shaking his fist. 'Sinner!' The bite of the serpent endured beyond death. Perhaps he had been wrong about Rachel. Had she been a whore too, like Eve a temptress of men, destined to writhe for all eternity in the flames of hell?

Caw, caw, said the rooks. Caw, caw.

CHAPTER TWO

It is marvellous what money in your pocket and a toehold in the world will do for a man's self-esteem.

There I was, James Marwood. Sleeker of face and more prosperous of purse than I had been six months earlier. Clerk to Mr Williamson, the Under-Secretary of State to my Lord Arlington himself. Clerk to the Board of Red Cloth, which was attached to the Groom of the Stool's department. James Marwood — altogether a rising man, if only in my own estimation.

That evening, Thursday, 2 May, I set out by water from the Tower, where I had been a witness on Mr Williamson's behalf at the interrogation of certain prisoners. The tide was with us, though only recently on the turn. The ruins of the city lay on my right — the roofless churches, the tottering chimney stacks, the gutted warehouses, the heaps of ash — but distance and sunlight

23

lent them a strange beauty, touching with the colours of paradise. On my left, on the Surrey side, Southwark lay undamaged, and before me the lofty buildings on London Bridge towered across the river with the traffic passing to and fro between them.

The waterman judged it safe for us to pass beneath the bridge. A few hours later, when the tide would be running faster, the currents would be too turbulent for safety. Even so, he took us through Chapel Lock, one of the wider arches. It was a relief to reach open water at the cost of only a little spray on my cloak.

London opened up before me again, still dominated by the blackened hulk of St Paul's on its hill. It was eight months since the Great Fire. Though the streets had been cleared and the ruins surveyed, the reconstruction had barely begun.

My mind was full of the evening that lay ahead — the agreeable prospect of a supper with two fellow clerks in a Westminster tavern where there would be music, and where there was a pretty barmaid who would be obliging if you promised her a scrap of lace or some other trifle. Before that, however, I needed to return to my house to change my clothes and make my notes for Mr Williamson.

I had the waterman set me down at the Savoy Stairs. My new lodgings were nearby in the old palace. I had moved there less than three weeks ago from the house of Mr Newcomb, the King's Printer. Since my good fortune, I deserved better and I could afford to pay for it.

In the later wars, the Savoy had been used to house the wounded. Now its rambling premises near the river were used mainly for ageing soldiers and sailors, and also for private lodgings. The latter were much sought after since the Fire — accommodation of all sorts was still in short supply. It was crown property and Mr Williamson had dropped a word on my behalf into the right ear.

Infirmary Close, my new house, was one of four that had been created by subdividing a much larger building. I had the smallest and cheapest of them. At the back it overlooked the graveyard attached to the Savoy chapel. It was an inconvenience which was likely to grow worse as the weather became warmer, but it was also the reason why the rent was low.

My cheerfulness dropped away from me in a moment when Margaret opened the door to me. I knew something was amiss as soon as I saw her face.

I passed her my damp cloak. 'What is it?'

'I'm sorry, master — your father went wandering today. I was only gone for a while — the night-soil man came to the door, and he does talk, sir, a perfect downpour of words, you cannot —'

'Is he safe?'

'Safe? Yes, sir.' She draped the cloak over the chest, her hands smoothing its folds automatically. 'He's by the parlour fire. I'd left him in the courtyard on his usual bench. The sun was out, and he was asleep. And I thought, if I was only gone a moment, he —'

'When was this?' I snapped.

She bit her lip. 'I don't know. Upward of an hour? We couldn't find him. Then suddenly he was back — the kitchen yard. Barty brought him.'

'Who?'

'Barty, sir. The crossing-sweeper by Temple Bar. He knows your father wanders sometimes.'

I didn't know Barty from Adam, but I made a mental note to give him something for his pains.

'Sir,' Margaret said in a lower voice. 'He was weeping. Like a child.'

'Why?' I said. 'Had someone hurt him?'

'No.'

26

'Has he said anything?'

Margaret rubbed her eyes with the back of her hand. 'Rachel.'

I felt as if someone had kicked me. 'What?'

'Rachel, sir. That's what he said when he came in. Over and over again. Just the name. Rachel.' She stared up at me, twisting a fold of her dress in her hands. 'Who's Rachel, sir? Do you know?'

I didn't answer her. Of course I knew who Rachel was. She was my mother, dead these six long years, but not always dead to my father.

I went into the parlour. The old man was sitting by the fire and spooning the contents of a bowl of posset into his mouth. Margaret or someone had laid a large napkin across his lap. But it had not been large enough to catch all the drops of posset that had missed his mouth. He did not look up as I entered the room.

Anger ran through me, fuelled by love and relief, those most combustible ingredients, and heating my blood like wine. Where was my father in this wreck of a human being? Where was Nathaniel Marwood, the man who had ruled his family and his business with the authority of God's Viceroy, and who had earned the universal respect of his friends? He had been a printer once, as good as any in Pater Noster Row, a man of substance. Politics and religion had led him down dangerous paths to his ruin, but no one had ever doubted his honesty or his skill. Now, after his years in prison, only fragments of him were left.

The spoon scraped around the side of the empty bowl. I took the bowl from him, meeting only the slightest resistance, and then the spoon. I placed them both on the table and considered whether to remove the soiled napkin. On reflection, it seemed wiser to leave it to Margaret.

Eating and the afternoon's unaccustomed exercise had tired him. His eyes closed. His hands were in his lap. The right hand was grimy. The cuff of his shirt protruded from the sleeve of his coat. The underside of the cuff was stained reddish-brown like ageing meat.

My anger evaporated. I leaned forward and pushed up the cuff. There was no sign of a cut or graze on his wrist or his hand.

I shook him gently. 'Sir? Margaret tells me you went abroad this afternoon. Why?'

The only answer was a gentle snore.

Four hours later, by suppertime, the posset was merely a memory and my father was hungry again. Hunger made him briefly lucid, or as near to that state as he was ever likely to come.

'Why did you go out, sir?' I asked him, keeping my voice gentle because it upset him if I spoke roughly to him. 'You know it worries Margaret when she cannot find you.'

'Rachel.' He was looking into the fire, and God alone knew what he saw there. 'I cannot allow my wife to walk the town without knowing where she is. It is not fitting, so I followed her to remonstrate with her. Did she not promise to obey me in all things? She was wearing her best cloak, too, her Sunday cloak. It is most becoming.' He frowned. 'Perhaps it is too becoming. The devil lays his traps so cunningly. I must speak to her, indeed I must. Why did she bear the mark of Cain? I shall find out the truth of the matter.'

'Rachel . . . ? My mother?'

He glanced at me. 'Who else?' Even as he spoke, he looked bewildered. 'But you were not born. You were in her belly.'

'And now I am here before you, sir,' I said, as if this double time my father inhabited, this shifting confluence of now and then, were the most natural thing in the world. 'Where did my mother go?'

'Where the lawyers are. Those sucklings of the devil.'

29

'Where, exactly?' The lawyers congregated in many places.

He smiled. 'You should have seen her, James,' he said. 'Always neat in her movements. She loves to dance, though of course I do not allow it. It is not seemly for a married woman. But . . . but how graceful she is, James, even in her kitchen. Why, she is as graceful as a deer.'

'Which lawyers were these, sir?'

'Have you ever remarked how lawyers are like rooks? They cling together and go caw-caw-caw. They all look the same. And they go to hell when they die. Did you know that? Moreover —'

'Rachel, sir. Where did she go?'

'Why, into the heart of a rookery. There was a courtyard where there was a parliament of these evil birds. And I followed her by a garden to a doorway in a building of brick . . . and the letters of one name were most ill-painted, James, and ill-formed as well. There was a great drip attached to it, and a poor creature had drowned therein, and I could have scraped it away but there was not time.'

'A creature . . . ?'

'Even ants are God's creatures, are they not? He brought two of them into the ark, so he must have decided they should be saved from the Flood. Ah —'

My father broke off as Margaret came into the room bearing bread. She laid the table for supper. His eyes followed her movements.

'And then, sir?' I said. 'Where did she go?'

'I thought to find her in the chamber with the ant. Up the stairs.' He spoke absently, his attention still on Margaret. 'But she wasn't there. No one was, only the woman on the couch. The poor, abandoned wretch. Her sins found her out, and she suffered the punishment for them.'

The fingers of his left hand played with the soiled shirt cuff. He rubbed the stiff linen where the blood had dried.

Margaret left the room.

'Who was this woman?' I said.

'Not Rachel, thanks be to God. No, no.' He frowned. 'Such a sinfully luxurious chamber. It had a carpet on the floor that was so bright it hurt the eyes. And there was a painting over the fireplace . . . its lewdness was an offence in the eyes of God and man.'

'But the woman, sir?' I knew he must have wandered into one of his waking dreams, but it was wise to make sure he was calm now, that he would not wake screaming in the night and wake the whole household, as he sometimes did. 'This woman on the couch, I mean. What was she doing there?'

'She was a sinner, poor fool. Displaying herself like a wanton for all the world to see. Tricked out in her finery, yellow as the sun, red as fire. With a coach and horses too. Oh, vanity, vanity. And all for nothing. I closed her eyes, I owed her that at least.'

Margaret's footsteps were approaching.

My father's face changed, scrubbed clean of every expression but greed. He turned his head to the door. Margaret stood there with a platter in her hand. 'Come, James, to table,' he said. 'Supper is served. Can't you see?'

I learned nothing more from my father that day. Experience had taught me that there was little purpose in talking to him after supper, not if you expected replies that made much sense. Nor was I convinced that there was anything more to learn.

Besides, why bother? My father's memory was unpredictable in its workings and, by and large, he was now more likely to recall events from the remote past than more recent ones. If he remembered anything at all. For much of the time he lived among his dreams.

'Come to me later in my chamber,' he

mumbled, when he had finished eating. 'We must pray together, my son.'

'Perhaps, sir.' I did not like to look at him. There was a trickle of dribble at the corner of his mouth and his coat was speckled with crumbs. He was my father. I loved and honoured him. But sometimes the sight of him disgusted me. 'I have business to attend to.'

My mind was busy elsewhere. Something might be salvaged from my plans for the evening. I calculated that if I took a boat from the Savoy Stairs, my friends should still be at the tavern. And, if fortune smiled on me, so would the pretty barmaid.

Accordingly, after supper, I left Margaret to deal with my father. I had grown prosperous enough to keep two servants — Margaret Witherdine and her husband Samuel, a discharged sailor who had suffered the misfortune of losing part of a leg in his country's wars against the Dutch. Samuel had fallen into poverty and then into debt, partly because of his country's inability to pay him what he was owed. Nevertheless he had done me a great service, and I had discharged his debt. In return, I believed, Sam and Margaret served my father and me from loyalty as well as for their board and lodging and a little money.

All this was agreeable to me. God help

me, it gave me a good opinion of myself. I was as smug as the cat who has found the larder door open and eaten and drunk his fill. And like the cat, sitting afterwards and cleaning his whiskers in the sunshine, I assumed this happy state of affairs would last for ever.

So I did not see my father after supper that day. Sometimes I went into his chamber when he was ready for bed, even if I had been out late. But not that night. I did not admit it to myself but I was irritated with him. Because of his folly, I had been obliged to forgo my evening on the river. To make matters worse, when I had reached the tavern, my friends were not there and the pretty barmaid had left to be married.

So Margaret must have settled him in his bed, listened to the mumbled nonsense that he believed to be his prayers and blown out his candle. She must have sat with him in the dark, holding his hand, until he fell asleep. I knew that would have happened because that was what she always did. I also knew that my father would have preferred his son beside him when he said his prayers, and that he would have liked his own flesh and blood to hold his hand, rather than a servant.

34

The following morning, I had arranged to go into the office at an earlier hour than usual. Mr Williamson wanted my notes from the Tower interrogations as soon as possible. Besides, I was behind in my task of copying his correspondence into his letter book, and there was also my regular work for the *Gazette.* The press of business was very great — the *London Gazette,* the twice-weekly government newspaper which Mr Newcomb printed here in the Savoy, was another of Williamson's responsibilities, and he delegated much of its day-to-day administration to me.

My father was already awake. He was in his chamber, where Margaret was helping him dress. As I left the parlour, I heard his voice, deep and resonant, booming in the distance; like his body, his voice belonged to a healthier, stronger man, a man who still had his wits about him. I persuaded myself that I could not spare the time to wish him good morning before I left.

I did not give my father another thought until after dinner, when my servant Samuel Witherdine came to Whitehall and knocked on the door of Mr Williamson's office. Sam was a wiry man with a weathered face and very bright blue eyes, which at present were surrounded by puffy eyelids. He wore a wooden leg below his right knee and supported himself with a crutch.

Something was amiss. It was unheard of for him to come to the office of his own accord. I thought the puffy eyes meant he was hungover. I was wrong.

CHAPTER THREE

The door opened.

'Mistress?'

On Friday morning, a woman lay on her bed in a new house on the north side of Pall Mall. She clung to the shreds of sleep that swirled like seaweed around her. Drown me in sleep, she thought, six fathoms deep, and let the fish nibble me into a million pieces.

The door closed, and was softly latched. Footsteps crossed the floor. Light and quick and familiar.

'Are you awake?'

No, Jemima thought, I am not. She fought the creeping tide of consciousness every inch of the way. To be conscious was to remember.

She had been dreaming of Syre Place, where she had grown up. It was strange that she knew it to be Syre Place because it had seemed not to resemble the real house. The real Syre Place was built of brick, of a russet colour like a certain apple that her father was fond of. As a child, she had assumed that the house had somehow been built to match the apples, which was all part of the rightness of things, of the patterns that ran through everything.

But the Syre Place in her dreams was all wrong. It was faced with stone, for a start, and designed after the modern fashion that Philip liked. (Philip? Philip? Her mind shied away from the thought of Philip.) It was a house in the modern fashion, a neat box, with everything tidy and clean both within and without, and a roof whose overhanging eaves made it look as if the building were wearing a hat.

'My lady? My lady?'

In Syre Place, the real one, there was a park where her father used to hunt before he lost his good humour and the use of his legs. Down the lane was the farm, whose smells and sounds were part of life, running through every hour of every day. In this Syre Place, however, the park was gone, and so was the farm. Instead there was a garden with gravel paths and parterres and shrubs, arranged symmetrically like the house. But — now she looked more closely at it — there was nothing neat about the garden in the dream because weeds had sprung up everywhere, and brambles criss-crossed the paths and arched overhead.

Nettles stood in great clumps, their leaves twitching, desperate to sting her. Her brother had thrown her into a bed of nettles when she was scarcely out of leading strings, and she still remembered the agonizing, unfair pain of it. How strange and unnatural it was, she thought, that a plant should be so nasty, so hostile. God had made the plants and the animals to serve man, not to attack him.

Nature was unnatural. It was full of monstrous tricks. Perhaps it was the work of the devil, not God.

'Come now, madam. It's past eleven o'clock.'

Time? What time of year could it be? In the garden at Syre Place, the gravel paths were carpeted with spoiled fruit. Brown apples and pears, and yellow raspberries, and red strawberries and green plums, as if all fruitful seasons existed at once. They lay so thickly on the ground that she could no longer see the gravel. The smell of decay was everywhere. Jemima raised her skirts — good God, what was she wearing? just her shift? But she was outside and in broad daylight, where anyone might see her — but the pulpy fruit splashed stickily against the linen and spattered the skin of her bare legs.

There were wasps, too, she saw, fat-bellied things cruising a few inches above the ground and feeding on the rottenness. What if one of them flew up inside her shift and stung her in her most private and intimate place?

In her fear, she cried out.

'Hush now,' Mary murmured, the voice floating above her. 'It's all right. Time to wake up.'

No, no, no, Jemima thought. Despite the wasps, despite everything, it was better to stay asleep, her eyes screwed shut against the daylight. She wanted to stay for ever in Syre Place where once, she thought, she had been happy.

What was happiness? Rocking in Nurse's lap as she sang. Sitting beside her brother Henry when, greatly condescending, he guided her as she stumbled through her hornbook. Or, better still, when he perched her up before him on the new brown mare, with the ground so far beneath that she had to close her eyes so she wouldn't see it.

'I'll drop you, Jemima,' her brother had said, his arms tightening around her. 'Your skull will crack like an eggshell.'

Oh, the sweet, delicious terror of it.

Someone she could not see called her name.

No. No. Go to sleep, she ordered herself: down, down, down into the deep, dark depths where no one can see me. To the time before that fatal letter, before the Fire Court, before she had even known where Clifford's Inn was.

Something was buzzing. It must be a wasp. She moaned with fear.

There was a sudden rattle of curtain rings, brutally unexpected, and she was bathed in brilliance. The bed curtains had been thrown open. It was as if someone had thrown a bucket of light over her. She squeezed her eyelids together but the light glowed pinkly outside them. A current of cool air swept over her, bringing the scents of the garden.

'Close the curtains, you fool,' she wanted to say, 'shut out the light.' But she couldn't, wouldn't speak.

She was lying on her back, she knew, on her own bed in her own bedchamber. If she opened her eyes she would see the canopy above her, blue and silver, silk embroidery; the bed was in its summer clothing; the winter curtains and canopy were made of much heavier material, and their embroidery was predominantly red and gold, the

41

colours of fire. The curtains were hers, part of her dowry. Almost everything was hers. Everything except Dragon Yard.

She didn't want to know all this. She wanted to be asleep in the dark, in a place too deep for dreaming, too deep for knowledge.

'Master's coming,' said the voice. A woman's. Her woman's. Mary's.

A wasp. Buzz, buzz, buzz. Why can't it go away?

'Any moment he'll be here. I can't put him off.'

Her brother Henry had had a waistcoat like a wasp: all yellow and black. Jemima wondered what had happened to it. Perhaps it had been lost in the fire. Or perhaps it was down, down in the deep, dark depths, where Henry was presumably lying himself. Anything the fishes had left. Philip had served with Henry in the Navy in the Dutch wars. That was how she had met her husband, as her brother's friend.

The latch rattled again, shockingly loud. The buzzing stopped.

'Isn't she awake yet?'

Philip's voice, achingly familiar, and horribly strange.

'No, master.'

'She should be awake by now. Surely?'

'The draught lasts longer for some people than for others.'

Heavy footsteps drew closer to the bed, closer to her. She could smell Philip now. Sweat, a trace of the perfume he sometimes wore, the hint of last night's wine.

'Madam,' he said. Then, more loudly: 'Madam?'

The voice made something inside her answer to it. Her body's response was involuntary, beyond control or desire. She knew she must continue to breathe, and that she must give no sign that she was not deeply asleep. Yet she wanted to cry out, to scream at him, to howl in agony and rage.

'Hush, sir. It's better to let her be.'

'Hold your tongue, woman,' he shouted. 'She's pale as a ghost. I'll send for the doctor.'

The buzzing returned. To and fro, it went, nearer and further. She focused her attention on it. A distraction. She hoped it was not a wasp.

'She's always pale, sir,' Mary said, almost in a whisper. 'You know that.'

'But she's slept for hours.'

'Sleep's the best cure. There's no physic can mend her faster. It's always been the way with her. I went out this morning and fetched another draught from the apothe-

43

cary in case she needs it tonight.'

'You left her alone? Like this?'

'No, no, master. Hester was watching over her. I wasn't gone long, in any case.'

'Devil take that fly,' Philip muttered, his attention fastening on another irritation.

The buzzing stopped abruptly. There was the sound of a slap, followed by a muffled oath.

'Hush, sir,' Mary said. 'You'll wake her.'

'Hold your tongue. Or I'll put you out on the street with nothing but a shift to cover your nakedness. Has she said anything yet?'

'No, sir. Not a word.'

'Stand over there. By the door.'

The heavy footsteps drew nearer. She kept her eyelids tightly closed. She heard the sound of his breathing and knew he must be stooping above the bed, bringing his face close to hers.

'Jemima.' His voice was a whisper, and his breath touched her cheek. 'Can you hear me?' When she said nothing in reply, he went on, 'Where were you yesterday afternoon? Where did you go?'

Philip paused. She heard his breathing, and a creaking floorboard, the one near the door, where Mary must be standing.

'What made you so distressed?' he said. 'What did you see?'

44

After a few seconds, he let out his breath in a sigh of exasperation. He walked away from the bed. 'Mary? Are you sure you know nothing?'

'No, sir. I told you — she left me in the hackney.'

'I'll whip the truth out of you.'

'That is the truth.'

The door latch rattled. 'Send for me as soon as your mistress wakes. Do you understand?'

'Yes, master.'

'Don't let anyone else talk to her until I have. Not Hester, not anyone. And not you, either. Is that clear?'

'Yes, sir.'

The door closed. The footsteps clattered down the stairs.

She listened to Mary moving around the room and the buzzing of the fly. After a moment she opened her eyes. Daylight dazzled her. 'I thought he would never go,' she said.

Jemima spent Saturday and Sunday in bed. Mary tended to her needs. Mary was her maid. She had come with her from Syre Place. Her father was a tenant farmer on the estate, a man with too many daughters. Sir George had charged Mary to take special care of her mistress when she married

45

Philip, and to obey her in all things, not Philip.

Mary sometimes slept with her when Philip did not come to her bed, especially in winter.

When Mary wasn't in the room, she sent Hester in her place. Hester was a stupid little girl, fresh from the country. When she was obliged to speak to her mistress, she blushed a cruel and unforgiving red that spread over her face like a stain. She blushed when her master was in the room too, but he never spoke to her.

'My lady?' Mary said on Monday afternoon. 'We need to change the sheets.'

She opened her eyes and saw Mary standing over her with an armful of bedlinen. She allowed herself to be helped out of bed and placed in an armchair by the window. It was a fresh, clear afternoon. Her bedchamber was at the back of the house. The trees at the bottom of the garden shielded the brick wall behind them and the fields stretching up to Piccadilly.

The window was open, and she heard hooves, hammering and sometimes distant voices. The trees blocked out most of the view, but occasionally she glimpsed a flash of colour through the leaves or wisps of smoke, rising higher into the empty sky until they dissipated themselves in the empty blue of heaven.

If one went to heaven after death, Jemima thought, how eternally tedious it would be if it were nothing but blue and infinitely empty. Better to be nothing at all oneself. Which was blasphemy.

Philip came up to see her while she was sitting there.

'Madam,' he said, bowing. 'I'm rejoiced to see you out of your bed at last.'

He glanced at the maids, who had continued at their work but were making themselves as unobtrusive as possible, as servants should. 'Mary says you remember nothing of your — your illness.'

'No, sir.' She and Mary had agreed it was wiser this way, wiser to bide one's time. 'I had pains in my head when I woke up.'

'The doctor called it a sudden inflammation of the brain. Thanks to his treatment, it came and went like an April shower. Can you remember how it happened?'

'No. It is all a perfect blank to me until I woke up in my bed.'

'You and Mary went out for a drive in a hackney coach,' he said slowly, as if teaching a child a lesson. 'After you'd dined — on Thursday. Remember?'

'No.'

47

'The fever came on suddenly. You were insensible, or very near to it, when Mary brought you home.'

'I remember nothing,' she said, though she remembered everything that mattered. She remembered every inch of the way to Clifford's Inn, every step up the stairs of Staircase XIV. For now, however, it was better to pretend to forget.

Philip's hand touched her arm. 'The doctor said that sometimes sufferers are much troubled by dreams when the fever is at its height, and believe all sorts of strange fancies. But thank God all that is passed now.'

'I am much better, sir,' she said. 'I feel quite refreshed.'

'Good. In that case, will you join me at supper?'

'I think not. I will take something here instead.'

Jemima watched him as she spoke, but his expression told her nothing. Her husband was tall, lean and dark-complexioned — like the King himself. He was not a handsome man but usually she found his face good to look at, because it was his. But now his face had become a mere arrangement of features, an array of hollows, projections, planes, textures, colours. He was a stranger to her.

A familiar stranger. A treacherous

48

stranger, and that was the very worst sort of stranger.

'Tomorrow, then,' he said, smiling. 'For dinner. We shall have guests, by the way — a brace of lawyers. One of them's Sir Thomas Twisden, the judge.'

It seemed to her that he spoke more deliberately than usual, enunciating the words with precision as if they were especially significant. He paused — only for a second, but she knew that the pause meant something, too. He knew that she didn't like people to come to the house.

The maids had finished making the bed. Hester left the room, her arms full of dirty linen. Mary remained, tidying the pots and bottles on the dressing table.

'And I've asked Lucius Gromwell to join us,' Philip said.

Jemima caught her breath, and hoped he hadn't noticed. Gromwell, of all people. The sly, twice-damned, whoreson devil. How dared they? She stared at her lap. She sensed he was looking at her, gauging her reaction to Gromwell's name. She was aware as well that, on the very edge of her range of vision, Mary's hands were no longer moving among the litter on the dressing table.

'It will be good to have you at the table,'

he went on. 'You must make sure they send up something worth eating. We must do our best to keep Sir Thomas amused. We want him to look kindly on us, after all, don't we?'

His voice sharpened towards the end, and she looked up. He wants me to twitch like a hound bitch, she thought, to the sound of her master's voice.

'Yes, sir,' she said.

'He's a Fire Court judge,' Philip reminded her. 'He's down for the Dragon Yard case.'

He smiled at her and made his way towards the door. He paused, his hand on the latch.

'Lucius is writing a book, by the way. He is mad for it. It's called *The Natural Curiosities of Gloucestershire,* and it will have many plates and maps, so it will cost a great deal to produce. I promised him I would pay for the publication, and he assures me it will make me a handsome profit when the edition sells out, as well as enshrine my name for posterity.'

Gromwell, she thought. I hate him.

'You remember him, don't you? My old friend from school and Oxford.'

She nodded. Gromwell will look at me tomorrow and know my shame, she thought, and I shall look at him and know that he knows it. He arranged it all. None of this would have happened without him. Gromwell, who dared to stand in my way at Clifford's Inn.

'Poor Lucius, eh?' Her husband lifted the latch and laughed with what seemed like genuine amusement. 'I doubt he'll ever finish the book. He is a man of many parts but he finishes nothing he begins. He was like that at school, and he's never changed.'

CHAPTER FOUR

My father had been run over in Fleet Street by a wagon bearing rubble removed from the ruins of St Paul's Cathedral. The weight had broken his spine, killing him instantly. It was a miracle that the pressure had not cut him in half.

Infirmary Close was full of wailing women. Margaret persuaded herself that his death had been her fault, for she had left him in the parlour while she was making dinner, believing he was no longer capable of managing the locks and bolts of the door into the lane. The neighbours' maids wept in sympathy. The laundry woman came to the house to collect the washing; she wept too, because tears are catching and death is frightening.

After he brought me home in the hackney coach, Sam went into the kitchen yard and chopped wood as if he were chopping down his enemies: one by one, with deliberation and satisfaction.

As for me, I went into my father's bed-chamber and sat beside him, as I should have done last night. He lay with his eyes closed and his hands folded over his chest. Someone had covered the great wound with a sheet and bound up his jaw. His face appeared unmarked. Sometimes the dead look peaceful. He did not.

I could not pray. I did not weep. The weight of his disapproval bore down on me, for I had strayed from the godly path he had ordained for me, and now it could never be put right. Worse still was the shame I felt about how I had behaved to him and how I had felt about him during the last few months, when he had become as vulnerable as a child.

Something shifted inside me, as an earthquake ripples and rumbles through solid earth and rock, bringing floods and ruin in its wake. Nothing would be the same again.

That was when the memory of Catherine Lovett came into my mind. She was a young woman with a strange and independent cast of mind. I had done her a service at the time of the Fire, though I had not seen her since; she was living in retirement and under an assumed name. As it happened, I had been with her when her father died, and I had seen what she had done. She had taken his hand and raised it to her lips.

I looked at my father's hand. Flesh, skin and bone. The fingers twisted like roots. The nails discoloured and in need of trimming. Death had robbed his hand of its familiarity and made it strange.

I lifted the hand and kissed it. The weight of it took me by surprise. The dead are heavier than the living.

'I am truly sorry for your loss,' Mr Williamson said the following morning.

I thanked him and requested leave of absence to bury my father and settle his affairs.

'Of course.' Williamson turned away and busied himself with the papers on his desk. 'Where will you lay him to rest?'

'Bunhill Fields, sir.'

Williamson grunted. 'Not an Anglican burial ground?'

'I think not. He would not have wished it.'

Bunhill Fields was where the Dissenters lay, and where my father belonged. Williamson returned to reading letters, occasionally annotating them. The two of us were alone in the Scotland Yard office, which lay just to the north of the Whitehall Palace itself.

Williamson had two offices, one close to my Lord Arlington's, and this one, which he used for the *Gazette* and for other concerns that required more privacy.

A few minutes later, he spoke again, and his voice sounded harder than before, closer to his northern roots, which was often a sign of irritation in him. 'You must look to the living, Marwood, as well as the dead.'

'Yes, sir.'

'You would not wish anything to reflect ill on this office. Nor would I.'

I bowed my head. I knew what Williamson intended me to understand. Before his mind lost its bearings, my father, Nathaniel Marwood, had been a Fifth Monarchist. As a result of his allegiance to that dangerous sect, he had been imprisoned for treason. He had considered the Church of England as the next best thing to the Church of Rome with its Papist ways and its foul plots against honest men. He had hated all kings except King Jesus, whose coming he had devoutly waited for.

'After all,' Williamson said, staring grimly at me, 'you would not want to lie in Bunhill Fields yourself when your time comes. At least, I hope you would not.'

'Of course not, sir.'

Nowadays I served the King; and it was

55

politic for me to have a care for what I did and said, and to choose wisely whom I associated with. I made sure the world knew that I went to church regularly and that I took communion when it was fitting to do so, according to the rites of the Established Church and the instruction of its bishops. But there was always the danger that, through my father, I might be considered guilty by association, by blood.

'So you will change your mind, Marwood? No doubt your father would have wished you to think of your best interests in these changed times.'

'Yes, sir. But I must also think of his.'

Williamson gave a laugh — short, sharp and mirthless, like the bark of a dog. 'You're obstinate in your folly.' He lowered his head over his papers. 'Like father, like son, I suppose.'

For some reason, that last remark comforted me as nothing else did.

Two days later, on Monday, we laid Nathaniel Marwood in his grave. There was no reason for delay — the death had been an accident; it was easy enough for an old man to stagger on the crowded pavement and fall under the wagon. He had been notably infirm in mind, if not in body, and quite possibly did not even know where he was. Such deaths happen every day.

We took the body to Bunhill Fields. Apart from the minister, the bearers and the diggers, the only mourners were Sam and myself. Margaret was debarred by her sex from coming, which was unkind, for her grief was in its way deeper and truer than my own. She still wept for my father at the slightest provocation, despite the fact that in life he had been a burden to her.

After the interment, Sam and I took a hackney coach around the walls of the ruined city, a wasteland of blackened chimney stacks, roofless churches and sodden ashes. I told the driver to set us down in Fleet Street. We went to the Devil, the big tavern between Temple Bar and Middle Temple Gate, where Sam stuffed himself with as much as he could eat and I made myself swiftly and relentlessly drunk.

Memory is a strange thing, fickle and misleading, as treacherous as water. My memories of the rest of the day are like broken glass — jumbled, largely meaningless and with sharp edges liable to wound. But I remember perfectly one snatch of conversation between us, partly because it happened early on, and partly because of what was said.

'Do you know the crossing-sweeper here, master?'

I was too busy drinking to reply.

'He knows you,' Sam went on.

'Do I?' Of course I gave the sweeper a penny occasionally. If you used a crossing regularly, you would be a fool not to. But I could not for the life of me remember what the man looked like.

'His name's Bartholomew,' Sam said. 'Like the prophet. Barty.'

I was not attending to what he was saying. I was trying to attract the attention of the waiter and order more wine.

'He's the one who brought your father home. The day before he died.'

I forgot the waiter and looked at Sam. 'Yes — I remember. Margaret told me. I should give him something for his trouble.'

Sam touched the side of his head with his forefinger. 'Barty said he didn't know the old man's wits were wandering. Not at first. I mean, seeing him from the outside, who would? He didn't look as if he had an addled brain.'

It was a fair point. Nathaniel Marwood had looked what he was — an old man in his sixties, but hale enough. It was only if you tried to talk to him, and you heard the nonsense that poured out of his mouth, making little more sense than the babble of an infant, that you realized his infirmity.

'There's an archway up beyond the church, sir. Barty said that was the way your father came.'

'An archway?' I thought he meant the great gateway that divided the City from Westminster, and Fleet Street from the Strand. 'You mean he came through Temple Bar?'

'No, no. This archway's off the street. To the north, by St Dunstan-in-the-West.' Sam leaned forward. 'It's the way into one of these lawyers' colleges. Clifford's Inn.'

Suddenly my father's words were in my mind. The last words, nearly, that I had heard from him, and possibly the last words that contained some fragmentary elements of lucidity. 'Where the lawyers are. Those creatures of the devil.' He had hated and feared lawyers since they helped to put him in prison and take away his property.

'Isn't that where the Fire Court is sitting? Why would he go there?'

Sam shrugged.

Have you ever remarked how lawyers are like rooks? They cling together and go caw-caw-caw . . . And they go to hell when they die.

So there had been, after all, a single fragment of fact among my father's ramblings, buried in all the nonsense about my mother. He had been to Clifford's Inn, among the lawyers.

'Did Barty say more?'

'He was weeping,' Sam said. 'Barty told me that. So he walked him home, but he couldn't make head nor sense of what your father was saying.'

I hammered my fist on the table. 'Then I shall go to Clifford's Inn and find out.'

The waiter mistook the gesture and was at my elbow in a trice. 'Beg pardon, master, didn't mean to keep you waiting. Another quart of sack, is it? You will have it directly.'

'Yes,' I said, frowning at him. 'Very well, a drink before we go, to godspeed us and drink to my father's memory.' I glared at Sam. 'He should not have been weeping. He should not have been unhappy.'

Sam stared at the table. 'No, sir.'

'And why in God's name did he go to Clifford's Inn? Did someone drag him there?' All my guilt, all my sorrow, had at last found an outlet. 'I shall have the truth of it, do you hear, and I shall have it now. Find me this Barty and I shall question him.'

'Yes, sir,' Sam said.

There was the waiter again, back already.

Before I was an hour older, I was too drunk to have the truth of anything.

Before I was an hour older, I was too drunk to know the truth of anything.

CHAPTER FIVE

The day after the funeral I woke with a headache that cut my skull in two.

My mouth tasted as it had in the first few weeks after the Great Fire when everything had turned to ashes, from the air we breathed to the water we drank. Every breath and every mouthful was a reminder of what had happened. Every footstep raised a grey cloud that powdered our clothes and our hair. The destruction of a city and the death of an old man tasted the same: ashes to ashes.

It was early. I wrapped myself in my gown and went down to the kitchen, tottering like an old man myself: in fact just as my father used to do when his limbs were stiff after sleep. Death, I think, must have a sense of humour.

The kitchen was at the back of the house, a gloomy room partly lit by a leaded casement which looked over the graveyard. Margaret was already there. She had lit the fire and was busying herself with the preparations for dinner. She took one look at me, pointed at the bench by the table and went into the pantry. The kitchen smelled of smoke and old meat. Now I was here, I wanted to leave, but I lacked the strength. In a moment Margaret returned with a jug of small beer and a pot to put it in. Without speaking, she poured a morning draught and handed it to me.

The first mouthful made me retch. I fought back the rising nausea and took a second mouthful. I kept that down and ventured cautiously on a third.

'I put juice of the cabbage in there too,' Margaret said. 'A sovereign remedy.'

I retched again. She went back to stirring the pot over the fire, the source of another smell. I watched a rat skim along the bottom of the wall from the larder and slip through the crack below the back door. I lacked the energy to throw something at it.

Taking my time, I drank the rest of the pot and let it settle. I felt no worse for it. At least my mouth was less dry.

Margaret refilled the pot without my asking. Sam had a tendency to take too much drink, and she knew how to deal with it.

I closed my eyes. When I next opened

them, Margaret was standing over me. She was a short, sturdy woman with black hair, dark eyes and a high colour. When hot or angry, she looked as if she might explode. She looked like that now but I wasn't sure why. My memory of the later part of yesterday was blurred. Clearly, I had been very drunk. That probably meant that Sam had been very drunk too.

'Master,' she said. 'Can I speak to you?'

'Later,' I said.

She ignored that. 'Your father's clothes, sir. I —'

'Give them to the poor,' I croaked. 'Sell them. I don't care a fig what you do with them.'

'It's not that, sir. I tried to clean his coat yesterday. The one he was wearing.'

I winced and looked away, reaching for the pot.

'It's a good coat,' she said. 'There's a deal of use left in it.'

'Then get rid of it somehow. Don't bother me with it, woman.'

'I emptied the pockets.'

Something in her voice made me look up. 'What is it?'

For answer, she went to the shelves on the wall opposite the fireplace and took down a small box without a lid. She set it on the table.

Inside was my father's frayed purse and a piece of rag. The purse contained two pennies — we had never given him more because his money tended to be stolen or lost, if he had not given it away first — and four pieces of type, the only surviving relics of his press in Pater Noster Row. His folding knife was there too, with its handle of wood, worn and stained with constant use. At the bottom was a crumpled sheet of paper, smeared with rust.

Not rust, of course. Dried blood. Just as there had been dried blood on the cuff of his shirt.

Yesterday's conversation with Sam flooded into my mind. The crossing-sweeper. Clifford's Inn. *Where the lawyers are. Those creatures of the devil.* And, before that, my father talking deluded nonsense about my mother, and the woman on the couch, and closing her eyes.

I picked up the paper and smoothed it out. It was a strip torn from a larger sheet. Written on it were the words 'Twisden, Wyndham, Rainsford, DY'.

Margaret refilled my pot. 'It wasn't there last week, master.'

'Are you sure?'

She ignored the question, treating it with the contempt it deserved.

My brain was still fighting yesterday's fumes. I screwed up my eyes and tried to focus on the words. First, the three names. Then two initials. DY — a name so well known that initials sufficed for it?

'Bring me a roll and some butter.'

She went away. I sat there, staring into nothing. Clifford's Inn. A scrap of paper stained with blood. A few names. It unsettled me that my father's ramblings had contained a grain of sense. He really had strayed into a place of lawyers. But he could have picked the paper up anywhere.

The door from the yard opened and closed. There were footsteps in the scullery passage, and the tap of a crutch on the flagged floor.

Sam appeared in the kitchen doorway. He jerked his head towards the scullery passage and the back door. 'Barty's in the yard.'

I stared at him.

'He won't get any scraps out of me at this hour,' Margaret said tartly. 'Tell him to come back after dinner.'

'Hold your tongue, woman.' Sam looked at me. 'Barty, master. The crossing-sweeper who saw your father. You told me to find

66

him for you. Do you remember? In the Devil?'

Suddenly I was sober, or I felt I was. I stood up, knocking over the bench. 'Bring him in.'

'Best that you go out to him, master.' Margaret wrinkled her nose. 'If you'd be so kind. He stinks.'

'You'll give him something to eat,' I said. 'Take it out to him.'

'Something you should know, sir,' Sam said. 'Barty says he saw your father again.'

'What the devil are you talking about?'

Sam's voice was gentle. 'On Friday morning. As well as on Thursday.'

There was a moment of silence. My mouth was open. Margaret stood with a pan in her hand, leaning forward to put it on the fire, as still as a statue.

I swallowed. I said slowly, 'Last Friday, you mean? The day my father died?'

Sam nodded.

'Did he see what happened?'

'He'll only speak to you. I'm no use to him. You're the one with the purse.'

Margaret whimpered softly. She set the pan on the fire.

'Why didn't he tell us sooner?'

'He was taken up for debt that very afternoon. It's only yesterday evening his

67

mother raised the money to get him out of prison.'

Sam hopped down the passage and into the yard. I followed. Over his shoulder, I saw the crossing-sweeper sitting on the side of the trough that caught the rainwater. He was huddled in a filthy cloak with his hat drawn low over his ears. He was a crooked man with a sallow countenance.

When he saw us, he sprang up and executed a clumsy bow. Then he shrank back into his cloak as if he wanted to make himself as small as possible.

'Sam says you saw my father on the day he died,' I said. 'As well as the day before, when you brought him back here.'

Barty nodded so violently that his hat fell off, exposing a bald patch covered in scabs, below which a fringe of greasy hair straggled towards his shoulders. He licked his lips. 'You won't make me go before a justice, master? Please, sir.'

'Not if you tell me the truth.'

'I done nothing wrong.' He looked from me to Sam with the eyes of a dog that fears a beating.

'Tell me,' I said. 'You won't be the poorer for it.'

'It was like Thursday, master. He came out of Clifford's Inn again, down to Fleet

68

Street. He was in a terrible hurry, and he knocked against a bookstall there, and the bookseller swore at him . . .'

Sam nudged him with his elbow. 'Tell his honour the rest.'

Barty screwed up his face. 'He was looking back over his shoulder. As if someone was chasing him.'

'What?' I snapped. 'Who?'

'Couldn't see, sir. There was a wagon coming down from St Paul's, and a coach coming the other way, under the Bar. But I thought I'd go over and give the old fellow a helping hand, like I done the other day.'

'Hoping it would be worth your while,' Sam said. 'You don't have to tell us all that. Go on.'

'Well . . .' Barty looked at me, and then away. 'That's when it happened. The old man tripped — fell into the road — in front of the wagon. But I heard . . .'

I seized his collar and dragged him towards me. Part of me wanted to shake the life out of him. 'What did you hear?'

'His screams, master. His screams.'

I let the wretch go. He fell back against the trough. I was trembling.

'And next?' I said.

'All the traffic stopped. I went over the road to see if . . .'

'If there were pickings to be had?'

He tried to give me an ingratiating smile. 'He was alive still, sir. Just. There was a crowd around him. But he looked up and he saw me there among them. I swear he saw me, master, I swear he did. He knew me. I know he did. He said . . . *Rook. Where's the rook?*'

'Rook,' I said. 'Rook? What rook?'

Barty stared up at me. 'I don't know what he meant, master. But I know he was scared of something.'

'What else?' I demanded.

'That's all he said, master. Then he was gone.'

Later that morning there was a knocking at the door. Sam announced that the tailor had come to wait on me.

I had quite forgotten the appointment, perhaps because I did not want to remember it. Death is a dreary business, time-consuming and expensive, and so is its aftermath. But it would not be right in the eyes of the world if I went abroad without visible signs of my bereavement.

Some of these signs were cheap enough to arrange — before the funeral, I had ordered Margaret to dull the metal of my buckles, attach black silk weepers to my hatband,

and blacken my best brown shoes — including the soles, on Margaret's advice, for they would be visible when I knelt to pray.

I had borrowed a suit of mourning for the funeral but I needed to have my own. On Saturday, I had visited the tailor's shop to be measured, and to choose the material and discuss the pattern. Now the man had come to fit the suit and to try to persuade me to buy a black silk sash to set off the new clothes.

By the time all this was done, my head was clearer, and my stomach had returned to something approaching normality, though the very thought of sack made me feel queasy.

Death has this consequence: it jerks a man from the rut of routine: it throws him back on his own company at a time when he wants it least. All this time, as the tailor prattled away and my mind became my own again, I could not concentrate on anything but the one word: 'rook'. There was nothing to distract me from it.

But what could I do? Find the nearest justice and lay the information before him? What was there to say? That a foolish old man had strayed into Clifford's Inn, and afterwards he had fallen under the wheels of a wagon in Fleet Street. A crossing-sweeper had told me that his last words had been to ask where the rook was.

What crime had been committed? Whom could I lay information against? But I had to do something, for my father's sake.

No. That was a lie. I had to do something for my own sake as much as his. In the hope of easing the grief, the guilt.

When the tailor was gone, I took the tray of my father's possessions upstairs to his chamber. The bed had already been stripped to its mattress and the curtains removed. The floor had been scrubbed and the room aired; Margaret was a vigorous housekeeper.

My father's clothes, such as they were, lay folded in the press. His smell clung to them, faint and unsettling. An old man's smell, musty and familiar. He had left little else behind him apart from his Bible and the contents of his pockets.

He had had the Bible as long as I could remember. It was a Geneva Bible, the old translation favoured by those of a Puritan persuasion. When he had been taken up for treason, he had had the book in prison with him and he read it over and over. When I was a child, he had ordered me never to touch it in case I sullied the sacred volume with the sinful touch of my grubby fingers. Until now, I had obeyed him.

Now the Bible was mine. I took it down to the parlour and laid it on the table, where the light fell on it from the window. I turned the pages, which were brittle and torn. Without my father there, the book had lost its significance. It was still a Bible, of course — the Holy Book, more precious than all the world. The Word of God. I did not dispute that. The volume was dense with wisdom, crammed with essence of holiness. But at the same time it was just a book, a small, shabby copy of something available in its tens of thousands across the country. It needed my father to lend it weight and value.

Fixed with a rusty pin to the back cover was a fold of paper. Inside, I found a lock of light brown hair, the strands twisted together and held in place with a knotted red thread.

Memory ambushed me, swift and vicious as a footpad. 'Rachel . . . how graceful she is, James, even in her kitchen. Why, she is as graceful as a deer.'

I touched the curl of hair, the fragment of my mother, a relic of someone who had been alive, whom my father had once loved and desired. I could not imagine him courting her. I could not imagine my parents being young together, younger than I was. But it seemed that her youthful self had remained so vividly alive in his memory that the image of her had lured him into Clifford's Inn, had lured him among the lawyers.

My father hated them. Lawyers were agents of Satan, servants of the Antichrist. They had helped to put him in prison. Yet desire for his dead wife had cast out all fear of them.

CHAPTER SIX

St Dunstan-in-the-West was partly clothed in scaffolding. The church projected into the street, forcing the roadway into a bottleneck before it passed under the Bar into the Strand. Shops and booths huddled as if for protection against the south aisle wall, blocking more of the pavement and constricting the foot traffic. Though the Fire had not destroyed the church, it had come close enough to cause minor damage and blacken the stonework, particularly at the east end.

The entrance to Clifford's Inn lay at the west end of the nave, squeezed between the square tower of the church and the wall of the neighbouring building. I walked along a flagged passage that took me past the churchyard to a gate. A small, dingy courtyard lay beyond, much wider than it was deep, surrounded by a series of buildings of different sizes and ages.

The hall was directly opposite, filling the right-hand half of the northern range. I followed the path to the doorway at its left-hand end, where people were standing and talking in low voices. Some were lawyers and their clerks. Others were ordinary citizens, both men and women.

They ignored me as I passed like a ghost among them, through the doorway and into the passage that ran through the range to another doorway. The passage was crowded too, though the people were much quieter than those in the courtyard. The door to the hall itself was on the right. It was closed. A porter with his staff stood in front of it.

'Hush, sir,' he said in a savage whisper. 'The court's in session.'

I went out by the further door. I found myself in a much larger courtyard, which had a garden beyond. Over to the left, through another gateway, was Serjeant's Inn, with Chancery Lane beyond, running north from the Strand. To the right was an irregular range of buildings, leading to a further court and then another gate, which gave on to an alley off Fetter Lane. The lane had marked the western boundary of the Fire last September, but the flames had left their mark on both sides of the road. One of the Inn's buildings had been gutted — a block just inside the gate on the north side of the court. The roof was gone and the upper storeys had been partly destroyed.

Clifford's Inn as a whole had an air of dilapidation like an elderly relation in reduced circumstances left unattended in the chimney corner. There was one exception to the general neglect: a brick range facing the garden, on the far side of the blackened ruin.

What had my father said?

'I followed her by a garden to a doorway in a building of brick.'

It was strange indeed. Here was another grain of truth among my father's ramblings on his last evening. First a place full of lawyers, and now a building of brick beside a garden.

The building had four doors at regular intervals along its length, with a pair of windows on either side overlooking the garden. I sauntered across the courtyard towards it in an elaborately casual manner. Each doorway led to a staircase, on either side of which were sets of chambers. The names of the occupants had been painted on a board beside each doorway.

I paused to examine the nearest one. There was something amiss with the lettering. I had spent my early life in the printing

house, and I noticed such things. My father
had made sure of that.

XIV

6 Mr Harrison
5 Mr Moran
4 Mr Gorvin
3 Mr Gromwell
2 Mr Drury
1 Mr Bews

'The letters of a name were most ill-
painted, James, and ill-formed as well.'
My skin prickled at the back of my neck.
It was extraordinary. The board was just as
he had described it. One name had obviously been added more recently than the
others, and by a painter with little skill, and
with no inclination to make the best of what
skill he had. Gromwell.
'There was a great drip attached to it, and
a poor creature had drowned therein.'
It was as if my father's ghost were beside
me, murmuring the words into my ear. Yes,
there was the ant, trapped below the last 'l'
of 'Gromwell', decaying within its rigid
shroud of white paint.
Horror gripped me. If my father had been
right about all this, then what about the
woman he had seen displaying herself like a

78

wanton in a chamber above? The woman with her coach and horses. The woman whose eyes he had closed in the chamber with the ant.

Gromwell's chamber?

I opened the door and climbed the stairs. I did not hurry, partly because I was scared of what I would find. On the first landing, two doors faced each other, numbers 3 and 4. I waited a moment, listening.

'I thought to find her in the chamber with the ant . . . up the stairs . . .'

I knocked on number 3. I heard movement in the room beyond. A tall, florid-faced man opened the door. He wore a morning gown of dark blue plush and a velvet cap. There was a book in his hand, with a finger marking his place. He frowned at me, raised his eyebrows and waited.

'Mr Gromwell?' I said.

It must have sounded like 'Cromwell' to the man's ears. Or perhaps he was merely oversensitive, which was understandable as Oliver Cromwell's head was displayed as a dreadful warning to traitors on a twenty-foot-high spike over Westminster Hall.

'It's Gromwell,' he said, drawing out the syllables. 'G-r-r-romwell with a G. I have no connection with a certain Huntingdonshire family named Cromwell. The G-r-r-

79

romwells have been long established in Gloucestershire. G-r-r-romwell, sir, as in the plant.'

'Whose seeds are used to treat the stone, sir?' I said, remembering a herbal my father had printed.

The eyebrows rose again. 'Indeed. A thing of beauty, too. As Pliny says, it is as if the jeweller's art has arranged the gromwell's gleaming white pearls so symmetrically among the leaves. Sir Thomas Browne calls it *lithospermon* in his *Pseudodoxia Epidemica.*'

I bowed in the face of so much learning. Behind Mr Gromwell was a table piled high with books.

'Forgive me for disturbing your studies.' I shifted my stance, so I could see further to the left. I couldn't see a carpet. All I could make out was an expanse of bare boards and a grubby rush mat. 'My name is Marwood. I wonder if my late father called on you last week.'

Gromwell frowned, and I guessed he was taking account of my mourning clothes for the first time. 'Your late father?'

Over the fireplace was a dusty mirror in a gilt frame that had seen better times, but no trace of a painting, lewd or otherwise.

'He died the day after he came here.'

'I am sorry to hear it.' Mr Gromwell did not look prosperous but he had a gentleman's manners. 'But I have been away. My rooms were locked up.'

He took a step back. His arm nudged the door, which swung further open, revealing most of the room. There wasn't a couch of any description, let alone one with a body on it. None of the furnishings could be called luxurious. I felt both relieved and disappointed. It was remarkable that my father had recalled so much. Once he had entered the building, his imagination must have taken over. But I persevered.

'I am much occupied with business at present,' Gromwell said in a stately fashion. 'I bid you good day, sir.

'Does the name Twisden mean anything to you, sir?' I asked. 'Or Wyndham? Or Rainsford?'

He shook his head. 'Forgive me, sir, my studies —'

'Or the initials DY?'

Gromwell's face changed. For an instant, he looked surprised, jolted out of his stateliness. His features sharpened, which made them look briefly younger. 'No,' he said, more firmly than he had said anything yet. 'Good day to you.'

He closed the door in my face. I knocked

on it. The only answer was the sound of a bolt being driven home.

CHAPTER SEVEN

The young woman sat in the gallery taking shorthand. Her real name was Catherine Lovett, but most of the time she tried very hard to forget that inconvenient fact. Now she was Jane Hakesby, a maidservant attending the Fire Court at Clifford's Inn to serve her master, Simon Hakesby, who was also a second cousin of her father's. She was a maidservant with accomplishments, equipped with some of the advantages of gentle breeding, though few of them were much use to her at present. In her new life, only Mr Hakesby knew her true identity.

She did not intend to be a maidservant for ever. On her knee was a notebook held flat with the palm of her left hand. A steadily lengthening procession of pencilled marks marched across the open page, meaningless except to the initiated.

In the hall below, the court was in session, dealing with the last of the day's cases.

There were three judges at the round table on the low dais at the east end. The clerks and ushers clustered to one side, making notes of the proceedings and scuttling forward when a judge beckoned, bringing a book or a letter or a fresh pen. The petitioner and the defendants, together with their representatives, stood in the space immediately in front of the dais.

There was a lull in the proceedings — perhaps five seconds — during which no one spoke, and the court seemed to pause to draw breath. Her mind wandered. Her pencil followed. *His wig's crooked,* she wrote. *Judge on left.* Then a lawyer cleared his throat and the talking and arguing began again.

The hall was cramped and shabby. Clifford's Inn was not a grand establishment on the scale of the Temple, its stately colleague on the other side of the Fleet Street. Even in May, the air was chilly and damp. In the middle of the floor, a brazier of coal smouldered in the square hearth. The heat rose with the smoke to the blackened roof timbers and drifted uselessly through the louvred chimney into the ungrateful sky.

Jane Hakesby was sitting in the gallery at the west end, though a little apart from the other women. Her notebook rested on a copy of Shelton's *Tachygraphy.* She was in the process of teaching herself shorthand, and the Fire Court provided her with useful practice. Most of the women were in a whispering huddle at the back, where the judges could not see them. Sometimes they glanced at her, their faces blank, their eyes hard. She knew why. She did not belong among them so they disliked her automatically.

'All rise,' cried the clerk. 'All rise.'

The court rose to its feet as the judges retired to their parlour to confer on their verdict. Jane Hakesby looked down at the floor of the hall. Below her was a bobbing pool of men's hats. Benches had been fixed along the side walls, and it was here that the elderly and the infirm sat. From her vantage point at the front of the gallery, she saw the brim of Mr Hakesby's best hat and the folds of the dark wool cloak he usually reserved for church and high days and holidays. Even his best cloak was shabby.

Hakesby did not have a direct interest in the case under consideration. He was here on behalf of the freeholder to keep watch over his interests. The dispute itself was an involved and bad-tempered affair between the leaseholder and three of his subtenants about which of them would be responsible

85

for rebuilding their houses after the Fire, and how the cost of doing so would affect the terms of their leases and sub-leases. The Government had set up the court solely for the purpose of settling such disputes, with the aim of encouraging the rebuilding of the city as soon as possible.

Mr Hakesby's white hand rested on his leg. Even at this distance, she made out that the fingers were trembling. A familiar sense of dread crept through her, and settled in her stomach. She had hoped that as the weather improved, his health would improve with it. But if anything his ague grew worse.

And if it grew so bad he could not work, what would become of her?

In a while the judges returned with their verdict, which found in favour of the subtenants but varied the terms of their leases in the leaseholder's favour. The judges departed and the hall began to empty.

Jane Hakesby allowed the other women to leave before her. She kept her head down as they filed past her to the stairs, pretending to study a page of *Tachygraphy*. It was improbable that any of them would recognize her, or rather recognize her as who she had been, but old habits died hard. In a moment she followed them down to the passage at the end of the hall.

There were doors at either end of the passage, one to the small court bounded by the Fleet Street gate, the other to the garden court that contained most of the other buildings of Clifford's Inn. Mr Hakesby emerged from the hall and touched her arm. She took his folder of papers and offered him her arm. He pretended not to see it. Leaning on his stick, he made his way slowly towards the north doorway, leaving her to trail behind him.

He was a proud man. It was one thing to show weakness to his maidservant, but quite another to show it to the world, especially to that part of the world that knew him. But she was learning how to manage him.

'The sun is out, sir,' she said. 'I found it so cold in the hall. Would you permit me to sit in the garden for a moment?'

But he wasn't attending to her. He stopped suddenly. 'Good God,' she heard him say.

She looked past him. Her eyes widened. Without thinking, she took a step backwards, ready for flight. Here was someone who belonged to her old life.

'Mr Marwood,' Hakesby said, his voice trembling. 'Your servant, sir.'

She recognized him at once, which was strange. James Marwood looked different

87

from before — he seemed taller, and he was dressed in mourning. He was also out of place at Clifford's Inn. He belonged among the clerks of Whitehall, not here among the lawyers. Most of all, though, her instant recognition was strange because she had seen him properly only once, and then by the light of candles and lanterns, and at a time when she had other things on her mind. She wondered who was dead.

Mr Hakesby glanced over his shoulder at her. He turned back.

'Good day to you, sir,' Marwood said, his voice cautious as though he was uncertain of his welcome. His eyes slid towards her but he did not greet her.

'And to you . . .' Hakesby hesitated and then went on in haste, as if to have the information off his chest as soon as possible. 'And here is my cousin Jane. Jane,' he repeated with emphasis, as if teaching a lesson, 'Jane Hakesby. She's come up to London to be my servant at the drawing office.'

She dropped a token curtsy. Four months earlier, Marwood had saved her life in the ruins of St Paul's. Apart from Hakesby himself, only Marwood knew that Jane Hakesby was really Catherine Lovett, the daughter of a Regicide who had died last year while plotting against the King.

'And what brings you here, sir?' Hakesby asked.

'An enquiry, sir. And you?'

Hakesby nodded towards the hall. 'The Fire Court has been in session.'

'Do you often attend?'

'As occasion requires. When I have clients whose interests are concerned.'

Marwood drew closer. 'I wonder — indulge me a moment, pray — do the names Twisden, Wyndham or Rainsford mean anything to you?'

'There's Sir Wadham Wyndham — he's a justice of the King's Bench, and he sits sometimes at the Fire Court. In fact, he was one of the judges sitting there today. Could it be him?'

'Perhaps. And the others?'

'I don't know the names. Could they be connected with the Fire Court as well? You should ask Theophilus Chelling. He's the Fire Court's assistant clerk. He will know if anyone does.'

'I'm not acquainted with him.'

'I'll introduce you now, if you wish.' Hakesby's eyes moved to his maid and then back to Marwood. 'I believe there can't be any harm in it.'

Marwood murmured his thanks, and Hakesby led the way to a doorway in the building that joined the hall range at a right angle. Marwood walked by his side. Jane Hakesby trailed after them, as a servant should.

They climbed stairs of dark wood rising into the gloom of the upper floors. Hakesby's trembling increased as they climbed, and he was obliged to take Marwood's arm. The two doors leading to the first-floor apartments were tall and handsome modern additions. On the second floor, the ceilings were lower, the doorways narrower, and the doors themselves were blackened oak as old as the stone that framed them.

Hakesby knocked on the door to the right, and a booming voice commanded them to enter. Mr Chelling rose as they entered. His body and head belonged to a tall man, but nature had seen fit to equip him with very short arms and legs. Grey hair framed a face that was itself on a larger scale than the features that adorned it. The top of his head was on a level with Jane Hakesby's shoulders.

'Mr Hakesby — how do you do, sir?'

Hakesby said he was very well, which was palpably untrue, and asked how Chelling did.

Chelling threw up his arms. 'I wish I could say the same.'

'Allow me to introduce Mr Marwood.'

'Your servant, sir.' Chelling sketched a bow.

'I am sorry to hear that you're not well, sir,' Marwood said.

'I am well enough in my body.' Chelling puffed out his chest. 'It's the fools I deal with every day that make me unwell. Not the judges, sir, oh no — they are perfect lambs. It's the authorities at Clifford's Inn that hamper my work. And then there's the Court of Aldermen — they will not provide us with the funds we need for the day-to-day administration of the Fire Court, which makes matters so much worse.'

Uninvited, Hakesby sank on to a stool. His maid and Marwood remained standing.

Chelling wagged a plump finger at them. 'You will be surprised to hear that we have already used ten skins of parchment, sir, for the fair copies of the judgements, together with a ream of finest Amsterdam paper. Scores of quills, too — and sand, naturally, for blotting, and a quart or so of ink. I say nothing of the carpenter's bill and the tallow-chandler's, and the cost of charcoal — I assure you, sir, the expense is considerable.'

Hakesby nodded. 'Indeed, it is quite beyond belief, sir.'

91

'It's not as if we waste money here. All of us recognize the need to be prudent. The judges give their time without charge, for the good of the country. But we must have ready money, sir — you would grant me that, I think? With the best will in the world, the court cannot run itself on air.'

Chelling paused to draw breath. Before he could speak, Hakesby plunged in.

'Mr Marwood and I had dealings with each other over St Paul's just after the Fire. I was working with Dr Wren, assessing the damage to the fabric, while my Lord Arlington sent Marwood there to gather information from us.' When he had a mind to it, Hakesby was almost as unstoppable as Mr Chelling himself. 'I met him as I was coming out of court just now. He has a question about the judges, and I said I know just the man to ask. So here we are, sir, here we are.'

'Whitehall, eh?' Chelling said, turning back to Marwood. 'Under my Lord Arlington?'

Marwood bowed. 'Yes, sir. I'm clerk to his under-secretary, Mr Williamson. I'm also the clerk of the Board of Red Cloth, when it meets.'

'Red Cloth? I don't think I know it.'

'It's in the Groom of the Stool's department, sir. The King's Bedchamber.'

Mr Chelling cocked his head, and his manner became markedly more deferential. 'How interesting, sir. The King's Bedchamber? A word in the right ear would work wonders for us here. It's not just money, you see. I meet obstructions at every turn from the governors of this Inn. That's even worse.'

Marwood bowed again, implying his willingness to help without actually committing himself. There was a hint of the courtier about him now, Jane Hakesby thought, or at least of a man privy to Government secrets. She did not much care for it. He moved his head slightly and the light fell on his face. He no longer looked like a courtier. He looked ill.

She wondered who was dead. Had there been a mother? A father? She could not remember — she had probably never known. For a man who had changed her life, she knew remarkably little about James Marwood. Only that without him she might well be dead or in prison.

'Mr Marwood has a question for you, sir,' Hakesby said.

Marwood nodded. 'It's a trifling matter. I came across three names — Twisden, Wyndham and Rainsford. I understand there is a Sir Wadham Wyndham, who is one of the

Fire Court judges, and —'

'Ah, sir, the judges.' Chelling rapped the table beside him for emphasis. 'Mr Hakesby has brought you to the right man. I know Sir Wadham well. Indeed, I'm acquainted with all the judges. We have a score or so of them. They use the set of chambers below these, the ones on the first floor, which are larger than ours. We have given them a remarkably airy sitting room, though I say it myself who had it prepared for them, and also a retiring room and a closet. Only the other day, the Lord Chief Justice was kind enough to say to me how commodious the chambers were, and how convenient for the Fire Court.'

'And do the judges include —'

'Oh yes — Sir Wadham is one, as I said, and so is Sir Thomas Twisden. Sir Thomas has been most assiduous in his attendance. A most distinguished man. I remember —'

'And Rainsford?' Marwood put in.

'Why yes, Sir Richard, but —'

'Forgive me, sir, one last question. Do any of the other judges have the initials DY?'

Chelling frowned, and considered. 'I cannot recall. Wait, I have a list here.' He shuffled the documents on his table and produced a paper which he studied for a moment. 'No — no one.' He looked up, and his small, bloodshot eyes stared directly at Marwood. 'Why do you ask?'

'I regret, sir, I am not at liberty to say.'

Chelling winked. 'Say no more, sir. Whitehall business, perhaps, but I ask no questions. Discretion is our watchword.'

Marwood bowed. 'Thank you for your help, sir. I mustn't keep you any longer.'

'You must let me know if there is any other way I can oblige you.' Chelling tried to smile but his face refused to cooperate fully. 'And if the opportunity arises, I hope you will not forget us.'

'You may be sure of it, sir.'

'If the King but knew of our difficulties, especially with our governors who —'

'Mr Gromwell, is it?' Hakesby interrupted, beginning to rise to his feet. 'Is he still putting obstacles in your way?'

'Gromwell, sir?' Marwood said. 'The name is familiar.'

'Then I pity you, sir.' Chelling waved his hand, as if consigning Gromwell to a place of outer darkness. 'It would be better for the world if he were entirely unknown.'

'Why? What has he done?'

'He is one of our Rules — that is to say, the members who are elected to govern the affairs of Clifford's Inn. He is particularly charged with overseeing the fabric of the place, and its maintenance. I regret to say that he's no friend to the Fire Court.'

'But you are paying something for the use of the hall, I suppose?'

'Of course we are — and for these chambers — but he thinks we do not pay enough for the privilege. He ignores entirely the *pro bono* aspect of the matter.' Chelling pointed out of the window. 'The other day I asked if we could use the fire-damaged staircase over there for storage. It would ease our lives considerably, and cost him absolutely nothing. It's no use to anyone else at present. But he refused point-blank.'

Marwood bowed again. 'I'm sorry to hear it, sir.'

Chelling returned the bow, and almost toppled over. 'If only the King were aware . . .'

By this time, Hakesby had managed to stand up. She came forward to offer her arm — he was often unsteady when he had been sitting down — but Marwood was before her. The three of them said goodbye to Mr Chelling and went slowly downstairs.

'Poor man,' Hakesby murmured. 'Clinging to his duties at the Fire Court as a drowning man clings to a straw. Chelling has many excellent qualities, but he's been unfortunate all his life, partly because of his stature.'

They emerged into the sunlight. Marwood looked at Jane Hakesby and, she knew, saw Catherine Lovett.

She stared back at him, hoping he would leave them.

Hakesby turned towards them. 'Will you dine with us, sir?'

CHAPTER EIGHT

The Lamb was in Wych Street, just to the north of the Strand and set back in a court. It was an aged building with blurred, blackened carvings along the bressumers supporting the upper storeys. It lay conveniently between Mr Hakesby's drawing office at the sign of the Rose in Henrietta Street and the house where he lodged in Three Cocks Yard. Shops lined the ground floor, and the tavern was above.

The landlord conducted them to a small chamber, poorly lit by a mullioned window overlooking a yard. Hakesby ordered their dinner, with wine and biscuits to be brought while they waited. Jane Hakesby worried about the cost.

Marwood slipped on to a bench that faced away from the light. She set down her basket and sat opposite, beside Mr Hakesby who took the only chair. She examined him covertly. His face was pale, the skin stretched tight over the high cheekbones and smudged with tiredness beneath the eyes.

He had agreed to come with them, but without much enthusiasm. It was as if it didn't really matter what he did. He ate a biscuit, and then another, which brought some of the colour back to his face.

He caught her looking at him. 'How do you do, mistress?' He left the briefest of pauses and added with a slight emphasis, 'Hakesby.'

The 'mistress' pleased her, however foolish of her that was. 'I do very well, thank you, sir.'

He turned to Hakesby. 'I don't wish to cause trouble. You don't mind being seen with me?'

'We've heard nothing to alarm us, sir,' Hakesby murmured. 'About the other matter.' They were quite alone but he shifted uneasily and leaned closer. 'I have no idea if Mr Alderley is still looking for Catherine Lovett.'

The men exchanged glances. The Alderleys were her cousins. She hated her cousin Edward more than anyone in the world.

'I've heard nothing either,' Marwood said. 'Nothing of any moment.'

'Catherine Lovett has become Jane

99

Hakesby,' Hakesby said. 'Why, I almost believe it myself. She makes herself useful at the drawing office.'

'I am still myself, sir,' she said sharply. 'And I am here beside you. I do not forget who I am and what is owed me. Nor do I forget who has harmed me.' She glared impartially at them. 'In this company at least, I am Catherine Lovett.'

Hakesby shied away. 'Pray don't upset yourself.'

She saw the alarm in his face. 'You mustn't mind me, sir. When I was a child, they called me Cat. I have claws.'

Marwood said, 'Are you content?'

'I am a maidservant, sir. I assist Mr Hakesby in his business. I live a quiet life. What more could I possibly want?' She heard the bitterness in her voice and abruptly changed the subject. 'Who are you in mourning for?'

Marwood seemed to huddle into his black cloak like a tortoise retiring into his shell. Hakesby cleared his throat, filling the silence. Her abrupt, unwomanly behaviour made him uneasy. He had grown used to it in private, but he did not like it when she spoke so directly to others.

'My father. On Friday.' Marwood finished his second glass of wine. 'He was run over by a wagon in Fleet Street.'

'I'm sorry to hear it, sir,' Hakesby said.

'I mustn't bore you with my troubles. Tell me about the Court where these three judges sit. Why would they be listed together?'

'Because the Fire Court usually consists of three judges to hear each case,' Hakesby said, a little stiffly because Marwood had rebuffed his attempt at sympathy. 'Perhaps there was a particular case that came before these three. Or there will be.'

'Three judges for a trial?'

'Not a trial, sir. The Court exists to resolve disputes arising from the Fire. Parliament and the City are anxious that rebuilding should begin as soon as possible, and that the costs should be shared fairly among all the concerned parties. In many cases the tenants and so forth are still liable to pay rent for properties that no longer exist. Not only that, the terms of their leases make them responsible for the rebuilding. Often, of course, they lack the means to do so because they lost everything in the Fire. So Parliament set up the Fire Court, and gave it exceptional powers to settle such disputes and set its own precedents.'

'There must be a list of forthcoming cases,' Marwood said. 'If I knew which ones were coming up before those three . . .'

Hakesby said: 'It depends which judges are available.'

'Mr Chelling would know,' Cat said. 'As far as anyone does.'

'Yes, but the selection is not usually made public until the last moment. To prevent annoyance to the judges. They don't want to be pestered.'

Marwood hesitated. 'I'd rather not trouble Mr Chelling again.'

Hakesby smiled. 'He has a loose tongue. And your . . . your connections impressed him mightily. He will try to make use of you if he can. He will tell the world you're his friend.'

'But if you were to make the enquiries, sir,' Cat said to Hakesby, 'and in a fashion that suggested the matter had to do with something quite different, one of your own clients . . .'

'Would you, sir?' Marwood said, his face sharp and hungry.

Hakesby hesitated. 'I am pressed for business at present, and I —'

'He means, sir,' Cat interrupted, impatient with this unnecessary playacting, 'would you do something for us in return?'

'Jane!' Hakesby said. 'This is not polite.'

'I don't care much about being polite, sir.'

'What do you want?' Marwood said, returning bluntness for bluntness.

'Would you lend Mr Hakesby some money?'

'Jane!'

Cat and Marwood stared at each other. Perhaps, she thought, she had made him angry by asking him a favour at such a time. But he looked prosperous enough. And there was no room for sentiment. Didn't one good turn deserve another? This was a matter of business, after all, an exchange of services.

'Well,' Mr Hakesby said uncertainly. 'Taken all in all, I can't deny that a loan would be most welcome.'

After dinner, Hakesby and Cat took a hackney back to Henrietta Street.

To be Jane Hakesby in Henrietta Street was Cat's refuge, for the Government did not care for her. The reputation of her dead father and her dead uncle clung to her like a bad smell, and her living cousin wished her harm.

But Mr Hakesby's drawing office was more than a refuge: it was a place where, if she were fortunate, she could pursue the one occupation she preferred above all others: like the great Roman architect Vitruvius, she dreamed of designing buildings that would be solid, beautiful and useful, 'like the nests of birds and bees'.

The hackney meant more expense, Cat thought, but it could not be helped. They did not speak during the journey until the end, when Hakesby turned to Cat.

'I wish you had not asked Marwood for money. And so bluntly.'

'Do we have a choice, sir?'

As they climbed the stairs, Hakesby reached for Cat's arm. Floor after floor they climbed, and the higher they rose, the tighter his grip and the slower his step.

The drawing office was on the top floor. It was a converted attic that stretched the width of the house, with wide dormer windows to make the most of the light. Two drawing slopes were set up at an angle to the windows, each one separate from the others, so they could be turned individually to increase or occasionally reduce the light that fell on them from the windows.

As Mr Hakesby and Cat entered the room, Brennan laid down his pen, rose from his stool and bowed to his master.

'Any callers?' Hakesby said, making his way to his chair.

'No, master.' Brennan's eyes strayed towards Cat. 'I've finished inking the north elevation if you care to inspect it.'

Hakesby lowered himself into his chair. 'Good. Bring it here.' His finger flicked towards Cat. 'Then I shall dictate a note to my lord.'

Cat hung up her cloak. In this case, my lord was the freeholder for whom Hakesby had held a watching brief at the Fire Court this morning. While she gathered her writing materials together, she watched the two men studying the elevation. Or rather she watched Brennan. He watched her so she watched him.

Brennan had been working here for less than three weeks. He had come with a letter of recommendation from none other than Dr Wren himself, with whom Hakesby had worked on several projects. He had been one of the men working on the Sheldonian Theatre in Oxford, helping to adjust the designs after discussions with the masons employed on building the theatre. He was certainly a good draughtsman, Cat gave him that, and a fast worker too.

In this next hour, Cat took dictation from Mr Hakesby for the letters, wrote a fair copy for him to sign, and copied it again into the letter book as a record. It was not work she enjoyed but it was work she could do. Afterwards her reward came: she was allowed to work on the plans for a house and yard in Throgmorton Street — routine work, but with details she could make her own, subject to Mr Hakesby's approval.

Brennan was behind her, and she felt his eyes on her. Her skin crawled. She twisted on her stool, presenting him with a view of her shoulder. The afternoon was drawing towards its end, and the light was changing. She took her dividers and pricked first one hole in the paper before her and then another. She laid the steel rule between them and, frowning with concentration, pencilled a line, a mere shadow, on the paper.

There. The base of the architrave. And now, at an angle of twenty degrees —

Her irritation faded as the lines of the east façade spread across the paper. In her mind, the same lines sprang up, newly translated from two dimensions to three, acquiring solidity as well as depth, existing in space and time. The miracle was familiar but no less astonishing for that.

While the two of them worked at their slopes, Mr Hakesby sat by the fire, reading and occasionally making notes in his crabbed hand. At present he was checking accounts and invoices, and scribbling notes on the margins of letters. He had caused a carpenter to fix a board to each arm of his chair, and these he used as a desk. His handwriting was now almost illegible, because of the ague. On a bad day, even Cat found it hard to read.

Time passed. The light faded. The bells of surrounding churches chimed seven o'clock, though not quite at the same time.

Mr Hakesby dismissed Brennan for the day. The draughtsman was due an extra fee for a piece of work he had done at home. Hakesby found the money in his purse himself and told Cat to make a note of the payment. She added it to the current sheet of sundry expenses. Glancing back, she saw an alarming number of entries already. She drew up a rough total in her head, and the amount staggered her. There were two months to go until the quarterly rent on the drawing office was due at midsummer.

The draughtsman came over to where she was sitting so she could pay him the money and initial the entry as a receipt. At that moment, Mr Hakesby retired to his closet to answer a call of nature.

Brennan took his time. He stood very close to Cat's stool. He was fair complexioned, with pink cheeks and a sprinkling of freckles on his nose. He wore his own hair, which was sandy in colour. Cat saw two grey lice squatting among the roots where it fell into a parting on the left-hand side of his scalp.

He laid down the pen and blew on his initials to dry them. Cat felt his breath touch her cheek. Involuntarily, she turned her head. He took up the paper. He stared at her with pale eyes, neither blue nor grey, that made her think of pebbles on a shingle beach.

She held out her hand for the paper, anxious for him to be gone. His hand touched hers. She snatched it away.

'Less haste,' he said, smiling, 'more speed. What's the hurry?'

He leaned on the table, resting on his right hand. His left hand touched her neck in a caress which was as light as a feather. She seized her dividers and jabbed them between his index and middle fingers, missing them by a fraction of an inch on either side. He snatched his hand away. The points of the dividers had passed through the expenses sheet and dug into the wood of the table.

He raised his hand. 'God damn you, you could have stabbed me. My right hand, too.'

'Next time I will stab you.' Cat tugged the dividers free from the table and turned the points towards him. 'And it won't be your hand.'

'Ah.' He lowered his arm and grinned at her, exposing long, yellow canines. 'A vixen. I like a woman with spirit.'

The closet door opened. Brennan sauntered over to the peg where his cloak was hanging.

'Why are you still here, Brennan?' Hakesby said. 'I thought you'd be gone by now.'

The draughtsman had recovered his composure. 'Talking to Jane, sir.' He bowed low. 'I wish you goodnight.'

'He promises well,' Mr Hakesby said as his footsteps sounded on the stairs. 'Particularly on the fine detail. Dr Wren was right.'

Cat busied herself with throwing another shovel of coals on the fire, keeping her face averted to conceal her rising colour. The fire was a luxury at this time of year. More expense. Hakesby craved warmth, a symptom of his illness. His blood ran cold nowadays, he said. Colder and colder. She stood up and looked at him.

'Come here,' he said.

She put down the shovel and stood beside his chair.

'This damnable question of money,' he said. 'I wish I had not taken yours.'

'Sir, you had no choice in the matter.

Neither of us did. If you hadn't taken it, both of us would have starved.'

Cat had lent him sixty pounds in gold on Lady Day, all the money she had in the world, taken from her dead father's body. Hakesby had been behindhand last quarter's rent and the wages for his employees. He had owed his own landlady for two months' board, and there had been a host of other debts. The commissions were flowing in but few clients paid promptly for the work. With luck, most of the money would come in its own good time, and they would be more comfortable, but in the meantime they all had to live.

'Money confers an obligation,' he said. 'I'm worried I may not be able to discharge it.'

'Of course you will. But at present we need ready money. Which is why Marwood was a gift from heaven, sir. If you go to a moneylender, they would rob you.'

'I can't get reasonable terms.' Hakesby held up his right hand. The bony fingers fluttered. 'This grows worse.'

'It's been a hard winter, sir. Everyone says so. But now summer is here, the warmth will soon —'

'I have seen the doctors. This ague of mine will not get better. In time, it may touch the mind, as well as the body. With your help, and Brennan's, and perhaps another draughtsman's, we shall manage for a few months, perhaps a few years. But then . . .'

'We shall contrive somehow,' Cat said. 'If you rest more and worry less, the ague will progress more slowly.'

'And how will I pay you back if I cannot work? Or Marwood?'

'You give me shelter, sir, and you give me work. That is repayment. We'll manage with Marwood. He looks prosperous enough to be kept waiting a little.'

After a pause, he said: 'What will become of you if I'm not here?'

A silence spread between them. Cat did not want to think about the possibility of Hakesby's death. It was not just the trembling that was growing worse, it was the depression of his spirits.

Hakesby straightened in his chair, squaring his shoulders as if for a fight. 'Fetch me the ledger, Jane. We shall reckon up the accounts. Let us find out how bad matters really are.'

CHAPTER NINE

'My husband,' Jemima said, sitting at her dressing table in Pall Mall and staring sideways at her reflection in the mirror, 'is a fortunate man.'

And Mary, whose own reflection shimmered and shifted behind her mistress's, murmured like a mangled echo, 'Yes, my lady, the master is very fortunate. I'm sure he knows it too.'

Yes, Jemima thought, and when my father dies and Syre Place and everything else is mine, he will be even more fortunate. Because of me. When her father died, her husband would have the management of Syre Place and everything that went with it. Including herself — unless she could learn the art of managing him.

When she was ready, she descended the stairs, one hand on the rail of the bannisters, the other clutching Mary's arm. She wore her grey taffeta, sombre yet elegant, and a pendant with a diamond the size of a pigeon's egg. Mary had dressed her hair and applied the patches and powders to her face.

Rather than go directly to the dining room, where there was already a murmur of voices, she went halfway down the stairs to the kitchen. The smells of their dinner came up to meet her, and made her feel queasy. For a moment her hand touched her belly. Was it possible she could be pregnant?

In the kitchen, the birds were turning on the spit over the fire, the fat sizzling as it dropped on to the hungry flames. The cook and the scullery maid curtsied, Hal the coachman doffed his hat and made his obedience, and the boy, Hal's son, tried to hide behind the scullery door until Hal dragged him into the open and cuffed him so hard he fell against the wall. The Limburys did not maintain a large establishment in London — all of their servants were in the kitchen, apart from Richard and Hester, who were serving at table upstairs, and the gardener.

Without speaking, Jemima stared at them. She had sent Mary down with her orders. But it was good to show oneself in the kitchen too, even if one didn't want to. Marriage was a contract, her father had told her, and she would fulfil her part of it, to the

113

letter, even if her husband faltered in his.

Faltered. What a puny, insignificant, inadequate word.

'Well?' she said.

The cook curtsied again. 'Yes, my lady. Everything as it should be.'

She held the cook's eye for a moment, as her mother had taught her to do all those years ago at Syre Place, and then let her eyes drift over the other upturned faces, from one to the next.

'The guinea fowl will turn to cinders if you don't have a care.'

The cook gave a strangled yelp and dived towards the fireplace. Without a word, Jemima tightened her hold on Mary's arm and turned. As they climbed the stairs to the hall, she felt as much as heard the rush of pent-up breaths escaping in the kitchen below.

In the hall, she hesitated. She had not seen Philip since he had come to her chamber the previous afternoon, though this morning he had sent up to make sure that she would dine with them today. She did not like meeting strangers, even in her own house. She did not want to see Philip, either.

As if sensing her mistress's anxiety, Mary touched her hand and murmured: 'You look very fine, my lady. I've never seen you look better.'

In the dining room, the gentlemen rose and bowed as she entered, and Richard moved forward at once to help her. Richard was Philip's servant, brought with him from his other life before their marriage. He wore his livery and had his teeth in, so he made a respectable show. Mary said he hated to wear his teeth because they hurt his gums.

Jemima curtsied to the gentlemen and allowed herself to be assisted to her chair.

'My wife has not been well these last few days,' Philip said, 'but she would not keep to her bed when she knew you would be dining with us, Sir Thomas. And our old friend Gromwell too.'

'What a charming diamond,' Gromwell said, staring admiringly but respectfully in the direction of Jemima's bosom. For all her dislike of him, she was forced to concede that he was a tall, fine-looking gentleman. He had once known great prosperity but his fortunes were now much reduced. 'My Lady Castlemaine was wearing one that was very like, only the other day, but it wasn't nearly so fine. Smaller, too.'

'It was my mother's,' Jemima said coolly, impervious to his attempt to charm her. The last time they had met, at Clifford's Inn, his

115

charm had been in short supply.

'Quite outstanding,' he murmured, leaving it discreetly ambiguous whether the compliment referred to her diamond or her bosom.

Sir Thomas cleared his throat and ventured into a complex and finely nuanced expression of opinion, which, though initially obscure, seemed to suggest that in this case the wearer adorned the diamond, rather than the other way round.

Philip smiled down the table at her, his brown eyes soft and adoring. It was a smile designed to melt the heart and during their courtship it had melted hers, against her better judgement. 'Lucius is right, my love,' he said, 'and Sir Thomas too — you look very well today, better than ever perhaps, if that can be possible.'

'How can one improve upon perfection?' Gromwell enquired; his manners were courtly though, like his yellow suit, they were a trifle old-fashioned. 'But my lady has. Behold, a double miracle, a miracle of both nature and logic.'

'You are pleased to jest, sir,' she said automatically, and twitched her lips into what could pass as a smile.

'I never jest on sacred matters, madam.'

You parasite, she thought, and smiled and

nodded her head while the gentlemen laughed and toasted her. Duty done, they went back to their conversation.

'I had no idea you would be sitting on the Dragon Yard petition,' Philip said to Sir Thomas. 'What a coincidence.' As Jemima knew to her cost, he had the knack of speaking the clumsiest, crudest lie with such assurance that it became a self-evident truth. 'It is so truly admirable that you judges sit for love of country, and for the city, and not for gold. You will be a pattern for future generations.' He raised his glass. 'A toast. Good health and prosperity to our Fire Court judges.'

They drank solemnly, and Hester came to the door with the guinea fowl, now dressed for table in their sauce. Jemima tasted a morsel and found the dish perfectly cooked, which pleased her, for she had pride in the food served at her table, as in other matters that belonged to her.

'I sometimes attend these hearings myself, sir,' Gromwell said. 'Not that I have a pecuniary interest in them, you understand, but for the sheer quality of the judgements.'

'You're a lawyer, sir?' Sir Thomas asked. 'I don't think I've had the pleasure of seeing you in court.'

'I've never practised, sir. As a young man,

however, I passed many profitable hours in the study of the law, and I believe I retain the ability to appreciate a well-argued case' — he bowed towards Sir Thomas — 'and a well-considered verdict.'

The gentlemen ate, and drank, and drank again. The room grew warmer. Sir Thomas was obliged to retire behind the screen to relieve himself. Jemima wanted to laugh at them, at their mockery of good fellowship, but instead she picked at her food and smiled at the compliments which were thrown her way like scraps to the bitch under the table; occasionally, as a well-bred hostess should, she threw in the sort of question designed less to elicit information than to allow the hearer to shine in his answer. But she said nothing to Gromwell.

Later — half an hour? an hour? — the conversation returned to the subject of the Fire Court. 'It is not a court of law,' Sir Thomas was saying, apparently to herself, 'though our judgements have the force of law, and have the ability to override such things that are usually considered sacrosanct. Leases, for example, and contracts relating to property.'

'And if I understand you correctly, sir,' Gromwell put in with the air of an eager student, 'your judgements do not set a

118

precedent, but apply only to the petition under consideration.'

'Precisely.' Sir Thomas nodded vigorously and held out his glass for more. 'You have understood me perfectly, sir.' He beamed at Gromwell. 'If I may say so, it is the law's loss that you decided to apply your energies in other fields of knowledge. Our powers are intended simply to help London return to its former glory as soon as possible, for the good of the City and the Kingdom as a whole.' He hammered his fist on the table. 'And indeed the world. For does not our trade encircle the entire globe and enrich all it touches?'

This led to another toast, after which Philip said, smiling, 'And if all goes well, sir, with the wise help of the judges, we shall do more than restore London. We shall increase its glories for centuries to come.'

'I suppose Dragon Yard will be a case in point,' Gromwell said. 'Eh, Philip? If the decision next week goes in your favour, that is.'

Here we are, Jemima thought, we have come at last to the point of this tedious meal.

Gromwell turned to the judge. 'I've studied the plans. It's a most noble development, sir, with houses of the first class, laid

119

out and built in a way that will make them proof against future fires. Safe, commodious and an ornament to the City. And also to the benefit of the public and of trade, I understand. It will provide another way to Cheapside, thereby easing the congestion of traffic there.'

Twisden's face became serious; he looked like a flushed owl. 'No doubt, sir, no doubt. Though all that would require considerable investment.'

'We must not weary Sir Thomas with talk of business.' Philip smiled round the table. 'Would you care for a hand or two of cards, sir?'

The judge brightened. 'If her ladyship would not object. And Gromwell too, of course.'

'I should like it above everything,' Gromwell said, smiling. 'What would you say to lanterloo? And perhaps a shilling or two on the outcome?'

'Why not? It adds a certain spice, does it not?'

'I think, sir,' Jemima said, 'if you would not object, and if Sir Thomas and Mr Gromwell would not think me discourteous, I shall leave you to your play.'

'Of course they will excuse you, my love,' Philip said. 'You are not fully yourself yet, and you must not overtire yourself. We can play with three as well as four. Richard? Send for Mary to help her mistress upstairs.'

A moment or two later, she withdrew. Sir Thomas bowed so deeply he stumbled against a chair and almost fell.

'All well, my lady?' Mary said softly as they climbed the stairs.

'Well enough.'

Jemima was tempted to add 'for your master', but held her peace. She would lay good money that Philip would have known beforehand of Twisden's taste for lanterloo, and that he would have arranged with Gromwell for the judge to win a pound or two from each of them.

When he was courting her, Sir Philip Limbury had seemed a creature of impulse, and his love for her had seemed as open and sincere as the sun itself. After their marriage, however, it had not taken her long to learn that he did little or nothing by chance. There was a purpose in almost everything he said and did. Sometimes more than one purpose.

When she was back in her chair by the window, and the chamber door was closed, she called Mary to her. 'The other matter. There's nothing? You're sure?'

'Yes, my lady.'

'The servants will know. They always do. Richard? Hal?'

'Hal Coachman would blab, madam. Richard, maybe.'

Jemima looked up at Mary. 'Talk to Richard. See if he will let slip anything about Thursday.'

'That one gives nothing for nothing, madam. He serves the master and himself. No one else.'

Jemima ran her tongue over her lips. 'Then make him desire you. See if that will open his toothless mouth. I must know who the woman was.'

Mary stared down at her mistress. 'Are you sure you want me to . . . ?'

Jemima stared back. 'Yes.'

CHAPTER TEN

After dinner at the Lamb, I went to collect a small debt I was owed by a man I had helped to find a job distributing the *London Gazette*. He lived in Leadenhall Street, on the opposite side of the road from the market, in the small part of the walled City that had survived the Fire.

When I had the money, I turned to my right and walked west towards what was left of Cornhill. The streets through the ruins were almost entirely clear now, and much of the ground on either side was parcelled out into building sites. In the meantime, in this hiatus of the City's life, weeds were colonizing the rubble and making wild gardens in lost corners.

At this time of day the ruins were safe enough, clothed with a fragile, provisional normality. After sunset, everything changed among the ruins, and only fools ventured into the burned areas of the city without lights and protection. Now, however, there were workmen labouring among the shattered buildings, preparing for the City's resurrection. Citizens hurried to and fro, going about their business, as they had in these streets for centuries past and no doubt would for centuries to come. Street-sellers plied their trade, for everyone needed something, and the urge to buy and sell was as tenacious as life itself.

Beggars stood and sat at every corner, straining to clutch the sleeves of passers-by, many claiming to be former householders who had lost everything to the Fire. Here and there, faded notices appealed for the missing. In Poultry I paused to read a weathered slate on which someone had scratched in faded, just legible capitals: MARY COME TO MOORFIELDS WEST SIDE PRAY GOD YOU ARE ALIVE. There was still a scattering of tents and sheds in Moorfields, though far fewer than there had been. Most of the refugees had melted away like snow in spring: a few remained, huddled in smaller, unofficial encampments; others had found lodgings in the houses of families and friends; and many had drifted away in the hope of making new lives in other parts of the kingdom.

I followed the road to Poultry and Cheapside, where some householders had already begun to rebuild their houses in defiance of the regulations and had set up stalls in the ruins of their homes. From the stone carcase of St Paul's Cathedral I went west through the blackened arch of Ludgate and down to the bridge over the Fleet Ditch. In Fleet Street itself, I paused by the stalls that clung like chicks to a mother hen to the south side of St Dunstan-in-the-West.

At that moment, a wave of grief overwhelmed me. It took me entirely unawares. I stumbled, and steadied myself on the side of one of the bookstalls. My father had died here, only a few feet from where I stood, crushed under the wheels of a wagon. But I felt more than grief, more than guilt. There was also a hard edge of anger that cut into me like a blade.

It was the ant that had tipped the balance. That tiny creature, entombed in white paint, had finally convinced me that there had been sense in my father's story, the dreamlike account he had given me during our last conversation on the last evening of his life. Everything else had fallen into place: Clifford's Inn, the lawyers, the brick building by a garden. But it was the ant that proved to me it had not been his waking dream.

125

If the ant had been real, and those other circumstances, then was it not probable that the rest of it was real too? In other words, that he had followed a woman who resembled my dead mother, at least from behind. And by the same token, did that mean his account of what had lain behind Mr Gromwell's door was equally real?

To my amazement, I found myself believing that there really had been a luxurious chamber where there was now a scholar's study. The bright carpet, the sinful picture and the wanton woman on the couch had been as real as this stall beside me, as real as the battered, damp-stained and fire-damaged volumes it offered for sale.

The wanton woman whose blood was probably on his cuff, and on the scrap of paper in my pocket. The dead woman whose eyes he had closed. There was no other conclusion.

'Sir,' said a deep voice at the level of my elbow, 'I believe I have the pleasure of addressing Mr Marwood? I am indeed fortunate.'

I started. Immediately in front of me was a large black hat. Its broad rim tipped backwards, revealing a small nose set in a broad face, red as the evening sun, and two blue, bloodshot eyes looking up at me.

'Good day, Mr Chelling,' I said. 'Forgive me, sir, I was wool-gathering.'

'You are come from Whitehall, no doubt. Is there . . . is there perhaps news from the King?'

'Not yet, sir. In fact, I have not been there this afternoon.'

'When you do, you will remember our conversation?' Chelling put down the book he had been examining and took my sleeve. 'About the Fire Court, and our difficulties with our bills? Not to mention with the authorities at the Inn.'

'Of course.' It occurred to me that this could be a fortunate encounter. If I could persuade Chelling to tell me what I needed to find out, it would remove the need for me to ask for Hakesby's help — and, in return, to make him a loan that would leave me almost penniless. 'Perhaps you would care to drink the King's health with me?' I said. 'We might step over the way into the Devil.'

'By all means, sir.'

Chelling bowed, which was not a success as he chanced to put his back foot on an uneven stone, which made him stumble. I caught his arm and steadied him. We crossed the road together with some difficulty, partly because of the traffic and partly because he was tottering along on two-inch heels. At the Devil, we went upstairs to the taproom. I ordered wine and found us a space at the end of a table at the back. The room was noisy — four law students were raising their voices in a ballad at the other end of the table, and two soldiers were arguing with passionate intensity about the disposition of the dragoons at an unnamed battle.

'Have you known Mr Hakesby long?' Chelling asked.

'No, sir. Only since last year — the business at St Paul's he mentioned.'

'Of course — you told me earlier. What do you think of this so-called cousin of his, eh? Jane. Who did he say she was?' Chelling stabbed his finger into my arm. 'The sly old dog. Keeps him warm at night, I'll be bound.'

I smiled politely. 'It was civil of you to help me this morning,' I said, trying to steer the conversation away from Catherine Lovett. 'You mentioned this man Gromwell. I —'

'Gromwell!' Chelling burst out. 'Always a maggot in his head about something. I cannot abide a man like that. We've all had our disappointments in life, but he bears his less gracefully than some I might mention.'

'Have you known him long?'

'Too long, sir. Far too long. I don't want to be unchristian about any man, but I fear he gives himself airs, though with little justification. After all, we are both members. We are equals.'

'Members . . . ?'

'Of Clifford's Inn, sir.' He paused as if to give time for me to digest the importance of this. 'I was bred for the law, you see, though at present I assist them at the Fire Court. But I have lived in Clifford's Inn for nigh on thirty years. Why, the Principal was good enough to say to me the other day that the place would be very much altered without me. But of course Gromwell is a Rule now, and by God he makes the most of it and carries himself very high with everyone. This business of the Fire Court is the perfect example. It's not as if Staircase Thirteen is of any use to anyone else at — ah! Is that the wine?'

'Staircase . . . ?'

Chelling was watching the waiter. 'Staircase Thirteen,' he said absently. 'I told you about it earlier. It's not completely ruinous. The ground floor is perfectly weathertight, and the use of it would make it so much easier to store the Fire Court's furniture and supplies and so on. As it is, we have to empty the hall when the court is not in session, so the Inn may have the use of it again. And that means — Dear Christ!'

The waiter was clumsy. The bottle tipped too far, and drops of wine spattered on the table.

'Blockhead!' Chelling snapped. 'Numbskull!'

'Beg pardon, masters, beg pardon.' The waiter began to wipe the table.

'Should we not drink His Majesty's health at once, sir?' Chelling said, seizing the bottle. 'Loyalty to the throne demands no less. Allow me, sir.'

He poured the wine — hastily but without spilling a drop. We drank the King's health, and then that of the other members of the royal family.

I set down my glass when we had drenched the monarchy in wine. 'Are there many other gentlemen who are Rules?'

Chelling smiled, comfortably superior. 'Clearly you were not bred to the legal profession,' he said with a touch of pity. 'In this Inn, there are twelve Rules under the Principal. Sometimes we call them the Ancients. They form the council that administers the affairs of the Society according to our statutes, as laid down by our honoured Founder.'

130

'But your members are all lawyers, I take it — like those of the Temple, for example, or Lincoln's Inn.'

'The case is not quite identical, sir. We enjoy a different status. We are an Inn of Chancery, whereas such places as the Temple and Lincoln's Inn are Inns of Court. In times past, our members were attorneys and solicitors who followed the Courts of the King's Bench or Common Pleas. Or they were young gentlemen from the universities or from our grammar schools, who came here to gain a grounding in the law before moving to one of the Inns of Court. And it is the Rules who decide who shall enter our fellowship, and who shall be admitted to a set of chambers within the Inn. We —'

'So Mr Gromwell is a lawyer?' I cut in.

Chelling puffed out his cheeks. 'I should hardly call him a lawyer.' He paused to drink more wine. 'One can hardly call him anything that's worth the name. True, as a young man, he was admitted to the Society, so he may have some scraps of legal knowledge, but that's all . . . He's a man of fits and starts and idle fancies. He tried the law, and failed in that. He calls himself an antiquary, which means he fiddles about among dusty old papers and grubs about in ruined places and preys on the generosity of

131

his friends.'

'If he's no lawyer, why is he here?'

'A good question, sir.' By now, Chelling was sweating profusely. 'In the last fifty years, Clifford's Inn has opened its doors to people our Founder would never have countenanced. Mr Gromwell's uncle was once a Rule, and he spent a great deal of money refurbishing his chambers, as a result of which he was granted the right to bestow them on an additional life after his own. He chose to bestow them on his nephew.'

'Number Three, on Staircase Fourteen.'

Chelling nodded but shot me a suspicious glance.

I said, 'It seems most unjust, sir, that such a man should benefit by his uncle's generosity, and in that way. And at the cost of others, too.'

'Precisely.' Chelling hammered his fist on the table, distracted from his suspicion. 'One could hardly have come up with a less appropriate choice.' He peered up at me, and wiped his brow with the trailing cuff of his shirt. 'We live in terrible times. Since the great rebellion against his late majesty, nothing has gone right for this unhappy country. Or for Clifford's Inn. We can't get the students now. Not in the numbers we used to before the war. They go elsewhere. Before the war, I tell you, the Ancients would never have sunk so low as to elect a man like Mr Gromwell as a Rule. It beggars belief! He claims to have influence at court, but he has no more influence than' — Chelling stamped hard on the floor — 'than my shoe.'

During this last speech, Mr Chelling's words had begun to take on a life of their own. They collided with one another. Consonants blurred, and vowels lengthened. Sentences proceeded by fits and starts.

My guest, I realized, was well on his way to becoming drunk on a mere bottle of wine. But perhaps this had not been the first bottle of the day. Or even the second. I doubted I would get anything useful about the Fire Court from him this afternoon. But at least he seemed happy enough to rant about Gromwell.

'My father called at Mr Gromwell's chambers last week,' I said, attempting to seize control of the conversation before it was too late.

'To see Gromwell? But why?'

'He called there by mistake. I'm not sure that he saw Mr Gromwell at all.'

Chelling drained his glass and looked mournfully at the empty bottle. I raised my hand to the waiter.

'Surely your father can inform you

whether he did or not?'

'Unfortunately he died on Friday.'

'God bless us, sir!' Chelling seemed to take in my suit of mourning for the first time. 'How did it happen? It wasn't plague, I hope, or —'

I shook my head. 'An accident.'

'The poor gentleman. We . . . we must drink to his memory.'

The second bottle came, and Chelling accepted a glass. His interest in my father had departed as rapidly as it had come, however, and we did not drink to my father's memory. Instead, Chelling returned to the subject of Gromwell, and worried at it like a dog scratching a flea bite.

'The trouble with Gromwell,' he said, 'is that he believes he's a cut above the rest of us. He was born the heir of a fine estate in Gloucestershire. His father sent him up to Oxford but he frittered away his time and his money there. Then his father died, and the estate was found to be much embarrassed — every last acre mortgaged, I heard, and the land itself was in a poor state. To make matters worse, his brothers and sisters claimed their legacies by their father's will, but there was no money left to pay them, so they all went to law against their brother. Gromwell is a fool, and fought them all the way rather than settle the business out of court. As a result he has nothing left but worthless old books and papers and a great heap of debts. I tell you frankly, sir, he has no more idea of how to manage his affairs than my laundrywoman.'

'Then how does he afford to live?'

'I told you: he's a perfect parasite — he preys on his friends.' Mr Chelling was still capable of relatively coherent thought, but his speech had now acquired an other-worldly quality, as if spoken with care by a foreigner who did not fully understand the meaning of the words or how to pronounce them. 'Gentlemen he knew in his prosperity. He has friends at Court, and one of his schoolfellows is even a Groom of the Bed-chamber. They say he's quite a different man when he's with them. Ha! No one could be more affable or obliging.' He shrugged, a mighty convulsion of the upper body that almost dislodged him from the bench on which he sat. 'He can make himself good company if he wishes, and he makes himself useful to them, too. He will find out their pedigrees for them, or keep them entertained with his conversation. In return, they lend him money and invite him to stay and lay a place for him at their tables. For all his airs, Lucius Gromwell is no more than a lapdog.' Chelling glared at me and shook his fist. 'Let him beware, that's what I say. No man is invulnerable.'

'That is very true, sir.'

'Believe me, I shall make him laugh on the other side of his face before I'm done. I have the means to wound him.'

Chelling paused to take more wine. His face was very red and running with moisture.

I said, 'You know something that will do him —'

Chelling slammed the glass down on the table so forcefully that its shaft snapped.

'A lapdog!' he cried in his booming voice, so loudly that the taproom fell silent for a moment. 'You must be sure to tell His Majesty when you see him. Gromwell is a damned, mewling, puking, whining, shitting lapdog!' His face changed, and he looked at me with wide, panic-stricken eyes. 'Oh God, I am so weary of it all.'

His body crumpled. He folded his arms on the table and rested his head on them. He closed his eyes.

For a small man, Mr Chelling was surprisingly heavy.

Once I had paid our bill, a waiter helped me manhandle Chelling down the stairs to the street door, a perilous descent because he twice made an attempt to escape, insisting that he had always stood on his own two feet and had no intention of changing his policy in that regard.

I had to bribe the servant a second time to help us across Fleet Street. With the lawyer dangling between us, sometimes kicking at our shins, we carried him safely past St Dunstan's to the gate of Clifford's Inn. At this point a porter came to our assistance.

'Been at it again, has he?' he said. 'He's got no head for it, sir. On account of his size, I reckon. Stands to reason: if you put a quart in a pint pot, it's bound to overflow.'

'I have the heart of a lion,' Chelling mumbled. 'That is what matters.'

'Yes, sir.' The porter winked at me. 'I just hope the Principal don't hear you roar.'

'Take him to his chamber,' I said.

The porter patted Chelling's pockets until he found a bunch of keys. 'Sooner he's out of sight, the better.'

He left a boy to mind the gate. He and another of the Inn's servants half-carried, half-dragged Chelling across the court, watched by a small but appreciative crowd of spectators outside the hall, where the Fire Court was still in session. I paid off the waiter and followed them.

Chelling lived in chambers on Staircase V, part of a range on the eastern side of the court that butted up against the north of St Dunstan's churchyard. The building was one of the oldest parts of the Inn, dating back to its days as a private house, and the staircase was cramped and ill-lit. At each landing there were two doors, one on either side, just as there were in New Building, but there were few other resemblances. The air smelled of damp and decay, and the stone steps were uneven, worn by generations of feet.

As luck would have it, Chelling's chambers were on the attic floor, which had been added to the building as an afterthought. The porter unlocked the door. They dragged him into a study with sloping ceilings and a sloping floor. It was sparsely furnished with a table, a chest, an elbow chair and a single stool. A dormer window looked east towards the ruins of the City. There was a broken pipe in the hearth and the study smelled of stale tobacco.

The porter dropped the keys on the table and glanced at me for guidance. 'On the bed, master?'

I nodded.

The servant unlatched the inner door, and

the pair of them manhandled Chelling into a chamber little larger than a cupboard. They dropped him on the unmade bed. His legs dangled over the side. One shoe fell with a clatter on to the floor. His round face was turned up to the ceiling, and his hair made a grey and ragged halo on the dirty pillow. His mouth was open. The lips were as pink and as delicate as a rosebud on a compost heap.

'Friend of his, sir?' the porter asked. 'Ain't seen you before, I think.'

'Yes.' I paused, and then, as the man was looking expectantly at me, added: 'Mr Gromwell will vouch for me. My name's Marwood.'

The porter nodded, giving the impression that he had done everything and more that duty required him to do. 'Will that be all, then?'

I felt for my purse. 'Thank you, yes.'

I gave the men sixpence apiece. I went back into the study and listened to their footsteps on the stairs. Snoring came from the bedroom, gradually building in volume. I glanced around the cramped chamber. It was very warm up here, directly under the roof. The windows were closed and the air was fetid. There were few books in sight. An unwashed mug and platter of pewter stood on the table.

Chelling had fallen on hard times. Perhaps Gromwell was not the only man at Clifford's Inn who survived on the kindness of friends. Everywhere I looked, there seemed to be unanswered questions, large and small. After the efforts I had made, the time I had spent, the money I had paid, all I had to show was a cloud of uncertainties.

Suddenly I was angry, and anger drove me to act. I could at least make the most of my opportunities while I was here. There was a cupboard set into an alcove by the chimney breast. It was locked, but one of Chelling's keys soon dealt with that. When I opened its door, the hinges squealed for want of grease.

The smell of old leather and musty paper greeted me. The cupboard was shelved. In the bottom section were rows of books in a variety of bindings. The upper section held clothing, much of it frayed and well-worn. On the very top shelf, a leather flask rested on a pile of loose papers an inch thick, with writing materials beside them.

I uncorked the flask and sniffed its contents. The tang of spirituous liquor rose up from it, with a hint of something else, perhaps juniper. So Chelling had a taste for Dutch gin as well as for wine. As for the

140

papers, they were notes, by the look of them, and written in a surprisingly fine hand, the letters well formed and delicately inscribed. I glanced at the top sheets. They were written in Latin. Every other word seemed to be an abbreviation.

I leafed further down the pile and found a page that was written in English. It was an unfinished letter, though its contents made no more sense than the others.

Sir,

It grieves me beyond Measure that my Conscience requires me to communicate this Distressing Information to you, not merely for the Good of our Fellowship and its Reputation in the World, but also to warn you of the Dangers of a too Generous and too Trusting Spirit. In Fetter Lane, by the Hal—

The last three words were smudged, suggesting the writer had pushed the letter into the pile of papers without troubling to blot it.

A door closed on one of the floors below me. I cocked my head. Someone was climbing the stairs. The footsteps drew steadily closer. I picked up the papers, returned them to the cupboard and put the flask on

141

top. The hinges shrieked as I shut the door.

The steps were on the landing now. There was no time to relock the cupboard. The door of Chelling's study was still ajar. There was a tap on it. The door swung open.

Lucius Gromwell entered the room, stooping because the lintel was so low. Once inside he straightened up. The crown of his hat brushed the ceiling at its highest point. He was dressed in a fine suit of yellow broadcloth, though the effect was somewhat spoiled by a large red stain on the chest and a hint of grubbiness about his shirt. His face was flushed with wine.

He frowned. 'I know you . . . You're the man who came to my chambers this morning with a cock and bull story about your father. What are you doing here?'

I nodded towards the open door of the bedroom. The snores were louder than ever. 'Mr Chelling was unwell,' I said. 'I had him carried to his bed.'

'But who are you?' Gromwell demanded. 'What right have you —'

'Hush, sir, he's only just fallen asleep. It would be unkind to wake him.'

'So you're a physician, are you? And he your patient? A likely story.'

'No. A friend.'

Gromwell laughed. 'Chelling doesn't have

friends. If you know him at all, you would know that.'

The words were offensive in themselves, but the man's manner was worse. This morning he had been at least superficially polite to me. Now, he radiated hostility.

Gromwell crossed the room and pushed the bedroom door fully open. He stared down at Chelling, his face twisting with distaste. He turned back to face me. He gestured to the outer door. 'After you, sir.'

I held his gaze, wondering why Gromwell had taken the trouble to come to call on a man he neither liked nor respected.

'You must leave,' Gromwell said. 'At once. I have authority in this place. Do not oblige me to exercise it.'

He left me no choice. I bowed and left the room. On the stairs, I paused to listen.

The building above was silent. Gromwell was still in Chelling's chambers. I heard, faint but unmistakable, the shriek of the cupboard door's hinges.

CHAPTER ELEVEN

A knock at the door. Hakesby looked up sharply, and a sheaf of papers slid from his lap to the floor.

It was Wednesday, early in the afternoon: the sky was overcast, and so was the mood in the drawing office. The stationer's apprentice had delivered an unexpected bill a few hours earlier.

The boy downstairs had brought up a letter. Hakesby tore it open and scanned the contents. He passed it to Cat. 'Marwood cannot complain that we do not keep our side of the bargain.'

The letter was from Chelling, in answer to an enquiry that Hakesby had sent to Clifford's Inn the previous evening. The next Fire Court case that was due to be heard before Judges Twisden, Wyndham and Rainsford was a week today, on 15 May. According to Chelling's notes, the case concerned a property known as Dragon

Yard, which occupied a site about halfway between Cheapside and what was left of the Guildhall. The petitioner was Sir Philip Limbury, the freeholder, and there were four defendants, whom Chelling had not named.

'DY,' she said quietly. 'Marwood asked about that. Dragon Yard.'

Hakesby nodded. 'That confirms it. Limbury? The name's familiar.'

'Sir Philip Limbury, sir?' Cat said, her memory providing an unwanted glimpse of her cousin Edward with one of his friends, a tall dark man. 'The courtier?'

'Very likely,' Hakesby said. 'Dragon Yard's a substantial plot, if I remember right. I wonder what he plans to do with it. We should look into it.'

His voice had sharpened, and he sounded younger. Hakesby had a nose for an opportunity, if not a head for balancing his accounts, and he was never slow to recognize an opening that might possibly lead to a commission.

Brennan put down his pen. 'It's off Cheapside. I could step over there, sir, if you wish. See what's what.'

Cat held her breath.

'I think I shall go myself,' Hakesby said. 'No harm, after all, the air will do me good.

145

Summon a hackney, Jane.'

'Would you like me to attend you, sir?' Brennan asked. 'In case you need to take a measurement or dictate a note?'

For a moment the decision hung in the balance. Cat's nails dug into the palm of her hand. Why couldn't Mr Hakesby see what Brennan was about? The draughtsman was trying to ease himself into Hakesby's good offices, to make himself indispensable.

She was learning cunning. 'In that case, master, should I finish Brennan's work? It's the north elevation of the warehouse on Thames Street.'

Hakesby frowned at her. 'That would never do. It is a fair copy, and the difference between your two hands would be obvious. Besides, you don't have the experience.'

She lowered her head submissively.

'No,' he went on. 'Brennan had better stay here. I suppose you must come with me instead.'

'Dragon Yard, master? That's Dragon Yard.'

The beer-seller leaned over the side of his stall and pointed across Cheapside at a jagged line of ruins, marked out by a row of white posts with lengthening shadows on their eastern side. It was early evening, but two labourers were still working at one end

146

of the site, shovelling rubble on to a barrow.

Hakesby slid a shilling on to the plank that served as a counter. 'Who owns it?'

'It used to be the Poultons — see, that's the old gentleman there.' The beer-seller nodded at a tall man wrapped in a cloak who was examining a blackened chimney stack at one end of the ruins. 'Lucky devil.'

'He doesn't look lucky,' Hakesby said.

The beer-seller leaned politely to his left and spat on the ground. 'Don't judge a book by its cover, master. Clothier. Rich as they come.'

Cat glanced in his direction. Poulton was a gaunt figure, stooping as if he had grown that way after a lifetime spent passing through low doorways. For a clothier, he was plainly, even shabbily dressed.

'Poulton — of course. I know him by reputation,' Hakesby said. 'He's a friend of Robert Hooke's. Indeed, I believe I may have met him once in Mr Hooke's company . . . You say he used to be the owner?'

'I suppose he still is, of what's left. But there's a gentleman from Whitehall who has the freehold. It's a sorry business, isn't it? Mr Poulton's been there nigh on forty years, over there: see, where he is now — that's where the big house was. And his brother's family was in the house next door, and some

147

cousins behind. A garden too, and a livery stable next to the paddock beyond. All gone now.' The man's eyes flickered towards Cat and back to Hakesby. He added the unconvincing piety, 'God has punished us all, high and low, for the sins of the City and the wickedness of the court.'

'What will they build there?'

'Houses for rich folk, that's for sure. Ask Mr Poulton if you want to know more. But I warn you, he'll bite your head off if you don't have a care. Or you could ask his niece if you can find her.' The beer-seller grinned. 'She's a widow. A merry one.'

Hakesby drained his beer. He seemed more vigorous than he had for days, if not weeks. Their expedition had acted as a tonic on him.

He took Cat's arm, and they crossed the flow of traffic on Cheapside. 'It's a big site,' he said as they reached the safety of the other side. 'Probably an inn at one time.' He led the way into what had once been a lane between two buildings.

'You! You there!'

Mr Poulton was brandishing his stick at them.

Hakesby let go of Cat's arm and picked his way towards the old man, navigating a zigzag course between a large heap of rubble and rows of blackened posts that might once have been a range of outbuildings.

'This is private property,' Poulton said. 'There is no right of way. I don't permit trespassers.'

Hakesby bowed. 'Of course not. Mr Poulton, I believe? My name is Hakesby. I think we met at my Lord Brouncker's two or three years ago.'

Instead of a wig and hat, Poulton wore a tight-fitting black cap which emphasized the shape of his skull. His eyes were sunk deep in their sockets. 'Perhaps we did. I don't recall it.' The words were abrupt but his tone was less aggressive. 'And what can I do for you, sir?'

'I'm a surveyor and a master draughtsman. I design buildings and oversee their construction. I'm a colleague of Dr Wren, who will speak for me, and of course Mr Hooke will too, and my Lord Brouncker. This is clearly a substantial site, and I wondered if my services might be of use to you.'

'I wish to God I knew.'

'Forgive me, sir — I don't understand your uncertainty.'

'Nor do I, sir, nor do I.' Poulton's bitterness forced its way to the surface. 'I tell you, sir, it's barbaric, unchristian. My family has

149

lived here since my father's time. We've built our houses here, and managed our businesses, and brought up our families. My lease has five years to run, and I expected to renew it when it fell due. And on reasonable terms, too, for our losses from the Fire have been enough to melt a heart of stone. But the freeholder will have none of it: if he has his way, he will cast us all into the street.'

'Surely he must compensate you?' Hakesby said.

'He has made an offer. The amount was an insult, and he must have known it.'

'But you have a legal recourse, sir. The Fire Court is sitting. I have spoken for several clients there in the last month or so. The judges are not unreasonable, and their priority is to see the City rebuilt as soon as possible — and to give every man his due.'

'Do you think I don't know that?' Poulton sat down suddenly on a fragment of wall. 'Forgive me. I see you know what you're talking about.'

Uninvited, Hakesby sat down beside him. 'These questions are not easy to settle, sir. There are so many sources of disagreement. But all parties must agree that the rebuilding should go ahead as soon as possible. It would be wise to negotiate a compromise.'

'Sir Philip is not interested in

compromise.' Poulton scowled. 'Nor am I, for that matter.' He raised his voice and shouted at the two labourers: 'I don't pay you to rest on your spades, you idle knaves. Dig!'

'Sir Philip is your freeholder, I assume?'

Poulton nodded. 'Unfortunately. He wants to build a street of new houses, eight, perhaps, or even ten. Three storeys high.'

Hakesby shook his head. 'That can't be right. Technically, that street over there would be classed as a yard or a lane. So new houses should have no more than two storeys, according to the Rebuilding Act. And they will insist on the regulations for a development of this type, I'm sure of that. They don't want another fire in the heart of the City.'

'That's the wicked part of it. Limbury wants to cut a street through the middle. To slice Dragon Yard in two. They say the Court of Aldermen likes the idea — another way into Cheapside from the north, thirty feet wide, and at no cost to them.'

'The first two storeys at ten feet high, the third at nine,' Hakesby murmured. 'Each house built of brick and fitted out for, say, three hundred pounds.' He raised his eyebrows. 'Two thousand, four hundred pounds to build eight houses. Plus fees and so on. A

151

pretty little speculation. And perhaps more could be squeezed on to the site, if it were better laid out, particularly at the Cheapside end. A wide frontage — ample room for shops.'

'Sir Philip Limbury is an idle spendthrift,' Poulton said. 'Like so many of these Whitehall parasites. I cannot imagine how he would bear the cost of it all. Unless his wife's father helps him. But I hear there's no love lost there.'

'It wouldn't be hard for him to sell new leases,' Hakesby said. 'Or he could borrow on the security of them, even before the building starts. If done well, the scheme could attract much interest. Say thirty-year leases, with deposits of a hundred and fifty pounds apiece at the start of them, plus an annual rent of sixty or even seventy. In two or three years' time, Sir Philip would cover his costs and start to make a handsome profit. And he and his heirs would retain the freehold.'

Cat, keeping her eyes lowered, murmured: 'And the existing tenancies, master?'

Poulton frowned at her.

Hakesby grunted. 'Always the difficulty.' He turned back to Poulton. 'You're not the only tenant, I think you said.'

'That's part of the problem.' Poulton's

head drooped lower. 'There are two main tenancies, sir, including mine, and a number of subtenancies. The main leases were granted around twenty-five years ago. As I said, they've only about five years to run. I hold the larger, and my niece the other, so effectively it is mine, unless she remarries. But the other two leases have been sub-leased over the years to people who have only the slightest connection to the family, and some who have none at all. They are a different matter. Some of them lost every-thing in the Fire, and they can't afford the cost of rebuilding. And I fear they will be easy prey for a man like Sir Philip. But I hope we shall have a fair hearing from the judges, my niece and I.'

'You plan to rebuild yourself?'

'Of course. And so will my niece. I shall have her sign the necessary papers . . .' A flicker of emotion passed swiftly over his face. 'When I next see her. Limbury will find that a man must get up very early if he wishes to get the better of me.' He pointed with his stick. 'My house stood here, with my niece's on the other side of the lane. The lane itself is over my land. So between us we can sink his entire scheme. Even if he redevelops the north part of the site, he can't put his road to Cheapside through if he doesn't have our land. He may have friends at Court but I have friends among the Aldermen.'

'What about your subtenants?' Cat said, as if to herself.

'They can be bought,' Poulton said, looking at Hakesby as if it were he who had spoken. 'Everyone can be bought. Limbury knows that, and so do I.'

CHAPTER TWELVE

I was early for the meeting with Hakesby and Catherine Lovett. I had frittered away the day, partly because I had drunk deep the previous evening after my encounter with Theophilus Chelling, which meant that I had slept long and heavily, though with confused dreams of flames, falling buildings and despairing searches for something I never found.

I should have gone into the office, but somehow I could not bring myself to walk the familiar road to Whitehall. I risked Williamson's anger — he had given me the indulgence of Monday and Tuesday away from the office, in order to bury my father and settle his affairs. I had taken today without his leave, without even sending word that I was ill. At present his disapproval seemed unimportant. Grief turns everything topsy-turvy.

Instead I sat in my father's chamber and

went through his meagre possessions again. I don't know why I did it, unless it was part of saying farewell to him. But part of him lingered in my mind, refusing to depart.

Later, after Margaret had made me eat something, I wandered along to Fleet Street and into Clifford's Inn. The Fire Court was in session. I stood in the body of the hall while three judges on the low dais heard a petition brought by a merchant who could not afford the rent on his destroyed house; a lawyer, defending the freeholder, the Dean and Chapter of St Paul's, methodically tied the poor man in knots. Mr Chelling was not there.

By the evening I felt more vigorous, and the internal fog that had filled my mind all day had dissipated. I set out for the Lamb. On a whim, I did not walk into Wych Street but passed under Temple Bar to the mouth of Fetter Lane. The fragmentary letter I had found yesterday in Chelling's cupboard was in my mind.

In Fetter Lane, by the Hal—

Fetter Lane ran north from Fleet Street towards Holborn and marked the western boundary of the Fire. To the east lay the ruins, with the blackened church towers where choirs no longer sang and prayers were no longer said. To the west, the buildings were largely undamaged, though here and there the flames had leapt across the road and devoured what they could before the wind had changed and driven them away.

The sun was out, but the shadows were lengthening. I walked slowly northwards, keeping to the western side. To the left was the square tower of St Dunstan-in-the-West and the roofs of Clifford's Inn. The Fire had reached a section of the buildings on this side, including part of the Inn. By this stage, however, its fury had been abating. Some of the damaged buildings had been made habitable after a fashion.

A beggar pursued me for a few yards until I shouted at him and waved my stick. The man fell back, grumbling. For all that, and against my better judgement, I felt a twinge of pity. I had known hunger myself, and the beggar was about my own age; the man had had the misfortune to lose an arm.

I came to the mouth of the lane leading from the east into Clifford's Inn. The gate was open. Black-clad figures moved in the court beyond, walking slowly as if in a dream world. To the right was the boarded-up ruin and the improbably green foliage of the trees in the garden. The tree trunks were dark with soot, like most of

London's trees, but the spring leaves glinted where they caught the sunshine.

Time was passing. If I wasn't careful, I would be late. I walked on, drawing level with the long roofline of the brick building in Clifford's Inn. It rode like the side of a tall ship over the humbler buildings between it and Fetter Lane. These belonged to a rambling house set back from the road, its frontage damaged by the Fire, with a yard and outbuildings behind it. The house was still inhabited, and a post stood before the door, signifying that there was hospitality within. A sign hung from the jettied first floor, but it was so blackened by the heat that there was nothing to be made out on it.

Somewhere a church clock began to toll the hour. One, two, three . . . I was late already.

The beggar drew level again. 'For the love of God, your worship —'

I swung round to face him. The man cowered and raised his one arm to cover his face.

Four, five, six . . .

'You there,' I said. 'What's the name of that house?'

Seven. Damnation.

The beggar blinked, taken off guard. 'The

Half Moon, master.'

'A tavern?'

'Yes. Good enough food, sir, if you can pay for it. For the love of God, sir . . .'

I felt in my pocket for a sixpence. It was a ridiculously generous amount for the service rendered. I dropped the coin into the man's palm and walked quickly away, ignoring two more beggars who were now moving towards us like wasps to a honeycomb. The one-armed man stayed put, calling down unwanted blessings on my head. I felt the familiar guilt: there, but for the grace of God, go I.

I turned into Fleet Street and set off in the direction of the Strand. The beggars dropped away, and with them went my guilt.

In Fetter Lane, by the Hal—

So did Chelling's unfinished letter refer to the Half Moon? Was the tavern connected to its promise of 'distressing information'?

Dear God, what murky business had my poor father strayed into?

After all that, I needn't have hurried.

'Mr Hakesby?' the landlord said. 'He's not here yet. Will you be wanting a private room, sir?'

'Yes. But I'll wait for him.'

I went back downstairs and stood in the

doorway. The street was full of people —
mostly men, mostly lawyers, who swaggered
about the neighbourhood as if they owned
it; which in a way they did.

Five minutes later, I caught sight of
Hakesby and Cat approaching: the tall, thin
man and small woman with the delicate
features. They made an unlikely couple.
Hakesby was slow and halting in his movements. Beside him, Cat was unnaturally
stiff, as if fighting to contain the vitality that
spilled out of her. I hardly knew her but in
my mind she was always in motion, darting
like a flame from one thing to another, her
outline constantly shifting. Not like a
woman at all. A sprite, perhaps, some
creature from another world where they
managed things differently.

The road was narrow, and it lacked the
posts along the sides that gave some protection to the pedestrians in wider thoroughfares. Hakesby and Cat were forced to step
into the roadway by a couple of law students, who were walking rapidly by in the
opposite direction, and arguing as they
went.

One of them jostled Cat, perhaps inten-
tionally. He paused, turned and leered down
at her. She spat at him, not at the ground.
His face contorted with anger.

160

Swearing under my breath, I left the shelter of the doorway and ran towards them. Why did the little fool have to be so indiscreet? I had no stomach for a street brawl.

But I wasn't needed. The man wheeled suddenly away and set off down the street. I reached Cat just in time to see the dying sunlight glint on a blade. The knife vanished under her cloak.

'You mustn't do that again,' Hakesby said to her, his voice trembling. 'You're too rash. It will be the death of us all one day. What if that man lays information against you? What were you thinking of?'

She did not reply. Nor did she curtsy. If she had been a real cat, she probably would have spat at me.

'I've ordered a room,' I said.

'We were delayed,' Hakesby said. 'But we have news.'

At the Lamb, we were shown to our private room. As soon as we were alone, I took out the leather pouch, secured with a drawstring. It chinked when I set it on the table, and the invisible contents shifted as if they were alive.

Hakesby sighed.

'Twenty pounds,' I said. 'Some gold, but mainly silver.'

'You will have it back within eight weeks,' Cat said.

'Jane!' Hakesby put his hand on her arm. 'You cannot say such things. It's not your place. Besides, you can't know whether we will be in a position to repay Mr Marwood so soon. Though of course I hope we will. What's your rate of interest?'

'I'm not charging interest. Just pay me back the principal.' I hesitated, reckoning up my more pressing debts and setting the total against my likely income in the next few months. 'Eight weeks would be most convenient.'

In that moment I was struck by an over-whelming sense of my own folly. I hardly knew these people. The service they were doing me was trifling. Yet I was lending them, without security, all the portable wealth I possessed. What in God's name was I doing? It was as if my father's death had removed something vital from me, something that had hitherto prevented me from acting like a credulous fool. Without it, I was as helpless as a child.

'I'm grateful for your kindness, sir.' Hakesby compressed his lips. 'And I wish the loan weren't necessary in the first place.'

'He doesn't do this for nothing, sir,' Cat said, flaring up. 'No doubt he has his reasons.'

I wanted to snap at her. Instead I said, 'You've heard from Chelling?' I didn't mention that I had seen him yesterday.

'Yes,' Cat said, even as Hakesby was opening his mouth to reply. 'There's a Fire Court case next week that will come before those three judges.'

'It concerns Dragon Yard,' Hakesby said. 'I assume that is your DY. Strange, isn't it?' He cocked his head. The waiter's step was on the stairs. 'One way or another, everything comes back to the Fire Court.'

When I returned to Infirmary Close, Sam met me at the door of my house. Margaret hovered behind her husband. Neither met my eye.

'What's this?' I said. 'A committee?'

The furniture and the panelling had been freshly polished. I sniffed. A smell of cooking was wafting up from the kitchen. My mouth watered. I had eaten nothing at the Lamb. I realized that for the first time in days I felt hungry.

Sam, who was wearing a clean collar, drew himself up and rapped the tip of his crutch on the floor. 'I hope I see your worship in good health.'

'Why so formal? Yes, I'm perfectly well.'

'There's a letter for you, sir.' Sam cleared his throat. 'I chanced to notice it bears the seal of Mr Williamson's office.'

'Give it to me, then.'

Irritated, I took the letter and turned aside to open it. It contained nothing more than a line scribbled by a clerk.

Mr Williamson expects yr attendance by 8 tomorrow.

I crumpled the paper and stuffed it in my pocket. By his lights, Williamson had treated me indulgently in excusing me from attendance at the office since Saturday. It wasn't as if I could plead that settling my father's estate required time, because there was nothing of consequence to be settled.

It was infuriating. The strange business of the Fire Court and Clifford's Inn filled my mind so much that there was little room for anything else, let alone for the routines of gathering information for Williamson's private ear and disseminating selections of it, suitably presented for the public, in the *London Gazette*. Whatever I felt about my father's death, however, I could hardly risk my employment, my main source of income — especially now, when I had given almost all the ready money I possessed to Mr

Hakesby.

'Begging your pardon, sir,' Sam said, implausibly obsequious, 'might I ask the honour of a word?'

'What the devil are you about, jackanapes?' I snapped, my irritation striking the nearest target like a bolt of lightning. 'Why are you talking like a gallant in a bad play?'

'It's this, sir,' Sam said, reverting to his normal voice, with an answering edge of irritation in his own. 'The wife and me are worried. And it's not right, you leaving us like this. Not knowing our arse from our elbow.'

'Sam!' Margaret whispered, her face filling with anguish.

'When you hired us,' Sam went on, scowling at me, 'it was because of your father needing us, Margaret especially. And that's why you took this house, so there'd be room for him and us all. You told me so yourself. So what's going to happen now, master? He's dead. He doesn't need us any more. Nor do you, for that matter, nor a house this size. For all we know, you're going to give up the lease come midsummer.'

I hadn't even thought about such things. But he was right. I no longer needed a house the size of Infirmary Close or two

165

servants.

'I don't know what I'm going to do yet,' I said. 'Damn your insolence,' I added, though without as much conviction as I should have done.

'We need to know if you're going to turn us out into the street, sir,' Sam said. 'That's all.'

Margaret sniffed. Her fingers plucked at her apron.

I understood now the reason for the gleaming woodwork and the smell of cooking, and for the care and patience that Sam and Margaret had lavished on my father, saving me from the burden of doing it myself. I also understood that by giving them employment and taking them into my family, I had somehow acquired an obligation as well as conferred one. I owed them a debt. Just as I owed my father a debt for not believing him on the last evening of his life.

'I don't know what I'm going to do,' I repeated, in a gentler voice. 'But — even if I move from the Savoy — I will not see you left without a roof over your head if I can help it.'

Margaret curtsied and said, as if this were an evening like any other, 'And when will you be wanting your supper, sir?'

'Later,' I said, coming suddenly to a decision. While I had loyal servants, I might as well make use of them. 'Sam, we're going out in a moment. Attend me.'

He followed me into the parlour and stood looking at me with his bright eyes. I heard Margaret retreating to the kitchen.

'Come armed,' I said softly, so Margaret wouldn't hear.

The light was ebbing from the sky, and the smoke from a thousand chimneys made a grey pall over London. I didn't need to adapt my pace to Sam's — he was extraordinarily agile, and with his stump and crutch he negotiated the streets as rapidly as most men did on two undamaged legs.

We walked along the Strand and passed under the Bar into Fleet Street.

Sam drew level with me. 'Clifford's Inn, sir?'

'Not exactly. Though it may have a bearing.'

I glanced at him. His face was alight with excitement. God's blood, I thought, he's enjoying this. When I had first met him, he had been surviving on his wits in Alsatia, the sanctuary in Whitefriars where thieves and debtors lived unmolested by the law. Sometimes I wondered if he was wearied by the respectability of his life at Infirmary Close.

We were on the north side of the street. As we drew level with St Dunstan-in-the-West, I threw a glance up the alley leading to the Inn. The gate was open. Beyond it was the stunted south court and the door of the hall. It seemed to me that there was something secretive about Clifford's Inn, about its untidy, close-packed huddle of buildings: it set itself apart from the world, drawing in its skirts like a prudish lady from the common crowds of Fleet Street.

We walked on and turned into Fetter Lane. Beggars have long memories, and two or three of them swarmed about us. Sam was ruthless and drove them away with his crutch and his sailor's vocabulary.

I paused outside the Half Moon. At the southern end of the building, towards Fleet Street, an alley little more than a yard wide wriggled between the gable wall of the inn and the side of the neighbouring building.

Sam glanced up at the sign over the door. His face brightened. 'You'll take a glass of wine, master?'

I lowered my voice. 'I've a fancy to see the back of the house. There must be a yard, outhouses perhaps. See that ruined building behind? And that long roof on the right?

That's part of Clifford's Inn.'

He wrinkled his nose. 'Are we going up that alley?'

'You aren't. Stay here. If anyone asks what I'm up to, tell them I have a powerful need to shit. Try and keep them away.'

I left him there, leaning against the wall and picking his teeth. The unpaved alley wound between the buildings on either side. Judging from the smell of it, many people had already used it as a makeshift necessary house. By this time the light was fading, and I had to watch my step.

The buildings gave way to the walls of the Half Moon's yard, which were topped with spikes. The alley seemed to be going towards the back of the new building, where Gromwell's chambers were. Then it swung abruptly to the left. After a few yards the path ended at a heavy door banded with iron, set in an archway of blackened stone. There was an extensive collection of turds of various ages on and around the doorstep. But the refuse had recently been scraped away from the centre, leaving a clear path up the alley and on to the step.

I looked up. The door was an entrance to the ruined staircase at Clifford's Inn, the one that had aroused Chelling's passions. He had pointed it out when we first met.

There was no sign of a latch or a keyhole. The threshold was worn to a deep curve, as if someone had taken a neat bite from it. I laid the palm of my hand on the door and pushed. It didn't move. That was when I heard the footsteps behind me.

Someone was coming up the alley. I heard men's voices, two of them. They appeared around the corner. One was a workman, wearing a stained leather apron over his breeches. The other was a tall, slim man in a dark cloak and a broad-brimmed hat. He was carrying a staff shod with iron.

'What are you doing here?' he said. He sounded as if he had his mouth full.

I pointed at one of the fresher piles of turds. 'What does it look like?'

The hat shielded much of his face, and in the poor light the rest of his features were a blur.

'It's private here.' The hard consonants were indistinct, but not his meaning.

There were more footsteps in the alley, and I recognized their halting rhythm.

The tall man turned towards the corner, just as Sam appeared. 'You're trespassing. Both of you. Get out.'

Sam stopped, his hand flicking back the edge of his cloak. I knew he had a pistol in his belt on that side. There was a dagger on

170

the other.

'As you please,' I said, as pleasantly as I could.

'And don't come back.' The tall man pointed his staff at Sam. 'Nor you, cripple.'

Because of the narrowness of the alley, he and the workman had to stand with their backs to the wall to let me pass. His head was bowed, the brim covering the upper part of the face. As I squeezed by, I glimpsed a small, compressed mouth overshadowed by the chin below and the nose above. That explained the articulation: he had lost all or most of his teeth.

As part of my mourning, there were black silk weepers attached to my hat, and they touched his shoulder as I passed. He brushed them away as if they were cobwebs.

I walked on, frowning at Sam to keep him from intervening. One of the men followed, at a distance. He wanted to make sure we had really gone.

We reached the street. A large handcart was waiting near the end of the alley, with a small boy guarding it.

'Who's old sourface then?' Sam said. 'I don't think he likes us.'

The boy with the handcart glanced incuriously at me. I ducked back into the alley. I did not go far — a few paces would bring me back to the safety of the crowded street.

But a few paces was all it took to reduce the sound of traffic on Fetter Lane to a fraction of its volume on the street. I waited a moment.

I heard three knocks in the distance — first one, then a pause, then two in swift succession. After another pause, the sequence was repeated. In my mind's eye, I saw the tall man standing among the turds and knocking the head of his staff against the door to Clifford's Inn.

Sourface. As good a name as any.

Chapter Thirteen

The sun, draped with fiery streamers of cloud, was sinking towards the horizon over Hyde Park. Jemima was in her bedchamber, sitting by the window overlooking the garden, with a novel by Mademoiselle de Scudéry lying unread on her lap.

The kitchen yard was to the side of their garden, divided from it by a fence. From her chair, she was able to look down slant-wise into the strip running along its far wall, which also served as part of the boundary wall between the Limburys' house and the one next door in Pall Mall. The hut over the cesspool, which the servants used as their privy, was in the yard, along with the midden, the gardener's shed and the kennels for the dogs.

The house around her was still. Two hours or so before supper, there always came a lull in the routine, a time for the household to draw breath. In the bowels of the building, the cook and the kitchen maid were at work, but they were out of sight and did not count.

Richard was the first to come out. He was a thin man, older than his employer by a good ten years, with the attenuated, overstated elegance of a greyhound. He dressed in dark clothes of good quality, as befitted his position as one who was seen in public with his master. But Philip was at Whitehall now, attending on the King, and his absence meant that his servant was at leisure.

In honour of the occasion, Richard was wearing his teeth. When he wore them, his face was passable, though no one would call him good-looking. Without the teeth, his face collapsed in on itself.

As Jemima watched, he took a turn about the yard, throwing glances in the direction of the door to the kitchen.

Mary glided outside. The girl looked well enough, Jemima supposed, quite a handsome creature in her way, and her green eyes would have adorned any woman's face. She appeared not to see Richard, but slipped between the kennel and privy. Here was a sort of alcove, framed by the side walls of the outbuildings and the boundary wall behind. He glanced back at the kitchen and followed her.

Jemima shifted her chair to the right, which gave her a clear view of most of the alcove. Though the window was open, she could not hear what the two servants were saying. But soon there was no need of words.

Richard's arms snaked out and tried to wrap themselves around Mary's waist. She sprang back. He hunched his shoulders and spread his hands in supplication.

Mary edged closer, extended her arm and let him take her hand. He raised it to those damp, mobile lips. He pulled her slowly towards him. She resisted at first, but allowed herself, step by step, to be drawn into his embrace.

Jemima leaned forward in her chair, trying to see more. Her book, volume ten of *Le Grand Cyrus,* slid from her lap to the floor, but she did not notice.

Richard's hand slid over Mary's hips. He pushed his knee between her legs. He gripped her gown and tried to lift it.

Suddenly it was over. Mary was walking briskly towards the house. Richard turned aside, his back to Jemima at the window, and appeared to be adjusting his dress.

Jemima sat back, leaving the novel where it had fallen. She closed her eyes. She did not bother to answer when there was a light tap on the door.

Mary came in, shutting the door behind her and sliding the bolt across. She crossed the room and stood by Jemima's chair.

'Did Richard tell you anything?' Jemima asked without opening her eyes.

'Something, madam. Only a little.'

'Comb my hair.'

She felt Mary's arm brush against hers as the maid leaned forward and took up the silver-mounted comb from the dressing table. The comb's teeth tugged at Jemima's hair. Mary steadied her mistress's head with her other hand. The tips of the teeth scraped the skin of Jemima's scalp. She felt her muscles relax, first in her face, then in her neck and then lower down her body, a gentle tide of well-being.

If I were a cat, she thought, I should purr.

'He was ready enough,' Mary said. 'He wants me.'

'I saw,' Jemima said softly.

'His breath stinks.'

'Did he answer you?'

'I asked where he'd been,' Mary said. 'Why he was always out these days. He said it's the master's business. So I said, what about on Thursday, when he was gone all day and most of the evening. I pretended I'd been mad with passion for him then. He

176

wouldn't answer at first, so I let him touch my breasts.'

'You wicked woman,' Jemima said.

'He said the master had a difficulty that he helped him deal with, and he'd been well paid.' The comb found a knot, and bit into it, tugging and pulling, loosening the strands of hair with delicious deliberation. 'A pound, he said.'

'A pound!'

'And in gold, mistress. He said he'd buy me a pair of gloves if I would grant him the last favour. That's what he wanted.'

'That's what men always want,' Jemima said. 'If they want you at all. It's either that or nothing.'

Mary snorted. 'He wanted it there and then, up against the wall. But I wouldn't let him. He wouldn't have told me, even if I had. He's hot for me, but he fears Sir Philip more.'

Jemima opened her eyes. 'Look at me.'

The comb stopped its work. Mary came to the side of her mistress and looked down at her.

'What do you think?' Jemima asked.

'About Richard? I think he's a bag of wind and piss.'

'No. About my husband's bitch in Clifford's Inn. Who is she?'

It was nearly midnight.

A single candle burned on the night table. Shadows crowded in the corners of the room. The mistress and maid were sitting in the bed, side by side, so close that their shoulders touched. They were both in their smocks. Jemima felt the warmth of Mary's body, seeping through the linen that separated their two skins. Their feet touched.

The bed curtains were tied back. Jemima thought they might be alone in the night in some far-off place — the Indies, perhaps, or Africa — sitting in their silken pavilion with the flaps raised. The candle was their campfire, its glow keeping them safe from the wild beasts that prowled about them, invisible in the darkness.

Mary turned her head. 'Why does master care so much?' she whispered, and her breath brushed Jemima's skin and made it tingle.

'About Dragon Yard? Because it's his, you foolish girl. Nothing else is. Only that freehold. His salary from the Bedchamber goes to pay the interest on his debts.'

'But why should he bother, mistress? He lives high, thanks to you and Sir George.

He wants for nothing, and never will.'

'Except his own money in his purse.'

'So this is his chance then? To have money he can call his own?'

'Even the clothes on his back and the food on his table comes from me and my father. And he won't have the use of the property I bring him until my father dies. Perhaps not even then. Father means to tie up everything in knots if he possibly can, to make it safe for his grandson.'

There was a silence. Mary had come to Syre Place when she was thirteen. Jemima allowed her a latitude she allowed no one else. Talking to Mary was like talking to herself. Her mind veered to her husband, and jealousy twisted inside her. Not just jealousy. Oh, Jemima thought, I would give anything to be with his child. How was it possible to love someone and hate them at the same time?

She said abruptly, to divert herself: 'I believe that Dragon Yard is not merely a matter of money.'

'What is it then, dear madam?'

'My husband does not care to be idle. Since he came back from the navy, he has done nothing except fritter his life away at court, or wander about here, or see his friends. He has no occupation apart from

179

warming the King's small clothes when it's his turn to serve him.'

Her father kept Philip on a tight leash like a distempered dog. Distempered dogs sometimes turned on those that fed them.

'But that's no reason for him —'

'Stop it, you foolish woman.' Jemima pulled away from Mary. She was tired of talking, tired of thinking bitterly familiar thoughts that led nowhere but endlessly back on themselves. 'Bring me my draught. I can't sleep properly at present.'

Mary laid her hand on her mistress's forearm. 'Madam,' she said softly, pleadingly. 'I know a better way than a sleeping draught.'

'Hush. Did you hear?'

Both women listened, hardly breathing. There were footsteps in the passage. Then a firm knock on the bedroom door, and the clack of the latch.

'Jemima. Are you awake?'

'Shall I say you're sleeping?' Mary whispered.

Jemima pushed her away. 'Open the door. Quickly.' She raised her voice. 'A moment, sir.'

Mary took up the candle and padded across the floor to the door. She drew back the bolt. The door opened sharply, banging into her.

'Be off with you,' Philip said to Mary.

Without looking at her, he pushed past and strode towards the bed, his leather slippers slapping on the floorboards. He was carrying his own candle, and the flame danced like a wild thing, throwing shadows around the room. He was wearing his bedgown and looked, Jemima thought, like an Indian prince striding into his harem. She had given him the gown; it was made of scarlet and gold silk, ankle-length, trimmed with fur at the neck and wrists, and padded against the chill of the night. He wore a silk kerchief around his shaved head.

'Mistress?' Mary said. 'Shall I —'

'Go away,' Jemima said without looking at her. 'Don't bother me.'

Mary left the room quickly, taking her candle with her. She closed the door with unnecessary emphasis.

'I'm glad I find you awake,' Philip said. He sat down on the edge of the bed, on her left side, and took her hand. 'You look very fine, my love. And quite restored, thank God.'

Despite everything he had done, despite everything she knew about him, and everything she was, she felt herself respond to his voice. She looked at her small white hand as it lay defenceless in the palm of his. She pulled it away and turned her face away from him.

'Are you sleepy?' he said.

'Not in the least.'

'Come, then.' He stood up and pulled back the coverlet and sheet. He stared down at her. 'Let us while away the time by entertaining each other.'

She sat up sharply. 'How can you come to me like this?'

He raised his dark eyebrows and chose to misunderstand her. 'Who better than me? You're my wife. You would want no one else, I hope.'

She tried to pull the sheet over her, but he would not let her. 'You come from another woman. I can smell your punk's stink on you. Your punk in Clifford's Inn.'

'What nonsense is this?'

'I know it all. I saw the woman's letter.' She spat out the name. 'This Celia.'

Philip stared at her. He forced a smile. 'You mean Gromwell's mistress?'

She stared at him. 'What? I thought —'

'Don't.' He pulled away from her. 'I should beat you for even thinking such slanders.'

'But the letter . . .'

182

Philip whistled. 'I remember now. Gromwell showed me the letter the other night. I left it on my desk when he and I walked over to watch the play at Whitehall. It named the time and the place of their meeting . . . So your little Mary was playing the spy?'

Jemima said, 'She — she has my best interests at heart. And as well someone has.'

'I'll have the jade whipped.'

'No, sir. You shall not.'

He held her eyes for a moment, and then shrugged. 'I'll let it pass this time.'

She tried to stand but he pulled her down. 'Let me go.'

'Full of passion, that letter, wasn't it? Full of my love this, and my love that. But think back — my name wasn't mentioned in it. You assumed that I must be the woman's lover because your jealous nature would have it so. But the letter was written to Gromwell, you goose, not to me. He brought it to show me. He was in raptures — she had agreed at last to meet him privately, in his chambers, and he thought he was as good as wed to her.'

'But — but that can't be true. I don't believe it.'

'Of course it's true.' He stroked her hand. 'Now, my dearest. Let us return to what

183

matters.'

He straightened and pushed the bedgown from his shoulders. The wavering flame of the candle converted his body into a map of hills and shadowed valleys; in places, the skin glowed as if a fire was raging across it. He was running to fat but she didn't care about that.

She stretched out her finger and touched his leg. It was warm and rough. Completely unlike a woman's. Tonight, she thought, perhaps God will at last permit —

'My love,' Philip said, sliding into the bed beside her. 'Oh — by the way — I had almost forgot: there is a small matter of business to discuss as well.'

Her excitement shattered.

'I should find it a great convenience if I had a little ready money. Two hundred would be enough, I think, and I shall soon be in a position to repay it and more.' His hand slipped over her left breast. 'Do you think Sir George might see his way —'

'You know what my father said last time.' Her nipple hardened under the smock, treacherously ignoring its owner's feelings.

'Yes, but this is different. It's an investment that cannot fail to yield a rich profit. See, I'm talking like a plump alderman already . . . If my plans for Dragon Yard go ahead — and there's no reason why they shouldn't — I'll even be able to repay his last loan.' He untied the neck of her gown and slipped his hand inside. 'I could borrow the money elsewhere, I know, but the interest would not be agreeable.'

She forced herself to think clearly, just for a moment, to float above the tide of sensation that was flowing through her. 'There's only one thing that will make him look kindly on you. You know what that is.'

He withdrew his hand abruptly. 'Yes, my love. An heir.' His voice had an edge to it. 'And we are doing what we can to achieve that most desirable aim at this very moment. But this other matter is important, too — not to him, perhaps, but to us. Now I think of it, we could avoid troubling your father entirely. You recall those earrings he gave you on your birthday before last? You never wear them — you told me they were too heavy, and ugly besides. And he wouldn't expect to see them on you, either, because he never leaves Syre Place now, and you would hardly wear such baubles in the country. So you wouldn't miss them, and nor would he.'

'How can you say this?' she said. 'Now, of all times?'

The room was almost silent around them.

She listened to the sound of their breathing and a faint scratching near the chimney piece. Mice, perhaps rats. A distant owl screeched among the trees of the park.

Was it possible that he had lied to her after all, and that he, not Gromwell, was the woman's lover? Why should she trust him?

'Well, well,' Philip said, and his voice had changed again: it was warm now, and soft as a caress. 'It is only business, like Dragon Yard. What do such things matter, after all, as long as we have each other?'

The hand was back. Only this time it was raising the hem of her smock. His fingers touched her inner thigh and she could not restrain a sigh of pleasurable anticipation. Her body was treacherous, her body was his ally.

'And we have this, my love,' he whispered. 'Always.'

His mouth hovered over hers, his breath brushed her skin. 'Let us give your father a grandson, my love. A little Henry who will have Syre Place when he is gone.'

Somewhere on the far side of the curtain windows, a distant church clock began to strike the hour. Her husband's fingers moved in time with the chimes as one day passed into another.

CHAPTER FOURTEEN

'Will you take some warm wine, sir? With spices to heat the blood?'

Mr Hakesby shook his head. He was huddled over the fire with a blanket draped over his shoulders. The ague was bad today.

The office was already uncomfortably warm. The morning sun streamed through the big windows of the drawing office at the sign of the Rose in Henrietta Street. Brennan was in his shirt sleeves, and there were patches of sweat under his arms. Cat thought he stank like a fox.

'I must see Poulton this morning,' Hakesby said. 'Is that the half hour already?'

'Yes, sir,' Cat said. 'You're engaged to meet him at ten o'clock in Cheapside.'

'I know, I know.'

They listened to the chime of a distant church clock.

'I could hire a coach . . .' Hakesby said. His deep voice quivered.

'You are not well enough to go abroad, master.'

He frowned at her and then looked away. A fit of shivering ran through him. 'I suppose I could send the boy downstairs with the plans . . .'

'Mr Poulton will have questions. The boy can't answer anything.'

'Or Brennan.'

She glanced at the draughtsman, who had his back to them and seemed absorbed in his work. 'But, sir, you need him here to finish the warehouse plans. That's as good as money in the hand.'

'Then it's hopeless.' Hakesby's eyes filled with tears; these sudden swings of mood were growing worse with the tremors. 'We've lost a possible commission. And Mr Poulton has the reputation of being a man who pays on the nail. He is exactly the sort of client we need.'

Cat wondered if Hakesby were right. Despite his wealth, Poulton might be the sort of client they didn't need. He was somehow mixed up in this dubious business that Marwood was concerned with. On the other hand, Hakesby might be right. Besides, they had already done the work.

'Send me instead,' she suggested.

'Think how it would look — sending a

maid in my place. Mr Poulton would take it as a slight.'

'He would take it as a worse slight if you sent the boy, who knows nothing about anything. If you send me, at least I know the plans, which is more than Brennan does. I should do. I drew them for you. And I know what's in your mind too. I could answer at least some of his questions.'

'Very well. It appears I have no choice.' Hakesby sighed. 'To think it has come to this. Let us hope he won't be insulted that I sent you in my place . . . But you must take the boy with you. You cannot wander the streets alone, particularly among the ruins. And even so . . .'

Cat had no wish to take the porter's boy with her. He had damp hands that left smudges on the letters he brought up to them. Despite his youth, she suspected him of trying to peep at her through the cracks of the necessary house in the yard.

But the boy's company was a small price to pay. Before Hakesby could change his mind, she put on her cloak, found her pattens and gathered up the plans into a folder.

She left the house with the boy, the plans under her arm. The clock struck the three-quarters as they passed St Dunstan-in-the-West by Clifford's Inn. Cat quickened her pace, and the boy straggled behind her, whining when she urged him to hurry.

When they reached Cheapside, Poulton was already at Dragon Yard, pacing over the site with a servant who was taking notes at his dictation. A hackney coach was waiting nearby, the driver refreshing himself at the beer stall on the other side of the road, and the horse, its head lowered, standing perfectly motionless apart from his tail, which flicked from side to side in a vain attempt to remove the flies.

Though he must have seen them approaching on the path that snaked through the rubble, Poulton ignored them until they were almost at his shoulder. He continued to dictate in a low, monotonous voice. The porter's boy stared openmouthed at him, as if at a prodigy of nature.

At last Poulton turned towards them. 'Well? What's this? Where's Mr Hakesby?'

Cat curtsied. 'He sends the most profound apologies, sir. He's unwell.'

'So there's an end to it.' Poulton turned away.

'But he has sent me in his stead with the designs, as he promised, and instructed me on the details.'

Poulton frowned down at her. He held out his hand. Cat gave him the folder. He took out the three sheets of paper and studied them — a sketch of Dragon Yard, marking the access roads and the locations of the houses, the front elevation of one of the terraced houses of three storeys, and plans of the principal floors.

'This is not unlike Limbury's design,' Poulton murmured, to himself rather than Cat.

'Mr Hakesby considered the matter and thought there was no reason why you should not follow a similar plan, with the new road to Cheapside. It would enhance the value, as you said yourself, and of course it would also be agreeable to both the Court of Aldermen and the Fire Court.'

His eyebrows shot up. He stared at her, Cat felt, in much the same way as he would have stared at the hackney coachman's horse if he had spoken.

'And did he say anything else?'

'Yes, sir. He begs you to consider that his scheme makes possible the building of twelve houses, rather than eight or ten, as Sir Philip intends.' She came closer and pointed at the plan. 'By inserting a crossroad there. And that would also make space — there — for a larger house at the southwest corner, which you might wish to reserve for yourself. All this is subject to a full survey, of course, as well as a favourable decision from the Fire Court. But if all goes well, it would increase your profits considerably.'

'You're Hakesby's maid, eh?'

Cat stared back at him. 'And his cousin, sir.'

Poulton grunted. 'Clearly he confides some of his business to you. I hope his work isn't conducted so eccentrically.' He paused. 'And what do you think about it all? You. Not your master.'

The question took Cat by surprise, and surprise made her answer with more honesty than tact: 'I think it all depends on the other leaseholders. I have watched other Fire Court petitions, and the judges try to act fairly to everyone. Or, failing that, to the majority of the interested parties.'

'So it will be which of us the others support that will decide the day — Limbury or me?'

'Perhaps. Assuming both of you either have or can borrow the necessary funds and can rebuild in roughly the same time. As Mr Hakesby said the other day, it shouldn't prove difficult to raise a loan if you need to.'

'Remarkable,' Poulton said, looking at her. 'Quite extraordinary.' His expression was grave but he did not speak unkindly. 'Tell Mr Hakesby that I have had a word with

Dr Hooke as to his suitability for employment in a work of this nature. He was most complimentary, and Dr Hooke is usually sparing of his compliments.'

'Yes, sir. Thank you, sir.'

'And tell him —' He broke off, frowning. 'No matter. There will be time for that later, if necessary. And one other thing. I should like to prepare a set of full plans as soon as possible. The hearing is next week, on Wednesday, so speed is vital. I've an accurate survey of the ground at my house, as well as several copies. It shows Dragon Yard as it was, including the vaults, and the route of an underground stream that runs down to the river. Mr Hakesby will find it useful to have a sight of it before he continues. You had better come back with me now, and I will give you a copy. And I shall write him a note, concerning the fees.'

Cat curtsied. 'Will it take long, sir?'

'Half an hour or so. An hour at most. My house is in Clerkenwell.'

'Then I'll send the boy back, sir. So Mr Hakesby knows where I am.'

Poulton nodded. He walked away towards the coach, leaving his servant and Cat to trail after him and, last of all, the porter's boy to follow everyone else.

There was no conversation on the journey

to Clerkenwell. The coach smelled like all hackneys, of sweat, horse manure, tobacco and stale perfume. Both Poulton and his servant were tall men, and the servant was fat as well. Cat felt surrounded by walls of masculine flesh.

The curtains were up, and she stared at the world as it jolted past. Cheapside was coming to life again — families were camping in shelters in the former cellars of their houses; makeshift stalls lined the street frontages; and there were even more permanent structures, built largely of wood, sprouting along the street in defiance of the new building regulations. You could not destroy a city merely by destroying its buildings.

Poulton's house was near the green in Clerkenwell. It occupied the wing of an old mansion. The porter admitted them to a hall that was open to the blackened roof timbers. He was big with news, his eyes bulging with excitement.

'Master,' he cried, 'it's Mistress Celia.'

For an instant, Poulton's chilly air of self-sufficiency faltered. 'Where is she? Is she here?'

'No, master, but — well, there's a Coroner's man to see you. In your study.'

'A Coroner's man?' Poulton's eyes widened. Then the self-sufficiency was back. 'Take this girl to Mistress Lee.' He glanced briefly at Cat. 'My housekeeper.'

He walked away. The servant opened a door for Cat but did not bother to bow to her.

The room was a parlour, sparsely furnished and hung with faded tapestries illustrating scenes from the Old Testament. An old lady sat in the only chair. Her head was turned away from Cat. She was doing nothing, though a pile of sewing lay on the table beside her. At first Cat thought she was asleep but, as Cat advanced slowly into the room, she turned her head. She was small and plump, with a face marked by time and smallpox.

'Who are you?'

Cat curtsied. 'Jane Hakesby, mistress. Mr Poulton brought me here about the Dragon Yard business.'

'He won't have time for that now.' Mistress Lee moved her head slightly, enough to catch the light from the single window. Her cheeks were wet with tears.

'Why?'

The housekeeper dabbed her cheeks with a handkerchief but didn't answer.

The door opened. Mistress Lee rose from her chair and flew to embrace Mr Poulton.

'My dear,' she said. 'Remember we don't know for sure.'

He was paler than ever, his face thinner, his shoulders more stooping.

'The foolish girl,' he said in a voice that did not seem wholly under his control. 'What was she about?'

'No, sir, you must not distress yourself. As I say, we must not jump to conclusions.'

'I cannot understand it. Among the ruins. Why would Celia go there?'

'Which is one reason why they may be mistaken.'

'And her clothes —'

Something in Mistress Lee's face stopped him in mid-sentence. A warning frown? A touch on his arm? A flick of the eyes towards the visitor?

Poulton stiffened, straightening his shoulders. He turned towards Cat, who was standing to one side of him and had been out of his line of sight.

'Ah — yes. I had forgotten . . . Hakesby's girl . . . Of course.' He swallowed. 'I can't attend to you now. Or to the Dragon Yard matter. Later, perhaps . . . We have had — well, it comes to this: you must go.'

'You can't turn the girl out, sir.'

He shook his head. 'We must go with the — the man. He has a coach waiting.'

'Where do you live, child?' Mistress Lee said.

'I am commanded to go to my cousin's drawing office, mistress. In Henrietta Street.'

'In that case we will take you up with us as far as Fetter Lane, and send you on in the coach. You'll never get a hackney here.'

'But, mistress — I can't cause you so much trouble. And at such a time —'

'I'm not letting you roam the streets by yourself.' The housekeeper was a foot shorter than Mr Poulton, but in her way she was as formidable as he was, perhaps more so. 'Especially now. When it seems there may be a monster roaming abroad.'

'A monster . . . ?' Cat said.

'I won't brook any argument.' Mistress Lee glanced from Cat to Mr Poulton. 'From anyone.'

CHAPTER FIFTEEN

On Thursday morning, I was at Whitehall by half-past seven. Under-Secretary Williamson was not there, but he had left word I was to work at the Scotland Yard office, copying out his private newsletter to a score of his correspondents scattered the length and breadth of the three kingdoms. It was tedious work in the extreme, and made my wrist and fingers ache.

Williamson himself looked in between eight and nine but he said nothing to me. He seemed not to see me. I knew his methods. He intended me to feel his displeasure, to brood on it, to wonder when and how the storm would break on my head. He was an artist in his way.

He went away to spend the rest of the morning with my Lord Arlington. I was worried. Williamson was careful, calculating and controlled. He did not rage at his clerks or at anyone, to my knowledge. But he demanded obedience and he was capable of nursing a grudge.

A few months ago, I had been in good odour with him — and indeed with my other master, Mr Chiffinch, the Keeper of the King's Private Closet and a useful ally at court. The King himself had looked kindly on me. But memories are short at Whitehall, and I did not fool myself into thinking I was invulnerable.

The summons came an hour or so after dinner, in the middle of the afternoon, at a time when even in the best-regulated office diligence tends to be on the wane. Williamson sent a servant commanding me to attend him by the Holbein Gate.

I seized my cloak and ran out of the office and into Whitehall. There was no sign of Williamson by the Holbein Gate or anywhere else. He kept me waiting a good twenty minutes before he strolled out of the Great Court. He waved me over to him.

'I'm going to the Chancellor's. Walk with me through the Park.'

The Chancellor's new mansion was in Piccadilly. We walked side by side into St James's Park. Williamson did not say anything until we were skirting the canal. He stopped suddenly and for the first time looked directly at me.

'Well, Marwood. What have you been up to?'

I could hardly tell Williamson the truth, not least because I did not know what the truth was. 'Settling my father's affairs, sir.'

'Your father was a trouble to us all in life. So now he will be a trouble in death too?'

'My father —'

'You've work to do here. What have you been up to? Why didn't you come into the office? I should have known better than to rely on a man from such cross-grained stock.' He scowled at me. 'A rotten tree produces rotten fruit.'

'I was distressed, sir, and I knew not what I was about.' My voice stumbled along, convincing neither of us. 'And there were debts to be paid, and so forth, and I quite . . .'

Williamson stared at me, wrinkling his nose as if I were a slug or a foul smell.

'Forgive me,' I said quickly, knowing that total abasement was my only hope of salvation, 'especially after all your kindness to me. It was . . . grief that prostrated me. I swear I shall mend my ways.'

His expression did not soften, but the anger left it. Williamson was a man who calculated everything in the most economical manner, even his outbursts of rage. 'I have a task for you now. Not an agreeable one.'

I bowed. 'Anything, master. Whatever you command.'

'A body has been found in the ruins. My lord is concerned that there are disaffected elements abroad.'

In this context, my lord meant my Lord Arlington, the King's Secretary of State and Williamson's superior. The security of the kingdom was in his charge.

'It's a woman,' he said. 'And she was stabbed.'

'A whore?'

'The Coroner thinks she's probably a widow by the name of Hampney. Perfectly respectable woman. Something of an heiress, in fact.'

That explained Lord Arlington's interest in the death. It was one thing for a woman of no account to turn up dead, her body abandoned in the ruins. But it was quite another for a wealthy widow to be found in a similar state. Wealthy widows had friends.

'But he's not convinced it is her,' Williamson went on. 'They say this woman is dressed like a whore, or the next best thing. Why would someone like Mistress Hampney dress like that?'

'Not a beauty,' the Coroner's clerk said. 'Though to be sure it's hard to tell.'

I said nothing. I was fighting the urge to vomit.

'She seems to have been well enough made if you like them on the skinny side. Me, I like my birds a little plumper.'

I turned aside, sickened. The clerk was hardly more than a boy, puffed up by his office and trying too hard to impress.

The woman had been placed on her side in a shallow grave. She was small and slight. Her body was lying in what had been the cellar of a house. It had originally been covered by a thin layer of rubble and ash. But it could not have lain completely hidden for long.

'See the calf of the leg, sir?' He was a ferret of a youth with a single eyebrow across his forehead. 'Looks like fox to me. What do you think?'

For a moment I lowered the cloth that covered my nostrils and mouth. 'Perhaps.'

'The jaw must have been quite a size. You see badgers sometimes at night, but I don't think the shape of the bite is right. Wild dog, perhaps? There's a good few of those out

202

here. All it would need is one animal to get a sniff of her and start scraping away with its paws.'

'How did she die? Can you tell?'

'Stab wound under the left breast,' he said. 'Probably hit the heart. Stabbed in the neck, too, in the artery. A lot of blood.'

'She must have been buried in haste. By night?'

'They'd have been seen if they'd brought her here during the day. Now look there, sir.' His fingers fluttered over the exposed forearm. 'It's not dog or fox did those. That's rat, and more than one of them. I'd put a crown on it.'

Unwillingly I stared down at the body. The horrors attending death have a dreadful allure. Black or very dark brown hair partly masked an unnaturally white cheek. Bled like a calf for veal.

'Someone found her before we did,' the clerk said. 'Someone with two legs, not four. See that hand?'

He pointed. My eyes followed. The woman had lost a finger from her right hand. Bone shone white at the stump.

'Probably a ring.' The clerk shrugged. 'Quicker to hack off the whole finger than work it loose, if it was a tight fit. As for the eye, I reckon a bird had that. A crow. They go for eyes, you know. They have a particular taste for them. My uncle keeps sheep, and the crows always go for the lambs' eyes. Living or dead, it's all the same to them. It's a delicacy, you might say.'

There was no sign of the woman's shoes. I stared at her feet. One was covered in a pale silk stocking, which had fallen to the ankle. The other was bare.

Somehow the worst thing was the loss of the eye. It made her look less than human. A velvet beauty patch clung to the corner of the empty socket, gaily mocking the bloody crater beside it. The patch was in the shape of a heart. You couldn't see the other eye, because she was lying on her side.

I said, 'How long has she been here? Can you tell?'

'Upwards of a week?' The clerk tapped his nose, to give himself a look of worldly wisdom: he looked like a smug little boy strutting through the kitchen with his grandfather's hat on his head. 'When you've seen a few, you can form an opinion. It's the smell, partly, and the way the skin goes.'

I climbed out of the cellar, partly to get away from the stink of putrefaction and partly to get away from the clerk. We were in a section of ruins to the east of Fetter Lane, in what had been a court off Shoe

Lane. The thoroughfares had been cleared in this area, but many of the buildings remained choked with their own debris.

From where I was standing, the blackened remains of houses, shops and manufactories stretched down the slope to the polluted waters of the Fleet Ditch. Beyond it, Ludgate Hill rose to the City walls and the taller ruins behind it, dominated even now by the hulk of St Paul's Cathedral. I turned the other way. There was the familiar tower of St Dunstan-in-the-West, with the roofs of Clifford's Inn to the north.

The clerk and I were alone, though another of the Coroner's men was trying to dissuade a knot of people from approaching. The news of the body had not spread far yet. But it soon would.

Why did it have to be here — so close to Clifford's Inn, to the Fire Court and Fetter Lane? I looked back at the corpse. It had been buried, if that was the right word, in a large, dark-brown cloak originally made for a man. But where it had been pushed aside you could see what she was wearing beneath. Some thin material, probably silk and certainly expensive; yellow in colour, almost golden, but badly stained with blood. The blood was rust-coloured now, but when it was fresh the contrast with the yellow must have been dazzling.

Yellow as the sun, red as fire . . .

For a moment I heard my father's weary voice on the last evening of his life, as he recounted his strange, fantastic dream. The dream that had turned out to have so many unexpected correspondences with reality.

A sense of foreboding crept over me. Yellow as the sun, red as fire . . . Had he been trying to describe the dress the woman had been wearing? But how could he have seen this woman in the ruins? As far as I knew he hadn't come here.

Unless he had seen her in Clifford's Inn.

'Jackson says she's a widow,' the clerk said. 'And wealthy, too.'

'Jackson?'

'The Coroner's coachman. He used to work for the woman's uncle before he came to his worship. But he's wrong, if you ask me. I know an old whore when I see one. This wasn't one of your tuppenny knee-jerkers, mind. Soft hands. Handsome gown. She'd been one for the gentlemen, though you wouldn't think to look at her now.'

'Turn her head,' I said.

'What?'

'I want to see the other side of her face.'

He shrugged. 'If you say so.'

'I do say so. Put her on her back.'

He spat on his hands and crouched beside the body. He thrust his hands and forearms underneath the shoulders and the waist. He made a half-hearted attempt to heave the body over. He glanced up.

'Easier if you'd lend a hand, sir.'

'No.'

I stared at the clerk until he looked away. I had shown him my warrant from Williamson, countersigned by Lord Arlington, and he dared not oppose my authority.

He applied himself a little harder, or at least with a great appearance of effort. The trunk of the body flopped over. He dragged up the legs and, careless of decency, left them splayed, with the gown and the smock below hoisted above the knees. Finally he pushed up the head, bringing the face towards the sky.

The smell grew worse. I gagged.

Underneath the woman's left breast was another rust-coloured stain of dried blood. Her face and her dress were smeared with ash. The left eye was still there, thank God. The ground beneath the body must have protected it from predators. It was closed.

I closed her eyes, I owed her that at least.

My father's words filled my mind. They were a reproach. He had done his duty to the dead. But I had not done my duty to him. I had not even believed him.

Ignoring the smell, I jumped down to the cellar's floor and stooped beside the woman's head. That's when I noticed the second patch on her face: a miniature coach and horses galloping towards the left-hand corner of her mouth.

With a coach and horses too. Oh, vanity, vanity.

The shock of it hit me like a blow. My father had spoken nothing but the truth to me, and in my folly I had ignored it and condemned him as an old man in his dotage. Who was the fool now?

Oh, vanity, vanity.

Shock comes in waves, like the sea. While I braced myself against the impact, part of my mind ran on undisturbed, dealing with my appointed task.

'I'm told her name may have been Hampney,' I heard myself saying.

The clerk nodded. 'We've sent for her uncle. We'll soon know.' He pointed towards Fetter Lane. 'That could be him.'

A coach was drawing up by the side of the road. As I watched, a tall, thin old man clambered out, followed by two women. A younger man came round from the other side of the coach.

'There's Thomas with them,' the clerk

said. 'The Coroner's man.'

The elder woman stumbled. The younger took her arm. The two men and the two women advanced into the ruins. The older woman was limping; perhaps she had landed awkwardly as she descended from the coach and twisted her ankle. She leaned heavily on the younger woman.

'Leave the body on this side,' I ordered. 'If she's the old man's niece, he shouldn't see her like this, with an eye missing. Not at first. And cover her up with the cloak. Make her decent, as far as you can.'

The clerk scowled at me. But he shrugged and obeyed.

The urge to parade his knowledge triumphed over his truculence. 'He's rich as the devil,' he murmured, eyeing the little party picking their way through the ruins towards us. 'So they say.'

'The uncle? What's his name?'

'Poulton.'

'The cloth merchant? Late of Dragon Yard?'

'That's him.'

All lines converged on the Dragon Yard case and the Fire Court at Clifford's Inn.

Then came another shock to add to the others: the younger woman was Catherine Lovett.

209

CHAPTER SIXTEEN

There are languages without words.

You may speak volumes with symbols, Cat knew, or gestures or hesitations or even silences. Your clothes may say what you cannot, and your eyes may plead, cajole or command.

These languages had never come naturally to her, but she had acquired a knowledge of them almost against her will in the days when she had lived in affluence and believed that her fate was to marry a courtier. Her Aunt Quincy had been a mistress of the sidelong glance or the twitch of a white, softly rounded shoulder.

'Patches,' said Mr Poulton. 'And paste. She looks like a woman of the court or those painted whores at the theatre. How could she have sunk so low?'

'And that gown . . .' murmured Mistress Lee, clinging to his arm; it was not easy to say who was supporting whom. 'Her

210

hair . . .'

Cat said nothing. What could you say to death? Besides, it was not her place to say anything. She was here against Poulton's will, because Mistress Williams desired to lean on her arm as they came across the ruins; and perhaps the old woman had wanted the support of one of her own sex, too.

'Patches,' Poulton murmured. 'Badges of sin.'

They seemed not to realize, Cat thought, that patches had their meanings, as precise and finicky as the chop-logical definitions of a scholar.

'Oh my poor Celia . . .' Mr Poulton sat down abruptly on the top of a wall. Tears coursed down his cheeks.

Mistress Lee sat and took his hand in both of hers. Cat stood to one side, watching, listening. The Coroner's clerk threw a glance at her and gave her a wink. Cat ignored him. At least the dead woman could no longer feel. Someone had valued her so little that they had dumped her here, carrion for the crows, a prey for the ghoulish. Even worse than death was the callousness of the living.

'Is that how she was found?' Mr Poulton asked.

211

'More or less, your honour,' the clerk said smugly. 'We made her look decent.'

'Decent?' said Mistress Lee in a faint voice. 'You call that decent?'

The clerk lowered his voice. 'There are . . . wounds, mistress. As I was telling Lord Arlington's man, the lady must have lain here for days.'

Mistress Lee whispered, 'No . . .' and looked away.

Poulton's head snapped up. 'My Lord Arlington?' he rasped. 'What's this to do with him?'

'He sometimes sends for further information when we report a body in the ruins, sir.' The clerk pointed down the slope to Shoe Lane. 'His man's over there.'

Cat followed the direction of the finger. A man in a suit of mourning stood with his back to them, talking to the Coroner's servant who had brought them from Mr Poulton's. She knew at a glance, and with a jolt of shock whose nature she did not care to analyse, that it was James Marwood.

Chapter Seventeen

'Madam,' I said, bowing to the elderly lady and the man beside her. 'Mr Poulton?'

Seated on the remains of the wall, they barely acknowledged my presence. I did not look at Catherine Lovett. She was standing to the side, watching me.

'Sir,' I persevered, 'my name's Marwood. I am come from my master, Lord Arlington.' I took a step forward, forcing the clerk to move aside. 'My lord commands me to convey his compliments of condolence.'

'Who did this?' Poulton said.

'I don't know, sir. The justices will spare no effort to find out, and nor will my lord.'

'What good will that do? Even if you find the monster who did it, it won't bring back my niece.'

The lady took Poulton's hand and squeezed it.

'How long has she lain here?' he burst out. 'Why is she dressed like a . . . like that?'

No one spoke.

'What was she doing?' he went on. 'Was she sleepwalking among the ruins when she was set upon? Was she alone?'

'Can we at least cover her face?' the old woman said.

'Of course,' I said, turning to the clerk.

He shrugged. His upper lip rose, increasing his resemblance to a ferret. 'What with?'

I took out my handkerchief, which was made of fine lawn edged with black; it was designed for display rather than use and, according to my tailor, it was absolutely indispensable for a decent appearance of mourning. I shook out the square and laid it over Mistress Hampney's head.

'Sir,' I said, 'forgive me, but may I ask a question? Had the lady been away from home? Had you seen her recently?'

Poulton's companion snorted. 'Chance would be a fine thing.'

He touched her arm and she fell silent. 'My niece didn't live with us. Until the Fire she lived in Dragon Yard, in the house she had shared with her husband. Afterwards, she found it convenient to lodge with a lady in Lincoln's Inn Fields. Mistress Grove.'

'You offered to take her into our house, sir,' the old woman said. 'You pleaded with her. But she was always headstrong. Ever since she was old enough to walk.'

'Elizabeth,' he said, his voice a low growl. 'Peace.'

'Then when did you see her last?' I asked.

'At church, the Sunday before last.'

'What will happen now?' the lady said, refusing to be repressed.

'There must be an inquest, mistress,' I said. 'And then the family may take away the body and bury it.'

'Indeed, sir,' said the Coroner's clerk, appearing at my shoulder and trying to seize the initiative, 'if you will permit me to say so, that is my —'

'Men will see her,' Poulton said, stumbling over the words. 'They will see her like this. It is not seemly.'

'Sir, the Coroner will see that her body is treated with all respect.' I wondered how true that would be, especially if the character of the Coroner's clerk was any guide to his master's. 'It's best you leave us now. The body must be removed.'

'I should stay with her. I . . . I owe it to my sister, her poor mother.'

'You will distress yourself needlessly if you stay.'

'And me,' the lady put in, tugging Poulton's arm. 'You will distress me, too. You needn't think I will leave you here alone.'

Poulton looked about him, a dazed expression on his face. He detached the old woman's hand from his arm. With painful slowness he knelt by the body. He peeled back the handkerchief and kissed his niece's cheek, his lips brushing the skin just above the coach and horses. He rose, even more slowly, to his feet, ignoring my attempts to help him. He took the old woman's arm and they walked a few paces towards Fetter Lane. She was still limping, and this time Poulton noticed her lameness and supported her.

She stopped and looked back at Cat. 'Young woman,' she said to Cat. 'Thank you. You mustn't go back to your master alone. The streets are too dangerous.'

Cat curtsied. 'It's broad daylight, mistress, and the streets are crowded. I'll come to no harm.'

'No, no, no,' Poulton said, his voice cracking on the last syllable. 'I will not permit it. Look what happened to my poor niece.' He stared wildly about us. 'There may be a monster abroad. I shall give you something for a hackney.'

'May I help, sir?' I asked.

Mistress Lee said, 'This young woman needs to be conveyed to her master at . . . ?' She threw a glance at Cat.

216

'Mr Hakesby,' Cat said, staring straight ahead at Fetter Lane. 'In Henrietta Street, by Covent Garden.'

'I'll make sure she's escorted there, mistress,' I said. 'You have my word.'

I dropped a coin into the outstretched palm of the man who had escorted them from the coach. He hastened after them.

I turned to the clerk, who continued to hover at my elbow, his lips tightly compressed and his single eyebrow crinkled into a frown. 'Lord Arlington particularly wishes that the body should be treated with the utmost respect, as if it were that of his own sister.' I paused to let the words sink in. 'You will take care that it is so. What's your name?'

'Emming, sir. But the Coroner —'

'The Coroner will not want to disoblige Lord Arlington, any more than you do.' I held his gaze until he looked away. I turned to Cat. 'Come.'

She scowled at me but obeyed. We walked in silence through the ruins until we were out of earshot.

'I'm sorry,' I said quietly. 'It can't be easy for you to play the servant.'

'Better to play the servant than the whore,' she snapped. 'But whatever that poor woman did, she didn't deserve to die like that.' She hesitated. 'You were gentle with the old man and his housekeeper. That was well done.'

I looked at her. 'I haven't always been gentle with old men.'

'Your father?'

I let the question hang but of course she was right. 'Why are you here? I could hardly believe my eyes when I saw you.'

'Thanks to you, Mr Hakesby saw an opportunity for work. Mr Poulton is a rich man, and Dragon Yard is a big site, and on Cheapside, too. I was at his house when he heard the news.'

'Who is the old woman?'

'Her name's Mistress Lee.'

'Poulton seems to depend on her. I thought at first —'

'That she was his wife?' Cat said. 'She carries herself like a wife. But their servant said she's his housekeeper. She's lived in his family for many years.'

We looked at each other. I dare say that Cat and I were thinking the same thought: that there was a certain irony in the old couple's disapproval of Celia Hampney's conduct.

'Did you examine the body before we came?' she said.

'I had the clerk turn the woman over

before Mr Poulton saw her.' I hesitated, a sense of decorum affecting me at the last moment. But Catherine Lovett was such a strange creature that to talk to her was not like talking to a woman — or to a man, for that matter. 'The right-hand side of the woman's face had been mutilated after death. The eye was gone.'

'Crows?' she said, in a matter-of-fact way that was a thousand miles away from the clerk's prurience a few minutes earlier.

'Probably.'

Poulton and the housekeeper were clambering into the coach in Fetter Lane. Cat and I hung back, not wanting to catch up with them. There was a small crowd opposite the Half Moon tavern, staring at the activity around the corpse. Theophilus Chelling was among them. It looked as if he was bobbing up and down in his excitement.

'The patches upset them,' I said. 'Almost as much as anything else. "Badges of sin" — that's what the old man called them.'

'There were more than one?'

'On the other side of the face. A heart.'

'Where?'

'At the outer corner of the eye.'

Il y a une langue des mouches.

I stared at her. 'What?'

219

'It means the flies have a language. It's what my Aunt Quincy used to say.' Cat looked up at me, and I saw mockery in her eyes. 'Did she never say that to you? You talked a good deal with her, I think.'

I shrugged and felt the colour rising in my cheeks. 'Never about flies. Why flies? There were flies around the body.'

'Not real flies. My aunt lived in France at one time. *Les mouches* — it's what the French call beauty patches. The point is, sir, they have their meanings for those who can read what they say.'

'The shape of the patch?'

'And its position and its name. For example, a patch that masks a blemish is known as *la voleuse,* because it steals away a blemish, and perhaps steals truth away with it.'

'And this lady's patches?'

'A patch at the corner of the mouth is called *la coquette.* It invites compliment or even a kiss. Then she has the coach and horses there — and at a hand-gallop towards her lips. You do not need me to parse you the sense of that. As for *une mouche* at the corner of the eye, that is called *la passionée.* In the shape of a heart, too. All in all, I know what my aunt would say about such a woman and her intentions.'

She gave me another mocking glance. At

one time, I had desired her Aunt Quincy beyond reason, beyond everything.

'What would my Lady Quincy say?' I said.

'She would say that there went a woman who was happy to give her lover everything.'

Fifty yards ahead, Poulton's coachman touched the horses with his whip and the coach wheels ground into motion, gradually picking up speed.

'I must go back to Mr Hakesby,' Cat said. 'You needn't trouble yourself to take me there. I'll manage perfectly well by myself.'

I laid my hand on Cat's arm. 'Wait.'

For a moment there had been a gap in the traffic passing to and fro. On the other side of the road were the sooty gables of the Half Moon, with the roofs of Clifford's Inn beyond. As Poulton's coach moved aside it revealed the entrance of the alley I had explored yesterday.

Standing on the edge of its shadows, by the corner of the inn, was a tall man in a dark cloak and a wide-brimmed hat. He was leaning on a staff. He was too far away for me to make out his face clearly, even under the hat, but I could see that he was looking into the ruins. I knew he was looking at me.

'What is it?' she said.

'That man over there.' Sourface. 'I think he knows me.'

'Which one?'

'On the far side of the road. Standing to the left of the tavern. The tall, thin man. Another man's just come up to him. A man with a cart.'

'Who is he?'

'It doesn't matter,' I said.

'Is that Clifford's Inn behind the tavern?' Her intelligence moved too quickly for comfort. 'Is this something to do with the Fire Court?'

I ignored the question. 'I don't want to meet him. We'd better go to Covent Garden another way. Back to Shoe Lane and down Harp Alley to the Fleet. We can cross the ditch and find a hackney on Ludgate Hill.'

'You won't meet him,' Cat said. 'He's gone now.'

I turned back to Fetter Lane. The carter was still there, but Sourface must have gone into the alley.

'Perhaps he didn't recognize you after all,' she said. 'Perhaps he was just looking past you at the place where the body is.'

I didn't reply. If Sourface had been watching me for any length of time, it was equally likely that he had no need to follow me. He would have seen me talking with the Coroner's men. He would just have to ask one of them who I was.

'Or,' Cat said, 'if I'm wrong and you're right, he can just ask the Coroner's men who you are.'

At Whitehall, I found Mr Williamson pacing arm-in-arm with Mr Chiffinch in Matted Gallery. That was both surprising and disturbing.

Neither man cared for the fact that I served the other as well as himself. It was an open secret that the two of them were not close friends. One served Lord Arlington and the other the King. They had few tastes in common.

Williamson caught sight of me first. 'Marwood,' he said, asserting a prior claim to me, 'are you come to tell me you've finished that copying at last? I hope you are, or by God, you shall pay for it.'

I bowed at the space between the two men, where their arms met. 'Yes, sir.'

I knew by this opening that the Shoe Lane murder was not something that Williamson wanted discussed in the hearing of Mr Chiffinch. For this I was grateful.

'I will look over the letters in a moment,' Williamson went on, 'and sign them. They must go down to the Post Office today.'

All the while, Chiffinch was looking at me, not directly but aslant, rubbing the great wart on his chin as if it were itching. His colour was always high, but his cheeks were more flushed than usual. I guessed that he had dined well. It was a curious fact that Chiffinch was capable of drinking steadily and in volume, yet he never seemed drunk.

Williamson flapped his hand at me. 'Go back to the office and wait for me.'

'To my lord's?' I asked, meaning Arlington's office overlooking the Privy Garden.

'No. Scotland Yard.'

I bowed to them and withdrew. Williamson did not keep me long. As he passed through the outer room where the clerks worked, he beckoned me to follow him into his closet.

'Is it the Widow Hampney?' he said.

I nodded. 'Her Uncle Poulton confirmed it. He came while I was there.'

Williamson sat down at his desk. 'And?'

I picked my words with care. 'It appears that Mistress Hampney had been lying in a cellar near Shoe Lane for some days. She had been covered in rubble.'

'Murder, then.'

'Yes. There was a stab wound below her left breast which probably hit the heart. And an artery in her neck had been severed.'

'Was she killed where she was found?'

'Probably not. There wasn't much blood around the body.' I didn't want to bring my

224

father into this, or Clifford's Inn. 'The body had been mutilated after death — by animals for sure, and probably by a thief as well. Someone had cut off a finger, perhaps to remove a ring.'

Williamson sat back in his chair. While I was speaking, he had taken up an ivory toothpick and was cleaning his teeth. He laid this aside and rubbed the bristles on his chin. 'And the rest of the report. Was that true as well?'

'Her gown, sir? Yes. And she was patched and painted as well.'

'And Poulton was quite sure of her?'

'Yes, sir. So was his housekeeper, who came with him. They were . . . distressed by the lady's clothing, as well as by her death. But they knew nothing of how she had come to be there, or of a lover, or any reason why anyone should wish her harm. She didn't live with them, but in lodgings in Lincoln's Inn Fields. They hadn't seen her since the Sunday before last.'

He grunted. 'So. Part of the matter is clear, at least. She was robbed, and that was probably why she was murdered, too. No doubt there were other things of value about her.'

He paused and stared at me. I had the sense he was testing me, though I did not

225

know why or even how.

'Why,' he said, 'it's clear enough. A secret lover. And if we ever lay the man by the heels, we shall find that he killed her and robbed her corpse. Not a pretty tale.'

'Then my Lord Arlington believes that her murder was merely a private crime? That it had nothing to do with affairs of state as he feared at first?'

'It's nothing to you what my lord believes, Marwood. As far as it touches you, you will bear in mind that this poor woman's death will bring much shame on her family and friends. No doubt the Coroner will deal with it as he thinks fit. As for us, we must do our best to ensure that there are no unseemly broadsheets and ballads on the subject. You must report any that you come across. I shall tell my lord that we will come down on the culprits very sharply.'

Everything printed in the country was subject to censorship. Both of us knew that tracing culprits and enforcing the law was often impossible, particularly for such things as ballads and broadsheets, which were here today and gone tomorrow. Still, his order was significant.

'Of course if you find any further intelligence about the murder,' he went on, 'make sure you bring it to me first. Don't spread it abroad.'

I bowed.

'Enough of that. Bring me the letters to sign.'

Williamson waved me from the room. Two things were now clear to me: he wanted to have sole control of any further information about the murder I might gather; and he was more concerned to quash publicity about it than to see the murderer on the gallows.

Which suggested that someone of considerable influence had put pressure on Williamson in the few hours since I had walked with him in St James's Park. And I could not help wondering whether that person had been William Chiffinch, the Keeper of the King's Private Closet.

CHAPTER EIGHTEEN

'You look very fine tonight, my love. I could drown in your eyes.'

'You are pleased to make fun of me.' Jemima smiled across the table, wanting to believe in his love though she could not be sure of it. 'You're a wicked man, sir, indeed you are.'

'True, I'm a sinner,' Philip said. 'But only you can forgive me.'

He raised his glass to her and drank a silent toast. The Limburys were having supper in the parlour. They were sitting at a table pulled up to the fire. Jemima's body glowed — Mary had washed her this afternoon, and then rubbed her down with perfumed oils and dressed her hair with especial care.

Philip enquired about this with delightful solicitude, and then made her cheeks glow too by suggesting that one day they should wash each other in all their private places.

'Or, even better,' he said, leaning towards her, 'we shall have a bath built for us — a stone trough, big enough for us to lie side by side and pleasure each other as fishes do.'

'But the cost, sir . . .' she protested, blushing all the more.

'What is money compared to love? Besides . . .'

She knew what his silence said. Besides, one day your father will be dead, his estate will come to us, and we may have a bath the size of a millpond if we should wish it, and fill it with milk and honey.

'Which reminds me,' he went on. 'You remember those earrings we talked of last night?'

Her happiness fell away, as she had feared it would. 'The ones from my father?'

'Yes. You offered to let me sell them or pawn them to assist me in our Dragon Yard venture.'

'You suggested I should, sir,' she said sharply. 'I did not offer.'

His smile did not falter. 'And you kindly agreed, from the sweetness of your heart. I know, my love. It must seem . . . What? Greedy of me? Unkind?' Philip's face was now so open, so frank, one could not imagine a devious thought could exist in his mind. 'But, as I explained, this is for us. And I have a particularly pressing need — an expense concerned with this business that I simply could not have foreseen.'

She delayed, for form's sake. But she knew from the start that she would give in, as in the end she generally did. When Philip had set his mind on something, who could resist his sugared words, his smiles and his caresses? In her limited experience, only her father: but her father was so obstinate he would argue with God Almighty at His judgement seat if he disagreed with God's verdict.

When at last she said yes, Philip rose from his seat, knelt beside her chair, took her hand and kissed it. She stroked his cheek.

'Tonight,' he whispered. 'May I come to you?'

'Yes,' she said. 'Oh yes.'

Then he leapt to his feet and, saying there was no time like the present, rang the bell. A few minutes later, Mary brought down the jewel box and set it on the table. Jemima unlocked it with her key and took out the earrings. She placed them on the table between them.

'I know you never cared for them, my love,' Philip said. 'They never pleased you. But what I do with them will please you.

230

That I promise.' His hand closed over the earrings, drew them towards him and tucked them away. 'I told you of my new street, did I not? It will cut through Dragon Yard into Cheapside, with my fine new houses on either side. I shall call it Jemima Street, in your eternal honour.' He paused, his eyebrows rising in comical consternation. 'Unless you would prefer Syre Street, in honour of your father and your family as well? It is too momentous a decision for me to make. It must be yours alone.'

So, by degrees, he expunged the sour taste the transaction had left behind. He made her laugh with a long, involved tale involving a squabble between pages in the Bedchamber. Philip could make a nun laugh on Good Friday if he set his mind to it. She was still laughing when there was a hammering on the hall door.

Her mood shattered. 'Who's that? And so late?'

'Only old Gromwell,' Philip said.

'What in God's name is he doing here?'

'I told him to call. Didn't I say?'

'No, sir, you did not.'

They heard the front door slam and the rattle of the bolts and bars. She frowned at her husband across the table. 'Twice in one week? You do him too much kindness.'

231

'Friendship is like a vine, my love. A man must cultivate it to increase the harvest and improve the grape.'

'Some old vines are not worth the trouble. They are better grubbed up to make way for new ones.'

He wagged his finger at her as if indulging a child. 'You turn a pretty phrase.'

'I shall withdraw.'

'No,' he said, smiling, as if this was a conversation about something frivolous. 'You shall stay.'

Footsteps crossed the hall. The servant announced Mr Gromwell, who bowed so low to her that for a moment she thought he might topple over.

'I am rejoiced to see you looking so well, madam. I hope you will forgive me for disturbing you at supper.'

'Not at all, sir,' she was obliged to say, though her voice was chilly and she did not look at him.

He had already supped, he said when Philip pressed him to eat something, but he joined them at the table and took a glass or two of wine with them.

'You are quite recovered from your indisposition, I understand?' he said, peering at her across the flame of a candle. 'There is no sign of it at all — indeed, if I may say so, madam, I believe I have never seen you look so radiant. Philip, will you allow an old friend to toast your wife, to worship with profound respect at your hymenal altar? And join me in raising a glass to her beauty?'

Afterwards, Philip pushed back his chair and glanced at his guest. 'Well, we must not linger in my wife's company, much as we would wish to.'

'Where are you going?' She noticed Gromwell look sharply at her; he had never heard that tone in her voice.

'Whitehall, my love. Didn't I tell you? Gromwell and I will stroll across the park and watch them at cards.'

'And will you play yourself, sir?' she asked, her voice cold.

'No — I've long since put away such childish things. I shall be as sober as a Puritan at prayer.'

Gromwell had risen too. 'I wish we could remain, my dear lady, but I confess I have work to do there.'

'Work? Is that what you call it?' Philip laughed as if he had not a care in the world. 'He hopes to find more subscribers for his great book. You remember, madam? His *Natural Curiosities of Gloucestershire*. Those who win at cards are easy game. Their generosity knows no limits.'

A moment later the men were gone, leaving her to stare at the fire while the servants cleared away the remains of their supper. What did Philip expect her to do with herself now? He would pay for his discourtesy, she told herself. Preferring Gromwell to her, and at such a time, and with so little regard for her feelings — it beggared belief! She would not be trifled with. Did she love Philip any more? Did she hate him? She hardly knew. Her feelings swung erratically from one side to the other, like a drunk man staggering home in the dark.

After a while, Mary came into the room. She made her curtsy and waited in silence.

'Well,' Jemima said at last. 'Why are you here? I didn't call you.'

Mary bowed her head on its long white neck. 'Forgive me, my lady. It was something I heard in the kitchen. I thought you would wish to know.'

'Why would I wish to hear servants' prattle?' Jemima hesitated. 'What was it?'

'A boy called before supper with a letter. Hester took it into the study and gave it to master. She said there were two letters, one sealed within the other. And he tore them open and swore as he read them. He kicked over a chair, he was so angry.'

'Who was it from?'

234

'She didn't know. He locked the letters away. Then he gave her sixpence and told her to pick up the chair and not to speak of what she'd seen.'

Coal shifted in the grate, and a flame spurted high, casting a flickering light into the room.

'There's something else, mistress. Hal heard it at the stables when he took the coach back. They've found a woman's body between Shoe Lane and Fetter Lane, somewhere in the ruins. She'd been stabbed . . .'

'Who was she?'

'I don't know. Perhaps a whore? But she was wearing a silk gown, they say, and so perhaps she was a lady.'

Celia, Jemima thought, could it be Celia?

The two women stared in silence at each other. By some trick of the light, Mary's green eyes reflected the glow and turned red.

CHAPTER NINETEEN

On Friday morning, Hakesby arrived late from his lodgings in Three Cocks Yard. He had hardly sat down before there was a knock on the door of the Drawing Office.

Mr Poulton was waiting outside, the crown of his hat brushing the low ceiling of the landing. His deep-sunk eyes were red-rimmed. He was already dressed in mourning, though his suit showed signs of wear. At his age, which Cat thought to be at least fifty-five if not sixty, she supposed that you must be hardly ever out of mourning.

'Mr Hakesby within?' Poulton demanded.

Cat curtsied and held the door wide. She began to murmur her condolences on the death of his niece, but he brushed past her. Hakesby rose to his feet, and bowed low. Brennan rose to his feet as well.

'I'm determined to build on Dragon Yard,' Poulton said loudly, ignoring Hakesby's attempt to speak. 'All the more so now. It will be a fitting memorial to my poor niece.' He shot a glance at Cat. 'We — that is, I — have decided to employ you about the business. If you are willing, and if you will press it forward as urgently and as swiftly as if it were your own.' He drew out a purse. 'You won't find me ungenerous.'

'I shall be honoured to give the matter my best attention,' Hakesby said.

'One question first. Forgive me, but I think you are not in the best of health.'

'It is but an ague, sir. It comes upon me sometimes, and then it goes away. It doesn't affect my ability to work, not where it matters.' Hakesby tapped his forehead. 'As for the rest, I employ a draughtsman to draw up my designs, and I hire others if I need them, while I remain, as it were, the presiding genius. But may I ask a question in my turn? What will happen to your niece's leasehold interest in Dragon Yard? The Fire Court petition may rise or fall because of that.'

'The leasehold comes to me. On my advice she made a will before her marriage. Had he lived, of course, her husband Hampney would have had everything. But he's dead, and there were no children. So, by the terms of her will, her estate falls to me.' He hesitated. 'Assuming that she did not make a later will.'

'You will need to make sure of that, sir.'

'Of course. But her lawyer is also mine — I saw him yesterday, and she hadn't asked him to draw up another will. But we must search her papers.' He paused, moistening his lips. 'I'm sending my housekeeper to my niece's lodgings after dinner, to pack up her things. If there's a later will, we shall find it there. Which reminds me, sir, I have a favour to ask.'

'Anything.' Hakesby spread out his trembling fingers. 'Anything within reason.'

'Reason? There's nothing reasonable about this business with my niece.' Poulton shifted his weight from one foot to the other. 'My favour is this: Mistress Lee is not as strong as she was, and she asks if you will allow your cousin to accompany her to my niece's lodgings this afternoon.' He glanced at Cat, who was pretending to busy herself with her work. 'She's taken a fancy to the girl, and it is good that she should have company at such a time.' His face looked gaunter than ever. 'I do not wish to go myself.'

Mistress Lee said barely a word in the coach that carried them to Lincoln's Inn Fields. They drew up outside the house where

Celia Hampney had taken lodgings. The coachman jumped down to talk to the porter, a heavy fellow shaped like an egg and dressed in faded brown and silver livery.

'I didn't want our friends to see this place,' Mistress Lee said, turning to Cat. 'Or our servants. It would lower Celia even further in their estimation, and give them more to prattle about.'

'Why, mistress?'

'Mr Poulton does not care for Mistress Grove — the woman who lets out the apartments. He does not think she is quite . . . He and poor Celia had words about it, but he had no control over what she did. No one had, once she was a widow, with her own property. That's why I thought it better that he did not come with us. It would only distress him needlessly.' Mistress Lee looked older than she had the previous day, and more frail. 'I would manage everything myself, but these days I lack the strength. So I asked for you. I hope you're not shocked.'

'No,' Cat said. I am a nobody, she thought, but a nobody she thinks she can rely on because of Mr Hakesby and the commission. On the whole, Cat liked being nobody. It was safer than being someone.

'Celia has a maid. Had, that is. Tabitha. A

sly creature. I shall pay her what's due to her and send her away.'

The coachman let down the steps. The house was newly built and well-proportioned, with a façade of brick. The porter showed Cat and Mistress Lee into the hall. He summoned a servant and sent word of their arrival upstairs. While they waited, he watched the two women as if he suspected they might pilfer something.

When the servant eventually returned, he led them to a lofty parlour overlooking the Fields themselves. They waited in silence, examining their surroundings. The curtains and the furniture were new but there was dust on the floorboards and cobwebs on the cornice.

The door opened, and a stout, middle-aged woman entered the room. She greeted the visitors with a stately lack of enthusiasm.

'Mistress Hampney murdered,' she said, rising from a token curtsy. She patted her formidable bosom somewhere in the region of her heart. 'I was never so shocked in my life. *Effroyable!*'

Her voice was modelled on the leisurely tones of the court, but her vowels belonged further east.

'I could hardly close my eyes last night for fear of being attacked in my own house,'

Mistress Grove went on, with all the excitement of a person describing the location of the necessary house. 'If I'd known this was going to happen, I'd never have let the apartments to her.'

Mistress Lee, formidable in black despite her short plump figure, drew herself up to her full height. 'And if Mistress Hampney herself had known what would become of her, no doubt she would have made other plans as well.'

Mistress Grove's pink features were too large for her face. Her eyes and lips had a sheen to them, as if varnished. 'I'm told that when she was found, she was dressed like a whore. She was gone for nearly a week . . . where was she? Her maid says she knows nothing, but you can't believe a word Tabitha says . . . Was there a lover? Was it he who —'

'Have you had Mr Poulton's letter?' Mistress Lee interrupted.

'Ah, poor Mr Poulton.' The bulging eyes stared into Mistress Lee's face. 'The shame of it. He must be so distressed.'

'You need not trouble yourself about Mr Poulton.'

'If only she had taken another husband, this would never have happened. Do you know what she said to me?' Mistress Grove arched her eyebrows in a parody of surprise. 'She said she wouldn't marry again for all the money in the world. She would rather live and die a merry widow than be at the beck and call of a man. Her very words!' Her lips pouted in horror. 'I fancy she would change her mind now.'

'We have come to make arrangements about Mistress Hampney's possessions,' Mistress Lee said in a voice as thin as a knife blade. 'If it would be convenient, we shall pack up what we can now and take it away. Mr Poulton will send a cart for the rest in the morning.'

'A cart? You'll need a wagon.'

'By the way, Mr Poulton has an inventory of his niece's possessions. It was made after the death of her husband.'

There was a momentary silence. Cat found that she was holding her breath. In her quiet way, Mistress Lee had told their hostess that she doubted her honesty.

'Mr Poulton must understand that I cannot repay the balance of the lease,' Mistress Grove said, returning to the offensive. 'It's true that our arrangement runs until Michaelmas, but I shall find it very hard to let the apartments after what has happened. Every kitchen maid in town is gossiping about this dreadful business.'

She conducted them upstairs to the apartments on the second floor where Celia Hampney had lodged.

'The whole house is newly furnished,' she told them on the stairs. 'Why, Sir Charles said to me only the other day, that he wished he had such things in his own house. Sir Charles Sedley? You know him? A great friend. He dined here only last month.'

Mistress Lee screwed up her lips as if to keep words from bursting out of her. She was climbing the stairs slowly, clinging to the rail and refusing to take Cat's arm. The whole world knew that Sir Charles Sedley was one of the most dissolute men at Court. He was not a man that a respectable woman would wish to see at her table, or indeed to have anything to do with.

'I suggested he bring his friend my Lord Rochester,' Mistress Grove was saying, 'but alas he was engaged. A most ingenious young man, don't you think? With quite a French twist to his wit as well. It's something I appreciate well — I lived in Paris for several years.'

Mistress Lee said she was not acquainted with his lordship, nor was she likely to be, so she was not in a position to judge his wit or its nationality.

Mistress Grove opened a door and led the

way into an apartment at the front of the house. Cat's first impression was of colour — too much of it; a deluge that drenched her eyes. She and Mistress Lee took a step into the room and stopped.

There were carpets, cushions, curtains and paintings, as well as a profusion of gilding on every surface that would take it. There was an empty wine glass on the table. There was also a smell in the air, a sour blend of perfume and spoiled food.

'Why hasn't Tabitha aired the room?' Mistress Lee said.

Mistress Grove shrugged her ample shoulders. 'I'm sure I can't tell, madam. I was in the country last week. My servants tell me that Mistress Hampney had an entertainment on Wednesday evening. Gentlemen were present, and there was a fiddler and dancing. They were at it until two or three of the morning.'

'Pray let us have some air in here.'

Mistress Grove did not move. Cat crossed the room and flung open the window.

'I do not like to speak ill of the dead,' Mistress Grove said, turning like a man of war to bring her majestic bosom broadside on to Mistress Lee, 'but she had proved a sad disappointment to me. There was a wildness about her that I could not approve.

I had already made up my mind not to renew my arrangement with her.'

'Would you send her maid to me?'

'Willingly, madam. Pray remove Mistress Hampney's possessions as soon as possible. And then I must insist that the apartments are returned to the state in which they were when she took possession. I shall send my account for sundries to her uncle.'

Mistress Lee made no answer. She turned away as if struck by the prospect from the window. Mistress Grove sniffed audibly and left the room. Cat closed the door behind her.

Mistress Lee turned to face Cat. 'That dreadful woman.' She paused. 'I hardly know you. But may I trust you not to speak of this? It would wound Mr Poulton so deeply if he knew how his niece lived in this house.' She made as if to take out her purse but, seeing Cat's face, stopped. 'You are a good girl.'

She ran her finger over the table and frowned at the thin layer of dust on it. They set to work. The bedchamber was in a worse state than the sitting room. The dressing table was strewn with cosmetics. Mistress Lee put aside the jewel box to take away with her. She told Cat to bring her any papers that she found.

'Pray God we do not find a later will,' she said. 'But if there is, we must obey its provisions. Mr Poulton will insist on that.'

There was a tap on the door, and the maid entered. Tabitha was a slender young woman with bony shoulders. She wore a dress that was too large for her. She curtsied to Mistress Lee and glanced at Cat.

'The floorboards are sticky,' said Mistress Lee in a querulous voice. 'What is it? Honey? Punch? What is the meaning of this?'

'Mistress had a party the night before she went. You should have seen it after that. I've done what I can.'

'Nonsense. When did you last see your mistress?'

Tabitha's eyes were small and narrow, and they grew smaller and narrower still. 'The day before she went away. At dinner.'

'Why not later?'

'She said I could go and see my mother, and stay the night there. And I needn't come back till evening the next day. And when I did she wasn't there.'

'But why did she send you away? Because of her party?'

The maid shrugged. 'I don't know.'

Mistress Lee's lips tightened. 'Did gentlemen call to see her?'

'Sometimes.'

'One in particular, perhaps?'

Tabitha's eyes opened wide. 'I'm sure I wouldn't know, mistress. Besides, she often went out without me.'

'You are concealing something,' Mistress Lee said. 'You will find it's in your interest to be frank with me.'

The maid stared at the old woman and said nothing.

'Your mistress is dead. You'll leave this house within the hour. Do you hear me?'

Tabitha curtsied, twisting her face into the mockery of a smile. She threw another glance at Cat, who was standing silently by the dressing table.

'Go and pack your box.' Mistress Lee was trembling. 'And I shall tell Mr Poulton how you have behaved.'

'It's already packed. And I don't care what you tell the old miser. That's what she used to call him, you know. The old miser.'

'You hussy. I shall have you whipped for your insolence.'

'You can't, and I'll rouse the house if you try. You're not my mistress.'

Without waiting to be dismissed, Tabitha flounced from the bedroom. They heard her slamming the sitting room door.

'Call the servants,' Mistress Lee said,

white-faced. 'I shall have that girl taken before a justice, I shall —'

Cat said softly, 'Madam Grove's servants won't obey you. And if you have Tabitha taken up, who knows what she'll tell the justice.'

The old woman sat down on the edge of the bed. After a moment she said in a calmer voice, 'But her insolence . . . How dare she?'

Cat held her peace. She would have liked the answer to a different question. Tabitha hadn't demanded her wages. Something or someone had changed her, had emboldened the girl to discard not only the respect she should show to her betters but also a servant's common prudence.

What? Or who?

CHAPTER TWENTY

My other master sent for me on Friday evening:

William Chiffinch, the Keeper of the King's Private Closet. There was something about him that made it difficult to be comfortable in his company: perhaps it was the cheerful air of good living that failed to correspond to the watery gaze of his cold eyes; or his reputation for infinite corruptibility; or perhaps merely the unsettling knowledge that this man had the ear of the King in his most private moments and could whisper whatever he wished to his master.

The servant brought me through a maze of apartments, passages and staircases to a small, dark chamber near the Privy Stairs. The room was empty, and he left me to wait.

The barred window looked out on the river. The tide was low, exposing the foreshore, an expanse of dank mud stained with the outflow from the palace privies and dotted with the sort of refuse that even the scavengers disdained. The slimy supports of the Privy Stairs marched down to the water's edge, where a four-oared skiff was pulling alongside the steps on the downstream side.

It was a dreary scene, and it matched my mood. My eyes were sore from copying, and my fingers ached from holding a pen for so long. The drudgery had filled the forefront of my mind all day. But now I wanted to be at my house, and at my ease. I needed time to mourn. To think.

The death of someone you love is bad enough. It creates an absence in your life, and your awareness of it rises and falls; its peaks and troughs are as unpredictable and as dangerous as the waves of the sea, whose rhythms work beneath the surface according to their own mysterious logic.

But my father's death came with a host of unanswered questions, and now with another body. Was his death somehow connected with the murdered woman half-buried in the rubble between Fetter Lane and Shoe Lane? Had he seen her lying dead in Clifford's Inn the day before he died? And what had all this to do with the Fire Court and Dragon Yard?

A movement caught my eye. Two men were descending the steps, deep in conversation. One of them, a tall, dark man I didn't recognize, scrambled nimbly into the skiff, where he sat in the stern, under the awning, and settled his black cloak around him. The other man raised a hand in farewell as the boat pulled away. He tilted his head up and I glimpsed the familiar profile beneath the hat. It was Chiffinch.

Ten minutes or so later, the door opened. My master entered.

'Marwood,' he said without any preamble. 'Your duties as Clerk to the Board of Red Cloth have not been onerous, have they?'

'No, sir.'

Chiffinch and I both knew that the Board of Red Cloth had no duties worth speaking of. Perhaps there had been duties when it had been instituted in the reign of Henry VIII. But now, more than a century later, it existed mainly to provide its commissioners, including Chiffinch, with generous salaries and its clerk with a much smaller one. The clerkship paid me about fifty pounds a year, and brought useful perquisites at Whitehall as well. I didn't want to lose it.

'Sometimes the Board requires its clerk to undertake commissions over and above his

251

usual duties. Which is the case now.' He ran his eyes over me, from my feet to my head; it was an oddly humiliating inspection that made me feel I was of no more significance to him than a hog or a pony. 'I see you're in mourning. Perhaps a change of scene will be a distraction from your grief.'

'What do you wish me to do, sir?'

'The King has commanded me to send a letter privately by a trusted bearer. You will carry it to the gentleman, and wait for his answer. Though there's no great hurry about it, discretion is essential. But that, of course, is always essential for those of us employed about the King's business. Wherever we are, whomsoever we consort with, we must never forget the need to be discreet.' He paused. 'Wouldn't you agree, Marwood?'

'Yes, sir. When should I go?'

'Tomorrow morning. Wait on me at nine o'clock, and I'll have the letter for you and a warrant for the necessary funds.'

'And where does the gentleman live?'

'About twelve miles east of Inverness. You should take the road to Nairn.'

For a moment I was too surprised to speak. Scotland? Everyone knew that Scotland was a land of mountains and barbarians, where the men did not wear breeches and acquired the rudiments of witchcraft with their mothers' milk. The further north one went, they said, the more savage the Scotch became.

'But, sir, Inverness must be nigh on six hundred miles.'

'At least that, I should think,' Chiffinch agreed. 'You will travel on public coaches, by the way. We must economize. Though that may not be easy once you reach the Highlands — I'm not sure there are public coaches up there. But there will be carriers' wagons, I'm sure, or ponies, or something of that nature.'

'It will take weeks. Wouldn't it be faster to go by sea?'

'Indeed. But, as I said, discretion is important in this matter, not speed. Besides, there will be letters for you to deliver on the way as well — did I mention that? — so going by sea would be impractical.'

'But Mr Williamson —'

Chiffinch dismissed Williamson with a wave of his hand. 'You needn't concern yourself with that. I will speak to him. Call at my lodgings in the morning, and my clerk will give you the letters and your warrant.'

He paused and looked at me, expecting me to acknowledge his instructions. I said nothing.

'I wish you a safe journey. I'll send some-one to show you out.' He turned to go, but stopped with his hand on the door. 'Don't disappoint me in this, Marwood. Discre-tion, eh? Discretion and obedience. Those are the virtues you should cultivate.'

I was full of rage.

First Williamson, now Chiffinch.

Astrologers find significance in the con-junctions of the stars. Those of us who work at Whitehall discover meanings in the con-junctions of great men. (And sometimes, in these changed times since the King's Resto-ration, the conjunctions of great women.)

Yesterday, I had seen Williamson and Chiffinch walking arm in arm in the Mat-ted Gallery. That was unusual in itself. Then Williamson had questioned me at length about the dead woman: his curiosity had been unusual too, and so had been his desire that the murder should be viewed merely as the accidental consequence of a robbery, and also his decision that the mat-ter required no enquiry on the Govern-ment's behalf. Which made it all the stranger that he had been concerned to stamp out any undue publicity about the crime.

Now Chiffinch had sent me from London on what was clearly a trumped-up mission.

It would probably take the better part of a month to complete and would bring me considerable discomfort into the bargain.

The conclusion was obvious. Someone had brought their influence to bear. If not influence, then money. It was said that Chiffinch would do anything if the price were right. As for Williamson, he wanted power: to be Secretary of State in Lord Arlington's place. To do that he needed allies in high places. Who better than Chiffinch, the man who had the King's private ear, who ministered to his pleasures and assisted his intrigues?

There are no friends at Whitehall. Only allies and enemies. Among the great, power ebbs and flows according to their conjunctions and oppositions. And the rest of us are tossed about in the current, helpless to direct our course, let alone navigate our way to safety.

I walked swiftly down to Charing Cross. In the Strand, however, rather than turning down to the Savoy, where Margaret and Sam were waiting in Infirmary Close, I veered away north towards the piazza of Covent Garden.

In Henrietta Street I knocked on Hakesby's door and sent a message up to him. A few moments later I heard several sets of footsteps on the stairs.

The first to appear was a plainly dressed young man of about my own age with a narrow, freckled face. He cast a curious glance at me.

'Master's on his way down, sir,' he said.

'Brennan?' Hakesby called. 'Come earlier tomorrow, will you? There is a great deal to do.'

'Yes, master. Good night.'

The young man disappeared into the gathering dusk. Hakesby reached the hall, his feet dragging as if he hardly had the strength to lift them. Catherine Lovett was by his side.

'I didn't expect to see you here, sir,' he said quietly. 'You're fortunate to find us — we were working later than usual.'

'I have to talk to you. Have you time?'

'Very well. Shall we go to the Lamb? What's it about?'

'I'll tell you there, sir,' I said. 'In private.'

Catherine Lovett said nothing. I was aware of her eyes on me, and I sensed her disapproval of my recklessness in coming here so openly, and thereby revealing our acquaintance unnecessarily to others.

My anger briefly spilled on to her. Be damned to her. What Mistress Lovett can't cure, I told myself, she must endure. Yesterday afternoon, when we had met over Celia Hampney's body, she had seemed almost friendly. She had instructed me in the language of the flies, the meaning of face patches, and she had teased me for my attachment to her aunt. All that was gone.

Hakesby walked between us, and we slowed our pace to his. My impatience was such that it spilled out into an absurd irritation with him and his halting gait. To make matters worse, he would not stop talking, rambling on, as old men do, as my father had once done, as if we had all the time in the world.

'We have such a quantity of business at present,' he was saying as we passed through the piazza. 'It is pleasing, of course, but I believe I may have to hire a second draughtsman to cope with it. Did you hear that Master Poulton has asked me to look at his Dragon Yard scheme? Interesting, especially if he can carry it through, but it's proving more complicated than I expected. Sir Philip Limbury's scheme is impressive, and he's in a position of strength as the freeholder, so we must study how best to counter the arguments his side will bring out at the Fire Court . . .'

'No, sir,' Cat said, gently tugging his arm.

'This way. And take care not to step into the gutter . . .'

'And Jane has been absent for most of the day,' he said, turning his head towards her as if he had only just remembered her presence. 'Most inconvenient. Mr Poulton asked for her this morning, as a particular favour, and I could hardly say no.'

I was so surprised I stopped at the corner of the arcade, causing a gentleman behind me to swerve and curse me loudly for a clumsy dog. 'Why? What did he want?'

'It wasn't Mr Poulton who wanted me,' Cat said. 'It was his housekeeper, Mistress Lee.'

'To help her at the lodgings of Poulton's niece,' Hakesby said. 'That poor lady.'

That was when I made up my mind to tell them the truth: partly because I wanted to know more about Celia Hampney and how she had lived, but more because I knew I would burst if I left my anger to fester inside me.

They gave us the same room at the Lamb, and I ordered wine to be brought.

'I have not been entirely open with you about this Fire Court business,' I said.

'What do you mean?' Hakesby demanded.

Cat just looked at me. She showed no surprise. Her face was grave.

So I told them everything, or almost everything, about my father's wanderings and what he had said to me about them; about his death and the bloodstains on his person; and about the scrap of paper with the judges' names and 'DY' written on it, which I had found in his pocket.

'So I think Mistress Hampney was killed at Clifford's Inn,' I said. 'And later they brought her body out and left it in the ruins. There's a private door from the fire-damaged building — it leads to an alley that goes to Fetter Lane. I went there with my servant on Wednesday evening.' I glanced at Cat. 'You remember that man who was watching us on Wednesday? The tall thin man by the Half Moon? He caught me in the alley. If Sam hadn't been there, God knows what would have happened.'

Hakesby waved his hand, brushing away my words. 'What is this business? I thought it concerned your father's death.'

'I don't know what it is,' I said. 'I've just come from Whitehall. They are sending me to Scotland on a fool's errand. It's to get me out of the way. It's to stop me asking questions that they don't want answered. There can be no other reason.'

'The dead woman your father saw,' Cat said. 'Was it Celia Hampney?'

'I think it must have been. Though God knows how it was done.'

Hakesby considered this. Then: 'So it's all connected. Does Mr Poulton know?'

'No. And he mustn't.'

'I tell you plainly, sir, I shall have nothing further to do with the intrigue. It's the sort of affair that leads to the gallows.' He began the slow process of standing up. 'Come,' Hakesby said to Cat. 'We're leaving.'

'Wait,' I said. 'I beg you. I understand — but, before you go, would you allow me to hear what Mistress Hakesby found in Lincoln's Inn Fields?'

'No.' He was on his feet now, wavering slightly like a tree in a stiff breeze. 'I'm sorry to hear about your father, of course, but there's an end to everything else. Come along, Jane.'

But Cat remained sitting on the bench. 'There's no harm in my telling Mr Marwood, sir.'

'No. We are going.'

'He helped me in the past,' she said. 'I should help him now. If only in this.'

'You must be quick,' Hakesby said harshly. 'I shall allow you a minute or two. No more.'

It was a surrender, but she was wise enough to allow him to cling to the appearance of victory.

'Yes, master,' she said, eyes cast down. 'Thank you.'

Hakesby sat down again. She turned to me and explained in a brisk voice that Mistress Lee had required a younger person to help her when she went to Celia Hampney's lodgings in Lincoln's Inn Fields. I heard traces of the old Catherine Lovett, secure in the arrogance that money and position bring:

'There was a most vulgar, greedy woman who called herself Madam Grove and gave herself the airs of a duchess. I wouldn't have her as my washerwoman.'

'Hush,' murmured Hakesby. 'You're too forward. And be quick about this.'

'The apartments were luxurious but disordered,' she said. 'And Mistress Hampney's maid was worse than insolent. Her name's Tabitha. She claimed to know nothing about her mistress's affairs or of any friendships with particular gentlemen. She also said that she'd been sent away on the day before her mistress disappeared, and told to come back the following evening.'

'By that time her mistress was dead,' I said.

Cat nodded. 'Celia Hampney held a party in her lodgings on the last evening of her life. For gentlemen. I suppose that's why she sent her maid away, to prevent her gossiping about what she saw. The Grove woman says she knows nothing, and in any case she was in the country all that week. She also said that Mistress Hampney desired to remain a widow, that she did not wish to lose her independence.'

I was watching Hakesby lifting his glass: it was cupped in his trembling hands and he guided it slowly towards his lips with a palpable effort of will. I said, 'So nobody knows anything?'

'Or if they do, they're not saying. Mistress Lee discharged Tabitha on the spot — the girl was asking for it, the way she behaved.' She moistened her lips. 'Tabitha didn't care.'

'Where did she go?' I asked.

'To her mother's. That's what she said. But I don't know where the mother lives.'

'Very well,' Hakesby said, setting down the glass and once more trying to rise. 'Let us leave, Jane. Now.'

Cat ignored him. 'Her impudence was strange . . . It was almost as if she had a protector, someone who made her invulnerable.'

'The Grove woman?'

She shook her head. 'There was no love lost there.'

'Do you think Tabitha knew about a lover?

Do you think he bribed her?'

'As plain as day,' Hakesby said impatiently. 'Of course there was a lover. Jane — come with me. This instant.'

I had to admit that he was probably right — and indeed everything I had learned this evening supported Williamson's view of the murder: a lovers' tryst and a robbery that had gone wrong and led to murder.

But there had to be more than that. There must be. My father had seen the woman lying dead in Clifford's Inn, not in the ruins east of Fetter Lane. Gromwell and Chelling had some knowledge that touched on the murder. It was even possible that one or both had been accessories before or after the fact of it. What of Dragon Yard, which linked Celia Hampney and Poulton to the Fire Court?

And what of my father? My poor dead father.

Something snapped in my mind.

I stood up, pushing back my bench so violently that it fell over. 'Stay here for a moment,' I said to Hakesby. 'Finish the bottle. I'm going.'

Hakesby sank into his chair. 'Have you considered, sir,' he said slowly, 'that sending you away might be a blessing in disguise?'

The wine I had taken on an empty stomach was loosening my tongue. 'Why in God's name?'

'Because sometimes it's better to let sleeping dogs lie.'

'Sleeping dogs be damned.'

'By sending you away, they have left you with no choice in the matter.' His voice was firmer now. 'Perhaps they have your best interests at heart.'

'They have no one's interests at heart but their own.' I had my hand on the latch. I looked back at them. 'I will not let this go.'

Hakesby said, 'Then it must be a matter for you alone. It is not my business.' He glanced at Cat. 'Nor hers. It is too dangerous. Remember, it doesn't concern you, and it concerns us even less.'

'That's plain-speaking,' I said, with an edge of anger in my voice, though I knew in my heart that Hakesby was right. 'I shall pursue this wherever it leads. And be damned to your cowardice.'

I flung out of the room. Even at the time, I knew I was being unreasonable, but I was so angry with the world I did not care.

I found the landlord and, with a lordliness I could ill afford, bought a bottle of Malmsey to take away with me and paid the score for what I had ordered already. I stormed down the stairs, half hoping that Hakesby would send Cat to call me back. But he didn't.

I emerged into the street. Night had fallen, and Wych Street was only dimly lit. There was a man on the other side of the road. As I appeared, he turned away and began to walk briskly westwards. By chance, he passed a lantern hanging over the doorway to a shop. For a second or two, I glimpsed the lower part of his face. He looked teasingly familiar.

Cradling the bottle under my cloak, I walked off in the opposite direction. It was only as I was turning up to the Fleet Street gate of Clifford's Inn that I realized why the face was familiar. For a moment, it had looked a little like the man I had passed in the hall at Henrietta Street: Brennan, Hakesby's draughtsman.

Chapter Twenty-One

The Fleet Street gate was barred. A lantern swung above it, shedding a dim light on the path beneath. My anger vanished. I watched a tall gentleman approach the gate. The porter came out to let him in, and they exchanged a few words. Afterwards the porter barred the gate again. At this hour of the evening, I realized, it might not be easy for me to enter Clifford's Inn.

Then a party of revellers blundered by me as I stood in the shadows by St Dunstan-in-the-West. They were half a dozen young lawyers, drunk as lords, innocent as children: they staggered up the path by the church, swearing affectionately at each other and laughing loudly for no reason.

The last of the party stumbled as he passed me. Suddenly I saw my opportunity. I stepped forward, took his arm and steadied him. He turned his head away from me and vomited politely in the gutter.

'Your servant, sir,' he said. 'Truly you are a good — a Good Samaritan.'

'Careful, sir,' I said. 'The path is treacherous in this light. Pray lean on me.'

'God bless you. We shall sink a bottle between us, damned if we don't. We must toast our everlasting friendship.'

'We shall!' I cried.

'We shall be the Damon and Pythias of Clifford's Inn. I'll be Pythias, shall I, because I must pith soon or I shall burst.'

The joke caught me unawares, and I burst out laughing. So did he. Side by side, the two of us staggered after the rest of the party, roaring with laughter.

Pythias patted the bottle in my hand. 'Ah! A man with forethought as well as wit. That is a friend indeed.' His fingers tightened on my arm. 'But it is wine, I hope? It is not a chimera? I am not dreaming this?'

'No, sir — it's Malmsey, as God's my witness. You need not fear.'

Our leaders started singing, if that is the word. After a moment, I guessed that the song was probably 'Come, Come Pretty Wenches, More Nimbler Than Eels'. On this assumption, I joined in. There was some confusion about the different parts and their harmonies, as well as about the precise wording, but what we lacked in musicality

267

we more than compensated for in enthusiasm and volume.

Our party bunched together as it passed under the archway and into the cramped court between the Fleet Street gate and the hall of Clifford's Inn. The porter on duty held up his lantern as we went through, but we must have seemed indistinguishable from one another in its feeble light — a wobbling, noisy cluster of dark hats and dark cloaks. Someone tossed him a few coins which sent him scrabbling to retrieve them on his hands and knees. He did not question my presence.

I disentangled myself from my new best friend and attached him to someone else. This was a success until they reached the hall doorway, where Pythias collided with one of the jambs and slithered to the ground. Two of his other friends tried to help him up.

Under cover of the excitement, I slipped away to the bottom of the staircase where Chelling lived. A faint light burned over the door, but otherwise the building on this side of the court was entirely in darkness.

If I didn't talk to Chelling now, it would be weeks before my next chance, and it might be too late. He knew something. I was sure of it. Perhaps something to do with

Gromwell.

In Fetter Lane, by the Hal—

The scrap of a letter I had found in his cupboard must surely refer to the Half Moon tavern, with the alley up to the locked door into the ruins. For all its fine words, it could be interpreted as the beginning of an attempt at blackmail.

The door swung open at my touch. Air swirled around me, cooler than the air outside. Drawing my cloak around me, I stood at the foot of the stairs and peered into the darkness above.

The voices in the court outside and the distant clatter of the traffic in Fleet Street ebbed away. Old stone buildings have a special form of silence, cold and dense. Gradually the darkness became less absolute, resolving itself into delicately graduated shades of black. Then the faintest of outlines appeared — the merest suggestion of the archway that led to the landing above.

As far as I was concerned, my surroundings were largely hypothetical. Faced with a hypothesis, the gentlemen of the Royal Society put it to the test. I could do no better than follow their example. I inched forward until the toe of my right shoe touched the riser of the bottom stair. I climbed the worn stone steps one by one, running the fingertips of my left hand along the cold, damp wall to keep me on course.

In this way, slowly, by trial and error, I climbed from floor to floor. On the second landing there was an uncurtained window which made my task easier. Some of the shades of black became shades of grey. There was an odd smell in the air, a blend of unexpected ingredients — linseed oil? Sulphur?

Up and up I went. None of the doors I passed showed a line of light beneath. Chelling, I remembered, had told me that the Inn had found it hard to attract students since the Civil War. And no one would wish to live in this decaying building except from necessity.

The steps were of stone until the attic storey where Chelling lived. This was a later addition of timber and wattle, reached by a narrow wooden staircase. Up to now my slow footsteps had made little sound, apart from the occasional scrape of leather on stone and the patter of dislodged dust. But now the wood creaked under my weight.

A current of air brushed my cheeks. The stairs rounded a corner. A few steps more and I was on the landing.

Chelling occupied the set of chambers at the back of the building. The other set was empty. I inched my way towards his door. The draught increased in force.

The door was ajar. The hinges groaned as I pushed it open. The study beyond was in darkness but there was a line of light under the inner door to the bedchamber.

'Mr Chelling?' I called. 'Are you there, sir? It's Marwood.'

There was no answer. At the same time a new smell reached my nostrils. Something was burning. The smell of sulphur was stronger.

'Chelling!' I cried.

In the near darkness I blundered across the outer room, jarring my thigh against the table. I threw open the door. A flickering orange light almost blinded me. For an instant I stopped. Fully clothed, Chelling was lying face down on the bed. On the floor lay a pewter candlestick. Beside it was a ball of fire, little larger than a tennis ball. The window was wide open. As I stood in the doorway, cradling the bottle, flames began to lick up the bed curtain.

I dropped the wine and lunged towards Chelling. I felt a tremendous blow on my skull. There was an explosion of blinding light. Somehow it managed to be both inside and outside my head.

The world fragmented. I was on my hands

271

and knees. An acute pain stabbed my side. Another savaged the back of my head.

The air stank of burning and Malmsey. The ball of fire was much nearer now, its flames licking my face. Consciousness was sliding away from me. I curled up, as a babe in the womb.

The bang of a door. Heat, growing hotter and hotter. Footsteps thundering down the stairs. Rough wood grazing my cheek. Hotter. Hotter.

An instinct for preservation cut in. I seized the nearest bedpost and hauled myself up. Coughing, I kicked the fireball aside. The room was thick with smoke. I stumbled through the fog towards Chelling. The flames were growing higher and higher, running up the bed hangings and along the sleeve of his coat.

I grabbed his ankle and tried to pull him on to the floor and through the doorway. He was a dead weight, and I couldn't shift him. I dived into the flames and pushed my hands under his armpits. I dragged him from the mattress and through the door.

The fire came with him.

Someone was screaming. Oh Christ.

The flames were dancing over me. I had long since lost my hat, the black silk streamers dissolving into fire. Chelling's hair had caught and so had mine. Our hair sparkled and shrivelled and blackened like a firework display. The stench made me cough even more. I noticed that my hands were dripping with blood.

Pulling my burden with a series of tugs, I staggered backwards across the study to the outer door. The flames followed us, filling the chamber with their gaudy, murderous light.

The outer door was closed, though I had left it open. I let Chelling fall to the floor and lifted the latch.

The door would not move, however hard I tugged. By now I was so desperate that I had almost forgotten poor Chelling. The air was now so hot it seared my lungs.

The door was a flimsy thing, a ledge-and-brace affair more suited to an outbuilding than a lawyer's chambers. I snatched up the elbow chair and swung it against the door with all my might. On the second blow, wood splintered and a gust of fresh air poured into the room, whipping up the flames like the blast from a pair of bellows.

After two more blows I charged at it with my shoulder. The first time I bounced back and tripped over Chelling's body, which reminded me that he was there. The second time, I plunged through splintering wood and sprawled on the floor, half inside and half outside the room. I tried to wriggle free, back to Chelling. I couldn't. I was trapped by the wreckage of the door, unable to go forward or backward. I couldn't even save my own skin.

So this, I thought, in a moment of clarity, is where it ends.

The last thing I remember was a flame that sent glowing tendrils dancing up to the landing. That and the screams. My screams.

CHAPTER TWENTY-TWO

With the fields on one side and the park on the other, Pall Mall by night was almost as quiet as the country.

Jemima turned over in the bed. After a while, Mary began to snore. The maid was lying on a mattress beside the bed. Jemima told her to be quiet, but the snoring continued. She parted the curtains, fumbled on the night table for her book, picked it up, and tossed it in the general direction of Mary's face. The snoring stopped.

Beyond the bed curtains, the room was in complete darkness. Philip was still not back. He had gone out after supper, just as he had the previous evening, saying he would not be late. She suspected that he was seeing Gromwell.

The snoring began again, building gradually in volume.

Jemima nursed her anger like a flame until it blazed up and made her swear aloud into the darkness. But then the fire died, leaving her cold and miserable. She wanted Philip back. She wanted Gromwell to go to the devil, along with his ill-omened name and his shabby finery.

Then it was three o'clock, announced by the watchman's hoarse voice in the street below and the sounds of distant church clocks. Dawn could not be far away.

Later, she heard footsteps in the street, which paused outside the house. Two people, she thought, Philip and a link boy to light his way. There was a knock at the street door, and soon another, louder one when the porter failed to stir.

Then came the rattle of bars and chains, and Philip's slow footsteps crossing the hall and climbing the stairs. He walked down the landing, passing her door without stopping, and went into his own room. He closed the door softly.

Time passed. The snoring stopped. Jemima tossed and turned. More time trickled painfully towards eternity, and suddenly she was seized by panic: soon she would be dead, and so would Philip; soon it would be too late for them all.

Jemima sat up abruptly. She dangled her legs over the side of the bed. She trod on Mary; the maid stirred in her sleep, whimpered softly and slept on.

The lantern that burned all night in the hall cast a faint outline around the door-frame. Jemima felt for her gown and wrapped it around her, drawing it tight against the chill of the night air. She pushed her feet into her slippers.

Jemima did not bother to light her candle. She made her way to the door, unlatched it and stood for a moment listening, while the draughts of the house swirled around her ankles.

She stepped on to the landing and closed the door. The house by night was dingy and unfamiliar. She padded along the passage to her husband's door. She did not knock. She raised the latch and went in.

Two candles burned on the mantle. Philip was sitting on the side of the bed. His wig lay like an untidy black spaniel beside him. He had thrown off his coat and waistcoat. A cap of short, black hair shadowed his scalp. He looked like a boy.

Something moved inside her, as if her heart twitched and twisted of its own voli-tion. She closed the door and crossed the room towards her husband. She perched on the bed, sitting to his right, leaving a few inches between them. He did not stir.

'Philip,' she said. 'What ails you?'

He raised his head and looked at her. His eyes were black pools. The heavy lids drooped over them. Why was he so troubled? She had never seen him like this. It must be something to do with the letter that had come this afternoon, the letter that had sent him into a rage, and with the woman whose body had been found in the ruins, the woman in the yellow silk gown. Had it been Celia? And did his sorrow mean that he had loved her?

Neither spoke. He was breathing very slowly. Gradually her own breathing slowed until it matched his, breath for breath.

After a while, Jemima put her arms around him. He didn't pull away from her. Holding her breath, she drew him down on her breast. When all was said and done, he was her husband.

She stroked his head as if it were a small, hard animal in need of comfort. Philip's natural hair was surprisingly fine and soft. Like a little boy's.

CHAPTER TWENTY-THREE

Brennan was as impossible to ignore as a bad smell. Cat couldn't see him but she heard his breathing. The hairs lifted on the back of her neck.

'Sunday tomorrow, isn't it?' he said.

'Yes.' Cat bent closer to her drawing board and hoped that he would take the hint.

'Thought I might take a boat on the river.'

She said nothing. With luck, Brennan would drown himself in the Thames. His footsteps drew nearer. She caught sight of him to the right, at the edge of her range of vision. He was closer than she liked.

'Old skin-and-bones gives you Sunday afternoon as a holiday, doesn't he?'

She glanced up, nodded and went back to her work.

He was directly in front of the window now, blocking her light. 'Want to come along with me? I know this tavern on the Surrey side. They have music there. Danc-

279

ing, too. You'd like it.'

'No,' she said. 'I can't.' Besides, she didn't like music much, or dancing, though she had no intention of revealing that much of herself to him.

He came closer. He was head and shoulders taller than she was. She put down her pen and pushed her right hand into her pocket.

He stretched out his hand and picked up her dividers. He smiled and showed his teeth, not a pretty sight. 'The cat's claws.'

Cat. The word jolted her. Brennan couldn't know that in her old life she was Catherine, known as Cat from childhood, especially to herself. But was it possible the man was more than he seemed?

'Give them back to me,' she said, keeping her voice low. 'If you please.'

'All in good time. I don't want you scratching me again, do I? What about it then? The river. It's going to be a fine day.'

She said nothing. Had her cousin or even one of her dead father's friends sent him here to find her? Perhaps this lure of an outing on the river was nothing more than a ploy to kidnap her, or worse.

'You're trembling,' he said. 'Why would you tremble? If you're cold, I know a way to warm a maid.'

'Go away.'

'Or what?'

'I'll tell Mr Hakesby that you are pestering me.'

'And I'll say you were imagining it, as silly girls do, and in any case old skin-and-bones won't want to believe you. He can't afford to lose me just now. You know that's the truth.'

Cat glared at him. 'Then he'll lose me instead.'

Brennan smiled. 'That's what I like about you. Your spirit. Come on the river tomorrow. You know you want to. I know you want to.'

'Give me the dividers.'

He slipped his left hand over her wrist, and his right arm encircled her shoulders. He drew her towards him. She felt the tip of one of the dividers press through her clothes, and touch the surface of her skin.

'Come on, my little sweeting. One kiss, eh?'

There was only one thing left to do so Cat did it. She snatched her right hand from her pocket. She was holding the unsheathed knife, given her long ago by an old man who used to call her Cat when she was a child. She stabbed it into Brennan's left arm where the shirt cuff met the wrist. He howled and leapt backwards, knocking over her drawing board with a great clatter. He dropped the dividers and clamped his right hand over the wound. Blood appeared between his fingers.

'You bitch, you punk, you devilish little quean —'

Knife in hand, she advanced towards him. He backed away from her. She saw fear in his eyes. She was glad of it. 'Next time I'll slit your throat,' she said softly. 'Or cut off your manhood.'

'You wouldn't dare,' he said. His eyes darted about the drawing office, looking for a weapon. 'I'll make you suffer, God's breath I will.'

Without warning, the door opened. Hakesby was on the threshold. He stared at them as if they were a pair of ghosts.

Brennan's mouth fell open. Cat's drawing board was on the floor. The plan she had been working on, she now saw, had detached itself from its clips. She was standing on it. Worse than that, she had a knife in her hand, and Brennan was bleeding, bright red splashes on the floorboards.

But Hakesby seemed not to notice. 'Chelling's dead,' he said in a voice that sounded like someone else's. 'It's all they could talk about in the coffee house. And Marwood will be dead soon too.'

Arm in arm, Hakesby and Cat followed the cobbled way from the Strand, passed under the archway where a porter sat dozing with a cat on his knee, and entered the precincts of the Savoy.

'It's not too late,' Hakesby said, tugging on her arm. 'We can turn back.'

Cat stopped. 'You may go back if you wish, sir.'

'This is folly. You know it is.'

'I don't care about that. I must know how he is. He may be dead.'

'In which case,' Hakesby said, scenting an opening, 'there's nothing we can do. So —'

'He saved my life once.' She looked up at him. 'I pay my debts.'

'Oh, be damned to it.' Hakesby rarely swore. 'You obstinate girl. Come then, but be quick about it. All we shall do is enquire after him.'

They walked on. Had she been by herself, Cat would have soon lost her way, for the old palace was a clutter of blind alleys, blank walls and dark courts. But Hakesby knew the place, as he seemed to know all of London, and he guided her into the winding lane near the foul-smelling graveyard, which led them eventually to Marwood's lodging in Infirmary Close.

Cat knocked. The door was opened by a wiry man with a weatherbeaten face and only one foot. He leaned on his crutch and scowled at them.

'We are come to enquire after Mr Marwood,' Hakesby said.

'He's not well.'

The man began to close the door. Cat put her foot in the way.

'Take it out,' he said. 'Or I'll squeeze it till you only have one foot worth mentioning. Like me.'

'Is he dying?' Hakesby said.

'You're Sam,' Cat said. 'He's mentioned you. You went to that alley by the tavern with him.'

His eyes widened. 'He told you that? You?'

'Why not? What's it to you?'

She held his eyes until the man shrugged and looked at Hakesby instead. But he relaxed the pressure of the door on the side of Cat's foot.

'We've been helping him in this matter,' she said. 'The alley off Fetter Lane? The tall thin man?'

He grunted. 'Sourface. That's what I call him.'

'Listen,' Cat said. 'Is that your master?'

The sound of screaming wasn't loud. But

it was unmistakable.

'He's not dead yet.' Sam grimaced, and the lines deepened on his face. 'He's got a good voice on him, even now, after hours of it.'

He opened the door more widely and stepped back. He hadn't actually asked them to come in but Cat took it as an invitation.

'What happened?' Hakesby asked.

Sam closed the door. He said in a hoarse whisper: 'Don't ask me. I don't know what's going on. We had a man down from Whitehall this morning, saying why wasn't master on his way to Scotland. To Scotland? What the devil was that about? And I said to the fellow, just you listen to him, that's why my master's not on the road to Scotland or anywhere else. He was howling even worse then. They could probably hear him the other side of the river.'

'What does the doctor say?' Cat said.

'We sent for him but he hasn't come yet. My wife's doing her best.'

Hakesby shivered. He sat down suddenly on a chest against the wall.

'Take me to your master,' Cat said.

Sam stared blankly at her.

'Now,' she snapped.

'Why?' Hakesby said, his voice querulous.

285

'What could you do?'

She rounded on him. 'I have some knowledge of how to treat burns.'

A door opened above them. A woman's voice called down the stairs, 'Sam? Is that the doctor?'

Before either of the men could say anything, Cat went quickly up the stairs, across the landing and into a small chamber whose door stood open. A figure swathed in white lay on the bed. For a second, she thought it was a corpse, because the face was covered.

But the figure was tossing from side to side. In the middle of the blank white head was the pink, open wound of the mouth. Dead men didn't moan, and this one did — continuously and loudly.

The servant by the bed was stout and red-faced, her skin shiny with sweat. She threw a glance at Cat and scowled. 'Get out. I don't want a nurse, I want the doctor.'

'I'm not a nurse,' Cat said. 'How bad are the burns?'

The servant frowned at her, but something in Cat's tone made her answer. 'The left side of his face is the worst, then the left arm and the leg. They pulled him out before his clothes went up. He's lucky to be alive.'

The figure on the bed screamed again.

'Lucky?' Hakesby murmured from the

286

doorway behind Cat.

'Go away,' the servant snapped.

'Beg pardon, master,' Sam said. 'Margaret doesn't know what she's saying. She's —'

'Those sheets won't do,' Cat interrupted. 'We need to wrap the burned skin in cerecloths.'

'None in the house,' Margaret said.

'Then send Sam out for them.'

'There's no money to pay for it.'

'We will pay,' Cat said.

Hakesby stirred. 'But —'

'Have you a salve?'

'No,' Margaret said. 'And how would I find time to make a salve now? God give me patience.'

Marwood was moaning now, the sound rising and falling.

'Poor devil,' Sam muttered to Hakesby behind Cat's back. 'And all for nothing. The other man died. You know — the one he tried to save.'

'The apothecary in Three Cocks Yard sells ready-made cakes of a salve,' Cat said.

Margaret threw a glance at her. 'What's in it?'

'Ground ivy simmered in deer suet. I've seen it used, applied with a feather. It helps.'

Margaret nodded. 'My mother used something like it.'

287

'Tell Sam what you need. What about rosewater? Honey?'

'I have both. We have houseleek as well. But he needs something for the pain.'

Cat said to Sam, 'See what the apothecary can offer. Your master needs opium, perhaps henbane as well. The apothecary will know.'

'Listen . . .' Mr Hakesby drew Cat aside. 'Is this wise?' he said softly. 'We don't wish our presence here to become known. It may be dangerous to us — and to Marwood, for that matter. And as for the money . . .'

Cat stared up at him, without speaking. For a few seconds, they fought a silent battle. She would not back down. Even then, she knew the battle's outcome concerned more than whether or not to help Marwood. It was about herself and Mr Hakesby.

After a moment Hakesby lowered his eyes and felt for his purse. 'Very well,' he said uncertainly. 'But pray God send a happy outcome. And how we pay Brennan, I —'

Cat said: 'There won't be a happy outcome to anything if we don't get the salve and the cerecloths soon.'

'The pain!' Marwood cried suddenly from the bed, his voice unrecognizable. 'For Jesus' sake, I beg you. Something for the pain.'

Chapter Twenty-Four

Four Days Later: Wednesday, 15 May
The case under consideration relates . . .

Cat watched the shorthand symbols marching in a stately fashion across her page in the manner prescribed by Mr Shelton in his *Tachygraphy*. The woman next to her on the gallery was trying to read what Cat was writing, craning her head while humming loudly and discordantly, in an attempt to suggest that her mind was on other things.

. . . to the extensive freehold known as Dragon Yard, situated immediately to the north of Cheapside between Lawrence Lane to the west and Ironmongers' Lane to the east . . .

Cat angled the pad towards the woman, who jerked her head away. A red stain spread up the woman's neck and across her face. There was a pleasure in shorthand, Cat thought, independent of its usefulness for making a rapid record: the symbols had their own beauty, and so had the secrecy of them: it offered a private language, for private thoughts, for private people.

. . . and in the possession of Sir Philip Limbury . . .

She could see Sir Philip himself in the body of the court, standing with his man of business beside the dais where the three judges sat at their round table, with their clerks behind them and the ushers against the walls, one on each side.

Theophilus Chelling would have been on the dais too, if he had been alive, taking notes and fussing with his papers. But Chelling was dead, and his chambers were reduced to charred timbers and shattered roof tiles. According to Hakesby, the authorities who controlled Clifford's Inn, the Rules, were not unhappy to have a reason to rebuild his staircase as well as Staircase XIII, damaged in the Great Fire. Also, Hakesby had said to her before the hearing, perhaps they were glad to see the back of Chelling too.

Limbury was whispering to the man of business, an attorney named Browning. Professional representatives were the exception rather than the rule at the Fire Court hearings — most people argued their own cases as best they could, not least because of the expense. But the major freeholders with many properties, such as the Dean and Chapter of St Paul's and the Livery Companies, employed lawyers or surveyors to do the work. Dragon Yard was a large, complicated site, a patchwork of freeholds, leaseholds, covenants and rights of way, so expert advice was sensible.

Besides, a gentleman like Sir Philip Limbury, a Groom of the Bedchamber, could hardly be expected to represent himself in such a matter. His presence here was unusual in itself, and had attracted some curious glances, both in the hall below and from the women in the gallery.

Limbury was dressed in black, in a sombre but magnificent suit of velvet. Beside him, Browning was small and dumpy, apparently insignificant. According to Mr Hakesby, it wouldn't be wise to underestimate Browning. He had his fingers in many pies — and he also represented the London interests of Sir Philip's father-in-law, Sir George Syre, a man reputed to have a very long purse.

'And who speaks for the defendants?' asked Sir Wadham Wyndham, who was chairing the proceedings.

Mr Hakesby shuffled towards the dais. 'I do, my lord. At the behest of Mr Roger

Poulton, who is one of the principal leaseholders.'

'But Mr Poulton is not the only defendant. Do you speak for the others?'

'Yes and no, my lord. There are many interests involved. It is a complicated matter to reconcile them all, which is why Mr Poulton begs the Court to defer the hearing for two weeks.'

Sir Philip stooped to Browning's level and murmured something in his ear. Browning approached the dais, bobbing up and down as if his irritation would not permit him to remain still.

'My lord, surely this is unreasonable? It is in no one's interest to delay the matter, let alone the City of London's. Here we have a well-thought-out scheme, providing a clear benefit to —'

Wyndham held up the palm of his hand. 'Enough, sir. You'll have your turn to speak in a moment.' He turned back to Hakesby. 'Sir, as you know, delay is the last thing that this court wants — we are here to speed things up, not slow them down. Why should we consider your request?'

'Because Mr Poulton and his family have an interest in Dragon Yard that stretches over three generations, as well as a smaller, adjacent freehold which he offers to merge with Dragon Yard. Their existing leaseholds still have years to run. And, on his behalf, I have drawn up plans for the site which will result in more houses than Sir Philip's development, without any loss of size, quality or amenities, and which will also allow better access to Cheapside. It is the City's preferred option — I have discussed the matter at length with one of their own surveyors, Mr Hooke, and I have a letter from him that —'

'But this is not to the point, my lord,' Mr Browning broke in. 'The truth of the matter is that the leaseholders cannot agree among themselves. Whereas Sir Philip is —'

'My lord, the reason for my client's request benefits Sir Philip as well. Indeed, a short delay may simplify the entire case in a way that will be in everyone's interest.'

Sir Thomas Twisden, sitting on Wyndham's left, leaned across the table and murmured something to his colleague. Wyndham nodded, and turned to the third judge, Sir Richard Rainsford, who shook his head.

Cat wrote in shorthand: *They can't agree among themselves?*

'After Sir Philip and Mr Poulton, my lord,' Hakesby went on, inexorable as death itself, 'the main interest in the Dragon Yard site is held by leaseholds in possession of the estate of Mr Poulton's niece, the late Mistress Celia Hampney.'

This led to a buzz of conversation below, that grew so loud that Hakesby was forced to stop. The clerk called for silence. The judges conferred among themselves. But it was not until Wyndham himself rapped his gavel on the table and threatened to clear the court that silence spread through the hall.

Wyndham beckoned Hakesby to approach the dais. 'Mistress Hampney, you say? You mean the lady who was murdered in the ruins last week?'

'Yes, my lord. After her death, her uncle instituted a search for her will, for she had an absolute right to convey her wealth as she wished, apart from the jointure she received on her marriage to her late husband. There is indeed a will, but it's an old one that was made at the time of her marriage. Under its terms, Mr Poulton would be her principal heir, since her husband had predeceased her and there were no surviving children of the marriage. But now, Mr Poulton learned only yesterday, there is the possibility of a later will. If that is true, and if the will is valid, its provisions may alter the circumstances of the case.'

As Hakesby was speaking, a tall man pushed his way through the crowd and joined Limbury and Browning near the dais. He glanced up at the gallery, surveying who was here. He had strongly marked features set in a thin, handsome face. Limbury turned as he approached and muttered something, accompanying the words with a slashing movement of his right hand. The newcomer nodded.

Gromwell? she wrote.

Sir Thomas Twisden was whispering something in Wyndham's ear, and gesturing towards Limbury. Cat wrote: *Twisden doesn't want to defer.*

Wyndham raised his head. 'I'm not minded to grant this request, Mr Hakesby, unless you can make a better case for the delay.'

'Thank you, my lord,' Browning said. 'Then may we proceed to outline our proposals?'

Hakesby drew himself up to his full height. Cat knew he was drawing on diminishing reserves of strength; he would pay later for this prodigal outburst of energy, and so in a different way would she. 'My lord, before we continue, may I beg you to read the letter my client has received from the agent employed by the Hampney family? It may materially affect your decision.'

Wyndham nodded wearily and beckoned an usher. 'Hand it up, sir.'

An usher stepped down into the body of the hall, took the letter from Mr Poulton, and carried it to the judges. Wyndham unfolded it and scanned the contents. He made no comment but passed it first to Rainsford and then to Twisden, who shrugged and returned it to Wyndham.

The hall was full of whispers and shuffling feet. The Dragon Yard case was unusual, something to feed the gossips that hung around the Fire Court. The judges conferred in low voices. Again, Cat thought, if the language of their bodies was any guide, Twisden was not in agreement with Wyndham and Rainsford. At one point, Twisden looked and glanced down the hall in the direction of Sir Philip, Browning and the man who was probably Gromwell.

At last, Wyndham rapped on the table, and the hall fell silent. 'The late Mistress Hampney's leases lie on the Cheapside boundary, and are therefore most important to the development of the entire Dragon Yard site. It appears that, two months before her death she visited Lincolnshire, where she had a lifetime interest in a house and farm under the terms of her jointure. While she was there, according to this letter, she signed a new will, drawn up for her by a local attorney. It is in Lincoln, with various deeds and other documents relating to the marriage settlement that need the signatures of her heirs. The contents of the new will are unknown. So it is necessary for it to be brought down from Lincoln and inspected by this court before we can assess with any certainty who has an interest in Dragon Yard, and indeed the precise nature of these interests.'

'Thank you, my lord,' Mr Hakesby said. 'My client is —'

'I have not finished,' Wyndham said, frowning at the interruption. 'But we cannot allow this to hold up the work of the court indefinitely. Therefore we shall set a term on this: the will and any other relevant documents must be presented to us within seven days. I shall give you an order of the court for your client to send to Lincoln, requiring that the will be brought before us. At the end of that period, using the extraordinary powers vested in us, we shall determine the case in the light of whatever information is available.' He rapped the table with his gavel. 'It's time for dinner. The court will reconvene tomorrow.'

■ ■ ■ ■

Cat found Hakesby outside the hall, leaning against a wall in the court between the hall and garden. His face was the colour of chalk. Despite his exhaustion, he was in a good humour.

'I didn't think we would do it,' he said. 'By God, it was close. If Rainsford or Wyndham had agreed with Twisden, it would have been all over in a moment. Limbury's plans are more advanced than ours, and everyone's wary of his Court influence, even if they pretend it doesn't matter here.'

'Do you think Twisden knows him?' Cat asked.

Hakesby's eyebrows shot up. 'Limbury? Why?'

'I thought I saw something between them.'

'Perhaps. Usually Twisden's a follower — he agrees with the other judges.'

A smell of roast meat drifted past them. A procession of waiters crossed the courtyard, carrying the judges' dinner up to their chamber.

'There was another man with Limbury as well as Browning,' Cat said. 'A tall man. He came in late.'

'That was Gromwell,' Hakesby said. 'Limbury's creature.'

'Is that the Half Moon?' Cat said, pointing at a group of roofs which were just visible beyond the buildings of Clifford's Inn.

Hakesby looked puzzled at the abrupt change of subject. 'The tavern? Yes, it must be. Why do you ask?'

Before Cat could reply, Mr Poulton joined them, rubbing his bony hands together. 'A week. It's not long, but you did well, Mr Hakesby. I'll send a man to Lincoln immediately.'

'Will there be time?'

'God willing. At least the roads are drier now. But of course we don't know what we shall find at the end of it.'

'The contents of the new will?' Hakesby said.

'Nothing would surprise me, the way Celia was since she went to live at Mistress Grove's. She was as predictable as a butterfly. But in any event it is better to know than not to know. Will you dine with me? We must plan for both best and worst.'

'With pleasure.' Hakesby glanced at Cat. 'You should go back to Henrietta Street.'

'But not alone,' Poulton put in. 'What if the monster who killed Celia is about?'

'It's only a step from here, sir,' Cat said.

Hakesby coughed and said he thought it

scarcely likely that Cat would be attacked in broad day.

Poulton pulled out his purse. 'I insist you take a hackney.'

He was obstinate as well as their client, so Cat took the money he offered her without argument.

'Come, Hakesby. Let us go across the way to the Devil. It's as near as anywhere, and I can get a coach in Fleet Street afterwards.'

Cat said to Hakesby, 'If you'll allow it, I'll correct my shorthand record before I go, while it's fresh in the memory.'

He nodded, his mind on Poulton and Dragon Yard. Cat stood in the sunshine and watched the two men moving towards the hall door on their way to the Fleet Street gate. It was true that it would be wise to check her shorthand as soon as possible. But her main reason for lingering in Clifford's Inn had more to do with the fact that Brennan was at Henrietta Street, and she had no desire to be alone with him in the drawing office.

The courtyard was now empty. The Fire Court was no longer in session. As for the remaining inhabitants of Clifford's Inn, it was time for dinner. The air in this sheltered place was as warm as summer. It was very quiet, as if the world were holding its breath.

On the other side of the courtyard was the green shade of the garden. It would harm no one if she sat on one of the benches for twenty minutes while she read back her shorthand. In normal circumstances, the use of the garden was probably restricted to members of the Inn, but now the Fire Court was here, the circumstances were no longer normal. If anyone objected, she would plead ignorance of the regulations. But at present there seemed no one about to object.

The garden was surrounded by railings, but the gate leading into it was unlocked. Once inside, Cat followed a gravel path that made a circuit of the enclosure. No one else was here. She found a bench in the sunshine, which was sheltered by a hedge of yew. There was a narrow gap in the hedge, which gave her a view of part of the new building, with what was left of Staircase XIII beyond, and then the gate leading to the approach to Clifford's Inn from Fetter Lane.

Yawning, Cat read through her notes, pausing every few lines to make a correction or insert a clarification. She had already made the unhappy discovery that it was far easier to write shorthand than to read it back. Her eyelids grew heavy, and she let the notebook fall to her lap.

As her body quietened, her thoughts ranged free and latched themselves on to Marwood. She wondered how he was doing. She had called at Infirmary Close on Monday afternoon, but had not seen him. Fiercely protective of her master, Margaret had told her he was sleeping like the dead. Perhaps she should visit him this evening. If he was awake and in a lucid state of mind, he would want to hear what had happened this morning at the hearing.

Everything came back to the Fire Court, she thought, and Clifford's Inn. Gromwell lived here, and he was Limbury's ally and he had been Chelling's enemy. Chelling had lived here too, and he had been a clerk to the Fire Court. Limbury had a case before the Fire Court. Gromwell's chamber was where Marwood's father believed he had seen a dead woman reclining in sinful luxury. Celia Hampney was the woman, and Dragon Yard linked her with Limbury and Poulton — and then back to the Fire Court and Clifford's Inn.

The thoughts danced erratically in her mind, chaotic as a cloud of flies, buzzing and wheeling and ducking and diving. But even flies, she thought sleepily, must obey the regulations of their kind, must follow mysterious patterns of their own.

The sound of footsteps tugged her back to full consciousness. Someone was crossing the courtyard behind her. She glanced to her right and saw Gromwell striding along with his hands behind his back and his nose in the air.

She expected him to enter Staircase XIV in the new building, where his chambers were. Instead, he made for the fire-blackened door to Staircase XIII. He took a key from his pocket and looked over his shoulder, first to the left and then to the right.

In the silence, the scrape and click of the key in the lock were clearly audible in the garden. But just as Gromwell was about to open the door, there was an interruption.

'Sir! Sir!' Hurrying footsteps crossed the courtyard. 'Thank God you're not at dinner — there's a difficulty between Mr Jones and Mr Barker. They're like to come to blows if they're not stopped. And the Principal is looking for you too.'

It was one of the Inn's servants, a wrinkled man with a shock of white hair below his hat. Gromwell snatched the key from the lock and stormed across the court towards the hall door. The servant scurried after him.

Cat acted on impulse. She stood up and made her way to the garden gate. When

Gromwell and the servant had gone, she walked quickly to the door leading to Staircase XIII. She lifted the latch. The door opened.

It was as easy, and as foolish, as that. Gromwell might return at any time. But it was such a golden opportunity — not just his absence and the temporarily unlocked door, but also the fact that it was the dinner hour and the open spaces of Clifford's Inn were as empty as they were ever likely to be in the hours of daylight.

She slipped inside and closed the door. A faint and musty smell of burning lingered from the Great Fire more than eight months ago.

This staircase was one of the older parts of Clifford's Inn. The ground-floor walls were three or four feet thick, pierced on either side of the door with pairs of mullioned windows in frames of dressed stone. These had lost their glass in the heat of the fire. The heavy shutters kept out all but a few cracks of light.

But it wasn't dark. Daylight filtered down from above, casting a hazy light that shifted and shimmered, as if underwater.

Cat looked up. The fire had gutted most of the interior, destroying floors and the partitions between the chambers. The

304

charred remains of some joists were still there, as well as the brick chimney stack, a relatively modern addition, which was standing to full height.

Less than a third of the roof remained intact, the section surrounding the chimney stack. Sheets of patched canvas, old sails, had been stretched over the remainder of the space. The breeze made the material ripple and flap lethargically, but the makeshift arrangement worked, and the interior was surprisingly dry.

On the floor above, pairs of planks rested on the joists, lashed in place with rope. They made a ledge along the back wall of the building. Cat took a few steps forward, so she could see the entire length of the run.

The planks stretched from one corner to the other. Archways were set in the thickness of the walls, facing each other along the two rows. The one to the right led to a stone staircase, buried in the thickness of the masonry at the north-east corner of the building, which rose in a spiral to floors that no longer existed.

At the north-west corner was a similar archway. It was impossible to see where it led. But the west wall must butt against the back of the new building where Gromwell had his chambers on Staircase XIV.

Cat made her way towards the staircase, her footsteps crunching on the layer of debris covering the flagged floor, a mixture of blackened tiles, plaster dust and ashes. It was only when she reached the arched opening that she realized that it also led somewhere else: to a short flight of steps rising to the right, branching away from the main staircase. There was enough light to make out a short passage ending in a door.

She felt a stab of excitement, followed by a less welcome sense of apprehension. Marwood was right: there was a private route between Fetter Lane and Clifford's Inn. He had been on the other side of this door last week.

Was this the way the murdered woman had come on the day of her death? Perhaps she had come by hackney to Fetter Lane and someone had met her in the alley and conveyed her here.

Cat climbed the steps. The passage was about three yards long. It was very dark here. She fumbled her way to the end. There was a door set in the east wall of the building, towards Fetter Lane and the Half Moon. It seemed undamaged by the fire. She felt the outlines of heavy bars, as well as the shape of a lock encased in a large wooden box.

As she turned back, she stubbed her toe on something resting against the wall by the door: something rigid that moved under the impact of her foot, making a scraping sound on the flagstones. She crouched. Her fingers touched a piece of wood. She explored it rapidly with her fingers, angling it towards what little light there was. A rectangle of carved wood, perhaps eighteen inches by two feet, with what felt like canvas within it.

A picture in its frame.

She picked it up and took it down the steps and into the watery brightness of the main building. She turned over the frame to bring it the right way up. She found herself looking at a painting of a group of naked women in the countryside. The picture was so absurdly lewd that it made her want to laugh.

Marwood had talked of the room where his father fancied he had seen the murdered woman: . . . a picture that disgusted him over the mantel . . .

The dead woman had turned out to be real enough. And now it seemed as if the rest of it had been true as well. In which case —

There was a crack like a gunshot behind her.

Cat bolted back through the archway and

into the welcoming gloom of the passage. Trembling, she set down the picture against the wall.

The sound had been the raising of the latch on the door. She heard the door closing. There were footsteps crunching over the dust and ashes and drawing closer. She cursed herself for showing no more sense than a startled rabbit: she had run into a trap. She felt in her pocket for the knife.

For a moment everything hung in the balance. The footsteps were at the bottom of the stairs. Then, slow and deliberate, they began to climb the stairs.

Cat let out her pent-up breath. She tiptoed towards the staircase. The steps climbed higher and higher. She stepped down to the archway. The footsteps were different — hollower, and even slower — the sound of them was louder. It was now or never.

Cat picked up her skirt and ran across the floor. She zigzagged round heaps of rubble. She tripped over a fallen beam and fell. She scrambled to her feet, and as she did so glanced upwards.

Gromwell was looking down at her from the walkway of planks. For a moment he was as still as an artist's model, his arms flung out in a strangely graceful pose, as if he had been frozen in the middle of a dance.

He turned and ran back towards the archway to the stairs.

Cat reached the door. She lifted the latch and pulled. The door did not move. Panic jolted through her. Gromwell had locked the door behind him when he came in. There was no escape.

She glanced back. Gromwell was stumbling through the archway at the bottom of the stairs.

In desperation she tugged at the door again. As she did so, she saw that Gromwell had thrown a bolt across when he came in. She slid it back and lifted the latch.

This time it opened, almost knocking her over. Then, God be praised, she was outside in the May sunshine and running across the courtyard towards the gate to Fetter Lane.

CHAPTER TWENTY-FIVE

In the afternoon, Jemima, Lady Limbury, had one of her fits of restlessness. Usually she preferred to stay at home, seeing no one apart from the members of her own household. But sometimes the house in Pall Mall grew oppressive and she had a craving for different air in her lungs and even a different life for herself.

I am a caged bird, she told herself, revelling in the sorrow of her plight, and I keep the key to my cage close to my heart.

Besides, she had a curiosity to see something. Something in particular.

She ordered the coach to be brought to the door at three o'clock. She summoned Mary, who dressed her mistress in the black, unrevealing gown that she usually wore when she went out for a drive. Despite the warmth of the day, Jemima insisted on her travelling cloak with the hood, as well as her veil.

310

When Mary ventured to suggest she might find herself uncomfortably hot, Jemima hit her with the back of the hand across her cheek. It was not a hard blow but the diamond she wore on her middle finger grazed Mary's cheek. Mary gasped and jumped back.

Jemima stared in fascination at the drops of blood oozing on to the surface of Mary's pale skin. Mary's eyes — those green eyes, her best feature — looked larger and brighter than ever, because of the tears.

'Come,' Jemima said, and beckoned her to approach her chair. 'Let me see your cheek. Closer, girl, closer.'

Mary bent nearer her mistress. A tear fell on to Jemima's bare forearm.

'Closer,' Jemima whispered. 'Closer.'

When Mary's face was only inches away from her, Jemima inclined her own head towards her. She licked the blood on Mary's cheek.

'There,' she said. 'That's better.'

A little later they went down to the coach. Richard escorted her outside, and handed her into the vehicle. He said his master had ordered him to attend them on their outing. But Jemima said that she did not require him, that they would take the groom from the stables where the coach was kept. She gave orders that Hal should drive to Hyde Park, and that he was not to stop for anyone.

The coach slowly climbed the hill to Piccadilly. The vehicle was new, a gift from Sir George, and it had windows containing glass above the doors rather than the usual openings covered by leather curtains.

The road surface grew rougher as the houses dropped behind. They turned left towards the park. The clatter of the hooves, the rattle of wheels and the cries and shouts of passers-by created a bubble of privacy. Jemima did not order Mary to lower the blinds to cover the windows. She liked to see the world outside, softened by the distortions of the glass and the material of the veil.

'I don't want to go to the park,' she said suddenly. 'I've changed my mind. Tell Hal to turn round.'

'Shall I tell him to take us home, my lady?' Mary said, her voice shaky from crying.

'No.'

Mary rapped on the roof. The coach slowed, and the groom riding behind drew level with the window to receive his mistress's orders.

'We shall go to Fetter Lane,' Jemima said.

Mary's head jerked round to look at her mistress.

'Tell them I want to see where the whore was found dead the other day. Tell them to drive as close as they can to the very spot.'

'Must we?' Mary whispered.

'Do it.'

Jemima stared out of the opposite window while Mary relayed the changed orders to the servants. She felt a thrill of excitement at her own daring. She had planned this outing carefully, ever since it had been confirmed that the murdered woman in the ruins was Celia Hampney. She had always intended to go to Fetter Lane, but she had not wished to alert anyone to this until they were well away from the house, in case Philip caught wind of it. He would have tried to stop her.

There was a good deal of traffic in Piccadilly, and it took an age to turn the coach round and set off eastwards. To avoid the crush at Temple Bar, they took the route that led up to Holborn and turned down Fetter Lane from the north. As they neared Fleet Street, Jemima looked out of the left-hand window at the ruins that spread down to the Fleet Ditch and then rose to the blackened City wall, with the gaunt remains of St Paul's beyond it.

Hal Coachman paused to ask directions from an apprentice, who guided them into a narrow entry on the left. The coach jolted along, straddling the central gutter, at less than a walking pace. When it drew to a standstill, half a dozen beggars appeared around them, all of them no more than children. Jemima stared into the freckled face of a street urchin.

The groom kicked the boy away and bent down to the window. 'If your ladyship pleases, Hal can't get any closer.' He hesitated, his tongue flicking out to moisten his lips. 'If her ladyship perhaps cares to walk? It's only twenty paces or less.'

Jemima sucked in her breath. She didn't want to leave the coach. But she wanted to see the place where the whore had lain. The exact place where she had made her last bed above ground.

'Tell them to make the people go away. Mary, give the man some pennies for them.'

The groom bribed the largest of the boys to point out the exact place where the body had been found, and to keep the others away from the coach. Hal made one of the smaller children howl with a flick of the whip on the girl's bare forearm. When the beggars had learned to keep their distance, the groom escorted Jemima and Mary down a path that led off the lane, swinging a staff in a manner that was sufficiently threatening to deter the other beggars from approaching too closely.

They came to a court surrounded by the remains of small, tightly packed dwellings. The groom pointed to one of the exposed cellars.

'In there, my lady.'

One of the beggars drew level. 'She was buried,' the boy said, glancing nervously at the staff in the groom's hand. 'In the rubble there. I saw her. But she wasn't buried well enough. The foxes and the rats had her.'

Jemima laughed. 'Give the boy a penny,' she said. 'Quickly.'

The groom held out the coin. The boy snatched it from him.

He tried his luck once more. 'And a bird had pecked out her eye.'

'And another,' Jemima said. 'Then make him go away.'

'See there,' the lad said, pointing. 'That's her blood.'

For a moment, Jemima stood there, staring into the cellar where they had found Celia. There was a darker mark on a heap of earth in the corner. It might be blood or it might merely be the boy's attempt to enter into the spirit of the occasion in the hope of a third penny. When Jemima said nothing, the groom cuffed the lad, who retreated to a safe distance.

The court was sheltered. Despite her cloak and her veil, Jemima felt the warmth of the sun. Yes, it had been worth the effort of coming here. The dead didn't feel the sun. All that was left for them was the cold of the grave and attention of the worms.

Celia Hampney. Who had owned one of the leaseholds on Dragon Yard, which must explain a good deal. Who had been Gromwell's lover, if Jemima's husband had spoken the truth. But had Philip spoken the truth? She tried to ignore the possibility but the pain of it stabbed her like a stitch in her side.

'Tell them we shall go home now,' she said to Mary. 'The long way round. By Shoe Lane and up to Holborn.'

She did not speak again until the coach turned into Pall Mall. Then she glanced at Mary. Her maid was weeping silently. Why? What had she to weep about? Servants were so mysterious.

Jemima leaned forward and stroked Mary's cheek. 'You're a good girl,' she said. 'You serve me well.'

She knew the value of a kind word in season.

CHAPTER TWENTY-SIX

My mouth was horribly dry and my tongue felt like a scrap of leather left by the heat of the fire. I lay for a moment, uncertain of why I was here or even where here might be. Some time later, and with a modest sense of achievement, I realized that I was in my own bedchamber in the Savoy.

I thought at first that it was early in the morning, for I would not be in bed when it was light outside. Sometime later, however, I realized that the window shutters were open, and the bed curtains were tied back. Nor did the light have the freshness of morning. Also, I could hear sounds that belonged to the other end of the day. Pans clattered below. A man was singing a ballad in the lane outside our lodgings in Infirmary Close. Children were shrieking, and someone was hammering something.

By degrees, I discovered that I was lying on my back, though tilted a little to the right with what felt like a narrow bolster running down the left side of my body. It was a strange and uncomfortable position to be in, though I lacked the energy to do anything about it. The skin on my face felt tight and hot. I touched my left leg with a finger and was rewarded with a stab of pain that briefly penetrated the clouds in my head, but then dissipated swiftly.

I tried to concentrate but my mind refused to cooperate. It drifted like a boat without oars or sails. I found myself thinking of my long-dead mother, remembering the cool touch of her fingers when I lay in bed with a childhood fever.

A new sound forced its way into my consciousness, a knocking below. Why did people have to make so much noise? There were footsteps, and voices raised in argument. Someone was coming up the stairs. The door of my chamber was flung open so violently that it collided with the side of the press.

'You can't do this, mistress.' Margaret's voice, loud and upset. 'I'll have Sam throw you out.'

'Peace, woman,' I said. Or rather that is what I intended to say. The words emerged in a soft mumble that even I could hardly hear. I closed my eyes.

'I'll do him no harm. Mr Marwood, are you awake?'

I knew the voice. Catherine Lovett's. My mind filled with a jumble of memories and impressions. Cat. Hakesby's hellcat. Long ago, she had bitten my hand and given me a wound that had not healed for days. Half woman, half child and wholly formidable: a person of many talents, whom I could not for the life of me understand.

'It's no use.' Margaret sounded resigned. 'He's been asleep since yesterday morning. Or having visions. He was talking to his father during the night. As if the old man was there beside him.'

'The laudanum?'

'It's a blessing.' The anger had left Margaret's voice, leaving tiredness and anxiety behind. 'God knows what we'd have done without it. That and the cerecloths — you were right about those.'

I tried to raise my right hand above the coverlet on which it lay. I made my fingers flutter. Then weariness overtook me.

'Look,' Cat said. 'He's awake.'

I opened my eyes. The two women were standing beside the bed, so close they were almost touching, and looking down at me. Cat covered her mouth with her hand, as if holding back words that were trying to escape.

'Master?' Margaret said, bending over me, her red face crinkled with worry. 'Master?'

'Margaret,' I said. 'Oh, Margaret, I've had such dreams.'

'I tried to keep her out,' she said. 'But she just ran up the stairs.'

I wanted to explain to her that it didn't matter, that nothing mattered. Instead I touched the left side of my face. Fabric of some sort covered the skin. But even that slight pressure from my fingers was enough to make me wince. That mattered.

'Help me raise him,' Margaret said. 'Might as well make yourself useful while you're here. But for God's sake be gentle.'

Cat went round to the other side of the bed. Between them, the two women lifted me in the bed so my head and shoulders were supported by pillows. The process was exquisitely painful. I cried out. My eyes filled with tears.

'Hush, now,' Margaret said, as if I were a whimpering child.

She turned aside and filled a mug from a jug on the night table. She held it to my lips. I sucked greedily at the liquid it contained. Small beer dribbled down my chin. But some of it found its way into the parched desert of my mouth and trickled down my throat. I had never tasted anything so wonderful.

When I had drunk my fill, she wiped the dribbles from my face and neck.

'Thank God,' she said. 'I thought you'd sleep for ever.'

Memories pushed into my mind, jostling each other in their haste. Fear rose in me like vomit. My mouth tasted sour. Friday evening, I thought. I was going to Scotland in the morning.

'What day is this?' I said, suddenly anxious. 'Saturday? Sunday?'

'Wednesday,' Margaret said.

I struggled with the arithmetic. 'But that means . . .'

'You've been here in this bed for five days.'

I looked from Margaret to Cat. 'The fire. I remember the fire.' More memories forced their way to my attention: a ball of flames by Chelling's bed; footsteps running down the stairs; a pain in my head. I raised my hand and felt the bulge of a bruise above the right ear. 'But then . . . ? Is he all right?'

I saw a glance pass between them. Cat said rapidly, 'Yes, you went to see Chelling. Do you remember? Before that you drank wine with Mr Hakesby and me at the Lamb and told us why you were interested in the

Fire Court. You were angry because they were sending you to Scotland on a fool's errand. Then you grew even angrier because we thought you should let the business alone.'

'They brought you back on a door that night,' Margaret said grimly. 'Shouting your head off.'

'But Chelling?' I said.

'He set fire to himself in bed,' Cat said. 'He was drunk — he overturned a candle probably, and the bed curtains went up. You tried to get him out, but it was too late. The top of his staircase was destroyed. They'll have to rebuild it.'

She fell silent. I remembered the dead weight of the man, small though he was. I remembered breaking open the locked door to the stairs. But the door had been unlocked when I had come up to Chelling's chambers — how else could I have got in? — and I had left it standing open. I remembered the pain in my head. And the fireball glowing malevolently by the bed, with the draught from the open window fanning the growing flames. And I remembered the footsteps running away down the stairs.

Cat went on, in a more hesitant voice, 'You've had opium for the pain. It gives you dreams, sometimes. Vivid dreams. Like visions.'

'But I didn't dream this. Chelling was murdered.' I looked up at their shocked faces. 'As Celia Hampney was.'

I was tired, and I closed my eyes. I heard the two women whispering to each other. I understood that they thought I had lost my wits, that the opium had so entangled me in my own dreams that they were more real to me than this living, breathing world with its rough edges and its hard corners. But I knew I had not imagined what I had seen. Opium brings dreams and visions; but it may also bring clarity of memory and precision of thought; if the angels have the capacity to think, they must think like this, always.

Something eluded me. Something I had seen. But when?

I opened my eyes. 'How badly am I hurt?'

Margaret's face appeared above me. 'There's a wound on your head, master. It's healing, God be thanked. But the fire caught you . . . it's the left side.'

'How badly?'

Margaret's features crumpled, and she glanced away. Then Cat was where Margaret had been.

'You were burned from your face to your knee. The doctor says there will be scarring.

So does Sam.'

I frowned at her, struggling to understand this strange world where Catherine Lovett talked familiarly of my servant.

Margaret misunderstood the reason for the frown, thinking I was dismissing Sam's opinion as worthless. She fired up — almost literally, because her face became even more flushed: 'He knows what he's talking about, master, and better than most. When he was in the navy, his frigate was caught by a Dutch fire ship. He's seen what fire can do to a man.'

She continued speaking, and then Cat said something too. But by that time their words had lost their hard edges; they were blurring into one another; they merged and became a soft, shifting susurration, like the humming of bees going about their business. The sounds rose and fell, mixing agreeably with the hammering and the cries of children, until I fell asleep.

'What are you doing here?' I said.

The bedroom was full of hard, clean light. I had already established that another night had slipped away, and now it was morning.

Cat said tartly, 'What does it look like?'

She poured the contents of the chamber-pot into the slop bucket, her nose wrinkling.

324

She rinsed the pot with water from the jug and covered the bucket with a cloth.

'Why are you in this house? Doesn't Mr Hakesby need you in Henrietta Street?'

She swung round to face me. 'Do you think I'd be here unless I had to be? Do you think I'd be doing this?'

'Then why?'

'Because I can't go back to Henrietta Street even if I wanted to,' Cat interrupted. 'People are looking for me.'

'Who?'

'I don't know who, exactly. But it's because I was foolish enough to let you drag me into your affairs.'

'What's happened?'

'I was at Clifford's Inn yesterday,' she said. She put down the pot at last and perched on the stool by the bed. 'The Dragon Yard case came up before the Fire Court. Mr Hakesby was speaking for Mr Poulton, and Sir Philip Limbury had his man of business there, as well as Gromwell.'

'Limbury?' The name was familiar.

She looked at me as if I were an idiot. 'You remember him, surely? The freeholder, who has his own scheme for the site — Mr Hakesby mentioned him to you on our way to the Lamb.'

I nodded with unwise vigour, and cried

out with the pain. 'What did the judges decide?'

'A deferment, as Mr Hakesby hoped, but only for a week. There's a possibility that Mistress Hampney made a new will, which would affect her interest in Dragon Yard. But that's not the problem. Afterwards, I went into Staircase XIII.'

It took me a moment to catch up with her. 'The fire-damaged building?'

She nodded. 'Gromwell was going into it. But he was called away suddenly, and he left the door unlocked, and like a fool I went inside.' She drew a deep breath. 'You were right about that door to the alley by the Half Moon. And on the floor above there's another archway that could well go into the back of the new building, to Staircase XIV.' She saw my dazed expression and added, 'Where Gromwell has his chambers.'

Fuddled by sleep and the lingering traces of opium, my mind needed a moment to grasp what she was saying. 'Do you think Mistress Hampney might have come in that way? And someone might have taken her body out by the same route?'

'I found the picture by the door to the alley,' Cat said.

'Picture? What picture?'

'The one you said your father saw. The

one over the mantel when he found the body.' Again the nose wrinkled. 'Women disporting themselves with satyrs.'

I twitched in the bed and was rewarded by stabs of pain. This too. My father, as honest a man as had ever lived, had spoken no more than the truth, and nothing but the truth, even in his dotage. And I had been stupid enough, arrogant enough, not to know it for what it was.

The pain subsided, steadying to an ache that ran from my left cheek down to the thigh of my left leg. 'I need another dose,' I muttered.

'Not yet,' Cat said. 'If you have too much, you'll need more and more, and then you will never stop.'

'The picture. Why was it there?'

'That puzzled me at first. But it was leaning against the wall, just by the door to the alley. What if they had piled all the furnishings your father mentioned by the door before taking them away?'

I nodded, remembering the handcart I had seen in Fetter Lane when Sam and I had found the alley by the Half Moon, and when the tall, toothless man had warned us away before he rapped on the door. Sourface. 'Why leave the picture behind?'

'They probably didn't see it. It would have

been concealed by the open door. It's not very big.'

'Did you bring it away?'

'No,' she said. 'Because Gromwell came back and he caught me there.'

My head snapped round. I forgot the pain for a moment, I forgot that I needed opium. Cat looked very small on the stool, huddling into herself like a child that fears chastisement. She stared at me.

'You fool,' I said, angry with her for putting herself in danger, and angrier with myself for dragging her into this business. 'You little fool.'

'I'm no fool, sir,' she snapped, 'though you are to call me one.'

There was a silence.

She said, 'I ran away. I was lucky. But he saw my face, and he'd seen me before with Mr Hakesby. That's why I've come here. To hide.'

Another day and another night drifted past me on a tide of sleep and fantastic dreams, coloured by the opium. It was not until Friday morning, all but a week since the fire that had killed Chelling, that I felt more like myself than I had for days. I was weak, partly from lack of food. But I was no longer possessed by that deathly tiredness.

For the first time, I refused the morning draught of laudanum when Margaret offered it. The pain was bad, but I thought I could bear it now, or at least try to do so for an hour or two.

I ordered Margaret to send Sam to me. He hopped across the room and hissed softly through his teeth, as he did when he was worried or confronted by a problem.

'I shall rise,' I said.

'Margaret says you must lie in bed for longer.'

'Who is master here?'

Sam shrugged and said nothing. With my good arm, I threw my mug at him but misjudged my strength. The mug fell short.

'You need to heal,' he said. 'That's what they both say.'

Both? Margaret and Cat?

I said, 'Have you heard from Whitehall?'

'I sent a boy with a message to your master's office. Mistress Hakesby wrote it, in my name. So they'd know you wouldn't be going to Scotland.'

Mistress Hakesby. Cat, despite her youth and her lowly position, had earned Sam's respect. Or he was afraid of her, which came to the same thing.

I said: 'That was well done.'

'They sent a man on Tuesday to ask how

you did. Margaret told him, and he went away.'

'They know about the fire?'

Sam nodded.

'But not . . . ?'

'No, master. Everyone thinks Chelling came back drunk as a lord and set fire to himself, and you were burned, trying to save him. That's what I hear, anyway.'

I pushed back the covers. I winced at the pain that even this effort caused me. I touched my face. The right side was itchy with stubble, almost a beard. A bandage encircled my head, masking the left cheek entirely.

Sam started forward. 'Master —'

'I'm getting up. Help me.'

Involuntarily, both of us glanced at my body. I was wearing a shirt of my father's, patched and frayed but wonderfully soft and familiar. Underneath the shirt were invisible dressings. My left leg was wrapped in a loose bandage, whereas my right leg was white and hairy, its normal condition.

I made an immense effort and dragged the right leg off the bed. It dangled towards the floor.

'Come along. Help me with the other leg or I'll turn you out on the street.'

Sam grinned at me, recognizing that I was

jesting. Probably. As jokes go, it wasn't amusing. But it lightened the mood.

He propped himself against one of the bedposts and helped me sit up. Ignoring my cries, he lifted my left leg off the bed. My bare feet touched the floor.

When the pain had subsided, I said, 'Now I shall stand.'

'You're a fool, master.'

I repeated, between gritted teeth, 'Now I shall stand.'

Sam crouched, and I put my good arm across his shoulders. Slowly he straightened up. I cried out, again and again. But afterwards the waves of pain moderated into ripples, and then at last diminished to the uncomfortable tranquillity of dull, steady agony.

I was standing upright, still supported by Sam. I had regained control over a tiny portion of my life. It was a small victory, and it might not last long, but it was a victory nonetheless.

'I will need the pot,' I said. 'Then tell Margaret I will take some soup.'

He stooped to fetch the pot from under the bed.

'First, though,' I said. 'Where's Mistress Hakesby?'

He stood up. 'In your father's

bedchamber.'

'At this hour?'

'She was up half the night, master,' Sam said with a hint of belligerence in his voice, as if ready to spring to Cat's defence.

'Why?'

'Because it was her turn to watch over you.' He stared pityingly at me. 'You didn't know? Margaret and me, we've taken it in turns to watch over you at night. And since she came here, Mistress Hakesby does the same. Margaret tried to stop her, said it wasn't fitting. Might as well have saved her breath.'

CHAPTER TWENTY-SEVEN

'Why so melancholy?'

Jemima looked across the table. She and her husband were dining alone. The servants were out of the room. The door was closed.

'Melancholy?' Philip said, barely raising his head to look at her. 'I'm not melancholy at all. I'm in a very good humour.'

'Then you keep it to yourself.'

'Your pardon.' He gave her a tight-lipped smile. 'The Dragon's Yard business drags on and on. Thanks to those old fools at the Fire Court.'

'Can't Browning do all that for you? My father wouldn't mind if he spends more time on your affairs.'

'There are some things, my love, that even Browning cannot do.'

He spoke lightly but she was not fooled. Of late, Philip had lost his taste for society. He had kept within doors for days — in fact, now she thought about it, ever since he had come back to the house in the early hours of Saturday morning, almost a week ago. She smiled, not so much at Philip now, sitting across the table from her, as at the memory of how she had gone to his chamber that night, and he had laid his head on her bosom. She remembered with particular tenderness the softness of the short, dark hair on his scalp. There had been no lice among them. He was fastidious about such things and summoned Mary to use the comb almost every morning.

She said, 'You mustn't trouble yourself so much. It's only money, after all.'

No longer smiling, he stared at her. 'Only money? It isn't always the money that matters.'

'No, sir.'

She shivered as memories crowded into her mind. Something cracked inside her, like an earthenware pot too close to the kitchen fire.

'You miss the whore, don't you?' she said. 'And now she's dead, and I'm glad of it.'

'What are you talking about?'

'I know it was you she was meeting all along. Not Gromwell. I was right all the time. You're sick with love for her, and you will never be cured.'

'You damned, stupid woman,' Philip

334

shouted in the sort of voice he used for the servants. 'How can you talk such nonsense? Hold your peace or I'll thrash you till you bleed for a week.'

They stared at each other. He had never talked to her quite so harshly before. Law and custom allowed him to treat her just as he pleased, short of murder. God had ordained that, if Philip wished, he could beat her, he could shout at her, he could lock her up. But they were different, Jemima had thought, she and Philip were the exceptions to the general rule and they always had been. Her father had seen to that when he arranged the marriage settlement with the lawyers.

'But you love me a little, sir — don't you?' she whispered.

'Love?' he said. Then, more loudly, 'Love?' He pushed back his chair and stood up. 'What do you know of love? What do you know of anything? You hide yourself away in this house like a snail in its shell.'

He left the room. Jemima listened to his footsteps in the hall and, a moment later, heard the slam of the study door. Minutes passed, as sluggish as the snail she was meant to be. Tears trickled down her cheeks, cutting tracks through the Venetian ceruse that caked the surface of the skin. Snail tracks.

After a while she heard the study door open and Philip's voice calling angrily for Richard. Then movements and voices in the hall, and the chinking and banging of bolts, chains and locks as the front door was opened and then closed. Afterwards, a silence settled on the house, heavy as a nobleman's pall on his coffin.

In a while, Jemima rang the bell. Mary came almost at once, as if she had been waiting for the summons.

'Mend this for me.' Jemima touched her cheek and laughed, a dry bark whose sharpness surprised even her. 'What can be mended.'

CHAPTER TWENTY-EIGHT

Cat was surprised to see Marwood out of bed. Not only that, but standing. A chair had been brought up to the bedchamber, and he was holding the back of it with his good hand and standing by the window. He was alone.

He turned to look at her as she came in. The gown he wore covered most of his body, though his body had few secrets from her now. But the bandages that obscured much of his face made him appear a stranger, or perhaps a corpse wrapped for the grave. What made him seem even odder was the absence of hair. The old Marwood had worn his own hair, and worn it long. But the fire had taken more than half of it, and Margaret had cut the rest while he slept one day to make him look less of a monstrosity. Cat wondered whether the hair would ever grow back on the left side of his head.

He said, 'I want a mirror.'

'Why?'

'When Margaret changes the bandages, I want to see what I've become.'

A sight for nurses to frighten children with. Or something you pay a penny to see at Bartholomew Fair. She said, 'Give it time. It will heal. Though I'm not sure that Margaret will ever recover.'

He frowned. 'What?'

'From the shock of seeing you out of bed and on your feet. She told me she was so cross she wanted to slap you.'

The trouble with the bandages was that they concealed so much of Marwood's face that Cat could read nothing from it. He turned his head, very slowly as though even the slightest movement required careful monitoring to lessen the pain, and looked out of the window. It was a bright day and the sky was blue beyond the smudges of smoke rising from the south bank of the Thames. The river sent its smell into the room, where it mingled with the darker, more disagreeable odours from the Savoy's graveyard.

'Have you any word of what's happening?' he said. 'Is anyone looking for you?'

'I don't think so. Sam says he's heard nothing. I think Limbury and Gromwell wouldn't want to let the world know their business.'

'But privately? Have they made enquiries?'

'I don't know. Probably. They might send one of their creatures to Henrietta Street. But they can learn nothing there.'

'I'm sorry,' Marwood said. 'I have brought you and Hakesby into this affair, and now you cannot escape the consequences. Will they threaten him?'

'It's possible,' she said. 'But he's not alone in the house, and he has powerful friends. And they must fear publicity.'

'If I had known, I would —'

'You can't undo what is done,' Cat said. 'Besides . . .'

Besides, she thought, Marwood had helped her at the time of her father's death; she owed him for that, and she always would.

After a pause, he said, 'Does he know where you are?'

'Hakesby? No.' She imagined the distress that he must be feeling but did not allow herself to dwell on it. 'There was no time. Besides, it's better that he doesn't know. I didn't want to risk Brennan finding out where I was. I don't trust Brennan. He's up to something.'

Brennan, she thought. Who stinks like a

339

fox. Who may be even worse than he seems.

'Brennan,' Marwood said. 'The draughts-man . . . Did I tell you that I saw him when I left you and Mr Hakesby? I can't remember.'

For a moment her courage failed her. 'No,' she said. 'When was this?'

'Last Friday. When I left you on my way to Clifford's Inn. He was waiting outside the Lamb.'

'So he followed us there,' Cat said. 'He saw us together that evening when you came to the Drawing Office. And he knows about the Fire Court case and Dragon Yard, of course, and Mr Poulton and Sir Philip Lim-bury. And God knows what else. Is he work-ing for —'

'Limbury,' Marwood said. 'He must be the key to all this.'

'Yes,' she said. 'Who else could it be? Celia's lover . . .' Cat paused, and out of nowhere came a bitter anger that filled her so completely she found it hard to breathe. 'The man she made herself beautiful for.'

'So.' Marwood's fingers tightened on the back of the chair, and the knuckles whit-ened. But when he next spoke his voice was level. 'Limbury needed Celia Hampney's support to ensure he gained the outcome he wanted for Dragon Yard. He sought out her acquaintance at Madam Grove's, and he wooed her. Did she even know who he is? Or that he's married? Perhaps she was so hot for him, she didn't care.'

'Of course she cared,' Cat said. 'Perhaps he gave her a verbal contract of betrothal. Who knows? Perhaps . . .'

He looked at her in silence, and she was aware that she had aroused his curiosity. Why did she care? She hardly knew the answer herself. Only that she did care.

'And then,' Marwood went on, 'did she refuse to do what Limbury wanted about her Dragon Yard leasehold?'

Cat stared at him, almost rejoicing in the vicarious anger that possessed her. 'So he flew into a passion and stabbed her.'

'In which case,' Marwood said, 'who was the other woman? The one my father followed? Did he have to die because he had seen a dead woman or a living one?'

'There's no one to ask,' Cat said. 'No one who will speak to us.'

Even as she was speaking, it occurred to her that there was someone who might talk, if she could be discovered.

'Speak to *us*?' He rubbed the bandage on his left hand. 'You must not do anything. I'll brook no argument. I've harmed you enough already.'

She curtsied, mocking his tone.

'I want a mirror,' he said.

When Cat went down to the kitchen, she found Sam at the table cleaning a pistol and whistling almost soundlessly between his teeth. Beside the pistol was a long, thin dagger, its blade recently silver-edged by the whetstone.

He was sitting on the bench with his back to the wall. Propped within easy reach was a heavy stick. Margaret was tending a pot over the fire. She had her back to the room. Backs cannot speak, but sometimes they may betray emotion: Margaret's showed fury.

Sam glanced up at Cat. 'How's master?'

'Out of bed.'

'More fool him,' Margaret said without turning round.

'He wants a mirror,' Cat said. 'He wants to see what he's become.'

'Better not. Not yet.'

Sam squinted down the barrel of the pistol. 'Be careful what you wish for. That's what I say.'

Margaret threw him a look. 'I wish you'd put that thing away. And the dagger.'

Cat said, 'I want to go out. Will you help me?'

Sam set down the pistol. 'How?'

'Hire a pair of oars to wait for me at the Savoy Stairs. And make sure that no one's watching out for me. I want to go into the City.'

'Does master know?' Margaret said bluntly.

'No.'

'Will you tell him?'

Cat thought of the poor apology for a man in the bedchamber upstairs, half desiring and half fearing to see his own face. 'No,' she said.

Long shadows danced among the ruins. Soon it would be midsummer, and there would be madness in the air, even more than there seemed to be now.

The boatman had dropped her at the stairs by the ruins of Barnard's Castle. Cat walked up to St Paul's, skirted the fence around it and turned into Cheapside. She threaded her way through the crowd, heading east.

The street bustled with life, albeit life of a makeshift kind. People clustered round the booths and shanties, following the old rituals of buying and selling, looking and wanting. In the surrounding alleys and lanes, it was a different story. Life was scantier here, more furtive, more precarious. Few people went there after dark unless they had no choice in the matter.

To the north of Cheapside, the Dragon Yard site was in a happier condition. Since Cat had last been here, the posts on the site's boundary had been replaced with a whitewashed fence designed to mark out the extent of Poulton's territory beyond dispute. The pathways were wider than they had been when she was last here, and some of the chimney stacks remaining from the former buildings had been taken down.

Four labourers, working in pairs, were shovelling debris into barrows and wheeling them into the north-west corner of the site, where there was already a great heap of spoil — stone, ashes, fragments of tile and timber, and broken bricks. Among them were clumps of green, for the weeds were colonizing the ruins.

Mr Poulton's angular figure was propped against the side of a horse trough. He was still wearing his skullcap, and his clothes seemed shabbier than before. He was talking urgently to a fifth workman, older and better dressed than the others. But when he saw Cat approaching, he dismissed the man and beckoned her to approach.

'I had Mr Hakesby's letter this morning,'

he said without preamble. His cheeks were flushed. His face was more haggard than before, and he spoke rapidly. 'He thinks I should stop the work until the Fire Court reconvenes. Tell him I will not wait. Why should I?'

'Sir, I haven't —'

Poulton cut her off. 'Why should I waste time because Limbury chooses to make a fool of himself? My foreman can't keep his men waiting indefinitely, unless I pay them for doing nothing. Good workmen can go where they please at present, there's such a demand for them. No, the sooner we start, the better for everyone. And we can't rebuild before the site is cleared.'

'But if the Fire Court decides for Sir Philip?'

'It won't. They are men of sense. He has Court connections, of course, and that's a worry, I won't deny it. But I have my own friends here in the City, and I have made sure they will speak for me in the right ears. Even in Whitehall.'

If the contents of Mistress Hampney's will went against Poulton, all this expense, all this effort, would be for nothing. But there was something admirable about Poulton's obstinacy. And something foolish too.

'Thank your master for his advice,' he

went on, 'but say I will not let my men stand idle. Was this why he sent you? To see if I had heeded what he said?'

'I don't come from him, sir.'

Poulton overrode her, his mind running ahead with feverish speed. 'He promised me a copy of the plans for one of my subtenants, and I told him he would find me here. Have you got it?' He seemed to see her properly for the first time, to realize that she had come empty-handed. He frowned. 'Where is it?'

'I don't have it. I don't come from Mr Hakesby.'

That caught his attention at last. He glanced at Cat, and the skin tightened over his face. 'What is all this? Is something amiss? Have you run away from your master?'

'No, sir.' Cat hesitated, for she had in fact done precisely that. 'Pray, may I ask you something? About Mistress Hampney.'

He frowned at her, and in that moment she saw herself through his eyes: a maidservant betraying an impudent and inexplicable curiosity.

She hurried on, 'Forgive me, sir, it's your niece's maid I'm looking for. Tabitha.'

Poulton's lips twisted and his face puckered, as if he had eaten something bitter. 'If your master's looking for a servant, I wouldn't advise looking in that direction. She's a lying jade.'

'It's not for Mr Hakesby.'

'Then why?'

'For the sake of your niece's reputation, sir.' In for a penny, Cat thought, in for a pound. 'And to do you a service.'

'How can you help poor Celia now?'

'As you said yourself, master, Tabitha is a lying jade. What if she told Mistress Lee a pack of lies about her mistress?'

'If she wouldn't tell the truth to Mistress Lee,' the old man said, 'why should she talk to you? A stranger.'

'That's exactly the reason. I'm a stranger to her. She has no reason to fear me. More than that, I'm just a servant, as she is, and servants like nothing better than boasting about how they cheated their masters.'

Poulton snorted. 'True enough.'

'Then where may I find her, sir?'

He hesitated. One of the workmen dropped his shovel with a clatter. Cat looked towards the sound. In the distance, a man was walking towards Dragon Yard — not from Cheapside but from the west, through the ruins. He was too far away for Cat to see his face, but she was almost sure she recognized the shape of him, and the way he walked, head down, swinging from side to side as if sniffing for a scent.

Brennan. The eternal fox. He was carrying something under his arm, perhaps the folder containing the copy of the Dragon Yard plans.

'Your pardon, sir,' Cat said rapidly. 'Tabitha?'

'Eh? Yes. With her mother, I suppose. That's why the girl came to Celia. Her mother had been our laundry maid before she married.'

'Where does the mother live?'

'On the Surrey side. Lambeth? I remember Mistress Lee saying there was a tavern nearby called the Cardinal's Hat, because we wondered if it had once belonged to Cardinal Wolsey, or to some other Papist. I wouldn't put it past the girl to be a secret Papist herself. She would murder us all in our beds, given half a chance.'

Brennan was walking more quickly now. He was looking towards them, shading his eyes.

Poulton was frowning at her. 'What ails you now, girl?'

Brennan shouted something, perhaps Cat's name, but the word was snatched away by the wind blowing off the river. She turned and ran.

■ ■ ■

Brennan cornered her in a ruined bakehouse somewhere between Walbrook and St Swithin's Lane. Cat had tried to throw him off her scent by ducking and diving among the ruins, on the assumption that she must know London better than a man from Oxford would do. But she had reckoned without his determination, his longer legs and, most of all, the fact that the London she had known before the Fire was gone for ever. In this wasteland, among the ash heaps and broken buildings, she was as much a stranger as he was.

No one else was in sight. They were alone in the heart of the City. The bakehouse floor was three feet below the ground level, and its brick walls were still high enough to prevent a quick escape. Brennan had stopped in the doorless doorway. He was panting. His face was red with the effort of running. He had lost the portfolio in the chase, and his hat as well. His pale eyes darted to and fro, assessing the nature of the trap he had driven her into.

Cat's hand slipped through her skirt and into her pocket. Her heart was beating wildly. Her fingers wrapped themselves around the handle of the knife. She backed against the curving breastwork of the oven. She drew out the knife, holding it so he could see the blade. She readied herself to duck, to dive, to spring.

'Don't. Pray don't, Jane. I beg you.'

'Leave me alone,' she said, her voice as ragged as his with lack of breath. 'I — I'll kill you.'

'You don't understand,' he said — almost wailed. 'You don't understand.'

Her fingers tightened around the knife. 'Understand what?'

'I wish you no harm. I swear it on my mother's grave.'

'Liar.'

'Please,' he said. 'I've no skill with women. I thought you would like a man to be masterful —'

'You? Masterful?'

'I don't know how to say sweet words, how to court a girl. But I — I admire you. Truly. From the bottom of my heart. And now you will hate me for ever.'

Cat stared at him, temporarily robbed of words. She was small, and she made nothing of herself; she knew that, thank God, she lacked the voluptuous charms that made men lust after a woman; nor did she smile at them and flutter and seek to trap their

350

attention: yet Brennan had tried to woo her. It was beyond understanding.

And it disgusted her. What he could not have known was that, however he had approached her, she would have hated him for the very fact of his trying to court her. The last time a man had spoken such words to her, he had ended by raping her. Then her only resource had been to use her knife on him. So naturally she had been prepared to use her knife on Brennan now. Or, to put it more plainly, she had wanted to use her knife on him.

Neither of them moved. The light was softening and fading. Slowly she lowered the blade.

'Why did you run away?' he said. 'Old Hakesby's beside himself with worry. Someone was asking for you at the drawing office this morning.'

'Who?'

'A man. Said he used to know you.'

Cat frowned. 'What was he like?'

'In his middle years.'

'You must have noticed more than that.'

Brennan shrugged. 'He was tall,' he said. 'No flesh on him, thin as a pole.' He paused for thought. 'Not many teeth in his mouth.'

Was that the man that Marwood had seen watching them from Fetter Lane when they

351

were in the ruins with the body of Celia Hampney? Sourface, Sam called him.

'Looked as if he had a mouthful of vinegar?'

'Yes. He said he was in a hurry. He didn't leave a name.'

'What condition?'

'Respectable. Well-dressed, even. Could have been a clerk or a shopkeeper or even a servant — a servant like you, I mean.'

He coloured again, the blood beneath the skin drowning the freckles. It was in its way a compliment that Brennan thought of her as a superior sort of maid, the sort with accomplishments.

'Was it you who talked to him?'

Brennan nodded.

'What did you say about me?'

'I told him you were away, and I wasn't sure when you'd be back.' He came a step closer to her. 'What's happened? Why did you run away? I don't understand. Nor does the master.'

'There are men who wish me harm,' she said. 'That's all you need to know.'

'Are you with that man?' Brennan demanded, taking a step towards her. His voice had acquired a surly edge. 'Is that where you went? To him.'

It was her turn to colour. 'What man?'

'The one I saw you with last Friday. He came to the office, and then you and Hakesby went to the Lamb in Wych Street with him. What is he to you?'

'You followed us,' she snapped. 'How dare you?'

He took a step backwards. 'I wanted to know if I had a rival.'

'A rival? Dear God, you give yourself airs. You're nothing to me.' She saw Brennan's face crumple. 'That man saw Mr Hakesby on a matter of business, and I chanced to be there.'

'I followed him,' Brennan said. 'I know all about him. After he left the Lamb, he went to Clifford's Inn, where the Fire Court is. Did you know that? They had a fire that night and he was badly hurt in it. I was there — they were shouting in Fleet Street for volunteers to help put out the flames. Another man was killed, burned to death. It's to do with the Fire Court, isn't it? The Dragon Yard case? And Marwood's lending master money, isn't he?'

Her old suspicions revived. 'How do you know his name?'

'Marwood,' Brennan said, as if the name were a curse. 'Marwood. The Temple Bar crossing-sweeper recognized him. I made enquiries. Nice little clerkship at Whitehall, eh? All perquisites and fees, I'll be bound, and not much work. How did he get it? Did his father make interest with someone? I bet he can afford a wife if he wants one. Burns and all. Do you know they're after him too?'

She heard the pleasure in his voice. 'I don't know what you mean.'

'I followed them when they took him home that night, to his lodgings in the Savoy. I thought he was dead at first. I wasn't the only one who was following him, either. That man was as well. I saw him that night.'

'Who?'

'What did you call him? Sourface? The one who's trying to find you.'

Cat squeezed the handle of the knife. 'I must go now.'

'Listen, Jane, now we're friends, why don't you come out on the river with me this Sunday?' Hope flared in Brennan's face. 'It's different now, so can't we —'

'No,' Cat said. 'No, no, no.'

CHAPTER TWENTY-NINE

The tide was on the turn, and the boatman had to pull hard to approach the shore. It was past ten o'clock in the evening when they approached the Savoy but the Thames was busy, with boats and barges moving in both directions. Most of them had their lanterns lit, and they bobbed like fireflies on the water.

Cat could be sure of this, if nothing else: it would be safer to approach from the river. Sourface had followed Marwood when they brought him back to the Savoy after the Clifford's Inn fire. He had also been to Henrietta Street to ask for her. Who was he? A hireling of Gromwell's? What scared her was the fact that he and perhaps others were looking for them both, for Marwood and herself, and they knew both where she worked and where he lived. They might well have seen her leave the house today.

She had left Brennan among the ruins,

plodding back towards Dragon Yard and Mr Poulton, assuming the old man had not already left in anger. The knowledge that she had somehow attracted his — his what? his devotion? his lust? his love? — made her feel physically queasy. She did not want to be the object of anyone's affection. But it was a relief to know that Brennan's motives were not more sinister.

The Savoy's river gate was still open. The only people about were going home to their lodgings, their minds on their own business, many the worse for drink. The porter was an idle fellow who took little notice of their comings and goings. He did not even look up as Cat passed under the archway.

Once inside, Cat did not make her way directly to Marwood's lodging in Infirmary Close, which would have meant going down the narrow cul de sac. If anyone were watching Marwood's house, it would be there, near the mouth of the alley. Instead, she took the path leading to the burial ground by the chapel.

Its ground level was several feet higher than elsewhere in the Savoy, rising to an irregular mound towards the centre. The graveyard had been filled several times over during the year before the Fire, when the plague had killed so many thousands. They had buried the dead on top of each other, layer upon layer, bringing wagon-loads of earth and quicklime to cover them. But the ground could not digest so many bodies: Margaret had told her that it vomited out what it could not consume: dismembered limbs and skulls, scraps of skin, clothing and rotten flesh.

No one went there by choice, even those who had recently buried a loved one. The smell was insupportable. Even to look at it, Margaret said, was dangerous, because the stink of the dead was so pernicious it insinuated its poison into a person through his organs of sight.

At the back of Marwood's lodgings, two small mullioned windows overlooked the graveyard, one above the other. Because of the smell, they were never opened, and the edges of casements were stuffed with rags and scraps of paper. The upper one belonged to the bedchamber where Cat slept, which had once belonged to Marwood's father. The lower window was in the kitchen, tucked into the alcove where Margaret kept pails and brooms.

The sky was not dark but a pale, luminous blue that shaded into grey. Cat paused to let her eyes adjust. Other windows overlooking the graveyard glowed with the murky flickering of rushlights.

She followed the line of the buildings around the graveyard, ducking in and out of the shelter of the buttresses that propped them up. Occasionally she stumbled on something protruding from the ground, and once something crunched beneath the sole of her shoe, and the ground gave way under her weight.

Better not to think too much about what lay beneath her feet. Better not to look down, either. She tugged her foot free and forced herself to plod on until she reached the back of Marwood's house.

The sill of the lower window was less than a foot above ground level outside. Cat crouched by the lattice and rapped with her knuckle on one of the squares of glass. Nothing happened. She looked round, suddenly convinced that someone was at her shoulder. But there was no one there, only the restless dead. She took up a fragment of stone and knocked harder.

A fingertip flattened itself against the other side of the glass. It rubbed the square with a circular motion, scrubbing away some of the grime. Cat spat on her finger and did the same on her side.

The pane cleared. The finger inside disappeared, to be succeeded by a distorted

358

eye. The glass was so impure that she could not hazard a guess to whom the eye belonged.

It vanished. Cat huddled in the angle between the nearest buttress and the wall. Time passed, long enough for her fears to breed furiously among themselves.

There were faint sounds — a stealthy scrape, a click, another scrape. With a creak, the casement swung outwards, but only by an inch.

'Margaret?' Cat whispered.

The window opened a little more. There was Margaret's face and shoulders. She was open-mouthed. Behind her, the familiar kitchen glowed like the promised land.

'What — what are you doing?'

'Let me in,' Cat whispered. 'Quickly.'

The window was less than two feet high, and the gap between the mullion and the side of the frame was narrower still. Cat tugged open the window as wide as it would go. She raised her arms above her head. Like a diver in slow motion, she inserted herself into the gap.

Her shoulders caught, and she wriggled on to her side, grazing her skin. Margaret seized her under the armpits and tugged. For a moment, their two straining faces were only inches away from each other.

Margaret's cheeks were red and slicked with sweat. Her breath smelled of onions.

Suddenly Cat was through. Her left hip bumped painfully over the sill, and her legs and feet followed rapidly after her. The speed of it took Margaret by surprise, and she fell backwards on to the flagged floor, with Cat sprawling untidily on top of her.

They rolled apart from each other.

'For God's sake,' Margaret gasped. 'The smell. Close the window.'

Cat scrambled up and pulled the casement shut.

'You're lucky I heard you,' Margaret said. 'God in heaven, what are you about? Why can't you come in at the door like a Christian?'

'It may not be safe.'

Margaret shot her a glance but said nothing. She opened the other kitchen window, the one to the yard, and also the back door. She turned back towards Cat. The room was lit by a single candle on the table, guttering in the draught, four rushlights and the glow of the dying fire.

Margaret's face was blurred and shadowed. 'This can't go on, mistress,' she said.

'I know.' Cat shook out the folds of her cloak.

'The master flew into a passion when he'd

heard you'd gone. Never seen him in such a rage.' Margaret sniffed. 'And him in the state he's in, too.'

'Is he worse?'

'No. But he's downstairs.' The words hissed with outrage. 'And that's your fault. I couldn't stop him. He's been in the parlour this last hour.'

'But the doctor said he shouldn't come down for at least a week. And not before he'd seen him again.'

'And master said the doctor's a fool who only wants to make another visit because it means another fee for him. And he says you're a fool, too.'

'I'll go to him,' Cat said. 'Try to make him see sense. About the doctor, anyway.'

She heard the weariness in her voice. The day had been a succession of terrors and crises, and here was yet another; she had no time to think, nor time to rest or even to eat.

'He won't thank you,' Margaret said. 'Especially smelling like that.'

Cat climbed the stairs to the hall. She straightened her back and went into the parlour. Marwood was slumped in the chair by the empty fireplace. He was wearing only a bedgown and a pair of slippers; and his head was bare, apart from a loose bandage,

361

which gave him the appearance of a slovenly Turk.

'What foolishness is this?' she said, more harshly than she had intended.

He winced. 'Where the devil have you been?'

'You should let us help you to bed. Have you taken your laudanum today?'

'No.'

'Then you shall have it now.'

'I shall not,' he said.

Suddenly she was furious with him and his obstinacy, and ready to blame him for everything that had gone wrong since their ill-fated meeting outside the Fire Court. 'Then you must look after yourself, you fool. I wish to God we'd never met. I shall go away. I shall leave you to your folly, I shall —'

'Peace, woman,' he snarled, without even looking at her.

'Don't you dare peace me!' Her voice was rising in volume, and she didn't care who heard her. 'Peace? I'll give you peace. I am not your servant or your sister, sir. You're nothing to me. Less than nothing.'

He raised his head and looked at her at last. They glared at each other. The bandage had slipped, exposing the left side of his skull and the livid skin that had been concealed by it. The nearest candle was on that side of him, and by its light she saw shades of mottled pink, from pale to angry red, shimmering with the movements of the flame. Pity, that treacherous emotion, ambushed her.

'Where have you been?' he said in a quieter voice. 'Why have you come back so befouled? And you stink like a dead thing.'

She answered the first question. 'I've seen Mr Poulton.'

'Where? Why?'

'At Dragon Yard. I want to find Tabitha, Celia Hampney's maid. I think she knows more than she's saying, and someone's bribed her to keep her mouth shut about her mistress's lover.'

'Who?'

'Why, the lover, of course. Poulton thinks the maid's mother lives over the river, near a tavern called the Cardinal's Hat, and the girl's probably there. I would have asked him more, but Brennan found me.'

'The draughtsman? He haunts us both.'

Cat's cheeks grew warm, but she hoped Marwood saw nothing. 'He was bringing plans to Mr Poulton. He told me a man asked for me at the drawing office. The one Sam calls Sourface. Not many teeth in his —'

Marwood made a sudden movement. He cried out.

She said quietly, 'Are you in much pain?'

He didn't reply. After a moment, he said, 'So. You mean the man I met in the alley by the Half Moon?'

'I think so. And there's worse. When they brought you back here after the fire in Chelling's rooms, Brennan followed. And he said that Sourface was there as well. He knows who you are, and where you live. And he must also know there is a connection between us. That's why I came back through the graveyard and in by the kitchen window. In case the house was watched.'

'Who's he working for?' Marwood said. 'If we —'

There was a hammering on the outer door to the lane.

'Who is it?' she whispered. 'At this hour?'

'Sam will send them away.'

They listened to men's voices rumbling in the hall. The parlour door was thick, and Cat could not distinguish the words. Then the door was suddenly flung open. Sam was on the threshold, propping himself on his crutch. Another, taller man stood in the shadows behind him, his hat on his head.

Sam drew himself up and announced in a loud voice, attempting to sound like a

364

properly trained servant in a respectable household, 'Mr Williamson, master.' Then he spoiled it by adding when he saw Cat, 'Oh God, where did you spring from?' He glanced from her to Marwood and jerked his thumb in the direction of Williamson. 'He just marched in as if he owned the place. I couldn't stop him.'

CHAPTER THIRTY

Joseph Williamson. Under-secretary of State. My master. The sight of him at my parlour door was like seeing a swallow in the depths of winter. It was against nature.

We stared at each other, and it would have been hard to say who was the more dismayed. He knew I had been injured in the fire at Clifford's Inn, but he had not seen what the fire had done to me. I was not a pretty sight, particularly without the protection of the bandage, and particularly to one taken unawares.

'Merciful God,' he blurted out, for once careless of his words. 'What have you done to yourself?'

Of all the many people I did not want to see at present, Williamson ranked high. My absence must have sorely inconvenienced him — and puzzled him, too, because of the business with Mr Chiffinch, my other master, and the plainly unnecessary journey to Scotland that only my injuries had prevented. Williamson had both the power and the intelligence to ask awkward questions about what I had been doing. Worst of all, he had now seen Cat.

She dropped him a curtsy, but it was the sort of curtsy that does not imply respect. Nor did she lower her eyes, as a maid should, to show becoming modesty. To compound the problem, her clothes were worse than shabby: they were filthy, as if she had dragged herself through a field of mud and ashes to be here. And then, of course, there was her graveyard smell.

'Jane,' I said sharply. 'Why are you dawdling there? Tell Margaret to send up a bottle of Rhenish and something to eat for our honoured guest. And put yourself under the pump.'

Cat sidled round Williamson and slipped out of the parlour.

I stood up. The effort made me cry out. Both Sam and Williamson started forwards. 'Sir,' I said between clenched teeth, 'pray do me the honour of taking the chair.'

'For God's sake, man,' Williamson said. 'Sit down.' He waved Sam forward. 'You. Help your master.'

Sam hobbled forward, took my right arm and made me sit. There was only one chair in the room and in normal circumstances Williamson would have taken it by right. We both knew that his very presence here in my house was an immense act of condescension, whatever the reason, and he had every right to expect it to be recognized. Why was he here? If he had wanted simply to know how I was, he could have sent someone to enquire.

He unclasped his cloak, dropped it on the bench by the table and sat down beside it. He was dressed with more care than usual in a dark-blue velvet suit, and he wore new gilt buckles on his shoes. I wondered whom he had been visiting. A clerk must notice such things about his superiors.

'Was that your maid?' he asked, wrinkling his nose.

'A new girl, sir.' I waved towards the flask of laudanum on the table, which Margaret had left at my elbow to tempt me. 'She fell in the gutter on the way back from the apothecary.'

Williamson shrugged, dismissing Cat from his mind. 'I chanced to be passing,' he said. 'And it wasn't out of my way to call to see how you do.'

'I'm very sensible of the honour, sir, and I'm truly sorry that I have been unable —'

He cut me off with a wave of his hand. 'I

give you one thing, Marwood, you're not usually shy of work.' He tapped his finger-tips on the table until the silence became uncomfortable. 'How badly were you burned?'

'It's my left side.' I swallowed, for my mouth had become unaccountably dry at the memory of the flames. 'My face and my hand are the worst. And the wrist. The burns are less on the rest of my body — my clothes gave some protection. I was lying on my right side and, thank God, that's barely touched.'

'You could very well have died,' he said flatly.

'I was fortunate. They were able to drag me out in time.'

Williamson looked down his nose at me. 'I heard the man who died was a clerk at the Fire Court.'

'Yes, sir.'

'How did the fire start?'

There was a knock at the door, and Margaret brought in wine and a dish of oysters. By now I was in worse pain, accentuated by every movement in the chair, and by the effort of talking. I was aware of a niggling desire to look at the apothecary's flask beside me, and perhaps uncork it and at least sniff the contents.

Margaret poured us each a glass of wine, curtsied and left the parlour. Neither of us drank.

'When will you be ready to return?' Williamson asked.

'I can't tell, sir.' I was terrified that I might lose my clerkship. 'I wish I could come back tomorrow. I will need a day or two, I think, perhaps three. Not a moment longer than —'

He held up his hand to stop me. 'You are no use to me unless you are well, Marwood.'

'No, sir. I will come as soon as —'

'I command you to make sure you are restored to health before you come back to Whitehall. However long that may be.' Williamson picked up his glass, held it to the candle flame as if examining the wine's colour, and set it down without drinking. 'I saw Mr Chiffinch in the Privy Garden today. He asked me how you did.'

I bowed my head, as if overwhelmed by such consideration.

'He said it was a pity you had not gone to Scotland after all. He said you were a rash young man, though you had abilities.'

'Sir — why did Mr Chiffinch want me to go to Scotland?'

For a moment I thought I had presumed too far. Williamson took an oyster from the dish, ate it, and tore off a piece of bread to ram it down. He swallowed a mouthful of wine.

'Have you heard of a man called Limbury?' he said.

'The courtier?'

Williamson nodded. 'Sir Philip Limbury. A Groom of the Bedchamber.'

Yes, I thought, and therefore a man with the King's ear. And therefore perhaps Chiffinch's ear too, for Chiffinch was rarely far from the King. Chiffinch who had wanted me in Scotland on a fool's errand, and who had told Williamson I was a rash young man.

'A good family, but impoverished by their support of the late King. Sir Philip served with courage against the Dutch — reckless courage, some would say — but he was nearly court-martialled when he came back. There was a scandal about the division of prize money. The King chose to let it go. They say Chiffinch had a word . . . and a month or two later Sir Philip was betrothed to Jemima Syre. The sole heir of her father, Sir George. He's worth eight or nine thousand a year, if it's a penny.'

I nodded, touching the left side of my face, which was stinging. I could not stop myself. Not that touching did any good.

'As it happens,' Williamson went on, 'Sir Philip is the petitioner in a case at present before the Fire Court.' He paused. 'Where that acquaintance of yours worked. Chelling.'

I took up my wine and emptied the glass in one.

'The principal defendant is a man named Poulton,' he continued in his steady, methodical way as if briefing a committee. 'A cloth merchant. A man of substance, and a good reputation in the City, I understand, where he has many friends. The dispute centres on a site near Cheapside known as Dragon Yard. Sir Philip owns the freehold, but the existing leaseholders restrict what he can do with it. Poulton's niece, Mistress Hampney, is another leaseholder — she's a widow, so she controls it absolutely. Strangely enough, she was found murdered the other day. As you know, because at my command you inspected the body where it was found: in the ruins to the east of Clifford's Inn.' He paused again. 'Clifford's Inn is where the Fire Court sits. Where Mr Chelling, the court's clerk, lived and died. It is like a dance, is it not, Marwood? Round and round we go. And always back to the Fire Court and the Dragon Yard.'

He looked at me. He wanted me to say

something, heaven knows what. His words were clear enough in themselves: but, like ripples on the surface of a pond, they also marked the presence of something beneath the surface.

'Something's going on here,' he said at last. 'We both know that, don't we? So does Mr Poulton.'

I began to understand. Poulton must have friends at Court as well as in the City. Including, perhaps, Mr Williamson.

'Will it heal?' he said.

The question took me by surprise, and I did not know how to reply.

He clicked his fingers. 'Your face, Marwood, your face. Will it always be badly scarred?'

For answer I took up a candle, holding it at arm's length because I was now afraid of fire. I turned my head so that Williamson could see the left side of my face by the light of the flame. He leaned closer, frowning, and then wrinkling up his nose when the smell of the apothecary's salve reached his nostrils. The inflamed skin was sticky with the thick paste, the preparation of ground ivy and God knew what else mixed into the deer suet. I pushed aside the loose bandage to show him what remained of my left ear.

'Good God,' he said, recoiling.

'This will not mend,' I said. 'As for the rest, the doctor thinks my cheek and neck will show the scars until the day I die. The question is, how badly . . . The hair may grow back on that side of the head, he says, or it may not.'

Williamson sat back on the bench. 'You must have a periwig. A good full one.'

'When I can afford it, sir.'

'You shall have it sooner than that. And you must live, too. I shall make an advance on your salary.'

I began to stammer my thanks.

'But the periwig,' he interrupted, frowning. 'That's another matter. If you are to be of any use to Lord Arlington in future, we cannot have you looking so monstrous.' He must have seen something in my expression, for he checked himself and then went on in a gentler voice. 'But we shall make the best of it. I shall advise his lordship that you should have a grant from the Special Fund. Five or six pounds should be ample. There's no point in wasting time — I'll send my perruquier to you. It's a pity you lost so much of your own hair in the fire but we shall see what the man can contrive.'

I thanked him. The kindness — if that's what it was — made my eyes fill with tears. I felt a great weariness and wished he would leave me. Instead, and to my surprise, he took another glass of wine and settled back, his elbow on the table, as if he had all the time in the world.

'And now, Marwood,' he said, 'let us talk confidentially.' He leaned towards me. 'But first you have to choose where your loyalties lie. No man can serve two masters, or not for —'

He broke off, for at that moment we both became aware of a commotion below, of raised voices and running footsteps. Margaret screamed.

Gripping the arms of the chair, I pulled myself to my feet. Williamson also stood up. For an instant, our eyes met, and I saw my own confusion mirrored in his face.

Then came the sound of a shot.

Leaning on Williamson's arm, I descended the stairs to the kitchen. Below us was the sound of Margaret shouting at Sam, upbraiding him, and his deeper voice making a quieter counterpoint to hers.

At the bottom of the stairs, I broke away from Williamson and flung open the kitchen door. Silence fell like a stone. Williamson held up the candle he had brought with him. The room smelled powerfully of gunpowder. Tendrils of smoke moved sluggishly, wreathing around Margaret and Sam. They were on either side of the table, their faces staring open-mouthed at me as if I were an apparition from the far side of the grave.

Cat appeared in the doorway to the larder, bringing more smoke with her. Her eyes widened when she saw me, with Williamson looming behind.

'You could have killed us!' Margaret said to her husband. 'You fool.'

'What would you have me do, woman?' Sam roared at her.

'Hold your tongue,' I shouted. 'Both of you.'

Williamson pushed past me. 'What's this?' he demanded. 'Are you all mad?'

Cat said, 'They were trying to burn the house down.'

I walked unsteadily to the table and lowered myself on to the bench. Sam's pistol lay before me. I touched the barrel. It was warm.

'I heard a noise in the larder.' Cat had changed her gown since I had last seen her. She was wearing what looked like an old gown of Margaret's, a patched and faded garment that hung on her shoulders like an overlarge sack and trailed on the floor. 'Someone forced the window.'

'A burglar?' I said. 'That window's hardly big enough for a cat.'

The larder was served by a north-facing window that looked on to the alley at the front of the house. It was less than twelve inches square and protected down the middle by a vertical iron bar the thickness of a man's thumb.

'Big enough for a firebomb,' she said.

Williamson strode across the room, pushed her aside and inspected the larder by the light of the candle. He prodded something on the larder floor with his foot. He stooped down to it.

'The girl's right,' he said, looking back at me.

'It was struggling to stay alight,' Cat said. 'I threw my apron over it. And then —'

'And then Samuel must seize his pistol and rush into the larder and fire in the darkness like a foolish, overgrown boy.' Margaret shook her fist in her husband's face. 'Scaring us out of our wits, and to no purpose.'

'Who did it?' I said.

They looked blankly at me. Cat said, 'I heard someone running away.'

Williamson returned to the kitchen, carrying a bundled apron. He set it on the table and carefully pulled back the scorched folds. There was a harmless-looking, dun-coloured ball with an acrid smell rising from it.

'Raise the alarm,' Williamson said to Sam.

'No, sir,' I said. 'It's too late.'

Whoever had done this was long gone. It was hopeless. The Savoy was poorly lit. Although the gates were meant to be locked in the evening, there were so many people coming and going that the porters did not trouble themselves overmuch and left the wickets open for latecomers until midnight and sometimes beyond.

Williamson raised his eyebrows at me. 'Why would . . . ?'

'I don't know.'

Someone meant us harm. But it also occurred to me that there was no better way than a well-placed firebomb to force the inhabitants of a house to flee in a panic. Perhaps someone had wanted to flush me out, and bring me into the open. Or, if not me, then Cat.

'Well?' Williamson said, when he had made sure the parlour door was fastened.

I said nothing. We had left Sam and Margaret in the kitchen, and climbing the stairs had exhausted me.

Williamson took my right arm and helped me to sit. He bent down, and I felt his breath on the skin of my undamaged ear as he whispered, 'I told you, Marwood. No man can serve two masters. So which is it to be? Chiffinch or me?'

'I choose you, sir.'

It was not only that I earned money through my connection with him, or that he was here in person to ask me such a question. It was that Chiffinch served no one but himself. He even served the King his master because he knew it was in his interests to do so. He would lie, cheat and bribe if it served his purpose.

So would Mr Williamson, perhaps. But there was more to him than a man of ability and ambition: there was also something as hard and uncompromising as his northern vowels and bluntness of speech; something private to the man himself; something I thought I could trust. I didn't think he would willingly break his word, even to a clerk who served him.

'Good.' He waved his hand as if sweeping the matter aside. 'I've no doubt that Chiffinch gave you that fool's errand to go to Scotland because Sir Philip Limbury made it worth his while. I don't know what you've been up to, but Limbury must think you a threat to his case before the Fire Court. And I had no choice but to permit it — Chiffinch showed me the King's signature on the warrant. I doubt the King knew what he was signing. He trusts Chiffinch, and will oblige him if he can without trouble to himself. I don't like Chiffinch interfering with the work of my department. But he's made a mistake, Marwood — he's over-reached himself. If the King hears what Chiffinch has been doing in his name, he won't be happy. He places a particular value on the Fire Court and the fairness of its judgements. He abhors anything that might harm its reputation, because that would lead to a rash of appeals against its verdicts. If the court loses public confidence, it affects the rebuilding of London.'

'What would you have me do, sir?'

Williamson didn't answer me directly. 'And there's more,' he whispered. 'As you know.'

I shivered. 'You mean Mistress Hampney?'

'Aye. So. If you wish to continue as my clerk, Marwood, now is the moment when you must speak frankly to me and conceal nothing. Agreed?'

I bowed my head. 'I think Limbury se-duced Mistress Hampney in the hope she would side with him in the Fire Court. They met in Clifford's Inn, in the rooms of a friend, a man named Gromwell. He and

Limbury had been intimate friends since their schooldays. There is a private way to go unseen into his building from Fetter Lane. I think she refused to do as he wished, and perhaps threatened to expose him when she realized what he really wanted. They quarrelled, and it ended in him killing her. Later her body was moved out and left among the ruins where it was found, in the hope that no one would connect it to Limbury or Clifford's Inn.'

'And the Fire Court clerk who was killed in the fire?' Williamson interrupted. 'What was his name?'

'Chelling, sir,' I reminded him. 'He knew something of this. He hated Limbury's friend, Gromwell. I believe he tried to turn the affair to his advantage, and Limbury decided that it was safer to kill than pay him off.'

'Can you prove it?'

'No.' My concentration was waning. 'I saw a letter in his room. It could have been an attempt at blackmail.'

'I need more than a theory, Marwood.'

'There was a fireball burning his bed-chamber where I found him.'

'Another fireball? Why didn't you mention it earlier?'

'And when I tried to drag him out, someone hit me on the head and locked the door from the outside. I heard footsteps running down the stairs.'

Williamson let out his breath in a long sigh. 'Ah,' he said softly, a smile of unexpected sweetness spreading over his face. 'So Chiffinch may be an accessory to murder twice over. An accessory after the fact of the Widow Hampney's murder. And quite possibly before the fact of Chelling's.'

He looked at me, as if expecting a comment on what he had said, or further information that touched on it. That was the moment when I might have said it: that I believed that another death was connected to this: my father's. If he had not fallen under a wagon, I should not have been here, now, scarred for life, and trading secrets like a conspirator with Mr Williamson.

The smile vanished abruptly. 'But we can't prove it, Marwood. It all rests on your word. And what is your word worth against Sir Philip Limbury's? Besides, you didn't see his face when Chelling died. We can't prove he killed Mistress Hampney, either. It's all speculation.'

I said, almost pleading with him, 'You saw what happened this evening, sir, with your own eyes. Someone tried to burn my house down. If it wasn't something to do with

Limbury, who else could it have been?'

'That's the question. Who else?'

A thought struck me. 'What manner of man is Limbury, sir? Tall, short — fat, thin?'

'He's tall and dark,' Williamson said. 'Not a handsome man, but vigorous. He has a taste for wearing black that sets him a little apart at Court. Why?'

'I saw such a man in conversation with Mr Chiffinch last Friday.'

'Where was this?

'On the Privy Stairs. Mr Chiffinch escorted him into a boat and then came back to see me. That was when he told me I must go to Inverness.'

'Then you must see Limbury, and as soon as possible. If he is the man, it is another scrap of circumstantial evidence. But it is still not enough. If you are to be truly useful to me, you must find evidence that Limbury is a murderer and Chiffinch is his accessory. Can you do that for me?'

I was on the verge of saying that no one could promise to do that and be sure of keeping his word. But Williamson's face was as unyielding as one of his northern mountains.

'I will do whatever I can, sir. I swear it.'

It wasn't good enough, and we both knew it. He tapped me on the right knee and said,

'You had two masters, Marwood. Now you have one. Take care you do not end up with none.'

CHAPTER THIRTY-ONE

Faith moves mountains. So do money and hatred.

Sam kept watch throughout the night, dozing for an hour or two in the kitchen and then patrolling the house. He had a sailor's ability to slip in and out of sleep and wake, cat-like, to the slightest sound that deviated from the ordinary.

I summoned him in the morning. 'Do you know a tavern called the Cardinal's Hat?'

He scratched the stubble on his chin. 'There's one over the river. Lambeth way — but not near the palace. Further upstream.'

'Have you been there?'

'I've drunk everywhere, master,' he said, with quiet pride.

'Everywhere?'

'As near as gets no difference. Cardinal's Hat used to get its main business in the summer. Not much of a place, but you can sit outside and watch the river.'

We were interrupted by a knock at the door. A messenger from Williamson's office had brought me the promised money. Later, after dinner, the perruquier called with his boy and showed me his samples. He was a Frenchman with a lined face. He darted about like a monkey and stroked his wigs as though they were living things in need of comfort. His hands were gentle on my head, and he caused me hardly any pain.

Nor did he refer to my injuries, except indirectly when he advised me to choose one of the fuller, longer wigs he had in stock, and when he advised that softer, finer hair would be less of an irritant to the skin. Then he and his boy bowed themselves out of the room, promising to return on Monday with the wig ready for the final fitting.

After they had gone, Cat came to me with a letter in her hand. 'Will you send Sam out with this, sir? It's for Mr Hakesby.'

'What have you told him?'

'Nothing. Only that I am safe and will return.'

'He may guess where you are.'

Her lips twisted, and for a moment her face looked years older than it was. 'He probably does. But guessing isn't the same as knowing.'

I gave her money for Sam. Rather than leaving me, she hovered by my chair.

'What did Mr Williamson mean last night? When he said no man can serve two masters.'

So she had heard his whisper in the kitchen. I was tempted to tell her to mind her own business. But of course I had made it her business, which was the reason why she was obliged to hide in my house, quite possibly at risk of her life.

I told her the gist of what Williamson had said on Friday night, and how I had thrown in my lot with him and undertaken the impossible task of finding proof of Limbury's guilt and Chiffinch's collusion with him.

'The King would not ignore that,' I said. 'He could not. Particularly because it touches on the Fire Court and could harm its reputation.'

'But how can you prove anything?' Cat said, glancing at me. She didn't mean to be unkind, but her look was almost contemptuous. You, it said, a man in your pitiable condition.

I should not have believed it possible that on Monday, a mere three days after Williamson's visit, I should be walking up and down my own parlour — slowly, it is true, and with great caution.

For the first time I was wearing my new purchase — a fine, full wig of lustrous brown hair that flowed down to my shoulders and masked my ears and much of my face from prying eyes. Its weight felt warm and unfamiliar on my head. It was also painful, despite the dressings that protected the burns on my scalp and face. But I was vain enough to think that a little more suffering was a price worth paying.

The perruquier stood back to admire his handiwork, flinging out his arms in wonder. *'Ah, monsieur,'* he said, *'que vous êtes beau! The ladies will flock to you, sir.'*

The boy mirrored his master's gestures exactly, and I swear his lips moved, as though he were silently echoing his master's words. Not in mockery, for his face was serious: he was learning his trade. Sam was standing behind me, near the door. I distinctly heard him smother a laugh.

When the perruquier and his boy had gone, I told Sam to bring my old cloak and hat. My new ones — made to show I was in mourning for my father — had been ruined by the fire.

'You're not going out,' he said.

'I am.'

'Then you're stark raving mad,' he muttered.

'And I'll whip you if you don't mend your manners.'

Sam glared at me. We both knew I was in no condition to whip anyone. But he could not stop me from doing as I pleased, though he attempted to enlist both Margaret and Cat to support him. I overrode them all. Margaret was particularly furious. I ordered her back to the kitchen with a passable imitation of anger.

Cat was harder to dismiss. She lingered in the parlour when the others had gone. 'Where do you want to go?'

'To find Mistress Hampney's maid. Tabitha.'

'It suits you,' she said.

I stared at her, unsettled by the change of subject. 'What does?'

'The wig. It makes you look older.'

I turned away. 'As long as it conceals at least part of my face. That's what matters.'

'It does. You may rest easy on that score.'

I swung back, thinking that Cat might be on the verge of laughing at me. But her face was as grave as a nun's on Good Friday.

'But you shouldn't go out,' she said. 'You're not well enough yet.'

'You will not tell me what I should do.'

She stared at me. My anger deflated like a punctured pig's bladder.

'I want you to come with me,' I said. 'You know what the woman looks like.'

'If they catch me outside —'

'I know.' She had not left the house since she had returned, foul-smelling and filthy, by way of the graveyard on Friday evening. 'But they can't be watching all the time. And in broad daylight there's not much they can do.'

'Do you want to get rid of me?' she said.

'Of course not. You can't go back to Henrietta Street because they will be looking for you there. But you can stay here as long as you need.'

'And how long will that be?'

'We know this,' I said. 'There have been two murders. And the Dragon Yard petition comes up before the Fire Court on Wednesday. In two days' time. That will bring matters to a head.'

We knew something else: that the murders and the Fire Court case interested my two masters, which suggested that in some way they affected the constant manoeuvring for power at Whitehall.

'But what can you do about it? You?' There was a world of scorn in Cat's voice, though I do not think that she meant to speak unkindly.

I said, 'I want to find out what happened to my father. I don't care about the rest.'

I was lying, of course. I did care about the rest. I cared about Cat's safety, because I was the one who had put her in danger. I cared about my Whitehall clerkships and feared to lose them. And I cared most bitterly that the fire had turned me into a spectacle that would sour milk and frighten babies in their cradles, into a terrified apology for a man who dared not show his face in public.

That's why I had to leave the house now. Because otherwise I feared I would never have the courage to venture out into the world again.

We took a boat from the Savoy Stairs. I found it exquisitely painful, particularly when, with the combined help of Cat and one of the boatmen, I crossed from the dry land into the swaying craft. What made it worse was a squall of rain that chose to come scudding down the river, making the boat's timbers slippery and soaking our cloaks in minutes.

We huddled under the awning in the stern, and the boatmen pulled away. I didn't envy their task. True, the tide was on the ebb, and we were going upriver as well as across it. But the gusts of the west wind fought us, making the water choppy. Sometimes I could not prevent a whimper from escaping me as I was jolted against the side of the boat or Cat's arm.

Neither of us spoke. We watched the clusters of wherries and barges, gigs and light horsemen that bobbed about the surface of the Thames, their oars twitching and rising and falling like the legs of insects. It was cold for May, especially on the water, and I wished I had worn my winter cloak. My hands were cold, and I could not warm them. The seat of my breeches grew damper and damper until I could not pretend it was anything other than wet.

Slowly the untidy huddle of Whitehall slid away from us, then the Palace of Westminster. The boatmen pulled across the river to Lambeth, towards the brick buildings of the archbishop's palace, with the tower of St Mary's church close by. To the south lay the settlement that had grown up in their shelter. Beyond it, orchards and gardens were scattered along the bank of the Thames, interspersed with dilapidated houses and other buildings. There were marshes here as well, and patches of waste ground. The area had a ragged, untended appearance.

Our boat was making for the stairs beside the palace. I leaned forward and directed the rower who owned the boat towards a landing place nearly a mile further south.

As I moved, the wind caught the periwig, and the hair lifted on the left side, exposing some of my face, and perhaps what remained of my ear. The man's expression changed, just for a moment. I thought I saw surprise, swiftly followed by disgust.

The moment passed. Upstream from Westminster, the river was much less busy. The men rowed on. I leaned against the back of the seat. No one spoke. Cat swayed towards me, and her left arm briefly touched my right arm. I knew that I would have to become used to this: to seeing my injuries reflected in the expressions on other people's faces, or at least imagining that I did, which in some ways was worse.

The boat's hull grated on the bottom. The tide had not yet covered the upper part of the foreshore. I paid the exorbitant fare the boatmen asked and told them not to wait. I did not want to see their faces again. Besides, the less they knew about us and our movements the better.

A walkway of old timbers stretched up the glistening mud of the foreshore to a small jetty, where there was a narrow flight of steps. There was room to walk abreast, and Cat took my arm, as if she needed my support; though God knows it was the other way round.

On the jetty a small crowd watched our approach. Perhaps it was the weather, perhaps it was my state of mind, but Lambeth seemed dreary beyond belief. There were beggars, scavengers and those who picked over the exposed mud in search of oysters and other delicacies. Their clothes were the same colour as the foreshore itself. At the top of the steps, they parted to allow us to pass among them, though three beggars, a woman with two children clinging to her filthy skirts, held out their palms.

The beggars followed us along the path, with the woman whining monotonously for alms. When we were clear of the jetty, I stopped and waited for them to draw closer.

'I beg you, master,' she said. 'A penny or two to get us across the river. My sister's there, she'll help us.'

'Do you know a tavern called the Cardinal's Hat?' I asked.

She pointed a finger that lacked a nail at a group of buildings a hundred yards away. I dropped two pennies into her hand. They vanished into the folds of her dress, and then her outstretched palm returned.

'And a young woman named Tabitha, who lives nearby with her mother?'

'Not now she don't, master. The old one died. Mean old bitch.'

'But Tabitha's here still?'

'Came back a week or two ago. That's her cottage.'

The beggar pointed to a house on the very edge of the hamlet. It lay on a parcel of waste ground, separated from its neighbours, including the tavern, by a shallow stream. It was little more than a wooden shed with a roof of rotting shingles. Shutters covered the only window. There was a brick chimney but no smoke was rising from it.

I gave the woman two more pennies and they vanished as rapidly as their predecessor.

We walked away, with the beggars trailing after us. I glanced back after a few yards, and they had stopped, but remained standing there in the rain, staring after us as if hoping against reason and experience that we might turn back and give them more money.

Cat said, 'How are you, sir?'

'I manage,' I said. 'It's easier on land.'

It was true that the damp discomfort of

the boat had been harder to bear. Now I was walking, the exercise seemed slightly to moderate the nagging pain. Even the rain felt refreshing on my face. It was good to remind myself that I was not entirely helpless now, that my limbs would obey my commands.

As we neared the cottage, a cur staggered from the shelter of a water butt beneath an overhanging eave. He circled us slowly, barking and showing his yellow teeth. His coat was matted with blood, and it had a wound on its side that oozed pus. I fended off the brute with my stick and it slunk away to the side of the house.

We made our way across water-filled cart-ruts to the door. I knocked three times. There was no answer. I gave another knock, then tried the door. The latch lifted. The door opened into the room beyond, scraping on the mud floor.

As the door opened, light poured into the single room of the cottage, picking out a pile of clothes, a blackened cooking pot, a straw mattress strewn with blankets, a servant's box, a partly broken-up barrel, and a pile of ashes in the grate.

Something moved in the corner beyond the door, where the light barely reached.

Cat pushed past me and stepped inside.

'God have mercy,' she whispered.

I opened the door as widely as it would go and followed her into the cottage. A tie beam ran across the building, preventing it from collapsing under its own weight. A large bundle dangled from it. It stirred slightly in the draught from the door. My first thought was that someone had hung it there to keep it clear of the rats.

And then I saw that it was a young woman. Her head was uncovered. Her neck was at an angle to the body, pulled there by the noose around her neck and her own weight. She was bare-footed. On the floor beneath her feet was an overturned stool and a wine bottle lying on its side.

The face was suffused with blood. The tongue poked out of the mouth. It looked blackened, as though charred by fire.

'Tabitha,' Cat said. She turned away and vomited on the floor. She went outside.

I fought a desire to do the same. I made myself examine her more closely. The arms hung at the side. I touched one and tried to raise it, but it resisted me. The stiffness that follows death had already seized her limbs. But my efforts made the body rotate slightly, bringing her face to face with me. I shuddered, and left her to death.

I tried the lid of the box. It wasn't locked.

Inside was a clutter of clothes and shoes. I stooped, wincing, and poked at them. It was too painful for me to bend so low and examine them properly. The clothes seemed well-worn but many were of good quality, perhaps cast-offs from Tabitha's mistress. They were worth good money on a second-hand clothing stall.

Cat returned and joined me. She knelt by the box and explored it more thoroughly. She fished out a darned woollen stocking with something hard in its toe. She pushed her hand inside and found a gold piece and a handful of silver.

I glanced back at the body, at the stool on the floor. 'Whatever happened here, it wasn't robbery.'

'Did she kill herself?' Cat said.

'It might have been designed to look like it. We should go before someone finds us.'

Cat looked up at me; she had a pair of women's shoes in her hand. 'And leave her hanging here?'

'She won't mind. Not now.' I felt callous for saying it, but it was true.

'Shouldn't we find a justice? We could ask at the tavern.'

'If we do that, there will be questions. Who we are. Why we came here.'

'But they will search for us after they find

Tabitha.'

'It's only the beggar who knows we were looking for her, and she was waiting for a boat. With luck they'll never find her, even if they try. It's a risk worth running.'

'It can't be right to leave her like this,' Cat said.

'Right or wrong be damned,' I snapped. 'What choice do we have?'

She shook her head but said nothing more about it. She was examining the shoes. They were of yellow leather, with blue embroidery, with high red heels, perhaps a cast-off from Tabitha's mistress, for the leather was scuffed and stained. While we were speaking, Cat had been extracting balls of paper which had been stuffed inside the shoes to keep their shape. Methodically, she smoothed them out.

There were perhaps half a dozen sheets. I looked over her shoulder at them. They looked crudely printed, some with woodcuts at the head. Ballads and broadsheets, I thought, nothing of interest. But something had caught her attention.

'What's that you have there?' I asked, hoping to divert her from uncomfortable questions of right and wrong.

She held up a sheet of paper. 'Look. This one was folded, not made into a ball. As if she was hiding it. A clever girl. She made the money easier to find than this.'

The first thing I noticed, with the printer's eye I owed to my father's training, was the quality of the paper, which was far removed from the cheap, coarse stuff they used for ballads and such. There were a few lines of handwriting on it. And, at the bottom right-hand corner, a large, curling capital L.

'Limbury?' Cat said.

There was no time to waste. We went back outside. The dog greeted us like old enemies and this time I hit him so hard that I stunned him. He fell on his side and for a moment lay there, panting, his eyes open and fixed on me.

It was then that I saw the wound on his side clearly. It was a small, neat puncture, flat and symmetrical, though the flesh around it was swollen with infection.

With painful slowness, the dog rose to his feet. He stared balefully at me. I raised my stick. He backed away. Weaving like a drunk, he slunk into the doorway of the cottage.

We dared not go back to the place where we had landed. Instead we followed a lane protected with high hedges, which ran north in the direction of the palace and the church. We did not speak of what we had seen. I was in considerable pain, and I could hardly drag one foot after the other. I leaned heavily on Cat as I walked. The lane was narrow and very muddy and the rain fell incessantly. But we met no one.

Near Lambeth Palace, the houses increased, and we met other people, passing to and fro. Few of them gave us a second glance. There was a little crowd waiting at the palace stairs for the common barge which with every tide passed up and down the river between London and Windsor. There were people of all sorts, many of them strangers to each other, and Cat and I lost ourselves among them.

We were fortunate — there was also a tilt boat taking passengers aboard to cross the river to Westminster Stairs. I paid our fares and we crossed to the other side. We were more exposed to the rain on the water, and the sudden gusts of wind made the boat sway and buck like a wild thing, throwing us to and fro and driving gouts of spray on board.

I felt more dead than alive by the time we reached Westminster. There was a cab stand in Palace Yard, but I was in acute pain and we were both cold, wet, weary and miserable. I could not face the prospect of the jolting hackney ride to the Savoy.

'Come, sir,' she said. 'We must find shelter for a while.'

I no longer cared what we did. Cat took my arm and steered me towards the Dog, a vast tavern on the north side of the yard, near the gate to King's Street. The noise of the place almost overwhelmed me — since Chelling's murder, I had lost the habit of moving freely in the world. The great barroom was crowded but Cat found us places on a bench at the end of one of the common tables. I called for aqua vitae and she, more wisely, ordered us soup, bread and a jug of ale. The waiter gave me a curious look. I turned my head away.

We ate and drank in silence. The spirit made me cough violently but its fire slid down to my belly. The soup gradually warmed and revived me. I had not realized how hungry I was.

Afterwards Cat fumbled with her dress while I poured the last of the ale. She took from her pocket the paper she had found among Tabitha's clothes. It was now crumpled and damp. She smoothed it out on the table before us. In places the rain had smudged the ink but the tall, slanting handwriting was perfectly legible.

Whenas in Silks My CELIA goes

Then, then (methinks) how sweetly flowes
That Liquefaction of her Clothes.

Next, when I cast mine Eyes and see
That brave Vibration each way free;
O how that glittering taketh me!

L

'Verses,' I said softly, though there was little risk of our being overheard in this crowded place. 'A love poem written by Limbury to Mistress Hampney in her silks. Her yellow silk gown?'

'He didn't even write it,' Cat said. 'He copied it, and changed the lady's name to hers.'

'How do you know?'

'The lines are by Mr Herrick. My Aunt Quincy set them to music once.' She glanced at me. 'You wouldn't think it,' she went on, 'but he's a clergyman.'

'If we match the writing to Limbury's, then —'

'Then we have him. Only as Celia's lover, true, but that's a great deal.'

'Tabitha must have taken the verses from her mistress's papers,' I said. 'After her murder, to use as a tool for extorting money. Which means she knew her mistress had a lover.'

'And Tabitha knew who he was, too,' Cat said. 'The way she behaved to Mistress Lee shows it, and her lack of interest in finding another position. She believed that Limbury would keep her, to ensure her silence.'

'Then he decided it was wiser to shut her mouth permanently.'

'But perhaps she did kill herself,' Cat said. 'When she's found, they may think that her mind was disordered — perhaps with grief from her mother's death — and that is why she did it. And you and I can't be sure that it wasn't like that. After all, there's nothing to show that Limbury was there.'

I stirred on the bench. 'Nothing?' I dug my nails into the palm of my right hand to distract myself from the pain. 'Not quite. Someone was there. A man, very possibly a gentleman.'

'What makes you think that?'

'The dog. I think it had been stabbed with a rapier and left for dead.'

CHAPTER THIRTY-TWO

Filled with joy, Jemima sat in her private parlour with a silver pencil in her hand. She was alone.

Flurries of rain tapped on the window pane. The sky was grey, streaked with the darker charcoal plumes of smoking chimneys. It was colder than it had been, and she had ordered a fire to be lit.

She had not been sure until this morning, though she had suspected it for more than a week. But, after discussing it with Mary, she believed that she could not be mistaken. Her courses were late this month, and the plain fact was that she was never late. The only explanation must be that she was with child.

She had tried numerous methods guaranteed to lead to conception and done everything the physicians advised. One of the methods must have worked. Had it been the fern roots and steel shavings warmed in

405

wine? Or perhaps the poultice of ram's dung applied to the belly?

No matter. She spread the palm of her left hand over her belly. Already she felt life stirring and twitching within her. She was sure of it.

Beside her was a list of names, arranged in two columns, one for boys and one for girls. Coming to a sudden decision, she scribbled out the girls' names, digging the pencil deep into the paper to erase even a hint of them remaining.

It was a boy. It must be a boy. Her father wanted him to be christened George Syre Limbury. She had no objection to the Syre — after all, the boy would sooner or later own Syre Place — but she had never cared for the name George. She had little doubt that she could bend her father to her will. As for Philip, she was confident that he would agree with whatever she wanted. If she gave him a son, he would allow her anything in his power.

Jemima wrote: Valentine; she laid down her pencil, folded her hands over her belly and sat back to consider the name. She picked up the pencil again and wrote: Christopher.

She had barely exchanged a word with Philip since their quarrel on Friday. But now she had the means to make all well between them — indeed, to make all better than it had ever been before.

She rose carefully from her chair. Her closet was on the first floor, next to her bedroom but overlooking Pall Mall at the front of the house, not the garden at the back and the fields beyond. She went on to the landing.

The house was silent. It was the hour after dinner. The servants were somewhere downstairs, living their mysterious lives and doing whatever servants did when they were not serving their masters. Mary would come if she rang for her. But she did not want Mary. She wanted Philip.

Somewhere below, a door closed. Footsteps ran lightly down the hall, and then down the stairs to the kitchen. She waited a moment until everything was quiet. Then she slowly descended the stairs, step by step, clinging to the broad bannister rail. She walked down the landing to the door of Philip's study. She tapped on the door, and entered.

He was at his desk, with a mass of papers before him — including, she noted, what looked like plans of houses. That wretched Dragon Yard.

Frowning, he rose and bowed. 'Madam,'

he said. 'This is unexpected.'

He set a chair for her. She found the study an oppressive room, though it overlooked the garden. It was small and square, dark and masculine. The walls were panelled with stained oak. There was a desk by the window and a book press within reach. On the opposite wall stood a tall cabinet richly carved with satyrs' heads. Only a turkey carpet lent it colour.

Joy bubbled up inside her. 'I'm with child.'

She had meant to lead up to it, to tease his curiosity, to prolong the enjoyment of it. But she could not restrain herself.

'I am with child,' she repeated. 'It's a boy. I know it.'

And all our troubles will be smoothed away, she thought. God be thanked.

'Again? Haven't we had enough of this foolery?'

She covered her ears with her hands, pressing them tightly against the side of her head. But she could not shut away his voice.

'Is this the fourth time you've told me this? Or the fifth? I lose count. And always these children of yours melt away like snow in spring. They are but fantasies, madam, the imaginings of a disordered understanding.'

There was a knock at the front door.

'It's not true!' She tore her hands away. 'How can you say such things? I've been unlucky. Why, I think I lost them before because I was cursed. It was the old woman, remember, the one who used to stand on the corner outside the house. She was a witch, Philip — you agreed with me, you know you did. In any case, she's gone now — Richard sent her away, though I wished she could have been burned — but all is well now.' She hugged herself. There were voices in the hall, and then footsteps. 'And I am bearing your son.'

He did not smile with joy. He did not take her in his arms. Instead he sat down at his desk and rubbed his eyes.

'Jemima, my love,' he said sadly. 'If this were true, no one would rejoice more than I.'

There was a tap on the door. Richard entered. He glanced slyly at Jemima, and she guessed he had heard something of what had been said.

'Mr Gromwell, sir,' he said.

Gromwell swept into the room in his shabby finery. His face lit up when he saw Jemima. 'Madam,' he said, 'you adorn this room as an angel adorns paradise.'

CHAPTER THIRTY-THREE

As the Hackney approached the southern end of Bedford Street, Cat raised the leather curtain above the door. She had taken a risk in coming here. As far as she knew, no one had followed her from the Savoy to the cabstand, but she couldn't be sure.

At first she thought Mr Hakesby wasn't there. Then a rider urged his horse forward, and she saw the old man's tall, angular figure on the corner. He had propped himself against one of the posts that protected pedestrians from the flow of traffic in the Strand.

Cat knocked twice on the panel that separated her from the driver. He drew up at the side of the road a few yards beyond the post. She felt a rush of relief as she watched him walk unsteadily towards them, leaning on his stick. Not just relief — affection, too. She had missed him, she realized, and missed the work of the drawing office as well. Infirmary Close was a refuge, but it was also a prison.

He opened the door. 'My dear —'

'Tell the driver to go on, sir.'

'Where?'

'It doesn't matter. Let him drive up to Holborn.'

When Hakesby climbed into the hackney, she took his arm and helped him to sit. It gave her a pang to see that he was frailer than ever.

With a jerk, the coach moved off, pulling into the traffic. Someone swore at them, and their driver swore back. Now the door was closed and the blind was down, the interior was lit only by the cracks of light between the curtains and the frames around them. Barely a yard away, Hakesby's face was a pale blur, the features smudged into shapelessness beneath his broad-brimmed hat.

'Thank you for coming. I thought perhaps you might not wish to . . .'

'I've been worried,' he said in a faltering voice that was barely audible above the clopping of hooves and the din of iron-rimmed wheels on the roadway. 'I don't understand why you went away. Brennan said he saw you with Mr Poulton the other day, but you ran off. It's something to do with the Fire Court, isn't it? It's Dragon

Yard and Mr Marwood's business, whatever that really is. How I wish I'd —'

'Sir,' she interrupted. 'You must not worry yourself about me.'

'It's been most inconvenient. We have such a press of work at present. Where have you been? You didn't say in your letter.'

She ignored the question. 'I am perfectly safe, and I hope to be with you again soon.'

'I should turn you off,' he said, suddenly petulant. 'You are my servant, after all — what right have you to leave me unless I send you away?'

'Forgive me, sir. I wish it were not so.' She leaned forward. 'Tell me, have you brought it?'

'And there's another thing! Why in God's name do you want this?' He was working himself into a passion. 'A specimen of Sir Philip's handwriting. I never heard of such a thing. No explanation — no reason — barely even a by-your-leave.'

The hackney swayed as it rounded a corner, and a wheel scraped against a kerbstone. The jolt threw Hakesby against her.

'That fool of a driver,' he snapped, his anger diverted. 'I shall have his licence taken away.'

Cat helped him back to his seat. 'No harm is done, sir.'

412

'Did I hurt you?' he enquired, his rage evaporating as suddenly as it had come. 'I'm such a clumsy brute and so much heavier than you.'

'Not in the slightest.'

There was a pause. Hakesby fumbled in his coat.

'I have it here . . .' He held out a folded paper. 'A letter from Sir Philip — it's very short . . . I shall need it back.'

She took the letter from his shaking fingers and slipped it through her skirt and into the pocket beneath. 'Thank you, sir. Tell me, has Mr Poulton heard anything from Lincoln?'

Hakesby shook his head. 'Not unless something came in these last few hours. There's so little time — we'll be before the Fire Court in two days. And I dread hearing from Lincoln in case it's bad news, and there's a new will, leaving Mistress Hampney's leases away from her uncle.'

'Pray don't be anxious.' She leaned forward and rapped on the panel. 'Forgive me — I must leave you now.'

'What? Where are you going?'

The hackney slowed. Cat took a couple of shillings from her pocket and pressed them into the palm of Hakesby's hand. It was shaking so much she had to hold it steady

413

and fold the fingers over the coins.

'What's this? Money? Why are you giving me money?'

'For the fare. Mr Marwood said I must be sure to pay it, as he would not have you out of pocket. I'll tell the driver to take you back to Henrietta Street.'

The coach stopped and she opened the door and jumped down. She looked back at his creased, bewildered face.

'I will come back, sir,' she said. 'I swear it. Everything will be as it was before.'

Cat closed the door and told the driver where to go. She waited, watching the hackney rattling up Drury Lane. It was still raining. The roadway was filthy with mud and horse droppings. The sky was dingy and drab. But the coach had been newly cleaned and its yellow cab and red wheels made a splash of colour in the street. It turned left into Long Acre and disappeared from her sight.

The alley to Infirmary Close was gloomy and slippery with rain. It was empty. If people were spying on the comings and goings at Marwood's house, Cat saw no sign of them.

Sam opened the door to her knock. He had a pistol in his belt and an iron-shod staff in his hand. Cat slipped into the house, unfastening her cloak. He slammed the door, drove the bolts home and put the bar across. As he was securing it, Margaret ran red-faced through the hall with a tankard in her hand, throwing Cat a glance and then ignoring her. She thundered up the stairs.

'Is he bad?' Cat said.

Sam turned to her. 'It started soon after you left. He's moaning away like a baby.'

'Has he had any laudanum?' Cat asked.

'He won't. He's as stubborn as his father. If he wasn't my master, I'd call him a fool.'

Cat followed Margaret upstairs and into Marwood's bedchamber. He was lying on the bed, on his right side. The moaning had subsided to the occasional whimper.

Margaret looked old and tired. 'He'll not let me dress the burns,' she whispered. 'When it's really bad, he acts like one possessed.'

'Has he taken anything at all?'

'He called for beer to quench his thirst, but he'll not touch it now it's here.'

'Let me stay with him for a while.'

Cat went over to the bed. Marwood was lying on his right side with his eyes open. His expression didn't change when he saw her. His head was bare — even the loose bandage was gone. The skin was livid and shiny. There was no sign that the hair was growing back. For the first time she saw clearly the wreckage of his left ear, reduced to a pink, misshapen thing, unfamiliar and strangely unsettling.

'I saw Mr Hakesby,' she said.

Marwood took a deep breath but said nothing. She sensed that he was willing himself to concentrate on what she was saying.

'He gave me a letter from Sir Philip. Where did you put the verses?'

'In the Bible there.' His voice was faint and hoarse.

The book was on the night table by the bed, along with the beer and the laudanum. It was a small, shabby volume whose binding was in poor condition. She riffled through the pages until she found the folded sheet of paper.

'Put them side by side,' he said. 'The letter and the verses. Oh Christ, have mercy. I am a sinner.'

'You need to take a dose, sir.'

'No,' he shouted. 'No, no, no.'

She carried the verses to the window and laid them on the sill. She took the letter from her pocket, unfolded it and placed it next to them.

'Well?' he said. 'Well?'

The letter was brief, curt and clearly written in haste. It was addressed to Mr Poulton. The contents informed him that Mr Browning of Gray's Inn was acting for Sir Philip Limbury in the matter of Dragon Yard, and should be allowed full access to the site at any time as the accredited representative of the freeholder.

'The verses are written carefully, and in a fine neat hand,' Cat said. 'The letter is a scrawl. But they look as if they were written by the same person.'

'Then we have him. It's Limbury who was Celia Hampney's lover. And more than likely worse. Her murderer too, and Tabitha's. Put both papers back in the Bible. I shall show them to Williamson. I shall — ah, dear God, stop it and —'

The words lost their shape and faded to a whimper.

Cat picked up the laudanum. 'Why won't you take this?'

'It will make me its slave. And there are bad dreams . . .'

'Better that than be a slave to your pain.'

'No. When I show Williamson —'

'You'll show him nothing at all unless you take some of this.'

'I shall not —'

She stamped her foot, driving him into

silence. 'You shall, sir. Or you will be no use to any of us, least of all yourself.'

His face was contorted. He was sweating. 'I — say — I — will — not.'

'And I say you will.'

'Leave me, you witch,' he shouted, his voice high and jagged. 'Leave me.'

'If you make me,' she said, 'I shall call Sam and Margaret to hold you down while I force it into you. The more you struggle, the more you will suffer.'

For a moment Marwood said nothing. She stared down at him. He bit his lip. A drop of blood appeared, reminding her of the dog they had seen in Lambeth. Tears filled his eyes and overflowed.

'By God,' he said. 'You're a devil. I believe you would do it and not think twice about it.'

'Take it,' she said, and picked up the flask.

The double knock on the door came after the candles had been lit. Cat was sitting upstairs with Marwood, who was now sleeping so deeply it seemed he might never wake. Perhaps, she thought more than once, it might be kinder if he didn't. Strange to think that before the fire at Clifford's Inn, she had envied his good fortune.

The chamber door was open. She heard

Sam's footsteps downstairs, and the click of the door shutter opening, allowing him to inspect who was waiting outside. For a moment she held her breath. Then came the rattle of bolts and the grating sound the bar made when it was removed from its sockets.

She took up the candle and went on to the landing. Williamson's harsh voice filled the shadowy space below, demanding to be taken to Marwood. She glanced back at the man on the bed. He was still dead to the world and its pains, his breathing as regular as before. She left him and went downstairs.

'Master's not well,' Sam was saying. 'He's sleeping, sir, and mustn't be wakened.'

'You'll let me decide that. Where is he? Upstairs?'

'Sir,' Cat said, taking the last few stairs at a run. 'May I speak to you first?'

Williamson frowned down at her. 'Who are you?'

'Jane, sir. You saw me the last time you were here.'

He ran his eyes over her. There was nothing lascivious in his stare. She might have been a column of figures to be added up or a horse to be assessed for its suitability for a task. 'Did I?'

'Yes, sir. In the parlour. I had fallen in the gutter on my way back from the

419

apothecary's.'

'Ah. I remember.' His expression was different now: he was comparing his memory of that filthy, dishevelled creature with the demure, neatly dressed young woman before him. 'The maid.'

'Yes, sir. Mr Marwood asked me to speak to you if you called.'

A puddle of rainwater was forming around him. He took off his cloak and tossed it to Sam. 'About what?'

The words were curt but his manner had subtly changed. He had adjusted his assumptions about her, if only by a trifle. There were maidservants of all conditions in London, some of whom had been gently bred. There were men who employed their unmarried sisters or cousins to serve them, often for little more than the cost of their board and lodging.

'There are two papers he wished you to see, sir.'

His eyebrows shot up. 'Where are they?'

'In the chamber where he's asleep. Would you come with me?'

Sam cleared his throat noisily but said nothing.

'But pray don't wake him,' she went on. 'He has had a large dose of laudanum. He went out today on your business, and now the pain is particularly bad.'

She led the way upstairs, with Williamson's heavy steps behind her, and took him into Marwood's room. Their shadows swooped drunkenly before them, thrown by the candle she had left burning on the chest by the door.

Cat went to the bed and held up her candle so the light fell on Marwood's face. He was snoring gently.

Williamson stared at him for a long moment. He nodded at the periwig on its stand at the foot of the bed. 'Has he worn that?'

'Yes, sir. When he went out today. With the wig and a hat on his head, you hardly notice the burns . . . most of the time, at least.'

He grunted. 'That's something, I suppose. Where are these papers?'

She took up the Bible on the night table, and removed the poem. She passed it to Williamson, who angled them to the light of the candle.

'What's this? Verses? Why did he want me to see this?'

'He found them in the possession of a woman called Tabitha, who was living in Lambeth.'

'He told you this?' Surprise battled with outrage in his voice.

'In case he could not talk to you if you called.'

'Very well. Who is this Tabitha?'

'Mistress Hampney's maid. But now she is dead.'

'How?'

'She hanged herself in her own cottage. Or someone did it for her.'

Williamson peered at the paper in his hand. 'Who wrote this?' he said sharply. 'Who is this "L"?'

'I don't know.' Cat turned the pages of the Bible and took out the letter that Hakesby had given her. 'He commanded me to show you this as well.'

Williamson read the letter, muttered something under his breath and then read it again. 'Addressed to Mr Hakesby, I see. The name's familiar.'

'He is the surveyor acting for Poulton.'

'How did your master get this?'

'I can't say.'

He took up the verses and compared them to the letter. 'By God, I believe they're in the same hand.' His eyes went back to the figure on the bed, still snoring. 'I must talk to him.'

'No, sir.'

He stared down at her. 'What did you say?'

'Pray don't wake him. He needs this sleep

more than anything.'

Williamson shook his head and took a step towards the bed. He laid a hand on Marwood's shoulder.

'Stop,' Cat said, more loudly than she had intended.

He swung back, his eyebrows shooting up.

'If you wake him, you'll get no sense from him. You'll distress him to no purpose.'

'What makes you so sure?'

'I've helped nurse him these last few days. I know the pattern of it.'

Williamson shrugged. 'Perhaps you're right.' He folded the two papers and slipped them in his pocket. 'When he wakes, tell him I came, and that I wish to see him as soon as possible. If he's too ill to come to Whitehall, then send word to my office.'

She bowed her head.

'Can you write?'

'Yes, sir.'

'Then, if he cannot come himself, or write to me, you must write on his behalf. Or at least give me a report on how he does.'

He gestured to her to light him downstairs.

Sam was waiting for them in the hall. As he was unbarring the door, Williamson turned back to her. 'What did you say your name was?'

'Jane, sir.'

'And your surname?'

'Hakesby, sir.'

'Like the surveyor?'

'I am his cousin, sir. He took me in when my father died. He sent me here to help with nursing Mr Marwood.'

Williamson clicked his fingers. 'Curious. Are they intimate friends?'

'I can't say, sir.'

To her relief, he did not probe further. He said goodnight and left the house.

'Thank Christ for that,' Sam muttered piously as he barred the door.

Cat went back upstairs. On the landing outside Marwood's room, there was a small, unshuttered window. Shielding her candle with the palm of her hand, she looked down into the alley below. A light burned on the corner at the end. She was in time to see Williamson marching slowly towards it, his outline wavering and indeterminate because of the lack of light and the distortion of the glass.

CHAPTER THIRTY-FOUR

'Bring me the box,' Jemima said. 'The one in the chest.'

Without a word, Mary curtsied and went away. The chest had a drawer with a false back, and it was behind this that the box was kept. It was a pretty thing made of ebony inlaid with silver.

At this hour, approaching midnight, the house was quiet. The other servants were in the kitchen or in bed, apart from Richard, who was attending his master at Whitehall; or so he said.

Jemima unlocked the box with a key she kept in her pocket. Among the litter inside were more keys, held together on a ring.

Mary did not need to be told what to do. She picked up a candle, opened the door for her mistress and followed her down the stairs, along the hall and into the study. Once inside, Mary closed the door behind them and stood with her back to it.

'Light another candle,' Jemima said. 'I don't want to be poking about in the gloom. Put it on the desk and then hold a light for me over here.'

Jemima had commissioned the cabinet with satyrs' heads for Philip, as a wedding present. Most of the woods used for the inlays and the veneers had come from the East Indies. It was probably the most expensive piece of furniture in the entire house — it had cost even more than her own bed.

She unlocked and opened its outer doors. Inside were three drawers above a cupboard. The top drawer had its own lock, but Jemima had a key for it too — that was the advantage of commissioning the cabinet-maker and the locksmith yourself.

The majority of the contents were familiar from earlier inspections. There was a small bag of gold and a few trinkets that had survived the shipwreck of the Limburys' fortunes during the Commonwealth when Philip had been abroad with the King and the court in exile. Beside these was a bundle of documents relating to the Pall Mall house, and another bundle dealing with the Dragon Yard property and the Fire Court case.

Underneath them all was a folder of letters and notes, most of them about Philip's debts and his attempts to pay them. Until the last few weeks, Jemima would have said that gambling, not women, was his weakness. Now she was not so sure.

All this was familiar, though at a quick glance the debts amounted to almost twice as much as they had before, despite the earrings she had given him to sell. One of the new bills was for thirty pounds owed to a printer, the Widow Vereker at the sign of the Three Bibles on London Bridge. That puzzled her for a moment — her husband was not a man who cared for the printed word, by and large — until she remembered Gromwell's book of Gloucestershire antiquities. Whatever the favour that Gromwell had done Philip, it was an important one, and he desired to keep his side of the bargain.

Another thing was new since her last inspection: a letter at the very bottom of the drawer. Or rather two letters, for the outer one had another folded inside it.

She carried them over to the desk. The first letter had a broken seal (an anonymous smudge of wax with nothing imprinted on it) and Philip's name on the outside, but no address. She took it to the desk and examined it by the light of the candle. It contained a few words scrawled in pencil. It was unsigned.

> This under my door by night. I will call on you at supper.

Jemima unfolded the second letter. It was much longer, and written in a fine, clerkly hand.

> Sir,
> It grieves me beyond Measure that my Conscience requires me to communicate this Distressing Information to you, not merely for the Good of our Fellowship and its Reputation in the World, but also to warn you of the Dangers of a too Generous and too Trusting Spirit. In Fetter Lane, by the Half Moon tavern, an alley leads to our Inn, to the Remains of Staircase XIII. I have had the Misfortune to learn that it is possible to pass between the two, and that it has been the means of conducting an Intrigue that will bring Shame upon our Fellowship.
> Pray advise me. Should I lay the Matter before the Principal and Rules at their next Meeting? Or would it be more prudent for us to deal with it privately,

to preserve the good Repute of the Inn?

T.C.

Was this the letter that Mary had told her about the week before last? The one the boy had brought, which had thrown Philip into a rage? Underneath the fine words there was an unmistakable hint of a threat. The letter must have been sent to Gromwell — who else did Philip know at Clifford's Inn — who had indeed called at Pall Mall that evening and taken Philip away from her. She did not know who 'T.C.' might be, though he was obviously a member of the Inn as well.

. . . the means of conducting an Intrigue . . .

Jemima knew what the intrigue was, if nothing else. No wonder Philip had flown into such a passion. A bubble of pain burst inside her, and she cried out.

'Madam,' Mary said. 'Oh madam.'

Jemima glanced at her. For a moment, she wondered whether to show her the letter — Mary could read quite well, though writing was another matter. Then she read it again, thinking about its implications, and decided not to.

The letter had been delivered to the house

429

on Thursday evening, eleven days ago. On Friday night — or rather in the darkest hour before dawn on Saturday morning — Philip had returned to the house and gone to his bedchamber; she had gone to him there and found him distraught; she had never seen him so distressed; and she had comforted him. Her heart melted within her bosom at the sweet memory of it. She found consolation there, at least: in his time of trouble, he had not turned her away.

A triple knock echoed through the house.

Both Jemima and Mary gasped. It could not be Philip at the street door — he had his own knock, which the porter knew as his master's. This was a stranger's knock. An uninvited caller at this hour was unheard of.

The knock would bring the servants into the hall. They could hardly help noticing that their mistress was in the study. There was no reason why she should not be here. On the other hand, there was no reason why she should.

Jemima folded the letters. She glided back to the cabinet. Already there were footsteps outside, and the sound of voices. She put the letters back in the drawer, locked it, closed the cabinet doors and locked them.

'What do we do, mistress?' whispered Mary.

Jemima dropped her keys in her pocket. 'Do?' She did not lower her voice. 'Why, we shall go back upstairs. Snuff that candle and open the door.'

Mary obeyed. She replaced the study candlestick on the mantle shelf and lighted Jemima into the hall. Hester glanced at them, and so did Hal Coachman, who was standing in the shadows near the stairs to the kitchen. He was not supposed to come up into the house, but it was a sensible precaution when there was an unexpected caller at this time of the evening. Besides, according to Mary, he lusted after Hester, though Jemima found this hard to believe. Still, you could never tell with servants.

'Who is it?' Jemima said.

'The porter says it's a gentleman called Mr Chiffinch, mistress.'

'Let him in.'

Jemima had never met Mr Chiffinch, but she knew that Philip counted him as a friend. Hester bobbed an awkward curtsy to her mistress while the door was opening. Hal edged further into the shadows. They must already have seen the candlelight around the study door.

Cold air rushed into the house. The bulky

431

figure of a man came into the hall, brushing raindrops from his cloak.

'Damn me,' he said. 'God rot this weather. Where's your master, girl?'

'He's out, sir.'

'Where the devil is he?'

Jemima advanced down the hall with Mary a step or two behind with the candle. 'My husband isn't at home,' she said. 'May I help you?'

The man turned to her, removing his hat, which sent a gout of water to the floor. His eyes ran swiftly over her, taking in the fur-trimmed gown and the maid at her elbow. He bowed. 'Madam, your pardon for disturbing you. My name is Chiffinch. William Chiffinch.'

'My husband has talked of you, sir. He's at Whitehall. He may be there still.'

'I couldn't find him there.'

'Then he's probably supping with friends. Will you leave a message?'

Chiffinch hesitated. 'I wonder, madam, if I might have a word in your private ear?'

'Of course, sir. In my closet, I think.'

He declined refreshment. Jemima went upstairs, with Mary padding almost silently behind her, and Chiffinch last of all, his steps heavy and deliberate. In the closet, she sent Mary away and sat down, waving

Chiffinch to the sofa. His face was shiny with moisture, though it was hard to know whether it was rain or perspiration.

He did not sit. 'Forgive me if I go straight to the point — I'm pressed for time. Your ladyship knows who I am, I think?'

She inclined her head. 'Indeed, sir.' All the world knew of Mr Chiffinch, the Keeper of the King's Private Closet. All the world that mattered.

'I've the honour to serve the King in his private affairs, which means that I cannot always explain the reasons for my words and actions as frankly as I should wish to do. But, believe me, madam, I'm here to do your husband a kindness. Tell him that I strongly advise him to beg leave of His Majesty to withdraw from Court for a month or so. My advice would be for him to take you down to Syre Court as soon as you can contrive it — after all, what could be more natural than for you than to pay a visit to your father? His health would furnish you with an excuse.'

She registered the fact that he knew so much about her family's circumstances. She said, 'I must give my husband some reason, sir, surely? He would be most reluctant to leave London just at present. He has a case before the Fire Court, for example —'

'My lady, hear me out,' Chiffinch said. His voice remained soft but he spoke with more deliberation than before, which gave his words an edge. 'You may tell Sir Philip this: that the reason has to do with the Fire Court. He'll understand me.'

Jemima shivered.

'Forgive me, madam,' Chiffinch said. 'I've kept you talking in a room without a fire. Let me ring for your maid. I'll leave you in peace now.' He took a step towards her and loomed over her. His voice dropped. 'Be sure to tell your husband what I've said as soon as he comes in. Tell him I will do what I can, but you two must go down to the country as soon as possible. Otherwise I can't answer for the consequences.'

He left the room without another word. She listened to his tread on the stairs. Then Mary was with her, urging her to retire to her bedchamber, where there was a fire.

Jemima allowed herself to be taken to her bedroom. But she would not get into bed, though it had already been warmed for her.

'Light more candles,' she said. 'Build up the fire and bring me a posset. I shall wait up for your master.'

Mary left her alone. Jemima hugged her belly. Was it larger than before? So it came back to the Fire Court. Chiffinch's warning must have to do with Clifford's Inn and Philip's intrigue, with the letters in the cabinet and the murder of the widow Hampney. The ugly whore was dead. But even now she had power to haunt them.

Jemima hugged herself, hugged her son. Now though, Mr Chiffinch had changed the rules of the game. If she played the cards she had in her hand with skill, she could have everything she wanted. At Syre Court, with her father standing by, Philip would be entirely hers and for ever. She would make him love her once more. And —

My son, she thought, my son. I do all this for you.

CHAPTER THIRTY-FIVE

Laudanum. A solution of alcohol infused with the juice of the poppy, to which the apothecary adds the ingredients that his skill and his judgement suggest.

To know what composes a thing is not to know the nature of that thing.

A body is a prison, within which the spirit dashes itself against bars of bone and walls of flesh until death unlocks the door and sets the spirit free.

Even in prison, a man may have visions that make him an emperor of time and space.

These thoughts, and others of a like nature, marched through my mind in a stately procession organized according to some logic of its own. I knew each of them was of profound importance. But when I tried to contemplate a thought, the next arrived and shouldered its predecessor out of the way.

Indeed, my mind was a lively place, busy but orderly in its organization and its transactions — not unlike, it occurred to me, a hive of bees. The metaphor pleased me, and I seemed to see the outer forms of my thoughts take the appearance of bees.

While this was going on, a part of me was aware that I was lying on my left side in my own bed in my chamber in Infirmary Close. My eyes were shut, not that it mattered because I appeared to be able to see perfectly well with them closed. My body was immobile. I thought it possible that this condition would be permanent. The prospect did not trouble me unduly. I noticed without surprise that I was not in pain. Or, if I was, the pain was somewhere remote from me.

While I had been thinking of this, the bees had begun to misbehave. Their yellow had become red and they were forming patterns, which I discovered were letters of the alphabet. In another moment they were combining into words. Four words to be precise, written in scarlet letters and repeated over and over again.

The mark of Cain. The mark of Cain. The mark of Cain.

'I think he's awake,' Margaret said. 'God be thanked.'

'His eyes are open. But that don't mean a thing.'

'Aren't they blue, Sam? I never noticed how blue they were.'

'His eyes are the same as they always were, you foolish woman. It's the opium. Makes the pupils smaller. I've seen it a hundred times.'

I tried to say, 'Of course I'm awake.'

My father was sitting beside me now. He was smiling.

On Tuesday morning, Sam brought me the letter. I was downstairs, though in my bedgown.

By this time the effect of the medicine had passed its peak. I had emerged strangely refreshed from the trance-like state which had paralysed me a few hours earlier. I was alert and capable of movement. I felt some discomfort, though the laudanum masked the worst of it. The pain was a sleeping tiger, its claws unsheathed and resting on my skin, but not as yet digging deep into it.

'It come by hand, master,' he said. 'Messenger's waiting for an answer in the kitchen.' Unable to contain himself, he spat in the empty fireplace. 'Proud as a cock on his own dunghill.'

The seal told me who had sent the letter.

438

I unfolded it.

Call at my lodging before midday. WC

There was a tap on the door, and Cat entered the room. Without a word, I handed her the letter.

She glanced at it, and then at me. 'Will you go?'

'I have to see him sooner or later. And the sooner the better. Tomorrow the Fire Court will meet, and they will settle Dragon Yard, one way or the other.'

'They say Chiffinch has the King's ear, and can make him do whatever he wants.'

'He has the King's ear,' I said. 'But the King isn't a fool, and Chiffinch won't want to tell him what he's been doing. I saw him with Limbury just before he tried to send me off to Scotland. I think he's been taking bribes from him.'

'Are you well enough to go anywhere?' she said. 'You should see yourself.'

Sam helped me dress. Despite his rough manner, he was deft and gentle in his movements. He hissed through his teeth as he brushed my coat.

'It's filthy,' he said. 'What were you doing with Mistress Hakesby yesterday? Rolling in

439

the mud?'

'Hold your tongue.' I saw the leer on his face and I would have thrown something at him if I had had the energy. 'Fetch a hackney. You'd better come with me to Whitehall.'

We were on our way in half an hour. The pain was worse — I had taken a second, though smaller, dose of laudanum but it didn't protect me from the jolting of the hackney. I didn't like leaving Cat and Margaret alone in Infirmary Close but I needed Sam in case my condition worsened — or in case I was attacked.

At Whitehall, I left him to wait for me in the Great Court. Chiffinch's lodgings were close to the Privy Stairs and the King's private apartments. I found him in his study, making up his accounts. When the servant announced me, he closed the book and beckoned me to stand before him.

He studied me. 'A periwig, eh? You are becoming quite the gentleman, Marwood. I suppose you'll soon be strutting about Whitehall with a sword at your side.'

'I lost most of my own hair in the fire, sir.'

'Ah. At Clifford's Inn. So I'm to understand that your injuries prevented you from going to Scotland?'

'Yes, sir.'

'You've failed me, then. And failed the King, too.'

'I'm sorry for it, sir,' I said. 'But what could I do? I was in such —'

'What could you do?' he interrupted, banging the palm of his hand on the desk. 'You could have done nothing! But you chose, from your own wilfulness, to poke your nose into affairs that don't concern you. And this is the price you pay.'

I stared at him.

'Enough of your insolence!' he roared, as if I had said something to contradict him. 'Well?'

'Forgive me, sir, but I don't understand what you want of me.'

'You understand well enough.' Chiffinch leaned forward and said in a soft, insinuating voice, 'Listen to me. I am a reasonable man, Marwood. Here is what we shall do. You will tell me everything you know, everything you have done, everything you suspect, that touches on this affair of the Fire Court and Clifford's Inn. I want know about the death of that clerk you tried to save, and about the murder of Mistress Hampney. You'll tell me what Mr William-son has been doing, too. Yes? And then you will do nothing more in the matter — you will put it entirely from your mind. And, in

441

return, we shall say no more about your derelictions of duty. You will recover from your injuries, you will remain as clerk to the Board of Red Cloth, and all will go on happily as before.' He hesitated, fixing me with his watery, bloodshot eyes, and went on, 'And perhaps we may find other emoluments for you, in the fullness of time. One thing leads to another for those who are obliging, and know how to fit in.'

He waited for me to reply. 'Well? Well?'

'You are very good, sir,' I said, fixing my eyes on a spot on the wall six inches above his head.

He sighed. 'You have to choose, Marwood.' His voice had lost its unnatural softness. 'Either you do as I wish, and take the consequences. Or you don't do as I wish, and you take the consequences of that. Remember, your clerkship at the Board of Red Cloth is not yours absolutely. You can lose it tomorrow, and all that goes with it.' He clicked thumb and finger. 'Like that. In the twinkling of an eye.'

To lose the clerkship and its perquisites would be bad enough. But there was worse: Mr Chiffinch had been my patron, and at a stroke he would become my enemy.

'You have to choose, Marwood,' he repeated. 'So be wise as the serpent.'

Williamson had told me that I had to choose as well, and it was the same choice: a man cannot serve two masters, so which was mine to be?

But I would not say the word to Chiffinch, any word.

In the end, he lost patience. 'God rot you, you son of a whore,' he said. 'Get out of my sight before I have them throw you out.'

By and large Williamson's face was not a useful guide to his feelings. Most of the time it was rather less expressive than a block of wood. But I had studied him for almost a year, trying to discover what lay behind the blank expression, the curt words and the many silences. I was almost certain that he was pleased with me.

I had gone to him at Scotland Yard immediately after I had seen Chiffinch, though I wanted nothing more than to go back to Infirmary Close and take another dose of laudanum. I stood before him in his private room, trembling slightly, and told him what had passed with my other master.

Williamson seemed unaware of my discomfort. 'Poor Mr Chiffinch,' he said. 'A man could almost feel sorry for him. I know it cannot please you to lose your employment at the Board of Red Cloth, but you will find it's for the best.'

It might be for the best as far as Williamson was concerned. It was different for me. No man feels unalloyed pleasure at being forced to resign almost half his income and acquiring a powerful enemy in the process.

'Nevertheless,' he went on, 'I don't quite see our way clear yet.'

'But Limbury must be behind the murders, sir.'

'Of course.' Williamson held up his right hand and counted off the points on the fingers. 'One, we have the verses in his handwriting, which show he was Mistress Hampney's lover. Two, the Dragon Yard case at the Fire Court was clearly his reason for courting her. Three, she rejects him — or more probably his wish for her support — and they quarrel. Four, he kills her to keep her quiet; it would not do for his wife to hear about it, for a start — they say he depends on her father's assistance to live in the manner he does. Perhaps, in her anger, she threatened to expose him. She had friends. She was not some tuppenny drab he could afford to ignore.'

I stretched out a hand and rested it on the back of the settle by the fireplace. I was afraid I would faint.

Williamson's eyes flickered. He said:

'Then the Fire Court clerk — Chelling, was it? — threatens to expose Limbury's assignation with Mistress Hampney in Clifford's Inn, and so he must be killed as well. We might have thought his death an accident, if you had not been there. Limbury knows this, and he persuades Chiffinch to manufacture a reason for you to be sent away. A bribe is usually the only argument that convinces Chiffinch. Then there's the attempt to burn down your house, which could have killed you all.' He paused, compressing his lips. 'And indeed myself, as it happened. It smacked of desperation. Finally, he kills Mistress Hampney's maid, the one person who knew him as her mistress's lover, to shut her mouth. Or perhaps he has her killed — it's all one.'

'There was a dog at the maid's cottage. It had been stabbed with a sword, I think.'

'Sit down, you fool,' Williamson said, standing up suddenly and taking my arm. 'Before you fall down.'

He helped me to the settle. 'The trouble is,' he went on, 'there's a world of difference between what we know and what we can prove. Chiffinch and Limbury are not common people. We have nothing we could lay before the King — or before a justice, come to that.'

445

'Dragon Yard comes up before the Fire Court tomorrow,' I said. 'If I were there . . .'

'You can do nothing in your present condition.'

'I will be better tomorrow, if I rest today. I'm sure Sir Philip Limbury will be at Clifford's Inn. I should like to see him, sir. And to have him see me.'

He raised his eyebrows. 'To test his nerve?'

I nodded.

'It can't harm, I suppose, in the want of anything better. If you are well enough. And it would be useful to have a report of what passes when the case is heard.' Williamson was still standing, and he moved a little to improve his view of the damaged side of my face. 'And it would show Sir Philip someone suspects what he's done.'

'There's also Mr Gromwell,' I said. 'The gentleman at Clifford's Inn, whose room was used for Limbury's assignation with Mistress Hampney. If he sees my face, it might unsettle him . . . he might even be persuaded to give evidence against Sir Philip.'

'A long shot,' Williamson said.

'As you said yourself, sir. For want of anything better.'

'Be with people at all times. Take your servant with you. The cripple. Better than

446

nothing. When's the case due to be heard?'

'In the morning.'

'Then you'd better come and find me afterwards and tell me what passes. I'll be at the Middle Temple. Ask at the lodge for Mr Robarts.'

Williamson sent me away. As I left, he offered to send someone to fetch me a hackney, another uncharacteristic kindness. I told him Sam was waiting and would do what was needed.

Clinging to the balustrade, I went downstairs, step by painful step. I wished I could sleep for ever. It was not just the pain that made me long for oblivion. My spirits were depressed. Since my father's death, nothing had gone right for me, and I could not see how matters could ever improve.

Sam was in the yard below. I saw him glance at me. Only a glance. He did not raise a hand in greeting or move towards me. Instead he turned his head and stared at the archway that led into the court where the Guard House was.

I followed the direction of his gaze. A tall, thin man was standing there. He looked up for a moment, perhaps catching sight of me, and I saw his face. It seemed to have collapsed in on itself, so that the tip of the nose almost touched the chin.

447

It was Sourface, the man I had seen at Clifford's Inn, guarding the private door to Staircase XIII from the alley beside the Half Moon tavern. I had also seen him in Fetter Lane, watching me when I had been into the ruins to see Mistress Hampney's body. According to Hakesby's draughtsman, he had also followed me back to the Savoy after the fire in Chelling's chambers.

Sam hobbled away to the gate leading to Whitehall, where the hackneys and the sedan chairs were waiting for hire. I waited a moment and then followed him, pretending to be oblivious of the watcher behind me.

I passed through the gate. The street was busy — people were always coming and going in Whitehall — but Sam had already brought up a hackney, which was waiting twenty yards away. He helped me up the steps and then scrambled in beside me.

The driver cracked his whip and we set off at a decorous pace in the direction of Charing Cross. For a moment, Sam put his eye to the crack of light between the blind and the opening it covered. With a grunt, he sat back in the gloom and rested his crutch against the seat.

'He followed us out of the gate,' he said.

'He's looking around. Not sure where we are.'

'Sourface,' I said. 'You remember?'

Sam nodded. 'He was talking to someone before you came out. A courtier.'

'What was he like?'

'A tall dark gentleman, in black. I asked the guard on the gate if he knew him. His name's —'

'Limbury,' I said. 'Sir Philip Limbury.'

CHAPTER THIRTY-SIX

Jemima waited all day for Philip to return. She had not seen him since their last bitter encounter in the afternoon of the previous day. He did not come. He did not even send word.

In the evening, Mary made her ready for bed as usual. She wanted to stay with her mistress — she was as shamelessly devoted as a puppy, and sometimes just as irritating — but Jemima told her to build up the fire and leave her.

She tried to read. But Mademoiselle de Scudéry failed to hold her attention, and after a few minutes she flung the novel in the corner and gave herself up to the unsatisfactory pleasures of brooding.

Just after midnight, she heard Philip's knock on the street door below. This time she did not wait for him to go to his room. Wrapping the bedgown around her, she took up a candle and padded to the door of

450

her chamber. She was waiting in the doorway when he came slowly up the stairs. Richard was beside him, lighting his way.

'Madam,' Philip said coldly as he reached the landing. 'Your servant.'

'I wish to speak to you, sir.'

'I'm not in the humour. I'm tired. Tomorrow.'

'It won't wait. Mr Chiffinch has been here. I have a message from him.'

Philip sighed. 'Go to my chamber,' he said to Richard. 'I won't be long.'

He followed Jemima into her bedroom. She sat by the dying fire. He stood on the other side of the chimney piece, looking at her.

'Chiffinch?' His voice was low. 'What the devil was he doing here?'

'Where have you been all this time? He said he couldn't find you at Whitehall.'

'I had business with Gromwell,' Philip snapped. 'Chiffinch. Tell me about Chiffinch.'

'He says that you must take me to the country to stay with my father. As soon as you can manage.'

'I've no wish to go to Syre.'

'But you must. Chiffinch says you must apply to leave Court for a while.'

'It is impossible. I have my duties at the

451

Bedchamber.'

'You're to say it is my father's health that is the reason. Or mine, I suppose. In any case, we must leave London.'

Philip scowled at her. 'If Chiffinch wanted to say this to me, he could have written a letter. Is this some nonsense of yours?'

'Ask the servants if you don't believe me. Chiffinch was here.'

'But what possible purpose would be served by our going away?'

'I don't know.' She watched him closely. 'But perhaps you do. He told me to say that the reason has to do with the Fire Court. Does that give you a clue?'

He winced. 'My case is coming up before the court tomorrow.'

'I know that. So does he.' She hesitated, and then decided that there was no need to skirt around the matter. 'I imagine this has to do with the scrawny old whore who was murdered. Whose mistress was she? Yours or Gromwell's?'

It happened so fast that she didn't see it coming. His right hand whipped out from his side. He slapped her cheek so hard that the force of it threw her against the arm of her chair, winding her. Her head snapped over, wrenching her neck. The pain of it was so sudden, and so acute, that she shrieked.

He turned and left the room without a word.

It was the first time in their marriage that he had hit her. All that she had wanted was for him to say that he loved her, only her, and that he was true to her. And this was his reply.

Jemima stood up, picked up her candle and walked unsteadily to the dressing table. She heard movement above her head and Mary's feet stumbling down the stairs from the attic where the maids slept.

Jemima sat down before her mirror. She was breathing rapidly, but she could not fill her lungs with enough air. She stared at her face in the glass.

At the marks on the left cheek and the marks on the right. Her face was all of a piece now.

Chapter Thirty-Seven

After the rain, the morning was bright with sun and unexpectedly warm under a cloudless sky. Clifford's Inn looked newly washed, though this was not to its advantage as the hard, unforgiving light revealed the shabbiness of the place, and left it nowhere to hide.

Cat arrived when the Fire Court was already in session. She climbed the steps to the gallery. She made her way to one end of a bench near the back.

Marwood had wanted her to stay in the safety of the Savoy, but she had argued forcefully that the Fire Court was such a public place that she would be as safe there as anywhere — and so, for that matter, would he. There was a risk that Gromwell would recognize her, but her cloak shielded her face and it was gloomy at the back of the gallery. Besides, she could use her shorthand to make a record of the proceedings for Mr Williamson. And what if poor

Mr Hakesby should have need of her?

Cat peered over the balustrade and down to the hall below. Hakesby was standing with Poulton, with Brennan nearby. They were looking towards the dais where the three judges were sitting at their table.

Marwood was further back; he was leaning against the wall with Sam by his side. He was watching Sir Philip Limbury, who was standing close to the dais, flanked by his attorney and the tall figure of Mr Gromwell.

Cat wrote in her notebook, the shorthand symbols recording what was passing around her. The same three judges as last week — Wyndham, Twisden and Rainsford.

The first case, which involved a messuage called the Artichoke, three lawyers, an irascible alderman and an aggrieved linen draper, wound its way to a conclusion that was, on the whole, in the latter's favour. The judges retired for a break. Many people left the hall. The dais remained empty, apart from a servant of the court who was laying out fresh paper on the judges' table and checking inkwells and shakers of sand.

There was a great bustle outside, and the sound of raised voices. The noise drew closer. Cat heard feet on the stairs. A man appeared in the doorway, and called back over his shoulder, 'Plenty of room, mistress. But we can clear it completely if you want.'

A maid appeared, and looked about her. Ignoring Cat and the other women, she looked out over the hall. Two women were sitting on the bench at the very front of the gallery.

'Move back,' the maid said to them. 'Both of you. My lady needs this.' She glanced at the rest of the women. 'You can stay where you are. But keep your distance.'

The women she had displaced muttered angrily. But the manservant came to stand beside the maid. He was a burly, silent man, one of the porters at Clifford's Inn. His presence was enough to reinforce the maid's orders. A boy appeared with an armful of cushions and shawls, which he arranged according to the maid's directions on the bench at the front.

While he was doing this, the judges returned to the dais, and the hall rapidly filled up again. This time there were more people than before.

A lady was ushered on to the gallery. She was heavily veiled, and wore a wide hat and a fine travelling cloak. Her arrival made a considerable commotion. The maid escorted her mistress to the bench at the front with as much care as if she were as frangible as glass.

Limbury's lady? Cat scribbled, the pencil travelling rapidly across the paper, less for Williamson than for herself. *Come to gloat with her cartload of monkeys?*

The judges had sat down, but one of them, seeing the lady's arrival, rose to his feet and bowed. The veiled lady inclined her head in reply.

Sir Thomas Twisden bows to her. Limbury looks up, then Gromwell, but both look away, and they mutter together.

Marwood had seen what was going on, too. But Poulton and Hakesby were still deep in conversation.

The clerk called the court to order, and Judge Wyndham reopened the Dragon Yard hearing by ordering those concerned to approach the dais.

Poor Mr Hakesby is so unsteady. Why doesn't Poulton or Brennan offer him their arm?

Browning, Limbury's lawyer, brushed Hakesby's shoulder as he passed, which made the old man clutch at Poulton's sleeve. Poulton, his face pale and haggard, glanced at Hakesby's hand as if he could not understand what it was doing there, or even what it was.

457

Limbury and Twisden seem to nod to each other.

'This matter should not detain us long,' Wyndham said. 'We have already heard the main points of the case, and the arguments on both sides. The Court wants to strike a balance between the interested parties. On the one hand, the freeholder, Sir Philip Limbury, wishes to cancel the outstanding leases on the site and rebuild over the entire ground on a new design. He offers compensation to the leaseholders. A minority of the leaseholders would accept the compensation. But many of the other leaseholders, notably Mr Poulton, desire to rebuild themselves and renegotiate the leases for longer terms and at lower rents, to take account of their investment in the property, which would be substantial. Both schemes have merits and can be put into action almost immediately.'

He paused, which gave Cat time to scribble *A fair summary, though Hakesby's scheme is more extensive and —*

'The decision now rests on a single point,' the judge continued. 'First we need to establish who now owns the leases formerly possessed by the late Mistress Hampney. They are long leases, which cover a substantial part of the Dragon Yard site along

458

Cheapside. The support of their new owner will shift the balance of our verdict to one side or the other, though of course we shall consult the interests of all parties in our settlement. The question turns on whether the lady transferred ownership of the leases before her death or altered the terms of the will she made at the time of her wedding to the late Mr Hampney. If neither of these is the case, then the old will applies. When we have established this, we shall be able to make our decision. Who speaks for Mr Poulton?'

'I do, my lord.' Hakesby shuffled closer to the judges' table, forcing Gromwell to step aside. He straightened himself and faced them. *It's not possible. He looks taller, broader and younger.* 'Mr Hakesby, sir, the surveyor.'

'I know who you are, sir. Continue.'

'My lords, my client Mr Poulton has caused his late niece's papers to be searched at her London lodgings.' Hakesby's voice was firmer than usual, and clear enough to be heard even in the gallery. 'There is no sign of a new will, or any mention of her Dragon Yard leaseholds. He has sent to Lincoln, as the court ordered last week, and I have here the letter from the attorney with whom she dealt about her late husband's estate. If you remember, it was suggested

459

that Mistress Hampney might have taken the opportunity to make another will while she was there. No evidence has come to light that she made a more recent will. Nor was there any evidence that she transferred ownership or control of her Dragon Yard leaseholds.'

'You can't prove that,' Gromwell shouted.

'Hold your tongue, sir,' Wyndham snapped, 'or I'll have you ejected from the court.'

'I have an affidavit from the attorney here confirming what I have told you,' Hakesby went on.

'Hand it up.'

An usher stepped forward to take the letter from Brennan.

'As you will see, my lord, the attorney writes that he asked Mistress Hampney if she would like him to draw up a new will for her, taking account of her husband's death and any other testamentary changes she might want, but she said there was no need for the expense and trouble of a new will as the old one would do perfectly well.'

'When will it be proved?'

Hakesby looked at Poulton, who gave him a sheaf of papers. 'As soon as possible — but I have here letters from two lawyers who deal mainly in probate giving as their opinion that the will is straightforward in its terms, and that on the face of it there is no reason to believe it could be successfully contested. So the fact of the matter, my lord, is that my client, Mr Poulton, has every reason to believe he controls the head leases for most of Dragon Yard. And — as we heard last week — many of those with an interest in the subleases will be glad to support him. As you know, he also owns an adjacent freehold, so his plans cover a larger area than Sir Philip's.'

Poulton turns his head — he's smiling, though he looks like death . . . he stares at Limbury.

Without waiting for an order, Brennan handed the letters to the usher, who carried them to the judges.

Wyndham reads the letters one by one and passes them to the others. Twisden writes something on a piece of paper and slides it to Wyndham. They put their heads together and whisper. Why are they so slow?

On the gallery, the porter was blocking the door to the stairs, preventing others from coming up. The maid and the boy were standing to one side. As for the lady herself —

Sitting bolt upright in the middle of the bench at the front. As if she's sitting under a preacher

461

in church, and daren't move an inch in case God strikes her dead. All alone. The maid keeps glancing at the rest of us.

Judge Wyndham signalled to his clerk, who called the court to order. Silence settled over the body of the hall.

'We are in agreement —' his eyes flicked towards Twisden and then back to the hall '— that, for the good of the City and in the best interests of the majority of those concerned in this case, Dragon Yard should be rebuilt according to Mr Poulton's plans, and at his cost, with newly drawn-up leaseholds of forty-two years, with rents to be fixed at —'

'By God, my lord, this will not do,' Limbury burst out.

Wyndham looked coolly at him. 'Sir Philip,' he said with cold courtesy, 'you may of course appeal, but not at this moment or in this way. As Mr Browning will tell you, you must set down your grounds for appeal in writing within seven days, as required by Section X of the Rebuilding Act. But I must warn you that we do not look kindly on appeals, any more than we look kindly on interruptions. They delay the work of the court. Costs may well be awarded against the appellants.'

Hakesby swayed on his feet. This time

462

Poulton noticed, and gestured to Brennan, who at last came forward to help his master.

Browning tugged Limbury's sleeve and whispered something in his ear.

Wyndham glanced at his notes and opened his mouth to continue, but —

— *the veiled lady rises to her feet so sharply that she knocks over the bench behind. The noise makes everyone stare up at her. And she stares down at them, as if she's in a box at the theatre. She starts to laugh —*

Once more, the usher called for silence. The lady stopped laughing. Her maid and the boy restored the bench to its position behind her. She gave no sign of noticing. She was standing almost motionless. Sitting behind her, Cat thought the border of the veil was trembling.

Judge Wyndham read out the terms of the verdict, itemizing the costs of the new leases, in an uninflected voice that made dull listening unless you were directly affected.

Cat continued her shorthand record, but she stopped when a movement distracted her. The lady had raised her right hand. The maid hurried to her mistress's side. There was an exchange of whispers. The maid gestured to the porter.

The lady drew her cloak around her. She

463

walked in a slow and stately fashion towards the door to the stairs, with the maid attending her. The boy gathered up her belongings from the bench.

Though the party did not make a great deal of noise, their departure aroused considerable interest in the hall below. Even Wyndham hesitated in his reading, his eyes rising to the gallery, though his face remained expressionless. Preceded by her maid, the lady began to descend the stairs.

Limbury turned abruptly and pushed his way through the crowd towards the door to the passage. Gromwell murmured something to Browning and then followed Limbury.

The judge resumed his reading. The porter and the boy left the gallery. Cat heard raised voices below. She closed her notebook and slipped on to the stairs.

'Well, madam,' Limbury was saying below, 'you've made a spectacle of yourself before the world. I hope you're satisfied.'

'Take your hands off me.'

'You are my wife. I shall lay my hands where I please.'

Cat went down the stairs. She hesitated in the archway at the bottom. Apart from herself, the Limburys and their servants were alone in the passage. Sir Philip had

464

grasped his wife by the wrist; he towered over her, his back to Cat. Gromwell stood between them and the maid and the boy. The porter had vanished.

'You make a fool of me at your peril,' Limbury went on, his voice low but hard.

'You do that yourself, without any help from me.' Lady Limbury's veil trembled. 'You and that whore.' She waved her free hand at the servants. 'Take me to the coach.'

The maid started forward. Gromwell blocked her path. The maid caught sight of Cat standing in the archway, and her eyes widened. Gromwell caught the movement and glanced in the same direction.

In the split second that followed, Cat registered the fact that there was a bandage wrapped around the palm of Gromwell's right hand.

Recognition spread over his face when he saw her. 'By God! It's the little thief —'

He broke off and plunged towards her. Lady Limbury's maid took advantage of the distraction and ran to her mistress. Cat darted past Lady Limbury to escape from Gromwell. She slipped her free hand into her pocket. Her fingers closed around the handle of the knife. She ripped the blade from its sheath.

'Philip,' Gromwell said urgently. 'It's that

wench I caught prying the other day.'

But Limbury was still talking to his wife. 'I've had enough. Enough of your clinging ways, your play-acting, your lies, your schemes' — his voice rose slightly — 'and most of all your damned ugliness.'

He let go of her suddenly. She slumped against the wall, her head drooping. Limbury snatched at the veil and tugged. The veil fluttered to the ground, along with the hat that had helped to hold it in place. His wife crouched, covering the side of her face with her hands.

'You'll hide no more.' Limbury pulled her hands away. 'Let the world see what you are.'

Cat was not aware of making a decision. Had she thought rationally, she would have run away from Gromwell, who was making his way towards her. But she was in a place beyond calculation, beyond thought even, where only action existed. Which was why, quite of its own volition, her right hand shot forward and lunged with the knife towards Sir Philip's thigh. The blade slipped through the black velvet of his wide breeches. The tip met the resistance of skin. Cat pressed harder.

It was little more than a pinprick, not even half an inch deep. Limbury screamed with pain. He released his wife and swung to face Cat, one hand dropping to his sword, the other to the wound in his leg.

Cat backed away. Lady Limbury ran to her maid. The door to the hall opened. Marwood was on the threshold. Behind him was the crowded hall.

For an instant, no one spoke or moved in the passage.

'Mr Gromwell!' Marwood said. 'How do you do?'

He moved smoothly between Cat and Gromwell. 'You remember me, sir, I hope? We met the other day when I knocked on your door to ask if my father had called on you.'

Sam followed his master through the door. 'Your pardon, sir. Not in your way, am I? Since the damned Dutch took off my foot, I've been as clumsy as a baby.'

The Fire Court session had finished. Others were now pressing to leave the hall. Cat swerved round Gromwell and escaped into the narrow court.

The lady and her maid had already left. They were almost at the Fleet Street gate, with the boy trotting after them, burdened with his mistress's cushions and rugs. They passed through the archway with Cat hard at their heels.

Lady Limbury looked back. She had her gloved hands clamped to the side of her face. The hands were too small to cover all that was marred. A claret-coloured birthmark stretched from the hairline to the neck, covering most of the right-hand side of the face. The left-hand side was untouched, the face of a plain, unremarkable woman with small eyes and a long, thin nose.

In Fleet Street, a coach-and-four was drawn up near the bookstalls by the church, half blocking the narrow roadway before Temple Bar. It had a gentleman's coat of arms painted on the door and a large coachman on the box, with a whip in his hand.

Lady Limbury climbed into the coach. She sat down facing the horses, presenting her left cheek to the world. She looked past the maid to Cat, who was standing irresolute on the pavement. 'You'd better come with us for now. God knows what they'll do to you if they catch you.'

The maid sat down beside her mistress. Cat scrambled inside and sat opposite them. Lady Limbury draped an Indian shawl over her head, masking most of her face. The maid looked blankly at Cat. The boy closed the door.

The whip cracked, and with a jerk the

coach moved off. The blinds were down over the glass windows. None of the three women spoke. Around them was the raucous, familiar din of London.

In the distance, a man was shouting, but the sound grew steadily fainter as the coach picked up speed. They were travelling east into the ruins of the City.

CHAPTER THIRTY-EIGHT

'Where is she?' Mr Hakesby said. 'Brennan says he saw her on the gallery.' He clutched Brennan's arm. 'You're sure it was her?'

'Sure as the coat on my back.'

'She went towards Fleet Street, sir,' I said. 'She was in a hurry. I doubt you'll catch her now.'

'Why would she run away? She must have seen me, and heard me speak.'

Mr Poulton came out of the hall behind them. He was smiling and looked ten years younger. 'Have you found your cousin yet, Hakesby?'

'No, sir. Mr Marwood saw her.'

Their words washed over me like water. Perhaps it was the opium, but I felt entirely removed from what was going on. I was more than happy to stay where I was, doing nothing except lean against the wall of the passage, while Poulton and Hakesby talked. The hall was now empty apart from a

470

solitary clerk clearing the papers and writing materials from the judges' table.

Gromwell and Limbury had gone. I had sent Sam to talk to the porter on the Fleet Street gate.

'It is most satisfactory,' Poulton was saying. 'Hakesby, you argued my case as well as any lawyer. And to be granted such long leases, and on such generous terms! There's nothing to prevent us starting tomorrow. You'll need ready money, of course, when you start in earnest. I shall arrange it in the morning.' He rubbed his hands. 'I can't wait to tell Mistress Lee.'

I noticed that the three of them — Poulton, Hakesby and Brennan — were looking strangely at me. 'What is it?' I said.

Mr Hakesby coughed. 'Your wig, sir, I — ah . . .'

I raised my hand. In the recent excitement, the left side of the periwig had been pushed back over the shoulder, exposing some of the fire-scarred tissue beneath. I rearranged it. 'Forgive me, sir,' Hakesby said. 'I — I had forgot. Poor Chelling — and you.'

'There's a difference,' I said sourly. 'Chelling's dead. I'm alive.'

'Yes, but I did not realize that —' He broke off. 'You poor fellow.'

Poulton asked Hakesby a question about

471

the drainage at Dragon Yard, perhaps as a kindly attempt to distract the conversation from my injuries.

I should be grateful to be alive, I reminded myself, unlike poor Chelling. A man who was prodigal with gossip. My unruly memory turned a somersault, and I remembered a crumb of information he had let fall while he was drinking himself into a stupor that day in the Devil.

'Marwood?' Hakesby said. 'Marwood?'

A crumb? Memory turned another somersault. No. Two.

I heard the tapping of Sam's crutch before I saw him. 'What news?' I said, turning away from Hakesby and lowering my voice.

'The porter's lad followed them into Fleet Street, in case he could earn something from them,' he murmured. 'But he was out of luck. Mistress Hakesby went off in a glass coach with the lady.'

'Which way?'

'East. Into the City. Shall I find us a hackney, master?'

'No. I want you to find someone first.'

'It was laden,' Sam said. 'The coach, I mean. And four horses. The lad said it looked like they were going on a journey.'

She was a snaggletoothed woman with a

freckled face and a fringe of greasy curls escaping from under her cap. She could have been any age from twenty-five to fifty-five. She rose from a curtsy, smoothing a patched brown skirt with grubby hands, and casting a longing glance at the pot of beer on the table.

'Miriam, sir,' Sam said, gesturing towards her with the air of a showman. 'As your worship desired.'

Miriam squinted up at me, trying to make out my features beneath the brim of my hat. We were in a yard behind the Half Moon, where the tavern's poorer customers could buy their drinks at a hatch in the wall.

I nodded at the beer. 'You'd rather drink good, strong ale, I'll be bound.'

She grinned unexpectedly. 'Who wouldn't, master?'

'Then you shall.' I turned to Sam, feeling for my purse. 'Fetch a jug of ale.' I saw his face and took pity on him. 'And a pot for yourself.'

He joined the knot of people at the hatch. I leaned against the wall. Miriam shifted uneasily under my gaze.

'Drink your beer. Don't let it go to waste.'

She seized the pot and swallowed what was in it as fast as she could.

I jerked a thumb in the direction of the

roof of New Building. 'I hear you work there.'

'Yes, master. Clifford's Inn.'

Sam was already returning towards us, dextrously managing his crutch, the jug of ale and a pot.

I said, 'Who do you work for?'

Her eyes were on Sam. 'Some of the gentlemen, sir. Staircase Fourteen.'

'What do you do?'

'Clean the chambers, make the beds.'

'What else?'

'I used to help with the staircase next door too. Thirteen. But that was before the Fire.'

That set my mind on another track. 'Is there a connecting door between the staircases?'

She nodded vigorously. 'It's in the servant's closet on Mr Gromwell's landing. Between his door and Mr Gorvin's.' Alarm spread across her grubby face. 'Is there something wrong? I never stole a —'

'Nothing's wrong. And here's the ale.' I motioned Sam to pour it. 'What else do you do there?'

'I empty the pots in the morning, and do the fires, and I bring up coals. I'm only there till dinnertime.'

I watched her bury her face in the pot of ale. I said, 'And who are these gentlemen?'

I already knew the answers to this and earlier questions. Sam had bought the information at the cost of sixpence from the aged and infinitely corruptible porter at the Fetter Lane gate, including Miriam's name and where to find her.

'There's Mr Moran, sir, and Mr Drury and Mr Bews. Mr Gromwell, Mr Gorvin and Mr Harrison.'

'Are the gentlemen kind to you?'

'I don't see much of them, sir. They're either asleep or out when I'm there. They all keep a man to serve them and look after their clothes, and give me my orders.'

'What about Mr Gromwell? Be open with me. You won't regret it.'

She glanced about her as if fearing we were overheard. She lowered her voice. 'He's rough in manner, sir. And he's not a generous gentleman. He goes weeks without paying, sometimes. He's got a temper, too. But he's one of the governors of the Inn, so we have to mind our step with him.'

'Tell me, about three weeks ago, when you cleaned his chambers, were they in any way unusual?'

Miriam looked blankly at me.

'I mean anything about them that was out of the common way.'

She smiled. 'Oh — you mean the day

475

when the furniture was all arsey-turvey? Is that it?'

I smiled and nodded to Sam, who refilled her pot and then his own. 'When was this?'

'Three weeks ago, maybe?' Miriam stared at me over the rim of her pot. 'It was a day I had orders to go in early, make everything especially neat and clean. He had some new furniture coming, they told me. But when I came in next morning there was nothing new there. All the old stuff was still there — but all out of place — huddled against one wall. I reckon he must have got merry with his friends, and they fancied a change, and then they thought they'd have another bottle instead when they were halfway through. Or they were playing a game that needed the space. God knows what they get up to when they're in their cups.'

'Was there a brightly coloured carpet there? Or a couch?'

'No. He never had anything like that.' Miriam's face brightened and she smacked her lips. 'But I found a couple of sweetmeats in the hearth that morning. He must have thrown them away. Nothing wrong with them. I rinsed the ash off and had them for breakfast.'

'Can you read?'

Miriam shook her head. 'I leave that to

the gentlemen.'

'You see, I need a piece of Mr Gromwell's handwriting. Anything will do.'

A doubtful expression crossed her face. 'I couldn't take anything from his room, master. More than the job's worth . . . And it would be wrong, wouldn't it?'

'No, no.' I smiled at her, fighting an urge to scratch the savage itching of healing skin under my periwig. 'I don't want you to take anything. I just want to see what his handwriting looks like. Perhaps you could borrow something. Or bring me a paper he's thrown away or left to use as a spill for the fire. Anything at all, as long as it has his writing on.' I took a shilling from my purse. 'Such a small service. And it will earn you this.'

'Why do you need it, master?'

'It's a wager,' I said. 'That's all. My friend and I have a wager about who wrote something, and when I know what Mr Gromwell's hand is like, I'll win.'

Her expression cleared. 'Will this do then?' She dug her hand into her skirt and took out a crumpled sheet of paper. Panic flared in her face. 'But I can't let you take it away.'

'Of course you'll have it back. I only want a sight of it. Just for a moment.'

The reassurance satisfied her. She smoothed out the paper and passed it to me.

'Mr Gromwell's man give it me so the porters let me in and out. It says I work for him and the other gentlemen. Like I said, he's one of the governors, and you need to have a paper from one of them or they won't let you pass through.'

I examined the pass while she drank, her eyes following my movements over the brim of her pot. It permitted her to come and go at Clifford's Inn when serving the occupants of Staircase XIV. It was signed by Lucius Gromwell in his capacity as one of the Rules, the men who directed the affairs of Clifford's Inn.

Gromwell. Lucius Gromwell.

I looked carefully at the writing. For a moment, the pain, the itching and the tiredness dropped away from me. Mr Williamson had kept both Sir Philip Limbury's note to Hakesby and the poem that Cat and I had found among the belongings of Tabitha, Mistress Hampney's maid. But their appearance was fresh in my memory. The three pieces of writing had been written at different times and in different circumstances. Nevertheless, they looked as if the same person could have been responsible for them all — though I knew for a fact that that was not the case: Limbury had written the note to Hakesby, and Gromwell had written Miriam's pass.

Was it so very strange that their handwriting should be similar? The two men had been instructed from childhood by the same teachers: they had grown up together and they had been intimate friends at school and the university. They had probably learned their letters from the same teacher.

In that case, the handwriting of the poem stolen from Herrick — 'Whenas in Silks My CELIA goes' — could belong to either of them. As for the 'L' at the bottom of the poem, that might signify Limbury, as we had assumed until now, or — just as easily — Lucius.

I returned the pass to Miriam. Sam gave her the rest of the ale. It was strong stuff, and her face had grown flushed and her breathing more rapid. I held up the shilling. Her eyes fixed on it, like a cat's on a mouse.

'I'd prefer Mr Gromwell not to hear that we've talked together.'

She shook her head violently. 'I won't tell, I swear it. He's got such a temper, sir. He'll beat a servant as soon as look at her. Why, yesterday he struck the man that serves him, knocked a tooth out, and all because he was in a passion about the pain in his hand and the mad dog, so he —'

'What?' I snapped.

At the harshness of my voice, she cowered like a dog herself.

I softened my tone. 'I didn't mean to speak so loudly, Miriam. What's this about a dog? Tell me.'

'The one that bit him on the hand. Down to the bone it was, his man said, and he bled like a stuck pig.'

'When did this happen?'

'The day before yesterday. Mr Gromwell feared the dog was mad, and he'd soon be mad too, and he'd run through the streets foaming at the mouth.' She shivered with a sort of pleasure. 'And he'd be screaming curses at respectable folks and biting them and making them mad too . . .'

The pleasure seeped away from Miriam's face. 'But he's not gone mad yet, so maybe the dog wasn't mad in the first place. Maybe it just hated him.'

Prudence was better than pointless self-denial, I decided, for everyone's sake, not just my own.

So, to be on the safe side, I stopped briefly at an apothecary's in Fleet Street and took a modest and carefully calculated dose of

480

laudanum. Sam looked askance at me, or I thought he did. I snapped at him, telling him to keep his eyes and thoughts to himself, and left the shop in a cloud of righteous indignation.

I ran Williamson to earth in the Middle Temple. He was dining privately with Mr Robarts, a man he often met on private business. He excused himself to his host and came out into the passage.

He led me to a deep window embrasure where we could talk unheard and largely unseen. I believe I made my report lucidly enough. I had measured the dose with great care: in moderation, I believed, the apothecary's mixture sharpened my mental faculties as well as eased the pain to a point where it was generally tolerable.

'Sir, this morning I recalled two facts that had slipped my memory. First, Gromwell's Christian name is Lucius. Secondly, Chelling told me that one of his schoolfellows is a Groom of the Bedchamber. That must mean Limbury, surely.'

Williamson frowned at me. 'Get to the point.'

'We assumed that the "L" on the poem to Celia stood for Limbury. But perhaps it stood for Lucius. And two men with the same schooling may well write a similar

481

hand. Gromwell and Limbury do — I've just put it to the test. And then today I heard that Gromwell has a dog bite on his hand, which could connect him to the wounded cur at the dead maidservant's cottage in Lambeth. The dog with a stab wound in his side.'

'What are you saying?' Williamson said. 'That Gromwell is the rogue in this affair? That he was Mistress Hampney's lover all along?'

'Why not, sir? He's better suited for the part. And it would make sense for Limbury to keep his distance from Mistress Hampney. Gromwell was acting for him, of course, though perhaps he had no objection to marrying her, if he could contrive it, thereby killing two birds with one stone. After all, she had money, he needs it.'

'And then he killed her when she would not do as he wished, and then killed Chelling when he threatened to unmask him. And the maidservant in Lambeth too — perhaps she tried to extort money from him as she knew he had been her mistress's lover. The poem could be taken as evidence of that.' Williamson hesitated, considering. 'You may be right, but what use is all this to me? You've given me nothing my Lord Arlington can take to the King. Chiffinch is in a strong position — as strong as any man's, because he knows the King's secrets. So if I am to hurt him, the evidence against him must be as strong as steel.'

I had expected praise from Williamson. I should have known that was almost always a vain hope. Besides, men who devote their lives to the strange, skewed world of Whitehall are not like the rest of us. They live by different rules. Williamson was less interested in finding the murderer than in gathering ammunition with which to attack Chiffinch.

I tried another line: 'Lady Limbury was at the Fire Court when the case was heard.'

'I thought she hardly stirred from her house.'

'There's no love lost between her and her husband. She came solely to mock him when he lost his case. And afterwards they met outside the hall, and the quarrel went beyond all bounds.'

'His passions outweigh both his understanding and his manners.' Williamson himself was a man who never let his own passions outweigh anything. As for his manners, they knew their place in his scheme of things and, like a good servant, appeared only when required.

'There's more,' I said. 'My lady has a large

birthmark on her cheek. She covers it with a veil, but Sir Philip was so angry he tore it away from her face.' Even the memory of that scene made me uncomfortable.

'A birthmark? That's it, is it? I'd heard she was ugly as sin. Limbury wouldn't have had her if she hadn't been her father's heir. Come to that, if she'd been unblemished, Sir George Syre wouldn't have let her marry a poor man like Limbury, especially one with his reputation. But beggars can't be choosers. Did she go back to Pall Mall afterwards?'

'I don't know for sure. She went off with her servants. The porter on the Fleet Street gate at Clifford's Inn said she had a glass coach waiting for her, and she drove away as fast as she could. Four horses, and the coach was laden with luggage. They were going east. Towards the ruins.'

'If she and Limbury have quarrelled, she's probably going to her father's. Where else can she go? He lives in Kent — Syre Place is beyond Seven Oaks, on the road to Tunbridge Wells.'

Williamson paused a moment to think. I watched the lawyers criss-crossing the paths below the window. I had come a long and uncertain way from my father's death to the shabby Court intrigues of Williamson and

Chiffinch.

'Talk to her, Marwood,' he said at last. 'That's the best thing to do. And do it soon, while the lady's passions run high against her husband. Tell her Lord Arlington desires to help her. Fan the flames in any way you can and she may blurt out what she knows of this affair. Does she know of an intrigue between Chiffinch and her husband? Try to persuade her to talk to me. I can be her friend in this.'

'She may be miles away by now.'

'I think not. If she continues in her own coach, they must go by the bridge. The traffic is so bad in the ruins, and it will take them an age to reach it. Once they get there, it will take at least an hour to cross to Southwark at this time of day, probably longer. If you don't catch her on the bridge, hire a horse at the Bear on the other side and go after her.'

'Sir, we can't be sure she is going to her father's house. Surely we should —'

He waved my objections aside. 'There's no time to be lost, and this is the best chance we have. You must go at once.' He found his purse. 'I shall advance you five pounds in case you have to follow her into Kent. Spare no expense to find her.' He blinked, and his familiar caution reasserted itself. 'I shall need an account of what you disburse, of course, and to whom and where.'

I nodded, wondering where I could buy laudanum on London Bridge. There must be an apothecary there or in the neighbourhood. I didn't need another dose now, but I would need more if I were riding down to Kent.

Williamson beckoned me closer. 'If we have her on our side,' he murmured, 'and if she knows something of her husband's scheming with Gromwell and Chiffinch, we may be able to persuade her to appeal to the King. If she could be persuaded to write a letter to him — a memorial about the business, petitioning him to intervene — that would carry real weight. Let her make the most of Limbury's cruelty to her. The King is tender-hearted — he doesn't like to see a woman cruelly used.' He gave me a thin smile. 'Even an ill-favoured one.'

CHAPTER THIRTY-NINE

'Old swan stairs,' I told the older of the two watermen. 'As fast as you can.'

I scrambled to the stern and sat down. Sam followed me, surprisingly agile despite his crutch. As an old sailor, he was comfortable in small boats. The two watermen pushed the boat out from Temple Stairs and began to row, swiftly picking up their rhythm.

The tide was behind us, ebbing fast, and we made good time downriver. The ruins of the city glided past us. At this hour there was plenty of activity, particularly along the wharves where gangs of labourers were clearing the rubble. Their shouts drifted across the water.

London Bridge grew steadily closer. Seen broadside from the water, the scale of it was even more impressive than it was from the land. It was about a hundred yards long, a straight, narrow street floating above the water. Though a fire — not last year's but an earlier one — had destroyed the houses at the northern end, most of its length was covered with towering buildings, distributed into three irregularly shaped blocks. In the middle, a drawbridge crossed the central arch. It was occasionally raised for tall vessels when the water was calm enough to admit them. Houses and shops lined both sides, and over the centuries they had sprouted higher and higher, and wider and wider, so they now seemed impossibly tall and unstable, like plants run to seed.

The backs of the buildings overhung the river, just as their fronts overhung the roadway along the bridge. They were encrusted with closets and balconies and bay windows, many of them a series of afterthoughts added over the years.

The sun came out. The river stretched around us, a glittering and swaying monster, panting with the effort of trying to squeeze itself through the nineteen arches of the bridge. The massive piers blocked almost half the width of the river. Here at water level you felt the power of the tide, especially at times like this when, twice a day, it raged at the manmade obstruction of the bridge.

When the tide was ebbing or flowing hard, the river backed up against the partial obstacle of the bridge. With their splayed bases, the arches were narrow enough in the first place. To make matters worse, wooden starlings had been built out around them to protect the stonework from the impact of the water, which had the effect of constricting the flow still further, as did the waterwheels at either end.

Our boat was low on the water, the gunwale less than a foot above the surface. The wind was blowing briskly and the curls of my periwig were flying about my neck. I turned my head so the scars would not be visible to the others and pulled up the collar of my cloak.

The river was creaming through the arches and the water gave off a steady, rustling roar as it poured down the lower level beyond, several feet down. There were some boatmen who, if you paid enough, would take you through an arch when the tide was in flood and bring you, soaked and shaking, to the calmer waters beyond. Every year, however, the river exacted its tribute of shattered boats and drowned men.

Sam nudged me. 'Master,' he whispered in my ear. 'Over there. Starboard.'

He was pointing to another boat with two pairs of oars, this one nearer the south bank. There were three passengers, two in the stern and one perched in the bows. I squinted at the little figures, finding it hard to see them clearly because of the sway and glare of the river.

'It's Limbury,' Sam muttered. His eyes were keener than mine. 'With his friend beside him. Don't know who's in the bows.'

I guessed that Limbury and Gromwell were on the same errand as I was, trying to intercept Lady Limbury's coach. They had made the same calculations as Williamson and I. Wiser than myself, perhaps, they were making for the south end of the bridge.

It was possible that the Limburys' coach had already crossed. But Williamson had been right: at this time of day, the lumbering vehicle would not have made good time. Four horses were a hindrance, not an advantage, in the crowded streets of a city. If I were a gambling man I would have put money on the coach still being on the bridge, especially if the traffic hadn't been moving for a while.

I came to a swift decision and leaned forward. 'I've changed my mind,' I said. 'Take us to Pepper Stairs.'

'Across the river with the tide running like this?' said the waterman, turning to spit over the side; a streak of silver whipped past my face, missing me by inches.

'Yes,' I said. 'And a double fare if you hurry.'

Our oars dug into the water, bringing the bow of the boat round towards the south bank. Pepper Stairs was the nearest landing stage to the bridge on the Surrey side. The rowers pulled hard, fighting the current pushing us downstream. The roar of the water was louder now, as it surged through between the piers of the bridge and plunged down to the lower level downstream.

Limbury's boat reached Pepper Stairs. I watched them disembarking and paying the boatmen. I recognized the third man now: Sourface, Limbury's servant, the man who looked as if he had a lemon in his mouth.

Sam nudged my arm again in the unmannerly way that he ought not to use to his master. He pointed up at the bridge.

'What?'

'The traffic, master. It's not moving.'

I followed the line of his finger. It was impossible to see what was going on among the buildings as they were packed so closely together, but in the clear spaces between the three blocks were stationary lines of wagons and coaches, head to tail. Even horsemen and sedan chairs had been brought to a halt.

'The stop's near the gatehouse,' Sam said.

491

The Great Stone Gate was at the southern end of the bridge, marking the end of the city's jurisdiction. A clump of buildings was attached to it, a hotchpotch of rooflines, turrets, balconies and windows. The queue of vehicles stretched along the visible sections of the bridge in one direction, from north to south. Traffic travelling in the other direction had been able to leave the bridge, but no more was coming on to it from the Surrey side of the river.

'There are always stops on the bridge,' the older waterman said with obvious satisfaction. 'Two or three times a day sometimes. Good for business. It's an ill wind, eh?'

Pepper Stairs was packed with people trying to hire a boat to get across. We landed there and left our boatmen holding an impromptu auction for their services.

The tower of St Mary Overie loomed over us as we followed Pepper Alley round to Borough High Street. A noisy queue of wagons and coaches stretched down the road. The Bear Tavern at Bridge Foot was packed, and its customers had spilled out on to the roadway. Tempers were souring as the queues grew longer and the crowd thickened. It wouldn't take much for people to start throwing things at each other.

I caught sight of Limbury and Gromwell,

standing at Bridge Foot, the approach to the Great Stone Gate, and staring through the archway that led to the bridge. There was no sign of Sourface. I pulled Sam into the shelter of a stall selling old clothes.

We waited, watching the archway. Above the gatehouse were the long poles holding the heads of traitors — no more than skulls now, picked clean by time and birds. No new ones had been added for years, but no one had cared to remove the old ones.

In a moment or two, Sourface came out of the yard of the Bear Tavern and joined his master and Gromwell. They held a quick conference and then passed through the gateway to the bridge beyond.

I guessed that Limbury had done what I would have done — sent his servant to ask at the Bear's stables if the Limbury coach had come through. Ostlers noticed everything that went to and fro, especially if it involved horseflesh. A glass coach with four horses was not exactly inconspicuous.

Sam and I walked up to the gatehouse. One of the traitors' heads above the battlements was loose on its pole, and the wind was playing with it. The skull nodded at me. I took that as an omen, a dead man's agreement that I was doing the right thing.

Beyond the gatehouse was the street running high above the river over the bridge. The traffic kept to the left in both directions. Each carriageway was barely six feet wide. The houses on either side were jettied outwards, so the upper storeys were within an arm's reach of their neighbours opposite.

Because there was so little natural light, the street was perpetually gloomy, a fetid, slippery tunnel full of horseshit and disgruntled people. Usually there were sweepers who sluiced the dirt into the river, but they were not in evidence today.

Among such a press of people and vehicles it was difficult to keep our quarry in sight without drawing attention to ourselves. It was hard enough even to push our way through.

Only the shopkeepers were cheerful. They were doing a brisk trade, enticing people who had too much time on their hands to spend money while they waited. We passed an alehouse so packed that people could scarcely raise their pots to their lips. Next door to it was a pastry cook's whose shelves were almost empty.

A few moments later, we passed out of this block of buildings and into the open air. The wind from the river buffeted me, but I was glad of it after the stench of the street. We hung back, taking shelter behind a portly merchant and his equally portly lady.

We went into the next block of buildings. The cause of the blockage was here — a wagon and a coach going in opposite directions had locked wheels, and then the horses had panicked. A gang of labourers was now working with axes and saws and ropes, trying to deal with the mess.

By the time we had negotiated this obstacle, I thought we must have lost Limbury and Gromwell. With relief, I caught sight of Gromwell perhaps sixty yards away. He was standing before a shop talking to a large, middle-aged woman in its doorway. There was no sign of Limbury or Sourface. As I watched, Gromwell followed the woman inside.

I told Sam to wait and advanced cautiously up the street. As I drew nearer I saw that the shop was a stationer's and bookseller's. In front of it was a row of red posts to which were nailed sheets advertising new publications.

It was a substantial establishment by the standards of the bridge. It occupied the entire ground floor of an ornate house whose upper storeys billowed over the street. Above the door was a sign displaying three Bibles.

I realized that I had been here before, when I was an apprentice printer. I paused beside the shop as if by chance, as if drawn to examine the pamphlets and sermons displayed on the shelf at the front. There were no ballads or cheap broadsheets among them. This establishment was reaching for a different class of customer. Inside, there were some large, finely bound volumes, as well as folders of engravings.

Two apprentices were attending to the customers — like everywhere else, the place was packed — but there was no sign of Sourface or the woman he had been talking to. I sauntered inside and pretended to admire an engraving of my Lady Castlemaine which hung on the wall in a prominent position to tempt the gentlemen.

No one bothered me. The shop was well lit, with a bay window overlooking the river on the upstream side. Behind the counter was a doorway. Gromwell must have gone through it. Did that suggest he was known here?

The Widow Vereker had inherited the shop and business at the sign of the Three Bibles from her husband. Their customers came from Whitehall, the Law Courts, and the wealthy families of the City . . . . Fine presswork, I gave her that, and prices to match.

I heard footsteps on the stairs, and Gromwell's tall figure filled the doorway. He was smiling. The middle-aged woman followed him.

'It's no trouble at all, sir,' she was saying, 'though the apartments are hardly fit for you. But I'll have them light a fire in there at least.'

He turned back to her. 'Madam, you are kindness itself. A veritable good Samaritan. We shan't trouble you for long, and I promise you won't be the poorer for it.'

'Oh — I almost forgot.' The woman was girlishly flustered by his attentions. 'The key for the outside door — going by the entry at the side of the house will save you the trouble of coming through the shop.'

He bowed and took the key she held out. Then he turned and strode towards the street door.

I had no time to escape. I examined Lady Castlemaine more closely, as if immersed like the King in the generous pleasures of her bosom, and prayed that Gromwell wouldn't look closely at me. He had seen me in my new periwig this morning, but not for long. I stooped closer and closer to my lady.

Gromwell's cloak brushed my arm as he left the shop. I let out my breath in a long sigh. I gave him a moment and then followed him outside.

There was no sign of him. I hesitated, wondering what to do. I cast my eyes up and down the street. When I stepped away from the shop, I felt a tug on my cloak. I turned, alarmed, fearing that Gromwell had noticed me in the shop after all.

The hem of my cloak had caught on a nail in one of the red posts outside the shop. The nail held in place one of Vereker's handbills. I glanced down at it, and a name leapt out at me. Thanks to my father's training, I knew that it was finely printed in a modern variant of Garamond, probably one of the new Dutch typefaces.

Lucius Gromwell, Esquire,
Master of Arts in the University of Oxford.

CHAPTER FORTY

The inside of the coach was hot and airless. Jemima grew increasingly impatient, increasingly worried by the delay.

'How long will this last?' she burst out. 'Why can't Hal find out? Let me see outside.'

Mary raised the blind. Jemima found herself staring into a shoemaker's shop. If the coach window had been down, she could have stretched out a hand and touched the hinged shelf at the front of it, on which was displayed an array of samples. Beyond the shelf was the front room, with a shopman bowing low to her.

'Tell the man to approach. Ask him what's keeping us.'

Mary lowered the window and put her head out. The shoemaker's man told her that a wagon and a coach had entangled themselves ahead, blocking the traffic in both directions.

'Could be another half hour, mistress,' the man said, smiling invitingly and craning his head to gain a better idea of who was in the coach; Jemima shrank back from his gaze. 'Perhaps your ladyship would care to while away the time by inspecting some of our shoes. I have imported examples of the latest Paris fashions, brought over at great expense —'

'Shut the window,' Jemima ordered.

'— which are the delight of many ladies of the Court, and —'

Mary obeyed, cutting off the man in mid-sentence.

'Lower the blind.'

Then they were in the stuffy gloom of the coach once more. Jemima peered at the strange young woman who had helped her at Clifford's Inn. The girl was sitting opposite Mary, their skirts touching.

'Who are you?' Jemima demanded. 'Who's your master?'

'Mr Hakesby, madam.'

'Who is he?'

'The surveyor employed by Mr Poulton at the Dragon Yard hearing.'

'Of course.' Jemima remembered the thin old man who had made such a fool of Philip. 'Why did you come to help me?'

'Because . . .' The girl's voice acquired an

edge. 'Because a man shouldn't treat a dog so, let alone his wife.'

Jemima warmed to her, though the words could have been taken as impertinent. She leaned forward and tapped her on the knee. 'You won't be the loser for it. I shall see you are rewarded.'

'Thank you, madam.' The girl sounded uninterested in the prospect of a reward, which irritated Jemima slightly.

'What's your name, girl?'

'Jane Hakesby.'

'The same surname as your master?'

'He's my cousin, madam. That's why he took me in.'

'We don't know her from Adam, mistress,' Mary interrupted. 'She could be a spy.'

Jemima knew, with the certainty of long and intimate acquaintance, that her maid was furiously jealous of the attention paid to the young stranger. 'How would you like to come to me instead?' she said, partly in gratitude and partly because she could not resist the temptation to torment Mary. 'I'll pay you more than Mr Hakesby. The work will be more fitting for you. I shall give you prettier clothes, too.'

Mary sucked in her breath. She twitched her skirt away from the stranger's.

The strange girl said nothing for a moment. Then: 'Thank you, madam. I —'

At that moment, there was a tapping on the right-hand window.

'What is it?' Jemima said. 'The fool will break the glass if he doesn't have a care.'

Mary leaned across and lowered the blind.

Philip's face was on the other side of the window. He took off his hat when he saw them and ducked his head in a parody of respect.

'Why don't they stop him?' Jemima wailed, shrinking back against the side of the coach. 'What's Hal doing? Why didn't he warn us my husband was here?'

Philip opened the door. His eyes glanced at Mary, then Cat. His eyes widened as he recognized her from the Fire Court.

Jemima wrapped the shawl around most of her face and neck. 'Go away, sir. I shall scream if you don't. I shall send for a constable. Where's Hal? I demand you send him to me.'

'Directly, madam. When Richard has finished giving him my orders.'

Jemima felt the ground sliding away beneath her feet. 'Why are you here?'

'I couldn't let my wife go unescorted to the country.' His voice was casual, as if their meeting here were no more unexpected than their chancing to pass on the stairs in the Pall Mall house. The anger he had shown at Clifford's Inn seemed to have evaporated. 'They won't clear the bridge for a while. But you can't stay here. I hoped we could hire a private room at the Bear, but they're all taken. Lucius is asking his stationer if she will let us use her parlour. If not, we may have to walk a little further.'

'Lucius . . . ? I don't want to see Lucius.'

'You can't stay in here. It's so stuffy.'

'I — I am quite comfortable as I am, thank you, sir.'

'No,' he said, his eyes moving from Jemima to Cat, and then back again. 'You are not. You must let me be the best judge of where you will be comfortable.'

For a moment, no one spoke. It was one thing for Jemima to slip away from her husband without telling him that she was going to her father's house. It was quite another to disobey what was clearly his command in public, and to his face as well. Things might have been different at Syre Place, with her father to throw his weight into the scales. But here — on London Bridge, in front of the servants and God knew how many strangers — his authority overwhelmed her. She guessed that Hal would obey his master if he had to choose between them.

503

'Ah — and here's Lucius coming up.' Philip turned his head. 'What luck!'

Gromwell appeared at the window, lifting his hat and smiling. 'It couldn't be better. Madam, your servant. Mistress Vereker's parlour would not be convenient — her aged mother is there. But there are apartments above that we can use — rather shabby, I'm afraid, but private and overlooking the river. They have lit a fire for us. We can send out for anything we need.'

'Admirable.' Philip held out his hand to Jemima. 'Madam. Pray let me hand you down.' He glanced at Gromwell. 'We have an unexpected guest. Look.' He nodded towards Jane Hakesby in her corner.

Gromwell's face changed. 'What's she doing here?'

'Perhaps my wife has taken a fancy to her.'

There was a flurry of movement. The girl flung herself at the opposite door, trying to open it, her hands desperately scrabbling for purchase on the handle.

'Stop her,' Gromwell snapped.

Mary's arm shot out and hooked itself around the girl's neck, dragging her back against Jemima's legs. Gromwell pushed the upper part of his body into the coach and wrapped the fingers of his left hand around the girl's thin wrist. This brought his face within inches of Jemima's. She smelled sour wine on his breath and turned her head away.

'Forgive me for incommoding you, madam,' he said to her. 'But this girl is a dangerous thief. She tried to stab your husband. We must take her before a magistrate.'

At this point, the Hakesby girl craned her head and bit Mr Gromwell's hand until he screamed like a girl.

CHAPTER FORTY-ONE

The natural curiosities of Gloucestershire.
The handbill outside Mistress Vereker's shop extolled the marvels of this forthcoming publication. It would be the first truly comprehensive account of the geography, history, antiquities and natural wonders of the county from the time of the Flood. The splendid, lavishly illustrated folio volumes would adorn any gentleman's library. The author, from a distinguished family long-settled in the county —

The clack of a latch made me look up. There was a door at the far end of the building, beyond the shop's frontage. As it opened I glimpsed a passage on the other side. Gromwell appeared, turning to lock the door behind him, which meant that he had his back to me. So that was how he had vanished so quickly when he left the shop.

He set off up the street, his sword swinging by his side. I stared after him. He was going in the direction of the City, towards the Limburys' coach probably, snarled up in the traffic. The handbill had given me an unexpected glimpse of a Gromwell I didn't know. I knew enough of antiquarians and their activities to know that such pursuits required dedication and scholarship — and, if they were to produce a book as handsome as the handbill promised — a good deal of money from someone. Was this strange obsession what had driven Gromwell to help Limbury in the first place? Underwriting the costs of a book like this would need several hundred pounds.

I walked back to Sam, who was where I had left him, loitering some fifty yards away.

'It looks like the coach is up ahead somewhere. Limbury's probably already there, and Gromwell's just gone up to join him. He went into the stationer's there, at the sign of the Three Bibles. I think they're going to let him use one of their chambers upstairs.'

'What for?'

'That's the question.'

'So what do we do?'

'We wait for the answer.'

In truth there was nothing else we could do. If I was to do what Williamson wished, I needed to talk to Lady Limbury when she was by herself. Sooner or later, I hoped, the chance would come, but it wouldn't while Gromwell and Limbury were here. If they went back to Pall Mall with Lady Limbury, I would have to give up. But if they let her travel on, or left her here, there might be an opportunity to reach her.

We didn't have long to wait — no more than ten or twelve minutes. Sam touched my arm. Further up the street, a knot of people was forcing a passage. They were tightly bunched together, despite the obstacles in their way. Two men of the party were wearing swords.

I recognized most of them. The small figure of Lady Limbury, her face almost entirely covered by a shawl, was hanging on the arm of her husband, Sir Philip. Supporting her on the other side was the maid who had attended her at the Fire Court.

Behind them was Lucius Gromwell with his arm locked around a small woman whose head and shoulders were covered by a blanket. She was flanked on her other side by Sourface, who was gripping her arm. Her wrists were roped together in front of her.

The woman was kicking impotently at the men on either side, though it was obvious she could not see them because of the blanket over her head. She had lost one of her shoes.

The crowd parted before them but one man, braver than the rest, asked what the prisoner had done.

Gromwell scowled at him, his hand dropping to the hilt of his sword. 'A thief caught in the very act of her crime.'

The man backed away, raising his hands as if to say that he meant no harm by the question.

I didn't need to see the woman's face to know who she was. Oh God, I thought, this is all I need.

CHAPTER FORTY-TWO

When they pulled the blanket away, the light blinded her. A figure loomed over her, its outline wavering as if the light were eating away at its darkness.

The blanket had been thick and stuffy, smelling of horses. Cat sucked in lungfuls of air. Water roared continuously, and the very air seemed to vibrate with its restless force.

'Tell Mary to find me something to bandage my hand.' It was Gromwell's voice, harsh and assured, speaking to someone she couldn't see. 'The hellcat bit me.'

Cat's eyes were adjusting rapidly to the light. She was in a tiny room with a big window criss-crossed with bars. She was huddled on the floor in front of a box. Her arms were bound tightly, the cord biting into the skin just above the wrists. There was a draught coming from somewhere and also the smell of the river: salt and sewage, mud and seaweed.

Gromwell was standing in the doorway, scowling at her and nursing his left hand. His right hand already had a bandage on it.

Gradually her breathing subsided to its normal rate. Her wrists were painful from the rope, and she knew there would soon be bruises on her arms and on her right cheek. He had hit her as he was dragging her from the coach.

To be fair, though, she thought he would probably have hit her anyway, even if she hadn't bitten him. This, she reminded herself, was the man who had almost certainly killed two women already, Celia Hampney and her maid, Tabitha, as well as Mr Chelling. She wished she had been able to bite him harder.

'Who are you?' he said.

She moistened her lips. 'Jane Hakesby, sir.'

He snorted. 'Kin to Mr Hakesby, by any chance?'

'His cousin, sir.'

Gromwell leaned against the jamb of the door. His hat brushed the lintel. 'That's frankness, at least.'

Cat said nothing. He wasn't to know it was in fact a lie, and that she was really Catherine Lovett, daughter of the notorious Regicide. That was a small mercy.

'But it doesn't explain anything,' Gromwell went on. 'I can believe that Hakesby sent you to spy on us, but it can't be the whole story. The way you went for me. Look at that.'

He held up his left hand: her teeth had made two punctures; the wounds were rimmed with dried blood. She had bitten James Marwood once, in the heat of the moment, and drawn blood; but that had been different. Even at the time she had regretted the necessity for it.

'You broke into property belonging to Clifford's Inn and you ran off when challenged. You attacked me and drew blood. You attacked Sir Philip Limbury outside the Fire Court — dear God, you stabbed him with a naked blade, and for no shadow of a reason. What's a justice going to make of all that? It'll be the gallows for you, my girl. Unless they show mercy and send you to Bedlam instead. But you wouldn't survive there long. Not on the common ward.'

There was a relish in his voice that made her shiver, however hard she tried not to show fear. The Bethlehem Hospital was in Bishopsgate, and viewing the miserable and often violent antics of the lunatics was a popular spectacle to the public and a lucrative source of income to the keepers. If you weren't insane when you were committed there, it wouldn't be long before you were.

'I was afraid, sir. I didn't know what I did in my fear. But I'm heartily sorry for it.'

'You take me for a fool?' He took her chin in his hand, squeezed it and raised it, forcing her to look at him. 'What is between you and Marwood?'

'I . . . I don't know him, sir.'

The timbers of the building creaked loudly, as if proclaiming the fact she was lying. She glanced over her shoulder. It wasn't a chest behind her. It was a bench with a hole cut in it. A privy.

'Of course you know him,' Gromwell said. 'You were acting together outside the Fire Court this morning. You were seen talking to each other a fortnight ago. Let me remind you. It was in the ruins, where they found a woman's body. You're working for him, aren't you? So is your cousin, I imagine, so far as he can, the state he's in. You're living in Marwood's house, aren't you? Is he your lover?'

Cat said nothing. He squeezed her chin more tightly. She tried to jerk it away. But he was too strong. The building groaned, and this time Cat felt it move slightly, as if twitching in its sleep.

Gromwell released her and stepped back

513

into the doorway. 'Pray be careful. I'd avoid sudden movements if I were you.'

She cleared her throat. 'Why?'

'This privy projects over the water, so the waste falls directly into the river.' He spoke with exaggerated patience, as though explaining something to a slow-witted child. 'But the house is old, and the timbers supporting the closet have rotted.' He smiled at her. 'I'm standing in the main house. I'm quite safe, in case you were concerned. But the people of the house don't use this privy now, because it's too dangerous.'

She wondered if he was speaking the truth or merely trying to terrify her more. Directly below her was the river. At this moment the tide was ebbing rapidly under the arches, pouring downstream with violent, noisy urgency. Suppose Gromwell spoke the truth: even if she wasn't battered to death in the torrent under the bridge, she couldn't swim.

She heard footsteps in an adjacent room and the soft, slushy voice of Sourface: 'Sir? My master would speak with you.'

Gromwell stepped aside. 'What do you think of our prisoner?'

Sourface appeared at his shoulder. 'Skinny little thing, sir.'

'Could she please you? Do you think she's pretty?'

The servant smiled. 'Well enough, sir. If she was willing.'

'And if she wasn't?'

'Well enough again. Even if she weren't.'

Gromwell laughed. 'Stolen apples taste sweeter.' He turned back to Cat. 'I'll be back soon. Think over what I said. Tell me the truth, and you will find I can be kind. Richard will stay with you while I'm gone.'

'Shall I put a gag on her?'

'In a moment. I haven't finished questioning her. If you stand in the doorway, she can't go anywhere, except to you. And if she screams, well — who is there to hear on this side of the house except us?'

Gromwell left. Cat heard his footsteps on bare boards. Sourface came to stand in his place.

In the distance was the sound of voices, including a woman's. Lady Limbury's, presumably, or perhaps her maid's. Sir Philip must be there too.

She heard heavy breathing a yard or two away from her, and a rustling, creaking sound.

They must be on an upper storey of one of the higher buildings of the bridge. On the way here, they had pushed and pulled

515

her up several flights of stairs. Unable to see, she had tripped and fallen twice. At the top of the stairs, they had walked across bare boards. How far? Ten yards? More than one room perhaps — the sound had changed. Then they had pushed her into the privy and on to her knees.

'Look at me,' Sourface whispered. 'You crafty slut.'

She squinted through her lashes. He was staring at her and rubbing himself, not so much for the pleasure of the thing itself as for the pleasure of seeing Cat's face as he did it.

She shut out the sight of him and fought harder to distract herself. Sourface was Limbury's servant. He had not been at the Fire Court this morning. Perhaps he had been at the Limburys' house, instead, and he had seen enough to realize that his mistress intended to leave for her father's house.

The rhythmical rustling in the doorway continued, just audible above the roar of the water beneath. Sourface must have warned his master about his mistress's plans, so Limbury and Gromwell could reach the coach in time, before it crossed the bridge.

'Oh, you doxy!' The whisper was soft as

slurry. 'Oh, you dirty doxy.'

The truth was, there was no one who could help her now. No one knew she was here. Even if Marwood learned that she had boarded the coach with Lady Limbury, he would think that either she was still there, with the lady in the coach, and therefore relatively safe, or she had left, in which case he would expect her to return to the Savoy, or possibly to Henrietta Street.

If Cat wanted help, the only person who could provide it was herself.

'Look at me,' Sourface said. 'Look at me.'

Instead she spat in the direction of his whisper.

CHAPTER FORTY-THREE

How dared they leave her like this, without even a servant to attend her, and amid such squalor?

Philip and Gromwell were whispering on the landing beyond the door to the stairs. Jemima had called for Mary, but no one had come. She was angry, miserable and afraid, all at the same time. Only pride stopped her from weeping.

At last the door opened and Philip came back. She heard Gromwell's heavy footsteps going downstairs.

'Why have you brought me here?' Jemima demanded.

'I told you,' Philip said calmly as if this were a conversation over their dinner table at Pall Mall. 'To rest and refresh yourself.'

'But it's so strange here. So dirty and old-fashioned.' She found it hard to breathe suddenly. Did they mean to murder her? 'Why am I here?'

He turned away and stared out of the window at the river. 'We must look after you, madam,' he said. 'You were distraught — exhausted — this morning. You didn't know what you were doing or saying. And then rushing off to your father's without any warning. Perhaps you're feverish?'

Jemima was scared — not so much of Philip, who was after all her husband and had an interest in her survival, but of Lucius Gromwell. She had always underestimated him, she realized, mocking his shabby finery and his elaborate manners, and disliking him purely because Philip liked him. But Gromwell was formidable, despite his handicaps. It was he who had brought them here, and he who seemed to be in command.

'Where is he?' she asked. 'Your — your friend.' She could not bear to say the man's name.

'He went back to deal with Hal and the coach. He won't be long.'

The air was dank and chilly. She glanced about her. They had brought her to a long, narrow chamber, almost a gallery, on the top floor of the building. There was another, smaller room beyond it, though the door to it was now closed. They had put the girl somewhere in there, with first Gromwell, then Richard to watch over her.

519

The walls were panelled in dark wood, splintered and cracked, and on the river side grey with mould. Plaster had flaked from the sagging ceiling, which was moulded with an old-fashioned pattern of roses and straps, and stained with the smoke of candles; damp was spreading from one corner. There was a tall, carved chimney piece, but the fireplace beneath was choked with a heap of soot and ash that had spilled out from the hearth. The only furniture consisted of three stools, a crudely built cupboard and the high-backed settle on which she sat.

'I'm cold,' she said pettishly.

Philip nodded towards the door of the second room. 'The chimney's clear in there — they've lit the fire, but we'll let it draw. It's smoking a little.'

'I don't want to see them. Richard or Gromwell.'

'Then you shan't. Or only in passing.'

'I want to go to Syre,' she said, trying to inject an imperious note into her voice. 'I want to see my father. Have them bring up the coach.'

'That's quite impossible at present.' He spoke patiently, as if to a child. 'You know that. Nothing's moving on the bridge. We shall go down there later if you wish, if the King will give me permission for a leave of absence from my duties. Perhaps at the end of the week.'

'Why's Mary so long? I need her.'

'She'll be back presently. I've sent her to buy food and wine. The shops on the bridge are picked clean, so she may be a while. In any case, I must talk to you first.'

Philip sat down beside her on the settle and lifted her hand from her lap. She let it lie in his, as unresponsive as a dead fish. She turned her head and stared through the window at the river, allowing her eyes to be drawn across the water towards the blackened stump of St Paul's tower.

'You must forgive me, my sweet,' he said, his voice low and gentle. 'I spoke to you most unkindly outside the Fire Court. I was in such a passion I didn't know what I was saying. I shall never forgive myself.'

'You were cruel, sir,' she said, feeling the itch of tears about her eyes. 'You insulted me before the servants, before strangers. You —'

'My love, it was that damned unjust verdict. Poulton must have bribed the judges. It overturned my reason — it let loose a devil inside me — my anger made such lies pour out of me.' Suddenly he raised her hand to his lips. 'Be my priest,' he said. 'I've confessed my sins to you, terrible though they are. I beg you, give me my absolution.'

His words were a caress. But she could not speak the words of forgiveness. He sensed her softening, however, and he covered her hand with kisses. She tried to delay her capitulation.

'What about that girl?' she said. 'What have you done with her?'

'She's quite unharmed. She's in a closet beyond the bedchamber where the fire is. Richard's keeping an eye on her.'

'He must be kind. She helped me.' She paused and then added pointedly, 'When others were unkind.'

Philip squeezed her hand. 'Your goodness does you credit. But I'm afraid the girl's a spy. She's Hakesby's cousin, which means she's in Poulton's pay.'

She shook her head. 'I don't care. She was kind.'

'She didn't help you from the goodness of her heart — it was from calculation.'

'I don't believe it, Philip. Even if it's true, you mustn't harm her.'

'We'll see. Lucius will get the truth out of her.'

'Lucius,' she said, seizing on another reason for complaint. 'Why is it always him?'

Philip's grip relaxed, and he pulled back

from her as if to see her face more clearly. 'He's a brave fellow. Fortune hasn't dealt kindly with him, but you wouldn't want a better friend when matters go awry.'

'A better pander, you mean,' she snapped. Pain flared up in her belly at the very thought of it. 'He pimps for you, Philip, and you call it friendship. Why, he even lent you his chamber in Clifford's Inn so you could meet your lover there.' She spat out the last words. She stood up, brushing away his hand. She backed across the room from him, holding up her hands as if to push him back. 'Your lover,' she repeated. 'You foul thing. Stay away from me.'

Philip was smiling, as if she had made the most excellent jest in the world. 'I told you, Jemima. Celia Hampney? That awful woman wasn't my lover. She was Lucius's.'

Her mouth opened, but no words came.

'I admit I had a hand in the business. If anyone acted the pander, I fear I did. I was trying to do Lucius a favour, and myself one at the same time. He's always known how to play the lover, even when we were lads. I asked him to try his luck with the Hampney woman. I lent him some money so he could make his chamber fit for an assignation. Why not? She looked like a half-starved horse but she was a rich widow, and she wanted amusement. If Lucius married her, he would restore his fortunes at a stroke. I hoped that he could at least persuade her to support me over Dragon Yard, even if she wouldn't wed him. It would have made all the difference. You heard what they were saying at the Fire Court today.'

'I — I don't believe you.'

'Nevertheless, it's no more than the truth.' He leaned back, still smiling. 'So he scraped an acquaintance with her —'

'Did you ever meet that whore yourself?'

'No, of course not. Why should I? Besides . . .' He stood up and approached her. He stopped within arm's length but made no attempt to touch her. 'How could I even look at another woman when I have you?'

His brown eyes were like a dog's, melting with devotion.

'Lucius won her affections easily enough,' he went on. 'But it turned out she didn't want a husband. She wanted a man to amuse her, to take her to bed. And when she began to think that he was only making up to her because of Dragon Yard and her money, that angered her. It was no more than the truth, of course, but she should have known that no one's motives are wholly pure.'

'And then,' Jemima said, 'and then . . .'

He wasn't smiling now. 'Then someone stabbed her to death.'

CHAPTER FORTY-FOUR

God was merciful, in a small way at least. Limbury called Sourface away to fetch more fuel for the fire.

'We're in the next chamber,' Limbury said to Cat. 'Remember that. No one will hear you if you call, no one but us. You have nowhere to go.' His lips twisted. 'I'd try not to move, if I were you, in case you end up in the river without meaning to.'

She stared up at him but said nothing. He shut her in. She heard the click of the latch, and then the scrape of a wedge driven in to secure it.

Her wrists were burning from the tightness of the rope that bound them. She tried in vain to move her arms. The rope had passed over her right-hand sleeve. She bent her head and tugged at the material with her teeth. In less than a minute she worked it free from the rope.

The pressure on her wrists instantly

slackened. Only a little, but it gave her hope. It also meant that she could move her wrists slightly, one against the other. She tried in vain to reach the pocket hanging at her waist beneath her skirt. They had not searched her, so she still had her knife. But she could not reach it, however much her fingers strained towards it.

There were footsteps in the room next door over the rushing of the water. She tensed. In a moment there was a bang that made the floor shudder, as if someone had thrown down a heavy weight. Then came the familiar scrape of a poker riddling ashes from a grate.

Behind her, on the seat of the privy, there was a flap of wood that had once covered the hole. Its hinges had rusted, and the flap was now detached and lay on the bench. The rusting halves of its hinges were fixed on the planking of the seat.

Cat knelt in front of the privy, with the water rushing below her, and rested her bound wrists on the jagged stump of the hinge on the left. She rubbed the rope to and fro, to and fro, over the rough edge of the metal.

The friction made heat, and the heat burned her chafed skin. Tiredness made her clumsy. The rusty iron dug into the soft skin above her inner wrist. She caught her breath, forced back a cry of pain and continued to work the rope to and fro over the hinge.

A strand parted. Spots of blood appeared on the seat of the privy. Then another strand separated. Her shoulders and arms ached but she dared not rest. Her throat was so dry she could no longer swallow.

A third strand broke, and the rope gave for the first time, slackening its hold.

She sat back on her heels, panting. Sourface might be back at any moment or — even worse, perhaps — Limbury or Gromwell. The sounds from the neighbouring room had faded away. All she could hear was the endless surge of the water below.

She set to work once more. Her muscles had stiffened already. She had been sweating hard, too, and the brief rest had given the moisture a chance to cool on her skin. She transferred her wrists to the remains of the second hinge, which was smaller than the first but unblunted by her rubbing of the rope.

Five minutes later she was free. She stared with something approaching disbelief at her two wrists. She raised her arms above her head and stretched. She swept the rope from the seat and into the hole. It writhed as it fell to the foaming water and disappeared under the surface.

Cat's knees shrieked with pain as she leaned against the seat of the privy and pushed herself into a standing position. She flexed her fingers. Both her forearms were smeared with blood.

She took out her knife. The familiar feel of it in her hand comforted her. She went to the door and listened. She heard nothing moving, though now — mingling with the noises of the river — there were muffled sounds that might have been voices. But not, she thought, from the room next door.

There were only two ways to leave the privy: through the window and into the river, or through the door and into a building full of enemies. As gently as she could, she tried the latch. It wouldn't move. She stopped to listen. Then she pushed the door outward. It shifted a little in the frame.

Cat took out her knife and poked experimentally at the jamb of the door, close to the latch. The tip dug itself into the wood, which was softer than it looked, perhaps rotting from the damp.

She didn't want to risk snapping the knife blade by using it as a lever. Instead, she picked up the flap of wood from the privy and worked it into the gap between the door and the jamb.

She leaned her weight against the flap and pushed as hard as she could. The door creaked and moved slowly away from her. The jamb splintered. Suddenly the door gave altogether. There was the sound of something falling to the floor. The door swung outwards.

'What was that?' a man's voice said.

She was in a square chamber hung with tapestries that sagged from their original fixings and in places trailed along the floor. They were so filthy and faded that their design was almost entirely gone. The room was empty, apart from a plain bedstead without either curtains or bedding. A newly lit fire blazed in the grate, throwing flames up the back of the chimney. The door opposite the privy was ajar.

'You make me the unhappiest woman in the world,' Lady Limbury wailed, her voice high and edged with hysteria. 'I'm your wife, sir. Promise me you'll never see that man again.'

Footsteps crossed the room beyond. Sir Philip Limbury paused in the doorway. He saw Cat. The logs settled in the grate, dislodging one of them, which rolled from the fire basket into the hearth.

'You cunning little bitch,' he said to Cat,

his hand dropping to the hilt of the sword.

'What is it?' Lady Limbury called. 'What's happening?'

He ripped the blade from the scabbard and advanced slowly into the room, with the tip of the sword dancing in front of him at the level of her eyes. Cat's knife was useless against a sword. She darted to the fireplace and took up the poker.

'Don't be a fool, girl. Put that down.' The blade swung briefly towards the privy. 'Get back in there.'

There was movement behind him and the dishevelled figure of Lady Limbury appeared in the doorway. Her birthmark was uncovered, glowing a deep, angry red.

'Drop your sword, sir,' she cried. 'I told you, you mustn't hurt that poor girl. I command you.'

Cat backed into the corner of the room.

'Put down the poker,' Limbury said to her, ignoring his wife. 'And that knife. Or I'll spit you like a pigeon.'

Lady Limbury screamed with frustration. She darted into the room, seized the tongs and took up the burning log from the hearth. 'Listen to me, sir.' She waved the log at him, and acrid smoke curled around them both. 'You shall listen to me, just this once. I will not be ignored!'

Limbury swung the sword towards his wife. She shied away, her face contorting with fear. The blade swept the tongs aside. She lost her grip on them and they fell to the floor. The log rolled towards the wall.

He waved the sword towards the privy. 'In there,' he said to Cat. 'N—'

He broke off as his wife flung herself at him, wrapping her arms around his neck, so for a second or two he was bearing her full weight. Her feet kicked at his legs. Her body hung over his sword arm. She was howling at him.

Cat leapt forward and lunged, driving the tip of the poker towards Limbury's eye. It missed by a fraction of an inch and jarred against the bony socket. He shouted and staggered back, half-carrying, half-dragging his wife with him. But he did not fall, and he kept hold of his sword. Cat threw herself between him and the wall, keeping Lady Limbury between them. He tried to block her but his wife impeded his movements so much that all he managed was a sideways stagger that nearly overbalanced him.

Cat stopped abruptly, knees flexed, poker in one hand and knife in the other. Gromwell was standing in the doorway to the room beyond. Behind her, Lady Limbury coughed. Then so did her husband.

The air was full of smoke. Her eyes stinging, Cat retreated towards the privy. The
log from the tongs had skittered across the
floor to the foot of the wall. Still smouldering, it had come to rest against the bottom
of one of the tapestries. They were as dry as
tinder. The flames were streaking up the
material with astonishing speed, bringing
the tapestries briefly and glowingly alive in
the moment of their destruction.

For an instant, only the flames and the
thickening smoke moved. Then Limbury
dropped his sword, tugged apart his wife's
arms and dropped her on the floor.

She fell awkwardly, missed her footing and
sprawled on her back, her arms waving,
where she lay helpless as an upturned turtle.
She cried out. Her hands clutched her belly.

The flames were spreading around the
walls. 'Stamp it out,' Limbury called. 'Stamp
out the flames.'

'Too late for that.' Covering his mouth
and nose with his cloak, Gromwell lugged
out his sword. He beckoned to Limbury.
'Quick — pull her out.'

Limbury scooped up his own sword and
dragged his wife towards the further door.
Gromwell waited by the doorway, sword in
hand, his eyes on Cat.

'What about the girl?' Limbury gasped,

coughing.

Gromwell stood aside to let them pass. He said — as much to Cat as to Limbury, 'Let her take her chances.'

Then he too left the room. He slammed the door. Cat heard the sound of a bolt driven home on the other side.

There was now so much smoke that the opposite door was invisible. Her ears were full of the familiar, dreadful crackling roar of the fire. Flames tore up the chimney; they danced along the old, dry wood of the bedstead; sparks rained on the mattress.

Cat ran back to the privy, pulling the door closed after her, though it would not latch. At least it was a barrier: it might grant her a few minutes' grace from the fire and the smoke.

Below her, the river roared between the piers of the bridge, pouring downstream towards the sea. She was caught between two roaring lions, the fire and the water, seeking whom they might devour.

The smoke leaked into the privy. She slashed the poker at the window repeatedly, poking out lozenges of glass and breaking down the lattice of lead. Air swept into the little room. A draught, she thought, suddenly realizing her mistake: a draught fans a fire.

The privy creaked on its supporting timbers. The floor shifted beneath her feet.

CHAPTER FORTY-FIVE

The laudanum dulled the edge of the pain,
but I wasn't comfortable standing still.
Movement was a distraction. Sometimes I
walked fifty yards or so away in one direction or the other, always keeping the stationer's building in sight. I didn't stand out —
other people were doing much the same,
moving aimlessly to and fro, trying to allevi-
ate the tedium of waiting until the blockage
was cleared.

I sent Sam into the alehouse we had
passed earlier to see if he could pick up any
information about the stationer's house and
its layout. With hindsight, that was a mistake: it was a long shot at best, and giving
Sam leave to go into an alehouse was asking
for trouble.

But I was growing desperate. Everything
had changed. I did not care about having a
quiet word with Lady Limbury on Williamson's behalf. Gathering evidence against the

murderer of the Widow Hampney, her maidservant and Chelling no longer seemed as urgent as it had. The only thing that mattered was Cat.

Somewhere in that house she was a prisoner, trussed like a turkey for the oven. It was my fault that she was there. I had to do something but I didn't know what. If I banged on the door beside the shop until somebody came, how would that help? Limbury and Gromwell were in the house as the lawful guests of Mistress Vereker.

I would need a magistrate's warrant to search the place for Cat. It would take hours even to apply for one, and there was no guarantee of success. A magistrate would demand to see strong evidence before he risked alienating a senior courtier like Limbury. As for Williamson, the last thing he would want was to draw publicity to himself. Why should he care about a young woman of no importance?

Early on, Sourface and Lady Limbury's maidservant came out. She had a basket over her arm. They set off up the road towards the Great Stone Gate. I would have tried to talk to the maid if she had been alone.

I watched them until they were blocked from my view by a hackney coach. Shortly afterwards, Sourface came back alone, carrying a wicker scuttle full of coals. I cursed myself for sending Sam away — I could have sent him after the maid.

Sourface let himself in the house. After a while, I went into the baker's shop over the road. A woman came to serve me, wiping floury hands on her apron. I had missed dinner so I knew I must be hungry, though I didn't feel it. The laudanum played the devil with my appetite. Besides, there wasn't much to buy. The rush of unexpected customers had bought most of the stock.

I asked for a roll and she offered me a misshapen thing, slightly charred at one end. 'All I got left, master. Take it or leave it.'

I said I would take it, despite its flaws. As she took my money, I said, 'Where does that door lead?' I pointed over the road. 'The one beside the stationer's shop. I think I saw a friend going in.'

'Widow Vereker's lodgings,' she said, handing me the roll. 'Her husband's aunt used to live up there. Dead now.'

The roll was so hard and heavy that it might have been fired from a cannon. The crust was as hard as plate armour. 'Who lives there now?'

'No one.' The woman's eyes looked past me. 'Look,' she said.

Both of us stared out into the road. The traffic was moving at last, albeit slowly. Someone applauded. A donkey plodded by, drawing a cart laden with someone's furniture.

'Shame,' the woman said. She shrugged. 'It was good while it lasted.'

I went outside. I waited, pressed against the wall of the baker's. Ten minutes later, the Limburys' coach rumbled along the road. The coachman was up on the box, and there was a boy beside him.

The coach stopped outside the stationer's. I tensed my muscles, ready to do something, though I had no idea what. There were angry shouts from the drivers behind, infuriated by yet another stop. The coachman pointed with his whip at the door of the lodgings. The boy jumped down. The coachman shook the horses' reins and the coach lumbered on.

The boy hammered on the door with the heel of his hand. No one answered. He looked around him for help, his face desperate. When he found none, he ran after the coach.

I lost track of time. Traffic moved sluggishly along the bridge in both directions. The pain was getting worse. I discovered that I was gripping the roll in my hand so tightly that my fingertips had made holes in the crust.

A throaty voice murmured in my ear, 'There you are, master. Thought I'd lost you for ever.'

Sam was at my shoulder, grinning at me.

I swung round. 'Where the devil have you been? You've been gone an age.'

'What could I do, master?' Sam put on an injured expression that didn't suit him. 'You get nothing for nothing, so I had to have a drink. But I learned something about the place.' He jerked a thumb at the sign of the Three Bibles. 'The tapster said the lease is running out and the building's falling apart. The word is that Mistress Vereker's moving off the bridge.'

'What use is that to me?' I snapped, taking my irritation out on him.

'I don't know. You said to find out anything I could about the place, so I did.' Sam stared over the roadway at the building opposite, running his eyes up the ornate but decaying façade. 'Mind you, anyone with a pair of eyes in their head can see it needs repairing.'

'You know I needed you here. You deserve a —'

'Master,' he interrupted. 'Look up there.'

He pointed at the top of the building.

Smoke was drifting into the air above it. Not a disciplined thread from a chimney, but a dark and riotous cloud, growing larger and denser even as we watched. I heard, faintly, far above the street noises and the muted roar of the river, the sound of broken glass.

Others had seen the smoke too, including the baker's wife, who was standing in the doorway of the shop.

'Fire!' she screamed. 'Fire!'

CHAPTER FORTY-SIX

Jemima lost one of her shoes on the stairs. Philip wouldn't let her stop for it. He held her arm — almost wrenching it from its socket — and dragged her down flight after flight. In his other hand was his naked sword.

She lacked the strength even to cry out. She had a pain within her.

Richard was running ahead and Gromwell's footsteps thundered after theirs.

Gromwell. If this was hell, there was the devil himself. Why in God's name didn't Philip protect her?

At the bottom, Richard fumbled with the door, his hands scrabbling in his haste at the bolts and the bar. He swung the door open just before they reached it, and slipped into the street in front of them.

There were cries of 'Fire! Fire!' People were everywhere, pouring out of houses and shops, abandoning their vehicles and struggling to escape from the bridge.

The door to the stationer's was open, and apprentices and journeymen and servants milled around the entrance. A middle-aged woman was in the doorway, shrieking at them to come back and carry out the stock.

'This way,' Philip said, waving with his sword towards the south end of the bridge. 'The Bear.'

'But the girl, sir,' she gasped, recoiling from Gromwell, who had joined them. 'The girl's inside.'

She saw a face she knew on the other side of the road, not five yards away. It was the man who had accosted Gromwell outside the Fire Court when Philip had been attacking her. Beside him was the man with the crutch who had lost part of his leg, who had also been there.

'Save her,' she cried to them, to anyone. 'For the love of God. Save her.'

Gromwell took her other arm. In a dream, she saw the man raise his arm and pitch a small dark object across the street. It caught Gromwell in the face and made him recoil slightly. But he kept his grip on her arm. The object fell to the ground. Automatically she glanced down at it. It was a charred roll.

He and Philip dragged her away. The crowd fell back from their drawn swords.

Behind them came Richard. Then her pain returned, worse than before.

CHAPTER FORTY-SEVEN

'Follow them,' I ordered Sam.

'But, master, what —'

'Go,' I roared, suddenly furious with him. 'Or go to the devil. It's all one.'

I pushed past him, forced my way through the crowd outside the stationer's and went into the building. Once inside, I glanced back. To my relief, I couldn't see Sam. With luck, he had obeyed me for once. A cripple couldn't run upstairs. I didn't want to be responsible for killing him as well as Cat.

The covered passage led to a staircase and a doorway beyond to a bookbinder's workshop. I ignored the workshop and climbed the first flight as quickly as I could. The pain from my burn and the stiffness of my limbs slowed me down.

There was smoke in the air, but not too much to make breathing difficult. The higher I went, however, the worse both the smoke and the heat became.

But no flames. Not yet. I can't face a fire, I thought, and then Chelling's face floated into my mind: as he had been in death, when I had last seen him, bathed in flames.

I wrapped my cloak over my mouth and nose. I climbed higher and higher until I could climb no more. On the top landing, there was a single door, closed. It was a stout affair, in its way, but it couldn't hold back the fire for ever. There was already an orange glow around the frame.

I touched the latch. The iron was so hot I had to wrap a fold of my cloak around my hand in order to lift it.

It opened into a tunnel of fire. Smoke billowed towards me. There was no sign of Cat. An almighty cracking sound filled my ears, and one of the windows burst outwards. The flames licked through the opening towards the sky.

Fear gripped me, squeezing my bowels. On one level, I thought that history was repeating itself, and I was back in Chelling's room, and this time the fire would do even worse things to me.

But on another level there was no time to think at all. My actions seemed to have little or nothing to do with the part of me that was terrified. With the cloak clamped over my face, I staggered across the floor of a long room, making for a door at the opposite end. God be thanked, the floorboards supported my weight. The door was bolted. When I drew the bolt back, I forgot to pad it with my cloak, and metal burned my hand. I screamed with the pain of it, losing what was left of the air in my lungs.

I smelled burning hair. The right-hand side of my wig was on fire, the hair frizzling and blackening in the heat. I tore it off my head, along with my hat, and tossed them to the flames.

This chamber was smaller than the first, with another door opposite me. The air was clearer here. The windows had gone and so had part of the ceiling. In one corner was the blackened skeleton of a bedstead. The beams above had caught fire, as had some of the floorboards. Looking up, I glimpsed the sky. Roof tiles cracked in the heat and showered down on to the wreckage of the bed. Lines of fire were streaking along the remaining rafters.

I drew the cloak over my bare head, trying to protect the damaged skin from the intense heat. The joists below, which had supported the floor, remained intact, though two near the fireplace were smouldering and charring. I took in another breath, coughed most of it out, and skipped from one joist to the next. The door at the end had lost its latch. I tugged it open.

There was Cat at last, turned away from me, leaning on the window sill. Relief surged through me. In my heart I had feared she must be dead already.

I said her name, as I crossed the threshold, drawing the door shut behind me. The flames hadn't reached here yet. The room was a privy. Cat had punched a jagged hole through the glass and lead of the lattice. Her head and shoulders were poking outside.

She was unaware that she was no longer alone. I touched her side. She spun round instantly. I saw the glint of the knife in her hand. She didn't look like herself any more. Her face was white, the skin stretched tightly over the skull, the teeth bared.

I heard a crash of falling timbers and tiles behind me, and the roar of the fire increased.

'The river,' I said, trying to keep my voice gentle, as one would to a frightened child or a nervous animal. 'It's the only way now.'

'No,' she whispered. 'I'd rather stay here.'

'We must jump.' I dropped the cloak, tore off my coat and let it fall to the floor. 'Kick off your shoes.'

She made as if to lunge at me with the knife.

I stepped back as far as I could in the cramped space. I felt the warmth of the fire on my back and heard the hungry crackle of the flames.

'Cat —'

'I can't do it,' she said. 'You go.'

'Don't be foolish.'

'I won't.' She stamped her foot, reduced to a child in a temper. 'I can't swim. And I hate water.'

I seized her right arm and twisted it. She tried to bite me. She kicked at my legs. But I kept up the pressure until she dropped the knife. I clamped my arms around her and forced her back to the window opening.

The privy groaned. With a snapping and a cracking of timber, it swung outwards over the river until it was hanging at an angle of nearly forty-five degrees. It threw the two of us against the outer wall beside the window. The wall sagged and creaked.

Hand over hand, Cat pulled herself along the bench until she could cling to the hole of the privy. I clambered around her. My hand appeared beside hers, our skin touching. We stared at each other, as close as lovers or mortal enemies. I watched our knuckles whitening.

The privy sighed. It broke asunder like a cracked walnut. It crumbled out into the river in a shower of debris.

I closed my eyes as we fell.

The fire, the river, the falling building wrapped me in their sounds. There was a smack as my body hit the water. Hard objects buffeted me. Someone screamed. The cold was vicious: it paralysed me. The river sucked me underwater and rolled me over and then —

Something struck my shoulder. The force of it drove me under the surface, where the current played with me like a boy torturing a cat, or a cat torturing a mouse. It turned me round and dashed me against the starlings. I curled myself into a ball, trying to protect my head with my arms. The current tossed and twisted me over and over. It let me free for a second and then threw me over the weir tumbling downstream from the bridge.

The water was so cold that it made me gasp. I took in a mouthful of it and tried to spit it out before it reached my lungs. I couldn't reach the surface. I couldn't breathe.

I felt a sharp pain in my right thigh, the one the fire hadn't scarred, slicing down the leg to the knee. A stabbing agony blossomed in my chest. There was another hammer blow, worse than the others, on my curved spine. The river was killing me slowly.

Then — with miraculous suddenness — it was over. I was bobbing about in calmer water, downstream from the bridge. I broke the surface and sucked fresh air in my lungs. The current was bearing me with it, but much more slowly than before. I rolled on my back. Over my head was the grey dome of the sky.

Where was Cat? I flipped over and turned my head this way and that. I was nearer the north bank of the river than the south. The houses of the bridge rose above me like a jagged cliff. People were pointing down at me, their mouths silently opening and closing. But I couldn't see Cat.

With growing desperation, I swam to and fro. I called her name. My chest was heaving, forcing me to rest. I trod water and drew in mouthfuls of air. The pain in my chest slowly subsided, but not the despair I felt. I had killed her. I had let her drown. If it hadn't been for me, she would not have been here in the first place.

Thank God. A boat was putting out from Billingsgate Stairs. A man in the stern was pointing in my direction.

The swell of the water briefly lifted me

higher. I saw a small hand poking above the surface. It vanished almost immediately.

With a sudden surge of energy, I swam towards the place where she had been. I dived. The water was murky, for the turbulence of its passage through the bridge made it cloudier and filthier than it was upstream. I waved my arms under the water, stretching my fingers out. I couldn't see her or touch her. I surfaced, filled my lungs and dived again.

My left hand found something. I swam further down. I touched what felt like an arm. It was sliding away from me. Before it could escape, I gripped it with my left hand, wincing as the tightening muscles increased the pain from the burns. I pulled it closer, and felt the outline of Cat's body with my other hand.

I kicked my legs and dragged her to the surface. Gasping for breath, I lay on my back in the water, kicking my feet. She floated inert beside me. I tried to pull her on to my chest.

Her eyes were closed. Her skin was broken on one shoulder, and there was a gash on the other arm. Her hair was floating free and bedraggled.

I shook her gently. I might have been shaking a wet mattress for all the response I had.

Desolation swept over me. Oh Christ, I thought, after all that she's dead.

CHAPTER FORTY-EIGHT

Jemima's pain grew worse as Philip and Gromwell dragged her along the street.

She was dimly aware of the crowd parting as they approached, of the murmur of voices, and people asking who they were and where was the constable. But no one was willing to interfere with two gentlemen with drawn swords.

They emerged from the gate passage at Bridge Foot. The approach of a fire pump forced them to stop. Men with buckets and hoses were running beside it towards the fire, caught up in their own drama. They had no eyes for hers.

Her legs collapsed beneath her. The pain was worse than ever. Philip glanced at her. He kept his grip on her arm. She saw the shock in his face before the pain distracted her even from him.

The pump and the firemen were gone.

'Come on,' Gromwell said. 'We'll have to

carry her.'

'No,' Philip said. 'Wait. She's ill.'

Gromwell would have none of it. He tugged at Jemima's arm.

She saw someone running towards them. 'Mary,' she cried, 'Mary. Help me.'

'Let her go,' Mary cried.

Gromwell barged into Mary with his shoulder, sending her flying. She dropped the basket she had been carrying. It toppled over and the contents cascaded over the slippery cobbles.

But not all of them. When Mary straightened up, she was gripping a wine bottle by the neck.

Gromwell was already moving away. He took Jemima's arm. Mary swung the bottle at him in a rising backhanded blow that slammed into the bridge of his nose.

He recoiled with a roar of pain. Blood spurted down his face. His wig was askew, covering one eye. He tried to bring up his sword, but the wheel of a cart was in his way.

Before he could recover, Mary hit him on his blind side. This time, the bottle caught him just in front of his exposed ear. His body crumpled. The bottle broke with the impact and showered him with wine and broken glass.

Mary turned to her mistress, stretching out her hand to her. Jemima stared at her.

It was then that Philip released Jemima's arm. She saw the point of his sword leap forward and upward, catching Mary under the chin. It pierced the skin and slid smoothly into the soft matter beneath. Blood appeared between Mary's lips. Her green eyes opened wide and fixed on her mistress.

Jemima closed her own eyes, squeezing the lids together to shut the world out, and surrendered entirely to her own pain.

Chapter Forty-Nine

It was Sam, Cat discovered later, who had taken charge of matters.

He had heard the cries of 'Man in the water' further up the bridge, and had rushed towards them. He had been in time to see Marwood in the water, and the boats rowing out from Billingsgate Stairs.

He reached them there, shortly after they had been dragged like large inert fish from the boats and laid on the tarred planking of the landing stage. Cat had been lying on her side, Sam told her later, bleeding like a pig, and puking the Thames out of her belly. She had been freezing cold and someone had wrapped a blanket around her.

As for Marwood, Sam said, he had been crouching over her, clutching her and crying like a baby, and shivering worse than poor Mr Hakesby when one of his fits was upon him.

'Thought the master had lost his wits,'

Sam said, seeming to find this possibility very amusing.

A little later, she and Marwood were still at the landing place, now sitting apart and wrapped in blankets. They were both conscious by this time, but they hadn't said a word to anyone — even each other. Neither of them had breath for words.

By his own account, at least, Sam had dealt with everything with speed and exemplary efficiency. By talking airy nothings about his master's lofty connections at Whitehall, he had persuaded the people of a nearby tavern to help. They had carried Cat and Marwood to a private room, set them before a fire, and swathed them in yet more blankets.

When Cat had stopped trembling, the landlady took her away to bathe her wounds and dress her in a cast-off shift, her maid's winter waistcoat and a thick cloak. The clothes were twice as large as she was and enveloped her like a tent.

Time must have passed, and a good deal of it, because when she came back to the room with the fire, Mr Hakesby had been there, holding his hands towards the warmth. But Marwood and Sam had gone.

Hakesby's skin was grey. His hair was uncombed. He had spilled gravy down his best coat. He looked ten years older than when she had last seen him, in the Fire Court this morning.

'How could you?' he demanded as she came into the room. 'You foolish, wicked child. Come and sit by the fire.' He waved a long, thin hand at the landlady, who was watching the proceedings with interest from the doorway. 'Bring broth for her. And wine . . . mulled wine? With ginger in it? Whatever you think will best revive her. But hurry, hurry, hurry.'

The landlady curtsied and left them alone. Cat sat on the bench beside him and stared at the fire.

'Is this Marwood's doing?' he asked. 'I thought he had more sense.'

She shook her head wearily. 'It no longer matters.'

'Of course it matters. You could have drowned. Or burned to death like poor Chelling.'

She said nothing. She was warmer, and beginning to feel drowsy.

'Has he dragged you into government business? Or is this just his mad folly about his father and the way he died?'

'I can't say, sir. I don't know the whole of it, and I don't want to.'

'They're saying downstairs that someone

was killed on the bridge,' he said. 'A woman. Run through with a sword. Was that part of it?'

'I tell you I don't know.'

He said nothing. Slowly his hand crept along the bench and laid itself over hers. She glanced at it. She wanted to snatch her hand away; she didn't care to be touched. Instead, she forced herself not to move.

Her mind drifted. It was an old man's skin, wrinkled like a lizard's and speckled with liver spots. His fingers trembled slightly. The nails needed trimming. She must do something about that. But not now.

Food and a long night's sleep repaired at least some of the damage. The following day, Thursday, she rose late. Hakesby fussed over her and tried to make her rest, but she resisted him. She felt perfectly well, she said. In fact, her bruises were painful, and her cuts would take weeks to heal, but she was desperate for distraction.

Towards the end of the day, when the light was going and it was becoming harder to work, there was a knock at the door of the drawing office.

Brennan went to answer it. Mr Poulton's portly manservant was waiting on the threshold. He was clasping a very small package to his chest.

Brennan made as if to take it. The servant stepped back. 'I'm to put this in your master's hands. And wait for a receipt.'

'Come in then,' Hakesby called. 'Bring it here.'

He was sitting in his usual chair by the fire. After dinner, Cat had refused to return to her closet and rest as he had wanted. For the last hour, she had been taking his dictation in shorthand, hoping that she would be able to read it back in the morning. He was in a strange humour, bright-eyed and full of feverish energy.

Poulton's servant brought the package to him. Hakesby weighed it in his palm. He broke the seals — there were three — and unfolded the paper. Inside was a leather pouch with a letter rolled around it. He read it and handed it to Cat.

To Mr Hakesby
By the hand of my servant I send you forty-five pounds in gold, in payment for your services to date in connection with Dragon Yard and as an advance on future payments, as itemized in the Memorandum of Agreement. Pray sign and date this letter to confirm your

receipt, and return it by the hand of my servant.

Roger Poulton

At a signal from Hakesby, she took the pouch, poured the coins into her hand and counted them. Brennan watched, his mouth slightly open, his eyes on Cat's face. He turned his head away when he saw that she had noticed him.

After Poulton's servant had gone, and the money had been locked away in the strongbox, Hakesby dismissed Brennan for the day.

'Will you pay back Marwood?' she asked when they were alone.

'We shall give him ten pounds at least.'

'Not more?'

'We must hold the rest of it back for ourselves. You can take the money to his house tomorrow, if you're well enough.'

'Of course I shall be well enough, sir,' she said. 'What about the rest we owe him?'

'Tell him he must wait a little. He gave us eight weeks, didn't he? After what he's done to you, the least he can do is be patient. And I have not forgotten the money I owe to you, either.'

Cat tried to change the subject. 'Talking of hackneys, you'll need one this evening when you go back to Three Cocks Yard. Shall I send the porter for one?'

'Wait — not yet. There is something I wish to say.' He stopped, and glanced furtively around the room, as if to make sure they were really alone. 'Something that concerns you. Sit here where I can see you.'

She obeyed. 'I am perfectly well, sir. I am quite capable of returning to my drawing board tomorrow. I —'

'It's not that,' he said. 'I've been uneasy in my mind about you.'

'There's no need, sir.'

He held up his hand, and they watched the tiny tremors that rippled through it. 'This doesn't get better,' he said. 'I don't think it will. What will you do when I'm gone?'

'That won't be for —'

'Or when I grow too ill to work? Indeed, what shall I do when I reach that point? How shall I keep body and soul together?'

'I shall find a way to support us both. Perhaps Dr Wren —'

'I've been turning this over, and I've come to a decision.'

Cat glanced sharply at him. His voice was sterner than usual.

'I wish to offer you a contract,' he went on. 'Purely as a matter of business, and with clear benefits, rights and responsibilities on both sides. An agreement, governed by law.'

'Why? We do very well as we are.'

'What I propose is that you marry me.'

'Marry you?' She stood up, knocking over her stool, and backed away from him. 'Marry you? Dear God, sir, have you gone mad?'

CHAPTER FIFTY

'Mistress?'

The voice insinuated itself into Jemima's dream, a desperate confusion of flames and screams and tumbling buildings.

Glad to be wakened, she opened her eyes. Hester's plain face, shiny with sweat, hovered above hers. She was frowning and biting her lip with anxiety. For a moment Jemima wondered where Mary was. Even as she was opening her mouth to ask, the memory of yesterday flooded back.

'Please, mistress, there's a gentleman below. You said to wake you.'

Jemima knew by the light that it was evening now — not late, for it wasn't dark: the colours were beginning to leach away, the outlines were softening.

'Who is it?'

'Mr Chiffinch. He's with master in the study.'

'Bring my gown. Sit me up.'

Hester was willing but stupid, and the fear of doing wrong made her even clumsier than usual. The pain in Jemima's belly grew suddenly worse. Her bandages were wet. They needed changing, and probably the sheets as well.

At the thought of all that this signified, her grief overwhelmed her, and her eyes filled with tears. Can you mourn the loss of someone who has not been born? Of course you can.

And of course she mourned Mary, too. But that was different.

Hester poked Jemima's arms into the armholes of the gown. Jemima bore the girl's clumsiness with patience she thought of as saintly. What did it matter now?

The midwife and the physician had separately examined her yesterday evening. Both of them had said in their different ways how sad her loss was, but neither could see any reason why she should not carry a healthy child to full term. The physician recommended he prescribe another course of treatment. The midwife, perhaps more usefully, promised to pray for her.

When Jemima was settled, her face washed with a sponge, the cosmetics applied and her book to hand, she sent Hester away with instructions to bring her a cup of chocolate.

'Make sure they tell my husband that I am awake, and I should like to see him.'

She waited, wondering why Chiffinch had come here, and turning over in her mind what she wanted to say to Philip. In the event she did not have long to wait before there were footsteps below and the sound of men's voices. The front door opened and closed. She heard Philip climbing the stairs. He walked more slowly than usual, and paused every few steps, as her father did, to rest and draw breath.

He tapped on the door and entered. He asked how she did. As well as could be expected, she said, given what happened to her yesterday. He nodded and went to stand by the window.

'Well, sir. What did Chiffinch want with you?'

Philip swung round. She couldn't see his face clearly because the light was behind him. 'He came to warn me that the King is angry.'

She stared blankly at him. 'What about?'

'Me. I am dismissed — I'm no longer a Groom of the Bedchamber. Which means I'm five hundred a year poorer, too. As well as everything else.'

She knew at least part of what 'everything else' meant: the position at Court; access to the King; the power to whisper words in the ears of influential people; the little presents from less influential ones; the ability to dazzle tradesmen into providing infinite credit.

'They will all start dunning me in a day or two,' he went on in a dull voice. 'I shall have to sell the freehold of Dragon Yard for what I can get. Unless your father . . . ?'

'I'm sorry for it, of course,' she said, sidestepping the question. 'But at least we will no longer be tied to the Court.'

'There's more. The King has banished me. I'm forbidden to come within twenty miles of London.' He walked from the window to the bed and glowered at her. 'It's this damned business with Dragon Yard,' he burst out. 'Poulton has been spreading poison at Court about me. Arlington and his creature Williamson are using it to undermine Chiffinch. Do you know what the gossips are saying? That I bribed Lucius to woo Mistress Hampney to get her support, and he killed her when she would not do as he wanted.'

Her fingers plucked at the embroidery on the coverlet. She kept her voice light. 'But isn't it true? That you asked Gromwell to woo her? Wasn't that why you were willing to pay the costs of his book and heaven knows what else? And have him here, in this house, at my table?'

'Well, yes — in a manner of speaking. I explained all this to you the other day, on the Bridge.' The confidence seeped away from his voice. 'But killing her? Why would he do that? He swore to me that he never laid a finger on her. Not in that way. Besides . . .'

Jemima studied his face. 'Besides what, sir?'

He swallowed. 'You can't still think that I was making love to her, can you? I —'

There was a knock on the door. Philip swore, stormed across the room and opened it. Hester was outside, carrying a tray. He picked up the jug of chocolate and threw it down the stairs. Hester scurried away, leaving her sobs in the air behind her.

He slammed the door and pushed the bolt across.

'I don't know what to believe,' she said coldly. In fact she was inclined to believe him now, but it was wiser not to tell him that. Not yet.

Philip made an effort to control his anger. 'I swear it was Gromwell who was Celia's lover, not me.'

'And what else did he do for you?'

'He helped Richard move her body, and

569

bury it in the ruins. If he'd left her where she was, he was afraid of being taken up for murder, and then the whole business about Dragon Yard would have come out.' He sat down on the bed. 'There's worse about Gromwell. You'd better know the whole of it. People have been whispering about the little clerk who died in a fire in his chambers at Clifford's Inn. He worked at the Fire Court, you know, so he must have known about Dragon Yard. People say he knew something about the widow's murder and tried to blackmail Gromwell about it.'

That was true enough, Jemima thought, about the blackmail at least: she had seen the proof of it locked away in Philip's cabinet, the blackmail letter that 'T.C.' had sent to Gromwell. And so, of course, had Philip. So he was not being entirely frank with her.

'And . . . and there was also some other folly about the widow's maid. It appears that the foolish girl hanged herself in Lambeth — from grief after her mother's death or perhaps her mistress's. But now they are saying that Gromwell killed her too, to stop her mouth about his wooing of the mistress.'

'Of course he killed the girl,' she said. 'And the clerk. And the whore.'

He shrugged. 'The King is persuaded that

570

all this is my fault. That I used Lucius as the monkey did the cat's paw, to scrape the nuts from the fire.'

'Gromwell's dead,' she pointed out, hoping she did not sound triumphant. 'They can't prove anything, and nor can he. Nor can the King. He can't blame you for what Gromwell might or might not have done.'

He shook his head. 'It's not a matter of proof. The thing that matters is what the King believes. According to Chiffinch, he thinks I tried to interfere with the running of the Fire Court, and that enrages him even more, because he wants the court to be seen as impartial. And the affray yesterday on London Bridge . . .'

'Affray?' she said. 'Is that what you call it? Gromwell is dead, killed by Mary, who was trying to help me. And you yourself killed my poor Mary.'

He reared away from her. 'I ran her through in self-defence, madam. I swear it. Even Chiffinch agrees with me there. What else could I have done? She lost her wits and ran mad. She could have killed you next.'

She almost laughed at such a ridiculous suggestion. She leaned forward and pointed at him. 'Why, sir, all this happened because of you and your friend Gromwell. I was only

571

there because the pair of you snatched me from my coach and held me in that dreadful place where I was nearly burned alive. As for your behaviour to me at the Fire Court —'

'Lucius thought —'

'Can't you think for yourself for once? You'll have to, now Gromwell is dead. He would have killed me if there had been any advantage in it to him. Between you, you made me miscarry our son. And so there's another murder to lay at Gromwell's door and yours. Your own child's.'

Exhausted, she sank back against the pillows. After a moment, and to her surprise, he sat down on the bed. He tried to take her hand, but she pulled hers away.

'I intended none of this,' he said gently. 'Not the first, not the last.'

'The murders, you mean?' she said. She felt the pain deep inside her, the absence. 'Our child's death?'

'I didn't want anyone to die.' Then Philip added, so quietly she had to strain to hear him, 'If I could live these last few weeks again . . .'

She watched the assurance flaking away from her husband like the shell from a hardboiled egg, exposing something white and flabby beneath. How different from this was the hero whom she had sworn to love, honour and obey in the church at Syre.

'And I — I'm sorry about the other thing,' he went on. 'I'm sorry that I didn't believe you when you said you were with child, and I'm sorry that you lost it.'

She turned her head away from him.

'Perhaps you're right — perhaps Gromwell killed Chelling and the maidservant in Lambeth,' Philip whispered. 'Indeed, he hinted as much to me . . . You remember that night when you comforted me?'

She nodded. Despite herself, her heart softened towards him. 'Was that the night when Chelling died?'

'Yes. They said it was an accident, but in my heart I knew it wasn't. I could see it in Gromwell's face when he told me of it, and I smelled burning on his clothes. He only meant to frighten the little man into keeping his mouth shut, not to kill him. It was an accident . . . But did he kill Celia Hampney, too? He swore that he didn't.' Philip looked at her, his face unhappy. 'Jemima, will you tell me what happened that day when Celia was murdered? What you did that afternoon? What you saw?'

The silence settled around them. Jemima stared at the blue and silver embroidery of the bed hangings. It was time to abandon the convenient fiction that fever had purged her memory of that afternoon when the Widow Hampney had died and all this had begun.

'Mary found me a hackney,' she said at last. 'I was angry with you — I own it. I thought you had gone to see that woman. I'd seen her letter, remember, and I knew where the meeting was, in Gromwell's chambers at Clifford's Inn. We went for a drive to Whitehall. It was hot and I had a fancy to go on the river because it was cooler.' She hesitated. 'And later we came ashore at the Savoy.' There was no reason to make this easy for him.

He persevered. 'Gromwell told me you went to Clifford's Inn. By yourself.'

'Then let us say that I did,' she said. 'I was distressed, of course, and it was on the spur of the moment. What did he tell you about me?'

'He said he saw you from the window when he was with Celia, and you came up his staircase, but he went out on the landing and stopped you from entering his chamber. He was half-undressed . . . He heard footsteps below so he bundled you out another way, by the fire-damaged staircase next door, to avoid scandal. You — you did not make it easy for him. When he came back, Celia was dead. Lying in her own blood.'

She stared at her husband. She had the measure of him now. For better or for worse, as the vows said. 'Gromwell told more lies than the devil, sir. He lied to you as he lied to everyone else. When the widow wouldn't do as he wanted, he fell into a rage and killed her as he did the others. Perhaps she threatened to betray your shabby little plot to the world. That's the long and the short of it. Whether he killed her after I went there or before is neither here nor there.'

He bowed his head. 'Perhaps you are right.'

After a moment, she surprised them both by taking his hand. 'What is done is done. We must make the best of it, sir. I suppose we shall give up the lease on this house and go to Syre. After all, we can afford to live nowhere else. We shall live very quietly, I expect, and perhaps our prayers for a child will at last be answered. My father will be pleased.'

CHAPTER FIFTY-ONE

So there was more laudanum, and another expensive visit from the physician.

Margaret nursed me when I allowed it, and Sam strutted about the house as if he were its master. In his own mind, he figured as the hero of the affair on London Bridge, on the grounds that he had rescued Cat and myself, and brought us to safety.

My patience ran out with him on Thursday. In practice, I told him, all he had done was spend money that wasn't his in the alehouse on the bridge, and spend more money at the tavern near Billingsgate, and bring me home in a hackney. And if he thought I hadn't noticed that he was more than half drunk by the end of it, he was even more of a fool than I thought he was.

By this time I had rebelled against Margaret's tyranny and come downstairs to the parlour. As a compromise, I wore a velvet cap on my head, as well as a gown and slippers. I also permitted Margaret to drape me with blankets. But at least I was no longer in bed. The laudanum kept the pain at bay, though it plugged up my bowels and gave me bad dreams. Still, the price was worth paying, at least for now.

I sent Sam to Whitehall with a letter for Mr Williamson. I gave him a brief and strictly factual account of what had happened, both at the Fire Court and on London Bridge, with certain omissions, particularly in relation to Cat. I did not receive a reply.

I also gave Sam orders to call at Henrietta Street and enquire after her. Hakesby told him that she was in her closet and he could not see her. According to Hakesby, she appeared very little hurt, apart from cuts and bruising, but no thanks were due to me, who had led her quite unnecessarily into the dangers that had nearly cost her her life.

'Tough as an old boot, that one,' Sam said when he passed on the message to me. 'Mark my words, sir, she'll outlive the lot of us.'

He also told me the news: that Lady Limbury's maid, the one I had seen at the Fire Court yesterday, had run amok on London Bridge and killed Gromwell with a blow to the head, and that Limbury had run her through with his sword before she could turn on himself and his wife. He had also heard that Lady Limbury had been in great pain, so probably the maid had attacked her as well.

I chewed over the information in my mind. From what I had seen of Lady Limbury's maid at the Fire Court yesterday morning, she had seemed devoted to her mistress, to the extent of risking her master's anger by trying to help her. Why would she attack her mistress? It was surely more likely that the maid had been trying to protect her from Gromwell and Limbury.

Not that it mattered. The dead cannot defend themselves. Besides, a gentleman's word weighs more heavily in the scales of justice than a servant's.

No more bad dreams, I promised myself in the small hours of Friday morning, no more laudanum, despite the pain from my burns and bruises.

I lay awake in the darkness. I heard the cocks crowing over the middens of London, and then the relentless chattering of the birds. I pulled back the bed curtains and watched the light, grey and dirty like the river on a cloudy day, returning to my chamber. I told myself over and over that I could bear the pain if I set my mind to it.

The sounds of the Savoy coming slowly to life gradually surrounded me. I heard Margaret crossing the hall and the rattle of the bolts on the door to the yard. I fell asleep. There were no more dreams, thank God, or not that I noticed.

When I woke, it was broad day. I lay there a moment or two, relishing the absence of pain all the more because I knew it would not last. I was at peace with myself for the first time in days, if not weeks. My mind was empty of clutter. Perhaps that was why those three words chose to float serenely through my mind like leaves on a stream, just as they had on Tuesday.

The mark of Cain.

My father's words, from the last time I had seen him, the last time we talked. Everything went back to there: to the day he had gone to Clifford's Inn and then, that evening, rambled on and on to me about what he had seen, until I was sick of his childish nonsense, and perhaps ashamed to own such a man as my father. If he was looking down on me from Paradise, perhaps my father was ashamed of me.

I swung my legs out of bed, ignoring the stabs of pain, and found my gown and slippers. I took up my father's Bible from the night table and went slowly downstairs, one step at a time. Sam and Margaret were arguing about something in the kitchen. I went into the parlour.

There was an old press cupboard in the corner. The open box containing my father's possessions was on the top shelf. I took it down and put it on the table, with the Bible beside it. I sat in the chair and picked through the contents. I was slow and clumsy. Both my hands were bandaged now.

Here was all that remained of a life. The pieces of type, the scarred folding knife and the rag looked smaller and shabbier than before. So did the Bible. I took up the book and it opened at the end to show me my mother's hair pinned to the back cover. I turned to the beginning.

In the beginning God created the heaven and the earth.

Genesis, chapter one, verse one. My father had read his Bible every day of his life, apart from his last weeks when he could no longer decode the black marks on the paper let alone find any meaning in them. Even then, though, he would hold the book open on his lap and turn the pages mechanically, as a Papist tells the beads of his rosary. He had known his Bible as intimately as a man knows the body of his lover. He had found comfort in touching it.

Genesis, chapter four. Cain kills his brother Abel. God condemns him to wander the earth as a fugitive and a vagabond. That is Cain's punishment for murdering his brother. God forbids anyone to shorten his punishment by killing him, by granting him the easier fate of a swift death.

And the Lord set a mark upon Cain lest any finding him should kill him.

Yes, I thought, I see what my father meant at last, and the knowledge shocked me. I closed the book, went to the door and shouted for Sam.

Sam and I took another jolting, painful ride in a hackney. With a heroic effort, he said nothing in the gloom of the coach's interior, but he stared reproachfully at me, and that was words enough. I was meant to be lying in my own bed, with Margaret fussing over me and Sam guarding me.

At Whitehall, I gave him money to pay off the driver and let him help me out of the coach. People stared at us as we made our slow way past the guards at the gate. One soldier made as if to stop us, but his sergeant knew me, and laid a hand on the man's arm to restrain him.

It was worse in the Great Court. People

581

pointed at us. I heard someone tittering. Sam and I made a moving tableau of infirmity — the cripple with only one leg and his crutch, and a man with a maimed face, shabby clothes and the gait of an old man. It must have been hard for them to tell who was supporting whom.

I sent Sam to enquire for Mr Williamson. We were directed to Lord Arlington's office. I waited in the yard, propped against a mounting block, while Sam took my message to Williamson, begging the favour of a word with him. I didn't think that Williamson would appreciate my calling at my lord's office. Those of us who worked for him at Scotland Yard rarely ventured to my lord's unless our master commanded us to wait on him there.

It was a fine morning, and the mounting block was in the sun. While I waited, I closed my eyes and let tiredness roll over me. I don't know how long I was there. I felt something poke my shoulder and opened my eyes with a start.

Williamson was in front of me, his back to the sun so his face was little more than a shadow under his hat. Sam hovered behind him, keeping a discreet distance.

'Forgive me, sir,' I said, trying to rise. 'I must have —'

582

'Sit down,' he said, running his eyes over me. 'God's wounds, you look even worse than before. Where's your periwig?'

'In the Thames, sir. Thank you for —'

'I might have known. You'll have to get another. You'll pay for this one yourself.'

I wondered how I would manage that.

Williamson sniffed. 'I don't know what you did on Wednesday, but it's the talk of the town. And the Court. Half the bridge burned down. A gentleman stabbed to death by a servant maid, who is then killed in her turn by a Groom of the Stool. Lady Limbury made to look a fool in public. Or worse. Good God, what a mess.'

'Yes, sir,' I said.

'And that business at the Fire Court earlier in the day. I hate to think what her ladyship's father will say when he hears the whole story. Sir George Syre has many friends at Court, and he dotes on his daughter.' Williamson made a noise in the back of his throat which was the next best thing to a dog's growl. 'The only mercy is that no one seems to have realized that you were my man. You're mentioned in two reports of what happened, but not by name.'

He paused. My eyes were adjusting to the light. To my amazement I saw that he was smiling.

583

'So,' he went on. 'God willing, it has worked out well, or it should do. Limbury is disgraced, and out of the Bedchamber. He and his wife have already left London. The King isn't at all pleased with Chiffinch. It won't last, but my Lord Arlington finds it particularly convenient at present.'

I felt a rush of anger. For Williamson, all this — the killings, the sufferings of the living — had been reduced to a squabble for power and influence over the King in the back stairs of Whitehall. 'But, sir,' I said, 'there are also the murders.'

'You said Gromwell was responsible for them. In that case, it's fortunate that he's dead. For all of us. The maidservant did us a favour.'

'It is possible that he didn't kill Celia Hampney.'

He scowled. 'You said she was killed in his chamber.'

'Yes, but —'

'Then who else could have done it?'

I opened my mouth and paused. The mark of Cain. But what did that amount to? And did I really want to explain about my father's part in this, which I had concealed for so long? I said, 'I'm not sure, sir. It's just that we have no actual proof that he

584

did. I'm sure he helped to move the body but —'

'Of course we have proof,' Williamson interrupted. 'You tell me she was killed in Gromwell's chamber. You also say that he was responsible for moving the corpse and leaving it for carrion among the ruins. You surely don't dispute that the threat of exposure led him to kill Chelling and the maidservant?'

He paused, and that was my last chance. I didn't take it.

'Of course Gromwell killed her as well as the others,' he said. 'The evidence we have would convince a judge and jury.'

I bowed my head.

'Go away, Marwood,' Williamson said, not unkindly. 'By the way, the King declined to sign the warrant that Chiffinch gave him.'

I looked up. 'What warrant, sir?'

'The one to remove you from your clerkship to the Board of the Red Cloth. Either he wanted to cross Chiffinch or he has a kindness for you. Though I can't think why that should be. Either way, the post is still yours.'

I stared stupidly at him, gradually absorbing the meaning of his words.

'Go home,' Williamson said. 'I'll see your salary is paid as usual. Restore yourself to health and make yourself look respectable. Then come back to work.'

He strode away without a backward glance.

Chapter Fifty-Two

To a tavern with Sam, for the poor man deserved something for his service and for my bad temper, and then home by water.

Cat Lovett was waiting for me in the parlour. She was talking to Margaret, and the smells of dinner rose from the kitchen.

I was glad to sit down, though I felt better than I had expected. Perhaps the ale I had taken in King Street numbed some of the pain. It helped with the craving, too. I wanted laudanum, but so far I had kept to my resolution during the night.

'Mr Hakesby has sent me with some money,' Cat said. 'Not all of it, but something on account.'

She laid a small paper packet on the table. I let it lie there. I was glad to have it. Though Williamson had promised to pay my salary, I was running short of ready money.

'Ten pounds,' she said. 'He wants a

receipt.' She added quickly, as if defending herself from an accusation I hadn't thought of making, 'That's why I waited for your return.'

'I need paper and pen.'

But Margaret said that dinner would be spoiled if she did not bring it now, so I told her to serve it. Without my saying a word, she assumed both that Cat would dine with me and that Cat was no longer to be considered merely as another servant.

When the food was on the table, she and Sam left us alone. Cat and I sat opposite each other. At first we ate and drank in silence, seeking refuge in food. The bandages on my hand made eating slow and messy. She studiously avoided watching me. She seemed more restless than usual, shifting on her stool and glancing about the room. I knew she must blame me for what had happened to her on Wednesday, and indeed for dragging her into the Fire Court affair in the first place.

When we had run out of silence, we talked like polite strangers, enquiring at length about each other's health. That didn't last long.

'Margaret said you went to Whitehall this morning,' she said, breaking the second silence, which had grown even more uncomfortable than the first.

I told her what Williamson had said.

'It's over?' Cat said. 'All of it?'

'I think so.' Without my intending it, my hand touched the scars on my cheek. 'For Williamson and Chiffinch, at any rate. And the rest of them at Court.'

'It's all to the good, sir, surely? You'll get another wig, and we may go on with the rest of our lives.'

'But what about my father?'

'What about him?' Cat was not a woman to mince words and make palatable nothings out of them. 'You can't bring him back to life.'

'There's something I didn't tell you. After the wagon went over him, as he lay dying, the crossing-sweeper told me he asked where the rook was.'

' "Rook"?' She stared blankly at me. 'The bird? Or the piece in chess? Or did he mean to cheat?'

'It was his word for lawyers. From their black plumage, I suppose, and because he felt they'd cheated him out of his liberty and life. He said Clifford's Inn was a rookery. A place of rooks.'

'And therefore you think one of them killed him?'

I shook my head. 'Not killed. Caused his

death. There's a difference.'

'You're chopping words and meanings, sir. What's the profit in that?' Cat glanced at the unopened packet of money on the table. 'I must go. Shall we finish our business?'

'In a moment. The sweeper thought that someone was chasing after my father. A rook, I think, if his last words meant anything. One of the lawyers, one of the people he had seen in Clifford's Inn.' I shrugged, which made me wince. 'It could have been Gromwell, who came from the rookery. You see, Gromwell wouldn't have realized my father's wits were wandering — he would have thought him a potential witness, someone who had seen the body of Celia Hampney in his chamber. But in his hurry my father stumbled and fell under the wagon. And then he wasn't a problem for Gromwell any more.'

'Let it go,' she said. 'This is madness. You're like a dog with a bone, except there's some purpose to that.'

'And there's another thing. The woman my father followed into Clifford's Inn. I told you. You remember? He thought she was my mother when she was young. But he told me that she bore the mark of Cain, and that confused him. Why would my mother have borne the mark of Cain?'

'What did he mean by it?'

I shrugged, and wished I hadn't because of the pain it caused. 'What does it mean to you?'

Cat said slowly, 'The Lord set the mark on Cain so no one would kill him. He was condemned to live and wander the face of the earth for ever.'

'You saw Lady Limbury's birthmark. Was that my father's mark of Cain? If there's any meaning at all to what my father said, it must surely be that he followed Lady Limbury into Clifford's Inn about the time of the murder.'

'Are you really saying that this means Lady Limbury killed Celia Hampney?' She laid down her knife and lowered her voice. 'And Gromwell committed two more murders to protect her? For God's sake, sir. If you say that abroad, they'll throw you into Bedlam. Or worse.'

'But don't you see? Even if it was Lady Limbury who killed Mistress Hampney, Gromwell faced ruin, and perhaps the gallows as her accessory. And if he saw my father following her to his chambers around the time of the murder, that explains why he chased after him the next day — to stop him talking, or at least find out who he was, what he had seen. My father fled from him,

591

as he fled from anyone he thought was a lawyer, and Gromwell pursued — and then came that cursed wagon.'

A church clock was striking the hour.

'It's one o'clock,' Cat said. 'Mr Hakesby will be worried.'

'I can't prove anything,' I said. 'So it doesn't matter. I can't tell anyone, except you.'

'And I shall do my best to forget it. So should you. We'll never know which of them killed that poor woman. And it doesn't matter now, not to you, not to me. Will you count the money?'

Her voice was hard and brisk. I pushed aside my plate. The little parcel of coins was secured with string. Hindered by the bandages, I fumbled at the knot.

'Let me do it.'

I shook my head. I was cross with her for the way she had brushed aside my confidence. Besides, I thought I heard in her voice the note of pity that she sometimes used to Hakesby. I could not bear her pity.

The knot resisted me. I stretched out my hand to the box of my father's possessions and drew it towards me. I took out his knife. After a struggle, I managed to open it. The blade and the corresponding slot in the handle were caked with a powdery substance. I scraped part of it with my nail, dislodging a shower of tiny rust spots. There was something else there, too, caught between the handle and the blade, just above the hinge that kept them together.

Yellow threads.

I stared at them, my mouth open, my face pricking with sweat. Perhaps Lady Limbury hadn't killed Celia Hampney, after all. Nor had Gromwell.

I looked up. Cat was watching me. I knew how fast her mind worked. Very slowly, I began to close the knife.

Perhaps Gromwell had chased after my father for another reason. Yellow silk, from a woman's gown?

'Stop,' she said. 'Let me see.'

The moment trembled in the balance. Perhaps I should have closed the knife and slipped it in my pocket. Perhaps I should have taken the money, signed the receipt and ordered Cat to leave the house. Instead I passed the knife across the table.

She examined it. 'Whose is this? Where did you find it?'

I could have lied. I could have tried to bluster it out. But I owed her something for all that had happened, and the truth was better than nothing. 'It was my father's. It was in his pocket when he died.'

Cat frowned. 'I don't understand. Why?'

I knew what she was asking: why would my father have stabbed Celia Hampney? 'Because his straying wits took him to strange places. Because he believed that she was a whore. She was a sinner, and he was punishing her for her sins. To prevent her leading men to sin. Because he felt it was God's will. His God was very terrible.'

God the father. We never really know our fathers. We think we do, but we don't.

'For God's sake, sir,' Cat said, closing the knife and pushing it across the table towards me. 'Throw it in the river and be done with it.'

After Cat had gone, I stayed in my chair with the box of my father's pitifully few possessions before me. The afternoon passed slowly. I tried not to think about laudanum. Margaret came to clear the table. I shouted at her, and she went away. Two flies buzzed among the remains of our dinner. Something scratched behind the wainscot.

Had I ever really known Nathaniel Marwood? I used to think so. First there had been the giant of my childhood, the next best thing to God, whose word was law and whose powers were limitless. When I was young, I had never entertained the idea that my father, or indeed his God, might be wrong. My father could be stern, even cruel — I bore scars on my back to attest to that — and he had often been as tyrannical and capricious as Jehovah. When he had seen sin in me, or in anyone else, he had been savage in his efforts to root it out, whatever the cost to the sinner.

Then came the broken man who had emerged from prison last year, drifting through his second childhood towards its inevitable end. During the years of his imprisonment our roles had imperceptibly reversed themselves, and it had become my duty to care for him. He had seemed greatly softened by his tribulations — almost a different man, capable of a sweetness I had never known before. At the same time, he had been a burden. He had irritated me. But I had loved him. I mourned his passing.

But a few threads of yellow silk changed all that, together with the shower of rust spots, dried blood. Yellow as the sun, red as fire . . .

Now, for the first time, I realized there had been no division between the two men in the same body, between the tyrant of my childhood and the gentle, decayed fool of his last years. When my father had stumbled into Gromwell's chamber, he had found sin in the person of Mistress Hampney, waiting for her lover, displayed on a couch in all her lewdness.

Celia Hampney had been a small woman. She had been taken by surprise. My father had been large and still vigorous in body. Had she tried to stand up? Had he thrown her back on the sofa? Had he held her down in her death throes, clamped his hand over her mouth?

Dear God, I thought, the ugliness of it, the horror, the sadness.

He had told me what had happened, just as he had told me everything else. *The poor, abandoned wretch. Her sins found her out, and she suffered the punishment for them.* He had taken out his knife and rooted out the sin. We had found blood on his shirt cuff that last evening, but no sign of a wound on him.

As so often in my childhood, my father had appointed himself God's agent and meted out the punishment to the sinner. Perhaps he desired the punishment of whores because he desired them too much. He had been a man of strong appetites. He punished his own lusts.

They say it's a wise father that knows his own child. Yes, and the contrary is also true.

CHAPTER FIFTY-THREE

When she left Marwood, Cat walked along the Strand with the receipt for the money in her pocket. She didn't hurry back to the drawing office, though it was perfectly true that Hakesby would be worrying about her.

The affair was over and done with, at last. Let the dead bury the dead. Marwood was probably right but, if he had any sense, he would forget what he knew and what he suspected. He would cover the more visible of his injuries with a new wig and go back to Whitehall to earn his living. What else was there for him to do?

For the moment, life went on. She would try to forget what Marwood had told her. She would push her own injuries deep inside her to join the others that lay there in the darkness. For most of the time, it was a simple matter to pretend that they weren't there.

As she waited to cross the road, she forced

her mind into a different direction. She thought with satisfaction of the plan for a set of stables at Dragon Yard that Hakesby had entrusted to her. If he would permit it, she would start work this afternoon.

Cat turned up towards Henrietta Street and Covent Garden. For a moment, another thought crossed her mind like a cloud drifting over the sun. She hadn't told Marwood her news, that she had agreed to marry Hakesby.

There had been other, more pressing things to talk about. If she saw Marwood again, she would mention it. In any case, there was no hurry. The marriage was purely a business matter between her and Hakesby, and there was no reason why the news should interest Marwood.

Besides, it was not something she cared to think about, let alone talk about, unless she had to.

Marwood, she murmured aloud. James Marwood.

ABOUT THE AUTHOR

Andrew Taylor is the author of a number of crime novels, including the ground-breaking Roth Trilogy, which was adapted into the acclaimed TV drama *Fallen Angel,* and the historical crime novels *The Ashes of London, The Silent Boy, The Scent of Death* and *The American Boy,* a No.1 *Sunday Times* bestseller and a 2005 Richard & Judy Book Club Choice.

He has won many awards, including the CWA John Creasey New Blood Dagger, an Edgar Scroll from the Mystery Writers of America, the CWA Ellis Peters Historical Award (the only author to win it three times) and the CWA's prestigious Diamond Dagger, awarded for sustained excellence in crime writing. He also writes for the *Spectator* and *The Times.*

He lives with his wife Caroline in the Forest of Dean.

The employees of Thorndike Press hope you have enjoyed this Large Print book. All our Thorndike, Wheeler, and Kennebec Large Print titles are designed for easy reading, and all our books are made to last. Other Thorndike Press Large Print books are available at your library, through selected bookstores, or directly from us.

For information about titles, please call:
(800) 223-1244

or visit our website at:
gale.com/thorndike

To share your comments, please write:
Publisher
Thorndike Press
10 Water St., Suite 310
Waterville, ME 04901

SOCIAL INSTITUTIONS AND SOCIAL CHANGE

An Aldine de Gruyter Series of Texts and Monographs

EDITED BY

Michael Useem • James D. Wright

Larry Barnett, **Legal Construct, Social Concept: A Macrosociological Perspective on Law**

Vern L. Bengtson and W. Andrew Achenbaum, **The Changing Contract Across Generations**

Remi Clignet, **Death, Deeds, and Descendants: Inheritance in Modern America**

Mary Ellen Colten and Susan Gore (eds.), **Adolescent Stress: Causes and Consequences**

Rand D. Conger and Glen H. Elder, Jr., **Families in Troubled Times: Adapting to Change in Rural America**

Joel A. Devine and James D. Wright, **The Greatest of Evils: Urban Poverty and the American Underclass**

G. William Domhoff, **The Power Elite and the State: How Policy is Made in America**

Paula S. England, **Comparable Worth: Theories and Evidence**

Paula S. England, **Theory on Gender/Feminism on Theory**

Richard F. Hamilton and James D. Wright, **The State of the Masses**

J. Rogers Hollingsworth and Ellen Jane Hollingsworth, **Care of the Chronically and Severely Ill: Comparative Social Policies**

Gary Kleck, **Point Blank: Guns and Violence in America**

David Knoke, **Organizing for Collective Action: The Political Economies of Associations**

Dean Knudsen and JoAnn L. Miller (eds.), **Abused and Battered: Social and Legal Responses to Family Violence**

Theodore R. Marmor, **The Politics of Medicare** (*Second Edition*)

Clark McPhail, **The Myth of the Madding Crowd**

Clark McPhail, **Acting Together: The Organization of Crowds**

John Mirowsky and Catherine E. Ross, **Social Causes of Psychological Distress**

Steven L. Nock, **The Costs of Privacy: Surveillance and Reputation in America**

Talcott Parsons on National Socialism (*Edited and with an Introduction by Uta Gerhardt*)

Carolyn C. and Robert Perrucci, Dena B. and Harry R. Targ, **Plant Closings: International Context and Social Costs**

James T. Richardson, Joel Best, and David G. Bromley (eds.), **The Satanism Scare**

Alice S. Rossi and Peter H. Rossi, **Of Human Bonding: Parent-Child Relations Across the Life Course**

David G. Smith, **Paying for Medicare: The Politics of Reform**

Martin King Whyte, **Dating, Mating, and Marriage**

James D. Wright, **Address Unknown: The Homeless in America**

James D. Wright and Peter H. Rossi, **Armed and Considered Dangerous: A Survey of Felons and Their Firearms**

James D. Wright, Peter H. Rossi, and Kathleen Daly, **Under the Gun: Weapons, Crime, and Violence in America**

Mary Zey, **Banking on Fraud: Drexel, Junk Bonds, and Buyouts**

CARE OF THE CHRONICALLY AND SEVERELY ILL

Comparative Social Policies

J. Rogers Hollingsworth and Ellen Jane Hollingsworth
EDITORS

ALDINE DE GRUYTER
New York

About the Editors

J. Rogers Hollingsworth is Professor of Sociology and History and Chairperson of the Program in Comparative History at the University of Wisconsin-Madison. He is author of several books on comparative medical systems. His most recent books on medical care are *The Political Economy of Medicine* and *State Intervention in Medical Care: The Consequences for France, Great Britain, Sweden, and the United States* (co-author).

Ellen Jane Hollingsworth, the Research Director of the Mental Health Research Center of the University of Wisconsin-Madison, is the author of several books and numerous articles on organizations providing social services to the underrepresented (e.g., welfare clients, those needing legal assistance, the severely mentally ill, etc.).

Copyright © 1994 Walter de Gruyter, Inc., New York.

ALDINE DE GRUYTER
A division of Walter de Gruyter, Inc.
200 Saw Mill River Road
Hawthorne, New York 10532

This publication is printed on acid-free paper ∞

Library of Congress Cataloging-in-Publication Data

Care of chronically and severely ill : comparative social policies /
   J. Rogers Hollingsworth and Ellen Jane Hollingsworth, editors.
        p.   cm. — (Social institutions and social change)
     Includes bibliographical references and index.
     ISBN 0-202-30485-X (alk. paper). — ISBN 0-202-30486-8 (pbk. :
alk. paper)
     1. Handicapped—Services for—United States.   2. Handicapped—
Care—United States.   3. Chronically ill—Services for—United
States.   4. Chronically ill—Care—United States.   5. Handicapped—
Services for—Great Britain.   6. Handicapped—Care—Great Britain.
7. Chronically ill—Services for—Great Britain.   8. Chronically
ill—Care—Great Britain.   I. Hollingsworth, J. Rogers, (Joseph
Rogers), 1932–   .   II. Hollingsworth, Ellen Jane.   III. Series.
HV1552.C37   1994
362.1'6—dc20   93-38398
                                                                      CIP

Manufactured in the United States of America

10 9 8 7 6 5 4 3 2 1

Dedicated with love, to
Pearl R. Hollingsworth and Richard A. Bywaters

Contents

Acknowledgments

Professor Jens Alber, now of the University of Konstanz, and Rogers Hollingsworth, University of Wisconsin, working together at the Max-Planck-Institute in Köln initiated a project comparing care for non-traditional groups across countries. The Directors of the Institut, Fritz Scharpf and Renate Mayntz, encouraged their interests through support of a international conference in November 1990. The papers included here (revised and updated) were among those presented at that time. We wish to thank many people for their assistance with this project: other conference attendees such as Christa Altenstetter, Nicholas Bosanquet, Marion Döhler, Willi Ruppert, Brigitte Schenkluhn, Malcolm Taylor, and Ernst von Kardorff; and people whose discussions and writings have been helpful, Odin Anderson, Lee Benson, James Bjorkman, James R. Greenley, Jerald Hage, Douglas Webber, and Burton Weisbrod. We are especially grateful to Jens Alber for the stimulating discussions about this project, both before and after the 1990 conference.

Foreword

THEODORE R. MARMOR

Broadly speaking there are two quite different reasons for comparing social policies across nations—each of which calls for a rather different research strategy. First, there is what is termed *policy learning* (Klein 1983; Marmor, Bridges, and Hoffman 1978). That is, one investigates the social policies of other countries to draw lessons that can be applied at home. This approach has a long history, such as the reports by American presidential committees and European royal commissions, which often draw on the experience of other countries. Good examples are the United States' Report of the Committee on Economic Security of 1935 and Canada's Royal Commission on Health Services of 1964–1966 (Committee on Economic Security 1935; Royal Commission on Health Services 1964: 482–91).

Second, there is what is called *policy understanding*. Here the emphasis is not so much on policy learning as on explanation. For example, if we are to achieve an understanding of the factors that shape the evolution of a social security system, it is unlikely that we can do so by looking at any one country in isolation. Are the key factors that explain policy the level of industrialization and the political mobilization of workers? The history of Britain, examined in isolation, might suggest they are, but comparative studies indicate otherwise (Wilensky 1975; Flora, Alber, and Kohl 1977; Carrier and Kendall 1977). Similarly, it has been argued that the power of the British medical profession rests on its access to Whitehall (Eckstein 1960), while comparative analysis shows that the nature of that power is largely independent of the precise relationship between doctors and bureaucracy (Marmor and Thomas 1972). American critics of Canadian health insurance, to cite a contemporary example, suggest that Canada's relative success in restraining medical care expenditures rests on its distinctive political culture, not its single-payer form of finance. Comparative research supports the latter interpretation. In short, comparative studies may be essential if misleading conclusions are not to be drawn from single-case studies about the making or evolution of public policy.

The research strategy associated with the first of these two approaches, policy learning, to judge from the literature, is a microstrategy with a focus on countries somewhat similar to each other and the concern is usually a single issue. This single-issue focus, of course, keeps the number of cases down. The primary interest of such investigations is not with the nature of the overall social policy *system*, since it is implausible to assume that a total system can be transplanted from one country to another, but with a discrete area of policy. In turn, this means comparing countries where similarity is understood in terms of economic development, social organization, and political ideology or culture. If the focus of concern is the transplantability of ideas, models, or specific policies, it is clearly essential that the compared environments not be too different.

The research strategy associated with the second approach, policy understanding, is more of a macrostrategy, sometimes using most different countries and variation in large numbers of variables. The nature of the analysis positively requires differences in the economic development, social organization, or political ideology of the countries being compared. It is obviously impossible to test the significance of a specific factor if it is common to the national cases being examined. Large numbers of cases, insofar as they allow a statistical analysis of the factors concerned, are an additional advantage of such studies.

A variant of the most-different-system approach addresses an admittedly contrasting sociopolitical community. It compares one set of practices (problems, or programs) with those of another country, and highlights the cultural and other factors that set the two societies apart. Comparing one's own society with a profoundly different one is a way of illuminating one's own national circumstances; we see ourselves more clearly by asking similar questions in different settings. Anthropologists do this for a living, but the anthropological practice has its own tradition of caution in drawing any policy lessons at all. The legitimate purpose of this analytical variant is intellectual illumination without any promise of policy transplantation.

The inclination to use cross-national research in attempts to find solutions to the increasingly serious problems in the field of health is growing. This partly results from concern about the costs of medical care in advanced industrial countries, and is clearly evidenced in the choice of topic and structure for this volume. Health expenditures constitute one of the most powerful sources of strain within contemporary welfare states, making matters of change and choice both urgent and important. Increases in the proportion of public expenditures spent on social welfare policies may make a preemptive claim upon government resources or, by straining the capabilities of states to meet them, may even trigger political transformations. It is this context that lends urgency to the evident international preoccupation with the structure of public health–related programs.

Sometimes comparative policy research reveals what is possible, not what is either normatively desirable or practically transplantable. Such work provides, as we have noted, illumination rather than indoctrination. Sometimes such research produces seemingly transplantable policies, but the effects are so difficult to disentangle from other forces that learning whether such a policy would be appropriate is quite difficult. This is a case of temptation without satisfaction.

Cross-national research is difficult, costly, and time-consuming (see, for example, Marmor, Bridges, and Hoffman 1983:Ch. 2). Only compelling, expected intellectual returns justify both the costs and the difficulty of identifying comparable circumstances and actually doing the cross-national research. When the expected benefits are policy learning, the issue is whether the prospects are favorable enough to warrant the expected costs of investigation. In other instances of cross-national policy research, the aspiration is for significant tests of social science theories that would be impossible within a single national research framework. Cross-national research in health reveals instances of all of these approaches.

The essays presented in this volume constitute a distinctive mix of the types of comparative policy studies discussed above. Individually, the essays are investigations of the systems of care for the frail elderly, the chronically mentally ill, and the homebound in both Britain and the United States. The issues addressed in each of the reports, in the context of coordination of the care systems, are (1) the number of clients and their needs; (2) the institutional and financial arrangements for care that prevail; and (3) the manner and types of client representation in the political process. However, the editors indicate that they have more in mind than simply description. The aim of these essays is also to discover, through cross-national comparison, whether certain factors are significant in explaining why these three vulnerable groups fare the way they do in the two countries. In particular, the essays seek to determine whether or not the type of medical system causes variation in the services that these groups receive. Britain and the United States have been chosen as case studies precisely because they have very different medical systems. Thus, studying them offers the chance to explore whether or not the type of medical system is a determining variable.

All three (Kane, Goldberg, Hollingsworth) of the papers on care for disabled groups in the United States call attention to the ways in which financing has shaped the provision of care, both by plan and by inadvertence. As well, the papers indicate the difficulties of providing both congregate and community-based care. For the frail elderly, for example, the nursing home remains the institution of choice not because of its desirable qualities, but because of a quirk of financing. Community-based care for the disabled has been very difficult to establish, and the gap between client need and client service is vast. Patchwork arrangements rather than well-coordinated systems are the result—brilliant here, abysmal there, mediocre and overburdened in the modal situation. Yet, as various scholars have demonstrated, the multiplicity of programs and purposes found in these social welfare programs are representative of the ways in which welfare policy is approached in the United States, where welfare policies have achieved much more than has commonly been recognized (Marmor, Mashaw, and Harvey 1990).

The trio of papers about Great Britain reinforces the pessimism of the American commentators. Epitomizing their theme, Bleddyn Davies argues that the British government—comparatively unified at the center and capable financially of devolving constraints on local actors—has been able to change the balance of care for frail populations away from institutional care toward home care. He gives great emphasis to the influence of "independent policy review bodies established by the government itself," implicitly highlighting the capacity of powerful central authorities to change existing policy. But he emphasizes as well the necessary dangers of such ample central authority. Where one body prescribes and others implement, the gap between promise and performance can be considerable. There is in Britain, Davies argues, a "wide knowledge gap: the absence among the managers of change of a *lingua franca* and body of evidence-based argument to guide their development of local systems." Preoccupied by the strains of "living with fiscal restraint," local authorities "underestimate the scale of the investments needed to make the community-based services bear heavier responsibilities." As a result, "beds in long-stay hospitals continue to be closed without satisfactory arrangements for those who had occupied them and without the transfer of sufficient funds for the development of alternative community-based services." And so it is clear to him that "the consequences of demographic and social changes are likely to make the balance of need and informal care resources progressively more adverse" in the years to come. Comparativists should heed Davies's pessimistic forecast. If a unified regime like Britain warrants such pessimism regarding the capacity to meet well-established needs for change, societies with less accountable political structures and equally compelling needs have no reason for optimism.

In summary, the papers on Britain and the United States show both great differences and similarities between the two countries. Historically, the British welfare state was far more ambitious than anything the Americans envisaged. Structurally, British politics lacks the extremely decentralized, fragmented features of American federalism and separation of powers.

The papers portray policy areas in both countries in which financial exigencies tend to overpower human ingenuity and flexibility. Services for the three vulnerable groups have been underfunded and inadequate. As the numbers of those who are frail elderly and have chronic health needs continue to increase, significant expansion of services seems unlikely. In neither country are social services and medical services sufficiently integrated. In both the United States and Great Britain, these disabled groups have had little opportunity to represent themselves, partly because they have little status and power.

From the standpoint of policymaking in the future, the import of comparative study is not simply understanding, or even sobriety. The purpose of study is not only to predict the future but, as Paul Starr once put the point, to "change it" (Starr and Marmor 1984:234). To do that requires going far beyond the description of the past. To make changes requires, at a minimum, understanding the determinants of change and the role of national policies (Marmor and Barr 1992).

This volume assumes that both policy learning and policy understanding are useful building blocks in the efforts to shape more desirable policy; it combines description and analysis as part of policy study. Its conclusions are toward the pessimistic: that institutional provision, however constituted, is difficult to alter in favor of community-based care; that community-based care settings are overwhelmed by demands and the lack of financial and human resources; that rhetoric and policy change take place somewhat apart from the realities of care for the vulnerable. The stagflation of the 1980s and 1990s underscores these difficulties.

A nation such as the United Kingdom, more familiar with systemwide welfare service thinking, may articulate client-responsive policies more clearly than the United States, a decentralized country with a different set of welfare sensitivities (Marmor et al. 1990). But in both nations, the reality is far from the ideal design for "best care." The ability to conceptualize an alternative care system for the disabled—even to have prestigious governmental documents addressing it over many years—means rather little in terms of making money available to get real services to real people in need.

Recognizing the difficulties of *increasing care* at any time, and especially in times of widespread discussion of privatizing health services and dismantling the welfare state, these authors have sought to develop interest among other social scientists and policymakers in services for disabled populations. They recognize that these and other disabled client groups, limited in their ability to advocate, require the support of others if their needs are to receive serious attention on the social policy agenda. This volume begins but does not finish that task in its special area within cross-national studies of the modern welfare state.

REFERENCES

Carrier, J. and I. Kendall. 1977. "The Development of Welfare States: The Production of Plausible Accounts." *Journal of Social Policy* 6:271–90.

Committee on Economic Security. 1935. *Report to the President*. Washington, DC: U.S. Government Printing Office.

Eckstein, H. 1960. *Pressure Groups Politics*. London: Allen and Unwin.

Flora, Peter, Jens Alber, and J. Kohl. 1977. "Zur Entwicklung des West-Europaischen Wohlfahrstsstaaten." *Politische Vierteljahrsschrift* 18:4.

Klein, R. 1983. "Strategies for Comparative Social Policy Research." Pp. 13–25 in *Health and Welfare States of Britain*, edited by A. Williamson and G. Room. London: Heinemann.

Marmor, T. R. and Michael Barr. 1992. "Making Sense of the National Health Insurance Reform Debate." *Yale Law and Policy Review* 10:228–82.

Marmor, T. R., A. Bridges, and W. L. Hoffman. 1983. "Comparative Politics and Health Policies: Notes on Benefits, Costs, and Limits." Pp. 45–57 in *Political Analysis and American Medical Care*, edited by T. R. Marmor. Cambridge and New York: Cambridge University Press.

Marmor, T. R., J. L. Mashaw, and P. L. Harvey. 1990. *America's Misunderstood Welfare State: Persistent Myths, Enduring Realities*. New York: Basic Books.

Marmor, T. R., and David Thomas. 1972. "Doctors, Politics and Pay Disputes: Pressure Group Politics Revisited." *British Journal of Political Science* 2:421–22.

Royal Commission on Health Services. 1964. *Royal Commission on Health Services*, Vol. 1. Ottawa: Queen's Printer.

Starr, Paul and T. R. Marmor. 1984. "The United States: A Social Forecast." Pp. 234–54 in *End of Illusion: Medical Care in Post-War Democracies, 1940–1980*, edited by V. Rodwin, J. Kimberly, and J. Kervasduoe. Berkeley: University of California Press.

Wilensky, H. L. 1975. *The Welfare State and Equality*. Berkeley: University of California Press.

Chapter 1

Challenges in the Provision of Care for People with Chronic and Severe Illness

ELLEN JANE HOLLINGSWORTH and
J. ROGERS HOLLINGSWORTH

In the twentieth century, the medical systems of most Western, industrialized countries have been predominantly oriented toward services for clients who are fully functioning or likely to become fully functioning once they have received medical care. Of course, the medical systems have long served more than these populations, but the provision of medical care for employees and their families has been the dominant paradigm. However, as a result of demographic and technological changes, there is now an increasing number of disabled people with chronic and severe conditions requiring long-term medical and social services. This population includes those with illnesses not sufficiently incapacitating to require hospitalization in acute-care facilities for long periods of time. To date, advanced industrial societies have not developed the financing mechanisms, the trained personnel, or organizational settings to provide adequate services for the expanding populations with chronic and severe illness.

For example, although the proportion of the population age 75 and over is rapidly increasing, there has been insufficient attention devoted to the types of institutional arrangements appropriate to cope with the health needs of a frail elderly population—whether they are in nursing homes, in other congregate living settings, or in their own homes receiving home care. The number of elderly 85 and over is projected to grow in the United States by 106% from 1986–1990 to 2016–2020 (Rivlin and Wiener 1988; also see Aiken 1987). There is another expanding population requiring various types of home care. Partly as a result of technological change, many people survive illnesses and accidents that would at an earlier time have been fatal. They have chronic and serious illnesses or disabilities, but also are not sufficiently ill or disabled to require long-term hospital care. For this population, as well, most

1

advanced industrial societies have failed to develop satisfactory care plans.

Similarly, as a result of various factors—including rapidly changing drug therapy—many people who suffer from serious mental illness have been discharged from hospitals or asylums, or do not enter them. However, they are in need of community-based medical and social services. In short, medical advances have reduced mortality but have resulted in an expanding population with serious disabilities (Rivlin and Wiener 1988:33; Gruenberg 1977; Kramer 1980).

Focusing on the United States and Great Britain, the essays in this volume are concerned with services to three populations with chronic and severe disabilities: the frail elderly, the homebound under 65, and the seriously mentally ill. They use a comparative analytical framework to examine the system of both medical and social services for these groups.

The following six essays employ a common conceptualization of service systems, by analyzing similar topics: the degree to which there is comprehensiveness in the social and medical services for each disabled group, the degree to which there are coordinated services, and the structure and performance of the systems. These three topics work themselves out differently according to the type of disability and the national system, but by being sensitive to these themes, we improve our ability to conceptualize the achievements and limitations of care arrangements. The strategy of this analysis permits a form of matrix analysis, so that readers can discern both whether (1) medical and social services are the same for a disability group in both countries, and (2) medical and social services are the same for all three disability groups in the same country.

Knowledge about the desiderata for providing services to these disabled populations is relatively well developed. For example, there are sophisticated studies demonstrating that increased home care for the frail elderly in the United States is both desirable and affordable. Indeed, there are studies that demonstrate that increases in home care lead to decreases in the need for, use of, and cost of nursing homes for the frail elderly (Kemper et al. 1986; Zimmer, Groth-Juncker, and McCusker 1985; Weissert, Wan, Livieratos, and Katz 1980; Skellie, Mobley, and Coan 1982; *Washington Post*, June 28, 1993:A9). There are comparable studies from Great Britain, for this and other disability groups (Barker 1987). Similarly, there are several studies demonstrating the efficacy of alternative strategies of care for the chronically mentally ill (Bachrach 1980; Beiser, Shore, Peters, and Tatum 1985; Braun, Kochansky, Shapiro, Greenberg, Gudeman, Johnson, and Shore 1981; Mechanic and Aiken 1989; Weisbrod, Test, and Stein 1980).

There is, however, virtually no literature analyzing patterns of service delivery across disability groups, much less literature employing a common analytical framework to examine services for several disability groups in more than one country. Thus, these essays have evolved in order to assist with developing a broader perspective on services for these three populations.

Because of the fiscal crisis of the state, it is especially important that we focus on these three populations now, as their numbers and needs are increasing. In recent years, there has been extensive discourse about the future of welfare services, partly as a result of the fiscal problems facing many countries. In a number of advanced industrial societies, there have been serious proposals to privatize public services, to decentralize the welfare state, and to reduce the level of social services. How have services for disabled groups been affected by these debates? As groups not recognized as traditional clients of the core medical system of each country, have they fared poorly during the 1980s, losing services? Or, have they held their own, or even managed to garner additional resources? To frame the issue differently, to what extent have the disabled been marginalized, increasingly treated only at the periphery of the existing service systems, with only small jots of service? The following essays are designed to shed light on these questions.

COMPREHENSIVE AND COORDINATED SYSTEMS OF CARE

Conceptualizing a System of Care for People with Chronic and Severe Illness

In twentieth-century Europe and North America, much of our public policy focusing on care for the severely chronically ill has provided a medical model of care. For example, in the United States, Medicare and Medicaid have provided substantial funding for many people with chronic illness, but the emphasis has been essentially on providing medical services. However, it is extremely important as we address the health needs of those with severe chronic illness that a system of care focus very much not only on the delivery of medical services but also on the delivery of social services. The failure to emphasize the delivery of both types of services is a major shortcoming of the care systems for these populations.

Obviously, the elements of a system of medical and social care are numerous. They range from care in particular types of institutions to community-based care, including home care. Increasingly, in both Europe and North America, the goal of many policymakers is to keep people out of hospitals, nursing homes, and other types of institutions, and to care for them in the community and in their homes, and to use institutional care parsimoniously over the long term, only if absolutely necessary. But if such a perspective is to gain widespread currency, we need to be much more concerned with the elements making up community-based and home care services. Thus, in Table 1, we briefly suggest some of the key elements of such a system (Barker 1987; Zawadski and Ansak 1983).

The establishment of community-based and home services can provide alternatives to costly, perhaps inappropriate, institutional care. Services provided in the community or in the home may result in lower costs and better outcomes for clients, expressed in terms of morbidity and satisfaction. Community services need to be very flexible: They may be provided in the home of the client, at a special facility (such as a day hospital, a day care center, or a nutrition center), or in everyday work settings (if clients receiving assistance hold jobs). Some community-based services take place during conventional work hours, but others need to be available around the clock (e.g., crisis services, safe houses).

Table 1. Selected Elements of System of Care for People with Chronic and Severe Illness

Institutional Care	*Community Medical Services*
Acute-care hospitals	Physician services
Intermediate-type care	Therapy
Long-term care (e.g., nursing homes, mental hospitals)	Medical supervision
Day hospital services	*Home Medical and Social Services*
Medical surveillance	Chore services
Rehabilitation emphasis	Personal Care (feeding,
Respite admissions	dressing, bathing, mobility)
	Portable meals
Community Social Services	Respite care
Adult day care	Shopping assistance
Group exercise	Socialization (conversation, walks)
Housing assistance	Surveillance
Information and referral	Various types of nursing
Nutrition	
Personal care	
Recreation	
Socialization	
Transportation	
Vocational assistance	

Assessing a System of Care for People with Chronic and Severe Illness: Comprehensiveness and Coordination

In the following papers, the authors are concerned with examining systems of care in terms of how comprehensive they are and how coordinated services for clients are. In assessing comprehensiveness, three types of issues are raised: the extent to which an array of programs exists, the availability of resources to the programs, and the access of clients to programs. Thus, the authors ask to what extent there is a broad array of medical and social services for the three disabled groups, as well as the extent to which disabled groups have access to existing programs.

Of course, it is not enough that these elements simply be present. It is vital that they be coordinated with one another, that systemwide planning be undertaken to provide flexible, client-appropriate care. If the system is poorly coordinated, elements operate in isolation from each other and are inefficient. If there is to be effective care, the various parts of the system should be linked together and well coordinated.

For example, a frail elderly person living in a private apartment using home health services may require hospital or nursing home placement until health problems can be stabilized. Once the client is hospitalized, communication between the hospital and community-based medical and social service personnel should continue, in order to permit aftercare arrangements suited to the inpatient experience of the client. Information acquired during the inpatient stay should be shared with community-based providers in preparation for discharge, and information from community-based providers should be available, when needed, for inpatient care providers.

There are various possibilities for coordinating the types of care in a system. Two of the most common models are those which are highly centralized and those which are part of a network structure. There is much variation between these two models, which are depicted in Figure 1. The centralized model (shown on the left) has many guises, but the two most common are that (1) various services are vertically integrated into a single organization and (2) there are many separate organizations, each highly dependent on a single budget authority for financing services. In the latter instance, high resource dependency on a single authority can provide a high degree of coordination among various organizations because of the power of the purse.

Network coordination (shown on the right) tends to provide more flexibility, innovation, and customization of service then other modes of coordination. Because of the high degree of complexity of a care system and the high level of specialization among caregivers, it is very difficult to coordinate them in a vertically integrated organization. Thus, net-

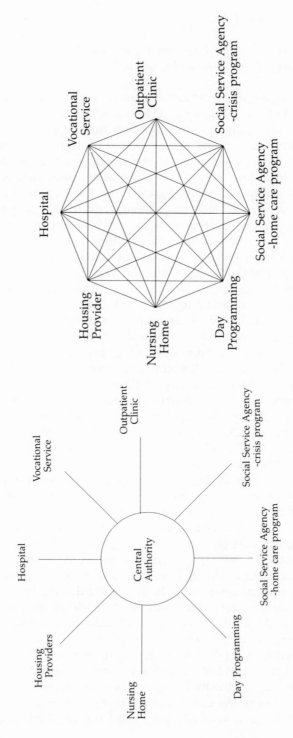

Figure 1. Ways of coordinating systems of care.

works are becoming more common for the delivery of these services. The characteristics of networks (i.e., the structural properties) may be shaped by environmental and task constraints, which in turn shape the performance of networks (Alter and Hage 1993). Because of the inadequacy of resources for care of those with chronic and severe illness, it often is difficult to attain a high level of coordination with a network model, as several of the following papers demonstrate. But whether coordination is by centralized control or though networks, the point to emphasize is the need for a coordinated system of care if the delivery of services is to be efficient and appropriate.

For many disabled people—be they frail elderly, homebound, or seriously mentally ill—who spend most of their lives in the community, episodes of institutional care may nevertheless occur. Such episodes may be few or numerous, brief or more long lasting. For all three of these disabled groups, effective community services should limit the need for institutional care, but its total avoidance is unlikely. Therefore, providing inpatient care in a manner sensitive to the long-term functioning of the client in the community is both therapeutic and humane.

Establishing and operating such a system of care, simple enough to conceptualize, is a tall order. The difficulties of establishing such a system have been particularly clear in both Great Britain and the United States with regard to the chronically mentally ill, as numerous psychiatric hospitals have closed and patients have been relocated to the community as the primary base of care. There have been efforts to have integrated management of resources, planning across the system, establishment of systemwide standards, need-based training and hiring of personnel, flexible and targeted budgeting. Here and there in the social welfare literature, there are descriptions of systems that work well (Stein, Diamond, and Factor 1990; Alter and Hage 1993; Barker 1987). But to establish any one of these elements is an enormous challenge. Simply to garner control of the revenue streams is a daunting proposition. The Robert Wood Johnson Foundation has fostered initiatives in nine major U.S. cities with regard to the seriously mentally ill, emphasizing coordinated budget management as the key to establishing care systems. The process of unifying funding streams has been extremely difficult, and the coordination of budgets across organizations has been even harder (Goldman, Morrissey, Ridgely, Frank, Newman, and Kennedy 1992).

All the essays that follow recognize the desirability of coordinating institutionalized care with care provided in the community. As sensitivity to coordination occurs, some psychiatric hospitals have developed day hospitals, and some community hospitals have developed home care programming (Richardson and Kovner 1987). At the same time, shifting more emphasis to community care requires developing accountability mechanisms for community organizations, with more emphasis on relating program activities to program goals and outcomes for clients. Since the provision of care in community-based settings is a relatively new paradigm, public authorities lack ways of implementing standard and meaningful measures of program performance even though there are a few sophisticated outcome studies. Not only must there be coordination between institutional care and community-based care, but within the community, medical and social services must be coordinated. For each of these three populations, a wide array of medical and social services needs to be provided, ideally in an integrated and comprehensively planned manner.

For example, for many people with serious mental illness, medical services should be integrated with social services, with the recognition that hospitalization, counseling, and medications should be provided with reference to services for activities of daily living, income maintenance, housing, and social and recreational programming. As an obvious example, it is probably not very useful to provide psychotherapy to someone with serious mental illness if the person lacks a home.

The issues of service integration tend to be more urgent in community-based settings, since institutional settings (1) require a less extensive array of types of services because of the severity of illness of clients, and (2) are likely to make fairly standardized provision of non-medical services. But in community settings, the issues of coordination and integration of services loom large. To communicate across organizational boundaries for people with serious mental illness about how changes in medications might affect vocational activities or to relate information about changes in living accommodation to those who prescribe medications may be costly in staff time. Because of the complexity of communication about care, involving so many individuals and specialties, important information about clients may not be properly factored into care plans.

Ideally, for each of these disabled populations (the frail elderly, those homebound with chronic illness, and the seriously mentally ill), services should be carried out by multidisciplinary teams, by specialists working together to provide individualized services for clients. The preferred service mode is for small teams consisting of different specialties to provide both medical and social services to disabled populations. Such ambitious programming of integrated social and medical services, necessitating the crossing of traditional disciplinary lines, and perhaps summoning into life new delivery structures, is difficult to achieve. It is especially difficult to integrate medical and social services when physicians, nurses, social workers, psychologists, and other professionals receive training in separate schools and are not socialized to pursue client needs without regard to specific academic disciplines.

United States and British Systems of Care for People with Chronic and Severe Illness

Traditionally, in Europe care for those with severe chronic illnesses has been provided through centralized state structures, whereas in the United States the central and local governments have been weakly involved in service delivery. Hence, in Britain the state has played a more important role in the coordination of services, while in the United States coordination has tended to be done more in the private sector. In the United States, many care services were long considered to be the responsibility of local voluntary organizations and charitable societies. And even after the federal government became more involved in financing care for the chronically ill, the delivery of services has been done by local authorities and private providers. Thus, the Americans have a care system consisting of a complex mix of governmental agencies, private nonprofit organizations, and for-profit agencies and clinics, all of which has led to more reliance on networks for the delivery of services. Whereas the British also use voluntary organizations, they have been less numerous and, as a result, the overall service system is less complex.

Overall, there is considerable variation in the care systems of these two countries. The Americans have historically placed more emphasis on being reactive, placing emphasis on curative and custodial care, while the British have placed more emphasis on rehabilitative services. In Britain, every citizen has a general practitioner (GP), and it is not uncommon for these doctors to make house calls, thus enhancing the capacity of the system to engage in preventive surveillance within the home. Moreover, the British have a long history of home nursing, which started with providing nursing for mothers in the home in the early twentieth century (Hollingsworth 1986; Klein 1983).

The following papers are very sensitive to these different traditions, and as they emphasize these traditions, they focus attention on three themes: (1) institutional and financial arrangements for care, (2) client numbers and needs, and (3) representation of clients in the political arena.

The problems related to institutional and financial arrangements for care and the consequences of these choices are numerous. The authors' discussions include the relationship between the arrangements for providing services in the traditional medical system and in community as well as home settings. As well, they analyze aspects of the care system such as the involvement of different levels of public authorities, the variety of funding sources, the ways in which personnel are appointed and standards set, and the mechanisms for quality control and accountability.

In addition, all of these papers are sensitive to the provision of care by public, for-profit, and voluntary organizations—a subject of increasing interest in the scholarly literature. Over time, as the authors indicate, the three sectors have varied in their roles, with services for the severely and chronically ill increasingly being provided in the voluntary and for-profit sectors, and diminishing services being provided by public authorities (see the papers by Davies, Goldberg, Hollingsworth, and Jamieson). In the financing of care, however, the papers demonstrate that the public sector is the major source of revenue. The papers also discuss how the level of expenditure influences how the delivery of services is organized and how clients fare.

A common theme in all the papers is the lack of adequate financial resources for providing the amounts and types of care needed for the three client groups. Beyond this, however, several papers discuss the ironies of financial arrangements: the continuation of funding for care in hospitals, nursing homes, and congregate care homes even if they do not provide the most suitable client care (see papers by Davies, Hollingsworth, Jamieson, and Kane). Sometimes the inability to handle funding flexibly, to divert it from hospitals to community-based care, results from the powerful political pressures generated by hospitals and nursing homes, as they seek to expand their budgets and programs. Increasingly, the provision of care in the community (through home care and other community-based programs) raises issues of accountability, such as who will ensure that care is actually needed, that needed care is delivered, and that those providing care are qualified. Ultimately home care providers are likely to develop their own powerful associations, certification programs, and enhanced legitimacy with government bureaucrats and insurance companies, but until this occurs the delivery of home services is likely to lag behind the need for such services.

Several of the authors discuss the prospects for adequate funding of services for the disabled in the 1990s, as fiscal shortfall and economic stalemate have characterized even the most vigorous of advanced industrial societies. They suggest that the resources necessary for closing the gap between service need and service provision may be fairly small (see papers by Davies, Hollingsworth, and Ramon). As Ellen Jane Hollingsworth demonstrates in her paper on the seriously mentally ill, even in times of greater prosperity, funding for the seriously mentally ill did not increase in constant dollars.

The type of care required by these three disabled populations is quite different from the services provided by the more traditional medical service sector. For example, the medical clinics and community hospitals that are the main sites for acute care are generally not the facilities and programs needed and used by the three disabled populations discussed in this book. Slowly and haphazardly, new types of community care arrangements are emerging in response to the needs of these three populations, incorporating different degrees of medical manpower and technology (see the papers by Davies, Goldberg, Hollingsworth, and Ramon). In these new organizational forms, there is often a tendency to substitute low skilled for highly skilled personnel, a practice quite different from the trends in the dominant form of medical care in the two countries.

The papers also focus on the number of people needing service and receiving service. Thus, an initial concern of the authors has been with how many people there are who are seriously mentally ill, homebound with chronic illness, etc. Because all of the disabled populations discussed in this book are quite heterogeneous, the fit between client needs and client services tends to vary even within disability groups. The following papers present comparable findings: Regardless of the definition of disability used, adequate services are provided only for small percentages of those who are seriously disabled and in need.

The papers are sensitive to the problem of whether there is an increasing segmentation between those, on the one hand, who have considerable resources and power and who receive the types of services the acute-oriented medical system provides, and those, on the other hand, who have long-term disabilities and need integrated social and medical services, who have few resources and are inadequately represented. In addressing this problem, the papers demonstrate that these populations often have inadequate representation in the contest for resources. These three populations are generally poorly mobilized and organized relative to those who are employed, especially those represented by unions and employer associations. Moreover, they tend to be low in status and to have few financial resources. And finally, because of their disabilities, they have limited physical capabilities to engage in political action. Because they are resource poor and because others have low incentives to represent their interests, there is good reason to be apprehensive that their needs will not be recognized and met, especially in an era of resource constriction. The papers highlight different, but complementary themes: the contest for resources at the national level, the development of community responsibility, the mobilization of consumers. All the authors express concern that representation of client needs and interests is inadequate to overcome financial shortfalls and political neglect.

Nevertheless, the papers demonstrate that many professionals and some policymakers have become increasingly sensitive to the problems of populations with severe chronic illness. In some instances, professionals have become advocates for the seriously chronically ill. However, the inadequacy of resources for care highlights a common, core problem of how to achieve fair representation for marginalized groups. There is substantial literature demonstrating that marginalized groups will not have their needs adequately met so long as their voices are excluded from policy deliberations (Young 1990; Beitz 1988; Sunstein 1988; Weale 1981; Williams 1992). This of course addresses an epistemological issue of what constitutes effective representation. It assumes that unless the voices and perspectives of those who are marginalized explicitly become part of the legislative and other aspects of the policy process, underrepresentation and grossly inadequate provision of services for their needs will occur. But since the three groups under consideration lack the physical capacity, as well as financial and political resources, to place their perspectives in the political process, their prospects for better services are bleak, despite their expanding numbers.

Performance of Systems of Care for People with Chronic and Severe Illness

The following essays are also concerned with the performance and outcomes of the various systems of care, using criteria such as access to care, appropriateness and quality of care, costs of care, patient outcomes, innovativeness and flexibility, and client satisfaction. In general, the emphasis in the papers is on the relationship between the overall institutional arrangements for care and the performance of the care systems. Despite the millions of disabled people needing services from specialized care systems, the authors point to the fairly dismal performance in the delivery of services, even allowing for the imperfections of mechanisms for evaluation. Even so, the papers convey the impression that services are less comprehensive and less well coordinated in the United States than in Britain. In particular, geriatric services in Britain appear to be somewhat more comprehensive than services for the other two populations. Despite their common theme, the concerns of the papers about performance vary somewhat: some give greater emphasis to targeting of services (Davies), some to issues of suitability of available services (Kane, Jamieson), and some to issues of insufficient services (Ramon, Hollingsworth).

INTERRELATED THEMES

There is an interrelated theme developed in the following papers: The institutional arrangements of the care systems shape the degree to which services are comprehensive and coordinated, while performance is very much shaped by the structure of the system, and its level of comprehensiveness and coordination. Moreover, these systems are not autonomous from the societies of which they are a part, as issues with regard to these three populations are played out according to fundamental societal choices and patterns.

Since the development of comprehensive and coordinated services with high levels of performance for the disabled requires linking both medical and social services, the greatest likelihood for realizing the desired modes and amounts of services would tend to be associated with universal access to medical and social service systems, and such systems would tend to be financed by common sources of funding. At the other end of the spectrum, when medical and social service systems are highly fragmented and are funded with many different types and sources of revenue, services tend not to be comprehensive, integrated, or well-developed for people with serious chronic illness.

When comprehensive medical and social services are funded by the national government, services are less subject to contraction and marginalization in eras of financial exigency than when services are fragmented, less comprehensive, and funded at multiple levels of society. Thus, when the pressures of privatization are exerted and dismantling of the welfare state is considered, more centralized systems of care are less likely to cut back on benefits for disabled groups. Changing the direction of centralized systems is difficult, with regard to either financing or programming. A more centralized system—such as that in Britain—may modestly reduce its yearly budget commitments, but to alter delivery systems materially is very complicated. On the other hand, fragmented and more decentralized systems—such as the United States—tend to decrease their attention to the disabled when the state and society are facing serious fiscal problems. And in such a system, it is easier to cut here and there, to allow historical patterns of scarce resources to prevail over more enlightened social policy choices (Hollingsworth, Hage, and Hanneman 1990). These generalizations, about the effect of centralization of medical and social service systems on care provision, are also themes in several of the following chapters.

Thus, Great Britain and the United States, two countries with very different types of medical systems, were chosen for analysis in order to profile the type of care for the same disabled people in two different settings, and to explore whether the different types of medical systems have led to variation in the services these three populations receive. A major strategy of the following papers is to assess the service provision for three needy and dependent populations and how provision varies according to the structure of the medical and social service delivery system in the two countries.

REFERENCES

Aiken, Linda H. 1987. "Extended Care: The Hospital's Perspective." Pp. 15–24 in *Medicare and Extended Care: Issues, Problems, and Prospects*, edited by Bruce C. Vladeck and Genrose J. Alfano. Owings Mills, MD: National Health Publishing.

Alter, Catherine and Jerald Hage. 1993. *Organizations Working Together*. Newbury Park, CA: Sage.

Bachrach, L. 1980. "Overview: Model Programs for Chronic Mental Patients." *American Journal of Psychiatry* 137:1023–31.

Barker, William H. 1987. *Adding Life to Years*. Baltimore, MD: Johns Hopkins University Press.

Beiser, M., J. H. Shore, R. Peters, and Ellie Tatum. 1985. "Does Community Care for the Mentally Ill Make a Difference? A Tale of Two Cities." *American Journal of Psychiatry* 142:1047–52.

Beitz, Charles. 1988. *Political Equality*. Princeton, NJ: Princeton University Press.

Braun, P., G. Kochansky, R. Shapiro, S. Greenberg, J. Gudeman, S. Johnson, and M. Shore. 1981. "Overview: Deinstitutionalization of Psychiatric Patients: Critical Review of Outcome Studies." *American Journal of Psychiatry* 138:736–49.

Department of Health, Social Services, Wales and Scotland. 1989. *Caring for People: Community Care in the Next Decade and Beyond*. London: HMSO.

Davies, B. P., A. C. Bebbington, H. Charnley, in collaboration with B. Baines, E. Ferlie, M. Hughes, and J. Twigg. 1990. *Resources, Needs and Outcomes in Community-Based Care. PSSRU Studies*. Aldershot: Avebury/Gower.

Goldman, H. H., J. P. Morrissey, M. S. Ridgely, R. G. Frank, S. J. Newman, and C. Kennedy. 1992. "Lessons from the Program on Chronic Mental Illness." *Health Affairs* 11:51–68.

Gruenberg, E. M. 1977. "The Failures of Success." *Milbank Memorial Fund Quarterly: Health and Society* 55:3–24.

Hollingsworth, J. Rogers. 1986. *A Political Economy of Medicine: Great Britain and the United States*. Baltimore, MD: Johns Hopkins University Press.

Hollingsworth, J. Rogers, Jerald Hage, and Robert Hanneman. 1990. *State Intervention in Medical Care: Consequences for Britain, France, Sweden and the United States*. Ithaca, NY: Cornell University Press.

Kemper, Peter, et al. 1986. *The Evaluation of the National Long Term Care Demonstration: Final Report*, prepared for DHHS. Princeton, NJ: Mathematica Policy Research.

Klein, Rudolph. 1983. *The Politics of the National Health Service*. London: Longman.

Kramer, M. 1980. "The Rising Pandemic of Mental Disorders and Associated Chronic Diseases and Disabilities." *Acta Psychiatrica Scandinavica Supplementum* 62, Suppl. 285:382–97.

Lindblom, Charles E. 1977. *Politics and Markets: The World's Political-Economic Systems*. New York: Basic Books.

Mechanic, David and Linda Aiken. 1989. *Pitfalls and Promises: Capitated Payment Systems. New Directions for Mental Health*, Vol. 43. San Francisco: Jossey-Bass.

Richardson, H. and A. R. Kovner. 1987. "Implementing Swing-Bed Services in Small Rural Hospitals." Pp. 91–107 in *Medicare and Extended Care: Issues, Problems, and Prospects*, edited by Bruce C. Vladeck and G. J. Alfano. Owings Mills, MD: Rynd Communications.

Rivlin, Alice M. and J. M. Wiener, with R. J. Hanley and D. A. Spence. 1988. *Caring for the Disabled Elderly*. Washington, DC: Brookings Institute.

Skellie, F. A., M. Mobley, and R. E. Coan. 1982. "Cost-Effectiveness of Community-Based Long-Term Care: Current Findings of Georgia's Alternative Health Services Project." *American Journal of Public Health* 72:353–58.

Stein, Leonard I., Ronald J. Diamond, and Robert M. Factor. 1990. "A System Approach to the Care of Persons with Schizophrenia." Pp. 213–46 in *Psychosocial Therapies*, Vol 5, edited by Marvin I Herz, S. J. Keith, and John P. Docherty. Amsterdam: Elsevier Science Publishers.

Sunstein, Cass. 1988. "Beyond the Republican Revival." *Yale Law Journal* 97:1539–90.

Vladeck, Bruce C. 1980. *Unloving Care: The Nursing Home Tragedy*. New York: Basic Books.

Weale, Albert P. 1981. "Representation, Individualism, and Collectivism." *Ethics* 91:457–65.

Weisbrod, B., M. Test, and L. Stein. 1980. "An Alternative to Mental Hospital Treatment: III. Economic Benefit-Cost Analysis." *Archives of General Psychiatry.* 37:400–5.

Weissert, W., Thomas Wan, Barbara Livieratos, and Sidney Katz. 1980. "Effects and Costs of Day-Care Services for the Chronically Ill: A Randomized Experiment." *Medical Care* 18:567–84.

Williams, Melissa S. 1992. "Memory, History and Membership: The Moral Claims of Marginalized Groups in American Political Representation." Paper presented at the American Political Science Association Annual Meeting, Chicago, September 3–6.

Young, Iris Marion. 1990. *Justice and the Politics of Difference*. Princeton, NJ: Princeton University Press.

Zawadski, R. T. and M. L. Ansak. 1983. "Consolidating Community-Based Long-Term Care: Early Returns from the On Lok Demonstration." *Gerontologist* 23:364–69.

Zimmer, J. G., A. Groth-Juncker, and J. McCusker. 1985. "A Randomized Controlled Study of a Home Health Care Team." *American Journal of Public Health* 75:134–41.

PART I

Care for the Frail Elderly

In both the United States and Britain, it is well-known that the number of frail elderly is increasing very rapidly. Estimates are that by the year 2000 the number of people over 85 in Britain likely to be disabled and have high demands for care will have increased by 50% over 1989 (*Financial Times*, December 18, 1989, pp. 11–12). The situation in the United States is similar. Although age is sometimes an imperfect index to impairment and disability, there is widespread recognition throughout the world that the number of aged, impaired people is a serious and growing problem (Kane 1990a).

The emphases of this volume are very important for understanding services for the frail elderly. Many of the frail elderly need a system that has community-based and institution-based elements working together to provide comprehensive, flexible, and coordinated care according to individual needs (for helpful discussion and diagrammatic presentation, see Brody 1987). Such systems exist to only a very limited extent in the public sector, especially in the United States, and thus are unavailable to many elderly.

During the last two decades there has been more and more interest, in both the United States and Britain, in delivering services outside nursing homes and group living situations. Rather, the emphasis has been on increasing the variety and amount of home care service for people who live in their own private residences in the community. Yet, it is necessary to improve congregate care facilities for the frail elderly at the same time that home care services are improved. Both settings—congregate care and home care—need to have medical and social service components. The necessity of upgrading group facilities and developing home care at the same time creates a fundamental financial tension; there has not been enough money to accomplish the changes needed (Kane 1990b; Amann 1980).

For many students of geriatric policy, a critical question is the extent to which societies can afford to provide the needed levels of comprehensive and coordinated health and medical services for the frail elderly. There are several studies of costs and benefits of home care, as opposed to institutional care. A number of analysts believe that community/home services could delay or possibly prevent admission to congregate facilities, or shorten length of stay in nursing homes, and at the same time improve the quality of life for the frail elderly (Kemper et al. 1986; Zimmer, Groth-Juncker, and McCusker 1985; Weissert, Wan, Livieratos, and Katz 1980; Skellie, Mobley, and Coan 1982).

During recent decades in both countries, spirited debates have taken place about the most appropriate care settings for the elderly. Often these debates have taken place as part of efforts to strengthen community-based care. At the same time, in both countries, there have been public policies in effect that have acted as strong incentives to provide care in nursing homes and group living arrangements for the frail elderly (see Kane and Jamieson papers), not in private homes. In other words, although there is increasing interest among providers and scholars in community-based care, in Britain at least there have fairly recently been changes in the direction of increasing the provision of congregate care, not reducing it.

Jens Alber (1992) has found that the number of places in group living arrangements for the elderly is about the same in the United States and the United Kingdom. Alber has based his conclusion on the number of places for care of the elderly, normed by the number of people over 65 years of age. These types of living situation are not identical for the two countries. In the United States, there is greater emphasis on nursing homes, whereas in Britain there is more emphasis on group and board-and-care homes. In both countries, according to Alber, there has been an increase in the numbers of places during recent years (Alber 1992). It is interesting that the normed number of congregate living places for the elderly has increased at the same time that there has been increasing belief that many of the frail elderly are best served if they remain in their homes.

In the United States, elderly people with needs for moderate (or more) amounts of medical services are eventually faced with the necessity of entering a nursing home. No fully developed system of alternatives to institutional care has emerged. Only quite limited amounts of home medical care are available to the frail elderly, and even then on a very restricted basis. Bruce Vladeck (1987) has pointed out that in the United States, as hospital stays have become shorter, the amount of home medical care has actually decreased, rather than expanding to meet needs of earlier-discharged patients. He terms extended care (the provision of medical care outside hospitals and doctors' offices) the undelivered benefit of the Medicare program. United States public policy to promote community-based social services for the frail elderly has been even more inadequate. Publicly financed nonmedical home services are very limited. Thus, for poor elderly people unable to pay for social services to enable them to live independently, nursing home care is virtually the only option. Some localities provide special means-tested public programs for supported living (in one's own home, or in special apartments), but such services are rare.

The way in which the debate about the most appropriate care for the frail elderly is framed in the United States is similar to the debate in Great Britain. In the United States, most discussion concerns the conditions under which the frail elderly can be adequately maintained outside nursing homes, and the extent to which home medical and social care, respite programs to provide relief for carers, and day programming can minimize use of nursing homes. In Great Britain, the issues are presented in terms of the balance between a broad array of group living arrangements on the one hand (i.e., nursing homes, residential or group homes, board-and-care homes) and care provided in the home (known as domiciliary care) on the other (see paper by Davies). In Britain, where there is more development of geriatric centers, some areas have developed comprehensive and balanced services (Barker 1987).

As our societies consider increasing the provision of care outside nursing homes, issues about coordination of medical and social services are becoming more salient (Aiken, Dewar, DiTomasco, Hage, and Zeitz 1975). Controlling for severity of illness, the concentration of people in the nursing home or in other types of group living makes service provision less costly and easier to manage than is the case if frail elderly people live individually. Coordination of services is thus more feasible in group living situations. Yet, as the number of frail elderly increases, the problems facing this population become ever more diverse, meaning greater need for diverse types of care (McCormack 1987). Such diversity exacerbates the problems of coordination of social and medical services. Both countries already have a diverse frail elderly population with a broad array of ailments, and this diversity of needs is one major difficulty in providing coordinated social and medical services.

The structures of the main caregiving modalities for the frail elderly in Britain and in the United States are discussed in the following papers by Robert Kane and Anne Jamieson. They discuss congregate caregiving settings—their ownership, size, funding, and regulation. As well, they discuss the shortcomings of these settings, and incentives for more appropriate care.

Both of the papers emphasize the importance of financing in shaping the organization and provision of care. Kane and Jamieson argue that whatever organizational or institutional form is funded by the state will become dominant, regardless of the suitability of such services. In the United States, the availability of Medicaid funding for nursing home care has led to enormous growth in nursing home beds. This policy was carried out at the same time that more and more people came to believe that advanced industrial societies could provide effective social and health services in the community, with nursing homes used only for the very impaired needing intensive nursing care. Although nursing homes in the United States do not provide the appropriate environment for many frail elderly, it has proved almost impossible to create organizational alternatives and to redirect funding streams. Similarly, in Britain, the inclusion in Social Security of grants for residential care has led to a virtual explosion in the number of such accommodations.

As Jamieson and Kane make clear, the performance of the existing institutions is far from high quality, almost regardless of the criteria applied. In the United States, with nursing home populations increasingly older, dependent, and more medically compromised, there is grave doubt that even minimally adequate medical care can be provided (Aiken 1987).

For the frail elderly, coordination among the components of the service system is vital. That coordination is poorly developed is hardly surprising, given the fragility of the community-based system. As Bleddyn Davies's essay in this volume indicates, the elderly in Britain have ready access to general practitioners. However, very few elderly report use of social services, aside from Meals on Wheels programs. Even those with rather severe impairments receive very few social services.

In both countries, the quantity and training of professionals for working with the frail elderly are severely deficient. There is a shortage of caregivers, and the skill levels tend to be below appropriate standards. Medical schools and schools of social work are independent organizations providing little integrated training of students, and thereby contributing to a low level of coordination of social and medical services.

Until these two societies value caring as much as they do curing, creating for the frail elderly a comprehensive, flexible institutional and community-based system with coordination of medical and social services, high-quality performance is a remote prospect. Even to improve the quality of existing institutions (see Kane, herein) is very difficult. And unless each society redirects or increases spending, these nations are not likely to have high-quality group living arrangements for the frail elderly, the right balance between community-based and home care on the one hand and nursing homes/group living arrangements on the other, or the right mixture of medical and social services.

REFERENCES

Aiken, Linda H. 1987. "Extended Care: The Hospital's Perspective." Pp. 15–24 in *Medicare and Extended Care: Issues, Problems, and Prospects*, edited by B. C. Vladeck and G. J. Alfano. Owings Mills, MD: National Health Publishing.

Aiken, Michael, Robert Dewar, Nancy DiTomasco, Jerald Hage, and Gerald Zeitz. 1975. *Coordinating Human Services.* San Francisco: Jossey-Bass.

Alber, Jens. 1992. "Care for the Frail Elderly: The United States, the United Kingdom, and Germany." *Journal of Health Politics, Policy and Law.* 17:929–57.

Amann, Anton (ed.). 1980. *Open Care for the Elderly in Seven European Countries.* Oxford: Pergamon.

Barker, William H. 1987. *Adding Life to Years.* Baltimore, MD: Johns Hopkins University Press.

Brody, Stanley J. 1987. "Continuity of Care: The New-Old Health Requirement." Pp. 25–36 in *Medicare and Extended Care: Issues, Problems, and Prospects*, edited by B. C. Vladeck and G. J. Alfano. Owings Mills, MD: Rynd Communications.

Kane, Robert L. 1990a. "Introduction." Pp. 15–18 in *Improving the Health of Older People: A World View*, edited by R. L. Kane, J. G. Evans, and D. MacFadyen. Oxford: Oxford University Press.

————. 1990b. "Perceived Progress in Aging: The Results of a Delphi Survey of International Experts." Pp. 1–6 in *Improving the Health of Older People: A World View*, edited by R. L. Kane, J. G. Evans, and D. MacFadyen. Oxford: Oxford University Press.

Kemper, Peter, et al. 1986. *The Evaluation of the National Long Term Care Demonstration: Final Report*, prepared for DHHS. Princeton, NJ: Mathematica Policy Research.

McCormack, J. J. 1987. "The Place of Extended Care in the Health System: The New York Experience." Pp. 45–52 in *Medicare and Extended Care: Issues, Problems, and Prospects*, edited by B. C. Vladeck and G. J. Alfano. Owings Mills, MD: Rynd Communications.

Skellie, F. A., M. Mobley, and R. E. Coan. 1981. "Cost-Effectiveness of Community-Based Long-Term Care: Current Findings of Georgia's Alternative Health Services Project." *American Journal of Public Health* 72:353–58.

Vladeck, Bruce C. 1987. "History of the Medicare Extended Care Benefit." Pp. 5–14 in *Medicare and Extended Care: Issues, Problems, and Prospects*, edited by B. C. Vladeck and G. J. Alfano. Owings Mills, MD: Rynd Communications.

Weissert, W., Thomas Wan, Barbara Livieratos, and Sidney Katz. 1980. "Effects and Costs of Day-Care Services for the Chronically Ill: A Randomized Experiment." *Medical Care* 18:567–84.

Zimmer, J. G., A. Groth-Juncker, and J. McCusker. 1985. "A Randomized Controlled Study of a Home Health Care Team." *American Journal of Public Health* 75:134–41.

Chapter 2

The American Nursing Home:
An Institution for All Reasons

ROBERT L. KANE

INTRODUCTION

The American nursing home (ANH) has come to occupy an uncomfortable place in the care system. It shows evidence of both mixed paren-
tage and confused mission. In many ways it is as much the victim as the
perpetrator of the problem. Like most American health care elements, it
has been shaped by the payment system, but its presence on both the
service and political agenda will have a great impact on future developments in chronic care.

As in most countries, the ANH has a mixed heritage. It is the mongrel
offspring of the almshouse and the hospital. Like the hospitals at the
turn of the century, it is a place associated with the care of the poor. In
large measure, the modern ANH is a creation of federal legislation in the
mid-1960s designed to purchase health care for the disenfranchised similar to that available for the more affluent. The elderly, who had been
gradually priced out of the private health insurance market by a process
of risk rating rather than community rating, were to be covered by a
virtually universal program appended to Social Security—Medicare,
while the poor were to be covered by a welfare program—Medicaid.
Most expected that the needs of the elderly would be met by Medicare;
but the Medicare program was modeled closely on what was available in
the private health sector at the time. Hence, its center was the hospital
and its epicenter the physician. Other modalities were considered to the
extent that they provided services to extend the period of recuperation
after hospitalization or offered services that might be used in lieu of such
care.

The Medicaid program was intended to fill a similar role for the poor,
who were thought of primarily as those eligible for categorical welfare
programs (families of dependent children, blind and disabled, chron-

ically disabled, needy elderly). The benefits under Medicaid were made a little broader because its founders recognized that (a) the recipients had no other means of purchasing care, and (b) they suffered from social as well as physical ills. No one at the time anticipated that Medicaid might be the major payer of long-term care, especially nursing home care.

Medicare is a federally operated program, administered through local fiscal intermediaries (often insurance companies). Its guidelines for both eligibility and benefits are constant across the country, except as they are inadvertently interpreted differently by the various intermediaries. It is paid for by a combination of direct taxes (paid by virtually all workers and their employers) and insurance premiums paid for by the beneficiaries. The latter are heavily subsidized. Medicare benefits utilize modest deductibles and copayments.

Medicaid, in contrast, is a welfare program operated by states and paid for out of tax revenues by a combination of state and federal funds (The relative contribution depends on the affluence of the state.). The federal government sets policies for the program but the states determine both benefit and eligibility conditions within those general parameters. Because the criteria of eligibility are linked closely to indigence, Medicaid has avoided any form of copayment. Under such an arrangement states have a strong incentive to try to use Medicare funds over Medicaid funds. In essence, they are using completely federal dollars in lieu of state dollars (even if highly leveraged). They therefore immediately pay the insurance fees, copayments, and deductibles for all elderly Medicare beneficiaries.

The Medicaid program had a sleeper. It contained a provision that permitted states to include among those eligible for the program persons who became medically needy by virtue of their high medical care costs. When their medical bills exceeded a certain percentage of their monthly income, they could be covered. In a number of states this eligibility criterion became a major vehicle for coverage of older persons with heavy health care expenditures. For many, the largest regular expenditure is nursing home care. Medically indigent elderly, many in nursing homes, became significant items in state budgets.

Because nursing home care's cost can be reasonably well estimated in advance (in contrast to home care, which may vary in intensity over time), it can be used as the basis for determining Medicaid eligibility in advance. Thus, a person in a nursing home where the monthly costs of such care can be calculated to exceed his or her income (especially if it derives exclusively from a Social Security retirement pension) can be deemed eligible for Medicaid, whereas a person accruing home care costs prospectively will reach the same state only after having spent all his or her own funds. This situation creates another subtle but real incentive to use nursing homes for those at or near medical poverty.

The framers of Medicare and Medicaid did not think much about nursing homes at the time. When they did, they pictured chronic-care facilities where elderly patients could recuperate after hospitalization at a lower daily cost. These sites were called "extended care facilities" to emphasize this role of providing posthospital service. The Medicaid program made provisions for "skilled nursing homes," which were intended, as the name implies, to provide care requiring nursing attention. Little thought was given to those needing chronic maintenance, but little had been given to them before.

The two major coverage programs of the mid-1960s brought with them regulations and conditions of participation. To be allowed to participate in the programs, institutions had to meet certain standards, which had a number of unanticipated consequences. Two forces shaped the standard setting: the pressure of time and the fear of catastrophes. Faced with the task of creating standards quickly for a modality of care that was largely unfamiliar, federal and state bureaucracies turned to models that were available. One of these was the small hospital. A federal program to support the construction of rural hospitals had created blueprints and standards for construction and staffing. Hence, there was a great temptation to envision these nursing homes as miniature hospitals, a view not at variance with that of the program's framers. At the same time, there was a great fear of headline-grabbing catastrophes, especially fires. Thus, the regulations placed strong emphasis on issues of life safety (wide corridors, fire doors, sprinkler systems). These were elements already incorporated into the hospital plans used as templates. Likewise staffing requirements were designed to provide an environment more akin to that of a small hospital with a strong complement of trained nurses, who might be expected to care for recuperating hospital patients.

The results were twofold. In the early years very few facilities could meet the standards set. The program was threatened with an embarrassing situation in which it promised coverage but excluded the places needed to provide it. By 1971, bureaucratic ingenuity found a way out of the dilemma by creating a new class of facilities, intermediate-care facilities, which would not have to meet such stringent requirements, especially around staffing. The second set of effects was less easily remedied. The strong emphasis on structural elements, especially life safety features, meant that many of the original supply of nursing homes, which had emerged out of boardinghouses, could no longer continue. The costs of rehabilitation were too high. The modern nursing home thus came to look and function much more like a miniature hospital than a home.

Ironically, today's nursing homes provide little of either implied attribute. There is only minimal nursing attention, especially from professional nurses, and rarely a homelike atmosphere. If anything, there has emerged a greater tension between these poles. Increasingly stringent standards for charting and documentational expectations of more aggressive care of a progressively more disabled clientele have been juxtaposed against client desires for a more livable environment. This trade-off has come to be called the dilemma between quality of care and quality of life considerations. At its heart, it is an artificial dichotomy.

I. NURSING HOME STATISTICS

The ANH network has emerged with several striking attributes. There are more nursing homes than hospitals in America. In 1985 there were 19,100 nursing homes in the United States housing 1.624 million beds, and 1.491 million residents (an occupancy rate of 92%). These numbers compare with 6,300 acute care hospitals with about 800,000 beds.

As shown in Figure 1, nursing homes, unlike hospitals, are primarily owned by proprietary firms. Whether counted by numbers of homes or beds, proprietary activity predominates, accounting for 75% of the homes and 69% of the beds. This suggests that the voluntary nonprofit and public homes tend to be larger. Many homes, in both the proprietary and nonprofit sectors, are part of chains or corporations that operate several homes.

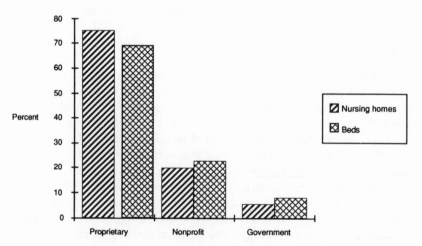

Figure 1.   Nursing home characteristics by ownership, 1985.
(*Source: Hing, Sekscenski, and Strahan 1989.*)

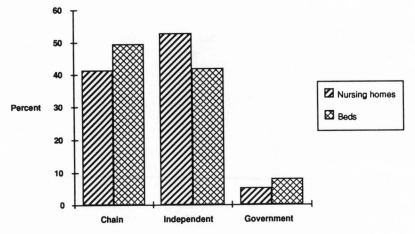

Figure 2. Nursing home characteristics by chain status, 1985.
(*Source: Hing et al. 1989.*)

Figure 2 indicates that 41% of the homes and 49% of the beds are part of chain operations. Again, the difference in these proportions reflects larger homes in the chains (Hing 1989). In addition, a growing number of nursing homes are part of vertically integrated health care corporations, which include hospitals, home health care agencies, outpatient facilities, and often housing.

Nursing homes are roughly divided into thirds according to bed size. One-third of the homes have less than 50 beds; another third have 50–99 beds. The remainder are split between those with 100–199 beds (28%) and those with 200 beds or more (6%). The homes in this latter group are very large, accounting for one-fifth of all the nursing beds.

The distribution of nursing homes does not directly follow the population. Although 76% of the American people live within a metropolitan statistical area (MSA; an indication of an urban setting), only 68% of the nursing home beds are in MSAs.

II. PAYING FOR NURSING HOME CARE

In 1988, the United States paid $43.1 billion for nursing home care out of a total of $540.6 billion spent on health care, including $88.5 billion on those age 65 and older. As shown in Figure 3, 48% of the costs of nursing homes comes from the purses of the individuals and their families. Government sources accounted for 49% of nursing home dollars, with only 2% from Medicare. Given the difference in funding responsibilities between Medicare and Medicaid (the former being a federal program

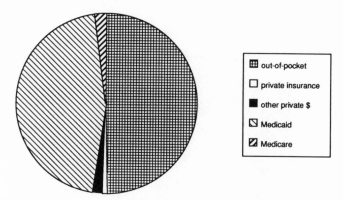

Figure 3.   Sources of nursing home financing, 1988.
(*Source: Office of National Cost Estimates, 1990.*)

and the latter a federal-state partnership), federal funds cover 29% of the nursing home costs and state and local funds 20%. Private insurance pays even less than the small amount covered by Medicare.

Medicaid is the major payer for nursing home care, but its influence is even more profound. Because Medicaid is a welfare program, its payments are made only after the client's personal resources are exhausted. Thus, a portion of the private out-of-pocket expenditures are really transfer payments from Social Security and other welfare programs that would otherwise have gone to support the older persons living in the community. Thus, Medicaid pays about half the nursing home bill, but covers about two-thirds of those in nursing homes. Again, because some persons are impoverished as a result of sustained nursing home costs, which eat up all of their savings, the longer a person is in the nursing home, the more likely he or she is to be on welfare. Liu, Doty, and Manton (1990) have suggested that the spend down rate is lower than many may have thought, but is about 14% per year. Table 1, taken from their work, shows how the proportion of persons on Medicaid increases with longer nursing home stays. Moreover, there is some concern that many older people use financial tactics to avoid consuming their assets before becoming eligible for Medicaid (Moses 1990).

The standards adopted for Medicaid shape the industry. Not only do a majority of nursing home residents use Medicaid at some time in their nursing home careers, it is inefficient for a facility to operate under two standards, one for Medicaid and one for its private-paying clients. Rather, Medicaid becomes at least a floor for many homes. Although private-paying patients are not examined by Medicaid inspectors, most facilities that serve both types of clients add amenities to their basic package for

Table 1. Proportion of Discharges of Each Medicaid Payment Group, by Length of Stay: 1985 National Nursing Home Survey

Length of Stay	Medicaid at admission (%)	Medicaid spend down (%)	Non-Medicaid (%)	Total (%)	Discharges (%)
< 2 months	23.8	2.5	73.7	100.0	473,338
2–6 months	35.8	8.5	55.7	100.0	194,539
7–12 months	46.1	10.8	43.1	100.0	119,627
1–2 years	48.0	9.6	42.3	100.0	100,703
2+ years	49.6	13.5	36.9	100.0	174,912
All stays	35.0	7.0	58.0	100.0	1,063,119

Source: Liu et al., 1990.

their private-paying clients. By federal law, Medicaid programs are forbidden from paying more than the private rates, but only one state (Minnesota) has passed a law that prohibits homes from charging their private-paying clients more than Medicaid will allow. Nursing home proponents and some regulators argue that this differential payment scheme is needed to subsidize the costs of caring for Medicaid residents who otherwise do not receive sufficient funds to cover their costs.

The $43.1 billion paid to nursing homes in 1988 represents 8% of the total health expenditures of $539.9 billion. The growth of health care costs has been very steep since the passage of Medicare and Medicaid 25 years ago, but the relative nursing home costs have been less severe than those of other sectors. Figure 4 compares the pattern of expenditures over time for nursing homes with those for hospitals and physicians; both show more rapid increases. Figure 5 shows the patterns of growth within the Medicare program, where the growth in nursing home expenditures is much less than that for hospitals (National Center for Health Statistics, NCHS 1990). Relative to either, hospice costs are very small, although increasing (NCHS 1990).

III. MULTIPLE ROLES

The ANH is at once expected to play many different roles. It serves a number of different types of clients: acutely ill persons recuperating from hospital care, physically impaired persons with chronic conditions, those with severe chronic cognitive deficits (primarily dementia), and those who are terminally ill. Moreover, the decision about whether to

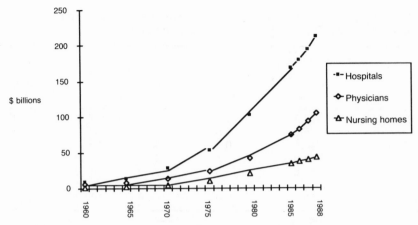

Figure 4.   National health expenditures, 1960–88.
(*Source: Office of National Cost Estimates, 1990.*)

treat such persons in a nursing home or in alternative settings often
seems arbitrary and sometimes capricious, influenced at least in part by
the availability of resources (Neu and Harrison 1988).

Several consequences result from this assorted clientele. First, it is
unlikely that a facility serving so diverse a population is ideal for any. At
a minimum, the presence of one group may adversely affect the quality
for another. Perhaps the clearest example of this problem is the cohabita-
tion of those physically and cognitively impaired. The quality of life for
the former is likely adversely impacted by the behavior of the latter

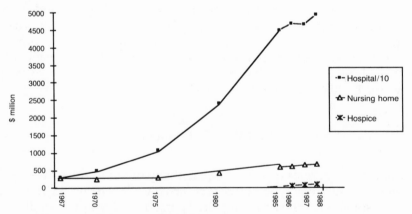

Figure 5.   Medicare expenditures, 1967–88.
(*Source: National Center for Health Statistics, 1990.*)

group, who may impose on their privacy in their seemingly aimless wanderings and who generally provide an ambiance that few would choose freely. Because the physically impaired are already compromised in their ability to exert control over their environments, it seems doubly cruel to expose them to this added burden. Some have argued that the recovery (or at least the slowed decline) of the cognitively impaired may be enhanced by keeping them in the company of more alert persons, but the social algebra involved in involuntarily taxing the latter in the hopes of such a benefit still seems misplaced.

Moreover, the basic physical design of a facility intended for cognitively impaired is different from that for physically impaired. The former need unrestricted but confined spaces where they can wander with as little confrontation as possible. Oval tracks and more inventive pathways are well suited for such patients. In contrast, the physically disabled need ready access to nurses' stations and more compact spatial designs. The more acutely impaired the person, the more one might argue for proximity to nursing care, whereas those more chronically impaired might do better with more private space set further apart from direct supervision.

In parallel with design considerations, it is unlikely that all types of patients need the same staffing arrangements in terms of either quantity or specialties. Certainly patients coming directly from hospital are likely to need more intensive nursing. Chronically cognitively impaired will need more socially oriented persons who are comfortable rechanneling their energies. The physically impaired may profit more from those oriented toward rehabilitation and functional independence. Social stimulation and activities will be quite different for those cognitively intact and those not.

IV. POSTACUTE CARE

The changes in the system for paying hospitals under Medicare has created new stresses on the posthospital care system (Morrisey, Sloan, and Valvona 1988). The Prospective Payment System, which gives a hospital a fixed amount for each admission, essentially according to the patient's diagnoses, encourages earlier discharge from hospital and hence, ironically creates the environment that the original extended-care facilities were designed to meet. This need for what has come to be termed postacute care (PAC) is currently being met by one of three major modalities of care covered under Medicare: rehabilitation, home health care, or skilled nursing facilities. Thus, the Medicare program may be expected to assume a larger role in nursing home care. At present, there is little evidence to permit distinctions between the major PAC modalities in terms of their relative efficacy, although there is a significant difference in their costs (Gornick and Hall 1988). There is some suggestion that one form of care is currently being substituted for another when there is a compromise in the supply (Neu and Harrison 1988). Work is currently under way at the University of Minnesota to examine the relative efficacy of these alternative modalities for a number of the DRGs (Diagnosis Related Groups; groups of conditions dealing with similar medical problems that have approximately the same average hospital length of stay) for which PAC is most often used.

V. HOSPICE CARE

Since 1983, the Medicare program has made special provisions for the care of those believed to be terminally ill. Persons with a prognosis of six months or less can opt to be treated in a specially designed hospice program. Such clients are then enrolled in a capitated program that pays the hospice a fixed amount for each day of coverage. (The amount actually changes depending on whether the client is living in the community or in an institution.) The hospice must assume responsibility for all care, although the client can opt to return to the usual Medicare system at any point. The intent of the Medicare hospice program is to promote less use of expensive high-technology care in favor of more humanistic personal service. The program is intended to promote home care; it requires that 80% of care be given in the community.

The hospice movement provides an interesting glimpse into what happens when a social movement is institutionalized (in the conceptual rather than physical sense). The hospice concept developed as a counter-cultural idea in response to the overly impersonal, technologically dominated approach to death in the modern hospital. Its founders sought to include better control of pain with more humane approaches to managing the dying patient, especially those dying from cancer.[1] The initial promises were that this type of care would lead to better outcomes, expressed in terms of less pain, less depression, more satisfaction with the time before death among both patients and their families, and less sequelae from bereavement. The results of both a large-scale demonstration program and a smaller study in which eligible patients were actually randomly assigned to receive hospice care and usual care both showed that hospice care did about as well as usual care, but the benefits (if any) were confined to those who preferred that approach (Kane, Wales, Bernstein, Leibowitz, and Kaplan 1984; Kane, Klein, Bernstein, and Rothenberg 1986; Greer, Mor, Morris, Sherwood, Kidder, and Birnbaum 1986). It seemed to save money only when the majority of care was given at home (Birnbaum and Kidder 1984).

Once hospice care became a reimbursable form of care under Medicare (actually before the results of the national demonstration were available), what had begun as a countercultural movement took on its own orthodoxy. A National Hospice Organization, which had been originally formed to promote the hospice concept, now became the official certifying agency for those programs that met its standards and were thus eligible for coverage under Medicare. Ironically, because the patient levels for hospice care were set low, many home health agencies determined that they would be better off financially providing hospicelike care services as fee-for-service activities under Medicare home health benefit (General Accounting Office, GAO 1989). Expenditures for hospice care under Medicare have grown from $4 million in 1984 to $210 million in 1989. The number of certified hospice programs has gone from 176 to 996. The total number of hospice programs has increased from 1,345 to 1,659, indicating a growing proportion of programs becoming certified.[2]

VI. MENTALLY ILL AND MENTALLY RETARDED

Although the nursing home was intended to house primarily the chronically physically disabled, it also served those with chronic mental problems. Spurred by the closure of state mental hospitals in the mid-1960s as part of a move toward community mental health care, the nursing home became the new back ward, housing large numbers of chronically mentally ill persons (Schmidt, Reinhardt, Kane, and Olsen 1977). The creation of intermediate-care facilities (ICFs) also led to the formation of a special class of care for the mentally retarded (MR). These facilities, labeled ICF-MR, included both small group homes (15 or fewer beds) and larger facilities. A longitudinal study of the growth of the ICF-MR facilities showed that between 1977 and 1982 the number of residents increased by about one-third, to 141,000, but from there to 1986 the growth was only about 2% (Lakin, Hill, White, Wright, and Bruininks 1989). Between 1986 and 1988 the number of residents in ICF-MR facilities was virtually constant (Lakin, Prouty, White, Bruininks, and Hill 1990). Although about two-thirds of the ICF-MR residents in 1986 were in large public facilities, there was substantial growth in private facilities, housing from 23 to 35% of ICF-MR residents between 1977 and 1986.

In 1989, a new federal program was introduced in response to concerns that nursing homes were inappropriately housing persons with chronic mental illness and mental retardation. The motivations were a combination of quality concerns and an effort to redirect Medicaid funds, which had unanticipatedly gone to cover the treatment of chronic mental illness. The Preadmission Screening/Annual Resident Review (PASSAR) program required that all nursing home residents covered under Medicaid with diagnoses indicative of mental illness (except dementia) or mental retardation be screened on admission and at least annually to determine (1) whether the resident's condition requires treatment in a nursing home or whether it would be better managed in a specialized facility, and (2) whether the resident requires active treatment for his or her condition.

VII. PATIENT CHARACTERISTICS

The diverse nature of nursing home residents makes it difficult to talk about the inhabitants of these institutions in any summary way. This problem is confounded by the epidemiology of nursing home care. Any descriptions must be careful to distinguish between residents and new admissions. Because there are several streams of persons entering the nursing home, the characteristics of the entrants will be quite different from those who are found on a cross-sectional study. Thus, while entrants seem to be comprised about evenly of those destined to stay only a few months and those who will remain for years, cross-sectional studies are likely to be dominated by those who remain for a long time.

These two populations have quite different characteristics. The short-stayers are a mixed group. Some who leave quickly return to the community, while others die. The short-stayers are more likely to have diagnoses associated with death (like cancer) and with recovery (like fractured hips), whereas the long-stayers will suffer from dementia. Short-stayers are more likely to be married and to have better social supports. For several of these reasons, they are more likely to be men. They are more likely to have come from the hospital (Keeler, Kane, and Solomon 1981; Liu and Manton 1983; Lewis, Kane, Cretin, and Clark 1985).

The hybrid produces strange statistics. About 5% of those over 65 are in nursing home at any time, but the lifetime risk of institutionalization for those at age 65 is about 40% (Cohen, Tell, and Wallack 1986). About half the persons admitted to a nursing home leave within three months, but the average length of stay is over a year (Spence and Wiener 1990).

Of those who return to the community, most will return to the nursing home at some time, but two-thirds of the time before their deaths will be spent in the community (Lewis, Leake, Leal-Soleto, and Clark 1990).

Similar caution must be used in trying to distinguish the characteristics that are associated with the risk of entering a nursing home. Summaries are misleading. The standard figure of 5% over age 65 hides the real variation by age. Among those aged 65 the risk is about 1%, compared to about 6% at age 75 and over 20% at age 80. Likewise, the preponderance of women in nursing homes reflects their longer life expectancy, their tendency to marry older men, and their poorer economic situation after retirement. The observation that nonwhites use nursing homes proportionately less than do whites has been interpreted to reflect both a stronger family structure among minorities and a lack of access to nursing home care. Table 2 contrasts data based on a cross section of nursing home residents and a sample of persons discharged from nursing homes in 1985. The sample of residents has a much longer length of stay (even measured at the assumed halfway mark in their stays). Those discharged are more likely to have been admitted from a hospital. Residents are older, more often female, and less often married. The pattern of primary diagnoses distinguishes the two groups. Residents are less often admitted because of cancer and hip fracture, but more often for dementia and psychiatric diseases. Mental retardation is uncommon in either group, whereas heart disease is prevalent in both groups.

Nursing home utilization has increased over the last decade. Figure 6

Table 2. Comparisons of Residents and Discharges in 1985 National Nursing Home Survey

	Residents	*Discharges*
Average LOS (days)	1059	307
Median LOS (days)	614	70
Admitted from acute hospital (%)	37	56
Female (%)	72	63
85+ (%)	40	30
Married (%)	13	23
Primary diagnoses (%)		
Cancer	2	7
Heart disease	14	15
Dementia	11	6
Hip fracture	3	5
Mental retardation	2	1
Psychoses/neuroses	6	4

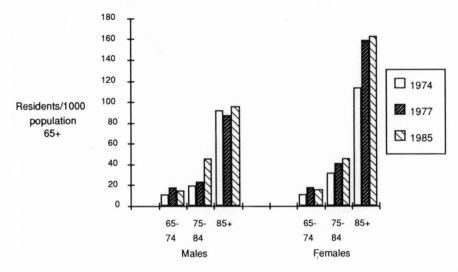

Figure 6. Nursing home utilization, 1974–1985.
(*Source: Hing et al. 1989.*)

shows the rate of nursing home use expressed as a ratio of residents per thousand persons aged 65 or more in the population. The rates increase with age and are generally higher among females than males, but there is also a pattern of increasing nursing home use with time. This pattern is all the more surprising given the picture shown in Figure 7, which compares the rate of dependency for each of a series of activities of daily living (ADLs). These data, taken from the National Nursing Home Surveys of 1973–1974, 1977, and 1985, show a general pattern of increasing dependency with time, but no clear evidence that the changes in hospital payment introduced in 1983–1984 had any profound effect on nursing home acuity.

Nursing home use seems to be the result of a combination of factors. Disability, usually reflected in some measure of ADLs, is a prime marker of risk (Morris, Sherwood, and Gutkin 1988). Often specific unpleasant problems, such as incontinence (especially fecal incontinence) or wandering (especially at night), trigger the need for institutional care. Social support has been mentioned as an attenuating factor, but its role is less likely to be felt until there is a precipitating need to consider entry (Wan and Weissert 1981).

The problem in determining precisely who is going to use nursing homes and under what circumstances has created a great deal of confusion. Programs developed to divert potential nursing home users have

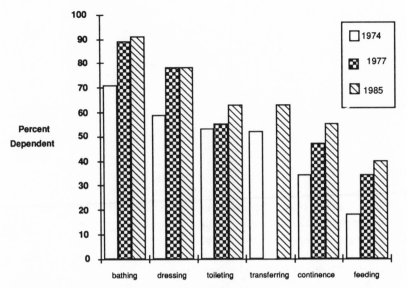

Figure 7. Change in ADL dependency levels among nursing home residents, 1974–85.
(*Source: Vital & Health Statistics 1978; Hing 1987.*)

been interpreted quite differently depending on their design. Many of those providing services to persons deemed eligible for nursing home care on the basis of disability levels or specific conditions have successfully maintained their clients in the community and claimed extraordinary savings (GAO 1979); but when the clients deemed to be at risk were randomly assigned to experimental and control groups, the benefits seemed to evaporate. The answer to the apparent paradox lies in the difference between eligibility and use. Only about 20% of those included in the control groups (all of whom were deemed eligible for nursing home care) actually took advantage of it (Weissert 1986). Until better means of establishing need for nursing home care are established, great caution needs to be exercised in talking about whether those who need such care get it and whether other means of care can displace nursing homes.

Because the definition of nursing home need is essentially arbitrary, it is very safe to say that other forms of care can displace it. Indeed, some of the newer modalities of care, which combine more of the elements of residential life with a more flexible package of care services, seem much preferable. Early experience with adult foster care and assisted living (Kane et al. 1990) suggests that it is possible to repackage nursing home services for many current users into alternatives that offer a better quality of life at no substantial risk to their quality of care. Ironically, in his now classic work on the ANH, Vladeck (1980) suggested a trichotomy of care among extended hospital use, community care, and a new institution for chronic care, which seems to be gaining favor today as we struggle for new models of care.

VIII. REGULATION

The nursing home has been called one of the most regulated industries in the United States just after nuclear power. The heavy use of regulation can be traced to a number of factors. Americans in general have a penchant for regulation. Unlike other nations, the United States seems to demand specific rules about how to govern itself. This level of specificity ironically leads to litigation where the rules are challenged and eventually made even more specific.

The situation is much worse, however, in the nursing home. Publicly funded services delivered by proprietary organizations are likely to be regulated, but nursing homes are much more controlled than are hospitals, even proprietary hospitals. In part, this heavy emphasis on regulation of the nursing home industry can be traced to its welfare heritage. Welfare agencies are not valued and are seen as unprofessional. At the same time, nursing home clients are usually there because of their vulnerability. There are strong pressures to protect them, even if it means robbing them of their independence.

Because of their clientele, nursing homes are potential catastrophes. Because disasters make headlines, much regulation occurs in response to such events. Routine neglect, which usually goes unseen, is less likely to elicit such concern. Thus, the aspects of care that can possibly create newsworthy material, such as fire protection, are actively attended to.

Nursing homes have a scandalous past. The early experience with Medicaid is checkered with stories of notorious operators who manipulated the system to reap large profits, often while providing inadequate care. The early fraudulent inflation of real estate values (Mendelson 1974) created a well publicized image of an industry committed to profit. State commissions exposing instances of terrible care led to federal hearings that uncovered similar patterns of neglect (Moss and Halamandaris 1977).

However justified the press for regulations was, the situation today is one in which the regulatory burden has become excessive. The steps taken to detect the few bad apples threaten the function of the rest of the barrel. The demand for ever more documentation can create a danger of healthy charts and sick patients. Moreover, the approach to regulation is exclusively punitive. Punishments for poor performance are not balanced by rewards for achievements. Rules developed by professionals on the basis of unproven beliefs can lead to a rigid set of orthodoxies that stifle creativity and innovation. Because long-term care is an area based on only limited empirical work linking the process of care to specific outcomes, such premature orthodoxy is counterproductive. Instead, one might hope for a system of regulations that addressed the achievements of care, wherein the outcomes of care, appropriately statistically adjusted to recognize differences in case mix, were used to define good care and commensurately rewarded or punished.

Mechanisms are available to estimate the expected course of care in nursing homes for use as a basis for comparing actual to expected care results (Kane, Bell, Riegler, Wilson, and Keeler 1983; Morris, Sherwood, May, and Bernstein 1987). There is broad consensus about the elements or domains to be including in examining outcomes (Kane, Bell, Riegler, Wilson, and Kane 1983), and even evidence of general agreement about the relative values placed on these domains, although the value weights will differ depending on the client's characteristics. (Kane, et al. 1986) It is thus possible to move from a regulatory system based heavily on predetermined methods of giving care to one that permits, even encourages, creativity by holding the providers of care accountable for achieving reasonable outcomes.

IX. STAFFING

Nursing homes have difficulty attracting adequate staff at all levels. They are generally perceived as low-prestige places to work. The pay rates are lower than those for comparable jobs in hospitals. The work is hard. Many of the clientele are confused; some are abusive. The care involves doing things that are both physically taxing and socially unpleasant (e.g., lifting heavy people, cleaning up incontinent messes). It is scarcely surprising that it is often hard to recruit staff.

At the same time, although nursing home patients are often portrayed as having little potential for improvement, studies have shown that even modest changes can often produce major improvements in function and affect. Perhaps a floor effect is often in place and these changes occur only in very deprived circumstances. Nonetheless, these findings suggest that progress is possible. The results of more specialized activities like geriatric assessment conform to the potential for making meaningful improvement even in more carefully selected groups of subjects (Rubenstein 1987).

The current shortage of nurses will exacerbate the problem. The nursing home is already at the lower end of the pecking order for recruiting professional staff. A shortage further up will make staffing even harder. Moreover, a case mix growing more acute demands more and better staff. Demanding more care from fewer people puts a still heavier burden on those who stay and threatens to drive them away as well.

The present supply of nursing home nurses seems to be composed of older women with modest amounts of training. Many are not college educated (Cotler and Kane 1988). As the standards for nursing are raised, this supply of nurses will disappear. The same pressures are being felt among the pool of persons who are now nursing aides. The competition for these service level jobs will undoubtedly drive up the costs and reduce the supply.

The antipathy toward working in a nursing home is also seen among physicians. Although regular examinations and certification of continuing need for care are required, it is sometimes very difficult to get physicians to visit their patients. Medicare payment rates are very low and steps taken to prevent billing for seeing multiple patients on a single visit to the nursing home will exacerbate the already precarious situation. Regulations requiring a minimum number of visits per months but refusing to pay for more, even when clinically needed, make nursing home care unattractive for most physicians. Not surprisingly the pattern of visits resembles the payments practices authorized, with clusters of visits around the time intervals at which a physician recertification is needed (Willemain and Mark 1980).

One promising development is the use of nonphysician practitioners as a source of primary care to nursing home residents. Both physician assistants and geriatric nurse practitioners have been shown to be effective in this capacity (Kane, Garrard, Skay, Radosevich, Buchanan, McDermott, and Arnold 1989; Kane, Garrard, Buchanan, Rosenfeld, Skay, and McDermott 1991).

X. TEACHING NURSING HOMES

One approach to stimulate improvement in nursing home care has been the effort to establish teaching nursing homes (TNHs). Modeled on the well-established relationships between hospitals and medical schools, these TNHs often rely on affiliations with schools of nursing (Mezey, Lynaugh, and Cartier 1989). In other contexts, they have proven valuable as the basis for both teaching and research (Schneider, Ory, and Aung 1987). The Veterans Administration has likewise experimented with a variant (Wieland, Rubenstein, Ouslander, and Martin 1986).

In virtually all cases, the reports have been positive. Students have been exposed to a positive model of nursing home care. Some have been successfully recruited into careers in that setting; others have at least been educated about the opportunities. The homes and their patients have shown indications of improved care as a result of the affiliation.

XI. A PROPOSAL

Although some see the nursing home as an efficient vehicle for providing both clinical attention and room and board, others have criticized it as providing too little of either nursing (technical care) or home (quality of life). The efficiency is achieved at real cost to client autonomy. Its institutional base places far more attention on doing the right things to residents than on offering them an opportunity to live out the remainder of their lives pleasantly. Rather than asking clients to adapt to the rules of the institution, reform should be directed toward insuring the client-centeredness of care.

One approach to planning for future long-term care (LTC) lies in abandoning the current fixation on the nursing home as the basic structure to be reformed and starting from a more basic premise that the goal of LTC is to provide those who need it with a package of services that meet their needs. The nursing services (which include support and rehabilitation) can be offered independently from the room and board functions. This separation has several advantages:

1. It emphasizes the client as the central focus. Services can be shaped around individual client needs and preferences. They can be brought/offered to the client in forms compatible with his or her life-style.
2. The services can be more creatively packaged, including more flexibility in intensity varying with changing client needs.
3. The universally covered portion can be restricted to the service component, leaving other funding approaches to cover room and board costs. This separation provides an incentive for persons to save for LTC because they could then afford a better standard of living but recognizes society's residual responsibility to support those without means to do so on their own.

Under this approach the distinction between institutional and home care would diminish greatly. It may be administratively necessary to require that some persons who live in inaccessible places relocate in order to receive services, but they could move into residences designed to allow them maximum personal autonomy. Regulations would be designed to assure appropriate provision of clinical services but without tightly specifying who provided them. Clients would have a greater role in choosing the intensity of service within maximums overseen by case managers. Quality could no longer be monitored in terms of adherence to fixed rules because innovation is encouraged. Instead of examining the orthodoxy of activities, emphasis would shift to the extent that reasonably expected outcomes were achieved regardless of the means used to accomplish this. The level of expectation could be based on either prior experience with similar cases or expert judgment. Its expression would reflect quality of life issues as well as more narrowly conceived functional outcomes.

Not all clients can be best served by this less institutional approach. Those totally physically and cognitively dependent (e.g., in a vegetative state) will continue to need some sort of modified hospital environment, perhaps best provided from the current excess hospital capacity. But most of those deemed eligible for LTC could be better, and probably cheaper (at least in terms of public outlays), served by an approach to care that permitted them first to live in an environment designed for living and second to receive services.

This proposal need not relegate nursing homes to the scrap heap. They can reorganize to provide a new brand of care. To the degree that they can offer both a more livable environment and more individualized care, they can compete effectively in the new care environment. Nursing homes have shown themselves to be extremely adaptable to an ever-changing regulatory climate. They should be able to rise to the challenge of more positive incentives.

XII. SUMMARY AND CONCLUSIONS

The nursing home is the result of many factors, including history, a close link to welfare, low status, and a difficult clientele. Workers in ANHs suffer in comparison to their hospital counterparts. They are less well paid, have less prestige, and have less pleasant places to work. Compared to several other countries, there is a greater gap between the nursing home and the hospital. Nonetheless, the United States has an excellent opportunity to create a new form of care to reach the clients previously served by nursing homes. New combinations of housing and long-term care services should be able to meet the needs of the future. American ingenuity will be taxed to create new systems of care with the appropriate incentives for better results.

NOTES

1. Hospice care may prove to be a modality with a limited market. It is best suited for persons who have predictable deaths. Cancer is probably the best case of this potential to diagnose and prognose with reasonable accuracy. Even then, the actual accuracy among so-called terminal cases has an error rate of at least 25%. Other conditions, where it seems reasonable to predict death in about six months, include some degenerative neurological conditions and some advanced forms of chronic cardiac and pulmonary disease, but many of these persons are too ill to appreciate the more social elements of hospice care.

2. Information supplied by the National Hospice Organization, Arlington, VA.

REFERENCES

Birnbaum, H. G. and D. Kidder. 1984. " What Does Hospice Cost?" *American Journal of Public Health* 74:689–97.

Cohen, M. A., E. J. Tell, and S. S. Wallack. 1986. "The Lifetime Risks and Costs of Nursing Home Use among the Elderly." *Medical Care* 24:1161–72.

Cotler, M. and R. L. Kane. 1988. "Registered Nurses and Nursing Home Shortages: Job Conditions and Attitudes among RNs." *Journal of Long-Term Care Administration* 16:13–18.

General Accounting Office. 1979. *Entering a Nursing Home—Costly Implications for Medicaid and the Elderly.* Washington, DC: Author.

———. 1989. "Medicare: Program Provisions and Payments Discourage Hospice Participation." Report to the Subcommittee on Health, Committee on Ways and Means, House of Representatives.

Gornick, M. and M. J. Hall. 1988. "Trends in Medicare Utilization of SNFs, HHAs, and Rehabilitation Hospitals." *Health Care Financing Review*, Annual Suppl.:27–38.

Greer, D. S., V. Mor, J. N. Morris, S. Sherwood, D. Kidder, and H. Birnbaum. 1986. "An Alternative in Terminal Care: Results of the National Hospice Study." *Journal of Chronic Disease* 39:9–26.

Hing, E. 1987. "Use of Nursing Homes by the Elderly: Preliminary Data from the 1985 National Nursing Home Survey." *Advance Data From Vital and Health Statistics No 135.* Public Health Service, Hyattsville, MD.

———. 1989. "Nursing Home Utilization by Current Residents: United States, 1985." National Center for Health Statistics, Public Health Service, Washington, DC: U.S. Government Printing Office.

Hing, E., E. Sekscenski, and G. Strahan. 1989. *The Nursing Home Survey; 1985 Summary for the United States,* Vital and Health Statistics Series 13, No.97 DHHS Pub No (PHS) 89-1758. Washington DC: Public Health Service.

Kane, R. L., R. M. Bell, and S. Z. Riegler. 1986. "Value Preferences for Nursing-Home Outcomes." *Gerontologist* 26:303–8.

Kane, R. L., R. Bell, S. Riegler, A. Wilson, and R. A. Kane. 1983. "Assessing the Outcomes of Nursing Home Patients." *Journal of Gerontology* 38:385–93.

Kane, R. L., R. M. Bell, S. Z. Riegler, A. Wilson, and E. Keeler. 1983. "Predicting the Outcomes of Nursing-Home Patients." *Gerontologist* 23:200–6.

Kane, R. L., G. J. Garrard, J. L. Buchanan, A. Rosenfeld, C. Skay, and S. McDermott. 1991. "Improving Primary Care in Nursing Homes." *Journal of the American Geriatrics Society* 39:359–67.

Kane, R. L., G. J. Garrard, C. L. Skay, D. M. Radosevich, J. L. Buchanan, S. M. McDermott, and S. B. Arnold. 1989. "Effects of a Geriatric Nurse Practitioner on the Process and Outcomes of Nursing Home Care." *American Journal of Public Health* 79:1271–77.

Kane, R. A., L. Illston, R. L. Kane, and J. Nyman. 1990. "Meshing Services with Housing: Lessons from Adult Foster Care and Assisted Living in Oregon." Final Report to John A. Hartford Foundation, Division of Health Services Research and Policy, School of Public Health, University of Minnesota, Minneapolis.

Kane, R. L., S. J. Klein, L. Bernstein, and R. Rothenberg. 1986. "The Role of Hospice in Reducing the Impact of Bereavement." *Journal of Chronic Disease* 39:735–42.

Kane, R. L., J. Wales, L. Bernstein, A. Leibowitz, and S. Kaplan. 1984. "A Randomized Controlled Trial of Hospice Care." *Lancet* 1:890–94.

Keeler, E. B., R. L. Kane, and D. H. Solomon. 1981. "Short-and-Long-Term Residents of Nursing Homes." *Medical Care* 19:363–69.

Lakin, K. C., B. K. Hill, C. C. White, E. A. Wright, and R. H. Bruininks. 1989. "Longitudinal Patterns in ICF-MR Utilization, 1977–1986." *Mental Retardation* 27:149–58.

Lakin, K. C., R. W. Prouty, C. C. White, R. H. Bruininks, and B. K. Hill. 1990. *Intermediate Care Facilities for Persons with Mental Retardation (ICFs-MR): Program Utilization and Resident Characteristics*. Minneapolis: Center for Residential and Community Services, Institute on Community Integration, University of Minnesota.

Lewis, M. A., R. L. Kane, S. Cretin, and V. Clark. 1985. "The Immediate and Subsequent Outcomes of Nursing Home Care." *American Journal of Public Health* 75:758–62.

Lewis, M. A., B. Leake, M. Leal-Soleto, and V. Clark. 1990. "First Nursing Home Admissions: Time Spent at Home and in Institutions After Discharge." *American Journal of Public Health* 80:22–24.

Liu, K., P. Doty, and K. Manton. 1990. "Medicaid Spenddown in Nursing Homes." *Gerontologist* 30:7–15.

Liu, K., and K. G. Manton. 1983. "The Characteristics and Utilization Pattern of an Admission Cohort of Nursing Home Patients (I)." *Gerontologist* 23:92–98.

Meiners, M. R. 1978. "Nursing Home Costs—1972, U.S. National Nursing Home Survey, August 1973–April 1974." *Vital and Health Statistics*, series 13, no. 38. DHHS Pub. No. (PHS) 79-1789. Washington, DC: Public Health Service.

Mendelson, M. A. 1974. *Tender Loving Greed*. New York: Knopf.

Mezey, M. D., J. E. Lynaugh, and M. M. Cartier. 1989. *Nursing Homes and Nursing Care: Lessons from the Teaching Nursing Homes*. New York: Springer.

Morris, J., S. Sherwood, and C. Gutkin. 1988. "Inst-risk II: An Approach to Forecasting Relative Risk of Future Institutional Placement." *Health Services Research* 23:511–36.

Morris, J. N., S. Sherwood, M. M. May, and E. Bernstein. 1987. "FRED: An Innovative Approach to Nursing Home Level-of-Care Assignments." *Health Services Research* 22:117–40.

Morrisey, M. A., F. A. Sloan, and J. Valvona. 1988. "Medicare Prospective Payment and Posthospital Transfers to Subacute Care." *Medical Care* 26:685–98.

Moses, S. A. 1990. "The Fallacy of Impoverishment." *Gerontologist* 30:21–25.

Moss, F. E., and V. J. Halamandaris. 1977. *Too Old, Too Sick, Too Bad: Nursing Homes in America*. Germantown, MD: Aspen Systems.

National Center for Health Statistics. 1990. *Health, United States, 1989*. Hyattsville, MD: Public Health Service.

Neu, C. R., and S. C. Harrison. 1988. *Posthospital Care before and after the Medicare Prospective Payment System*. Santa Monica, CA: Rand Corporation.

Office of National Cost Estimates. 1990. "National Health Expenditures, 1988." *Health Care Financing Review* 11:1–41.

Rubenstein, L. Z. 1987. "Geriatric Assessment: An Overview of Its Impacts." Pp. 1–16 in *Clinics in Geriatric Medicine*, edited by L. Z. Rubenstein, L. J. Campbell, and R. L. Kane. Philadelphia: Saunders.

Schmidt, L., A. M. Reinhardt, R. L. Kane, and D. M. Olsen. 1977. "The Mentally Ill in Nursing Homes: New Back Wards in the Community." *Archives of General Psychiatry* 34:687–91.

Schneider, E. L., M. Ory, and M. L. Aung. 1987. "Teaching Nursing Homes Revisited." *Journal of the American Medical Association* 257:2771–75.

Spence, D. A., and J. M. Wiener. 1990. "Nursing Home Length of Stay Patterns: Results from the 1985 National Nursing Home Survey." *Gerontologist* 30:16–20.

Vladeck, B. G. 1980. *Unloving Care: The Nursing Home Tragedy*. New York: Basic Books.

Wan, T., and W. Weissert. 1981. "Social Support Networks, Patient Status and Institutionalization." *Research on Aging* 3:240–56.

Weissert, W. G. 1986. "Hard Choices: Targeting Long-Term Care to the 'At Risk' Aged." *Journal of Health Politics, Policy and Law* 11:463–81.

Wieland, D., L. Z. Rubenstein, J. G. Ouslander, and S. E. Martin. 1986. "Organizing an Academic Nursing Home." *Journal of American Medical Association* 255:2622–27.

Willemain, T. R., and R. B. Mark. 1980. "The Distribution of Intervals between Visits as a Basis for Assessing and Regulating Physician Services in Nursing Homes." *Medical Care* 18:427–41.

The independent sector is regulated by either the health districts or the Local Authorities, depending on whether they are nursing homes or residential-care homes.

Residential homes with less than four residents have not until now been subject to registration and regulation. The figures presented in the following therefore do not include these homes. It is estimated that as many as 20% of all homes have less than four residents and are thus outside any public control (Hudson 1990).

III. BALANCE OF PROVISION AND FUNDING

A. Present Provision and Funding

Nursing and residential care is provided by the public, private, and voluntary sectors, but the balance among these varies among the care groups. For elderly, chronically ill, and physically handicapped the private sector is the largest provider, accounting for 47% of all places, compared with 43% from the public sector. The private sector provides relatively more residential places (60%) than nursing home places (40%). Voluntary provision is modest, accounting for only 10% of all places. Provision for mentally ill and mentally handicapped people is still dominated by the public sector, which provides about 80% of beds for each of these care groups. The remaining 20% is shared almost equally between the private and voluntary sectors (Laing and Buisson 1990).

Of the three care groups, the first—elderly, chronically ill, and disabled people—is by far the largest in terms of total number of places, accounting for about 80% of all places. For this reason, and because care of mentally ill and mentally handicapped people raises more issues related to the different hospital sectors, this paper will concentrate primarily upon the former group, the vast majority of whom are elderly people.

The sources of finance for the different sectors providing care for elderly and disabled people are shown in Table 1. Public finance is by far the most important source of funding, first through direct provision, out of NHS or local social services funds, and secondly through central government social security payments for clients in the independent sector. Local health districts and Local Authorities also finance the independent sector through the contracting out of services, but so far this type of activity is of minor importance. It is worth noting that although a great deal of private and voluntary provision is publicly funded, about 60% of the income of this sector comes from private and voluntary contributions. More than half the residents in private institutions pay their own charges, and many pay charges above the rate of social security payments, topping up the deficit through family contributions.

Table 1. Public/Private Expenditure on Nursing, Residential, and Long-Stay Hospital Care of Elderly, Chronically Ill, and Physically Handicapped People, England and Wales, 1988

	m£	%
Public supply and finance[a]	1,729	44
Public supply and private/voluntary finance[b]	279	7
Private/voluntary supply and finance[c]	1,146	29
Private/voluntary supply and public finance[d]	770	20
Total	3,924	100

[a] Local Authority net revenue expenditure £529m; NHS geriatric hospitals £770m; ESMI in NHS hospitals £430m.
[b] Local Authority charges to residents.
[c] Personally paid fees.
[d] Central government income support ("social security") £743m; Local Authority support of people in independent homes £16m; NHS contracts £11m.
Source: Laing and Buisson, 1990.

B. Changes in the Balance of Provision

In the last decade the number of residential and nursing home places for older people has grown faster than the number of older people in the population. The growth has been mainly in the private sector of provision; indeed the supply of publicly provided places has decreased in relation to the proportion of older people. Thus, while at the beginning of the 1980s Local Authorities provided about 70% of residential places for people over 65, by the end of the 1980s their share of provision was less than half. In absolute terms, the number of Local Authority residential places has increased very little during the 1980s and it is likely to decrease through the selling off of homes to the independent sector in line with central government policies (see below). For elderly and disabled people the number of places in the private sector increased dramatically in the 1980s: by about 600% for residential-care places, and more than 400% for nursing home places. It is noticeable for this care group that the voluntary sector has not expanded. For mentally ill and mentally handicapped people, the increase of the independent sector is also visible, although less dramatic.

C. Variations in Provision

The variations in provision between different geographical localities are considerable and have been exacerbated by the growth of private provision. For residential care, Local Authority provision in 1984 ranged from just over 30 beds per thousand people 75+ in the lowest provided region (Southern) to 52.6 beds per thousand people 75+ in the highest provided region (Northern). Variations in private and voluntary rates of provision are considerably higher. The number of private beds per 1000 people 75+ in the Inner London region was 5.6 and in the South Western region nearly 50. Furthermore, differences within regions are large. In 1984 for example, nine Local Authorities had no private homes; Devon and East Sussex alone had nearly 11,500 beds in private homes (Larder, Day, and Klein 1986).

Public provision tends to be higher in the poorest parts of the country, whereas private provision is concentrated in the wealthier areas. But despite such equalizing tendencies, total provision is most heavily concentrated in the southern—well-off—parts of the country, where the rate of private provision has increased the most in the last decade. Although the proportion of elderly people is higher in these areas, the concentration of private homes in certain areas, in particular seaside resorts, is a function more of availability of suitable and less costly accommodation rather than any pattern of need. Thus along the south coast guest houses and hotels have been converted into homes for older people, whereas in inner London for example, property prices and the cost of living have discouraged any significant expansion of private provision.

IV. RESIDENTIAL/NURSING HOME PROVISION IN RELATION TO NEED AND DEMAND

A. Extent of Use of Institutional Compared with Home Care

About 5% of people aged 65 and over live in institutions (nursing and residential-care homes). Thus by far the large majority of older people live in their own homes. Of those 65 years and over living at home, 9% are in receipt of home help service at any one time. Most people receive home help on a permanent basis, unlike home nursing, which is provided for short-term episodes of acute need. The question of whether home care is being effective in containing demand for institutional care is dealt with elsewhere in this volume (by Davies). However, there is no doubt that, irrespective of the quality and efficiency of home care services, the structure of funding has had a major impact upon the pattern of service use, encouraging institutional care. This will be discussed in more detail below.

B. Patterns of Provision

As already pointed out, the provision of private homes, although it can to some extent said to be demand led, by concentrating supply in areas with a relatively high proportion of elderly people, is influenced as much by supply factors such as availability of property. Public provision, being concentrated more in poorer areas, could be said to reflect differences in need. But even for this sector variations cannot be totally accounted for by reference to need and to availability of alternative services. Several studies suggest that a relatively low level of provision of Local Authority residential care is not associated with high levels of provision of geriatric hospital provision or indeed home help provision. In other words, services do not appear to be planned as part of a system of substitution between individual services. The financial and organizational separation between health and social services has always posed constraints upon any attempts at overall planning. But even within Local Authorities that are responsible for both residential and home help provision one study pointed out that between 1979 and 1983 there was no correlation between the increase in the amount of home help provision and the decrease in the provision of Local Authority places (Bebbington and Tong 1986). As far as Local Authority provision is concerned, at least part of the explanation of variations is to be found in the political priorities of individual Local Authorities (Sinclair 1988).

C. Clients of Residential/Nursing Homes

Is the provision of homes adequate in relation to the need of the population? For a number of reasons there is of course no simple answer to this question. Demand in the 1980s certainly increased, but the extent to which the increased demand reflects real needs is debatable. In an attempt to answer the question let us briefly consider the characteristics and circumstances of those admitted into residential/nursing care compared with those who are not.

As far as formal admission criteria/procedures are concerned, for the private/voluntary sector there were, until recently, no regulations stipulating criteria for admission or procedures for entry into a home. Only financial criteria operated as a rationing device in that people either had to pay for their own care or they had to qualify for social security benefits, paid on the basis of financial means testing and not on any assessment of needs for care. For the public sector, admission is based on needs criteria, and in practice is left to the judgment of the professionals.

Studies of applicants and residents in residential care point to a constellation of factors leading to application and admissions to institutions. The number of applications and admissions to institutions rises with increasing age, and the average age has been rising in the last decades. The age distribution of residents in Local Authority residential care is roughly the following: 20% less than 75, 40% aged 75–84, and 40% 85 or over (Sinclair 1988). For nursing homes it is estimated that about three-quarters are aged 80 or over. Patients in hospital long-term care are younger: Only 65% of them are over 80 years old (Challis and Bartlett 1988). Women outnumber men, partly because of the age distribution, but also because older men are more likely than women of the same age to have a spouse. The ratio of women to men in Local Authority homes is about 7:3 (Sinclair 1988), in nursing homes about 5:1, according to one study (Challis and Bartlett 1988).

By far the largest majority of those applying for institutional care have some problems of physical and/or mental disability, and could be said to be somehow at risk or in need of surveillance. However this does not necessarily mean that the needs of many of these people could not be met outside institutions. It is estimated that even at the highest levels of incapacity there are about three or four times as many people in the community as in residential care (Bebbington and Tong 1986). Residents in voluntary homes tend to be less disabled than those in Local Authority and private homes. The main difference between Local Authority homes and private residential homes is that the former tend to have a higher proportion of confused elderly people (Sinclair 1988). Although overall the proportion of physically disabled people in private residential homes appears to be similar to that of the Local Authority homes, there is considerable variation within the private sector in the degree to which they are geared to coping with dependent people, and therefore in the composition of their clientele.

The overall picture as regards the distribution of clients between different types of care (home care compared with institutional care; residential compared with nursing home; public compared with independent sectors) is one of considerable overlap. In other words, the level of dependency does not adequately predict the type of care a person receives; many are inappropriately placed, receiving either too much or too little care.

Other factors besides disability therefore affect the likelihood of a person entering an institution. As already indicated, the degree of informal support can often be decisive. People living alone, and especially people who are bereaved, are more likely to apply for care than people living with others, the majority of whom are married people. Availability of help from others—neighbors, friends, etc.—is also influential. While carers can to a large extent substitute for formal services, they can also be the main force behind applications for residential and nursing care. Thus the attitudes of relatives can work both ways, and often relatives who appear to push an elderly person into care have been providing care over a long period and have come to the end of their tether.

There is some evidence that income and class affect the choice of institution and the timing of the decision to enter an institution. Old people from professional/managerial classes are more likely than others to use nursing or private homes than Local Authority homes. Furthermore, people of relative affluence are more likely to postpone entry into an institution and to avoid entry altogether. Income affects decisions to enter care indirectly through housing. Homeless people, and people who do not rent or own their own homes are more likely to enter institutions. Often a combination of functional disability and inappropriate housing precipitates entry into care (Sinclair 1988).

Finally, the nature of the services and system of services, as opposed to the needs and characteristics of the clients themselves, probably have the most decisive influence on the likelihood of entry into an institution. First, the spectrum of services available sets the parameters within which any choice is possible. Lack of home care services is one example. Studies of applicants to residential care show that many very vulnerable people in this group receive very little or no home care at all. While there is little doubt that the present supply of home care services is inadequate in meeting existing needs, it is also argued that the services available are not allocated according to need and that better assessment and allocation processes—better case management—would help to overcome some of these problems (Davies, Bebbington, and Charnley 1990). Several studies show that admissions, whether to Local Authority residential care or to private nursing homes, are often arranged in a hurry in response to a crisis, and without any thorough assessment of social, medical or functional needs (Sinclair 1988; Challis and Bartlett 1988). Irrespective of such managerial problems, another factor that influences care decisions is the interests and needs of the various organizations themselves. For example, the wish by home managers to balance their intake of clients can often be more decisive than the needs of the clients (Hunter, McKeganey, and MacPherson 1988). Similarly, pressure from hospitals to free beds is likely to precipitate entry into institutions. Thus, while on the one hand lack of contact with appropriate services may contribute to people entering residential care, on the other hand, contact with services can in itself be a factor behind admission. Doctors and social workers may persuade people to apply for admission, and this applies in particular to people admitted to hospital. One study of nursing home residents showed that more than one-third were admitted from hospital (Challis and Bartlett 1988), and studies of applicants to residential care found that those applying from hospital were more likely to become residents than those applying from their own homes (Sinclair 1988).

One of the most important, and most widely debated, factors underlying the increased use of residential and nursing home care is the structure of provision and the modes of financing, which has created incentives in the direction of institutional as opposed to community care, and private as opposed to publicly provided institutions. This whole issue will be discussed further below. From the point of view of consumers, the point worth noting is that older people who qualified for basic welfare (income support) have been able to enter private homes and receive funding for this from central government funds, thus—in theory—giving them the choice between a publicly provided Local Authority home and a private home. (From the point of view of Local Authorities it presented an opportunity to offload some of their burden on to central government, see below.) In practice however, it is doubtful whether the majority of people in residential and nursing homes are there out of choice. As far as Local Authority residential homes are concerned, the Wagner Report (produced by a commission set up to provide an independent review of residential care) concluded that older people often enter into residential care as a result of other people's decisions and actions; they know little about where they are going, and they are mostly resigned or ambivalent about entry, only a minority appearing to make a positive choice. The report concludes that although the existence of private homes should widen the choice for older people, in practice studies of clients in the private sector show that "the proportion of residents exercising choice is so small that consumer choice serves no regulatory function" (Sinclair 1988:265).

V. THE CARE PROVIDED IN RESIDENTIAL AND NURSING HOMES

The care setting offered in residential and nursing homes varies enormously, in terms of size, location, facilities, organization, and staffing levels. For private homes the charges also vary considerably.

The vast majority of staff in both types of homes are unqualified and female. The majority of Local Authority residential homes are managed by a qualified person, most often a qualified nurse, or sometimes a social worker. In smaller private homes the proprietors themselves often provide the main staffing input including night cover. As far as nursing homes are concerned, they all employ at least a qualified nurse, as this is a condition of their registration. But less than half of the nursing home staff are qualified nurses. About 60% are untrained auxiliaries, many working on a part-time basis. Staffing ratios vary, from a mean of 1.25 staff to every resident in small homes to a mean of 0.6 staff per resident in large homes (Challis and Bartlett 1988).

The quality of life offered in residential and nursing homes does of course vary, yet the picture painted by many observers for most homes is fairly bleak. To quote the Wagner Report; "It would, for example, be exceptional to find a Local Authority home in which most residents can lock their own rooms, or have their own furniture, or get up when they please, or bathe when they want" (Sinclair 1988:269). Added to this are criticisms of inactivity and lack of stimulation. Observers of private nursing homes came to very similar conclusions, stressing the sameness of daily life and regimes, many homes "offering little more than what could be described as basic 'servicing' of patients" (Challis and Bartlett 1988:68).

VI. REGULATION OF STANDARDS

A. Formal Regulations

In formal terms nursing homes have existed since 1927, when the first Nursing Home Registration Act was passed. The concept of residential-care homes was introduced two decades later, in 1948, in order to distinguish old people's homes from nursing homes, the latter being a place for nursing whereas the former was seen to provide accommodation. This distinction still applies in the present system of legislation, the Registered Homes Act of 1984, which introduced the concept of personal care for residential homes as distinct from nursing. Part I of the act deals with residential-care homes, Part II with nursing homes and mental nursing homes, Part III with registered homes tribunals, and Part IV with offenses.

The act stipulates that residential-care homes catering to four or more people must register with the Local Authorities, which are also responsible for inspecting these homes twice a year. Nursing homes must register and be inspected by the local health authorities. The conditions and procedures for registration are set up in very broad outlines in the act. More detailed specifications are listed in two codes of practice: *Home Life* for residential-care homes (Working Party on a Code of Practice for Residential Care 1984), and for nursing homes a handbook produced by the National Association of Health Authorities (NAHA 1985), a nongovernmental body. In order to allow the widest possible range of care to be provided in one home, dual registration, that is, registration with both social services and the health authority, is required for nursing homes that have four or more patients who do not need nursing care and for residential-care homes that have one or more residents who need nursing care.

The regulations concerning registration and inspection set out in this act do not cover publicly provided services. Health services in general are subject to inspection by the Health Advisory Service, created in the 1970s, and Local Authority social services have since 1985 been inspected by the central government Social Services Inspectorate. The requirements that have to be met in order to qualify for registration are only very broadly defined in the legislation. For nursing homes the requirement for a qualified nurse to be on duty is the main one, as regards staffing. No staffing ratios have been stipulated, as this is seen to be variable depending on size and clientele of individual homes. The interpretation of what constitutes "adequate" staffing is left to individual authorities. The NAHA handbook lists a number of requirements related to areas like accommodation and general services, food service and facilities, waste disposal, and control of infection, and for homes specifically for older people it lists occupational and recreational facilities to be provided. In *Home Life*, the guidelines for residential-care homes pay more attention to quality of life issues and to dignity and independence, and devotes less space to matters such as requirements for food preparation. These differences in emphasis reflect the different concerns of the health as opposed to the social professions. What is common to both sets of guidelines is the lack of precision in the requirements, which are often phrased in terms of adequacy, leaving it to individual authorities or inspectors to interpret the meaning of this.

One of the problems in having a different set of guidelines for residential and nursing care is that homes that have dual registration have to fulfill both sets of criteria. Furthermore the distinction between personal care and nursing is not entirely robust. It could be argued that what is listed among so-called nursing duties are tasks that are often performed by caring relatives. In practice the question of definition is decided by a professional nurse from the health authority, who, according to the NAHA guidelines, will decide whether a particular person needs nursing care that is over and above that provided by the community service.

B. The Principles and Practice of Regulation

What is the rationale behind regulation in Britain? One of the keys to the answer to this question is the fact that historically the public sector has been the main provider of health and social services. Public provision has been seen as the norm: The very fact that it was public has been assumed to be a guarantee of quality, and therefore the need for any nationally controlled regulation has been assumed to be superfluous. The need for regulation and quality inspection was seen to apply mainly to the independent sector, and the growing concern with regulation can in part be seen on the background of the growth in private provision, especially since an increasing proportion was funded by public money. However, it is interesting to note that the first Nursing Homes Regulation Act in 1927 was passed as a result of pressure from the nursing profession, which was concerned with competition from unqualified staff (Day and Klein 1987). The 1984 legislation came about as a result of a number of pressures: the emergence of a wide disparity of private boardinghouses, the sheer growth in numbers, and the publicizing of various scandals in private homes. Yet the scope of the regulation has remained limited in certain respects, which reflects the British attitude to regulation. Thus Day and Klein (1987) in their comparison of the British and American systems of regulation argue that the British requirements are of a more persuasive and informal nature than the American ones, which tend to be much more rule bound. Staffing input requirements tend to be much more specific in the American system as do, similarly, process requirements. For example, regulations in the British system contain very little on how care should actually be organized, in contrast to the American requirements for managed packages of care and detailed specification of services that have to be available. What both have in common is a lack of outcome requirements. The differences between the two systems reflect the difference in the styles of strategies of regulation, whereby the British style has more elements of a *compliance model* in contrast to the *deterrence model*, which is closer to the practice in many American states. The compliance model emphasizes the prevention of problems and encourages improvements, and the process of inspection is more like a process of negotiation and bargaining. The deterrence model is more punitive and rule bound and makes more use of legal proceedings. This means that in the British system the actual enforcement of regulations through the statutory inspection of nursing homes takes the form less of policing than of discussions between peers. Nursing homes are inspected by nurses, who see their role mainly as improving professional practices and providing support and advice. This professional model of inspection is even more evident in the Health Advisory Service, which monitors the care provided for elderly and mentally ill people. As the name suggests, its role is advisory. Its reports carry no mandatory force, and are produced by teams of professionals who visit health and social services (Day, Klein, and Tipping 1988).

C. Criticisms of the System of Regulation

In recent years criticisms of this system have been mounted in several respects. First, a number of scandals in publicly provided homes have raised doubts as to the self-regulatory abilities of this sector, and have led to calls for some independent inspection of these homes. In the latest reforms in connection with recent community care legislation, inspection of Local Authority homes remains the responsibility of Local Authorities themselves. They are, however, asked to create independent inspectorates within their authorities, which should be able to keep at arm's length from the providers, but many still see this as an unsatisfactory solution. The response of the present government to the whole question of quality control and value for money has been to let the market solve these problems. Thus there is now pressure on Local Authorities to contract out more of its services to the private and voluntary sectors, and to reduce the stock of homes it runs. This is parallel to the government's policies in relation to the health service, where the creation of internal markets through the separation of funding and provision—but not (yet) through the selling off of public services— has been the main response to the problems of cost containment, prioritization, and quality.

A second criticism that has been raised against the 1984 act is the exemption from registration of residential homes with less than four clients. As already mentioned, these are estimated to constitute about 20% of the market of private residential care. This criticism has come from a number of quarters: the professional bodies, trade unions, associations of social services directors, metropolitan authorities, and county councils, as well as consumer associations such as Age Concern. The government has now responded to this pressure by including these small homes, although requirements will be less stringent than for larger homes. It is left to the discretion of Local Authorities to monitor the fitness of those in charge of these smaller homes.

Third, the issue of the inspection process has been raised in several ways. Existing practices have been criticized as being inadequate, with visits being too brief, the absence of feedback to proprietors, and the application of standards that can be assessed quantitatively rather than attempts to assess quality. One of the problems associated with the inadequacy of the inspection process is the lack of resources available for health authorities and social services to undertake this task. This problem is likely to become more acute with the increasing number of homes that social services are having to inspect. Another issue relates to the problem of enforcement. Homes found wanting on the requirements can be struck off the list, but in practice there is reluctance to do this, not only because of the British tradition of regulatory enforcement, but because it presents problems of finding suitable alternatives for the clients.

VII. FUNDING OF RESIDENTIAL/NURSING HOMES

A. The Role of Social Welfare Payments

The most dramatic change in the 1980s in the supply of homes for elderly people is the vast increase in the number of private homes. One of the keys to an understanding of this development is to be found in the nature of the financing system and in the regulations for social welfare payments. First it is important to bear in mind that Local Authorities have been responsible for providing and funding their own social care facilities, whether domiciliary or institutional, for those individuals considered to be in need. For health care similar responsibilities belong to the local health authorities. A private/voluntary sector has always existed alongside this public sector—indeed Local Authorities would refer people to private and especially voluntary homes and provide the funding as well. In the 1970s with the growing demand arising from demographic pressures, Local Authorities made increasing use of the independent sector to meet the shortfall in their own supply of accommodation, which has not increased substantially since 1977. This to a large extent explains the beginning of the upward trend in supply of private provision that happened in the late 1970s. Alongside Local Authority funding, however, the independent sector had always been able to take in people who received social welfare benefits, which could include allowance for board and lodging if needed. In 1980 changes in these welfare payments were made that effectively enabled people staying in independent homes to pay whatever was the local rate from social welfare payments. Social welfare payments come out of central government funds and are administered by local officers, who were enabled to exercise a great deal of discretion in setting the local allowances. These social security officers have been the only gatekeepers into residential/nursing homes. Their role has been to assess the financial means of clients. Thus people have been able to enter homes without any assessment of their care needs whatsoever. In the light of the funding made available from central government welfare payments, and in the light of the financial squeeze on Local Authority budgets, these authorities began to realize that there was no need for them to provide or fund residential care. As long as people agreed to enter a voluntary or private home the cost could be covered by welfare payments. Thus in the 1980s the number of Local Authority–supported residents in private and voluntary homes fell dramatically.

This development, whereby the private sector of providers has expanded, might be seen to be totally in accordance with the principles and ideologies of the Thatcher government, and has therefore at times been construed as a deliberate policy on the part of the government. However, given the reactions later by the government and given that this expansion led to a dramatic increase in public welfare expenditure, a more likely explanation is to be found in a combination of circumstances mentioned, i.e., demographic changes, scarcity of resources in Local Authorities, and a demand from the voluntary sector to increase the rate of welfare payments to cover costs of board and lodging. The explosion of the private sector following the 1980 regulations was not really foreseen or planned. When it became clear what was happening, the government began to take action, and through various regulations began to try to limit social welfare payments. Without here going into detail regarding these changes, it can be said that the main change that took place since the mid-1980s is that ceilings were set on the amount of welfare benefits that can be paid to individuals in residential and nursing homes. Thus, in addition to the regulation of standards (the 1984 Registered Homes Act) regulation through price was introduced. Although the rates of welfare payments given to individuals vary depending on the type of home they live in (residential care or nursing care for example), there has been no real attempt to link the two in the sense of addressing the question of value for money. Indeed, it could be argued that any attempt to link them and to exercise too rigorous criteria of quality might reveal the inadequacy of the funding made available. The independent sector and Local Authorities alike have now for some time been protesting that welfare payments are inadequate, and that an increasing number of homes are going out of business.

B. The Private and Voluntary Sectors Compared

It is worth noting that the voluntary sector appears to have responded differently from the private sector to the opportunities offered through welfare payments. Compared with the vast increase in the number of places in private homes, the increase in the voluntary sector has been almost insignificant. Although it is difficult to find hard evidence to explain this difference, a number of possible explanations have been suggested (Parker 1990). First, the proportion of poorer residents in voluntary homes may be smaller; second, voluntary organizations may be less able to respond to the availability of welfare allowances because of their administrative structures, which tend to be larger, more bureaucratic, and more traditional than private organizations; third, their cost structure is different and they tend to operate in high-cost areas like inner London; fourth, because they are not driven primarily by a profit incentive, their approach to investment may be different. For example, private organizations are likely to be more attracted to investment in property in order to capitalize on rising property prices. Finally, attitudes in the voluntary sector could be said to be guided more by professional opinion, which would emphasize community care rather than an expansion in residential care.

Whatever the reasons behind the differences between the two sectors, the important point is that there are differences: "Certainly, the incentives or disincentives to which they respond appear to be different; the beliefs and convictions that they hold may vary; their financial circumstances are unlikely to be the same, and their constituencies may also be markedly different" (Parker 1990:309–10). In light of the recent policies whereby the "independent" sector is to be given a more prominent role, it is important to bear in mind that this is not a homogeneous sector, which responds in the same way to a specific set of incentives.

VIII. THE 1990 NHS AND COMMUNITY CARE ACT

It is impossible to discuss residential and nursing homes without considering developments in relation to community care. No one would dispute that there ought to be a link between institutional care and community or home care, just as there ought to be a link between health and social services—from the point of view of policymaking, planning, and operation of services—and that therefore what goes on in one sector will affect the other. But even at the level of theoretical speculation the relationships between these sectors is complex and not at all obvious. Looking at practices, however, it is not difficult to point to the absence or inadequacies in the relationships. In the British context the organizational separation of health and social services has always presented a barrier to any integrated policies, although attempts to bring the two sectors together, through joint planning and joint finance, have been going on for a long time, but with limited success. As far as residential and home care is concerned, the two are to some extent closely linked in that they are both the responsibility of the Local Authorities, and funded and organized within one body. The complicating element, however, has been the availability of central government funding for independent homes, and thus a financial fragmentation, which has created perverse incentives. Although in principle these arrangements could be seen to have created an incentive for Local Authorities to substitute their own institutions for home care, in practice this has not happened. The incentive has been not to expand services at all. In light of this, the government decided to set up an inquiry (the Griffiths inquiry) to consider community care policies in a wider context. Some of these recommendations were incorporated in the government white paper *Caring for People* (Department of Health 1989), which formed the basis of the most recent legislation, passed in 1990, the NHS and Community Care Act. Three major aspects can be highlighted as of particular relevance to residential and nursing home provision. First, one of the key changes will be the transfer of financial responsibility for all residential care to Local Authorities. The government will transfer to Local Authorities the resources that it would otherwise have provided to finance care through social welfare payments to people in residential and nursing homes. People already in institutions will continue the existing arrangements, and the change therefore will be phased in gradually for new clients. Thus the financial incentive for Local Authorities to refer their clients to institutions will be removed, since all social care provision will be funded from one budget. Furthermore, all potential clients have to be assessed, not only in terms of financial means but in terms of their need for care. Thus the scene has been set for a more controlled system of referral.

A second aspect of the new legislation is the emphasis that the government puts on the role of the independent sector. Local Authorities are being told to promote the development of a "flourishing independent sector," by developing their purchasing and contracting role to become "enabling authorities" rather than direct providers. They are given no choice in this matter, but must show in their plans that they are working toward this goal. Thus the responsibilities of Local Authorities are to consist mainly in strategic planning, "case management," and regulation/control of quality.

Third, it is important to note that the separation between health and social services is being preserved. Health authorities continue to be responsible for the input and control of health-related care, for example, community nursing, provision of terminal care, and inspection of nursing homes. In order to improve coordination, health and social services are told to cooperate closely, both at the strategic and operational levels. They must produce coordinated plans, which clearly show the interrelations between health and social services, and in the day-to-day allocation of services all relevant professionals must be involved. Case managers must be allocated to individuals, and they will be responsible for the coordination of the input from the different professionals.

The measures taken in regard to regulation and inspection have already been mentioned. The existing division of responsibilities between health and social services will continue, but Local Authorities will have the added responsibility of setting up independent inspectorates that can undertake arm's-length inspection of all residential services, including Local Authority ones, and of applying the same criteria to these homes as to independent residential homes. The existing code of practice for residential homes is to continue to be the basis, but some further guidance is to be issued by central government.

IX. FUTURE PROSPECTS FOR RESIDENTIAL
AND NURSING HOME PROVISION

The new legislation was passed in 1990, but the implementation has been happening in stages, and the most important stage, the transfer of central government funds to Local Authorities, has only recently taken effect (i.e., from 1 April 1993). The period between enactment and implementation has been one of frantic debate and uncertainty, a period during which a number of ministerial circulars have been issued and announcements made, clarifying—and at times—confusing the situation. During all this time, referrals to independent homes, paid for out of central government money, have continued to increase. Indeed there has been a positive incentive to increase referrals in order to place people in homes before the changes in the funding mechanisms took place, since those already in social security–funded institutional places will continue to be paid for by central government.

At the end of 1992 the government announced how much money would be transferred to Local Authorities. This transitional grant is supposedly based on what the government estimates it would have had to spend in social security money on institutional care. The sum announced fell short of what Local Authorities themselves judged to be needed, although it is generally considered to be a significant amount. This transitional grant will be ring fenced for the first four years, i.e., earmarked for care of disabled people. After that, the money could in theory be spent by Local Authorities on anything from schools to road sweeping. However, there are strings attached to this money. One of them is that 62% of it must be spent in the independent sector, i.e., on private or voluntary services, thus encouraging authorities to contract out services rather than providing them themselves (Hudson 1992).

So, what are the likely implications of these changes for institutional care? As far as the balance of provision between independent and public providers is concerned, the reduction in the role of the public sector (Local Authorities) is set to continue. A growing number of Local Authority residential homes are being closed or contracted out to private providers. This is partly because of the directive from central government to change the balance, and partly because, ironically perhaps, many of these homes do not measure up to the new quality requirements, and authorities cannot afford to upgrade them. As for nursing homes, these have predominantly been taking people funded by social security grants. Health authorities are encouraged to take over this funding responsibility, but they are likely to want to limit expenditure in this area, and attempt to refer people to Local Authority–funded institutions or home care (Henwood 1992; Byrne 1992). It must be remembered that the main rationale behind the act is to encourage a shift in the balance of care from institutions to home care. The merging of the residential and home care budgets will undoubtedly make Local Authorities think twice before referring a person to residential care, and indeed the whole procedure of assessment is aimed to achieve this. Shortage of financial resources has already been felt by the private residential and nursing homes, where the rates paid by social security clients have become increasingly inadequate to meet costs. When Local Authorities take over the financial responsibility, they might be faced with the choice between paying adequate rates for a smaller number of institutional places or paying lower rates, thereby eventually squeezing some homes out of business. Most of the private homes that sprang up during the 1980s have very small profit margins because of the high interest rates and the collapse in property prices. It is therefore highly likely that many homes will go out of business. In short, there will be fewer institutional places in the system, and resources for home care are likely to be inadequate to make up for this.

Thus the 1990s are likely to be a period of contraction of both public and private institutional care, although the overall balance will continue to shift toward private provision. This will have implications for older people and their carers, who will have to take even more responsibility. It will also affect the hospital sector and put more pressure on acute beds. The aim of the Community Care Act was to stem the tide of institutions, but already many are beginning to doubt whether this is possible without causing a great deal of hardship. Whatever happens, the 1990s are likely to be a period of change, experimentation, and uncertainty, and the continued separation between health and social care budgets will continue to make clients pawns in the game between health and social services. Whether we will eventually see a satisfactory balance between institutional and home care remains to be seen. It is perhaps doubtful whether one will ever see a satisfactory balance, since there is no agreement and no clarity about what is the right level of institutional care provision.

REFERENCES

Bebbington, A. and M. Tong. 1986. "Trends and Changes in Old People's Home Provision over Twenty Years." Pp. 67–81 in *Residential Care for Elderly People: Research Contributions to Policy and Practice*, edited by K. Judge and I. Sinclair. London: HMSO.

Byrne, A. 1992. "Private Lives." *Health Service Journal* (19 November):22–23.

Challis, L. and H. Bartlett. 1988. *Old and Ill*. Surrey: Age Concern.

Davies, B. P., A. C. Bebbington, H. Charnley, in collaboration with B. Baines, E. Ferlie, M. Hughes, and J. Twigg. 1990. *Resources, Needs and Outcomes in Community-Based Care. PSSRU Studies.* Aldershot: Avebury/Gower.

Day, P. and R. Klein. 1987."The Regulation of Nursing Homes: A Comparative Perspective." *Milbank Quarterly* 65:302–47.

Day, P., R. Klein, and G.Tipping. (1988). *Inspection for Quality.* Bath Social Policy Papers, No. 12, University of Bath.

Department of Health. 1989. *Caring for People: Community Care in the Next Decade and Beyond.* London: HMSO.

Henwood, M. 1992. "Twilight Zone." *Health Service Journal* (5 November):28–30.

Hudson, B. 1990. "The Rise and Rise of Private Care." *Health Service Journal* (11 October):1520–21.

———. 1992. "Pawn Again." *Health Service Journal* (26 November):26–28.

Hunter, D., N. McKeganey, and I. MacPherson. 1988. *Care of the Elderly.* Aberdeen: Aberdeen University Press.

Laing and Buisson. 1990. *Laing's Review of Private Health Care 1989/90.* London: Laing & Buisson.

Larder, D., P. Day, and R. Klein. 1986. "Institutional Care for the Elderly: The Geographical Distribution of the Public/Private Mix in England." Bath Social Policy Papers No. 10, Centre for the Analysis of Social Policy, University of Bath.

National Association of Health Authorities. 1985. *Registration and Inspection of Nursing Homes: A Handbook for Health Authorities.* Birmingham: NAHA.

Parker, R. 1990. "Care and the Private Sector." Pp. 293–331 in *The Kaleidoscope of Care,* edited by I. Sinclair, R. Parker, D. Leat, and J. Williams. London: HMSO.

Sinclair, I. 1988. "Residential Care for Elderly People." Pp. 241–91 in *Residential Care. The Research Reviewed* ("Wagner Report"), edited by I. Sinclair. London: HMSO.

Working Party on a Code of Practice for Residential Care. 1984. *Home Life: A Code of Practice for Residential Care.* London: Centre for Policy on Ageing.

PART II

Care for the Homebound under Sixty-Five

This book, in discussing care for three disabled populations, focuses on a set of overarching, related ideas: the development of comprehensive systems of care with both institutional and community-based elements, the coordination of medical and social services, and the structure and performance of the care system. These emphases inform this section, which analyzes home care for the severely chronically ill under 65, but they work themselves out somewhat differently from the patterns in care of the frail elderly.

As long-term institutional care for disabled clients has declined, and the locus of care has shifted to the community level, the provision of home care for those with chronic and severe illness has become an accepted aspect of welfare services during the last 25 years. More and more, it has become widely recognized that it is desirable for chronically ill people to receive integrated home services—both medical and social services—to enable them to live in the community most of the time. Certainly, people with chronic health problems may need recourse to hospitals (or other congregate residential arrangements) from time to time, but most of the time they can live in their own homes. Home care thus is conceptualized as an alternative to costly institutionalization, delaying, averting, or shortening institutionalization (Melin, Hakansson, and Bygren 1993; Bishop and McNally 1993). It is also widely believed that home care is more humane and more likely to lead to client satisfaction.

The structure of the home care system is extremely diverse, since the system encompasses different target populations, different types of service with different time frames, different types of staff, etc. (see Goldberg in this volume). Sometimes home care is needed after hospital discharge; at other times, in lieu of hospital entry. Both of these are instances of need for home care related to medical purposes, but for many people with chronic and severe illness, there are also substantial needs for home care social services. For some clients, needs are extensive and continuing; for others, needs may be more modest and variable in quantity over time. Provision of home care may involve highly specialized organizations (giving only a few types of services based on sophisticated technology) or may be provided by organizations with very general services. Home care is a congeries of services, far from homogeneous. Therefore, discussions about the structure of the system (e.g., at what levels care is provided, what the sources of funding are, who regulates and monitors care, who trains and certifies personnel) quickly become very complex. Since clients with extensive, complex needs usually require both medical and social services, coordination among caregivers is important.

In recent work, Jamieson (1992) has argued that the theoretical distinction between the medical and social services in the home has been counterproductive and has prevented the implementation of a coordinated, efficacious system of care. Her emphasis is on the desirability of conceptualizing home care as integrated, blending medical and social services, rather than making distinctions between the two. Since home care includes a large number of services and many types of staffing, coordinating services around client needs over time requires extensive boundary-spanning communication.

Most home care for those with chronic and severe illness is privately provided, often without remuneration and without formal regulations and training. Often family members are the care providers, with women bearing disproportionate responsibilities in this regard (Kemper 1992). In the last two decades, however, there has been increased willingness in public programs to provide home care. In the United States, Medicare conditions for home health care coverage have become slightly less restrictive, and under the Medicaid program, several states have obtained waivers to permit modest Medicaid payment for home care services (*New York Times*, November 20, 1992). Even though Medicare was designed to provide medical services for the elderly, only 28% of home and community services for the elderly were financed by Medicare. On the other hand, more then 40% of those over age 85 in the United States receive at least one type of home service, financed from many different sources (Brickner, Lechich, Lipsman, and Sharer 1987).

The following two papers are concerned both with home care provided through public initiatives, and with home care in which actors other than those in the public sector provide services. Both papers, however, emphasize the desirability of focused public authority action to make home care more widely available and of higher quality.

At present, home care for people with chronic and severe illness is not well developed in either the United States or Britain. The following papers (Bleddyn Davies on Britain, Allen Goldberg on the United

States), with somewhat different frameworks, explore some of the serious conceptual and policy questions that relate to home care.

The issues Davies raises are macrolevel issues generic to discussing home care regardless of the specific target group. He centers his analysis on a set of general issues, relevant to other target populations and to much social welfare policy discussion. He suggests, first, the need for making a separate calculus for each different disability group in terms of the costs and benefits of downsizing institutional care and increasing community-based care by emphasizing home care. Thus, he contends the argument for substitution of community-based care instead of institutional care should be made with reference to a well-specified target group. Arguments across the board are not useful.

Second, he turns to targeting: the difficulty (and desirability) of focusing home care services on those most at risk for hospitalization or institutionalization, rather than distributing services fairly evenly among all applicants. Assessing the amount of targeting as inadequate in Britain, he notes that standardization of care across a large population, which has been easy for the British to accomplish, is inimical to the goals of both clients and society. Standardization provides large numbers of people with small amounts of service but does very little to affect the use of expensive hospitals and nursing homes. Targeting would be likely to be more successful in decreasing hospital/nursing home use. Davies discusses whether redistributing the already-committed home help resources could decrease hospital/institutional use, whether the targeting of home help resources on fewer people (those most at risk for institutional placement) could prevent institutional placements. His conclusion is that existing resources are insufficient for such a goal.

The third issue Davies raises is the possibility for substituting lower-cost staff for high-cost personnel, as care systems become less reliant on institutional provision of care and more reliant on skills almost everyone can master. Substitution of personnel, he indicates, offers prospects for lower unit of care costs, and thus for providing additional units of service. Finally, he turns to the types of evidence necessary to convince policymakers to reallocate funding in Britain. To develop persuasive cost-benefit evidence about home care, evidence that will be convincing in an era of scarce public funding, he suggests a combination of approaches: (1) singling out the populations for whom deinstitutionalization is most likely to be cost efficient and (2) ensuring that home care services are targeted on the specific subpopulations most at risk for expensive institutionalization, but able to be appropriately cared for in a home setting.

Goldberg raises an additional important theoretical problem in his paper on home care. Focusing on ventilator-dependent patients in the United States, he points out the importance of technology in shaping types of home care for those with severe and chronic illness. Certainly, as the technology becomes more complex and expensive, the level of training for home care providers with some kinds of responsibilities must also increase, and the standardization of services declines.

In both countries, there is an array of people who are dependent on life-supportive technology: people with spinal cord injuries, severe muscular dystrophy, and numerous other muscular, pulmonary, and neurological diseases. As Goldberg and Faure (1984) have pointed out, many nursing homes are reluctant to accept ventilator-dependent patients because of the lack of adequately trained staff and reimbursement problems. At the same time, most community-oriented programs are also unable to provide appropriate services, because of both fiscal limitations and lack of personnel trained for high-technology care. With both nursing homes and community programs unable to provide services, only the upper-income groups with private funds for individualized arrangements have access to such technologies.

Sharing Davies's concerns with the quality of home care personnel and with influencing policymakers to provide more support for home care, Goldberg also emphasizes the way in which cultural and historical variations at the level of the nation state have shaped home care development. Home care, he contends, is embedded in a new approach to medical care, one in which patients, families of patients, social workers, and medical professionals are all stakeholders in the provision of care. With such an approach, medical and social services should ideally be coordinated and integrated, and at the same time individualized.

Clearly, demands for home care for populations with chronic disabilities will increase in the future. Not only does technological change make it possible for populations to survive traumas and various diseases, but it has become too costly for advanced industrial societies to provide care in hospitals and nursing homes. Yet, creating home care systems, with comprehensive and coordinated medical and social services, has been difficult for a variety of reasons. So far there is a relatively small amount of home care available in both the United States and Britain, given the population in need (Short and Leon 1990). There have been difficulties convincing politicians and policymakers to support the development of home care networks, especially for social services. There also are awkward problems in monitoring the quality of care with some kinds of home care: Large numbers of cases in thousands of separate homes are difficult to oversee effectively. Funding and services are often poorly coordinated, manpower recruitment and training are problematic, and the overall supply of service is often limited.

REFERENCES

Bishop, E. E. G. and G. McNally. 1993. "An In-Home Crisis Intervention Program for Children and Their Families." *Hospital and Community Psychiatry* 44:182–84.

Brickner, Philip W., A. J. Lechich, Roberta Lipsman, and Linda Sharer. 1987. *Long Term Health Care: Providing a Spectrum of Services to the Aged.* New York: Basic Books.

Goldberg, Allen and Eveline Faure. 1984. "Home Care for Life-Supported Persons in England: The Responaut Program." *Chest* 86:910–14.

Jamieson, Anne. 1992. "Home Care: Denmark, Germany, the United Kingdom and the United States." *Journal of Health Policy, Politics and Law* 17:879–98.

Kemper, Peter. 1992. "Availability of Informal Home Care Crucial for Elderly Persons with Disabilities." *Research Activities: Agency for Health Care Policy and Research* 159:7–8.

Melin, A. L., S. Hakansson, and L. O. Bygren. 1993. "The Cost-Effectiveness of Rehabilitation in the Home: A Study of Swedish Elderly." *American Journal of Public Health* 83:356–62.

Short, P. and J. Leon. 1990. "Use of Home and Community Services by Persons Ages 65 and Older with Functional Difficulties." DHHS Publication No. (PHS) 90-3466. National Medical Expenditure Survey Research Findings 5, Agency for Health Care Policy and Research. Rockville, MD: Public Health Service.

Chapter 4

Home Health Care for the Chronically Ill in the United States: The Market-Oriented System

ALLEN I. GOLDBERG

INTRODUCTION: THE CONCEPTUALIZATION OF HOME HEALTH CARE

Major interest and activity in home health care is a worldwide phenomenon in developed and developing nations and involves multiple sectors of society: business, labor, consumer, government. Growth is being driven by health needs of two expanding populations: the elderly and persons with chronic conditions not sufficiently ill to require hospitalization. How it is evolving in each country is influenced by political, social, demographic, economic, and cultural forces that play out differently at each level: national, regional, and local.

A new wave of home health care is emerging that reflects a more fundamental social transformation of medicine (Starr 1982). Its features were predictable in the evolution of the industrial age society (second wave) to our postindustrial, information-based way of life, the third wave (Toffler 1980). Home care represents a new paradigm, which enlarges the mindset about the meaning of health and requires a new conceptualization recognizing the difference between curing and caring, the medical and the social model, illness and wellness, professional control and family-centered care, and person/family dependency and self-help, mutual aid, and personal independence. As a result, home health care development requires shifts of thinking with new definitions of organizational culture and new responses in organizational development, structural and functional design, and operations management.

Unfortunately, much that is traditional about home care up to now was established according to old (second wave) health care models. This is true for many organizational principles and management functions, including approaches to cost accounting, marketing, finance, operations, and human resource management. For example, some hospitals consider home health care only as a product line, part of competitive strategy to improve utilization of existing institutional capacity that represents high invested sunk and fixed costs. It is operated with a factory mindset regarding human capital and material resource management. Although community-based home health care models exist as an alternative approach, they are currently fragmented in structural, operational, and financial ways.

What should evolve in the United States is a new model—a totally integrated management system whose design considers *all* participants as stakeholders in the delivery channels of home health care: *from* producers, providers, suppliers of products, services, and resources *through* distribution networks *to* multiple end users (Stern and El-Ansary 1988). All beneficiaries *including* consumers must be involved in the evolution of their system: planning, design, implementation, evaluation, feedback, and continuous improvement.

Although home health care may be considered to be generic with common generalities, its evolution is better understood when seen as targeted to meeting specific, differentiated needs. Home health care can be designed for the elderly or disabled (simple/complex health and personal care); infants and children (developmental focus); medical specialties (hematology, oncology, surgery, endocrinology, nephrology); or technology-specific needs (home oxygen, mechanical ventilation, intravenous therapies, dialysis). In this context, home health care represents a wide spectrum, with multiple segments of a matrix defined by:

- degree of medical technology: none, simple, complex
- degree of support: none, intermittent, part-, full-time
- duration of time: acute, transitional, chronic (see Figure 1).

Matrix analysis reveals that home health care can be an option for acute vs. chronic conditions, posthospital stay (short extension), intermediate, transitional, or long-term care. It can represent care by trained, prepared family members alone with or without personal attendants (nonprofessionals), intermittent visits from professionals, or major support services from shift nursing (including round-the-clock critical-care professionals). It can feature no, low, or high technology. It can be designed or coordinated as a comprehensive total service-oriented system or it can be provided in a differentiated, partial-service (niche) approach.

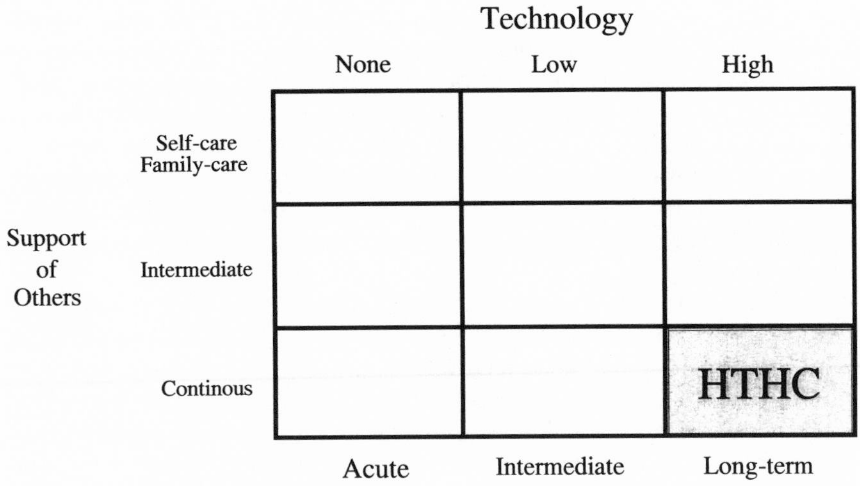

Technology

	None	Low	High
Self-care Family-care			
Support of Others Intermediate			
Continuous			**HTHC**

Acute   Intermediate   Long-term

Figure 1. The home care matrix.

I. HISTORICAL OVERVIEW OF HOME CARE IN THE UNITED STATES

Home health care has strong traditional roots in the United States. In the earliest years of our nation, the customary site for providing care for acute illness or chronic disability was home. Only those without economic means required institutional care. Middle- and upper-class families converted bedrooms into sickrooms, babies were delivered at home, relatively uncomplicated surgery was conducted in the home, and patients received care from physicians who made daily house calls (Ginsberg, Balinsky, and Ostow 1984:6). Institutional care for poor families was not even their only option. Indigent families could avoid entering institutions due to home care services organized by religious orders and secular groups. A home nursing service was established in Boston as early as 1796 (Spiegel 1987). By the end of the nineteenth century, visiting nurse associations (VNAs) supported by philanthropy were the major source of home care in the United States (Ginsberg et al. 1984).

The modern hospital era began with late-nineteenth- and early-twentieth-century scientific advances of asepsis, anesthesia, surgery, and medical technology created in response to the exigencies of war.

This led to the possibility of safely and efficiently conducting complicated procedures not possible at home. Although the hospital became the site for treating seriously ill patients, most people still preferred to remain at home with self- or family-provided care supplemented by privately funded VNAs. Experiences of the Second World War and postwar era continued to stimulate demand for community-based care, which now exhibits explosive growth (Ginsberg et al. 1984). Although home health care is growing in the United States, its thrust is not simply a return to the past.

To illustrate the new-wave home care concept and system evolving, the initial focus will be through one specific segment as a window to home care in general: high-technology home care (HTHC). The case example will be home mechanical ventilation (HMV), which represents complex, catastrophic-cost home care. HTHC requires extensive human resources at a time of challenging labor economics (Arewine 1990) and expensive technology at a time of cost containment, but has been recognized as applicable to more general needs of larger populations (U.S. Department of Health and Human Services 1983).

Before concentrating at some length on the market-oriented home health care system (United States), the stage will be set by reviewing HTHC care in the United States briefly and then briefly examining HTHC solutions in other nations' health finance systems: National Health System (England) and national health insurance (France). The political, social, economic, and cultural factors will be considered that led to the evolution of successful HTHC programs in these countries (Goldberg 1989). The following major theme will be developed: Home health represents a new mind-set that should be considered an alternative to hospitalization for more than organizational, management, and financial reasons. It represents a new culture with different attitudes, beliefs, values, and norms of behavior. What must be put in place represents a new model that can be designed according to general principles but must be adapted to cultural differences and adjusted to national, regional, and local realities.

II. HIGH TECHNOLOGY HOME CARE AROUND THE WORLD

The birth of HTHC was the outcome of technological and organizational advances in health care responding to the poliomyelitis epidemic of the 1950s (Faure and Goldberg 1982). During this worldwide crisis, every nation had survivors who, prior to the development of modern respiratory care, would have died. They remained chronically ill and required prolonged hospitalization because of the lack of alternatives.

Among them were the first generation of ventilator-assisted patients, some of whom remained for years in "polio" centers. HMV was a direct outcome of efforts by medical leaders and ventilator users in these centers. Whether such patients were ever discharged home depended on what happened in and to those polio centers. The evolution of HTHC followed similar patterns in different countries but also reflected some uniqueness in each nation's experience.

A. United States

The polio centers were phased out in the mid-1950s after the discovery of the polio vaccine. The voluntary organization (National Foundation–March of Dimes) that had been responsible for establishing and operating the polio centers redirected its mission to birth defects. With several notable exceptions, the United States was not to see a direct continuation of the HMV experiences from that period to present-day practice. There was to be a hiatus until progress in medicine, surgery, anesthesia, and critical care created a second generation requiring HMV.

The U.S. exceptions were publicly financed polio centers that remained open: Goldwater Memorial Hospital, New York; Rancho Los Amigos, Downey, California; Institute for Research and Rehabilitation, Houston (Goldberg 1983a). Each developed respiratory rehabilitation and HMV programs for polio and other neuromuscular diseases. The experiences in such centers and with other isolated individual cases in the United States and around the world were documented by a unique consumer network in the publication *Rehabilitation Gazette* (Laurie 1962–87). This documentation was to provide the inspiration for a new generation of medical leaders and intensive-care unit (ICU) ventilator users for new HMV demonstrations.

In 1982, U.S. Surgeon General C. Everett Koop brought the issue of developing programs for ventilator-dependent children to national prominence as a case example of children with special needs (*Report on the Surgeon General's Workshop* 1983). In 1983, the U.S. Department of Health and Human Services (DHHS), Public Health Service, Division of Maternal and Child Health, sponsored four Special Projects of Regional and National Significance to create and evaluate HTHC models for these children (Aday, Wegener, Andersen, and Aitken 1989). In 1984 and 1985, two major studies of the current status, issues, and dimensions of life-sustaining technologies were authorized by the U.S. Congress, Office of Technology Assessment (1987a, 1987b). In 1986, the DHHS secretary convened a major task force to study the needs of technology-dependent children (U.S. DHHS 1988b). In 1989, the Health Care Financing Administration (HCFA) designated several demonstrations for elderly persons requiring prolonged mechanical ventilation (U.S. DHHS 1988a).

The United States has not yet developed an integrated-systems approach to HTHC. Funding for HMV is often determined on an individual case basis. Most programs are based at experienced centers whose leaders have attempted to develop local solutions. Home care services and funding are fragmented and poorly coordinated. Many agencies, voluntary associations, and proprietary organizations are involved, but no uniform systems management exists to take advantage of scale economies, learning curve efficiencies, and quality improvement technologies (Goldberg 1992).

B. France

Because polio vaccination was not initially mandatory, the need for polio treatment centers continued and new polio cases were admitted well into the 1960s (Goldberg 1986). These centers were eventually incorporated into ICUs and became home to patients who filled them. In Lyon (Croix-Rousse) and Paris (Raymond Poincaré, Garches) polio survivors (consumers) and physicians took initiatives to establish home ventilator care (Goldberg 1984).

Many early leaders of intensive-care medicine in France were students of directors of the original polio centers. Their early experiences with prolonged mechanical ventilation made them comfortable with the concept of HMV. They were motivated by social concerns and the need to make acute-care resources available to new patients. They enlisted the involvement of regional governmental officials and finance authorities who were interested in new and better ways to extend the value and range of health care budgets (Goldberg 1986).

France has a cultural tradition of serving the public good with voluntary associations established under the law of 1901. Regional associations developed home care programs from the original polio centers, initially for social reasons and medical purposes. They then extended services to new patients with other conditions but related needs. Prominent political figures were included among the leaders who directed the establishment and growth of these associations. The original associations (ALLP, ADEP) became models for other regions, which adapted them to similar problems in their unique localities (Goldberg and Faure 1986). A major government-sponsored study recommended this approach to meet a larger and growing demand for home oxygen, the extension of regional associations to all of France, and the creation of a national federation of the regional associations, ANTADIR (Goldberg 1986).

As of 1990, nearly 18,000 ventilator-assisted and/or oxygen-dependent patients obtained home care from community-based regional associations linked to local associations serving other social needs and to centers of expertise at regional (university) medical centers. These programs compete for public reimbursement and are contracted with regional funding authorities. They provide equipment, supplies, and comprehensive surveillance with quality and cost-control. They have been established through the collaborative efforts of health care professionals, patients and families, funding authorities, and governmental officials. They coordinate/integrate the required social, technological, informational, and health care services (Goldberg 1989). More recently long-term oxygen has been provided by a private system (Muir, Voisin, and Ludot 1992).

C. England

The Responaut program evolved (in the 1960s) from England's first ICU at St. Thomas Hospital, London (Goldberg and Faure 1984). Incorporated into this original ICU was a former polio unit with beds occupied by polio survivors who still required mechanical ventilation. Home care was established through the cooperative ingenuity and tireless efforts of these patients and their physician. The dramatization of their cause to political leaders led to a major national study: the Responaut Study (Responaut Panel Research Team 1974). The Responaut program enabled these original patients to return with personal attendants to the community (or their families). Services were then extended to other patients with neuromuscular diseases whose lives were being sustained by medical technology.

The Responauts also created a voluntary, consumer-led association responsible for the development of a home care program from the base unit at St. Thomas. From this base unit of expertise, the Responaut program provided a growing number of patients throughout England and beyond with a comprehensive home maintenance service that met health, social, and equipment needs. The Responaut program is linked to other voluntary organizations in England that serve persons with disabilities; this network makes comprehensive support and informational services available to ventilator-assisted persons in the community. The Responaut's leadership has advocated for many reforms that today benefit all persons with disability in England (Goldberg and Faure 1984).

D. Lessons from HTHC

HTHC program solutions in different countries all have required demonstrations and studies that were prerequisite to determining public policy and authorizing health care financing needed to stimulate new major program development (Goldberg 1986). Model systems existing today were designed in ways that were appropriate to the cultural traditions of each country. They fit the political, economic, and social realities of each country and regional peculiarities of each locality (Goldberg 1989). In addition, there were preconditional, evolutionary patterns before new concepts could become established as new operational systems.

Medical techniques and technologies had to develop to a point where patients with critical illness could be saved, stabilized, and offered home care for their chronic conditions. A critical number of patients were required to make program considerations worthwhile and necessary. Although isolated cases may, for humane reasons, qualify for home discharge, projected costs savings were required before programs were considered. Acute care capacity had to become constrained due to prolonged occupancy, and hospitals had to face economic difficulties due to inadequate reimbursement. Financial authorities had to anticipate sufficient economic returns for funding program development.

Many categories of people and organizations required for successful program development had to reach a critical level of awareness about and comfort with the realities of HTHC. They had to accept the home care concept as possible, safe, and preferable, and they had to become committed. All beneficiaries had their own requirements for participation. A mechanism had to be established for joint program planning, implementation, and evaluation. Most HTHC programs were the outgrowth of local leadership efforts of key persons (doctors, patients, families, hospital administrators, governmental officials) who saw the potential and dedicated enormous time and energy. Programs often benefited from insights and skills of political leaders. Once home care advantages became clear, collaboration was required, with participation of all essential persons and organizations at the decision-making, action-taking level. All had to be involved from the outset for "ownership."

Although some HTHC programs happened due to the tireless efforts of founders, more often a special trigger event occurred unexpectedly or was designed to raise public policy interest. The need for home care was sometimes made evident by a person achieving notoriety or by a planned crisis. Programs then only grew after model development, initial trial, demonstration, reevaluation, and modification. All key persons and organizations had to participate at each step, and formal studies and major investigations were required. A major commitment to education was necessary for HTHC to proceed. Patients, families, and professional care providers had to know what was required at home. Participating persons and organizations needed understanding to motivate involvement.

As isolated experiences were demonstrated and documented, program considerations began. Each time the same questions were asked:

How many patients were involved? Where were they? Who was taking care of them? How much did it cost? What were the desired outcomes? What were the alternatives? Information had be collected, processed, and reported to satisfy those responsible for program development. Then, through advocacy efforts, information was used to elicit proper attention and support.

Although similarities exist in the evolution of HTHC, programs between and within nations have not developed in the same way nor extent. Although what must be accomplished may have been similar, the means may not. Much can be learned from the degree of home care development and how and why programs vary.

The number of patients requiring HTHC reflects levels of progress in critical and rehabilitative care. With more trained professionals and established units, more patients needing technology survive. As a greater number of expensive-care beds become occupied, bed utilization and economic issues eventually attract the attention of physicians, hospital administrators, governmental officials, and health care financial authorities. Leaders have different attitudes regarding long-term management of patients who require life-sustaining technology. Even among experts, agreement on concept definitions, care standards, and practice guidelines are hard to establish. Difference in management preference reflects professional disciplines and background. How programs develop depends on medical orientation.

Medical practice norms among nations vary dramatically (Payor 1988). How a nation views a person with a chronic condition that requires technological support is a dramatic example of how culture and tradition affect the value judgments of doctors, patients, and other members of society. Culture determines whether people think it is worthwhile to live on a ventilator, whether a ventilator-assisted person is sick, and whether such a person's needs are appropriately served outside the hospital.

Attention-attracting and awareness-building strategies have been used to a different extent but have always been appropriate to each nation. They have included media events (the Responaut's invasion of 10 Downing Street; Goldberg 1983b) and securing the involvement of an important public official (Katie Beckett/President Reagan; *New York Times*, November 11, 1981). Sometimes attention has been less dramatic but effectively captured by a major study (Lebreton, Ludot, and Tripier 1981) or by convening a major workshop (*Report on the Surgeon General's Workshop* 1983). To elicit interest and involvement of leaders and key officials, broad-based education initiatives must be undertaken. A key physician, ventilator user, or official in a position of power must recognize the need and plan a major conference, publication, or other information-generating activities (O'Donohue et al. 1986). Strategies to create awareness and stimulate local and regional activities to learn more about the issues have included project grants (Aday et al. 1989), technology assessment studies (U.S. Congress, Office of Technology Assessment 1987a, 1987b), special-purpose workshops (American Association for Respiratory Care, Food and Drug Administration, and Health Resources Services Administration 1989; Plummer, O'Donohue, and Petty 1989), and designated task forces (U.S. DHHS 1988b).

Nations with HTHC accomplishments have networking mechanisms to share experiences and disseminate information by major studies, publications, and international conferences (for example, ANTADIR, Home Care for Chronic Respiratory Insufficiency Conference, Lyon, France, March 14–15, 1985; Webb-Waring Lung Institute, Home Mechanical Ventilation Conference, Denver, CO, March 3–4, 1988; Journées Internationales de Ventilation à Domicile, Lyon, France, January 26–27, 1989; Gazette International Networking Institute, Fifth International Post-Polio Conference, St. Louis, MO, May 31–June 4, 1989). Program leaders and managers understand and practice advanced principles of organizational development (Peters and Austin 1985). Programs have grown because team members serve needs of all beneficiaries (shareholders) with deep and sincere commitment to people. Each successful program has adapted organization development practices to reflect and respond to national culture/tradition (Drucker 1988). Leaders and managers also understand and apply advanced practices of systems management in their operations (Stern and El-Ansary 1988; O'Toole 1985).

Because of the complexity of HTHC, social structures and political constituencies must be considered. Nations with advanced approaches benefit from insights of efforts to find and develop appropriate alliances. Programs were designed by leaders and political officials who subsequently shared a sense of ownership and made certain systems mesh with acceptable norms. Each nation's HTHC fits financing and delivery mechanisms unique to that country and peculiarities of regional/local settings. In some cases, the program extends from a hospital base unit (Responaut; Goldberg and Faure 1984). In others, community programs integrate centers of expertise and regional funding authorities (French Associations; Goldberg and Faure 1986). In contrast, in the United States, sources of patients, distribution of equipment and supplies, and mechanisms of health care financing are fragmented and difficult to integrate (Goldberg 1989). As a result, scale economies of a comprehensive systems operation do not exist, and alarming cost inflation endangers HTHC future in the United States.

In summary, HTHC programs around the world are rather similar. The elements and evolutionary steps are variations on a theme, but the mechanisms are unique to each nation's experience. The necessary and sufficient conditions fundamental to the successful realization of home care concepts and their implementation into systems are:

- involvement of a broad-based constituency
- representation of committed leaders
- implementation of program development in stages
- consideration of political, economic, and social preferences of each locality
- design to reflect the values, beliefs, attitudes, and behavioral norms of each nation and specific region
- response to unique cultural traditions
- utilization of advanced concepts of organizational development and management practice to meet the conflicting challenges of universal access, quality improvement, and cost containment.

III. CURRENT STATUS OF HOME HEALTH CARE IN THE UNITED STATES

A. The Size of the Market and Population in Need

In a market-oriented system such as the United States, growth projections for demand are often financial and provided in terms of revenue or numbers of providers rather than in size of population. For examples, HCFA stated that the *total home health* (vs. total health) care market in 1983 was $9.9 (vs. $355.1) billion; HCFA estimated that *total home health care* growth would range between 12.0 and 13.5% per year through 1990, when it would equal $22.7 (vs. $649) billion (HCFA 1983). Sales of total HTHC services/products were estimated at $1.2 billion in 1985 and projected to increase by 17% to $1.4 billion in 1990 (Kane 1989). Estimates by market research firms of core home services accounted for $5 billion expenditures in 1986, with high-tech services accounting for an additional $1.2 billion, anticipated to increase to $2.3 billion by 1991 (Foundation for Home and Hospice Care 1988). In 1983, approximately 2,500 patients in the United States received parenteral nutritional therapy at home at a cost of $200 million/year; the American Society for Parenteral and Enteral Nutrition needs estimate for 1990 was between 150,000 and 200,000 home parenteral patients at expenditures of $1.6 billion per year (Donlan 1983). The home drug delivery industry was valued at $265 million in 1983; the growth estimate was 34% per year until 1990 when it was projected to be worth $2.8 billion (Rucker 1987). The home care/DME industry in 1983 had 12% annual revenue growth; the five following years revealed actual volume growth ranges between 17 and 22% (1984, 22%; 1985, 21%; Stephenson and Cron 1987). However, there was a projected reduced growth for 1987 and thereafter which has been recently confirmed (Stephenson and Cron 1989; *Healthweek*, August 13, 1990).

Although HTHC has grown astronomically over the last decade, there is also evidence of growth in other segments of home care. Skilled home health care agencies grew rapidly between 1981 and 1986 after 1980 Medicare legislation removed reimbursement restrictions that required prior acute-care hospitalization and a 100-visit limit and that allowed proprietary home care agencies in states without licensure laws to participate in Medicare for the first time (Hughes 1986). As of December 1987, there were 10,848 home health agencies in the United States accounting for expenditures of $5.8 billion (Foundation for Home and Hospice Care 1988). The growth in home care agencies began during 1981–1983 and preceded the Prospective Payment System implemented in 1983, which anticipated "quicker and sicker" discharges of Medicare patients to home (Ruther and Helbing 1988). As of June 30, 1990, 8,105 home health agencies were operating nationwide: 12% more than 1988, 53% more than 1986. Most agencies were small businesses (73% with annual sales revenues less than $1 million; Marion Merrell Dow 1989). Based on 1987 dollars, growth projections for future *total* home care spending from 1986–1990 to 2016–1920 were from $8.6 billion to $21.9 billion (154% increase) (National Association for Home Care 1990).

Low-tech home care (long-term maintenance, custodial home care) does not have as reliable data available. The estimated range is as low as 45% of home care agencies identified by NAHC in 1989 that do not participate in the Medicare program to as many as 30,000–45,000 (Hughes 1990). The majority of providers are publicly held, multiunit, proprietary chains (Kane 1989).

Estimates of the growth of the industry do not truly give reliable indication of the size of the population receiving vs. needing home care and the proportion increasing or decreasing over time. Social science research and public policy analysis have determined that 32% of the nearly 3 million persons 85+ years need personal care assistance: 5–10% must rely totally on paid formal care; another 16–25% require additional formal care to supplement services provided by informal caregivers (Scanlon and Feder 1984). Forty-six percent of Medicare home care users must purchase additional services beyond Medicare and informal caregivers (General Accounting Office 1987); much of the care purchased out of pocket is unskilled (Soldo 1985; Liu, Manton, and Liu 1985). Seven million elderly (24% of total elderly population) need some long-term-care assistance. Twenty-two percent of them reside in institutions; the remaining 78% live in the community with a spouse, others, or alone (Scanlon 1988). Impairment levels and current and future service needs are not known (Hughes 1990). Needs estimates for skilled home care must take into consideration that demand increases sharply with age. In 1986, the rate of Medicare enrollees served was 26 per thousand (65–66 years) vs. 97 per thousand (age 85+ years), an increase of 273%; the number of visits per thousand enrollees increased from 578 (65–66 years) to 2352 (85+ years), an increase of 307% (Ruther and Helbing 1988).

Congressional desire to obtain national data on the size of the pediatric and elderly chronically ill populations dependent upon medical technology resulted in two initiatives by the Office of Technology Assessment (U.S. Congress, Office of Technology Assessment 1987a, 1987b). Data obtained regarding technology-dependent children varied according to definition and, after five years of debate, no satisfactory definition existed. Furthermore, the range of estimate was extraordinary: 680–2,000 children per year on mechanical ventilation; 600–9,000 on intravenous therapy, 1,000–6,000 dependent on some device-based respiratory or nutritional support. These three categories meant that there were approximately 2,300–17,000 technology-dependent children per year; the range was 11,000–68,000 if apnea monitoring and dialysis were added, and up to 100,000 if ostomy and urinary catheter care were considered (U.S. DHHS 1988b). Obtaining the data regarding the elderly on mechanical ventilation provided to be nearly impossible due to barriers to collection (U.S. Congress, Office of Technology Assessment 1987a); the experience collecting data regarding ventilator-assisted children and adults at the state level confirmed these observations (Goldberg and Frownfelter 1990).

B. The Organization and Influence of Home Care Providers

Although home health care has a strong community-based tradition, services have evolved less in response to client baseline and changing needs and more in response to the complexity of existing funding sources and divergent eligibility criteria (Hughes 1990). Prior to Medicare, home care was provided mainly by not-for-profit and voluntary associations. In 1969, VNAs and public health home care agencies still accounted for 89% of all providers (Hughes 1986). The creation of a market was due to reimbursement for home health services as a specified benefit in the 1965 Medicare legislation as well as the creation of financial incentives (growth in hospital costs, 1980 repeal of Medicare requirements) and technological innovation (design of products for home use). By 1987, VNA and public health agencies market share had dropped to 28%, with hospital-based agencies accounting for 25% and proprietary agencies accounting for 32% of all certified agencies (Foundation for Home and Hospice Care 1988). The organization of home care that has evolved in the United States is an unintentional effect of our system of financing; this is true of high-tech, skilled, and low-tech/custodial home health care (Hughes 1990).

High-tech services (oxygen, ventilation, intravenous therapies, home dialysis, enteral/parenteral nutrition) are available from for-profit organizations, which are giant pharmaceutical or hospital supply corporations or durable (home) medical equipment [D(H)ME] providers. In this category, over the past few years, the industry has consolidated with mergers and acquisitions, many under foreign ownership. Recently, hospitals and home health care providers have been forming joint ventures with each other and pharmaceutical/medical supply companies (Hughes 1990). Major competition comes from smaller regional-based medical equipment suppliers, local traditional mom-and-pop shops, and independent hospital-based for-profit ventures undertaken as strategic business units or value-added service, to augment the hospital's referral and revenue base and utilize excess existing capacity (Lutz 1990).

Skilled home health care can be obtained from VNA, public health nurse, community- or hospital-based nonprofit and for-profit organizations. It is available from Medicare-certified and (since 1980) noncertified agencies, which offer skilled nursing care on an intermittent or continuous basis in addition to physical, speech, nutritional, and occupational therapies and medical social services (Hughes 1986). Home health aide and housekeepers can be provided as an adjunct to skilled care.

Low-tech (maintenance, custodial) home care is provided by agencies that offer paraprofessional homemaker and chore/housekeeping services to persons of all ages in conjunction with or independent of high-tech or skilled home care. As previously stated, the majority of providers are non–Medicare certified and proprietary.

Personal care can also be provided by personal attendants who are recruited, selected, hired, trained, and managed by those individuals who need their support. This arrangement is preferred among self-directed persons with disabilities who have created their own cost-saving programs.[1]

Home health care providers are organized as trade associations.[2] Major studies, publications, information campaigns, promotional activities, and lobbying have had minor impact on public policy as far as finance and delivery (Cooper 1990). Limited resources and member participation, fragmentation of internal politics, and lack of solidarity from conflicting interests have all resulted in reduced credibility and influence.

The home care provider segment is small relative to global health care interest groups as can be seen in contributions to PACs (Wagner 1990d). New health care professional organizations that advocate home care have yet to develop their political influence. This contrasts sharply to traditional hospital and professional organizations rooted in established health care models.[3] They represent years of experience and influence with major effective organizational power.

C. Financing Home Health Care and Effects of Cost Containment

Although quality regulatory mechanisms have not yet adversely affected the numbers of providers, funding regulations have significantly affected financial performance, innovation, and the feasibility of services. Home care has evolved as a largely unintentional effect of our system of financing (Hughes 1990). Modern expansion of home care was initiated by the Medicare program and stimulated/constrained in past years by Medicare regulatory modifications (Hughes 1986). In HTHC, financial performance reflected increased regulations and administrative costs, resulting in reduced profitability and growth (Stephenson and Cron 1987 1989) that has recently stabilized or expanded (Stephenson and Cron 1992).

Prior to the 1980s HTHC was not a category of care covered by public or private payers because it was not considered by policymakers. Case-by-case funding was negotiated; creative financing combined monies from a variety of public/private, medical/social sources. Difficulties began after a few successful cases created fear of increased demand (the "woodwork" effect). The issue gained national attention when President Reagan took special notice of the Iowa Medicaid "bureaucracy," which denied home care to a ventilator-dependent child (Katie Beckett; *New York Times*, November 11, 1981). As a result of the Katie Beckett exception, DHHS Secretary Schweiker convened a task force to determine future funding policy for technology-dependent children. This activity and that of Congress (particularly Representative Henry Waxman) resulted in a series of waivers to Medicaid policy that restricted Medicaid funding to programs submitted by states meeting HCFA approval (*HHS News*, May 6, 1982, U.S. DHHS). The waivers strictly limited the number of beneficiaries, significantly reduced financing flexibility, and dramatically increased the bureaucratic process in funding cases. Not all states applied for waivers, and funding features varied dramatically depending upon perspectives of bureaucratic authors. Families were fortunate if they could live in states with creative and sensitive public officials; they dared not move if they did. The waiver (exception to policy) approach has remained the major mechanism for funding catastrophic-cost HTHC despite alternative recommendations (*Report on the Surgeon General's Workshop* 1983; Aday et al. 1989; U.S. Congress, Office of Technology Assessment 1987a, 1987b; U.S. DHHS 1988b).

There have been special funding policies established in HTHC for adults as well. To create a fixed reimbursement system (and control growth of profits of DME providers) 1987 Medicare legislation mandated HCFA funding regulations to put in place a six-point program to create payment for home oxygen based on utilization rates, an historic period, and local and regional fees rather than "reasonable charges."[4] The program required elaborate medical certification of necessity and established rental vs. purchase policies. The six-point plan clarified guidelines that had previously reduced payments and created financial risk for dealers due to cash flow uncertainties (Lutz 1988). However, it provided government regulators with the authority to determine rental prices that created significant financial disincentives (Stephenson and Cron 1989).

The private funding sector, alert to past practices of cost shifting, was sensitive to financial risks of catastrophic-cost HTHC. They initiated case management review (Aetna in 1983; Blue Cross in 1985) in-house or by contract. Similar approaches were used by other health care concepts: managed-care programs (HMOs, PPOs) and self-insured companies. Efforts were taken to involve managed-care professionals and to contract discounted rates for services. The combined effect of private and public funding strategies to contain costs has constrained the growth of HTHC by subjecting claims to intense utilization review and payment delays resulting in competitive disadvantages for smaller operations. This has created risk of reduced availability of HTHC to a new disadvantaged group: the high-cost home care candidate who must remain institutionalized. Hospitals, seeing opportunities in long-term care, have extended to utilize excess capacity (Kenkel 1987); proprietary organizations have seen windfall profit potential in this (diagnostic related group-exempt) niche and established cost-saving institutional alternatives.

Skilled and low-tech home care is financed by a combination of public programs. Skilled care is now Medicare eligible. Until 1981, services were only eligible if prescribed following acute hospitalization; this severely limited the availability of home care for chronic illness. After the Omnibus Reconciliation Act of 1980, this requirement as well as a 100-visit limit was ended (Hughes 1986). Low-tech services are reimbursed by a variety of sources including Medicaid waivers, state block grants, Older Americans Act Title III funds, state/local revenues, and private out-of-pocket pay (Hughes 1990). Inadequacy of coverage is revealed by the 46% of Medicare home care users who must purchase additional services beyond what Medicare and informal caregivers provide (General Accounting Office 1987).

Cost containment is a mandate since the United States faces global health care disaster as health expenditures grow toward 15% of the GNP and our non- and underinsured approach 50 million (20% of our population). Expenditure curtailment (probably slower growth) will be part of the inevitable change. Although cost containment will be a major thrust, HCFA leadership provides hope also for managerial reform (Wilensky 1990).

The U.S. budget *is* the U.S. health policy and the *only* policy that will affect home care. Cost containment limits service provision and growth and probably impacts resource availability/access and quality of services. Without outcome measures we cannot know how much for certain.

The home care system is in general a reflection of funding policy. If expenditures are curtailed or redirected, so will the system. Cost containment will cripple operating programs and limit new development; services will be eliminated or delayed. Private-sector niche development will target remaining funding.

Not only will the organizationally weak have reduced access to adequate supply of services. *Home care for all* may be a prime target of curtailments since home care needs must compete with alternatives for finite resources in *every* health care funding system.

D. Quality Management in Home Health Care

At present, home care services can be provided by unlicensed, uncertified providers; the quality of care is unknown; and it is not clear who is ultimately responsible for quality among the multiple providers involved (Hughes 1990). However, due to the desire for quality management and need to reduce risk, recent initiatives have created mechanisms for quality review. For examples, task force–generated guidelines help practitioners desiring to care for patients requiring mechanical ventilation in the home or at an alternative community site (O'Donohue et al. 1986). In addition, providers and consumers can refer to recommendations resulting from invitational consensus conferences (American Association for Respiratory Care, Food and Drug Administration, and Health Resources Services Administration 1989; Plummer et al. 1989). Manufacturers and distributors can relate to standards for home care devices (American Society for Testing and Materials F29.09.03; Eiserman 1990), and providers can follow home care practices created by voluntary consensus (American Society for Testing and Materials F31.01.02).

Home care accreditation review has been available from the Joint Commission on Accreditation of Healthcare Organizations (JCAHO) since 1988 (Joint Commission of Accreditation of Healthcare Organizations 1988). The standards apply to hospital-based *and* independent home care firms that supply nurses, equipment, pharmaceutical, and personal care aides. They provide quality review mechanisms that have been previously absent in skilled and low-tech care sectors in all but agencies that have been hospital based and subject to previous JCAHO accreditation (JCAHO 1993). Recent studies sponsored by foundations and government agencies (HCFA) to review home care utilization and determine quality/outcome indicators complement these initiatives in quality management.[5]

E. Personnel Resources for Home Health Care

Home health care represents a new paradigm that features a different culture than traditional medical models. Personpower recruited for home care must understand/accept this culture. In the past, major educational and public awareness initiatives have been undertaken to enhance awareness and understanding about home health care (*Report on the Surgeon General's Workshop* 1983; Faure and Goldberg 1982; ANTADIR, Home Care for Chronic Respiratory Insufficiency Conference, Lyon, France, March 14–15, 1985; Webb-Waring Lung Institute, Home Mechanical Ventilation Conference, Denver, CO, March 3–4, 1988; Journées Internationales de Ventilation à Domicile, Lyon, France, January 26–27, 1989; Gazette International Networking Institute, Fifth International Post-Polio Conference, St. Louis, MO, May 31–June 4, 1989). Conferences, postgraduate courses, and publications have failed to generate major interest or program development focused on recruiting and training future home health care personpower. At present, there is little formal opportunity for education to train health care students and professionals in high-tech and skilled home health care. This has been recognized and strong recommendations for basic and postgraduate education have been made by professional associations (American Association for Respiratory Care, Food and Drug Administration, and Health Resources Services Administration 1989; Council on Scientific Affairs 1990); there have been policy discussions to redirect medical education (Paige 1990; "Doctors Need Larger Role in Home Health Care" 1990).

Although home health care is getting more recognized by physicians and other health care professions (O'Donnell 1988), the United States faces a general health care personpower shortage relative to demand. One analysis of the shortage is that there is a maldistribution. Some professionals have left institutional care for other options including home care, where the challenges, autonomy, and opportunities for personal satisfaction and professional advancement are greater. Despite such preferences, there may not be enough people for high-tech/skilled care, and escalating costs may not permit all care to be provided directly by professionals. Personal attendants have proven to be appropriate alternative care providers (Goldberg 1983b; Alba, Goldberg, Oppenheimer, and Roberts 1990; also see note 1).

Low-tech home care features nonprofessionals in capacities as personal attendants, homemakers, and chore/housekeeping. If the greatest demand for low-tech home care exists among the very old, impaired elderly, the outlook for the future is cloudy (Hughes 1990). Five out of the seven largest U.S. low-tech home care chains operated at a loss during 1984–1986 (Kane 1989). This is in part due to the poor economic level of persons over 75, who cannot afford out-of-pocket expenses, and in part due to state reimbursement policies pooling Medicaid and other funding streams, establishing cost-based hourly rates, capping overhead allowable costs, and delaying claims processing (Hughes 1990). As a result of limited financial resources devoted to low-tech home care, the field is unattractive at the entry level to providers or unskilled workers. Low-tech home care is characterized by high worker turnover, low morale, and variable quality (Hughes 1990).

F. Evaluation and Consumer Preferences
in Shaping Public Policy

Several major federal initiatives have been undertaken to evaluate the health care needs and outcomes of care of persons with chronic illness who might benefit from HTHC. The U.S. Congress authorized two major studies to address outcomes as part of overall concerns for medically technology-dependent people on life-sustaining devices (U.S. Congress, Office of Technology Assessment 1987a, 1987b), and the DHHS secretary convened a task force to evaluate these issues (U.S. DHHS 1988b). In addition, U.S. Surgeon General C. Everett Koop convened a national workshop to address these concerns for disabled children and their families (*Report of the Surgeon General's Workshop* 1983). One result of Dr. Koop's initiatives was granting four projects to establish and evaluate operational programs at the state level for children with special needs (Aday et al. 1989; Lis, Goldberg, Monahan, and Murphy 1987). Recently, an Illinois study determined the health needs of ventilator-assisted individuals. This study recommended that communities establish tracking systems and documentation centers for ongoing evaluation of needs, services, and outcomes (Goldberg and Frownfelter 1990).

There has been federal inquiry regarding skilled and low-tech home care as well. At a workshop sponsored by the National Institute on Aging (National Institutes of Health) and Administration on Aging (DHHS), important knowledge gaps were identified regarding the case mix of Medicare clients served by skilled home care, including functional status and unmet service needs at both entry to and discharge from care (Hughes 1990). Current Medicare reimbursement policy permits care until a beneficiary has reached "maximum feasible rehabilitation potential," after which claims for payment are disallowed by designated financial intermediaries. At that point, patients have the option of self-pay or supportive maintenance with low-tech home care. Thus, the status of patients at discharge from Medicare home care is unknown (Hughes 1990). Little is known about users of low-tech home care as well. The Administration on Aging awarded ten grants to states to promote state-level quality assurance for low-tech home care (Hughes 1990). Future findings may shed some light on this sector.

U.S. studies have determined the status of the elderly in long-term care alternatives as an attempt to evaluate health needs. These include evolution of case mix severity in home health agencies (HHA) after the introduction of prospective payment (Guterman, Eggers, Riley, Greene, and Terrell 1988); review of utilization rates of HHA vs. skilled-nursing facilities (SNF) by census regions (Guterman et al. 1988; Gornick and Hall 1988) and age (Ruther and Helbing 1988); and analysis of diagnoses in HHA vs. SNF (Neu and Harrison 1988). Recent studies sponsored by HCFA and the Robert Wood Johnson Foundation have focused on increased needs of patients in nursing homes and patients receiving home health care (Shaughnessy and Kramer 1990). Information addressing home health status/conditions of the elderly is available from the pharmaceutical industry (Marion Merrell Dow 1989) and trade associations (NAHC 1990). Recent foundation grants focus on home care outcomes (see note 5), and HCFA expert panels are determining outcome indicators.[6] A comparison of outcomes of care before/after Medicare prospective payment has been released (Kahn, Keeler, Sherwood, Rogers, Draper, Bentow, Reinisch, Rubenstein, Kosecoff, and Brook 1990). It is too early to determine the effect of outcome analysis on public policy.

Consumers who must advocate for home care for chronic health conditions represent two major constituencies: the elderly and persons with disabilities. Their health conditions fall into heterogeneous categories of illness represented by voluntary associations classified by diagnosis, directed by professionals, and focused on traditional health models and research. Unfortunately, these associations do not always understand or encourage home care. The elderly have a major political impact regarding the future directions of home care, which has not yet been fully manifested. Potential impact was seen in the elderly's reversal of the Medicare Catastrophic Health Bill and influence on current budget debates regarding changes in Medicare contributions and benefits (Wagner 1989; Brazda 1990; McIlrath, W. 1990). Analyses of the outcomes of the long-term care debate and Pepper Commission activities do not clarify how (or even if) the interests of the elderly have been yet fully represented (Wagner 1990e, 1990f). Since issues of the elderly differ by decade (65–75, 75–85, 85+ years old), the very old may not have the same opportunity for need articulation as young elderly.

Disabled persons have only in 1990 achieved a desirable level of civil rights legislation to provide access to employment, transportation, and housing.[7] There remains major discrimination in access to health care (United Way of Chicago 1990). There has been a renaissance of the self-help movement recognized and encouraged by U.S. Surgeon General Koop. Grass roots organizations and networks exist for HTHC,[8] but they are legally constrained and not organized for political action. They are somewhat effective in activities of public/professional awareness, education, and stimulating research; they lack some of the influence of the more traditional professionally dominated voluntary associations.[9]

Consumer self-help/advocacy groups are limited in affecting public policy. Their greatest influence is networking and building awareness by public information campaigns. They have minor impact because of insignificant financial contributions (political action campaigns—PACs), limited voter participation, and disunity. However, institutional mechanisms indirectly exist to advocate for client groups. Health care reform is a major grass roots movement being represented in local United Way community needs assessment initiatives (e.g., United Way of Chicago, Health/Disability Priority Grants Program, and Health/Disability Needs Assessment Committee). Concerned citizens can write position papers recommending policy change that can be disseminated via government liaison activities.

A health care revolution was predicted more than 20 years ago (Rutstein 1967). Evidence of a crisis is the unabating escalation of global health care costs within statutory budget reduction constraints and consumer dissatisfaction with our health care system (Blendon and Taylor 1989; Eddy 1990). Although need for health care reform in general is evident, no consensus exists regarding the solution. Concerned persons and organizations have provided recommendations for consideration for public policy (Shortell and McNerney 1990; Wagner 1990a, 1909b, 1990c). Behind these reform activities very little active consumerism is evident except for some elderly advocating for national health insurance (Grey Panthers Task Force for a National Health System, 1990). There is no integrating mechanism to include the client/user in the reform process. Never before has the time been better for long-term care reform ("Survey Shows Public Support for Spending on Children's Health" 1990; "Public Backs Increases in Medicare Spending" 1990; McIlrath, S. 1990). Within the upcoming debate, home care must compete with other global health and social issues.

IV. PROSPECTS FOR NEW-WAVE HOME HEALTH
CARE IN THE UNITED STATES

The major theme of this chapter is that home health care requires a new conceptualization based on defined needs by multiple beneficiaries. HTHC around the world demonstrates the sufficient conditions and gradual step-by-step implementation process necessary to meet those needs. This process demands involvement of *all* participants (*including* consumers) before the new community care concept and alternative system can be realized. By this process, the perspectives of *all* stakeholders (providers, payers, consumers) can be identified and clarified so that the system put in place can be adapted to their needs and those unique to each region and locality.

In each nation, home care has evolved to whatever extent possible within limitations of available resources (technical, human, financial) in ways understandable as a reflection of culture. The current situation with home care in the United States provides evidence that services can be delivered *without* a system or full recognition of a new conceptualization. This is due, in part, to our culture, which encourages free enterprise and full opportunity. In the market-oriented United States, home care must be provided in response to a health care policy as determined by funding priority and public policy regulation. Many initiatives have documented unmet needs and proposed ways to develop a community care system that can serve *all* beneficiaries. The following analysis of the current situation in the United States reveals the major constraints to and rationale for the realization of a new-wave home care concept.

Neither public policy experts, voluntary and public agency planners, nor private sector market researchers have adequate information to determine with certainty the numbers of persons who could potentially benefit from home health care. The lack of reliable data on the size of the population receiving and needing home care results from the perspective of the surveyors and barriers to data collection in a competitive market environment. Descriptive information is provided in monetary terms required by proprietary and not-for-profit organizations to determine profit and/or financial survival; projections by public/private third-party payers are based on the need for cost containment. The funding/payment policy that results from reimbursers' projections has a major impact on the growth of home health care market and the proportion of population receiving/needing home care increasing/decreasing over time.

The United States does not represent a marketplace under the influence of free market forces; health care in general is a highly regulated industry. This is evident in the commentary of analysts who believe that the growth in high-tech expenditures could have been higher in recent years but have been constrained by Medicare and private payers who have subjected claims to intense utilization review resulting in extreme payment delays (Kane 1989; Selz 1990).

Home care organization reflects home care payment policy. Due to fragmentation and variability of funding rules, regulations, and restrictions, a home care nonsystem has evolved that is ever-changing in response to public and private reimbursement policies. Home care is an invisible industry built by an variety of organizations (manufacturers, distributors, agencies) providing products and services (*Modern Healthcare*, February 5, 1988). Although 70% of hospitals started to provide home care by 1988 (*Modern Healthcare*, February 5, 1988), this was often managed as a "product line" by hospital administrators with low priority and professionals who do not understand the home care culture. The diversity of community-based providers presents to the client a diversity of partial services uncoordinated with other health care and social service segments and difficult to comprehend and use.

Some service coordination is offered from providers and/or funders (agency-based case managers). Clients are fortunate if given access to collaboration with an independent managed-care professional who can advocate for the client while maintaining accountability to provider and payer. There are concerns that case management puts the client at risk for reduced access when this concept is used as an excuse for cost containment ("Case Management and Home Care" 1990). Furthermore, there are those that are feel that it creates a meddlesome and needless layer of bureaucracy ("Case Management and Home Care" 1990). However, an industry of professional case managers has evolved (Mullahy 1990; Sager 1990; see also journals for continuing care professions and case managers). Alternatively, public policy recommendations based on informed consumer input support family-centered case management as a means to overcome the chaos of fragmentation of services (U.S. DHHS 1988b).

In an effort to respond to (and control) growth of home health care in the United States, the public sector has attempted to create complex health care financing mechanisms outside public funding policy programs (Medicaid waivers) and within (Medicare). Bureaucratic interpretation has added discretionary regulation to statutory intent and a funding process that varies by locality, skill, interest, understanding, and caring of public officials. The net effect has been to limit home care growth and service development. Although home care organization should reflect client need, fragmentation of the funding system has caused fragmentation of the delivery system. All this must be considered in light of the overall *total health care* financial situation and the risk that health care reform may favor traditional health care and further limit the evolution of the home care alternative. A conflict of influence/power exists between associations supporting hospital/traditional health care and home care. This will escalate with limitation of the growth of the total health care financial budget and global capitation.

Prior to 1980, there were few mechanisms to assess, control, or regulate health care quality at home other than Medicare certification and state licensure. With growth of the home care industry, concern grew for quality, safety, appropriate care, and cost control. Some activities were voluntary consensus standards and guidelines that became "standard of care" and determinants of quality considered in medical liability cases. Other activities were "regulatory" in the sense that accreditation by the JCAHO determined operational and financial viability due to implications for licensing and funding authorities (HCFA). Accreditation was an expensive time and financial investment. Initial concern was raised that "increased regulation" would influence the number of providers. In practice, the accreditation process has only been undertaken by larger national or regional corporate entities now as a "marketing strategy." It has not been possible or desirable for "mom and pop" operations to become accredited; local operations well-known to users can still successfully obtain referrals from affiliated hospitals, discharge planners, and health professionals. This may change as decision-making is transferred directly to the payer and managed care programs. All know that if quality is not determined voluntarily by consensus or negotiation, the government will take necessary regulatory actions as part of cost management strategies. This is evident with recent HCFA sponsored activities in outcomes research (see note 5).

The human resources required for health care exceed current available personpower. Home care will have to compete with other sectors within the health industry which, in general, ranks high for future growth of employment opportunities. Needs have not been met for the identification, recruitment, selection, training, education, preparation, and certification of health care professionals, nonprofessionals, and others who formally and informally support individuals and their families at home.

There are no well-established mechanisms to evaluate on an ongoing basis health needs of clients to determine where care would be best provided. Efforts to date include federal initiatives (workshops, conferences, demonstration projects, studies), which have provided information on utilization and quality of life. None have provided rigorous analysis of care outcomes in long-term-care alternative settings (Hughes 1985). There is need for an integrated tracking system and designated registries to collect, analyze, and disseminate information regarding needs/outcomes. Documentation centers could be useful for education, research, and the coordination of existing/future investigational/evaluation activities for health systems research, trade associations, and consumer organizations. They explain HTHC success abroad (Goldberg 1983b; 1986).

For home care to legitimately represent needs of direct users, there must be major consumer input. Although consumer representation is necessary for the realization of the new-wave home care concept, self-help groups' advocacy activities do not yet have the recognition, resources, or strategies for major influence on traditional institutions. They do not yet affect voter registration/participation essential for political impact. Strong consumer-based leadership does not yet exist with the skills and means to influence public policy. Those advocating for home care as an issue must compete for attention and resources with other health and social concerns on the public policy agenda.

In the United States, people claim to be concerned about the disadvantaged, but policy change is disjointed and incremental, reflecting our pluralistic society and political expediency (Kinzer 1990). U.S. culture values individualism and the strong ("the fastest gun in the West!"), but also recognizes community support in times of critical need (town hall meetings, the frontier spirit). We are now facing such a crisis of demand for universal access to our health care system within constraints of global budget control. Technological advance and resource limitations are universal in our society (Toffler 1980). The future health care agenda is quality and cost control (Herzlinger 1989; American College of Healthcare Executives and the Arthur Andersen Company 1988). Both are achievable for home care by management (Herzlinger 1989) that reflects culture (Drucker 1988) and responds to change that is incremental and then consolidated (Kinzer 1990).

For home care to survive the inevitable changes of the future, it must be incorporated and integrated into comprehensive health reform. In the recent past, home care development only required definition of mission and desired outcomes; description of specific operational mechanisms; determination of required human and material resources; delineation of roles, responsibilities, and relationships among all actors; and description of essential communication and linkages. Today, much more vital considerations for organizational design and development are external environmental factors. Paramount is the need for containment of health care costs which is present in every nation as demonstrated by the top priority given to this issue in the United States by the Clinton administration and individual states (Somerville 1993).

In the past few years, the call for health care reform has become universal and home care is at risk in each nation no matter what the finance system: national health, national health insurance, market-oriented/regulated. No country can afford to divert funds designated for social needs to an ever-demanding health care system. Total health expenditures will be capitated and growth of expenditures controlled. Home care will have to compete for limited resources with established and influential traditional models.

How can home care survive health reform? What will it look like? How will it be established?

1. Home care will operate within finite predetermined fiscal constraints. The financial risk to manage these resources and respond to the needs of all beneficiaries will be the burden of the home care system. Home care cannot survive if it costs more than institution-based alternatives.

2. Home care must be operated by in integrated-management approach that involves and links all stakeholders in its evolution and development: health care professionals, patients, payers, community-based providers. Operational conflicts can be resolved by a process of planning, implementing, evaluating, and modifying the system that respects multiple viewpoints and perspectives. In this way, the system will be flexible, adaptable, meeting the individual needs of each participant and group while maximizing the utilization of resources. Home care will not survive if fragmented, inflexible, and unable to be innovative.

3. Home care must be designed intelligently by utilizing available technologies of management information systems and advanced communications, which can extend the impact of each player. A central role must be given to the person/family, who has valuable insight and skills in self-management and management of his or her own home care program.

4. Home care must be integrated into a variety of levels of care: primary, secondary, and tertiary; acute, intermediary, and long-term; community-based and institutional. It must be part of a total package offering options depending upon the needs of individual situations. Such a vertically integrated system must be designed and operated locally since home care is based on the dedicated collaborative efforts of doctors and patients, providers and payers, who all benefit if given the opportunity to work together within the constraints of regional/national policy.

5. Home care must responsibly accomplish goals of patient safety, medical necessity and appropriateness, quality, and cost containment. It must prove itself by presetting desirable outcomes and suitable indicators of variance. Only by achieving desired results as determined by rigorous outcomes research will home care justify resources required for survival.

ACKNOWLEDGMENTS

The author wishes to acknowledge invaluable input from the following contributors of information, publications, or personal viewpoints: Susan L. Hughes, Center for Health Services and Policy Research, Kellogg Graduate School of Management, Northwestern University; P. Ronald Stephenson, Department of Marketing, Graduate School of Business, Indiana University; Jeremy M. Jones, President/CEO, Homedco, Fountain Valley, CA; Carole Cullen, President, Americare, Naperville, IL; Jim Retel, District Manager, Glasrock Home Health Care, Atlanta, GA; Jill L. White/Bob Moyers, Legislative Affairs, National Association for Home Care, Washington, DC; Jo Holtzer, President, Center for Disability Rights, Chicago, IL; Margaret Pfrommer, Director, Technical Aids and Assistance for the Disabled, and Former President, Illinois Congress of Organizations for the Physically Handicapped, Chicago; JoAnne G. Schwartzberg, Director, Geriatric Health, American Medical Association.

NOTES

1. In Chicago, personal attendants to enable independent living are promoted by Access Living; *Independent Living* is their publication. In New York, Concepts for Independence, Inc., is a client-maintained personal attendant care program directed by and for persons with severe disabilities. *Concepts Voice*, their publication, is published by Concepts for Independence, Inc.
2. NAHC is the National Association of Home Care; NAMES is the National Association of Medical Equipment Suppliers; HIDA is the Health Industry Distributors Association.
3. American Medical Association, American Hospital Association, American Nursing Association.
4. Omnibus Budget Reconciliation Act of 1987 (PL100-203), effective January 1, 1989: HCFA Medicare Six Point Payment Plan for Durable Medical Equipment and Prosthetic Devices.
5. *AMA News*, October 5, 1990, p. 14, reports Kellogg Foundation evaluation of home care quality; *Modern Healthcare*, August 6, 1990, p. 38, reports Robert Wood Johnson Foundation evaluation of long-term care quality.
6. Personal communications with J. Keenan and R. Kane, University of Minnesota.
7. Americans with Disabilities Act, July 26, 1990.
8. Two such organizations are Sick Kids (Need) Involved Persons, Inc. (SKIP), and Gazette International Networking Institute, Inc. (GINI).
9. March of Dimes, Easter Seals, United Cerebral Palsy.

REFERENCES

Aday, L. U., D. H. Wegener, R. M. Andersen, and M. J. Aitken. 1989. "Home Care for Ventilator Assisted Children." *Health Affairs* 8:137–47.

Alba, A., A. I. Goldberg, E. Oppenheimer, and E. Roberts. 1990. "Caring for Mechanically Ventilated Patients at Home." *Chest* 98:1543..

American Association for Respiratory Care, Food and Drug Administration, and Health Resources Services Administration. 1989. *Consensus Conference on Home Respiratory Care Equipment.* Dallas.

American College of Healthcare Executives and the Arthur Andersen Company. 1988. *The Future of Healthcare: Changes and Choices.* Chicago.

Arewine, D. 1990. "Health Resources Managers Should Prepare for 'The Big One.'" *Modern Healthcare* 20(34):38.

Blendon, R. J. and H. Taylor. 1989. "Views on Health Care: Public Opinion in Three Nations." *Health Affairs* 8:149–57.

Brazda, J. F. 1990. "Catastrophic Insurance Law Hammered Out Too Hastily." *Modern Healthcare* 19(34):60.

"Case Management and Home Care." 1990. *Caring* 9:7–8.

Cooper, S. 1990. "Home Med Device Firms Fail to Win Fed Sympathy on Reimbursement Cuts." *Healthweek* (13 June):11.

Council on Scientific Affairs. 1990. "Home Care in the 1990's." *Journal of the American Medical Association* 263:1241–44.

"Doctors Need Larger Role in Home Health Care." 1990. *AMA News* 33:27.

Donlan, T. 1983. "No Place Like Home." *Barron's.* March 21.

Drucker, P. E. 1988. "Management and the World's Work." *Harvard Business Review* 66:65–76.

Eddy, D. M. 1990. "What Do We Do About Costs?" *Journal of the American Medical Association* 264:1161–70.

Eiserman, J. E. 1990. "Committee F31 on Health Care Services and Equipment." *Standardization News* 18:52–53.

Faure, E. A. M. and A. I. Goldberg (eds.). 1982. *Proceedings of an International Symposium: What Ever Happened to the Polio Patient?* Chicago: Northwestern University Press.

Foundation for Home and Hospice Care. 1988. *Basic Home Care Statistics. The Industry, 1988.* Washington, DC: Author.

General Accounting Office. 1987. *Medicare: Need to Strengthen Home Health Payment Controls and Address Unmet Needs: 1986 Report to the Chairman, Special Committee on Aging, United States Senate.* GAO HRD-87.9. Washington, DC: Author.

Ginsberg, E., W. Balinsky, and M. Ostow. 1984. *Home Health Care: Its Role in the Changing Health Services Market.* Totawa, NJ: Rowman and Allanheld.

Goldberg, A. I. 1983a. "Home Care for a Better Life for Ventilator-Dependent People." *Chest* 84:365–66.

———. 1983b. *International Exchange of Experts and Information in Rehabilitation Fellowship Report. Home Care Services for Severely Physically Disabled People in England and France. Case Example: The Ventilator Dependent Person.* New York: World Rehabilitation Fund.

———. 1984. "The Regional Approach to Home Care for Life Supported Persons." *Chest* 86:345–46.

———. 1986. "Home Care for Life Supported Persons—Is a National Approach the Answer." *Chest* 90:744–48.

———. 1989. "Home Care for Life-Supported Persons: The French System of

Quality Control, Technology Assessment, and Cost Containment." *Public Health Reports* 104:329–36.

———. 1992. "Home Mechanical Ventilation—The Free Market System (USA)." *European Respiratory Review* 2(10):422–25.

Goldberg, A. I. and E. A. M. Faure. 1984. "Home Care for Life Supported Persons in England: The Responaut Program." *Chest* 86:910–14.

———. 1986. "Home Care for Life Supported Persons in France: The Regional Association." *Rehabilitation Literature* 47:60–64,103.

Goldberg, A. I. and D. Frownfelter. 1990. "The Ventilator Assisted Individuals Study." *Chest* 98:428–33.

Gornick, M. and M. J. Hall. 1988. "Trends in Medicare Use of Post-Hospital Care." *Health Care Financing Review* Annual Suppl.:27–38.

Grey Panthers Task Force for a National Health System. 1990. *Wake Up. It's Time for a National Health System Now!* Philadelphia.

Guterman, S., P. W. Eggers, G. Riley, T. F. Greene, and S. A. Terrell. 1988. "Special Report: The First Three Years of Medicare Prospective Payment: An Overview." *Health Care Financing Review* 9:67–77.

Health Care Finance Administration. 1983. *Projections.* Washington, DC.

Herzlinger, R. E. 1989. "The Failed Revolution in Health Care—The Role of Management." *Harvard Business Review* (March–April):95–103.

Hughes, S. L. 1986. *Long Term Care: Options in an Expanding Market.* Rockville, MD: Aspen.

———. 1990. "Home Care: Where We Are and Where We Need to Go." Invited paper presented at Workshop on In-Home and Supportive Services, National Institute on Aging (NIH) and the Administration on Aging (DHHS), Bethesda, MD, April 19–20.

Hughes, W. L. 1985. "Apples and Oranges? A Review of Evaluation s of Community-Based Long-Term Care." *Health Services Research* 20:461–88.

Joint Commission on Accreditation of Healthcare Organizations. 1988. *Home Care Standards for Accreditation.* Chicago.

———. 1993. *JCAHO Accreditation Manual for Home Care.* Oakbrook Terrace, IL.

Kahn, K. L., E. B. Keeler, M. J. Sherwood, W. H. Rogers, S. S. Draper, E. J. Bentow, L. V. Reinisch, L. V. Rubenstein, J. Kosecoff, and R. H. Brook. 1990. "Comparing Outcomes of Care Before and After Implementation of the DRG-Based Prospective Payment System." *Journal of the American Medical Association* 264:1984–88.

Kane, N. M. 1989. "The Home Care Crisis of the Nineties." *Gerontologist* 22:24–31.

Kenkel, P. J. 1987. "More Hospitals Enter Long-Term Care Business." *Modern Healthcare* 17(24):30–34.

Kinzer, D. M. 1990. "Universal Entitlement to Health Care. Can We Get There from Here?" *New England Journal of Medicine* 322:467–70.

Laurie, G. (ed.). 1962–87. *Rehabilitation Gazette* 1–23.

Lebreton, G., A. Ludot, and A. Tripier. 1981. "Les Insuffisants Respiratoires Chroniques Graves Pris en Charge à 100% par le Regime Général de la Securité Social." *Revue Médicale Assurance Maladie* 3:3–6.

Lis, E. F., A. I. Goldberg, C. A. Monahan, and K. E. Murphy. 1987. *The Children's Home Health Network of Illinois (CHHNI)*. *Pediatric Home Ventilation: A Model of Discharge and Home Care Planning*. PHS, MCH #MC5172262. Rockville, MD: DHHS.

Liu, K., K. Manton, and B. M. Liu. 1985. "Home Care Expenses for the Disabled Elderly." *Health Care Financing Review* 7(2):51–58.

Lutz, S. 1988. "HME Dealers Await Changes in Reimbursement Policy." *Modern Healthcare* 18(10):40.

———. 1990. "Hospitals Reassess Home Care Ventures." *Modern Healthcare* 20(37):22–30.

Marion Merrell Dow. 1989. *Long Term Care Digest. Home Health Care Edition*. Kansas City.

McIlrath, S. 1990. "Poll: Taxpayers Willing to Fund Insurance Plan." *AMA News* (October 5):5.

McIlrath, W. 1990. "New Budget Eases Medicare Cuts: Retains $30 Billion in Pay Curbs." *AMA News* 33:1.

Muir, J.-F., C. Voisin, and A. Ludot. 1992. "Home Mechanical Ventilation (HMV)—National Insurance System (France)." *European Respiratory Review* 2(10):418–21.

Mullahy, C. M. 1990. "Empowering the Case Manager." *Continuing Care* 9(7): 14.

National Association for Home Care. 1990. *Public and Private Expenditures for Postacute Care*. Washington, DC.

Neu, C. R. and S. Harrison. 1988. *Posthospital Care Before and After the Medicare Prospective Payment System*. Cooperative Agreement No. R-3590-HCFA. Santa Monica, CA: Rand Corporation.

O'Donnell, K. P. 1988. "Savvy Physicians Are Beginning to Realize Benefits of Home Care." *Modern Healthcare* 18(6):34.

O'Donohue, W. J., et al. 1986. "American College of Chest Physicians. Long Term Mechanical Ventilation: Guidelines for Management in the Home and at Alternate Community Sites." *Chest* 90:1S–37S.

O'Toole, J. 1985. *Vanguard Management*. New York: Doubleday.

Paige, L. 1990. "AMA Suggests Emphasis on Home Health Care." *AMA News* 33:10.

Payor, L. 1988. *Medicine and Culture: Varieties of Treatment in the United States, England, West Germany, and France*. New York: Holt.

Peters, T. and N. Austin. 1985. *Passion for Excellence: The Leadership Difference*. New York: Random House.

Plummer, A. L., W. J. O'Donohue, and T. L. Petty. 1989. "Consensus Conference on Problems in Home Mechanical Ventilation." *American Review of Respiratory Diseases* 140:555–60.

"Public Backs Increases in Medicare Spending." 1990. *AMA News* (July 27):6.

Responaut Panel Research Team. 1974. *The Responaut Study: Final Report*. London: St. Thomas's Hospital.

Rucker, B. B. 1987. *The Home Drug Delivery Industry: An Outlook*. San Francisco: Hambrecht and Quist.

Ruther, M. and C. Helbing. 1988. "Health Care Financing Trends: Use and Cost of Home Health Agency Services Under Medicare." *Health Care Financing Review* 10(1):105–8.

Rutstein, D. D. 1967. *The Coming Revolution in Medicine*. Cambridge, MA: MIT Press.

Sager, D. 1990. "The Business of Case Management." *The Case Manager* 1:36.

Scanlon, W. J. 1988. "A Perspective on Long Term Care for the Elderly." *Health Care Financing Review* Annual Suppl.:7–15.

Scanlon, W. J. and J. Feder. 1984. "The Long Term Care Market Place—An Overview." *Healthcare Financial Management* 14:18–36.

Selz, M. 1990. "Home Healthcare: Companies Learn a Painful Lesson." *Wall Street Journal* (March 26), p. B2.

Shaughnessy, P. W. and A. M. Kramer. 1990. "The Increased Needs of Patients in Nursing Homes and Patients Receiving Home Health Care." *New England Journal of Medicine* 322:21–27.

Shortell, S. M. and W. J. McNerney. 1990. "Criteria and Guidelines for Reforming the U.S. Health Care System." *New England Journal of Medicine* 322:463–66.

Soldo, B. J. 1985. "In-Home Services for the Dependent Elderly." *Research on Aging* 7:281–304.

Somerville, J. 1993. "States Pave Way on Managed Competition." *AMA News* (March 15).

Spiegel, A. D. 1987. *Home Health Care*, 2nd ed. Owning Mills, MD: National Health Publishers, Rynd Communications.

Starr, Paul. 1982. *The Social Transformation of American Medicine*. New York: Basic Books.

Stephenson, P. R. and W. L. Cron. 1987. *HIDA Financial Performance Survey for Home Care/DME Dealers*. Alexandria, VA: Health Industry Distributors Association.

———. 1989. *HIDA Financial Performance Survey for Home Care/DME Dealers*. Alexandria, VA: Health Industry Distributors Association.

———. 1992. *HIDA Financial Performance Survey for Home Care/DME Dealers*. Alexandria, VA: Health Industry Distribution Association.

Stern, L. W. and A. I. El-Ansary. 1988. *Marketing Channels*, 3rd ed. Englewood Cliffs, NJ: Prentice Hall.

"Survey Shows Public Support for Spending on Children's Health." *AMA News* (July 27):10.

Toffler, A. 1980. *The Third Wave*. New York: William Morrow.

U.S. Congress, Office of Technology Assessment. 1987a. *Life Sustaining Technologies and the Elderly*. OTA-BA-306. Washington, DC: U.S. Government Printing Office.

———. 1987b. *Technology Dependent Children: Hospital vs. Home Care—A Technical Memorandum*. OTA-TM-H-38. Washington, DC: U.S. Government Printing Office.

U.S. Department of Health and Human Services. 1983. *Report on the Surgeon General's Workshop. Children with Handicaps and Their Families. Case Example: The Ventilator Dependent Child*. Publ. PHS-83-50194. Washington, DC: Author.

————. 1988a. *Federal Register* 53(December 14):240.

————. 1988b. *Report on the Task Force on Technology Dependent Children*, Vols. 1 and 2. HCFA 88-021271. Washington, DC: U.S. Government Printing Office.

United Way of Chicago. 1990. *Report of the Needs Assessment Committee on Discrimination.* Chicago.

Wagner, L. 1989. "Catastrophic Collapse: Is It a Millstone or a Milestone for Health Policy Evolution?" *Modern Healthcare* 19(42):20–23.

————. 1990a. "AMA Proposes National Healthcare Reform Plan." *Modern Healthcare* 20(10):2.

————. 1990b. "Coalition to Develop Proposals to Overhaul Healthcare System." *Modern Healthcare* 20(11):4.

————. 1990c. "Framework for Reform. Now Comes the Hard Part—Reaching for Consensus." *Modern Healthcare* 20(35):31–34.

————. 1990d. "Health PAC's Modest Donors." *Modern Healthcare* 20(38):4.

————. 1990e. "Pepper Panel's Healthcare Blueprint Omits Funding, Bipartisan Support." *Modern Healthcare* 20(10):20.

————. 1990f. "Pepper Report Obscured by the $66 Billion Question." *Modern Healthcare* (Eldercare Business Supplement):12–13.

Wilensky, Gail. 1990. "Steering Health Care Policy Along the Potomac: An Interview." *Healthweek* (July 30):22–25.

Chapter 5

Divisions of Labor and Home Care in Great Britain

BLEDDYN DAVIES

INTRODUCTION

The subject of this paper is the division of labor and resources between hospital and social care services, and the divisions of labor between home care and residential modes of provision whosoever provides it. I have focused on the main long-term care groups used in the general analysis of long-term care policy—what we in Great Britain have for many years called community care policy.

The argument is based on the premise that changes in the division of labor are substantially the outcomes of competition. Perhaps ultimately the most important form of that is the competition for the support of policymakers who determine the broad structures of policy and the allocations of resources among broad needs. The ideas about means and ends that count at this general level are the rationales that justify public policies to the broader body of informed opinion, which adjusts up or down the allocations of effort and resources to policy areas in the light of priorities. The changes in expectations, assumptions, and conscious choices have opened long-established arrangements to the possibilities of new forms of competition during the last 30 years, and particularly during the last 15 with large effects on resource flows and professional influence.

The priority has become to tailor resources and how they are used for individual needs in a way that reflects new normalization-related philosophies. The feature of the philosophies from which a discussion of divisions of labor should start is their implications for the outcomes expected from the policy process, those ultimate evaluative criteria that win or lose support for arrangements among those higher policymakers and spokespersons of public opinion who influence grand priorities in policymaking.

What the new weighting of ends and means has done is to make some of our favorite and best established categories for thinking less appropriate for the analysis of the new situation. In particular, an outcomes-led discussion must focus more on handicap than disability, disability than impairment, and impairment than disease category. We are increasingly trying to allocate more than a trivial amount of resources directly to reducing the diswelfares created by handicaps rather than countervailing disabilities or impairments or curing diseases.[1]

However, giving a high weighting to such outcomes in evaluating the success of policy has clear implications for resource flows. Whatever the pattern of variation in costs of inputs per unit of time, the greater proportion of the total cost of care for most potential beneficiaries is accounted for by inputs that do not require long professional training in highly technical areas or the use of machinery of such capital cost that the efficient use of it must dominate the care program. Looking at the clientele as a whole, these inputs are often essential for other inputs to be effective, but often are most effective when they are carefully coordinated with the other inputs (acting supportively or independently), and usually account for a small proportion of the total costs of care. That is not to say that many of the causal processes that produce the newly desired outcomes are necessarily simple and that they require no more than the routine application of simple skills. However, the complex skills required are often those in which the normal processes of acculturation make many people highly skilled, or at least the required skills are sufficiently like those in which many people have become highly skilled, that for the extension of existing skills to cover the new contexts is neither difficult nor expensive.

Several things follow for discussions of the divisions of labor:

- Changes in the prioritization of outcomes have created potentially innumerable ways of producing the mix of welfare outcomes desired. Likewise, there are innumerable sources of the person input that can be mobilized to perform tasks in the process.
- The range of possibilities for input substitution is enhanced. So therefore are the possibilities of variety and competition.
- The relative costs and benefits of combinations, and thus the most cost-effective choice, will vary more among contexts. The patterns of relative prices of similar inputs will differ greatly geographically as well as through time. Indeed, a system that in all contexts applied the same input mixes to persons in similar circumstances would be highly inefficient. Efficiency more than ever requires responsiveness to local circumstances, and a willingness to change through time.
- Arrangements that can efficiently deliver the mix of outcomes that were most highly valued 30 years ago but that are less efficient in

delivering the mix now desired have a comparative disadvantage and face a narrowing of role. Professions whose values and skills make them more effective in the production of the older output mix are likewise at a comparative disadvantage and are likely to face competition that will narrow their roles.

Section I provides some statistical description of the need-related circumstances of the population of England, Wales, and Scotland; and descriptions of the consumption of service. Section II discusses community-based home care in the context of achieving success in changing the balance of care, with greater cost-effectiveness in the use of public funds. Section III discusses recent legislation for changes in community care. Section IV provides empirical evidence about community care alternatives, and Section V is the conclusion.

I. NEEDS, PROVISIONS, AND RESOURCES: STATISTICAL DESCRIPTION

A brief paper must balance between inclusiveness and focus, between coverage of the broad categories that consume most resources and selection of types of groups for whom developments best illuminate current causal processes. The broad long-term care groups selected for this analysis are:

- elderly persons whose circumstances typically require substantial care over a long period
- persons with long-standing mental health problems who require either continuous or episodic deployment of resources of considerable cost and whose lifetime consumption is large
- persons with learning difficulties who likewise require large resources over their lifetime
- younger persons with physical handicaps

The introduction argued that the new structure of priorities for policy goals puts a greater emphasis on reducing the diswelfares of handicap than on offsetting the effects of disability, and more on these than on care or cure for the chronically ill or impaired as such. So a brief outline of relevant data about needs and utilization should logically focus on handicap and impairment. Since there are better British data on disability than on handicap or impairment, the empirical definitions of the groups will reflect disability more than handicap. The outline will necessarily be brief and so omit much that is important.

A. Disability

The two most general sources are (1) the national survey of disability whose results for adults are reported in Martin, Meltzer, and Elliot (1988), Martin, White, and Meltzer (1989), and related volumes; and (2) the General Household Survey (GHS), particularly for 1980 and 1985, when a fuller range of questions about disability and handicap was asked. The analyses allow us to distinguish (1) forms of disability, (2) degrees of severity of disability, and between (3) persons resident in private households and persons resident in communal establishments.

The design of the study reported in Martin et al. aimed to cover the areas of disability included in the *International Classification of Impairments, Disabilities, and Handicaps* (hereinafter ICIDH; WHO 1980). The classification reflects that in the ICIDH, though with differences of detail. The ten main areas distinguished were locomotion; reaching and stretching; dexterity; seeing; hearing; personal care; continence; communication; behavior; and intellectual functioning.

The design of the study was based on ratings by experts. The criterion they were asked to apply was how disabling several types of disability were in relation to individuals' performance. They were asked to consider the impact of the disability on a typical day, assuming that there would be no one available to help with the activity (Martin et al. 1988:52). Each individual with disability was rated from 1 to 10 (with 10 representing the greatest severity of disability). Thus they defined the criterion partly in relation to handicap, judges being required to assess the likely effect on people's performance of roles and lives in general, though not in relation to specific circumstances or with respect to norms for any particular group (p. 10). So the method of deriving severity scales makes this suitable for describing the diswelfare consequences of disabling characteristics.

The data and analytic methods used by Martin et al. yield a higher rate of increase of the proportions disabled as age increases than the proportions yielded by combining general questions in the GHS. However, the more general (and so inclusive) GHS question elicited a higher estimate of the proportion disabled: 399 per thousand of the population aged 60 and over, compared with 355 by Martin et al.

Among persons in private households, approximately equal proportions of adult disabled persons are in each of three age groups: those aged less than 60, those aged 60 and over and less than 75, and those aged 75 and over. However, whereas the proportion in each of the two younger age groups decreases with severity, the proportion in the oldest age group increases with severity. Almost half of those in the two high-

Table 1. Prevalence of Disability among Elderly Persons by Age and Severity Category for Men and Women (Cumulative Rate per Thousand Population)

	Men			Women		
Severity category	60–74[1]	75 and over[1]	Total[2]	60–74[1]	75 and over[1]	Total[2]
Private households						
10	3	10	2	2	20	3
9–10	14	48	7	14	61	11
8–10	27	86	13	27	105	20
7–10	42	128	21	45	171	34
6–10	57	167	29	68	238	49
5–10	82	226	41	100	314	68
4–10	112	287	54	130	376	86
3–10	149	349	69	166	442	105
2–10	202	425	88	208	510	125
1–10	278	521	117	258	586	151
Total population including establishments						
10	5	21	3	4	45	6
9–10	17	64	9	18	102	17
8–10	31	107	16	31	154	28
7–10	46	150	24	50	224	42
6–10	62	191	32	73	293	58
5–10	87	250	45	106	369	78
4–10	117	309	58	136	431	97
3–10	155	369	73	172	495	115
2–10	207	442	92	213	561	135
1–10	283	533	121	264	631	161

Notes:
[1] Rate per thousand of age group in question.
[2] Rate per thousand of population age 16 and over.
Source: Martin, Meltzer and Elliot (1988), Table 3.7.

est severity groups are elderly. The increase in the proportion aged 75 and over with high severity is greater for women than for men.

Table 1 shows the cumulative rates per thousand persons of disabled persons in each age group over 60 years. The rates of disabled persons per thousand of the population rise with age, though because of the attrition of the population at higher ages and the increased proportions living in communal establishments, the actual numbers in private households increase for each severity category and in total only up to age 70–79. The prevalence in the two most severe groups (9 and 10) is low until people are in their late 60s, after which there is a steep rise (Martin et al. 1988).

Most disabled persons living in communal establishments are elderly. Two thirds are aged 75 and over and just over one-half are aged 80 and over. Disabilities most likely to be associated with mental impairment or mental illness showed a decrease with age, either because of people leaving institutions and moving back into the community or because of relatively high mortality rates associated with some of the conditions that cause these kinds of disabilities.

Table 2 summarizes the rates yielded by the disability survey for persons of working age with mental health problems and/or learning difficulties. In the population of disabled persons living in private households, all three types of disability are associated with disabilities of other kinds, especially with inability to perform personal care tasks, reaching and stretching, and dexterity. Some kind of mental dysfunction is the most common kind of complaint among those in communal establishments, disabled intellectual functioning affecting four-fifths of residents.

Martin et al. (1988) also reported on persons of working age with physical disabilities. Among those in private households, the most common disabilities were related to locomotion, seeing, and personal care;

Table 2.   Percentage of Disabled Persons Aged 16 to 59 with Mental Health Problems Living in Private Households and Communal Establishments, by Overall Severity Level

| Severity category | Type of disability | | |
	Communication	Behavior	Intellectual functioning
Private households			
1–2	9	11	12
3–4	15	32	25
5–6	21	48	44
7–8	30	56	53
9–10	51	62	62
Total[1]	18	33	30
Communal establishments			
1–2	28	32	49
3–4	48	35	73
5–6	49	65	64
7–8	74	76	88
9–10	83	74	91
Total[1]	66	65	80

Note: [1] Percentage of all disabled persons.
Source: Martin, et al. (1988), Tables 4.6 and 4.12.

those in communal establishments were most likely to have disabilities in personal care, seeing, locomotion, and hearing.

B. Service Provision and Expenditures

We next pursue the analysis of utilization and contact by disability. Tables shown below describe provision and expenditures by broad groups.

1.   Contacts with Health Professionals among Elderly Persons in Private Households.   Table 3 describes the contacts with health professionals and services reported by the elderly persons interviewed in private households. The proportion of elderly disabled persons who had seen their general practitioners (GPs) during the past year was 82%, illustrating the potential of the function. The proportion differed little with the age group of the elderly person, but varied more with the degree of the severity of disability. However, approximately 10% of disabled persons in severity categories 7–8 seemed not to have had contact with their GP during the previous year—though the results might have been depressed by faulty recall by respondents. Older disabled persons had less contact with GPs than younger disabled persons.

The proportion who had stayed in hospital as an inpatient was strongly correlated with the severity of the disablement. It varied from 11–12% among the elderly persons in categories 1–2 to 36–38% of those in categories 9–10. Both the number of stays and the average length of stay increased with severity. For those in severity categories 9–10, the most common length of stay was between 1 and 3 months.

Contacts with chiropodists and community nursing were both age-related among elderly disabled people. Severity was associated with contact particularly for community nursing and primary care professionals.

2.   Contact with Home Care Services among Elderly Persons in Private Households.   Only 1% of disabled adults of all ages received a service other than Local Authority home help, Meals on Wheels, or private domestic help. Among the elderly, other more specialized services are not received by high proportions. The proportions by age group and severity category are described in Table 4.

Unsurprisingly, the proportions receiving the home care services were associated with age group, allowance being made for specific disability. The association between seeing a social worker and severity of disability was weaker among the older than younger elderly. Most of the more important home care services are both age and severity related.

C. How Well Is Social Service Targeted?

Among the need-related circumstances that make the use of these data difficult for the discussion of resourcing and targeting are the living

Table 3. Percentage of Disabled Elderly Persons Who Had Seen Various Health Professionals during the Last Year by Age Group and Severity of Disability, Living in Private Households

Health professional seen	Aged 65–74						Aged 75 and over					
	Severity category					All disabled	Severity category					All disabled
	1–2	3–4	5–6	7–8	9–10		1–2	3–4	5–6	7–8	9–10	
Consultant or hospital doctor	38	44	47	64	58	45	29	38	42	41	58	39
Hospital nurse	15	19	24	29	34	20	13	16	19	22	28	18
Physiotherapist	6	8	12	18	28	10	3	5	8	11	19	8
Occupational therapist	1	1	2	8	7	2	0	0	2	4	7	2
Radiologist (inc. radiographers and radiotherapists)	14	19	22	25	18	18	10	13	12	14	16	12
Dietician	3	4	4	6	8	4	1	2	2	3	6	2
Speech therapist	—	0	1	2	3	1	—	—	0	1	1	0
Hearing therapist (inc. audiologists and hearing technicians)	3	3	2	5	1	3	3	2	2	4	7	3
Optician or oculist	4	5	5	10	2	5	7	7	6	5	2	6
Hospital social worker	1	2	2	3	7	2	1	1	1	3	6	2
Artificial limb/appliance fitter	1	3	2	4	3	2	0	1	1	1	3	1
Psychologist/psychotherapist	1	1	2	1	1	1	—	0	1	0	1	0
General practitioner	77	82	88	88	95	82	76	84	82	90	92	84
Chiropodist	6	8	12	17	21	10	9	19	26	33	32	22
Health visitor	3	5	8	14	20	7	5	7	11	13	19	10
Community nurse	6	9	18	27	56	14	9	18	26	42	64	26
Osteopath/homeopath (inc. acupuncturists, chiropractors, and reflexologists)	3	3	3	7	3	3	2	2	2	2	2	2
Any of the above	83	88	94	96	99	89	84	90	92	95	98	90
Base[1]	1,017	622	462	288	144	2,533	864	719	715	566	317	3,181

Note: [1] Base is the number of disabled elderly by age group and severity category per 10,000 in private households.
Source: Martin, et al. (1989), Table 4.14.

Table 4. Proportion of Disabled Elderly Adults Living in Private Households Who Had Received Various Home Care Services, by Severity of Disability

	Aged 65–74						Aged 75 and over					
	Severity category					All disabled	Severity category					All disabled
Type of service received	1–2	3–4	5–6	7–8	9–10		1–2	3–4	5–6	7–8	9–10	
LA home help	6	8	20	20	28	12	17	28	41	43	30	31
Meals on wheels	0	2	2	5	2	2	15	6	11	17	11	9
Laundry service	0	1	0	1	4	1	—	1	2	2	5	1
Incontinence service	0	0	1	1	4	1	—	—	1	2	5	1
Night-sitting service	—	—	—	—	1	0	—	—	0	1	1	0
Mobility/technical officer for the blind	—	0	0	1	1	0	—	1	1	0	3	0
Social worker	2	3	8	12	22	6	2	4	7	10	12	6
Voluntary services	1	1	1	2	2	1	1	2	2	2	—	1
Visiting service	0	0	1	1	1	0	0	0	0	1	—	0
Private domestic help	3	3	3	4	4	3	6	7	7	7	4	7
Private nursing help	0	—	0	—	2	0	0	—	1	2	3	1
Other services	1	1	1	2	3	1	0	1	1	2	2	1
Any of the above	12	15	29	36	55	21	27	38	51	58	50	42
Base[1]	1,017	622	462	288	144	2,533	864	719	715	566	317	3,181

Note: [1] Base is the number of interviews weighted to take into account nonresponse and undersampling. (See Martin, et al. 1988: 68.)
Source: Martin, et al. (1989), Table 4.19.

arrangements of the disabled persons. There are higher probabilities of consuming some services among those living alone, particularly the standard social services, home help, and Meals on Wheels. But the proportions of disabled persons receiving the services are low whatever their household situation.

The relationship between disability, household composition, and the need-related circumstances that influence who receives what community-based service has been the subject of great policy concern. Since the early 1980s, it has increasingly been argued that the main way in which the equity and efficiency of the outcomes of the community-based services could be improved would be by better targeting: concentrating resources better and more consistently on those with higher priority needs and achieving a pattern of variations in amounts received that better reflected need-related circumstances and the likely benefits.

Davies, Bebbington, Charnley, and colleagues (1990) show greater consistency in the amounts of services received than would be inferred from some of the most trenchant criticisms in the policy analyses of public bodies. Their findings are that weekly hours of home help, home care, and warden services are associated with dependency characteristics (e.g., critical interval needs), life events (e.g., death of spouse, recent hospitalization), social interaction, and substitute services (e.g., social work, nursing services). Using these dimensions, and controlling for area, they were able to explain 43% of the variation in such services.

Summarizing their research on targeting community-based services for elderly people, they wrote:

> Home help/care consumes most expenditure on community social services. Estimates for a range of target criteria show horizontal target efficiency to be lower than vertical target efficiency: that is, the proportion of persons in need actually receiving service is lower than the proportion receiving service who are not in need. . ... The analysis of average consumption of home help/care by need type suggests that the patterns are more rational than has been suggested by some on the basis of cruder analyses. However, variations in needs are not precisely matched by variations in consumption. . ...
>
> Some of the same generalizations apply to the consumption of meals-on-wheels. In particular, there is a mismatch between self-care abilities and the pattern of consumption. . ...The same generalizations are valid *a fortiori* for the patterns of day care, whose utilization is also characterized by a high proportion of those recommended for service not taking it up. (Davies 1991:13)

Martin et al. (1989) also reported whether disabled adults thought that they needed help that they were not getting. Among all disabled adults, some 14% thought that they needed help that they were not getting, approximately one-half of them being recipients of services. The proportion increased with the severity of their disability. Allowing for severity, the proportions thinking needs to be unmet were higher among those aged 75 and over. The types of help most desired were chiropody, home help, and community nursing. Yet there is evidence that since 1985, more health authorities have contracted their community nursing activities for the elderly than expanded them (Davies et al. 1990).

Bebbington and Davies (forthcoming) report estimates of unmet need using a different methodology. The method used was to apply criteria of need reflecting allocation decisions to define conditions for membership of the target group for services. The sets of definitions varied in stringency and reflected differing priority to circumstances, e.g., to carer relief. Then the data of the GHS were used to estimate the extent of unmet need and the proportion of recipients who satisfied the need criteria. Estimates were made for 1980 and 1985. The results suggested that vertical target efficiency—*the proportions of resources consumed by those in need*—was high compared with horizontal target efficiency—*the proportion of those in need receiving service.* So the reallocation of resources from those served but not in need would be insufficient to provide what would be required to achieve coverage for those in need.

Analysis of the relationship between the severity of disability and capacity to undertake tasks showed a closer relationship between severity of disability and capacity to carry out self-care than between severity of disability and capacity to undertake household care tasks. Severity category was strongly related to the amount of help required. The relationship holds for all age groups. Indeed, no age effect was apparent.

D. User Charges and the Health/Social Care Divide

It is part of the argument of this paper that in Great Britain the general principle of funding health care is that it is provided from general tax revenues, but the general principle for the social services is that it is subject to subsidy only among those of low income. Among disabled adult recipients of all ages over 16, 12, 4, and 26% (respectively) had paid something for physiotherapy, occupational therapy, and chiropody. Likewise, Table 4 shows that the consumption of private nursing help is not negligible, care for which 92% of its recipients paid. Among the social care services, financed under different general principles, some 57% claimed not to have made a payment for it, and that was also true for 45% of persons receiving laundry services.

There are national policies for charging for health services. However, other than for residential care, the policy for charging for the social services is at the discretion of individual Local Authorities. Davies et al. (1990) show policies about charges to vary with the political characteristics of the authority and to some degree the socioeconomic circumstances of the populations most likely to need service.

E. Informal Carers

Most of those who needed help with a self-care activity received it informally from a relative or a friend, usually from somebody living in the same household as the disabled adult. Only a low proportion required self-care help from formal agencies. Somewhat higher proportions received formal agency help with household activities. Yet only 28% of disabled adults who needed a lot of help throughout the day and night received help from voluntary or formal services. Again research that looks at the costs and quantities of resources confirms the increased importance of informal carers among the most disabled.

The economic and above all the psychosocial costs to informal carers are high. Davies et al. (1990) have shown that one-fifth or so of the principal carers of elderly persons receiving community-based social services had a score on a Malaise scale (based on the Cornell Medical Index Questionnaire) on or above the threshold at which psychiatrists would expect a high probability of need for psychiatric assessment.

F. Persons Living in Communal Establishments

Tables 5–7 provide information about (1) residents of communal establishments for the disabled and (2) services received by the disabled adults residing in them.

Table 5 shows the location of disabled adults in residential modes of care by age group and type of establishment. It illustrates the overall importance of elderly people in all types of establishments, but particularly the social care facilities. Higher proportions of the populations of National Health Service (NHS) establishments are of working age because of the numbers of mentally handicapped and mentally ill people in long-stay wards.

Table 6 for 1984 is reported in order to maintain comparability with the data reported by Jean Martin and her colleagues. However, the numbers of persons in NHS hospitals and private (for-profit) homes are changing. There are substantial time lags in the publication of statistical data, and trends continue. Some, like bed closures in hospitals, may have accelerated.

By 1986, the number of beds occupied daily in geriatric wards and units for the younger disabled was 50,000. The number of persons of working age in private homes increased by 25% between March 1984

Table 5. Disabled Persons in Communal Establishments

Percentage of Disabled Residents in Each Age Group by Type of Establishment, 1985[1]

| Age group | Type of establishment | | | |
	NHS	LA	Vol. org.	Private (for-profit)
16–49	27	5	14	2
50–64	13	4	13	4
65–74	14	13	14	11
75–84	28	40	32	40
85 and over	19	38	27	43

Percentage of Disabled Residents with Disabilities in each Area, by Age[2]

Age group	Physical disability	Mental disability
16–64	77	85
65–74	86	76
75–84	95	69
85 and over	98	76

Percentage of Disabled Residents, by Type of Disability and Establishment[3]

Type of establishment	Physical disability	Mental disability
NHS	92	89
Local authority	91	73
Voluntary organization	84	63
Private (for-profit)	94	70

Sources: Martin et al. (1989). [1] Table 9.4. [2] Table 9.18. [3] Table 9.20.

Table 6. Number of Persons in Residential Care Funded by the Public Sector, England and Wales, 1984

	Elderly	Mentally handicapped	Mentally ill	Younger physically handicapped	Total
Hospital inpatients	54,100	40,600	70,700	1,400	166,800
Local Authority homes	109,100	12,100	2,400	5,200	128,800
Private and voluntary homes	45,500	7,500	3,300	4,700	61,000
Total	208,700	60,200	76,400	11,300	356,000

Source: Audit Commission for England and Wales (1986).

Table 7. Proportion of Disabled Adults Living in Communal Establishments Using Different Professional Services, by Severity Category and Age

Professional services	Ages 65-74						Age 75 and over						Aged 85 and over					
	1-2	3-4	5-6	7-8	9-10	All disabled residents	1-2	3-4	5-6	7-8	9-10	All disabled residents	1-2	3-4	5-6	7-8	9-10	All disabled residents
Consultant or hospital doctor	59	58	61	58	70	63	44	51	49	53	69	58	41	43	38	53	60	53
Hospital nurse	24	12	16	14	10	14	1	7	4	4	12	8	6	4	3	3	6	5
Physiotherapist	12	9	15	16	32	21	3	9	10	19	34	21	12	7	11	18	30	22
Occupational therapyst	20	16	7	21	28	21	1	5	5	14	26	15	6	5	4	7	17	12
Radiologist (inc. radiographers and radiotherapists)	12	9	4	9	16	11	11	13	12	12	18	14	9	5	11	9	13	11
Dietician	2	1	1	2	6	3	2	2	3	2	7	4	—	—	—	2	4	2
Speech therapist	2	4	1	4	7	4	—	—	—	2	5	3	—	1	—	0	1	1
Hearing therapist (inc. audiologists and hearing technicians)	8	5	8	7	3	5	5	2	3	6	4	4	—	3	7	7	5	6
Optician or oculist	29	27	8	31	14	20	19	20	24	20	17	19	9	23	20	25	16	19
Hospital social worker	12	11	9	11	13	12	1	3	3	6	12	8	6	2	2	4	6	5
Artificial limb fitter	4	1	—	1	2	2	—	1	0	1	1	1	—	—	—	1	0	0
Psychologist	6	4	11	4	3	5	3	2	3	1	3	2	3	—	—	1	1	1
Psychotherapist	—	—	—	4	2	2	—	—	1	1	2	1	—	—	—	1	2	1
General practitioner	39	61	57	56	50	52	76	74	78	69	49	63	74	81	76	81	63	71
Chiropodist	53	38	48	45	58	50	26	37	32	41	55	44	26	27	36	44	57	48
Health visitor	2	1	1	2	1	1	1	3	3	3	2	3	—	—	3	2	1	2
Community nurse	17	15	20	14	16	16	16	19	19	24	19	20	18	18	25	27	22	23
Dentist	26	9	15	14	12	14	2	7	3	4	10	7	—	2	2	2	5	4
Osteopath/homeopath (inc. acupuncturists, chiropractors, and reflexologists)	—	—	—	—	—	—	—	—	—	0	—	0	9	1	—	—	—	0
Any of the above	89	88	91	96	98	94	87	89	90	93	97	96	85	89	89	95	97	96
Base[1]	63	82	72	100	195	512	101	168	221	322	593	1,405	33	97	179	313	642	1,264

Note: [1]Base is the number interviewed of disabled elderly in communal establishments by age group and severity category.
Source: Martin, et al. (1989), Table 11.11.

and March 1988. There is no reason to assume that the proportion who are substantially publicly funded diminished during that period. The number of elderly persons increased by no less than 83% during the same period. It is guesstimated that the cost of the social security payments for supported residents in private homes has risen to £1 billion per annum. The uncontrolled third-party financing mechanisms that have powered the increase will remain in place until 1993, although the social security rates have been allowed to fall behind inflation, and the increases in rates for nursing home beds have been greater than those for social care beds, perhaps to provide an incentive to suppliers to specialize in the areas where the demand after 1993 is likely to be directed. (The issue is discussed again below.)

Table 7 describes the use made of professional services by residents of communal establishments. We have seen the extent of the contact disabled persons in private households have with GPs. Despite the importance of long-stay hospitals among the communal establishments, the GP is seen by a high proportion of residents. The table illustrates that residents have contacts with many health personnel.

Table 8, drawing on the data presented in Tables 1–7, informs one of the main topics discussed in Part II of the paper: the balance of publicly supported care by client group and sector of service. We discuss its content again at the beginning of Part II.

Table 8. Balance of Public Expenditure and Care by Client Group, 1984/1985

	Elderly	*Mentally handicapped*	*Mentally ill*	*Younger physically handicapped*	*Total*
National Health Service (£m)	1060	500	1090	50	2700
Personal social services (£m)	1380	320	60	140	1900
Social security (£m)	460	30	10	190	690
Total (£m)	2900	850	1160	380	5290
Residential care (%)	52.7*	79.0	86.2	34.6*	
Community care (%)	47.3*	21.0	13.8	65.4*	
Total	100	100	100	100	

Note: *Orders of magnitude only.
Source: Audit Commission for England and Wales (1986), Tables 3, 6, and 8, Appendix B; and Department of Health and Social Security (1988), Table 2.8.

II. HOME CARE AND DIVISIONS OF LABOR: ON MAKING A SUCCESS OF CHANGING THE BALANCE OF CARE

The main theme in the changing division of labor is changing the balance of care toward greater provision of community care and less residential/institutional care. Exactly what forms of care will work most cost-effectively is still being worked out. So also are the orders of magnitude of the flows of spending, the purchase of physical resources of various kinds, and the investments in human and physical capital, bricks and mortar, system components, and personnel.

A. The Orders of Magnitude of the Balance of Care: Medical and Social Services

Tables 6 and 8 have described the balance of care between health and social services for the main client groups. The data are for a year immediately preceding the current drive to change that balance. The important changes between 1984/1985 and 1988 have been mentioned at the end of Part I.

For the elderly, the tables illustrate a British phenomenon: the quantitative importance of the residential home for the elderly compared with residential medical and nursing facilities. The relative scale of residential homes compared with medical and nursing facilities (mainly the long-stay bed) was later to increase even more. The figures for hospitals cover only geriatric beds (and in other columns, younger disabled units), and so exclude persons in a wide range of acute beds. Some 45% of all acute beds were occupied by elderly persons. But these are short-stay beds, and are properly excluded from a description of the anatomy of long-term care systems. So for the elderly, changing the balance of care means reducing the probabilities that someone will receive care in residential homes, not in nursing homes or hospitals. Home care for the elderly would, in other words, be an alternative to care in residential homes more so than to care in hospitals or nursing homes.

For those with mental health problems or learning difficulties, the position is quite the reverse. Except among the younger physically handicapped, the number of hospital inpatients dwarfs the numbers in other residential facilities and the numbers receiving community-based care. For the mentally ill and the mentally handicapped, changing the balance of care means reducing the number of hospital beds and increasing either the supply of modes mixing care services with residential accommodation and/or the supply of modes mixing care services with other forms of community-based shelter.

Table 8 illustrates that although public expenditures are associated with client numbers, differences in the balance of care and the functions performed by facilities cause the association to be looser than the most efficient allocations would yield.

For the elderly, the higher cost per inpatient bed and the inclusion of costs incurred by the primary health care and community nursing services on the one hand, and the greater recoupment of service costs from user charges in the social services on the other, make the total spending on the elderly by the NHS similar to that on personal social services.

The predominance of costly care in long-stay hospital wards for the mentally ill and the inclusion of other health services make the costs of mental health services larger compared with spending on the elderly than the numbers of consumers of health and social services suggest.

The spending for personal social services on the mentally handicapped is larger compared with health service spending than would be suggested by numbers of recipients.

Social Security support for long-term care is dominated by the elderly and the younger disabled. The scale of this support grew rapidly in the late 1980s, as indicated in Part I.

Long-term care accounts for a high proportion of the total spending of each of the main institutions: one-third of all spending on the NHS, and approximately three-quarters of spending on Local Authority social services.

B. Critiques of the Balance and Development of Community-Based Social Care

Community services have been built up slowly and unevenly. For groups like the mentally ill for whom the task is the replacement of long-stay care in hospital wards by care in the community, the build-up of services has been slower than the closure of long-stay beds, 25,000 of which disappeared during the decade prior to the mid-1980s. The fate of many of those discharged from long-stay hospitals was not monitored. The results included imprisonment, vagrancy, and an unsatisfactory way of life in boardinghouses, familiar effects in the international literature. The low spending of some Local Authorities on services for those with mental health problems, less than £1 per head of the general population per year in many authorities during the mid-1980s, was seriously inadequate. In general, there was a shift from residential care in hospitals to residential care financed by social security payments in other facilities, without sufficient use of flexible and cost-effective forms of other community-based services.

The distortions and barriers to development of an effective and efficient community care system include the following:

- Inadequate mechanisms for securing the shift in funds from expenditure on hospital care by the NHS to expenditure on community services, mainly by the Local Authorities (though also by health authorities, particularly for mental health services). The expenditure on inpatient services had increased by more than 1% per annum during the decade ending in the mid 1980s. Since central government finance is separately distributed to the health and social services, it was impossible to adjust the budgets of the individual local health authorities to take account of the expenditure consequences of community care development. The system of allocation of health service funds was not designed to influence the distribution of local expenditures between areas of activity.
- Grant systems to Local Authorities that penalized authorities for expanding community services. As in the health services, the formula for the allocation of central government grants to Local Authorities takes no account of individual authorities' expansion of community care services in response to the contraction of health service provision of long-stay hospital beds or indeed community services. Also the grant formula has been used to penalize Local Authorities that increase their expenditures. In recent years, the central government has used legislative powers to fix the total expenditure of authorities that spend the most.
- Inadequate funds to bridge the transition period while hospitals were being contracted and community services built up (Webb and Wistow 1985). Various mechanisms have been developed. In one, joint finance, health services funds are temporarily transferred to provide pump-priming funds for projects agreed upon by Local Authorities and others with the health services. However, the system of local government finance strongly discourages authorities from negotiating schemes rather than providing pump-priming, and it became an ineffective mechanism for transferring responsibilities and the funding to accompany them. Direct transfers of funds, usually linked to patients discharged from hospitals, with the provision of dowries, were introduced in the mid-1980s, but they were small in scale, and linked only to persons discharged from hospitals, not to the new demand that would have been accommodated in the hospital beds had they not been closed. The funds are paid only after the closure of hospitals and so do not provide the necessary transitional double-funding, take no account of the costs to Local Authorities of persons placed by health authorities in independently provided accommodation, and are often smaller than the sums saved by the health authorities, who use the

remainder of the money to upgrade standards in their long-stay wards or to improve various acute services, mostly for quite different populations (Renshaw, Hampson, Thomason, Darton, Judge, and Knapp 1988). Also there are large interregional differences in dowry policies; differences which seem not to have diminished much during the last decade. As we shall see below, evidence is emerging that for those with learning difficulties, the costs of good care in the community exceed hospital costs; so dowries could not totally finance good community care (Knapp and Beecham 1990a). However, the same source suggests that the opposite may be the case for patients discharged from mental illness hospitals. The arrangements provided an incentive for authorities to delay their development of community services until the health authorities pay and until the long-run consequences of the financing arrangements for central government grants are clarified.

- Policies governing the payment of social security benefits that create uncontrolled demand for residential care by independent (but not Local Authority) providers, diverting to residential care many who could be more appropriately and cost-effectively maintained in private households (Firth 1987). Those policies also increased disparities in the services consumed in different areas (Larder, Day, and Klein 1986). Attendance allowances and invalid care allowances are made to carers of dependents, the latter for those who give up work to care for a dependent. Both are paid only for the care of those who have satisfied a test of disability. However, no test of disability is required for payment of the board and lodging allowances to low-income entrants to independent residential homes, save for those claiming the special rate for very dependent elderly. In the mid-1980s, the average value of the board and lodgings payment for residents (reflecting costs of care including shelter) was twice as great as the sum of the average value of attendance and invalid care allowances. The incentive to carers was clear, particularly if the space occupied by the person cared for at home had an opportunity cost. Both health authorities and Local Authorities began to transfer some of their residential provision to independent bodies so that the costs of care could be passed to the central government, and to provide residential alternatives to hospitals that were so designed as to pass costs onto the social security system rather than being cost-effective to public funds as a whole. This was so even among centrally funded demonstration projects provided under the Care in the Community Initiative (Renshaw et al. 1988). But most seriously, the system generates powerful incentives for individuals pursuing their own interests as carers and dependents to create the demand to fuel a system based on residential forms of care.

- Fragmentation of responsibility for the development of community services and for implementing local community care policies (Webb and Wistow 1985). The agencies have different priorities, styles, structures, and budgets. They have had to rely on organizational altruism to achieve complementary policies and working: a rare condition. There are few incentives to do so in the context of bureaucratic barriers and perceptions that change threatens jobs and turf influence and so professional standing. The distortions and barriers operate at all levels of the system. To achieve joint planning in such circumstances requires large staffs. The implications for field personnel of fragmented organization without effective arrangements for coordination are well known in many countries. Community care for persons living in private households often requires the coordination of services provided by different sections of departments and different agencies. Residential care provides most services under one roof and one management. There is therefore a powerful incentive to admit to residential care.

- Inadequate arrangements for staff training, retraining, development, and redeployment. Compared with persons working in hospitals, community care staff are required to be more capable of working on their own, being able to make decisions and adjust their patterns of working to fit in with the varying needs of clients. They need to be more flexible, and have more capacity to make judgments, a wider range of skills, and greater capacity to adapt. That requires adaptation of the training of traditional professions and perhaps the development of new ones, and the training of new kinds of workers, able for instance to combine personal and other forms of care. There has been great resistance from professional and other training bodies to the changes needed, and a lack both of clarity about what is needed and of the funding required from the employing authorities.

Seeing the whole of long-term care as a single pool of funds, the context seemed to present a window of opportunity. The increase in the number of very aged persons at high risk of need for long-term care could be coped with in part by reducing the inappropriate occupancy by other groups of costly long-stay hospitals, it was implied (Audit Commission for England and Wales 1986:4). However, there were few who believed that a community care policy could be cost-neutral even for the mentally ill and handicapped, for whom the savings due to hospital closures could be greatest; not, for instance, the Select Committee on the Social Services of the House of Commons (House of Commons Social Services Committee 1985). Not to make the community care policy effective would result in a new pattern of care based on for-profit residential homes, not a flexible mix of services including the appropriate use of residential care.

III. LEGISLATIVE CHANGE: THE GRIFFITHS REPORT, THE WHITE PAPER CARING FOR PEOPLE, AND THE COMMUNITY CARE ACT

Like the Griffiths Report (Griffiths 1988), the white paper proposed and the act legislated for:

The clarification of responsibilities for field operation: case management as "the cornerstone". Local social service authorities are to be responsible for performing the core tasks of case management: "assessing individual need, designing care arrangements and securing their delivery within available resources." So case management arrangements are to secure cost-effectiveness in the use of public funds. The authorities that have applied in experimental projects a model of case-managed community care giving case managers a pool of funds against which all the publicly financed social care substitutes and complements are charged are commended by the white paper. The emphasis of the policy documents is on consumer responsiveness and working with informal carers and other mediating structures of society. The white paper commended the work of authorities that had adopted variants of a prototype model for case management practice and a case management system. The model applies these principles through case managers and case management teams operating with budgets against which the costs of services commissioned were set at a rate determined by a menu whose prices reflected opportunity costs (Davies and Challis 1986; Challis, Darton, Johnson, Stone, Traske, and Wall 1989; Challis, Chessum, Chesterman, Luckett, and Traske 1990; Davies 1990a; Davies et al. 1990). These were the only authorities commended anywhere in the white paper. In short, assessment and case management are described by the white paper as crucial for a consumer-responsive system of long-term care, and the replacement of a command control by an incentive-led economy, an essential component of the British equivalent of the Shalyatin plan for community care.[2] Assessment and case management are described as "the cornerstone of high quality care." Assessment is not necessarily to be undertaken by social care staff alone, but the Local Authority case managers are to have the responsibility for coordinating it within a framework of policy and interagency agreements.

The clarification of the responsibilities of agencies within a planning framework. This again developed the Griffiths theme of clarifying responsibilities. The Griffiths Report argued for an integrated system of needs-based planning from the top of the central government Department of Health to the case management team. The government has chosen not to make an exception to the principle of general grants, but is proposing to implement a mechanism for the transfer of the care element of social security payments from April 1993. So the structure advocated by Griffiths does not apply at the national level.

The removal of the distortions in financing mechanisms. The handling of funds by case managers will remove the incentives bias toward admission to residential care. It will end the system of third-party payments by the social security system without gatekeeping by persons able to advise on, arrange, monitor, and in cases of financial need, commission alternative service. Thus it will correct the bias against home care. The health authorities dominated the resourcing of services for persons with mental health problems and Local Authority provision remains small. The act makes arrangements for mental health specific grants to encourage authorities to create social care capacity.

The concentration of Local Authority attention on its role as enabler. By *enabler* is meant funder of persons of low incomes, watchdog, and coordinator and developer of the system. This provides an incentive to Local Authority to place persons in residential care provided by independent providers.[3] (The Griffiths Report supported the same ends, but did not propose a departure from the principle of the level playing field to do so.) By this means, the separation of the provision and procurement roles being canvased throughout government will be applied. Three concepts were used in the Griffiths Report and the white paper: competition, variety, and choice. The first was to create the second, and the first and second were to enhance the third. The first owes some of its potential to two features described in the opening paragraphs of the paper: (1) The nature of the technology for the production of many of the desired outcomes permits a wide range of substitution opportunities, and the complex variations in the relative prices of substitutable inputs make the effectiveness of the processes by which substitutions are made important for the efficiency of the overall system; and (2) the vast variety of the relevant expectations, values, and need-related circumstances of consumers and their informal carers.

The concept of the authority as enabler is broad enough to allow it to make imaginative leaps, though without providing it with a policy metaphor that conjures up analogs for analysis and action. The better British Local Authorities are ready for this. For 20 years, they have been evolving from their historic role as provider of a narrow range of standard services of low quality mainly for the poor. The heuristic separation of supply from procurement for system development and control could presage a new period of intellectual growth.

The context is the shift from what has been wrongly assumed to be a command control economy of care to an incentives-led economy. A traditional area of British social policy has been conceptually redefined as an area of microeconomic policy. With it must surely come at least the partial replacement of analyses around the traditional concepts—for example, unmet needs, top-down budget planning, quantitative norms for service provision—by the conceptual tools underlying trade and industry policy, the analysis of actual and potential market failures, and a new repertoire of policy instruments and policies to address them (Davies 1986, 1990b). Already, there are discussions of contract forms and structure- and process-focused regulation developed directly from microeconomic analogs (Flynn and Common 1990; Davies et al. 1990; Kettner 1987). It is this, how the American states attempt to tackle market failures in what is premised to be a mixed economy of care, that is of such contemporary interest to British observers and to Europeans in general.

The emphasis on concentrating resources on the neediest and, by developing community-based services, changing the balance of care. The development of community-based services is stated as the first of the key objectives in implementing the new community care policy in the key Department of Health policy guidance (Department of Health 1990:para. 1.1.). Concentrating resources is argued to be a key aim whose achievement through better case management will attain the higher goals of community care policy (para. 3.5). The implementation papers describe the cultural and ultimately structural changes required for success as "profound," and rightly so, for reasons explained below. So the white paper and its supporting documents have a logic with features that can reasonably called radical.

The development of domiciliary day and respite services. The white paper associated this with the targeting of services on those whose needs are greatest.

The provision of practical support for informal carers as a high priority.

The introduction of a new funding structure. One objective is to transfer funds to Local Authorities. The Griffiths Report argued for specific grants for community care. The white paper provided specific grants only for services for those with mental health problems, the group for whom the Local Authorities had provided least. The other objective is to establish a funding structure that does not bias decision-making about the choice of technique. The level playing field excluded places in long-stay hospitals, not all of which are for assessment and acute treatment; and an incentive was created to choose independent provision of residential modes of care.

IV. EMPIRICAL EVIDENCE ON COST-EFFECTIVE ARRANGEMENTS

Putting first things first implies a different ordering of research questions for the main client groups. For clients with learning difficulties and with mental health problems, the first questions must be about *decanting* patients into the community. We have shown why in our description of the present balance of resources and client numbers. If the fashionable assumption is correct, and a better use of resources can be achieved with fewer in long-stay hospitals, we must use the resources freed thus to provide community-based care. The questions are partly about what patterns of community-based service for hospitalized persons in different circumstances would match resources to their needs in ways that make the best use of the total resources available, and partly about how to establish the arrangements for matching the resources to needs. Only if we assume that the outcomes allow the closure of many of the long-term hospital beds and that devices are found for channeling the resources so released (and others) into community-based modes will the most important questions be about the costs and outcomes of alternative community-based modes for persons in different circumstances.

However, for the elderly, the first questions are about *diversion* into community-based modes from residential/institutional care. Too many of the resources may still be used to provide custodial and general nursing care in long-stay beds. But the life expectancy of the occupants is too short to make decanting reasonable to contemplate.

A. Studies of the Relative Costs of Satisfactory Care and Outcomes in Long-Stay Hospitals and in Community Settings

In addition to reviews of experience elsewhere (Thornicroft and Bebbington 1989) and to reviews of secondary and restricted data (Wright and Haycox 1985), there is now some British evidence about the costs of satisfactory care and outcomes for patients discharged from long-stay wards. For the same persons, there are also comparisons of what their care actually cost in community-based modes and what it could have been expected to cost in long-stay hospitals.[4] What we do not seem to know is the cost of care of equivalent satisfactoriness between that achieved in the community and that in long-stay hospitals!

The Department of Health and Social Security commissioned the PSSRU to monitor the outcomes of the demonstration projects sponsored under the Care in the Community Initiative of 1983. These were established to relocate the patients of long-stay hospital wards in community settings. The results of the study are now available. They suggest a complex picture which differed between client groups and schemes. The study adopted a comprehensive definition of costs which included the opportunity costs of capital and estimated the long-run marginal costs required for economic appraisal (Knapp, Cambridge, Thomason, Beecham, Allen, and Darton 1990).

People discharged from mental handicap hospitals.   On average, the community care packages were estimated to be significantly more costly, 16% greater, than the hospital care the people had left. Moreover, the hospital costs for those who had been discharged to the community were likely to have been below the average for all patients, so that the discharge of the remaining patients is likely to increase the additional funding required more than proportionally to their numbers.

The estimated difference between cost in hospital and cost in the community was greater for some kinds of living arrangement in the community than others. The cost difference was greatest for staffed group homes, whose costs were estimated to be 34% higher. In contrast, the cost in residential care was estimated to be 21% less. Some of the difference is probably due to the difficulties of allowing for variations in cost-raising circumstances of clients in the modeling, but the estimates do suggest big differences in the costliness of alternative modes of care (Knapp et al. 1990:Table 3).

However, the higher costs were compensated for by important improvements in the quality of the lives of those discharged. Indeed, there was a small but statistically significant association between service package costs in the community (expenditures on services) and improvements in client welfare and quality of life: Higher spending produced greater welfare. Likewise Korman and Glennerster (1990) and Wing (1989) found for one hospital that a smaller informal setting appeared to have produced more improvements in social behavior and greater client contentment; but the PSSRU evaluation found these to be more costly.

People discharged from mental illness hospitals.   The evidence is stronger. It also suggests the converse conclusion: Community care need not be more expensive than the provision being replaced (Knapp et al. 1990; Knapp and Beecham 1990a, 1990b). In the Care in the Community demonstration projects, community care costs were lower by about 24% on average (Knapp et al. 1990:Table 2). Again there were big differences between types of housing arrangement, though community care costs were on average lower for each of the main types of arrangement. It seems that:

- Community care is less costly for the early leavers under most reprovision plans, because the early leavers tend to require less support.
- A study of at least two hospitals suggests that future community care costs for all patients will be lower than their hospital costs (Knapp et al. 1990).
- The quality of life of the patients in the care in community demonstration schemes is no worse than in hospital, and is in some respects better.
- The costs of community packages of services are weakly but significantly associated with better client outcomes.

However, all the costs are based only on the first year following hospital discharge.

Elderly persons discharged from long-stay geriatric wards. There is much less evidence. The Care in the Community demonstration projects yielded few schemes providing costs information, but for physically frail elderly persons accommodated in sheltered housing, the costs were estimated to be some 23% lower than they would have been in hospitals, and for elderly persons with mental impairment, the costs were estimated to be 60% less (Knapp et al. 1990:Table 4).

Additionally, one of the PSSRU experiments in case-managed community care in which the case managers held budget control was directed at persons discharged from acute wards. It found community care to be less expensive (Challis et al. 1990), and there were larger and more pervasive gains in welfare.

So, judging from the Care in the Community demonstration projects, (1) the worst consequences of badly executed change in the balance of care by the closure of long-stay hospital beds are avoidable, and (2) on average, worthwhile, and for some, substantial gains in welfare are attainable at affordable costs. For clients in some circumstances and some community-based settings, the costs of these improved outcomes can actually be less. However,

- There is great interscheme variation.
- There is even greater interpersonal variation. For instance, there was a twelvefold difference in costs among the first 145 persons leaving hospitals in the Care in the Community program.
- The relative costs of hospital and community care for persons being decanted from long-stay hospitals could be expected to be entirely

different from the relative costs for persons being diverted from hospital to community-based care. Perhaps the most general reason directly reflects the proposition argued in the first section of the paper. There are many sources for the most important inputs required in community-based care. However, one of the most important forms is informal care. But the cultivation of it has been unsystematic and too little thought through. It is to the evidence about this form of diversion that we now turn.

B. The Costs of Maintaining in the Community Persons Who Would Otherwise Require Residential (Including Long-Stay Hospital) Care

We have observed that for the mentally ill and handicapped, this is a secondary question for the strategy for changing the balance of care. (No doubt, it is partly for this reason that projects are only now being evaluated for costs and welfare outcomes.) However, it is the first question for changing the balance of care for elderly people.

There are two kinds of evidence: (1) evidence about the costs of packages of standard home care, combined with research into the impact of varying levels of input on outcomes, and (2) evidence from experiments in case-managed community care where the case managers work in a structure designed to provide incentives and the other preconditions for improving outcomes more efficiently.

The largest amount of evidence is for experiments with case-managed community care in which the case managers pay for the social care—goods and services procured from agencies and commercially, directly mobilized helpers and volunteers—from pooled budgets: the PSSRU community care experiments.

Two projects (Thanet and Gateshead) were targeted at a population for whom the most likely alternative is residential, not hospital, care. So the substitution effects on which the cost differences largely depend are between modes of social care, not between health and social care.

The main cost-affecting substitutions for the two projects included the replacement of residential social care by social care at home; the substitution achieved cost neutrality: an approximate equivalence of costs in both modes of care.[5]

The two experiments had cost outcomes that were budget neutral to the health and social services. Cost savings were not the main benefits. The Thanet experimental and control groups were followed for four years, and during that time, the discounted present value of the cost savings was only 20% of the combined annual opportunity costs to the health and social services (Davies et al. 1990).

However, one should not consider the cost savings of PSSRU community care experiments apart from the other outcomes. The logic on which they were based assumed benefits to be affected by costs, and so a trade-off between cost savings and benefits. What is most interesting is the wide range of benefits that were statistically established despite the small numbers of cases. So in the balancing of cost savings against other benefits, the reductions of costs of residential care caused by large reductions in the utilization of residential modes of care were used to finance inputs that created much higher levels of quality of life, and for those not in residential homes, higher quality of most aspects of care.

Budget neutrality has become a fetish in the evaluation of long-term care experiments. There is no reason why achieving budget neutrality should result in the optimal balance of care. It so happened that, in the context, setting the case management parameters at levels that would achieve budget neutrality also typically gave incentives to take due account of the social opportunity costs of care as the fieldworkers influenced individual choices between residential and home care modes. So by happy coincidence, setting the parameters at a level that by good luck produced a comforting budget neutrality also improved the choice of mode of care by fundamentally more important evaluative criteria.

However the experimental inputs of the PSSRU community care projects are not mainly (or even necessarily) the input of more standard home care services. They are the creation of assumptive worlds and arrangements that create the conditions for achieving greater equity and efficiency in the production of welfare. They are predicated on investments in changing policies, procedures, expectations, and skills. We must look elsewhere for evidence about the effects merely of concentrating standard services, of changing targeting without directly changing the other parameters of the production of welfare. Evidence about that is the subject of the next section.

C. Evidence about the Substitution of Community-Based for Residential-Based Care with Standard Provision of Services

The research on targeting community-based services for the elderly suggested greater consistency than has sometimes been argued. However, it also shows that *intensity* (the quantities allocated per recipient) has been sacrificed to maintain *cover* (the proportion of those in the target group allocated service) at a time of rapidly rising unit costs (Davies et al. 1990). That few recipients of home care services, even those most at risk of admission to institutions for long-term care, receive more than small amounts of services reduces the effectiveness of the home care services in making unnecessary admission to institutions for long-term care. Since the costs of community-based social and community nursing care are so small compared with costs of residential care, much of the emphasis in policy analysis has been on the improvement of targeting.

However, Davies et al. also found that controlling for need-related circumstances, inputting larger rather than smaller amounts of services made insufficient difference to the probability of admission to institutions for long-term care to be evident in the results of the modeling, despite the richness and scale of the data. On average, some 15% of new recipients of community-based care were admitted to residential care during the study period. However, the frontline personnel did not rate prevention of admission to be a major consideration in their care provision, mentioning it in fewer than one case in five. Davies et al. likewise showed low marginal productivities for other outcomes of importance for satisfactory quality of life at home, and also for stress on informal carers.

So one challenge is to make community-based services that have not been directed substantially at making unnecessary admission to institutions for long-term care effective for this. The experiments combining case-managed community care with the case managers facing the opportunity costs of care decisions and supported with a systems framework show how it can be done by targeting better and raising productivities (Davies and Challis 1986). They also show the benefits of resourcefulness by case managers in mixing resources. American and British evidence alike illustrates how field circumstances vary in ways that cause the pattern of resources tapped by resourceful case managers to differ greatly between areas (Davies and Challis 1986). And of relevance to managerial responsibilities at higher management levels, the evidence illustrates the complexity and variety of geographical variations in the relative prices of substitutable inputs. So the second challenge is to replace the command control economy with structures that encourage flexible responses to varying local and client circumstances.

V. CONCLUSIONS

In Great Britain, the history of changing divisions of labor has been dominated by the emergence of a powerful critique. This has had widespread publicity and influence partly because of the influence of independent policy review bodies established by the government itself. The critique has stimulated radical change in policy and arrangements. Many of the developments are changing the balance of care.

However, there are serious dangers. Beds in long-stay hospitals continue to be closed without satisfactory arrangements for those who had occupied them and without the transfer of sufficient funds for the development of alternative community-based services. The providers and procurers of care have continued to respond to perverse financing incentives, even in high-profile nationally commissioned demonstration projects. Local Authority and other local managers are not so much smug as preoccupied by problems of living with fiscal constraint, and unaware of who in fact benefits in what way from the services they provide. They are only vaguely aware that marginal productivities are low. So they underestimate the scale of the investments needed to make the community-based services bear heavier responsibilities. There is a wide knowledge gap: the absence among the managers of change of a lingua franca and body of evidence-based argument to guide their development of local systems. And there is a reluctance to see that the modernization of long-term care requires large investments now, if the targeting propensities and productivities of community-based services are to be transformed for the late 1990s and the new century. It is clear that the consequences of demographic and social changes are likely to make the balance of need and informal care resources progressively more adverse.

NOTES

1.   The distinction between handicap, disability, impairment, and disease category will be familiar: by *handicap* we mean "a disadvantage. . .resulting from an impairment or disability, that limits or prevents the fulfillment of a role. . ."; by *disability* we mean "any restriction or lack. . .of ability to perform an activity in the manner or within the range considered normal for a human being"; by *impairment* we mean "any loss or abnormality of psychological, physiological or anatomical structure or function": parts of the system of the body that do not work (Martin, Meltzer, and Eliot 1988:7).
2.   The Shalyatin plan was the radical blueprint for making the Soviet economy capitalist proposed by the radical advisor in the later Gorbachev period. Gorbachev himself supported a rival and less radical plan.
3.   The enabling authority is not primarily concerned with direct provision. Focusing on the purchase of services, quality control, and system development, and with an arm's-length relationship with suppliers, the enabling authority does not face the conflict of interest between its role as representative of the service user and of the citizen and its role as direct employer of service employees. That is hypothesized in British policy argument to allow the authority to be more customer responsive and better able to improve effectiveness and efficiency in the system.
4.   This evidence is in addition to the estimates of costs of alternative packages for hypothetical patients.
5.   The Gateshead project was basically a replication of the Thanet project. The workers were sent to observe policy, procedures, and practice at Thanet,

and the basic style and arrangements which they adopted were similar in comparison with other home care provision (Davies and Challis 1986; Qureshi, Challis and Davies 1988). Due to differences in political culture and community mobilization, the ratio of home care costs to residential care costs was higher in Gateshead (Davies, Bebbington, Charnley and colleagues 1990).

REFERENCES

Audit Commission for England and Wales. 1986. *Making a Reality of Community Care*. London: HMSO.

Bebbington, A. and B. Davies. Forthcoming. "Target Efficiency of the Home Help Service in 1985." *Journal of Social Policy*. Also available as PSSRU Discussion Paper 619/3 (1991), PSSRU, University of Kent at Canterbury.

Benthall, J. and T. Polhemus (eds.) 1975. *The Body as Medium of Expression*. London: Allen Lane.

Challis, D. J., R. Chessum, J. Chesterman, R. Luckett, and K. Traske. 1990. *Case Management in Social and Health Care*. PSSRU monographs, PSSRU, University of Kent at Canterbury.

Challis, D. J., R. Chessum, J. Chesterman, R. Luckett, and B. Woods. 1988. "Community Care for the Frail Elderly: An Urban Experiment." Pp. 13–42 in *The Production of Welfare Approach: Evidence and Argument from the PSSRU. British Journal of Social Work: Supplement*, edited by B. Davies and M. Knapp.

Challis, D. J., R. Darton, L. Johnson, M. Stone, K. Traske, and B. Wall. 1989. *Supporting Frail Elderly People at Home*. PSSRU monograph, PSSRU, University of Kent at Canterbury.

Davies, B. P. 1986. "American Lessons for British Policy and Research on Long-Term Care of the Elderly." *Quarterly Journal of Social Affairs* 2(3):321–355.

———. 1990a. "New Priorities in Home Care: Principles from the PSSRU Experiments." Pp. 47–72 in *Community Care Policy and Practice: New Directions in Australia*, edited by A. Howe, E. Ozanne, and C. Selby-Smith. Clayton, Victoria, Australia: Monash University Press.

———. 1990b. "The 'Trade and Industry' Policy Metaphor and Community Care." Pp. 14–27 in *Welfare and the Ageing Experience*, edited by B. Bytheway and J. Johnson. Aldershot: Avebury.

———. 1991. "Resources, Needs, and Outcomes in Community-Based Care: The Messages Distilled." Discussion paper 728/2, PSSRU, University of Kent, Canterbury.

Davies, B. P., A. C. Bebbington, H. Charnley, in collaboration with B. Baines, E. Ferlie, M. Hughes, and J. Twigg. 1990. "Resources, Needs and Outcomes in Community-Based Care: A Comparative Study of the Production of Welfare for Elderly People in Ten Local Authorities in England and Wales." *PSSRU Studies*. Aldershot: Avebury/ Gower.

Davies, B. P. and D. Challis. 1986. *Matching Resources to Needs in Community Care*. Aldershot: Avebury/Gower.

Davies, B. P., R. A. Darton, and M. Goddard. 1988. "The Effects of Alternative

Targeting Criteria and Demand Levels on the Opportunity Cost of SSD Care in Local Authority Homes." PSSRU Discussion Paper 484, University of Kent at Canterbury.

Department of Health. 1990. *Community Care in the Next Decade and Beyond: Policy Guidance.* London: HMSO.

Department of Health and Social Security. 1988. *Health and Personal Social Services Statistics 1985.* London: HMSO.

Douglas, M. 1973. *Natural Symbols: Explorations in Cosmology.* Harmondsworth: Penguin.

————. 1975. *Implicit Meaning.* London: Routledge and Kegan Paul.

Elias, N. 1978. *The Civilizing Process: Vol. I. The History of Manners.* London: Blackwell.

Ferlie, E., D. Challis, and B. Davies. 1989. "Efficiency-Improving Innovations in Social Care of the Elderly." *PSSRU Studies.* Aldershot: Gower.

Firth, J. 1987. *Public Support for Residential Care.* Report of a Joint Central and Local Government Working Party, DHSS, London.

Flynn, N. and R. Common. 1990. *Contracts for Community Care. Caring for People: Community Care in the Next Decade and Beyond.* Implementation Documents, London Business School, London.

Griffiths, Sir Roy. 1988. *Community Care: An Agenda for Action.* London: HMSO.

House of Commons Social Services Committee. 1985. *Second Report: Community Care with special reference to Mentally Ill and Mentally Handicapped People.* Session 1984/5. London: HMSO.

Kettner, M. L. 1987. *Purchase of Service Contracting.* Beverly Hills: Sage.

Knapp, M. R. J. and J. Beecham. 1990a. "The Cost-Effectiveness of Community Care for Former Long-Stay Psychiatric Patients." Pp. 201–27 in *Advances in Health Economics and Health Services Research,* edited by R. Scheffler and L. Rossiter. Greenwich, CT: JAI Press.

————. 1990b. "Costing Mental Health Services." *Psychological Medicine* 20:893–908.

Knapp, M. R. J., P. Cambridge, C. Thomason, J. Beecham, C. Allen, and R. A. Darton. 1990. "Care in the Community: Lessons from a Demonstration Programme: Care in the Community Newsletter." *PSSRU.* University of Kent at Canterbury.

Korman N. and H. Glennerster. 1990. *Hospital Closure: A Political and Economic Study.* London: Milton Keynes, Open University Press.

Larder, D., P. Day, and R. Klein. 1986. "Institutional Care for the Elderly: The Geographical Distribution of the Public/Private Mix in England." *Bath Social Policy Papers* No. 10, Centre for the Analysis of Social Policy, University of Bath.

Martin, J., H. Meltzer, and D. Elliot. 1988. *The Prevalence of Disability Among Adults.* London: HMSO.

Martin, J., A. White, and H. Meltzer. 1989. *Disabled Adults: Services Transport and Employment.* London: HMSO.

Mauss, M. 1935. "Les techniques du corps." *Journale de la Psychologie* 32.

Netten, A. and B. Davies. Forthcoming. "Community Services and the Social Production of Welfare." *PSSRU Studies*. Aldershot: Avebury.

Qureshi, H., D. Challis, and B. Davies. 1988. "Helpers in Case-Managed Community Care." *PSSRU Studies*. Aldershot: Gower.

Renshaw, J., R. Hampson, C. Thomason, R. A. Darton, K. Judge, and M. R. J. Knapp. 1988. "Care in the Community: The First Steps." *PSSRU Studies*. Aldershot: Gower.

Thornicroft, G. and P. Bebbington. 1989. "Deinstitutionalisation—From Hospital Closure to Service Development." *British Journal of Psychiatry* 155:739–53.

Webb, A. and G. Wistow. 1985. *Studies in Central-Local Relations*. London: Allen and Unwin.

Wing, L. 1989. *Hospital Closure and the Resettlement of Residents: The Case of Darenth Park Mental Handicap Hospital*. Medical Research Council, Social Psychiatry Unit, Institute of Psychiatry, London. Aldershot: Avebury.

World Health Organization. 1980. *International Classification of Impairments, Disabilities, and Handicaps*. Geneva: Author.

Wright, K. G. and A. Haycox. 1985. *Costs of Alternative Forms of NHS Care for Mentally Handicapped Persons*. York: Centre for Health Economics, University of York.

PART III

Care of People with Chronic Mental Illness

In both the United States and Great Britain, as well as other Western nations, there have been efforts during the last three decades to implement the same paradigm: to provide care for people with chronic and severe mental illness in the least restrictive settings (Freeman, Fryers, and Henderson 1985; Hannibal and ten Horn 1987; Mangen 1985). At an applied level, this has meant both relying less on specialty psychiatric hospitals and more on community acute-care hospitals, and, more vitally, creating a range of alternatives in the community for people with serious and chronic mental illness.

Both the United States and Great Britain have relocated to the community substantial numbers of long-term psychiatric hospital patients. For example, in the United States, the census of state mental hospitals has fallen from over 500,000 patients in 1965 to just over 100,000 in 1992 (Lamb 1992). The peak in British hospitalization occurred in 1954, with smaller census figures ever since (Wing 1991). As well, it has become much less likely in both countries that people with chronic and severe mental illness will receive long-term care in psychiatric hospitals. Rather, hospital admissions tend to be short-term.

In both countries, it is widely accepted that hospital psychiatric care should be coordinated with a comprehensive roster of services provided in the community (e.g., crisis care, routine monitoring, psychotherapy, medications provision and review, vocational opportunities, housing, social and recreational activities). Some of the community-based services should be medical, others social. Of course, opinion varies as to how much support should be given to the various elements of the system, to how much emphasis and resources should be set aside for specific types of activity (e.g., vocational services, social/recreational programs, psychotherapy).

Impelled by court orders, desires to economize, and new technologies, societies have made quite uneven progress toward the goal or providing appropriate services in the least restrictive setting. In the United States, the large number of homeless is one indicator of the inadequacies of the care system for people with chronic and severe mental illness. Some commentators suggest that the situation in Great Britain may not be markedly different (Thornicroft and Bebbington 1989). As both nations have decreased reliance on long-term inpatient care in public psychiatric hospitals as the keystone for policy for the chronic and severely mentally ill, the number of seriously mentally ill people living in the community but with no care or inadequate care has increased (Klerman, Olfson, Leon, and Weissman 1992). With regard to children and the elderly, lack of services is even more severe (Burns, Wagner, Taube, Magaziner, Permutt, and Landerman 1993).

As the two papers that follow indicate, however, efforts in both societies to create comprehensive and coordinated community-based systems have foundered, despite fairly widespread agreement among professionals on the desirability of the approach. In both countries, there are extensive reports, symposia, etc., setting forth these goals (U.S. Department of Health and Human Services Steering Committee on the Chronically Mentally Ill 1980; National Institute of Mental Health, NIMH 1991; Department of Health and Social Security 1975). As the following papers show, both countries have moved haltingly and imperfectly toward the creation of systems coordinating medical and social services, with each country using rather different mechanisms for system coordination. The Americans have begun creating systems at the local and state levels to capture control of several streams of funding and to use funding control to shape service system structure and performance (Mechanic and Surles 1992). The British, most recently through the Community Care Act of 1990, have placed responsibility for system coordination on Local Authorities (see Ramon). However, reports from the mid-1980s enumerate literally dozens of problems with implementation (Social Services Committee of the House of Commons 1985).

The two nations have had serious problems with creation of a coordinated system of care, but for rather different reasons. In the United States, pockets of excellence aside, the elements needed for a system of care do not exist in most communities, and where they do exist, coordination is poor among them. The system of care is so fragmented, with funds and services at different levels of government and in different sectors, that it is quite difficult to create a coordinated service system. Efforts to move from efficacious model programs to effective systems in many locations have been hampered by the fragmented structure of the system, especially the financing mechanisms (Cutler, Bigelow, and McFarland 1992). In Great Britain, efforts to center services in Local Authorities (poorly funded and variable in quality from place to place) are proving awkward. Although there are some reports that Community Mental Health Centers are moving to rectify their earlier neglect of services to clients with severe and chronic mental illness (Sayce, Craig, and

Boardman 1991), as one expert puts it, "there is no doubt that services for the mentally ill are in a great state of flux" (Seager 1991).

The structure of the system of care, described in the two following papers, gravely inhibits emergence of a coordinated institutional/community based system with medical and social services. Especially important in retarding the development of a coordinated, comprehensive system are the (1) provision of financing by different levels of government, (2) provision of services by different public administrative authorities (central, regional or state, county and local governments), as well as the private sector, and (3) lack of adequate funding.

The Hollingsworth and Ramon essays also address the performance of the care system for those with chronic and severe mental illness. They demonstrate that neither system performs well. Access to some basic medical service (the general practitioner) is ensured in Great Britain through the National Health Service, but access to specialists such as psychiatrists is limited (as in the United States). Some local areas in Britain have programs excelling in provision of comprehensive and full services, providing crisis care and keeping clients stabilized in the community for long periods of time. However, such examples are rare. Lack of money for community-based care inhibits adequate staffing, training is inadequate for the skills that are needed, and public authorities often find themselves with so few options that the seriously mentally ill are left to fend for themselves.

Unlike the other groups with serious and chronic illness discussed in this book, the chronically mentally ill suffer acutely from social stigma, and, to a certain extent, from blaming the victim. Although survey data in both the United States and Great Britain indicate increasing acceptance of mental illness as an illness, such attitudes are relatively new. In the contest for rewards obtained through the public policy process, the chronically mentally ill have real difficulties in competing with the frail elderly, not to mention chronically ill children who are homebound. At local levels, it has often been remarked that the chronically mentally ill are the last to receive services, after other groups of disabled people have been served.

REFERENCES

Burns, B. J., H. R. Wagner, J. E. Taube, J. Magaziner, T. Permutt, and L. R. Landerman. 1993. "Mental Health Service Use by the Elderly in Nursing Homes." *American Journal of Public Health* 83:331–37.

Cutler, David L., D. Bigelow, and B. McFarland. 1992. "The Cost of Fragmented Mental Health Financing: Is It Worth It?" *Community Mental Health Journal* 28:121–33.

Department of Health and Social Security. 1975. *Better Services for the Mentally Ill.* Cmnd. 6233. London: HMSO.

Freeman, H. L., T. Fryers, and J. H. Henderson. 1985. *Mental Health Services in Europe: 10 Years On.* Copenhagen: World Health Organization Regional Office for Europe.

Hannibal, J. U. and G. H. M. M. ten Horn. 1987. *Mental Health Services in Pilot Study Areas.* Copenhagen: World Health Organization Regional Office for Europe.

Klerman, G. L., M. Olfson, A. C. Leon, and M. M. Weissman. 1992. "Measuring the Need for Mental Health Care." *Health Affairs* 11:23–33.

Lamb, H. Richard. 1992. "Is It Time for a Moratorium on Deinstitutionalization?" *Hospital and Community Psychiatry* 43:669.

Mangen, Steen (ed.). 1985. *Mental Health Care in the European Community.* London: Croom Helm.

Mechanic, David and R. C. Surles. 1992. "Challenges in State Mental Health Policy and Administration." *Health Affairs* 11:34–50.

National Institute of Mental Health. 1991. *Caring for People with Severe Mental Disorders: A National Plan of Research to Improve Services* (ADM) 91-1762. Washington, DC: U.S. Government Printing Office.

Sayce, L., T. K. J. Craig, and A. P. Boardman. 1991. "The Development of Community Mental Health Centres in the U.K." *Social Psychiatry/Psychiatric Epidemiology* 26:14–20.

Seager, C. Philip. 1991. "Management of District Psychiatric Services Without a Mental Hospital." Pp. 33–38 *The Closure of Mental Hospitals*, edited by in Peter Hall and Ian F. Brockington. London: Gaskell.

Social Services Committee of the House of Commons. 1985. *Community Care with Special Reference to Adult Mentally Ill and Mentally Handicapped.* Second Report of the Committee. London: HMSO.

Thornicroft, G. and P. Bebbington. 1989. "Deinstitutionalisation—From Hospital Closure to Service Development." *British Journal of Psychiatry* 155:739–53.

U.S. Department of Health and Human Services Steering Committee on the Chronically Mentally Ill. 1980. *Toward a National Plan for the Chronically Mentally Ill.* Washington, DC: U.S. Public Health Service.

Wing, J. K. 1991. "Vision and Reality." Pp. 10–19 in *The Closure of Mental Hospitals*, edited by Peter Hall and Ian F. Brockington. London: Gaskell.

Chapter 6

Falling through the Cracks: Care of the Chronically Mentally Ill in the United States

ELLEN JANE HOLLINGSWORTH

INTRODUCTION

"Falling through the cracks," or (inappropriately) "between the cracks" is terminology unpleasantly familiar to those studying the system for services to the chronically mentally ill. These terms have become shorthand, in the last 15 to 20 years, for a general perception that all is not well in the care system for the mentally ill, that more than half of the seriously mentally ill do not receive adequate specialty care (Torrey 1988; Shapiro et al. 1984), and that community-based programs do not provide the resources and safety desired for clients once placed in state mental hospitals.[1]

The United States has, the argument goes, deinstitutionalized most persons with chronic mental illness (discharged them from hospitals) or diverted clients from entering mental hospitals, and has expected fledgling facilities located in the community to take up the burden of providing medical and social care. Community-based care, meaning that clients live in the community rather than in institutions, has been developed as part of providing treatment in the least restrictive setting. The assumption, of course, is *not* that clients live in the community without care, but rather that community-based services, as part of coordinated systems, can provide appropriate care. Many community-based programs, with notable exceptions, have been unable to provide the desired and needed types of care. The literature reflecting this perspective is abundant. Some of the literature includes important qualifications of the deinstitutionalization argument, demonstrating that some care in nursing homes is a proxy for care in state mental hospitals, and thus that

145

institutional settings continue to have a prominent role as service providers (Kiesler 1982). In article after article, we are told, however inaccurately, that a major cause of homelessness is deinstitutionalization.

Inadequate medical and social care for the chronically mentally ill—the lack of a coordinated system of care—however closely associated with deinstitutionalization, has its roots in fairly pervasive cultural tastes and values. These values and habits have shaped the structures (the institutional arrangements) and resources for care delivery, with markedly poor results. This is our mental health history (Grob 1983, 1987). Community-based services, now beginning to be based on a good understanding of what does work, suffer so much from the constraints imposed by the institutional arrangements and the dearth of resources that prospects for achievement are very limited. The extant gains in terms of service provision at the community level are even threatened with erosion.

I. INSTITUTIONAL ARRANGEMENTS FOR CARE

There are four central aspects of the institutional arrangements for care that influence the ability of the system to provide adequate levels of service for the chronically mentally ill. These aspects, in essence the political economy of mental health care, pervasively shape what happens in the system.

First, the system of care has historically had a strong statist component to it (commonly the system is called the public mental health system). Second, the state-oriented system, administered by the 50 American states or their subunits, has been very decentralized. Third, in the last 20 years quasi-public agencies (voluntary-sector organizations, generally) have become important parts of the delivery system, although the state sector still supplies the majority of services. This trend toward the incorporation of quasi-public organizations into the delivery system is often called the privatization of the mental health system. Fourth, services to the seriously mentally ill provided in the traditional private sector are modest, especially in the profit-making organizations in the private sector, so that the main institutions of health care provision in the United States are essentially apart from the mental health care institutions.

A. Governmental Services for the Mentally Ill

It is quite unremarkable to point out the low place on the political agenda that care of the mentally ill has today—and for that matter has long had in the United States (Marmor and Gill 1989). Although there may be modest differences from country to country in the place mental health care has on the political agenda, the differences are minor. The chronically mentally ill have historically been a group without esteem. Many other disability groups have also lacked influence in the care and treatment system, but the chronically mentally ill have been the most stigmatized disability group. As a result, they have been unable to affect the contours of the system.

The reasons for this lack of esteem are complex: Familiar are the allegations that the mentally ill have failed to take responsibility for themselves, that parents (mothers) were to blame for illness, that mentally ill people were dangerous to well society. Although historically the explanations for mental illness, and its insistent persistence, were numerous, there was little disagreement in American society about where the locus of responsibility for care should lie. Most chronically mentally ill people did not have money and could not pay for their own treatment; care expenses often extended over many years, as recovery seemed rare. In such circumstances, the private sector would not be responsible for undertaking long-term care.

As part of the obligation of society to do something—although not much—it was expected that governmental authorities should be responsible. State authority should shield society from "crazy people," who might threaten or frighten other citizens. This was a part of the expectation that social control was a part of police power. Police power was expressed through emphasis on protection of society (and thus, incarceration for those with serious mental illness) rather than through services for the mentally ill. So it was the state that early on assumed responsibility for paying for care (at a very low level) and for providing most of the services. Historically, physicians (psychiatrists) sensitive to the world of the mentally ill preferred a medical model of treatment, which was hospital-based. The only possibilities for providing hospital care for the chronically mentally ill lay with the state, but most of the rest of the American health system was in the private sector.

B. Fifty States

Once it was understood that services to the chronically mentally ill should be provided by the state, the lead agencies were the 50 state mental health authorities. The pattern adopted for the mental health area followed the pattern for virtually all health care: There was very little role for the central government, and thus there was very little centralization at the nation-state level. Within the 50 states there was considerable variation in the power given to the mental health agencies, whether they were freestanding agencies, and whether they were single-purpose agencies or agencies overseeing several disability groups. The locus of legal responsibility varied considerably from state to state, with some states giving more authority to county or regional units, and others maintaining central mental health department authority over programming. One of the effects of the decentralization of authority among the 50 states has been to increase the potential for preventing action or policy change, and for lack of coordination between financing and program administration (Marmor and Gill 1989). The patterns for care, and the dynamics for making mental health policy, varied from state to state. Some states integrated long-term institutions for mental illness (state mental hospitals) with mental health services delivered in the community; many did not. There were thus many different approaches used by states. Policies of the 50 states have varied markedly, as have systems of care (Torrey and Wolfe 1986, 1988, 1990).

Over time, the federal government has reserved to itself rather modest roles—research, providing care to a modest number of veterans of military service in veterans hospitals, providing limited funding to community mental health centers, providing money through the Medicaid program for inpatient (for the most part) care.[2]

There are interesting variations in institutional arrangements within states, and these arrangements also affect care. Briefly, there has been increased emphasis on regionalization and localization of mental health care (moving administration to the substate level), to create even further decentralization. Legislative rearrangements have created situations in which substate political authorities have become the locus of care. The most familiar example of this is California (Surber, Shumway, Shadoan, and Hargreaves 1986; Elpers 1989). Wisconsin also vests responsibility for care of the mentally ill at the county level.

These very decentralized institutional arrangements—using within-state regions or counties—have merits such as putting program responsibility at the level of impact, requiring local inputs into planning, and involving a larger number of citizens in decision-making about mental health. But decentralization within states is not all on the plus side. For one thing, decisions about mental health are made in many different governmental units (in Wisconsin, for example, there are over 50 different mental health authorities—counties or groups of counties). Mental health issues, usually very low in political priorities, are processed at local levels; the types of services are chosen at the local level. Thus there is ample opportunity for decision-making to reflect the strength of local organized political forces (which often revolve around the preservation of existing institutions).

C. Quasi-Public Agencies (Privatization)

The main change in the last 20 years, in terms of the institutional arrangements for care, has been the inclusion of more quasi-public private agencies as care providers. Quasi-public agencies are private sector agencies carrying out public functions, with public funding. Public organizations and quasi-public organizations exist now in a symbiotic set of relationships, to deliver care for those with chronic mental illness. To some extent, the lines between public and private activities have been blurred as a result of this change. Formally, the role of the state government has diminished, inasmuch as services are no longer delivered exclusively by those employed by the state. As deinstitutionalization and diversion of clients from state mental hospitals have proceeded, it has become obvious that if clients were to have any services, organizations based in the community would have to provide the care for the chronically mentally ill. Many communities have turned to existing private organizations to provide the needed services, to what are often called quasi-public organizations. Private mental health clinics, sheltered workshops, and church-based social services organizations already in existence were examples of programs with staff resources and community legitimacy. Many states/regions/counties turned to these programs in order to have services delivered. In other instances, new organizations emerged to provide community services. This reliance on quasi-public organizations has been termed by some the privatization of care. Private nursing homes and private board and care homes are familiar examples of this privatization (Shaddish, Lurigio, and Lewis 1989).[3]

These new care arrangements, involving private organizations functioning in a quasi-public manner, have not replaced activity by governmental actors. Rather, the system of care by governmental units has been augmented by the inclusion of new organizations. But government-employed staff continue to provide most services in most areas. Unfortunately, accurate data with which to establish the percentage of mental health workers in government employment are not available. Nor are there good data on the size of the mental health work force in quasi-public private agencies.

The term *quasi-public agency*, as used here, refers to a private (usually voluntary sector) agency providing care paid with government dollars. The quasi-public agencies may have only chronically mentally ill clients or may work with several different disability groups; income may all be from the public pocketbook or it may be from other sources as well; staff specialties may vary, but staff are not public employees.

How did it happen that quasi-public agencies were drawn into service provision, rather than public authorities retaining all of the responsibility and providing all the care? The answers lie in (1) the very strong role of the voluntary sector in providing services for public purposes, such as the historical provision of hospitalization for the needy in the United States (Hollingsworth and Hollingsworth 1987), (2) the reluctance of public authorities to hire more public employees (always a sensitive issue in the American context), and (3) beliefs that the voluntary sector was more flexible and imaginative, more able to move rapidly into areas of need. There were strong arguments to the effect that a more pluralistic, diverse system would offer benefits to clients (Paulson 1988; Schlesinger and Dorwart 1984; Kamerman 1983).

There is great variation among the fifty states in terms of the choice to adopt the quasi-public model. Some states have been more hesitant; some have hired personnel onto public payrolls, creating large new public organizations for care provision. This choice is not a dichotomous one; rather the blend of public and quasi-public organizations lies on a continuum (Frank and Goldman 1989).

D. The Private Health Care System

The final institutional arrangement to be described is the relationship between, on the one hand, the public and quasi-public system, and on the other, the private system for care for the mentally ill. The private mental health care system includes the specialty mental health outpatient clinics (operating on a profit-making basis), private psychiatrists and psychologists, private for-profit psychiatric hospitals, and modest numbers of other for-profit facilities. Although there is some interface between these two systems, this has been rather limited.

It is in the private system that much acute health care is provided; it is the private system to which most consumers prefer to look for services; it is in the private sector that most health professionals aspire to have their professional lives. It is often (perhaps usually) the private system that is the focus of concern in the United States when there are discussions about cost containment. But the private health care system, which involves large amounts of resources and personnel, is far from the lives of most persons with chronic mental illness. The main private health system providers serving the chronically mentally ill are hospitals, both community hospitals (voluntary and for-profit) and psychiatric hospitals (usually for-profit psychiatric hospitals). Since the Medicaid system will pay for psychiatric care in community hospitals, many patients are directed to such hospitals. Community hospitals, of course, may be public, voluntary, or for-profit. Thus, private sector hospitals do provide inpatient services to the seriously mentally ill in many communities.

Another way in which the private health care system has accommodated the chronically mentally ill has been in nursing homes. Over time,
some privately owned nursing homes (usually voluntary nursing
homes) accepted patients with mental illness. For-profit nursing homes
accepted such patients less commonly. The number of chronically mentally ill persons in private nursing homes has been in a state of flux since
the 1987 Omnibus Budget Reconciliation Act, but it is fairly clear that one
effect of the bill has been to reduce the presence of seriously mentally ill
persons in privately owned nursing homes.

Most private mental health outpatient clinics have very few seriously
mentally ill clients. Such clients are considered difficult to treat and the
fact that they pay their bills with Medicaid (which has notoriously low
fee scales) makes them unattractive as clients.

By and large, the private mental health system—which involves about
$9 billion annually in expenditures—is rather distant from the public
system, which provides care for the seriously mentally ill. Specific data
on the provision of care for the seriously mentally ill in the private sector
are incomplete, but 1986 National Institute of Mental Health (NIMH)
studies provide some useful information.[4] Examining both all clients
receiving care on a single day in 1986 and all clients admitted over the
course of a year to eight types of organizations specializing in mental
health services, NIMH authors found less than 2% of those diagnosed
with schizophrenia were served by private facilities (Rosenstein,
Milazzo-Sayre, and Manderscheid 1989; Crumpton, Stolp, and Warner
1990; Redick, Stroup, Witkin, Atay, and Manderscheid 1990).

Later in this paper there will be discussion of how these institutional
arrangements—the primacy of state responsibility, decentralization to
state and even local levels, the use of quasi-public organizations, and the
lack of private mental health system involvement—affect funding and
services.

II. RESOURCES

The types and amounts of resources for care of the seriously mentally
ill are related closely to the political economy of care, and thus to the
institutional arrangements discussed above. Two types of resources will
be discussed here: funding resources and human resources. Although
there are problems with some of the data about financial resources for
care, efforts by the National Association of State Mental Health Program
Directors (and their research institute) to standardize reporting systems
and categories of expenditures have produced quite good information
about funding for the seriously mentally ill during the 1980s.

Briefly, expenditures controlled by state mental health authorities for mental health totalled approximately $9.3 billion in 1987 (this figure includes the federal government's contributions to the Medicaid program). These are the monies that are available for care of the chronically mentally ill (contributions from other sources for care of chronic mental illness are very limited). This is $37.97 for each person in the United States. The overwhelming majority of this funding is used for persons with chronic mental illness. Approximately 5% of this spending is for geriatric care, and 8% is for the care of children and adolescents (National Association of State Mental Health Program Directors, NASMHPD 1990).

An alternative way of examining government expenditure for chronic mental illness is to divide the total expenditures for care $8,296,419,160 (the figure excludes prevention, research, training, administration, and unallocable expenditures), by the most likely estimate of those with chronic mental illness who are serviced (50%, or 1.25 million persons). Using these figures, the annual expenditures would be $6,637 per client. If one is willing to rely on these estimates of expenditure and client numbers, this figure may be useful as a crude estimate of costs per client for mental health care.[5]

For purposes of perspective, it should be noted that the best data we have on the whole mental health system (governmental, quasi-governmental, and private) reveals that for 1986 the cost was over $18 billion. These dollars were used for care for about seven million Americans (Scallet 1990).

State mental health authority expenditures (which *are* the expenditures for the chronically mentally ill) increased between 1981 and 1987 by 53% (in current dollars). However, in constant dollars (1981) state mental health authority expenditures *decreased* by 2.8%. Baldly put, governmental funding for the chronically mentally ill is decreasing in American society, not increasing, in terms of constant dollars.

Funding for care for the chronically mentally ill comes primarily from the state level—that is, 80% of funding comes from the 50 American states. The federal government provides about 15% of the total funding (8% through Medicaid and the other 7% through other programming). Local governments provide 2% of funding, and other sources provide 3%. These figures support the point made earlier: Services for the chronically mentally ill are state level responsibilities (NASMHPD 1990).

Sixty-two percent of funds controlled by state mental health authorities in 1987 is expended on inpatient care (56.9% on state mental hospitals, and 5.2% on other hospitals) and 33% is spent on community programs (administration, research, and training account for the balance). Adjusted for inflation, expenditures for state hospitals declined

9% between 1981 and 1987, while community services expenditures—similarly adjusted—increased by 8.4% over the same period. Thus, there have been some modest shifts in this time period from hospital to community care, but it should be noted that these shifts have occurred in the context of *decline* in overall funding. The pie may be cut differently, but it is a smaller pie.

Some crude measures of the amount of variation associated with decentralization in the system of care for those with serious mental illness can be drawn from data on state spending for services (NASHMPD 1990). There is considerable variation among states in the percentages of money used for inpatient care, which has clear implications for the amounts available for community-based care (see Table 1). These data on care expenditures do not include spending for federal Social Security Disability Income (SSDI) and Supplemental Security Income (SSI) programs for persons disabled by mental illness ($3.8 and $1.64 billion, respectively). Nor do they include the $42.7 million spent for housing subsidies to persons handicapped by mental illness. The federal expenditures for special education for mentally and emotionally disturbed children are excluded, as well as state-level expenditures for education, vocational, rehabilitation, health, criminal justice, transportation, and social services. These data are simply not available except for a few small, but excellent research studies of participants in small programs (Scallet 1990; Alcohol, Drug Abuse, and Mental Health Administration 1987; Wolff and Diamond 1990; Dickey and Breslau 1990; Shern, Coen, Wilson, and Vasby 1990).

The effect of decentralization of state programming to the local level, of making local units the locus of legal responsibility for providing programming to the chronically mentally ill, has been the reduction of state

Table 1. Range in State Spending for the Chronically Mentally Ill

	Amounts States Spent		
	Highest state	Lowest state	All states
Per capita expenditure ($)	98.93	11.76	37.97
Percentage of expenditure on inpatient care (%)	91.45	6.13	63.28
Mental health expenditures as percentage of all state spending (%)	4.9*	0.5*	NA

Source: NASMHPD 1990.
Notes *Individual state figures are from "State Expenditure Report: 1989," by the National Association of State Budget Officers, 1989.
NA: not available.

expenditures for the mentally ill. Although the 50 state governments have remained the main source of funding for care since programming responsibility was shifted to the substate level, states have tended to reduce their expenditures. For example, in California, the impact of regionalization was a decline in mental health budgets at the state level (Elpers 1989; Surber et al. 1986).

Finally, the delivery system for services to the mentally ill, with its extreme fiscal constraints, faces situations in which court and federal mandates for care cannot be realized. For example, one of the effects of federal-level nursing home legislative reform in 1987 was to discharge some chronically mentally ill persons into the community, introducing into the service system clients with complex and expensive care needs. These relocations took place largely because states lost Medicaid funds with which to provide nursing home care for some chronically mentally ill persons. But states have had great difficulty finding adequate funding with which to provide services for these very vulnerable people.

A second kind of resource in mental health care is human resources. Obviously, the supply and type of personnel are responsive to the amount of money available for creating positions and to salary levels (and both of these characteristics are shaped by the terms of employment for health and other professionals in the private health care system). The significant underfunding of the public mental health system has made it extremely vulnerable in terms of human resources. Considering the demand for services, there are not enough funded positions for trained mental health workers for working with the seriously mentally ill in much of the United States. Moreover, for the positions that do exist, in some areas there are not enough workers to fill them. When the numbers of those trained for work in mental health specialties decline, workers are more able to pick and choose among positions and are even less willing to accept low-paying positions in public mental health. Professionals completing their training are much more likely to recruit into up-scale professional settings, not into organizations providing services for those with serious mental illness.

The laments about the lack of psychiatrists for government-provided mental health services are too familiar to require reiteration. Salaries are lower in governmental programs and work conditions are stressful. Moreover, recent data indicate that the number of psychiatrists completing training is declining, creating a very acute problem in child and geriatric psychiatry for the severely mentally ill (Judd 1990).

The United States, like most advanced industrial societies, has a shortage of nurses, though the number of nurses completing training annually has generally increased since 1975. Of course, only a small fraction of either new or experienced nurses provide services to the chronically mentally ill, in either institutional or community-based settings. More-over, the number of social workers completing degrees has decreased in the last decade. The number of master's degrees granted in psychology for counseling or clinical psychology has been about 2,500 yearly for most of the 1980s.

The fields in which there are the most serious personnel shortages are psychiatry and social work. It is necessary to recognize, however, the differential effects of downturns in the production of persons with specialty skills. Public mental health authorities and organizations working with the seriously mentally ill are less able to compete for talent. When the number of new entrants into fields declines, these agencies are affected more adversely than private organizations.

These difficulties are exacerbated in two ways: in subspecialties within specialties such as child psychiatry, and in certain types of geographical areas. Rural areas particularly cannot compete for providers. The under-supply of physicians in rural areas has been often noted, and is variously explained as deriving from (1) the lack of a stimulating professional community of psychiatrists, (2) the lack of certain desired cultural amenities, such as museums, concerts, and restaurants, and (3) the lack of adequate salaries (Murray and Keller 1986). Only one of these can be altered directly: salaries. Although some psychiatric training programs (cf. the residency programs of the University of Maryland and the University of Wisconsin) have made conscious (and successful) efforts to introduce physicians-in-training to public mental health settings, these efforts are more novel than widespread. Difficulties with shortages have been temporarily alleviated in some areas through federally funded programs such as the National Health Service, but the funding for such programming was greatly reduced during the 1980s.

Where, then, do rural areas find psychiatric care for the chronically mentally ill? They have turned to sharing (one doctor or a team serving several mental health clinics on a rotating schedule), or tried to set up satellite clinics closely linked to hospital-based doctors in larger cities nearby. Neither of these models provides the kind of continuity of care needed and desired.

There is yet one more discouraging aspect to the provision of human resources for the care of the seriously mentally ill: the amount of burn-out. Research on burnout rates in the human services is only a decade old, and so far we lack systematic approaches to assessing the causes of turnover, rates of turnover, and the effects of turnover on clients and organizations. There are several tests and scales for measuring burnout and several studies concerned with the organizational context from which burnout arises. In recent years, a body of literature has discussed burnout among frontline care workers, in types of organizations comparable to those delivering services to the chronically mentally ill (Maslach and Jackson 1982; Pines and Maslach 1978). From these studies and from extensive surveys of mental health workers in Wisconsin, there is reason to believe there may be serious burnout problems, with many workers contemplating career changes (Schulz 1990).

The overall problems of human resources then lie both in the smallness of numbers of staff (due to lack of candidates with degrees, inability of the public sector to compete for candidates, and the lack of funding for positions) and in the burnout/turnover among workers due to the highly stressful nature of the work.

III. TECHNOLOGY

In assessing the role of technology in the provision of services, there are two related questions: To what extent are there demonstrated technologies for care, and to what extent are these technologies used? In referring to the first question, David Mechanic's definition of technology is helpful. Discussing the role of technology in caring for the chronically mentally ill, he has written:

> The concept of technology refers to much more than hardware. It applies to a process of organizing inputs—people, machines, materials, or whatever—in order to achieve desired results. In this sense, the care of the seriously mentally ill involves a variety of technologies that have been proved to be effective in diminishing pain and disability and in enhancing the quality of patients' and families' lives. We, of course, have medications of enormous utility. . . .. We have innovative community programs. (Mechanic 1989:74)

Here the types of technology to be discussed are the use of antipsychotic drugs and the organization of care.

A. Antipsychotic Drugs

The widespread use of antipsychotic medicines stems from American medical cultural traditions—belief in a medical, technically based model of treatment—and enjoys the endorsement of a highly esteemed group (the medical profession). Drugs are widely perceived as an efficient and economical means of treating patients, desirable insofar as they reduce needs for sizable financial and human resources. Antipsychotic medications are a relatively inexpensive resource, easy to mobilize in an area in which diagnosis, treatment, and outcome are poorly understood. While there is no implication intended herein that antipsychotic medications are always desirable, they are a technology that has permitted many clients to manage their illnesses in less restrictive settings.

B. Organization of Care

There are two conceptual approaches for organizing care that have emerged in the literature about community-based services in the United States. Leading professionals are often advocates of one or the other of these models, or of some blending of the two. These are models known to have worked successfully. One is the assertive community treatment (ACT) model, and the other is the coordinated system of services model.

Briefly, features of the ACT model are:

1. The integration of virtually all aspects of client living in the community—vocational, housing, medications, general and mental health care, activities of daily life, social and recreational activities—into a treatment plan usually carried out by a single organization.
2. Assertive outreach by staff to keep the client involved with the organization.
3. Delivery of services in the community as well as in the organization's facilities. Staff may meet clients or provide supervision at the grocery store, laundry, etc.

Of course, there are many refinements and variations of ACT, but most programs adhere to these principles. The key item in this listing is the first item: The organization personnel provide virtually all services to clients. It is the ACT staff who assess whether clients have the capability for some type of vocational activity, and then undertake training and coaching to prepare clients for work settings. ACT staff find employment for some clients, and once clients are employed, ACT staff visit work settings to provide medications and to work out job site problems if necessary. It is ACT staff who help clients find housing, emphasizing the desirability of having the most independence possible for clients in housing situations. ACT staff work with landlords or roommates to minimize change in residence for clients. ACT staff may assist clients in handling their finances, train clients to use public transportation, give assistance in time of crisis, provide assistance with personal hygiene, assist with food selection and preparation, and organize social activities. Of course, there are some things ACT does not do: It does not provide inpatient care (though ACT staff interact with clients in the hospital, provide information to the hospital staff, and work with the hospital to develop after-care plans); it does not provide primary health service.

Overall, the premise of ACT is that virtually all care (and very comprehensive care, often vocationally oriented) is best provided by the same
team of people. The general approach of ACT is to provide a seamless
web of services affecting most aspects of clients' lives.

ACT is not a program preparing people to be, after some months, fully
responsible for independent lives in the community. Rather, the assumption is that for many clients, there will be need for continuing
(lifelong) services. This approach, usually reliant on a multidisciplinary
staff with clinical backup, is expensive. It does not always work—people
still commit suicide and have troubles serious enough to require hospitalization. But there is increasing evidence (Test 1990; Bond 1984; Bond,
Miller, Krumwied, and Ward 1988) that such programming can assist
clients to have stable lives in communities over long periods of time.
ACT is not a technology needed by all persons with severe mental illness. Stein (1990) estimates that it is appropriate for only about twenty
percent of chronically mentally clients.

The ACT model is shown in Figure 1. In a system with several ACT
programs, the client enters one organization and that organization is the
locus of his/her services. Not shown in the figure are inpatient facilities,
inasmuch as ACT does not provide them.

There is an alternative type, the coordinated system of services model.
In this model, there is a case manager working with all clients, but most
services are provided by specialized organizations (the case manager is a
staff person in one of the organizations, in all likelihood). Thus, a client
would have basic community support services in program A, work services in program B, housing through program C or D, social/recreational

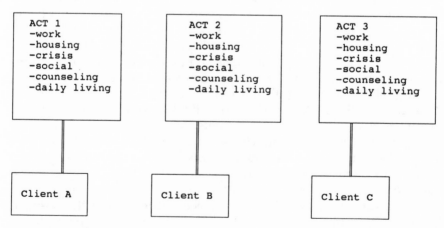

Figure 1. ACT model.

activity through program E, counseling through program E, crisis assistance in program F, inpatient care through program G. Of course, one program might provide more than one function.

The coordinated system of services is illustrated in Figure 2. The critical element in the coordinated system of care is the provision of effective systemwide case management.[6] There needs to be careful assessment by someone who knows the client well, of exactly what mix of programs is right for the clients at different points in time. This mix is subject to change, as client situations stabilize or disintegrate. The systemwide case manager has important responsibility for staying in touch with the various program elements serving the client, to make sure the client is not falling into the cracks in the system. In highly pressured work situations, with numerous clients and great change in client situations, it is not easy to effect coordinated systemwide case management. There is a substantial literature concerned with coordination of case management (Fisher, Landis, and Clark 1988; Gowdy and Rapp 1989; Harris and Bergman 1987; Lehman 1988). In this model, the client may participate in one or more of several programs. Each program has relatively discrete tasks (goals differ; staff training is related to goals), and each program is expected to carry out a part of the overall treatment plan for the client.

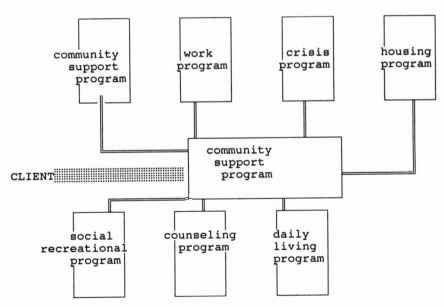

Figure 2. Coordinated system of services model.

Many case managers are staff in community support programs, which tend to be important providers of services for clients. But some clients vote with their feet, attaching themselves more firmly to work or other programming rather than to community support programs. Thus, each program must have capacity for providing systemwide case management.

This model is not just a collection of services. Rather, it presumes the active collaboration of managers and staff of the organizations, embracing the concept that care is coordinated, that there is an identifiable site at which responsibility is lodged. Otherwise, it is too easy for clients to be lost. If a client were attached to a work program and a counseling program, but used the counseling program only quarterly, the work program might bear the day-to-day responsibility for case management. If the client left the work program, he/she could easily be lost, because the counseling program contact was relatively infrequent. Communication costs (i.e., the cost of time required to exchange information) are high in this system, because of the time required for sharing information across organizational boundaries. And it is not clear how many clients can be served before it becomes more efficient to clone the system than to expand it. Finally, this kind of coordinated system of services will not work unless there is overall system consensus about the types of services that should be present, and unless each service element enjoys credibility. Each service program has to be capable of working with referred clients.

There is a fairly considerable literature about the ACT and the coordinated system of services models (Test 1981, 1984, 1990; Test and Stein 1980; Stein, Diamond, and Factor 1990; Stein and Test 1980; Bond et al. 1988). And of course, the models can usefully be commingled, so that clients needing ACT services are handled by ACT programs set in a coordinated system of services also used by clients with fewer service needs. What is important is the conceptualization of the service system as having an integrated focus, with well-understood links among system elements, and with considered use of inpatient care.

How common is the use of these models? How common is this technology? Although these programs are diffusing rapidly, with state after state adopting programming along these lines, most clients receiving service are probably not in an ACT program (even if they should be) and most care programming cannot be termed a coordinated system. It may be that "widespread proliferation of case management and community-based services has narrowed the differences between assertive community treatment and 'standard' care" (Olfson 1990:640), but systematic data do not exist. And even if many programs have accepted these models, there is the need to be aware that many persons with chronic mental illness receive no services at all (see below).

IV. CLIENTS

There is one additional type of input into the mental health care system to consider before turning to other aspects of the system: the client.

Most of our estimates about mental illness stem from the Epidemiological Catchment Area (ECA) studies involving about 18,000 individuals in five communities. Individuals were interviewed with the Diagnostic Interview Schedule (DIS). These studies, replicated in many other countries and widely accepted, indicate that about 1% of the population suffers from schizophrenia or a schizophreniform disorder. This 1% figure has diffused widely as the expected number of persons with severe mental illness (Shapiro et al. 1984).

The well-recognized demographic changes in the United States (the baby boom of 1947–1964) have meant an increase in the age group vulnerable to the onset of serious mental illness (persons 18–35 years of age). We know from epidemiological studies that the incidence of mental illness is fairly invariant, so that the number of potential new entrants to the care system is very much a function of the age distribution of the population. Simply put, the larger the number of people 18–35 in the population, the larger the number of persons becoming ill with schizophrenia for the first time.

Since most of the ECA studies were conducted in metropolitan locations, it is unclear whether the rates for rural areas differ substantially from the ECA findings. The NIMH takes the position that rates of mental illness (overall) are higher in rural areas. Others, reviewing regional evidence about the variation in the health of military conscripts, speculate that there may be considerable regional as well as urban/rural variation in incidence of illness (NIMH 1990).

The customary estimates are that approximately 2.5 million people suffer from chronic mental illness (Frank and Goldman 1989). The earlier-described very decentralized nature of the delivery system has meant that accurate figures could be produced only with state cooperation, and most states have been unable and unwilling to devote resources to locating and counting those with serious mental illness.

There are many other reasons that the United States lacks a good tally of those with chronic mental illness. Diagnosis is complex, and often clinicians prefer not to label clients as chronic. Some clients seem to be able, after acute episodes over many years, to live in the community with little or no mental health support. Although there are efforts by the NIMH to obtain information on the number of clients served by provider organizations, the accuracy of the information is questionable.

As indicated, the large number of clients alone places great stress on the mental health care system. There are also client characteristics that bear on the need for services and the ability of organizations to provide adequate services. The general problem is the increase in the number of difficult to serve clients.

The discharge of chronically mentally ill persons from nursing homes has already been mentioned, although reliable national data do not exist on the number of chronically mentally ill persons discharged from nursing homes into community care contexts. But these are clients with very complex care needs.

Second, it is widely believed that there are high levels of drug and alcohol use among younger clients with chronic mental illness. This use complicates treatment considerably. There are many variations in use patterns—more alcohol and fewer drugs in rural areas, differential substance abuse by gender, substitution of alcohol and drugs for psychotropic medications—but the overall effect has been to make some clients even more resistant to treatment.

In the United States, the homeless mentally ill—perhaps the most difficult population in terms of treatment—have been the focus of much concern. Estimates of the percentage of the homeless with serious mental illness vary widely, but the consensus is that about one-third of the homeless have severe mental illness. It goes without saying that these clients pose extreme challenges to the care system (Torrey 1988).

In sum, there are very large numbers of people with serious mental illness, actually or potentially in the public systems, and some of them are very difficult to work with. Few clients exit from the system, although some reject services or manage without services. Finally, some persons with serious mental illness have children, and care systems find themselves trying to coordinate services for the children as well as for parents.

V. ACCESS TO CARE

How do the configuration of the care system and the resources available to it influence the ability of clients in need to obtain care? The ECA studies provide data on the extent to which persons with mental health problems of different types have recently used the care system. Only one-fifth of persons with recent mental disorders of any type report mental health visits in the past six months. Among those with schizo-phrenic/schizophreniform disorders, between 38 and 53% report mental health visits in the past six months. The term *mental health visit* included care provided both by mental health specialists and by general medical providers (Shapiro et al. 1984).

A recent director of the NIMH basing his perspectives on these data, strongly indicted the system of care for its inability to serve most persons with mental illness. He also emphasized the discriminatory health insurance practices that create barriers to adequate mental health care and the public mythology that mental disorders are uncommon and less real than other illness. These factors, he argued, result in underfunding of services and stigma for those with severe mental illness (Judd 1990).

In Texas, there have been recent efforts to estimate the need for mental health services and the use of mental health services, reinterpreting the ECA data in terms of the Texas classification of the seriousness of mental illness. The majority of those with chronic major disorders, who are also dangerous and/or dependent have never been hospitalized. In this group (the most disabled of the Texas groups), only 24.65% of those with major affective disorders and schizophreniform spectrum disorders have ever been in a psychiatric hospital. If substance abusers are grouped with persons suffering from major affective disorders and schizophreniform spectrum disorders, only 18.95% have ever had mental hospital treatment. About 38% of those with chronic major disorders have had mental health services other than hospitalization in the last six months. The figure falls to 29% for people who have chronic major disorders or problems of substance abuse (Holzer, Swanson, Ganju, Goldsmith, and Jackson 1989). In simple terms, of those with the highest level of need, the mental health care service system serves only a minority.

In Wisconsin, information carefully assembled by mental health authorities in ten different county-level systems indicates that fewer than 0.3% of the population is receiving public services for serious mental illness. To put it differently, about three-tenths of the people with chronic mental illness obtain services. Presumably the remaining seven-tenths of the chronically mentally ill in Wisconsin receive no state-provided services. This may be for many reasons: They may not trust services involving medications, they may have had their fill of services, or they may simply reject involvement with bureaucracies. And Wisconsin has a reputation for having one of the best state mental health systems in the country.

Obviously, there are a few people with severe mental illness served exclusively in the private system. The number of persons in the private care system, given the high costs of care and the penury of insurance coverage, is quite small. And there may be some persons with serious mental illness who are served in other programs (programs for the developmentally disabled, the elderly, etc.). But this cannot be a large number. The most reasonable conclusion is that a substantial fraction of those with mental illness are not in the system of care.

Why are so many people with serious mental illness not in the care system? The lack of care for them (setting aside the number who have rejected care, refuse it, or do not require it) is a measure of the responsiveness of the care system. The care system, with very limited financial and human resources, is full. Field-level workers would take a stronger position: that the care system is overflowing. Program after program reports waiting lists and diversion strategies.

The ability of programs to accept new clients is shaped in part by the extent to which established clients need services. Caregiving organizations commonly report that new clients (in a state of crisis) require very large amounts of time, but in fact continuing clients also require considerable care. Some analysis in urban and rural counties suggests that clients longer in the service system actually use much more service than new entrants (Hollingsworth 1990; Hollingsworth and Covaleski 1990). New clients, after initial crises are resolved, may not get settled in the care system for a year or more. After a year or two, clients are firmly attached to the care-providing system, and the system has often developed multifaceted treatment plans.

Most service systems, in the relatively brief time in which community-based care has existed, have had to cope with providing both considerable crisis care to new clients, and considerable continuing care to established clients. The implications of this high level of demand for services have been fairly staggering: Clients have had to wait for admission (in many instances) and programs have been unable to make time to conduct outreach to find new clients.

Since access is one of the care system performances on which we have the most information, it appears that the institutional/resource system does not provide well, given client levels of need.

VI. QUALITY OF CARE

The fundamental point about using quality of service as an output measure for assessing services systems is that careful and imaginative attention needs to be given to the choice of indicators about service quality. Although there is a fairly vast literature touching on the issues of quality of services, and seeking appropriate measures, there is little agreement among scholars as to how best to measure quality. And even when there is some recognition of preferred strategies for measuring quality, the data do not exist for mental health.

The most familiar indicator of quality of community-based service has been the extent to which clients required hospitalization. Indicators of service quality, in the 1970s, were usually somehow related to the prevention of inpatient care, with the implicit contention that the better the community-based services the fewer the days of inpatient care needed for persons with serious mental illness. The inadequacy of this measure is obvious, but it has been difficult to move beyond it.

In her extensive and impressive body of work, Mary Ann Test has argued that good indicators of the quality of care and quality of life for clients would be (1) living arrangements of clients—both the degree of independence clients have in their living settings, and the stability of living arrangements over time, and (2) amounts and type of vocational activity. Her perspective suggests that for persons with serious mental illness, both symptomatology and hospitalization episodes follow an up-and-down zigzag pattern over time, and therefore may not be wholly useful as indicators. In longitudinal studies of persons with schizophrenia, she has found that measures of housing and vocational activities are useful indicators of community adjustment (Test 1981, 1984, 1990). Quality of service and community adjustment are not identical concepts, but inasmuch as community adjustment (living in the least restrictive circumstances possible) is the preferred goal for most treatment planning, it seems appropriate to set them equal.

Unfortunately, client-level measures on outcomes such as living arrangements and vocational activities are available only under very special circumstances. We simply do not know in any detail about the living arrangements of clients, their participation in vocational/educational activities, their social/recreational behavior, their adherence to medications, etc. The data are not available with which to assess the quality of client life as an outcome of the system. Therefore, to pursue questions of quality, it is necessary to look elsewhere.

Other possibilities for examining the quality of service are measures of inputs into service, for example, the number of treatment care persons and the qualifications of staff. The lack of established relationship between training and client outcomes, as well as the lack of information about the number and training of treatment caregivers make this approach difficult to pursue.

Finally, the quantity of services delivered and the complexity of the programming for clients are very useful indicators of quality. To use these indicators requires client-level data on the hours and days of service in the following categories: case management, counseling, medications, community support, social-recreational programming, crisis care, vocational, day treatment, housing, and inpatient care. This is an area in which a great deal is known for a few thousand clients. For small numbers of clients in Wisconsin, Massachusetts, and Colorado, there are careful studies of the volume and cost of services (Wolff and Diamond 1990; Dickey and Breslau 1990; Shern et al. 1990). And for approximately 2,000 clients in ten rural mental health systems in Wisconsin, data are now available on hours and days of various types of service (Hollingsworth 1990b). These types of information can help to put some floor under our quantity and quantity as quality discussions. The step from analysis of quantity to quality is, however, a large (and potentially ill-chosen) one. Moreover, the collection of client-level service data, given the lack of computer technology in many mental health delivery systems, is arduous and impractical.

VII. PERSPECTIVES

The findings of this analysis are rather bleak. The political economy of mental health care places very severe constraints on the ability of a coordinated system to respond to client needs by providing access or by applying the known technologies. There is no reason to expect that the patterns of resources or technology will change substantially, especially in an era of health cost control emphasis. Although there are some modest prospects for changes in service delivery for the seriously mentally ill, these are not impressive.

Some scholars have suggested that greater integration between general health care and mental health care could make for a different level of discourse about mental health programming, and thus more sense of entitlement for clients of the system. Social welfare functions of the state may be expressed through state policy favoring more service system integration, even in eras of expenditure containment (Ruggie 1990).

Other scholars note the ascendance of management and financing in mental health policy making, speculating that rethinking management and financing systems could lead to improved delivery of services. These efforts, too new for systematic evaluation, are reflected in stress on case management, centralization of service systems, and capitation approaches (Rochefort 1989).

As clients (consumers) and their families have become more active in asserting their demands for resources and their roles in treatment plans, there are new political and personnel resources drawn into the processes for making decisions and exercising power. As mental illness comes out of the closet, there are some possibilities that the context in which mental health policy is set will be less negative, and that the political economy of mental health policy may be freed from some of its historic restrictions and limitations. The National Alliance for the Mentally Ill, with 60,000 members in 900 chapters throughout the United States, works actively to influence appropriations. The example of developmental disability is noteworthy, showcasing a situation in which advocates for a disability group were able to influence power configurations and resource allocation.

There is modest, and contradictory, evidence that cultural perceptions of mental illness are changing, and that advocacy groups may be able to influence institutional and resource allocations. The traditional advocates of better services for the chronically mentally ill—psychiatrists in community mental health centers, the NIMH, some state mental health administrators—have been unable to garner resources on the scale that they are needed. The strong medical professional organizations have been ready with calls for action and rhetoric, but most professionals prefer to remain distant from care of the chronically mentally ill. And the courts, once very instrumental in reshaping the contours of the mental health system, seem unlikely to be a source of much advocacy in the near future (particularly at the federal level).

As social scientists and clinicians become better informed about the types of service provision that are more effective, the opportunities for introducing more of the much-vaunted concepts of efficiency and efficacy into programs may be realized. There is considerable debate in circles concerned with mental health services about the extent to which model programs can diffuse, but overall many scholars and policymakers agree that there is very strong interest in knowing what kinds of programming are associated with better outcomes for clients, and there is increasing scholarly research underway on these issues.

Finally, there are some interesting efforts to obtain and analyze systematic client-level data with which to assess behavior in organizations delivering services. With such information, it would be possible to discuss quality of services much more meaningfully, and to provide much more accountability of the mental health care system. The nationwide surveys carried out by the NIMH have provided some extremely basic information about services, but only in very aggregate terms. To have any adequate sense of the services clients actually receive, and the effects of these services requires a standardized longitudinal data system, used on a regular basis by staff. Such a data system, in order to assure any levels of quality, would have to be useful for multiple purposes: in day-to-day delivery of services, for research, for administrative record keeping. Most of these designs are only in the pilot stage, but writ large they could offer very exciting possibilities. Since data management in human services has so far promised so much and delivered so little, it seems a very slender reed on which to build any expectations.

That the just-mentioned types of change and study can reshape the established system of public underfunding for care of those with chronic mental illness is most unlikely. Creating the bricks of a coordinated system of care with such straw seems impossible. The institutional arrangements of the system facilitate underfunding. The results, services with severe deficiencies in access and care, are not susceptible to change in an era of budget deficits and stagflation (Marmor and Gill 1989).

NOTES

1. A chronically mentally ill person is "a person afflicted with a mental illness that is severe in degree and persistent in duration, causes substantial diminished level of functioning in the primary aspects of daily living, an inability to cope with the ordinary demands of life and may lead to an inability to maintain stable adjustment and independent functioning without long-term treatment and support which may be lifelong in duration" (State of Wisconsin definition, adapted from National Institute of Mental Health definition).

2. Medicaid is funded by both the federal government and the state governments. State governments have some discretion in the benefits, and are influential in setting eligibility criteria. Medicaid, a government health insurance program for the needy, covers inpatient and outpatient mental health care of many types, although it has a strong inpatient bias (Marmor and Gill 1989).

3. Obviously, not all private organizations delivering services previously handled by public authorities should be regarded as quasi-public organizations.

4. The mental health specialty organizations included in the study were state and county mental hospitals, private psychiatric hospitals, multiservice mental health organizations, Veterans Administration medical centers, nonfederal general hospitals with separate psychiatric services, residential treatment centers for emotionally disturbed children, freestanding outpatient mental health clinics, and freestanding partial care organizations. Not included were general medical services and nursing homes.

5. These estimates of cost are for mental health services only, not for income maintenance programs, criminal justice programs, or family contributions to care. Nancy Wolff's work has shown total living/support costs for relatively low functioning persons with chronic mental illness to be in excess of $20,000, and Barbara Dickey's work has shown figures ranging from $12,000 to $30,000 (Wolff and Diamond 1990; Dickey and Breslau 1990).

6. Systemwide case management refers to the concept of an overall case manager, coordinating and brokering the services from all providers for an individual's treatment plan.

REFERENCES

Alcohol, Drug Abuse, and Mental Health Administration. 1987. *Mental Health, United States, 1987.* Department of Health and Human Services Publication No. (ADM) 87-1518. Rockville, Maryland: Author.

Bond, G. R. 1984. "An Economic Analysis of Psychosocial Rehabilitation." *Hospital and Community Psychiatry* 36:356–62.

Bond,G. R., L. D. Miller, R. D. Krumwied, and R. S. Ward. 1988. "Assertive Case Management in Three CMHCs: A Controlled Study." *Hospital and Community Psychiatry* 39:411–18.

Brekke, John S. and Mary Ann Test. 1987. "An Empirical Analysis of Services Delivered in a Model Community Support Program." *Psychosocial Rehabilitation Journal* 4:51–61.

Crumpton, Laurie, C. Stolp, and D. Warner. 1990. "California Discharge Data: Letter to the Editor." *Hospital and Community Psychiatry* 41:1026–27.

Dickey, Barbara and Joshua Breslau. 1990. "Data-Based Capitated Rates for Public Mental Health." Paper presented to American Psychiatric Association, May 15, New York.

Elpers, John R. 1989. "Public Mental Health Funding in California, 1959 to 1989." *Hospital and Community Psychiatry* 40:799–804.

Fisher, Gloria, Dan Landis, and Karen Clark. 1988. "Case Management Service Provision and Client Change." *Community Mental Health Journal* 24:134–42.

Frank, Richard G. and Howard H. Goldman. 1989. "Financing Care of the Severely Mentally Ill: Incentives, Contracts, and Public Responsibility." *Journal of Social Issues* 45:131–44.

Gowdy, Elizabeth and Charles A. Rapp. 1989. "Managerial Behavior: The Common Denominators of Effective Community-Based Programs." *Psychosocial Rehabilitation Journal* 13:31–51.

Grob, G. N. 1983. *Illness and American Society, 1875–1940.* Princeton, NJ: Princeton University Press.

———. 1987. "Mental Health Policy in Post–World War II America." *New Directions for Mental Health Services* 36:15–32.

Harris, M. and H. C. Bergman. 1987. "Case Management with the Chronically Mentally Ill: A Clinical Perspective." *American Journal of Orthopsychiatry* 57:296–302.

Hollingsworth, Ellen Jane. 1990. "Two Rural Systems for Delivering Services to the Seriously Mentally Ill: Wisconsin Cases." Paper presented to the National Rural Mental Health Association, Lubbock, Texas.

Hollingsworth, Ellen Jane and Mark Covaleski. 1990. "Kinds of Care for the Seriously Mentally Ill." A paper presented to American Psychiatric Association. May 15. New York.

Hollingsworth, J. Rogers and Ellen Jane Hollingsworth. 1987. *Controversy About American Hospitals: Funding, Ownership and Performance.* Washington, DC: American Enterprise Institute.

Holzer, Charles E., Jeffrey W. Swanson, Vijay K. Ganju, Harold F. Goldsmith, and David J. Jackson. 1989. "Estimates of Need for Mental Health Services in Texas Counties." Pp. 149–81 in *Community Care of the Chronically Mentally Ill,* edited by C. M. Bojean, M. T. Coleman, and I. Iscoe. Austin, Texas: Hogg Foundation for Mental Health.

Judd, Lewis L. 1990. "Putting Mental Health on the Nation's Agenda." *Hospital and Community Psychiatry* 41:131–34.

Kamerman, Sheila B. 1983. "The New Mixed Economy of Welfare: Public and Private." *Social Work* (January/February):5–10.

Kiesler, C. A. 1982. "Public and Professional Myths about Mental Hospitalization: An Empirical Reassessment." *American Psychologist* 37:1323–39.

Lehman, Anthony F. 1988. "Financing Case Management: Making the Money Work." Pp. 67–78 in *Clinical Case Management,* edited by Maxine Harris and Leona L. Bachrach. New Directions for Mental Health Services, Vol. 40. San Francisco: Jossey-Bass.

Marmor, Theodore R. and Karyn C. Gill. 1989. "The Political and Economic Context of Mental Health Care in the United States." *Journal of Health Politics, Policy and Law* 14:459–75.

Maslach, C. and S. E. Jackson. 1982. "The Burnout Syndrome in the Health Professions." Pp. 227–51 in *Social Psychology of Health and Illness,* edited by G. Sanders and J. Suls. Hillsdale, NJ: Lawrence Erlbaum.

Mechanic, David. 1989. "Community Care of the Chronically Mentally Ill. III: Summary Comments." Pp. 73–80 in *Community Care of the Chronically Mentally Ill,* edited by C. M. Bojean, M. T. Coleman, and I. Iscoe. Austin, TX: Hogg Foundation for Mental Health.

Mechanic, David and Linda Aiken. 1987. "Improving the Care of Patients with Chronic Mental Illness." *New England Journal of Medicine* 317:1634–38.

Murray, J. Dennis and Peter A. Keller (eds.). 1986. *Innovations in Rural Community Mental Health.* Mansfield, PA: Mansfield University Rural Services Institute.

National Association of State Mental Health Program Directors. 1990. *Funding Sources and Expenditures of State Mental Health Agencies: Revenue Expenditure Study Results Fiscal Year 1987.* Alexandria, VA: Research Institute, Inc., of National Association of State Mental Health Program Directors.

National Institute of Mental Health. 1990. "Program Announcement: Research on Mental Disorders in Rural Populations." Mental Health Research Grants. Bethesda, MD: Author.

Olfson, Mark. 1990. "Assertive Community Treatment: An Evaluation of the Experimental Evidence." *Hospital and Community Psychiatry* 41:634–41.

Paulson, Robert I. 1988. "People and Garbage Are Not the Same: Issues in Contracting for Public Mental Health Services." *Community Mental Health Journal* 24:91–102.

Pines, A. and C. Maslach. 1978. "Characteristics of Staff Burn-Out in Mental Health Settings." *Hospital and Community Psychiatry* 29:233–37.

Redick, Richard W., Atlee Stroup, Michael J. Witkin, Joanne Atay, and Ronald Manderscheid. 1990. "Private Psychiatric Hospitals, United States: 1983–84 and 1986." *Mental Health Statistical Note 191.* Rockville, MD: NIMH Division of Biometry and Applied Sciences.

Regier, D. A., J. K. Myers, M. Kramer, L. N. Robins, D. G. Blazer, R. L. Hough, W. W. Eaton, and B. Z. Locke. 1984. "The Epidemiologic Catchment Area Program." *Archives of General Psychiatry* 41:934–41.

Reinke, B. and J. R. Greenley. 1986. "Organizational Analysis of Three Community Support Program Models." *Hospital and Community Psychiatry* 37:624–29.

Rosenstein, Marilyn J., Laura J. Milazzo-Sayre, and Ronald W. Manderscheid. 1989. "Care of Persons with Schizophrenia: A Statistical Profile." *Schizophrenia Bulletin* 15:45–58.

Rochefort, David A. 1989. "Mental Illness and Mental Health As Public Policy Concerns." Pp. 3–20 in *Handbook on Mental Health Policy in the United States*, edited by David A. Rochefort. New York and Westport, CT: Greenwood Press.

Ruggie, Mary. 1990. "Retrenchment or Realignment? U.S. Mental Health Policy and DRGs." *Journal of Health Politics, Policy and Law* 15:145–67.

Scallet, Leslie J. 1990. "Paying for Public Mental Health Care: Crucial Questions." *Health Affairs* 9:117–24.

Schlesinger, Mark and Robert Dorwart. 1984. "Ownership and Mental-Health Services: A Reappraisal of the Shift toward Privately Owned Facilities." *New England Journal of Medicine* 311:959–65.

Schulz, Rockwell. 1990. "Burnout Among Mental Health Care Personnel." Grant funded by National Institute of Mental Health, Bethesda, MD.

Shaddish, William R., Arthur J. Lurigio, and Dan A. Lewis. 1989. "After Deinstitutionalization: The Present and Future of Mental Health Long-Term Care Policy." *Journal of Social Issues* 45:1–15.

Shapiro, S., E. A. Skinner, L. G. Kessler, Michael Von Korff, Pearl S. German, Gary L. Tischler, Philip J. Leaf, Lee Benham, Linda Cotler, and Darrel A. Regier. 1984. "Utilization of Health and Mental Health Services: Three Epidemiologic Catchment Area Sites." *Archives of General Psychiatry* 42:971–78.

Shern, David L., Anita Coen, Linda A. Nelson, Nancy Z. Wilson, and Kyle O. Vasby. 1990. "Chronic Mental Illness: Cost Estimates in Two Cities." Paper presented to American Psychiatric Association, May 15, New York.

Shern, David L., Richard C. Surles, and Jonas Waizer. 1989. "Designing Community Treatment Systems for the Most Seriously Mentally Ill: A State Administrative Perspective." *Journal of Social Issues* 45:105–17.

Stein, Leonard I. 1989. "Wisconsin's System of Mental Health Financing. " Pp. 29–41 in *Integrating Mental Health Systems Through Capitation. New Directions for Mental Health Services*, edited by David Mechanic and Linda Aiken. San Francisco: Jossey-Bass.

———. 1990. "Comments by Leonard Stein." *Hospital and Community Psychiatry* 41:649–51.

Stein, Leonard I., Ronald J. Diamond, and Robert M. Factor. 1990. "A System Approach to the Care of Persons with Schizophrenia." Pp. 213–46 in *Psychosocial Therapies*, Vol. 5, edited by Marvin I Herz, S. J. Keith, and John P. Docherty. Amsterdam: Elsevier Science Publishers.

Stein, Leonard I. and Mary Ann Test. 1980. "Alternative to Mental Hospital

Treatment, I: Conceptual Model, Treatment Program, and Clinical Evaluation." *Archives of General Psychiatry* 37:392–97.

Surber, Robert W., Martha Shumway, Richard Shadoan, and William A. Hargreaves. 1986. "Effects of Fiscal Retrenchment on Public Mental Health Services for the Chronic Mentally Ill." *Community Mental Health Journal* 22:215–28.

Test, Mary Ann. 1981. "Effective Treatment of the Chronically Mentally Ill: What Is Necessary?" *Journal of Social Issues* 37:71–86.

———. 1984. "Community Support Programs." Pp. 347–73 in *Schizophrenia: Treatment, Management, and Rehabilitation,* edited by A. S. Bellack. New York: Grune and Stratton.

———. 1990. "The Training in Community Living Model: Delivering Treatment and Rehabilitation Services through a Continuous Treatment Team." Pp. 153–70 in *Rehabilitation of the Seriously Mentally Ill,* edited by R. P. Liberman. Oxford: Pergamon Press.

Test, Mary Ann and Leonard I. Stein. 1978. "The Clinical Rationale for Community Treatment: A Review of the Literature." Pp. 3–22 in *Alternatives to Mental Hospital Treatment,* edited by L. I. Stein and M. A. Test. New York: Plenum.

———. 1980. "Alternative to Mental Hospital Treatment, III: Social Cost." *Archives of General Psychiatry* 37:409–12.

Torrey, E. Fuller. 1988. *Nowhere to Go: The Tragic Odyssey of the Homeless Mentally Ill.* New York: Harper and Row.

Torrey, E. Fuller, and Sidney M. Wolfe. 1986. *Care of the Seriously Mentally Ill, 1986.* Washington, DC: Public Citizen Health Research Group.

———. 1988. *Care of the Seriously Mentally Ill, 1988.* Washington, DC: Public Citizen Health Research Group.

———. 1990. *Care of the Seriously Mentally Ill, 1990.* Washington, DC: Public Citizen Health Research Group.

Weisbrod, Burton, Mary Ann Test, and Leonard Stein. 1980. "Alternative to Mental Hospital Treatment: II. Economic Benefit-Cost Analysis." *Archives of General Psychiatry* 37:400–5.

Wolff, Nancy and Ronald J. Diamond. 1990. "The Cost of Patients in Assertive Case Management." Paper presented to American Psychiatric Association, May 15, New York.

Chapter 7

Community Mental Health Services for the Continuing-Care Client

SHULAMIT RAMON

INTRODUCTION

This paper, providing both an overview and a critique of the system of care for clients with persistent mental illness, begins with defining and estimating the client population, an essential aspect for evaluating and analyzing services. The diversity among continuing-care clients has important implications for the nature of appropriate services.[1] The analysis then turns to the legislative and political environment for providing for continuing-care clients, in which the shift to community-based services rather than hospital services is highlighted, as well as some of the ambiguities surrounding revision and implementation of care policies. The existing services are presented in the third section of this analysis. They are very much shaped by the legislative and political environment as well as, but to a lesser extent, the characteristics of clients. The best characterization of the system is that although it may appear comprehensive and coordinated, in many places some of the crucial elements are missing. The final section of the paper turns to the prospects for realizing a more satisfactory care system, assessing both the reasons for optimism and the barriers preventing such a system from developing fully.

I. THE CLIENT GROUP

A. Size and Definitions

It is impossible to suggest a precise number of people coming under the category of the continuing-care client in mental health. The difficulties arise in part from the imprecision in the definition of either chronicity or continuing care, and in part due to lack of relevant national statistics in Britain. Wing and Furlong have defined the client group as "mentally disordered adults, in addition to those with mental handicap and dementia, who are highly dependent on others and have a high all-round need for care which hitherto has been equated with a need for long term residence in hospital" (1986:449). While factually correct, this definition does not pay attention to nonillness factors, which are likely to contribute to the degree of dependency, such as the impact of long-term segregation and the consistent lack of comprehensive alternatives to hospitalization. Furthermore, there is nothing in the definition to direct us to look at the abilities of these people and hence at their differentiated need for care, rather than at the "high all-round need for care." The definition does not take account of the likelihood that a number of people in this category have suffered in the past from mental illness but do not necessarily suffer from it at present, yet nevertheless need continuing care as a preventive measure.

Existing statistics provide information on hospital admissions, focused on the total number of admissions, whether these were first admissions or readmissions, age, sex, diagnostic categories, duration, and whether people have been admitted as day cases, ward cases, or received outpatient services in the hospital. No national statistics are published on those attending mental health services in the community. There are several district case registers that offer partial information.

Studies on the use of family practitioners for mental health consultations indicate that about 140 new people per thousand in a given year have psychiatric symptoms, though only 17 will become users of the psychiatric services (Goldberg and Huxley 1980). Therefore, the number of new people within the category of the continuing-care client would be somewhere between 140 and 17 per thousand, leaving us with a rather unsatisfactory information basis from which to structure a service system.

To complicate matters even further, as of 1987 the Department of Health (DoH) is not providing the number of people who were hospitalized, but only the number of admissions, leaving it to us to guess how many people there actually were in our hospitals.

The following calculation of the number of continuing-care clients of mental health is therefore not more than a guess, based on the assumption that being admitted once does not constitute a state of continuing-care need, even though epidemiological studies have demonstrated that the likelihood of readmission after the first admission is much higher than before. In 1986, the last year for which the average number of people was calculated, there were 61,500 people in hospital in England and Wales, with 197,251 admissions, of which 51,673 were first admissions [Department of Health and Social Services, (DHSS) 1990]. By calculating the percentage of repeated admissions it would appear that 75% of the people admitted were in need of continuing care. Out of these we can subtract all of those admitted for one year or more, no more than 4%, as likely to remain in hospital and therefore not be making use of community service. This would bring us to the figure of roughly 43,000 people who have been in hospital during that year but left it and who most definitely would be in need of community service. To this figure we may add the estimated 100,000 long-term ex-patients now resettled in the community (Groves 1990b).

The Salford case register has indicated that out of a general population of 50,000 people, 200 known to the health services were living in the community and in need of long-term care related to mental illness, whereas the figure for Camberwell was 400 (Goldberg and Huxley 1980). The Salford register has also demonstrated an increase in the number of people treated in the community and a decrease in the number of inpatients during the ten-year period 1968–1978 (Wooff, Freeman, and Fryers 1983). The increase (from a ratio of 9.52 to 13.44 per thousand) is attributed to the introduction of two community services: the injection-only nurse contact and the community psychiatric nurse domiciliary contact. A recent survey in Nottingham has listed 1,740 such people known to the services out of a population of 600,000 (J. Cohen, Nottingham Social Services, personal communication, October 1990). Differences in figures per area need to be related to levels of social deprivation and service availability, both of which influence the likelihood of having a recognized need for long-term care.

If anything, the number of people in need of continuing care has increased since 1978, with the beginning of the closure of psychiatric hospitals from the mideighties. According to the National Schizophrenia Fellowship (NSF information cited in Groves 1990b), 30 psychiatric hospitals have closed down between 1980 and 1989, and another 38 are due to close by 1995. This would result first in a reduction of the estimated current bed numbers from 64,000 to 47,000 (NSF information, cited in Groves 1990b). That these figures would not be published or confirmed by the DoH is an intriguing point. Second, more of the people currently staying in hospital for a year or more will be living in the community, even though many of them would be living in sheltered accommodation. Third, fewer of those currently readmitted frequently for short periods will be hospitalized, raising the issue of the need for alternative asylum and refuge facilities.

B. Characteristics of the Inpatient Population

To judge from the available information, we are aware that there are more women in this client group, more people over 75 and 65 than in other age groups, yet also more people in the age group between 25 and 44 than either below 25 or between 44 and 65. The age division, accompanied by observations in community services, has led to the conclusion that there are two major groupings within this client group: the *old long stay*, who are now coming out of hospital plus people who suffer from dementia on the one hand, and the *new long stay*, namely, the younger group of people who have relatively short, yet repeated hospital stays.

Concerning diagnostic categories, depressive disorders and schizophrenia top the list, each with roughly 26,000 such admissions, followed by affective psychoses with 22,000. If the two categories related to depression are put together—as affective psychoses are likely to include a large proportion of depressive psychoses—they would outnumber considerably the category of schizophrenia. No breakdown of diagnostic classification is available by age, though this could have been helpful in understanding the nature of the psychiatric disturbance of the older vs. the younger group. However, the number of admissions because of dementia is available, and this usually applies to the older age group: 20,858 such admissions took place in 1986, of which 6,239 were first admissions. Between 1976 and 1986 the number of readmissions for dementia has more than doubled (from 5,000 in 1976 to 14,000 in 1986) while the number of first admissions remained very similar (5,207 and 6,239, respectively). Are they readmitted due to their deteriorated state? Due to lack of alternative solutions? Due to the inability of community services to meet their needs without hospitalization? Due to lack of support in the community to their informal carers? Is the psychiatric hospital a suitable place for people with dementia? These are some of the issues that this paper cannot tackle, but that require consideration.

Personality and behavior disorder is a classification rarely attached to people above 40, and thus offers an interesting comparison with the older group. Between 1976 and 1986 there was a decrease in the number of readmissions related to this category, from 13,234 to 9,812 respectively, while a smaller reduction took place in first admissions (from 5,333 to 4,386).

On the whole it would therefore appear that the younger group is kept in the community, as the number of first admissions and readmissions for people in the age group 25–44 has gone down between 1976 and 1986, while that for people above 65 has gone up.

The psychiatric symptomatology of the younger group and its family ties differ from those of many of the nondementia group of older clients.

The younger group shows more florid symptomatology, is more vocal, less overtly depressed, more aggressive, assertive, and tends to retain family ties. Hence this group is more likely to be perceived as a burden and a threat to informal carers, and perhaps to the person on the street, than the older group.

In terms of ethnic composition, proportionally more Irish people are hospitalized than people from other ethnic groups, followed by white British-born working-class people, with West Indians coming third on the list (Cochrane 1983). A disproportionate number (in relation to their proportion in the general population) of young black men are hospitalized, often at the request of the police (without committing an offense) and kept under a compulsory admission order. This has led to concern as to the racist element in the judgment of the police and of mental health professionals (Barnes, Bowl, and Fisher 1990).

C. Nonpsychiatric Characteristics of the Client Group

A recent survey of 500 people who use the services of Mind (the largest voluntary mental health organization, described below) indicates that they are primarily poor people living on meager government benefits, mostly men, who have been ill for more than 10 years, have neither held a job nor been in unpaid employment for a long time, often without any other activity than those on offer in the day center that some of them attend, without close contacts with their families of origin, unmarried, without children, living in sheltered accommodation due to lack of choice, without a hobby, hardly going out (to see a film, to a football match, to a restaurant, to visit a friend; Rogers and Pilgrim 1990). Some have a small number of friends, often other people who have suffered from mental illness. Most of them do not exhibit overt symptomatology, but look and act as depressed, listless, people. An earlier survey (Goldie 1988) that interviewed 50 people five years after discharge from a long spell in a psychiatric hospital found even greater isolation, but no wish to return to the hospital. Often service providers were the only people to knock on the ex-patients' doors.

A more recent participant-observer study of people who left two psychiatric hospitals after a long period of hospitalization has found that most of them preferred living in the small group home to which they were allocated than to remain in the hospital. When asked informally they cited privacy, choice, greater contact with family members, and greater everyday stimulation as the reasons (McCourt-Perring 1993). Tellingly, their reminiscences about the past skipped through the long period spent in hospital, going back to their childhood, adolescence, young adulthood, and their interpretation of the reasons for entering hospital in the first place. There was a strong sense of a life unlived in hospital, of people capable of describing in details that life when specifically asked, but choosing not to when possible. None of them expressed the wish to go back for a visit, to invite people from the hospital to their new residence; yet they were clearly touched when a nurse from the hospital came to visit them. Alas, she was the only staff member who has chosen to do so.

The differences in living conditions, level of social interaction, and satisfaction are explained in part by the differences in the way the resettlement of the various subgroups of clients has taken place, which will be outlined below.

D. The Life-Style of Different Subgroups

1. The Resettled "Old Long Stay." We have much more information on those defined as the *old long stay*, who are the target of the resettlement programs in operation since 1984, as part of the government's attempt to close large psychiatric hospitals. Only they are eligible for the new and better financed schemes, which will be mentioned below.

Considerable time and thought have gone into assessing the needs of this group, an area investigated in particular by the team for the assessment of psychiatric services based at the Maudsley, Friern, and Claybury hospitals (TAPS 1989). The minority among the professionals interested in particular in getting a sense of the patients as people with a preillness history and abilities opted for the "getting to know you" methodology adopted from the field of learning difficulties and the normalization approach (Brost and Johnson 1982).

Furthermore, it is mostly they who have been moved out in small groups rather than one by one, following a more concerted effort of preparation at the institutional level. The degree of choice in the move to the group homes was rather limited, as they were not presented with alternatives and were told that it was unclear when other choices would become available. This reflects the underlying belief that they would be unable to make a reasonable choice, as well as the wish to act according to administrative convenience. Yet this process represents also the narrowness of the preparation and the readiness to miss a golden opportunity of training people to make real choices and decisions, even though such an opportunity could have implied a longer and messy process. The new group homes offer a much more pleasant physical environment than the hospital wards. Although most of the self-care is carried out by the residents, not much is asked in terms of sharing the household duties. Residents are expected to comply with the house regulations, to attend day centers, and at times go to medical appointments. It would be fair to describe the routine in the homes as that of benevolent parenthood, even though the parents are 30–40 years younger than the children. Attempts not to follow the routine are usually interpreted as signs of pathology, and medication taking is strictly adhered to.

Overall, for a population of 357 such residents monitored over three years there is no deterioration in terms of psychiatric symptomatology coupled with a slight improvement in self-care and social behavior (Dayson 1990). The contacts with the ordinary community are usually either extremely superficial or nonexistent, with the exceptions of those who have rebuilt their family contacts since leaving hospital. This is in part due to the policy of keeping as low a profile as possible in fear of rejection and creating trouble; in part due to lack of contact between people in a formal residential establishment and those living in ordinary accommodation; and in part reflecting on the isolation of older people in Britain if they are new to an area or have no close ties with either groups or individuals in the community.

It is important to remember that this group constitutes only 4% of all hospital residents.

2. Older People Living in the Community. Many of these people who have not come out of the hospitals in the last five years are likely to live on their own, in adult foster schemes, and in warden sheltered flats, or be homeless.

Most of those living with others are likely to attend day centers. There is great reluctance in ordinary services for older people to allow people with mental illness in, on grounds of unsuitability and/or of being unwanted by other service users. In a large multidisability day center that I have recently visited, where most of the users are elderly people, those with mental illness have a separate unit. This enables them to join in the activities of the whole day center while having their own space. It is difficult to tell how many of the elderly clients with physical disability suffer also from long-term depression, which is usually untreated. Yet on average the people with long-term mental health problems were considerably younger than those in other components of the center, raising the issue of the usefulness and risk in making them socialize in an inappropriate age group.

Older people with dementia still in the community are more likely to live with their spouse or adult children.

3. The Young New Long Stay. When living in the community, people in this subgroup are likely to be living either with their parents, or in hostels, in therapeutic communities, in sheltered flats, in adult foster schemes, or among the homeless. As a rule of thumb, the more middle-

class they are the more likely they are to be in a therapeutic community, in a sheltered flat, or at home. Although offered places in day hospitals and later in day centers, many of them are likely to decline such possibilities in favor of more vocationally oriented centers, or just stay at home. Some may return to education and training, but not many. The level of compliance with prescribed medication frequently drops off with this subgroup; the once per month appointment with the consultant does not seem to offer much of a bolster. Service users argue that they are not offered a frank discussion on medication at the point of leaving or on the process of gradual and very lengthy withdrawal from the use of drugs. The risk of drifting into drug and alcohol abuse is more prominent in this subgroup than in others.

The task of resuming one's life after a long spell in a psychiatric hospital while continuing to take a not inconsiderable dosage of medication is largely left to that individual and his or her network and resources. Some may be helped by a social worker or a psychotherapist, and those living in collective accommodation may be helped by the new group and its regime. Elsewhere I have argued that professionals tend to underestimate the enormity of the task in terms of self-presentation and the presentation of oneself to the world, and/or to write off the possibility of this client group leading an ordinary life in the future (Ramon 1990).

4. The Older New Long Stay.   People above 35 are included in this grouping. There are fewer collective solutions for this subgroup, though most of the solutions cited above for the younger group would be available to this group too. There is certainly a greater sense of despondency in relation to this group, though this varies from one individual to the other and from one service provider to the other. In both groups people may have to wait for a place in any of these settings for some time, may have to go through the experience of being rejected by some schemes, and may feel forced to opt for the least desirable solutions from their point of view.

II. THE LEGISLATIVE AND POLITICAL CONTEXT

Services for the continuing-care client are influenced by all welfare legislation, which is not going to be looked at in this paper. References to eligibility for financial benefits and housing are made below in the section on universal services.

Two acts will be singled out for discussion here, as they are the most specific and central in their impact on services for this client group, namely the 1983 Mental Health Act and the 1990 National Health Service (NHS) and Community Care Act.

The 1983 Mental Health Act is an amendment of the 1959 Mental Health Act. It deals mainly with the arrangements for compulsory admission and discharge from such an admission. As such, it focuses on 5% of the inpatient population, or on less then 1% of the total population seeking psychiatric consultation. However, many people in the continuing-client group have been thus admitted to psychiatric hospitals. Presently, there is a need for a thorough assessment by both a psychiatrist and a social worker prior to any compulsory admission, though there are instances when a person is brought to hospital first or to a police cell before an assessment has taken place. The social worker's brief is to look for the least restrictive environment in which the person can be safe and receive appropriate treatment. Given the lack of asylum placements outside hospitals, the social worker will have no alternative but to agree to hospitalization when there is a risk of harm to the person and to others, and the person refuses to go in on a voluntary basis.

There are clear rules as to the length of time of such admissions, depending on whether they are for observation or treatment. Yet it is easy to change the status of an admission from being voluntary to being compulsory, as well as the length of stay (by changing the section under which the person is detained). There is an appeal procedure open to patients once every six months; the rate of success for appeals has been constant at 12% since their inception in 1961 (Gostin 1976; Peay 1989).

The major innovations in the 1983 legislation have been the introduction of a mandatory right to services in the community for discharged people and the right to a second professional opinion in the case of intervention deemed as potentially having irreversible effects. However, the first right does not specify the type of services that need to be provided, and the government has not developed a set of regulations to provide such a specification, the quality control assurances that need to go with it, or the sanctions to be used in the case of noncompliance by local authorities and health services. In the absence of a binding British constitution, unless a legal case is presented in the European Court, the British government, local authorities, and health authorities cannot be held responsible in law for lack of adequate services.

The second right has been put into effect in relation to hormonal therapy only; the debate on ECT (electroconvulsive treatment) has been deadlocked and left unresolved for the last three years. No such debate is taking place in the Mental Health Act Commission (the body that recommends to the minister of health on the application of the law) on major tranquilizers, even though users groups are adamant in their view of the damage created by the overuse of these drugs. A proposal to include laypeople in such a decision was strongly objected to by the Royal College of Psychiatrists in 1979 and taken out of the proposed legislation.

The 1990 NHS and Community Care Act was hastily passed through parliament only for its community care component to be delayed in implementation, primarily for financial reasons. However, the only client group for whom the full legislation is to be applied from April 1991 are people with long-term mental illness. This decision highlights the political sensitivity concerning this client group and is primarily due to pressure from relatives of people with schizophrenia and allied psychiatrists. The NHS component of the act is to be implemented also from that date, leading to a number of major changes in the way the NHS is to be funded and structured. These include the allocation of budgets and budgetary responsibilities to family doctors (general practitioners, GPs), hospitals becoming independent trusts within the NHS, and health districts having to divide into service-purchasing and -providing sections, both with balanced budgets annually.

The main features of the community care element of the act include the following:

- The overall responsibility for services in the community for people with long-term disabilities will be with the local authorities. This is not to be interpreted as their becoming the major service providers, but as having the planning and overseeing responsibility primarily.
- People with long-term disabilities will have the right to be assessed by professionals. People in institutions will not be discharged without a care package agreed on between the health and local authority.
- A system of case management will be introduced, in which the case manager will take the overall responsibility for the assessment and the implementation of the care plan, though not necessarily for direct service delivery.
- Local authorities will receive a specific grant earmarked to develop new services in the community for the continuing-care client group in mental health.

All of these features represent a radical shift within the British context from previous traditions of structuring services for this client group. It remains to be seen how the act will be in fact interpreted and implemented, the level of resources committed to its implementation, the response from professionals, the public, the users, and the carers.

A. The Politicians' Perspective

Among politicians mental illness currently has a higher profile than in the past (Ramon 1985). This is primarily due to the impact of two contradictory factors. For its own financially motivated reasons, the Conservative government came to the conclusion in the early 1980s that most psychiatric hospitals should close down. Existing American and European evidence on the quality of life and costs for the continuing-care clients in the community suggests that they will not be worse off outside the hospital, provided a gradual process takes place and alternative services are established (Test and Stein 1980; Mosher and Burti 1989; Ramon 1988). Thus the government's view was based on professional opinions, too. However, a number of eminent British psychiatrists and many of the relatives of people diagnosed as suffering from schizophrenia strongly objected to the adoption of this policy, inferring from the North American and Italian experiences that such a direction could only fail. This lobbying alliance has been successful in convincing politicians that unless they pay attention to ensuring the containment of the continuing-care client, drastic aggression and neglect will follow.

The current government, like all previous governments, did not have plans of its own as to the desirable structure and content of the mental health system. Instead, successive governments have relied heavily on professionals for ideas, and traditionally have been more ready to accept psychiatrists' ideas than those coming from other disciplines, let alone users. This has been one of the main reasons for the lack of development of a comprehensive community mental health service in Britain. However, as the Conservative government of the 1980s prided itself on being radical it took a more sanguine approach to the dominance of professionals, including doctors, promoting managers and a managerial approach throughout the welfare system.

This checkered scene of contradictory influences explains some of the ambiguity toward its own policy which the government has demonstrated since 1982. It has financed a relatively large number of demonstration projects in this field and their evaluation, but it has not really moved firmly to establish nationwide services in the community, even though the projects were largely successful in achieving their objectives and were modest in costs (Cambridge and Knapp 1988).

The concession in the NHS and Community Care Act that no one would be discharged without an agreed package of care illustrates the ambivalent commitment to community services. Nowhere is it mandatory to *implement* an agreed-upon care plan—it remains obligatory only to plan.

The overall cut in welfare expenditure that has been another hallmark of the present British central government has also had an impact on what is available in terms of meeting basic needs for income and housing for the client group under discussion in this text.

The government's preference for nonstatutory services has led to an initial expansion of the voluntary (not-for-profit) sector, and a much smaller expansion of the commercial sector. Both are now at risk of contraction if resources previously channeled to them were not earmarked.

The mental health system continues to be an unattractive political objective; efficient junior ministers are moved very soon from this brief as a reward, giving the impression that staying with the brief does not count as a positive step in one's political career.

III. EXISTING SERVICES

A. Overview of Services

Universal services that also offer a service to this client group include the family doctor, general hospitals, and libraries. For the time being, clients do not have to pay at the point of receiving a service.

Up to one-fifth of family doctor firms employ a consultant psychiatrist on a sessional basis (Strathdee and Williams 1984). A smaller number also have social workers, even though there is evidence to demonstrate that the involvement of social workers is not only welcomed by the clients but helps to reduce the burden on the doctor for people with mental health problems (Clare and Corney 1984). Some social workers are employed by the Local Authority (the largest employers of social workers), others by voluntary organizations (e.g., the Family Service Unit and the Family Welfare Association). I know of only one firm that employs its own social worker. However, with the introduction of family practitioner budgets, those firms wanting to have social workers but unable to get them from overstretched local authorities could easily become the direct employers, should they wish to do so. Some GP firms (mainly in London) now employ counselors coming from a variety of disciplinary backgrounds, who primarily use the cognitive-analytic therapy (CAT) method.

Following the 1990 NHS and Community Care Act, GPs could become the case managers, i.e., care coordinators, of people with long-term disabilities, including mental illness. However, doctors are unwilling to undertake such a task, and all other professions doubt their ability to carry it out adequately should they undertake it.

GPs vary considerably in their readiness to provide the necessary attention and care to people with long-term mental health problems. It is their decision whether to take on a client, or a group of clients. GPs also participate in the process of compulsory admission, in which they can be the initiators and among the main participants. As a rule, they are difficult to get hold of and engage for long.

All people with a proven disability judged as unemployable are entitled to financial benefits, and some of their carers are also entitled to a
carer's allowance (weekly basic benefits are about £40; carers allowance
is about £25). In principle, people with a long-term disability have the
right to decent housing. However, the increasing shortage in Local Authorities housing stock and cuts in their maintenance budget imply that
priority is given over any other group to families with young children.
As many continuing-care clients require supported housing rather than
an ordinary accommodation, specialized solutions are needed. These
may include core and cluster services (warden-supervised flats around a
day center or without a day center), group homes, adult foster placement, or a small residential-cum–nursing home setting. The cost of
sheltered accommodation (which is paid currently by the Department of
Social Security for people without incomes) varies considerably, from
£40 to £200 per week (1987 figures). Inevitably, the degree of individual
choice is limited and waiting for these solutions to materialize may take a
long time. Some hostels exist, providing temporary solutions of varied
length.

More selective services, even though statutory, are offered by the
Local Authorities' social services departments, which may provide home
aides, social work contacts, day centers, group homes, community mental health centers, and some employment projects. Social workers act as
gatekeepers in a number of instances, such as when compulsory admission and guardianship are considered; and also in sorting out welfare
rights, financial benefits, accommodation, and day centers, and in recommending home help service. They may also offer counseling. With
the exception of carrying out legal duties as laid out in the 1983 Mental
Health Act, all Local Authority services are in much shorter supply now
then they were at the beginning of the 1980s, due to the change in the
position taken by central government toward any aspect of the welfare
state. At the same time, since the late 1980s, there are more specialist
mental health services in social services departments, resulting from the
reorganization of these departments into services that focus on client
groups and perhaps also from to the ripple effect of hospital closure and
joint financing with health authorities.

According to the NHS and Community Care Act of 1990, Local Authorities should be taking the lead role in ensuring services for people
with disabilities, yet to do so primarily through *purchasing and inspecting*
services, rather than continuing to be service providers as they are
presently.

Specialist health services include psychiatric consultation often in an
outpatient clinic either in general hospitals or psychiatric hospitals, and
more recently in mental health centers, primarily run by the health

district. Day hospitals exist too (though the number of places is decreasing after an increase during the 1970s), or people may use the hospitals' rehabilitation facilities after discharge.

A district-based community psychiatric nurse (CPN) service exists as well, which may offer depo-clinic appointments, home visits, and some counseling.

With the recent planned closure of psychiatric hospitals some health authorities have established their own group homes and/or established nonprofit organizations responsible for sheltered housing. Short admissions for psychiatric reasons take place in either small psychiatric wards in general hospitals or in psychiatric hospitals. The plan is that the wards in the general hospital will replace all acute beds currently located in the psychiatric hospital. There are virtually no nonhospital asylum facilities, with the interesting exception of two facilities (Brindle House in Thameside, Cheshire, which successfully combines a mental health center with a number of beds in a house in the community, and a refuge flat in Basetlaw district general hospital).

A number of voluntary (not-for-profit) organizations offer a range of services to this client group, usually either in the form of sheltered accommodation or a day center, or both, and some also run employment initiatives. The two largest nonprofit organizations in mental health— Mind and the NSF—differ considerably in focus and in constituency. Mind—the National Mental Health Association—originated in 1946 as an umbrella organization of all mental health nonprofit groups, with a view to campaigning for a better deal for people with mental health problems. It has local branches that are autonomous from the national office, as it is up to each association to decide whether it wishes to be affiliated at the national level and to decide on its local policy and services. Most of the services on the ground are offered by the local branches. The national office is more into campaigning, legal representation, acting as a pressure group, and initiating pilot projects. Mind has a bimonthly journal and a long list of short, popular publications, and recently has developed Mindlink, a network of users coordinated by a worker who is herself an ex-user of the psychiatric services. The current vice-chairperson of Mind (an elected post) is a user, too.

Members of Mind are usually middle-class people with an interest in mental health, often due to personal encounters with people who have suffered from mental illness. Service coordinators are usually professionals (social workers, occupational therapists, nurses), whereas the rank-and-file workers are often unqualified. Branch members may often offer support by voluntary work in the different facilities, in fund-raising, and in administration.

Mind's underlying philosophy concerning mental illness is that it is a multifaceted illness, with more than one etiological base, and that most people who suffer from it require a comprehensive psychosocial and medical approach. Mind has concentrated on the social, legal, and political issues in particular. The NSF is largely an organization of relatives, which started 20 years ago. It also has a section of people diagnosed as suffering from schizophrenia. It has 6,000 members and 150 local groups. Its underlying philosophy is that schizophrenia is a physical disease, from which very few people recover, though with adequate medical treatment and psychosocial support many of them can lead an ordinary life for long periods. Like Mind, it has local, but less autonomous branches and a national directorate that carries the campaigning mantle. Local branches differ considerably in their views and activities. The more active ones are now into establishing and managing group homes and day activities, besides the more traditional relatives' and sufferers' groups. The national office organizes training events, short publications, and lobbying. With the accelerating process of hospital closures, the NSF has become a prominent lobby group first against the closure and second for legislation that requires assessment and a care plan to be agreed upon before people leave hospital. The NSF has the active support of psychiatrists opposing the closure. Although the NSF has highlighted the difficulties faced by informal carers if community services do not operate properly, it has not come up with an alternative plan for a comprehensive service, as Mind did in the early 1980s.

In all, at present the private for-profit sector is active in housing provision for people with long-term mental illness, but hardly at all in other components of the service system. Though in 1987 its share in housing provision was only 6.5 per 100,000 of the adult population, in terms of the places available, it now offers more places than the voluntary sector. A number of these homes are run by ex-employees of the health service, mainly nurses. The other main activity of this sector lies in establishing hospitals for people in need of a secure, closed facility (e.g., St. Andrews Hospital in Northampton). Both the housing provision and the secure hospitals are largely financed by the statutory public sector, which covers the cost of places for clients who are hard to place.

Although the existing service structure may look comprehensive, in many places some of the crucial elements are missing. The developments in relation to community mental health centers illustrate this point. Unlike the United States, such centers were not developed in Britain before the 1980s. Even as late as 1987 the official DoH line was not to have a policy concerning their desirability, but to let each district and each Local Authority decide whether to have such centers. Yet from 20 centers in 1984, the figure has jumped to 80 in 1987, and 146 in 1990 (Sayce 1989). However, even 146 centers in a country the size of Britain

(56 million citizens) do not offer that much, if the intention is to have these centers as the backbone of the mental health services.

Moreover, as has been observed in the United States, the natural-drift direction has been to offer services for people with neurotic symptoms, followed by some crisis work with people in acute psychotic episodes, and only lastly to attempt to offer a service for people with long-term mental health difficulties (Patmore and Weaver 1991). The unattractiveness of this client group for the professionals needs to be acknowledged and dealt with as effectively as possible if community mental health centers are to offer them effective service.

To complicate matters even further, there are several types of mental health centers. Centers that are part of a Local Authority are likely to employ only social workers, and offer individual and group counseling and social work service, often with a drop-in facility, and more recently with a day activity component. Centers run by health authorities are multidisciplinary, usually headed by a psychiatrist who works there on a sessional basis, as may the psychologist too, with nurses as the largest staff group, and at times with social workers attached too. These centers are unlikely to offer drop-in and day activities, but are likely to offer individual appointments for medication control, counseling, and scheduled group activities.

Some centers have been established to offer principally a service to people about to leave the hospital after a long period there. Staff members are involved in assessing and preparing residents to move out of the hospital, in deciding who will go to which group home, and in continuing to offer support to this subclient group. Yet I have personally witnessed the pressure put on one such center by the management to offer a more generic service even before the center became fully operational.

Furthermore, the likelihood of having a Local Authority social worker go beyond the stage of sorting out a specific short-term difficulty in areas such as financial benefits, housing, and compulsory admission is low, as long as most social services area teamwork is focused on child protection. For the time being, people in hospital have a greater chance of having a social worker than those who live in the community.

The number of CPNs is extremely small, and consequently teams are often unable to offer more than a skeleton service. There is some evidence to indicate that CPNs prefer to provide counseling rather than the more traditional forms of nursing, even though many of them lack adequate training in counseling (Wooff and Goldberg 1988). For the time being most CPNs work independently of mental health centers; this provides a fertile ground for conflict and overlap between the CPN service and that of the mental health center.

It is a matter of luck, geography, and personal attraction whether a person will get the benefit of a wide range of service or only the minimal level of provisions.

It is assumed that a number of clients in this group would not attend any service in the community on a voluntary basis. It is impossible to quantify the size of this subgroup, which includes both younger and older people, more men than women, more people from ethnic minorities than from the British white majority, more poorer and less well educated people, more of those isolated than those in contact with their families. In short, the group most in need of continuing care is the one less likely to seek it, less likely to be given care, and more likely to be unearthed at the point of severe deterioration and crisis.

Yet there are very few outreach services and liaison between voluntary services for homeless people and the statutory mental health services, even though it is estimated that one-third to one-half of all homeless people suffer from long-term mental distress. It is also relevant to note that the few existing outreach services do not form an integral part of a more comprehensive service, but function administratively and professionally on their own, staffed mainly with nurses.

For a variety of reasons, very little work is carried out with relatives, some of whom are informal carers. In fact, one of the reasons is that many of the people in this client group not only do not live with their relatives but have lost touch with them. Another reason is the lack of professional workers able and willing to take on this work when it would be most useful to do so, namely at the early stages of a psychotic breakdown, before the person has become a continuing-care client.

B. Methods of Work

So far in the description of available services reference has not been made to methods of work. It would be fair to state that medication tops the list of methods, followed by practical support in meeting basic needs (income, housing). Day activity, some forms of counseling, behavioral programs, psychotherapy, and employment projects follow with considerably reduced frequency and range. When asked for their views, users were particularly unhappy about day programs, which they found uninteresting and irrelevant to their lives (Mangen 1988). The more vocal users are also unhappy with the overreliance on medication, as opposed to the use of electroconvulsive treatment (ECT), and feel patronized by service providers in general. The need for employment initiatives on the one hand and counseling on the other hand is also expressed by the younger group of users, yet these are the services in very short supply. Although the efficacy of behavioral methods in self-care skills and coping strategies has been demonstrated (Hudson 1982), programs following these methods are also not available across the services. The reasons for these gaps have to do in part with the use of medication as an expediency, the belief in the disease model for severe mental illness, and above all the lack of adequate training of the professional and semi-professional service providers.

C. Service Providers

Given the degree and pace of change during the last decade in the British mental health services, it is important to take account of how the service providers have reacted to and have fared in this process. Only a brief outline of this issue will be attempted in this paper, due to space limitation.

Workers were alarmed by the prospect of closure, in particular psychiatrists and nurses. Decisions as to which hospital to close were taken without consultation with the workers or their representatives. Although future plans were formally discussed at various levels of the hierarchy, no attempt was made to involve workers in the planning process. Contrary to all of our knowledge concerning the importance of involvement of the direct participants in an innovative change process, the policymakers seem to have assumed that the work force will comply and that the process requires no more than compliance. The likelihood of intentional and unintentional sabotage was not even contemplated, and administrators seemed genuinely surprised to discover how angry workers were. Although initially there were plans to shed workers due to closure, the administration accepted a no-redundancy policy of permanent staff. This implies that workers apply for posts within the district to which they are attached and are interviewed like everyone else, but that the district ultimately has to find them a post should the hospital close before they have found one for themselves.

Contrary to expectations, only a small group of nurses has opted to move into private for-profit care; most hospital nurses are still working in the hospital sector, even though the hospital for which they initially worked has been closed. Those working in the community are on the whole nurses who chose not to work in the hospital some time ago.

Psychiatrists, psychologists, and social workers are not threatened with loss of job due to closure, as there is demand for them in the community. However, psychiatrists are heading the lobby that opposes the closure, even though relatives are made to appear as the spearhead of this lobby.

We have yet to see in Britain a reevaluation of professional activity, conceptualization, skills, and values in the light of the changes in the system. It is as if the professionals believe that only the location of their activity is changing, but not its focus or direction.

Although there are some studies on the work load of nurses working in hospital in comparison to those working in the community, no research on the professional response to the change process exists, apart from my own research of three social work teams in a hospital due for closure (Ramon 1992). The professional response is not seen as worthy of research.

There is now a considerable increase in the number of unqualified workers, concentrated in the residential sector of the mental health system. We lack information on the numbers involved, their background, the type of in-service training and supervision that they are receiving, the degree of satisfaction, and the quality of service that they provide. It is too early to assess their impact on the professional work force, but there is no doubt that in the current economic climate employers prefer to pay as little as possible and to have a compliant work force.

D. Cost

The British health service spends £2 billion per year on its psychiatric services; two-thirds of which goes into the hospital sector, despite the declining numbers of inpatients and the decrease in length of hospitalization in the last decade. This is explained as due to the bad state of the Victorian-era buildings and the lack of reduction in unit costs unless a whole unit, or ward, is closed (e.g., staffing levels have to be maintained even if the number of people is reduced). Traditionally much less has been spent on psychiatric hospitals than on general hospitals, even on items such as catering (Ramon, 1985).

The Local Authorities spent in 1987 only £42 million on mental health services, or 2% of their social services budget (Mahoney 1988). The new specific grant to be given to Local Authorities in the 1988 fiscal year as part of the implementation of the NHS and Community Care Act amounted to £30 million, though it is to increase up to £100 million by 1993. The grant is aimed at developing new services in the community; with each Local Authority receiving about £100,000 in 1991 it is difficult to envisage that viable new services will be established.

Previously, new services in the public sector were developed through mechanisms of either joint financing between health and social services, or by each of these services separately. Voluntary organizations applied for funding to the statutory sector and to charitable trusts. The resettlement of old-long-stay residents from the psychiatric hospital is financed through a dowry system, in which each of them is allocated between £12,000 and £20,000, which is given to the authority undertaking the responsibility for their care in the community. Recently the government announced the establishment of a bridging loans fund, to enable health authorities to complete the closure and resettlement process, when it became clear that a number of them were unable to do so for financial reasons. It is unclear whether this fund is merely a loan on future alloca-tion of resources to these authorities, or a one-time grant.

It is only in the last five years that comprehensive calculations of the cost of enabling continuing-care clients to live in the community have been attempted in a systematic way in Britain. The main impetus to do so seems to have come with the closure of psychiatric (and mental hand-icap) hospitals, when the DoH had to justify its policy.

The Kent Personal Social Services Research Unit (PSSRU) has carried out a considerable part of this pioneering work in the United Kingdom with successive cohorts of long-stay patients leaving the psychiatric hos-pital (Knapp and Beecham 1990). The following items have been in-cluded in the costing: accommodation and living expenses, hospital outpatient, hospital day patient, other day care, education services, po-lice, general practitioners, injections, nursing services, psychiatrist, so-cial worker, other professionals, travel, volunteer inputs, hospital inpatient stays.

The overall cost of living in the community with considerable support has been £271 per week in 1987 prices, compared to £354 for those remaining in hospital. The variations in costs for the first group run between a minimum of £47 and a maximum of £568; while those for the second group run between £119 and £882. The most expensive item in community living is accommodation and living expenses, followed at considerable distance by hospital day care.

It could be argued that it may be more expensive to resettle the re-maining long-stay inpatients in the community, on the assumption that a creaming effect has taken place, namely, that the less dependent inpa-tients have come out first. This may be the case, but it is necessary to take into account that those remaining in hospital of the old-long-stay group constitute only 2% of the total inpatient population. It would cost much less to maintain the majority of those currently coming for short periods of hospitalization, who have much lower levels of dependency. Yet remarkably little is being spent on preventing this large group from drifting into the costly life of the highly dependent client.

E. The Current Fortune of Innovative Projects

The pioneering work carried out by the Barnet interdisciplinary team (in Napsbury and Barnet General hospitals) responds to mental distress crisis by focusing on family work. It uses a variety of methods such as long home visits, discussions with all family members, offering individual support to the family members as well as to the one identified as the patient in the attempt to prevent his or her expulsion from the family system, besides employing the usual range of rehabilitative measures (Mitchell, 1990).

Although the team has been successful in lowering considerably the rate of first admissions, it has been less successful in preventing readmissions and in establishing a nonhospital asylum facility. Its work has hardly been adopted elsewhere in the country, and the reluctance of the staff members to use interventions such as ECT has led to threats of withdrawal of training status from established professional bodies. It might be useful to look at this example in the context of change-promoting and change-blocking factors below.

Some family work schemes have been more successful in attracting professional support and acclaim, notably the one pioneered by Boyd, Falloon, and McGill (1984). This is based on a combined behavioral and a disease management program, systematically carried out primarily by nurses and psychiatrists. Yet this scheme too has not been adopted throughout the country.

The only attempt to implement the Madison, Wisconsin, PACT program in Britain, within a project called the Daily Living Programme, was discontinued after three years. This is not the place to go into the reasons for this decision, but it is relevant to report that the American workers did not think that the British program was indeed following the American project closely enough, even before it folded up.

To date, there are no users-only run services for this client group in the community, despite discussions over the last five years on such possibilities, and the close contacts with American and Dutch users groups. Some mutual support initiatives originated by professionals have taken off, notably in groups such as Contact. Contact is a group of about 300 users which has its own constitution and budget, working from the base of a mental health resource center located within an ordinary community center. The group decides on its activities and on the allocation of responsibilities, but professional group workers are available. The group also has a number of small satellite groups in nearby more rural areas, set up jointly by users and workers (Hennelly 1988).

Patients councils exist in two health districts, Nottingham and Newcastle. Following the Dutch model these operate in hospital wards in an advisory capacity and are initiated by a group of ex-patients. They are useful in promoting a dialogue between patients and service providers, in empowering patients to debate and communicate their views, and in giving them the skills to do so. There is a larger number of users forums that have a similar role outside hospitals, primarily in cities and towns ruled by Labour Local Authorities. They have been set up initially by professionals and local service users, at times with local Community Health Councils (a national advisory body with local branches, funded by the DoH, aimed at representing the general public). Apart from offering some mutual support, the forums differ in the ability of their membership to present their views, to agree on the structure and methods of the services they would like to see, and in the clout they are able to master vis-à-vis the power holders in the area.

Most of the active members of these organizations are middle-class, young, and articulate. Although atypical of the majority, these people are bona fide continuing-care clients. They too have been hospitalized for long periods of time, have been diagnosed as suffering from schizophrenia or affective psychoses, and have had considerable difficulties in finding employment, training, housing, or a circle of friends. The element that seems to have made the difference, apart from the level of articulation (and hence of personal attraction to service providers), is that they have managed to sustain a greater measure of both autonomy and support, either from family members or one friend, and through psychotherapy and/or through being activists in the users movement have been able to find a more satisfying way of living. Interestingly, though some continue to be on medication, most of them went through a long withdrawal process from medication.

IV. PROSPECTS FOR CHANGE AND BARRIERS TO CHANGE IN THE BRITISH CONTEXT

The above broad description has been of necessity somewhat incomplete. In assessing the prospects for change toward a more appropriate care system, I now turn first to the barriers to change, and then to the more favorable developments suggesting that positive change, if unlikely in the short term, is more likely in the long term.

Although the itemization of barriers is potentially very extensive, the following are among the more important impediments to a more desirable system:

1. The ambivalent attitude toward community care by professionals, the politicians, and the general public has many consequences: the lack of an acceptable and comprehensive psychosocial model with which to understand what is happening to the continuing-care client and how best to support him or her and the lack of a good enough database with which to plan services.

2.   Without a full and well-coordinated service program, there is a lack of support services at the pre-continuing-care process to identified clients and their relatives, a lack of nonhospital asylum and refuge facilities, coupled with a lack of outreach services. To this should be added a lack of interest in and services to match the need for meaningful day activity and employment and lack of mechanisms to ensure good standards of care in the community across the country.

3.   There are also problems with personnel: an astonishing lack of training to work in and with the community across most professional disciplines, including a lack of conceptual and research knowledge, as well as skills; considerable difficulties in achieving multidisciplinary work as well as cooperation and coordination across service sectors; and a lack of consultation with grass roots workers or attempts to motivate them toward changing the current system.

4.   Finally, an important barrier to change is the habit of approaching the continuing-care client as only possessing disabilities; approaching relatives in the same way as clients are approached, and consequently, making insufficient attempts to consult users beyond the individual level and to make them participate in running those elements of the services to which they can contribute.

Factors tending toward system change tap many levels of society:

1.   The sense of public outrage at the level of neglect of this client group.

2.   The readiness of some politicians to change the service system.

3.   The readiness and dedication of some professionals, across the different disciplines, to work with this client group even though it is deemed unattractive by the majority of the professionals.

4.   The emergence of a new group of service managers interested in the success of mental health services.

5.   Positive program experience, such as the increasing number of innovative projects focused on this client group.

6.   The positive examples provided by activists in the users movement and by other users in projects that encourage users participation.

7.   The greater flexibility of services in the voluntary sector and the signs of increased flexibility in approach and methods of work among nurses and social workers should also be noted.

8.   There has been reasonable success to date in the resettlement of the old-long-stay patients in the community in terms of clinical and personal indicators, as well as in reducing costs, and in the overall development of mental health centers.

9.   Benefiting from the considerable success of the resettlement of

people with learning difficulties and the application of the normalization approach to them, there is (slow) development of evaluation and quality assurance mechanisms.

A list, whether of barriers or possibilities for change, no matter how long, can never be exhaustive. It requires more in-depth explanation than has been possible to provide in this text. I hope that the paper has conveyed not only the interdependency of the different components of the services for people in need of continuing care, but also the interdependency with the political and economic systems, and ultimately with our social beliefs about mental illness and health.

The summary indicators outlined above were based on the belief that comprehensive care in the community for the continuing-care client is both desirable and attainable. Given the right encouragement, many members of this highly dependent group can become not only more capable of self-care but able to contribute to the welfare of others, especially those they live with. This approach endorses the application of the normalization and social role valorization to this client group (Ramon 1991). I am aware that my beliefs, in particular the last one, are not shared by the majority of psychiatrists and nurses in Britain, though they are more likely to be shared by psychologists, social workers, and the growing number of community psychiatric nurses and the unqualified workers in residential and day care.

NOTE

1.   I prefer to call the client group *the continuing-care client*, rather than *the chronically ill*. With Lavender and Holloway (1988) I would like to suggest that the difference is not only semantic: The first term is less stigmatizing; more open-ended as to the reasons why people with mental illness are in need of long-term care; and more open-ended as to the belief in the potential of these clients to benefit from community services and lead a more ordinary life than before. Focusing on the need of some clients for long-term care does not imply that this should be provided in any given setting, or that clients should always be receiving active service provision. In the context of this paper, community services include residential arrangements, as long as these are not in large institutions or hospitals.

REFERENCES

Barnes, M., R. Bowl, and M. Fisher. 1990. *Sectioned: Social Services and the 1983 Mental Health Act*. London: Routledge and Kegan Paul.

Brost, M. and T. Johnson. 1982. *Getting to Know You.* Madison, WI: Coalition for Advocacy and New Concepts for the Handicapped Foundation.

Cambridge, P. and M. Knapp (eds.). 1988. *Demonstrating Successful Care in the Community.* Canterbury: University of Kent, PSSRU.

Clare, A. and R. Corney (eds.). 1984. *Social Work in Primary Care.* London: Tavistock.

Cochrane, R. 1983. *The Social Creation of Mental Illness.* London: Longman.

Dayson, D. 1990. *Clinical and Social Outcomes after One Year in the Community.* Paper presented at TAPS Annual Conference, London, July 5.

Department of Health and Social Services. 1990. *Health and Personal Social Services Statistics,* London: HMSO.

Falloon, I., J. Boyd, and C. McGill. 1984. *Family Care of Schizophrenia: A Problem Solving Approach to the Treatment of Mental Illness.* Guilford: Guilford Press.

Goldberg, D. and P. Huxley. 1980. *Mental Illness in the Community: The Pathway to Psychiatric Care.* London: Tavistock.

Goldie, N. 1988. *"I hated it there but I miss the people." A Study of What Happened to a Group of Ex-Long Stay Patients from Claybury Hospital.* London: South Bank Polytechnic, Health and Social Services Research Unit.

Gostin, L. 1976. *A Human Condition.* London: Mind Publications.

Groves, T. 1990a. "Who Needs Long Term Psychiatric Care?" *British Medical Journal* 300:999–1001.

———. 1990b. "What Does Community Care Mean Now?" *British Medical Journal* 300:1060.

Hennelly, R. 1988. "From Mental Health Centres to Resource Centres." Pp. 208–18 in *Psychiatry in Transition,* edited by S. Ramon. London: Pluto Press.

Hudson, B. 1982. *Psychiatric Social Work.* London: Tavistock.

Knapp, M. and J. Beecham. 1990. "Predicting the Community Costs of Closing Psychiatric Hospital: The TAPS Project." PSSRU Discussion Paper 640/2, University of Kent, Canterbury.

Lavender, A. and F. Holloway (eds.). 1988. *Community Care in Practice: Services for the Continuing Care Client.* Chichester: Wiley.

Mahoney, J. 1988. "Finance and Government Policy." Pp. 75–90 in *Community Care in Practice: Services for the Continuing Care Client,* edited by A. Lavender and F. Holloway. Chichester: Wiley.

Mangen, S. 1988. "Dependency and Autonomy." Pp. 79–81 in *Psychiatry in Transition,* edited by S. Ramon. London: Pluto Press.

McCourt-Perring, C. 1993. *The Experience of Psychiatric Hospital Closure.* Aldershot: Arebury.

Mitchell, R. 1990. "Mental Health Social Work Practice: The Barnet Model." Pp. 41–50 in *Social Work and the Mental Health Act,* edited by J. Cohen and S. Ramon. Birmingham: BASW Publications.

Mosher, L. and L. Burti. 1989. *Community Mental Health: Principles and Practice.* New York: Norton.

Patmore, C. and T. Weaver. 1991. *Community Mental Health Teams— Lessons for Planners and Managers.* London: Good Practices in Mental Health.

Peay, J. 1989. *Tribunals on Trial.* Oxford: Clarendon Press.

Ramon, S. 1985. *Psychiatry in Britain: Meaning and Policy*. London: Croom Helm.

———— (ed.). 1988. *Psychiatry in Transition*. London: Pluto Press.

————. 1990. "The Relevance of Symbolic Interaction Perspectives to the Conceptual and Practice Construction of Leaving a Psychiatric Hospital." *Social Work and Social Sciences Review* 1(3):163–76.

———— (ed.). 1991. *Beyond Community Care: Normalisation and Integration Work*. London: Mind-Macmillan.

————. 1992. "The Workers' Perspective: Living with Ambiguity and Ambivalence." In *Psychiatric Hospital Closure: Myths and Reality*, edited by S. Ramon. London: Chapman Hall.

Rogers, A. and D. Pilgrim. 1990. *The People First Project*. London: Mind Publications.

Sayce, L. 1989. *Community Mental Health Centres*. London: Research and Development in Psychiatry.

Strathdee, G. and G. A. Williams. 1984. "A Survey of Psychiatrists in Primary Care: The Silent Growth of a New Service." *Journal of the Royal College of Psychiatrists* 37:615–18.

TAPS 1989. *Preliminary Report on Baseline Data from Friern and Claybury Hospitals*. London: TAPS.

Test, M. A. and L. I. Stein. 1980. "Alternatives to Mental Hospital Treatment: 1. Conceptual Model, Treatment Program and Clinical Evaluation." *Archives of General Psychiatry* 37:392–97.

Wing, J. K. and R. Furlong. 1986. "A Haven for the Severely Disabled within the Context of a Comprehensive Psychiatric Community Service" *British Journal of Psychiatry* 146:449–57.

Wooff, K., H. L. Freeman, and T. Fryers. 1983. "Psychiatric Service Use in Salford." *British Journal of Psychiatry* 142:588–97.

Wooff, K. and D. Goldberg. 1988. "Further Observations on the Practice of Community Care in Salford: Differences between Community Psychiatric Nurses and Mental Health Social Workers." *British Journal of Psychiatry* 153:30–37.

Chapter 8

Comprehensiveness and Coordination of Care for the Severely Disabled

J. ROGERS HOLLINGSWORTH and
ELLEN JANE HOLLINGSWORTH

This concluding chapter undertakes two tasks: to draw together the papers in this volume using the themes of comprehensive and coordinated systems, and to move beyond the papers presented here to suggest policy implications for care of the disabled. In connection with the first task, we discuss (1) terms for assessing the systems of care, (2) an overview of the system of care for each of the three disabled groups in both countries, and (3) overall assessments of the systems of care, comparing them across disability groups and nations. Policy implications are discussed in the final part of the chapter.

I. ASSESSING SYSTEMS OF CARE: COMPREHENSIVENESS AND COORDINATION

As argued in the introductory chapter to this volume, as well as many of the individual papers, central to provision of adequate care is that services have two characteristics: that they be both comprehensive in meeting the needs of clients and coordinated into a system.

In thinking about comprehensiveness, we identify three separate dimensions: (1) the extent to which there is an array of programs involving medical and social services, (2) the availability of resources, and (3) the extent to which clients have access to needed services. The separation of these dimensions recognizes that establishing (or announcing) programs is quite different from providing funding for them, and that these are different from making services available to all clients who need them. Thus, there might be formal creation of programs for services, but such meager levels of funding that services are available to only a fraction of the needy. Similarly, resources and access are not the same.

Programs can be established and well funded, yet they may direct their services to few clients, restricting intake and discouraging efforts by many clients to receive services.

Systems should also be assessed in terms of coordination. The meaning of coordination is fairly obvious, that organizations or programs and the staff within them work together to accomplish the overall goals of client services. To do so, they must share an understanding of the task at hand, have similar values and goals, and be able to work in harmony rather than pursuing program-specific orientations.[1] It is also often important that there be proper links and sequences for elements of the service system, elements that flexibly incorporate feedback. Coordination also refers to the linking of local, regional, and national levels of service.

Obviously, these two concepts (comprehensiveness and coordination) overlap and are interrelated. If services are very low in comprehensiveness—for example, if there were just one service for only a small number of clients, so that the needs of clients were not met—then there would be no need to be concerned with coordination among different types of organizations. And the more comprehensive programs are in meeting needs—i.e., the larger the number of programs, the greater the funding, and the more accessible programs are to clients—the greater the need for coordination. But the two concepts are distinct. A complex system with many services for large numbers of clients (high in comprehensiveness) might be low in its ability for the various parts of the system to work together.

II. INVENTORY OF SERVICES

We now provide a brief overview of the services needed for the frail elderly, the seriously disabled homebound, and the chronically mentally ill for both Britain and the United States. The emphasis is on comparing the major appropriate modalities for delivery of services to these clients.

A. Frail Elderly

For the frail elderly, several types of services are required: acute hospital care, intermediate to long-term care, ambulatory medical services, community-based social services, medical services in the home, and social services in the home. Each of these elements has substantial utility in meeting need (see Table 1).

In Britain all citizens (including the frail elderly) have access to acute-care hospitals under the National Health Service (NHS). But in both

Table 1.   System of Care for the Frail Elderly: Great Britain and the United States

Array of Services	Services Relative to Need
	A. Great Britain
Acute-care hospital	Universal access through NHS. Increasingly, hospitals have well-organized geriatric units.
Intermediate to long-term care facility: skilled to intermediate nursing facilities as well as custodial homes	For the less severely ill, nursing and residential care homes available. These vary by size, level of staffing, and type of ownership (e.g., public, proprietary, voluntary nonprofit), with payment based on a sliding scale dependent on resources.
Ambulatory medical services: day hospital, clinic	Universal access through NHS to GPs. GPs receive small annual supplement for each elderly person on their patient list. There has been widespread development of geriatric day hospitals for medical treatment.
Community-based social services	Day centers established by Local Authorities and voluntary agencies provide social facilities, meals, and other services.
Home care: medical services	NHS provides GPs who visit patients' homes, as well as district nurses and auxiliary nurses. Patients pay only a small proportion of the cost for prescription drugs.
Home care: social services	Local Authority social services departments provide the vast majority of home help/care services, which are funded mainly by central government and local taxes, with some user contributions. There is considerable inequality in the distribution of resources; many with extensive needs receive less than those with more modest needs. There is great variability in the delivery of home social services. Some Local Authorities provide services free of charge, some charge a flat rate, and some charge according to the means of the individual. There is no formal eligibility criterion for home help service. Services are more widespread in the north than in the south, and in urban areas.
	B. United States
Acute-care hospital	Universal access through Medicare.
Intermediate to long-term care facility: skilled to intermediate nursing facilities as well as custodial homes	The dominant mode of provision of care is the nursing home, which provides both skilled and intermediate nursing care. Approximately half of nursing home patients have their expenses paid by Medicaid; the other half of

(*continued*)

Table 1.   *(Continued)*

Array of Services	Services Relative to Need
	patients pay for themselves. Under Medicaid, long-term care in nursing homes is provided for the very poor, though eligibility varies from state to state. Medicare prohibits payments for most long-term and custodial care. Most private insurance excludes payment for long-term institutionalized care.
Ambulatory medical services: day hospital, clinic	Virtually universal access for physician visits through Medicare. Because deductibles and copayments apply, a substantial proportion of the elderly carry supplementary private insurance. Unlike Britain, there are few geriatric day hospitals. Also unlike Britain, most outpatient care is by specialists, not GPs.
Community-based social services	Very limited supply of day centers. Most of those which exist are means tested.
Home care: medical services	Home care medical services are very poorly developed. Under Medicare, payment is primarily for the treatment of or convalescence from short-term acute illness, but rarely for medical care for severe chronic illness. Unlike Great Britain, there are not widespread community-based nursing services for home care for those with severe chronic illness. As a result, a number of proprietary home care organizations have emerged that market costly and profitable skilled services for those who can pay for them. Because Medicare provides very limited incentives for doctors to supervise or provide home care for the frail elderly, their involvement in the delivery of home care services is severely restricted. Patients pay most of the cost for prescription drugs.
Home care: social services	Publicly financed social service programs in the home are virtually nonexistent in the United States, meaning that such services must be financed by the patient. Title 20 of the Social Security Act provides very limited home care social services for the indigent.

Great Britain and the United States, many frail elderly are not in hospitals and not at home. They reside in intermediate to long-term care facilities. As the Kane and Jamieson papers point out, although the vast majority of the elderly live in their own homes, at any one time in both Britain and the United States, at least 5% of those 65 and over live in institutions. In both countries, the overwhelming majority (over 80%) of residents in intermediate to long-term facilities are over 75. British residents in such establishments may be private-pay or receive means-tested public support; 64% of payment for long-term care is from the public sector. About 47% of those in nursing and residential beds are in for-profit organizations, and 43% are in public sector institutions.

In Britain, there have been serious efforts to reduce the sharp distinction between acute and chronic care and to provide more of a continuum of care, to bring the dynamics of hospital care to chronic care institutions. Throughout the country, hospitals now have geriatrics departments that attempt to provide continuing care for elderly patients who are confined to beds in long-term care institutions (Carboni 1982; Smith and Williams 1983; Brocklehurst and Andrews 1985; Brocklehurst 1984). Moreover, general practitioners (GPs) have increasingly developed strategies designed to care for patients in long-term care facilities. In Britain, extremely high percentages of the elderly see GPs every year. And the GPs are often in a position to coordinate the care of the elderly who have many health problems (Barker 1987; Dunn and Patel 1983; Evans 1983). Even though physician care is much better developed for British patients in long-term care institutions than for those in United States institutions, the underfunding of the NHS results in delivery of physician services that is less than ideal (Barker 1984, 1987; Kayser-Jones 1981; Hollingsworth 1986; Hollingsworth, Hage, and Hanneman 1990).

In Great Britain, geriatric day hospitals operated by general hospitals as part of the NHS provide an extensive roster of services to the frail elderly: physical therapy, nursing care, dentistry, chiropody, and other medical-related activities. There are several million attendances annually by patients, the vast majority of whom suffer from stroke, severe arthritis, or serious mental and neurological disorders. Brought to the center by special transport, many patients spend four to eight hours a day in the day hospital, receiving lunch and afternoon tea. There are also large numbers of community day centers that provide social services (including meals) for the frail elderly, operated by Local Authorities and voluntary agencies (Barker 1984, 1987; Kayser-Jones 1981).

As the numbers and levels of disability of the frail elderly increase in both Britain and the United States, there are additional needs for home medical and social services (Jamieson 1991). These needs are exacerbated in both countries by hospital discharges of elderly patients earlier than in the past. Because Britain has a longer tradition of publicly funded social and medical services for those confined in the home, these services are more extensively developed there than in the United States. But even in Britain, the availability of services—particularly social services for the frail elderly—leaves much to be desired (Davies, Bebbington, Charley, Baines, Ferlie, Hughes, and Twigg 1990; Lawson and Davies 1991).

The NHS, by making a GP available to all citizens, has long provided doctors for the frail elderly, doctors who in principle do make house calls. But the more important delivery of medical services in the home is by home nursing services of district health authorities (DHAs), funded by the central government from general taxation. All frail elderly are entitled to community nursing at no cost to themselves, and each DHA has a number of senior nursing officers who supervise district nurses, auxiliary nurses, health visitors, and school nurses. District nurses provide treatment and monitor patients in their home, while auxiliary nurses tend to be more involved in providing personal care (e.g., getting patients out of bed, as well as dressing and bathing them). Health visitors are more concerned with providing services to children, but in some DHAs, they too provide services to the frail elderly.

Nursing services in the home tend to be provided on a shorter term basis than social services, being discontinued once clients seem to be able to cope on their own. However, care given by auxiliary nurses tends to continue longer than care by district nurses (Davies et al. 1990; Lawson and Davies 1991). Davies (in this volume) indicates that a very small proportion (approximately 2%) of the severely disabled elderly over age 75 pay for private nursing.

In all advanced industrial societies, the frail elderly have greater need for social than for medical services in the home. But there are serious problems in assessing need and in financing such social services. In Britain, the main providers of social services in the home are the Local Authority social services departments, which are funded by the central government, by block grants, and by local taxes. While Local Authorities are required by statute to provide social services in the home, the individual client has no statutory right to receive a service. Hence there is considerable variation among Local Authorities in the degree of access to these services, in the type of services provided, and in the extent to which clients pay for services (Hedley and Norman 1982). For example, in 1986–1987, 25% of Local Authorities provided these services without any charge to clients, 25% charged a flat rate, and the others provided services on a means-tested basis. Increasingly, the British people are being charged for these services when they can afford to pay (Lawson and Davies 1991).

As the numbers of the frail elderly have increased, Local Authorities are increasingly attempting to target the elderly who are considered most in need. For example, in 1985, 78% of those with the greatest disabilities, living alone, and socially isolated received social services in the home (Lawson and Davies 1991:79). Although Great Britain has a system for providing social services to the disabled frail elderly, the annual amounts of care provided to users are modest. Moreover, there are data demonstrating that elderly people needing services are twice as numerous as those receiving services. Many services are distributed in an inefficient manner. For example, many social services are not regularly reassessed, so that some clients continue to receive services long after they are needed.

In recent years as many British firms have developed employment-related pension schemes and many citizens have higher incomes in retirement, private home help firms have emerged on a for-profit basis, particularly in the more affluent parts of the country. These private agencies (for-profit and nonprofit) both supplement and complement the public sector, but also substitute for it. And in increasing numbers of cases, the public authorities reimburse clients who receive services from for-profit organizations or pay the firms directly. Indeed, the British government has recommended the extension of private services in order to promote choice and competition between the private and public sectors. As Local Authorities increasingly charge for home help social services, it is anticipated that the for-profit sector will expand. The voluntary sector is not heavily involved in the provision of home help social services, though some voluntary organizations do provide Meals on Wheels. Some of these services are financed primarily by Local Authorities (Lawson and Davies 1991; Griffiths 1988).

In the United States, as in Great Britain, the frail elderly have access to acute-care hospitals. But in the United States this kind of care is provided under Medicare, which is primarily for the elderly, and there are deductibles the frail elderly must pay. However, if elderly clients are indigent and therefore eligible for Medicaid, such deductibles may be covered by Medicaid.[2]

Because of the prevailing payment system by Medicare for hospital care, American hospitals have an incentive to discharge patients after short stays. For some early-discharged patients, there are inadequate postdischarge care arrangements, though some postacute care may take place in skilled nursing homes.

The main arrangements for providing intermediate to long-term care for the American elderly are nursing homes, which vary in the amount of nursing they provide. As in Great Britain, residents of nursing homes tend to be over age 75. Indeed, about one-quarter of those aged 85 or more are in nursing homes in the United States (Lawrence and Gaus 1983). In the United States, 49% of nursing home payments are by the government, with 47% from Medicaid. But Medicaid pays only after personal resources of patients are virtually exhausted. Forty-eight percent of nursing home fees are paid by clients. Sixty-nine percent of

American nursing home beds are in the for-profit sector, whereas the public sector provides less than 10% of the beds. In contrast to the British frail elderly, patients in American nursing homes have limited access to physician services. Because Medicare payments to doctors are low, physicians visit nursing home patients infrequently (Vladeck 1980; Johnson and Grant 1985; Burton 1985). Overall, however, a high percentage of the elderly regularly see physicians under the Medicare program, but they are much more likely to see specialists than general or family doctors, and are likely to have less coordinated care than the elderly in Britain.

The elderly in the United States have limited recourse to geriatric day hospitals. While there are a few centers in the United States comparable to the British institutions, these geriatric day hospitals are not at all pervasive (Barker 1987; Somers 1976; Kayser-Jones 1982).

There is also a limited number of day centers for the elderly in the United States, although this type of programming is also much less common than in Great Britain. Most American day centers offer social services on a means-tested basis, though there are a few experiments (financed by Medicare and Medicaid) with waivers for rehabilitation, medical, and social services in varied settings (Zawadski and Ansak 1983; Zawadski 1983; Barker 1987).

Despite the fact that the elderly are living longer, they are being discharged earlier from hospitals in the United States, particularly as the result of payment mechanisms like Diagnostic Related Groups (DRGs). Yet, the supply of government-funded home health services is extremely restricted. Although there is increased recognition of the need for such services, budget shortfalls and efforts to control growth in Medicare and Medicaid spending have prevented development of home health care on a scale adequate to respond to need (Vladeck 1987:5).

Since its creation in 1965, Medicare has given very low priority to home care. As a result, in 1984 only 3.1% of Medicare dollars were spent on home care services, and this entire sum was spent for people who had recently been discharged from an acute-care hospital. In other words, home care under the Medicare program has been designed to be an extension of acute services, not to provide long-term health care, as has generally been the case in Britain. As pressure grows to deliver more medical services in the home through Medicare, home health agencies increasingly find that they have rendered physician-ordered services to a patient, only to be denied payment (Langley 1987; Mundinger 1983; Koren 1986).

In addition to Medicare, there are four other public programs providing home health care for the frail elderly in America, though their coverage is also extremely restricted: Medicaid, Veterans Administration (VA) home care services, the Older Americans Act, and Title 20 of the Social Security Act. Medicaid uses approximately 2% of its budget for home care. In the Omnibus Budget Reconciliation Act of 1981, Congress agreed that Medicaid could respond to the needs of the homebound elderly with waiver of some legislative requirements. The home health services under Medicaid must be ordered by a physician, and the physician must review orders every 60 days. There is great variability in the distribution of these services among states, with New York state alone receiving half the funding. Thirty-eight states share the other half of the funding, while 11 states have no funding for such home services (Brickner, Lechich, Lipsman, and Sharer 1987).

The VA is authorized to provide home health services for the treatment of disabled veterans. The VA has considerable discretion in defining eligibility and tends to provide services only for the 12 months following hospitalization. Where this program exists, multidisciplinary teams make visits to veteran's homes within a 30-mile radius. This program is very limited in terms of the number of people receiving services, but it is significant in establishing the principle of home health care. Title 20 of the Social Security Act and the Older Americans Act also provide for home services for the elderly (including home health care), but have benefits that are very small in scale (Brickner et al. 1987:Chap. 7; Mather and Abel 1986; Lawrence and Gaus 1983).

Because home care follows an acute medical model in the United States, the services are very limited and oriented toward medical care. For long-term care needs, benefits are very small, and home social services are very rare. Therefore, there is gross inequality in the distribution of home services (medical and social), since clients must usually make personal payments and only a small percentage of the frail elderly can afford to purchase services.

In sum, the more successful societies have been in conquering acute disease and extending life, the greater the need to care for people with severe chronic diseases by providing both medical and social services, often in the home. In advanced industrial societies, chronic disease has become the dominant pattern of illness, so much so that the overwhelming majority of deaths are due to chronic conditions (Somers 1982; Hollingsworth, Hanneman, and Hage forthcoming).

No advanced industrial society has an adequate system for coping with this population, though the British system is better prepared to cope with the needs of the frail elderly than the American system. The NHS provides extensive and virtually free health and medical care to all citizens, meaning that the individual British elderly citizen encounters fewer problems in obtaining medical care than in the United States. And although the NHS has generally been underfunded, virtually every community has social services provided by the Local Authority operating in rough parallel with district health services. In Britain the medical and social services available for the care of the geriatric patient at home are much more developed, enjoy higher status, and are somewhat better financed than in the United States. Some of this is due to variation in the way the welfare state has evolved historically. Britain has had a long tradition of providing nursing and social services in the home, with services developed in the early twentieth century to meet the needs of expectant mothers and their newborns. Over time these and other services became widespread, providing visiting nurses, social workers, and home helps for other client groups in the home. In the United States, the welfare state developed much later and has never developed such extensive programs (Hollingsworth 1986; Nepean-Gubbins 1972; Connolly 1980).

But much of the difference is also due to the fact that the British developed a geriatric service shortly after the establishment of the NHS in 1948. A major goal of this service was to provide specialized medical care to the elderly and to make it feasible for them to stay at home and independent as long as possible. In the early 1980s, Great Britain was the only country that had developed geriatrics as a medical specialty. And, it has been the influence of this specialty that has contributed to Britain's having some of the largest volume and broadest range of home care services in the world (Kayser-Jones 1981, 1982; Pegels 1980; Barker 1987).

In contrast, geriatric ambulatory care and home services in the United States have been relatively neglected. Prestige, influence, and money have been overwhelming concentrated in research centers, medical centers, and hospitals. As a result, medical education in the United States has become more and more specialized, with less and less concern for the patient as a whole human being (Cherkasky 1987). In recent years, some American medical centers have developed training programs in geriatrics.

B. Homebound with Severe Disabilities under Age 65

Here we are concerned with the provision of services to the population under 65 who have severe chronic illness and who are for the most part confined to the home. This population is very heterogeneous in terms of disabilities: It includes, among others, people who are paraplegic, people with severe respiratory conditions requiring ventilator therapy, people requiring nasal gastric intubation over long periods, and people with severely limited motor and other functions due to congenital conditions. The population also varies greatly by age (U.S. Bureau of the Census 1986; U.S. National Center for Health Statistics 1987).

As Allen Goldberg's paper indicates, the care needs of this population vary in the extent to which they require complex machinery in the home. As well, the training of those providing care varies in response to differences in need. Some people require assistance with eating, bathing, dressing, and other activities of daily living, while others also need intermediate to skilled nursing.

Over time, there is also variation in the health conditions of these patients. While for the most part they are in their homes, from time to time they have episodes requiring admission to acute hospitals or skilled nursing facilities. Similarly, the type of home care needed for an individual patient may vary over time.

Some of these patients are confined exclusively to the home, while others may be able to attend schools with special programs, to undertake vocational activity in and out of the home, etc. Table 2 presents the major types of service for severely disabled homebound. The needs of the homebound do not usually include intermediate or long-term care (by definition), and their needs for community-based social services are fewer than those of some other disability groups.

As we have already indicated, Britain has highly institutionalized medical and social services for those confined to the home. Homebound patients needing medical services have free access to NHS benefits on an inpatient or outpatient basis. Moreover, each Local Authority has a social services department, and there are also district health authorities that provide a variety of nursing services in the home. Given the heterogeneity of the needs of this population, no single specialty (like the geriatrician for the frail elderly) can serve all clients. Each British citizen, of course, has a GP, but the adequacy of GP care varies according to the severity of the illness of the individual and the experience of the particular GP. Nevertheless, the British system does provide a GP, who is in a strategic position to link the client to hospital and district nursing services.

After evaluation of the medical condition, if it is appropriate, physician and nursing services through the NHS may be provided to patients in their home. Patient needs are regularly reassessed in order to determine the duration and nature of these services. There is variation among district health authorities in the extent to which nursing in the home is available, though nursing care provided by district health authorities is free to clients.

Most home help services are focused on the elderly, with approximately 10% of home help services provided to those under 65. As with the elderly, there is great variation among Local Authorities in the extent to which home help services are made available and in the extent to which patients are expected to make some payment for services.

Three long-term dynamics influence British home care for the home-

Table 2. System of Care for Homebound with Severe Disabilities under 65: Great Britain and the United States

Array of Services	Services Relative to Need
	A. Great Britain
Acute-care hospital	Universal access through NHS.
Intermediate to long-term care facility: skilled to intermediate nursing facilities as well as custodial homes	Nursing and residential care homes are available.
Ambulatory medical services: day hospital, clinic	Universal access through NHS to GPs. There are a number of day hospitals primarily concerned with providing therapy, rehabilitation, and physical maintenance. Patients are usually brought to day hospitals by publicly financed special transport.
Community-based social services	Provided through Local Authorities social services departments
Home care: medical services	Universal access through NHS. Complex medical equipment is provided in the home for those with respiratory, kidney, and other diseases.
Home care: social services	Social services departments of Local Authorities and voluntary consumer-led organizations provide services for care. In practice, social services consist of meals, home helps, some types of rehabilitation, and a variety of other services.
	B. United States
Acute-care hospital	Public programs providing payment for hospital care are Medicare, Medicaid, and the VA. Each program has complex and different eligibility criteria.
Intermediate to long-term care facility: skilled to intermediate nursing facilities as well as custodial homes	Government programs providing payment for skilled to intermediate nursing facilities are Medicare, Medicaid, and the VA. Each program has complex and different eligibility criteria.
Ambulatory medical services: day hospital, clinic	Public programs providing payment for ambulatory health care are Medicare, Medicaid, and the VA. Medicaid requires all states to provide payment for specified basic services, but states vary in the provision of optional services.
Community-based social services	Very limited services. Federal funds facilitate school programming for school-aged people in this group.

(*continued*)

Table 2. (Continued)

Array of Services	Services Relative to Need
Home care: medical services	Government programs providing payment for home care medical services are Medicare, Medicaid, and the VA, but services are very limited. Some limited services are also provided by Visiting Nurses Associations and public health nurses, though services are distributed inequitably. A very small number of people purchase services out of pocket.
Home care: social services	Public benefits are extremely limited. On a very small scale, under Title 20 of the Social Security Act and U.S. government–approved exceptions to the Medicaid program, there is very modest provision for a few Americans for social services in the home. The VA provides cash benefits for a few home-and-bed-bound veterans to purchase home care services.

bound under 65. First, as the momentum for deinstitutionalization continues, there is rising demand for home care services (both medical and social). Because of the size and heterogeneity of the population needing services, however, it is difficult to decide which patients will receive the limited available benefits. Second, the vast majority of home care is for the frail elderly, a population growing very rapidly. Thus, for other disabled groups to garner a greater share of home care is becoming more difficult. Third, the recent Community Care Act of 1990 came into being partly in response to criticisms that Local Authorities had been inefficient in their provision of home care, sometimes providing care when it was no longer needed. Under the legislation, there is now more emphasis on targeting aid on the truly needy, and more on personal services rather than housekeeping. As well, Local Authorities are reducing their role in the delivery of services and contracting with other providers—mostly for-profit firms—to deliver social services in the home. Such changes may permit opportunities for providers of more specialized services (both for-profit and nonprofit organizations) to compete for public funds for targeted care for the homebound (Lawson and Davies 1991; Griffiths 1988; Davies et al. 1990).

Unlike Great Britain, there is no national health insurance in the United States, nor are there Local Authorities or district health authorities providing medical and social services in the home on the same scale. As a result, in the United States, there are considerable eligibility gaps, inappropriate mixes of services, and fragmented and uncoordinated services for homebound clients. As is the case with most populations with severe chronic illness in the United States, there is a preponderance of acute illness services, but inadequate development of home care services for the severely chronically ill. There is evidence suggesting that the overwhelming majority of this population receive home care from members of their families, that less than one-third of the functionally disabled receive government assistance (Lawrence and Gaus 1983). For those who do receive government assistance, there is a patchwork of separate programs. In the United States, there are many more types or provider agencies and financing sources than in Britain, Each American program has separate benefits, as well as eligibility and reimbursement structures, meaning that the individual must generally negotiate with a multiplicity of agencies.

In the United States, the major governmental programs providing medical services in the home are Medicare, Medicaid, and the VA. Medicare includes home health benefits that are quite limited and generally confined to acute rather than long-term care. There are no social service benefits under Medicare. Services in the home covered by Medicare are usually given by skilled professionals, are for intermittent rather than continuing care, and have benefit ceilings. Hitherto, Medicare would cover home care services only after hospital stays, but this provision has recently been changed.

Medicaid, which pays provider fees considerably lower than those of Medicare, provides some medical services in the home. Home medical services are one of several basic types of service covered by the Medicaid program, along with care by physicians and clinics, hospitals, and skilled-nursing facilities. Home health services under Medicaid closely resemble home medical services under the Medicare program and account for only a small percentage of Medicaid spending.

As noted earlier in our discussion of the frail elderly, a small number of homebound disabled veterans receive home medical services from the VA for up to 12 months after acute-care episodes (Brickner et al. 1987; Mather and Abel 1986). Medical, social work, and rehabilitation services are available under this modest program.

Publicly funded social services in the home for the homebound are extremely limited. However, information about these services is in short supply. Under Medicaid waivers, some states provide social services in the home, services that include rehabilitation, housekeeping and chores, and personal care. These services are generally means-tested, and usually they are needed by many more people than can be aided

(Brickner 1978). New York state has taken the lead for home services for the severely chronically ill under age 65 (Caro and Blank 1985).

C. The Chronically Mentally Ill

The types of services needed by the frail elderly, the homebound under 65, and the chronically mentally ill are not alike. The chronically mentally ill have much greater need for community-based social service, some need for home social services, and very little need for home medical services (see Table 3). Care in acute hospitals or ambulatory settings must be available, and sometimes care in intermediate to long-term facilities is appropriate (Hollingsworth 1992).

Community-based social services for the seriously mentally ill in Britain are the responsibility of the Local Authority social services departments. Group homes, vocational programming, and social and recreational activities are generally arranged at the local level, with financing for such services derived from central government grants and local taxes. There is considerable variation in the types and amounts of such service, and in the extent to which social services appropriate to patient rehabilitation and independence are available at all (Ramon, in this volume; Carrier 1990; Jones 1987, Mangen and Rao 1985). With the Community Care Act of 1990, reforms have been planned, but funding and implementation have been delayed. Community-based social services are, to date, in very short supply and highly variable among regions (Yellowlees 1990; Knapp 1990).

Ambulatory mental health services for the chronically mentally ill in Britain are available through a variety of NHS programs. As Ramon points out (in this volume), services are provided by community mental health centers and GPs, some working with psychiatrists and community nurses). Access to specialized psychiatric care is severely rationed by the structure of the system, but is in principle freely available through the NHS.

Access to acute mental health services in Britain for the mentally ill, that is, services in general hospitals, has developed slowly during the last two decades. So long as the seriously mentally ill were in long-term mental hospitals, there was little need to provide access for them in acute-care hospitals. However, as deinstitutionalization has taken place, the process has begun under which seriously mentally ill people living in the community make use of acute-care hospitals of the NHS when they require inpatient care (Thornicroft and Bebbington 1989; Wing 1991).

Intermediate to long-term care in Great Britain for the chronically mentally ill is provided, for the most part, in mental hospitals. Although

Table 3. System of Care for Chronically Mentally Ill: Great Britain and the United States

Array of Services	*Services Relative to Need*
	A. Great Britain
Acute-care hospital	Universal access through NHS.
Intermediate to long-term care facility: skilled to intermediate nursing facilities as well as custodial homes	Universal access to long-term mental hospitals through NHS. Care in residential care facilities (limited in scale) is provided by Local Authorities and supported by central government/Local Authority funding.
Ambulatory medical services: day hospital, clinic	Universal access to GPs through NHS, which also provides for limited access to specialists (physicians and nurses). Limited number of day hospitals provided by NHS. Through NHS, community mental health centers provide services.
Community-based social services	Social services departments of Local Authorities provide or coordinate limited assistance with housing, vocational training, educational programming, and social/recreational activities. Sources of payment vary according to the type of social service, with central government and Local Authorities sharing responsibilities.
Home care: medical services	NHS provides payment for home health care services (a minor service).
Home care: social services	Social services departments of Local Authorities provide or coordinate home care social services on a very modest scale for this group.
	B. United States
Acute-care hospital	Government programs providing payment for acute-care hospitals are Medicaid and state/local welfare, with Medicare providing some funding.
Intermediate to long-term care facility: • skilled to intermediate nursing facilities as well as custodial homes • mental hospitals	Long-term stays in mental hospitals are funded by state government and local mental health authorities. The limited use made of nursing homes is paid by Medicaid.
Ambulatory medical services: day hospital, clinic	Payment for ambulatory medical services is provided by Medicaid and by state/local mental health authorities. These same sources provide payment for medications.
Community-based social services	Most payments for rehabilitative services such as housing, vocational and educational activities,

(*continued*)

Table 3. *(Continued)*

Array of Services	Services Relative to Need
	and social-recreational programming are from state/local mental health authorities. Only very limited support for community-based social services is available through Medicaid.
Home Care: medical services	These services (little needed or used) can be provided under very limited circumstances through Medicare, and on a less limited basis by Medicaid, public health nurses, and state/local mental health authorities.
Home Care: social services	These services are rare. Most home care of a personal care or housekeeping nature is provided and paid by state/local mental health authorities, with a very limited amount covered by Medicaid.

mental hospitals are slowly being closed and down-sized (see both Ramon and Davies, in this volume), they continue to serve patients to a considerable extent. Some long-stay patients may not be suitable for discharge, while other long-stay patients could be discharged if community-based services were in more ample supply. The policy of the British government, since 1959, has been to emphasize community care and to decrease long-term institutional provision of care. The realization of these goals, however, has proved elusive, and the provision of expensive long-term hospital care in mental hospitals continues. Some mental hospitals, as well, provide care for clients on a short-term stay basis.

Home social services, unlike home medical services, can be very useful to some people with serious mental illness. Home social services personnel can assist people in carrying out activities of daily living (e.g., cooking suitable food, maintaining personal hygiene, and performing home chores). Some clients with chronic mental illness have difficulty transferring learning from one situation to another: They are able to cook adequately at a day center but are unable to do so at home, and home social services may assist with the transfer of training. The responsibility for home social services in Britain falls on the Local Authority social service departments, organizations mainly accustomed to working with the frail elderly. Although the Community Care Act aims to link all aspects of client care for the seriously mentally ill, to date home social services have been very limited.

The situation in the United States with regard to the provision of community-based social services for the chronically mentally ill is not dissimilar from the picture presented for Great Britain. Programming at the local level is sometimes ample in quantity and imaginative (or at least adequate) in quality (Shaddish, Lurigio, and Lewis 1989). But this is rare. Geographical areas with stronger traditions of social service, with more public funds available for care of the disabled, attempt to provide more housing, more vocational/educational activity, more social-recreational programming for those with chronic illness. However, most areas in the United States have few or even no community-based reha-bilitative services. Existing services are overwhelmed with clients. In many areas, even crisis services to assure client safety are quite inade-quate, not to mention more specialized programs such as family respite (Mechanic and Rochefort 1990; Mechanic 1983, 1989a, 1989b; Mechanic and Aiken 1987).

The availability of ambulatory medical services for mental health care in the United States depends very much on local and state public pro-gramming (see Hollingsworth, in this volume). With the private medical sector providing almost no care for the chronically mentally ill in an ambulatory setting, it is the public authorities that have assumed the responsibility for supplying psychiatrists, psychologists, counselors, medications, etc. Since these ambulatory services are highly decentral-ized, and in many different programs, there is no effectively coordinated provision of care (Rochefort 1989). Client demand overwhelms the treat-ment resources, so that services are in short supply, and many of those needing services are unable to obtain them (Mechanic 1989a).

In the United States, where deinstitutionalization is an accomplished fact in all states, the use of acute-care hospitals by the seriously mentally ill is highly variable. In some states, clients routinely use general or community hospitals for inpatient mental health stays, especially if the hospital can be reimbursed by Medicaid for the costs of care. Yet, in other states, clients make little use of acute-care hospitals for inpatient mental health care and instead use state mental hospitals.

Long-term public mental hospitals in the United States have a census of under 100,000 patients (Barker et al. 1992), a decline from more than 500,000 in the 1960s. Some clients are clearly too symptomatic over time to permit community release to be safe. Moreover, some state mental hospitals have become long-term institutions in which forensic patients outnumber other clients. The number of patients in other types of long-term mental hospitals is relatively small.

Some chronically mentally ill people in the United States, perhaps as many as a million, are estimated to live in nursing homes (Barker, Man-derscheid, Hendershot, Jack, Schoenborn, and Goldstrom 1992). These clients are permanent residents of the nursing home, not there for short stays. In very recent years, as part of nursing home reform, nursing homes receiving federal funding have been required to assess residents and potential residents, so as to exclude many people with chronic mental illness. Under the terms of the recent legislation, those with a primary diagnosis of chronic mental illness are usually to be cared for in institutes for mental disease, rather than in nursing homes.

In terms of social services provided to clients in the home, the American record is essentially parallel to the British in its poverty. Some programs in a few communities provide staff who visit the home, to provide instruction, to assess how the client is doing while living in the community, and to provide social contact. But this is exceptional (Wegner 1990). Telephoning clients in their homes in order to stay in touch with them is more frequent.

Services for the seriously mentally ill in Great Britain and the United States are not vastly dissimilar. Both countries are deeply invested in deinstitutionalization; both speak the language of community care; both recognize the appropriateness of providing medical services in tandem with social services; both have some programs of excellence; both have tremendous shortfalls in service in most areas. Whereas the British have at least the standard GP service available to all, the United States has no commonly available resource. The United States has no parallel to the carefully developed British language about community care. Yet the United States, with its strong tradition of voluntary organizations and its literally thousands of communities trying to solve problems, has more innovation in its programming (Hollingsworth 1992; Hollingsworth and Hollingsworth 1992).

III. LEVELS OF COMPREHENSIVENESS
AND COORDINATION OF SERVICES

In the preceding section, we have presented a relatively brief inventory of the major types of services relative to the needs of each of the three disability groups in the two countries. Now we turn to a more explicit comparison of the services for the three disabled groups. To make these comparisons, we rely on the strategy that we set forth early in this chapter. The services for each group are assessed by examining the comprehensiveness of services (defined in terms of programs, financial and staffing resources, and client access to services) and the coordination among different agencies and professionals in the delivery of services. For each country, we compare both the level of comprehensiveness and level of coordination in the delivery of services for each group. With this kind of analysis, we can compare groups within and across countries.

For each disability group, we measure the degree of comprehensiveness and coordination of services in terms of high, medium, and low. And within each of these categories we make a further distinction of high and low (e.g., high medium, low medium). We make these assessments based both on the materials presented in the previous chapters and on other literature about each of these three groups. Of course, there are readers who would prefer a more quantitative assessment of the degree of comprehensiveness and coordination. Hence, we also add numerical values to each of the qualitative distinctions (high, medium, low), using a scale ranging from 6 (high high) to 1 (low low).

A brief discussion of the measurement of comprehensiveness and coordination of services for the frail elderly in the two countries will assist in understanding the data presented in Table 4. Public programs for the delivery of medical and social services for the elderly are quite well defined in Great Britain. Not only are all the elderly entitled to medical care under the NHS, but the Local Authorities have an extensive set of policies providing for social services in the home. Hence, we conclude that the British have highly developed public programs for medical and social services to the frail elderly, and we score them in terms of program comprehensiveness as low high, or 5. However, these programs historically have been somewhat underfunded. And the underfunding of services has meant that there is less access to services than would be the case were the systems better funded. Thus, we have evaluated the resources for and access to services for the frail elderly in Britain to be neither high nor low, but medium (e.g., high medium or 3.5 for resources, and low medium or 3 for access to services). Coordination among central, regional, and local officials within the NHS is quite impressive. However, there is somewhat less coordination between the NHS and Local Authorities. Moreover, there is also inadequate information exchange between the medical personnel who are employed by the NHS and the social workers who deliver social services to the elderly under the Local Authorities. Because these services are structured within the state and are not so fragmented as in the United States, we have coded the level of coordination among various agencies and personnel as being high medium, or 3.5.

This is very much in contrast with the United States. The U.S. Medicare program provides extensive hospital and office-based visits for the elderly, but other programs needed by the frail elderly are not well developed—especially home medical and social services. Hence, in terms of comprehensiveness, programs for the frail elderly are scored as high medium—a ranking much influenced by program development for services outside the home. The resources for and access to home care and nursing care are scored as medium level (low medium) in the United States.

Table 4. Comprehensiveness and Coordination of Services for the Chronically Ill

	Comprehensiveness				Coordination among Agencies and Personnel in Providing Various Services
	Programs (a)	Resources (b)	Access (c)	Average of Comprehensiveness Scores (d)*	
	A. Great Britain				
Frail elderly	Low high 5	High medium 3.5	Low medium 3	High medium 3.8	High medium 3.5
Homebound under 65	High medium 4	Low medium 3	Low medium 3	Low medium 3.3	Low medium 3
Chronically mentally ill	Low medium 2.5	High low 2	High low 2	High low 2.2	High low 2
Mean	High medium 3.8	Low medium 2.8	Low medium 2.7	Low medium 3.1	Low medium 2.8
	B. United States				
Frail elderly	High medium 3.5	Low medium 2.5	Low medium 2.5	Low medium 2.8	Low low 1
Homebound under 65	Low medium 2.5	High low 2	High low 2	High low 2.2	Low low 1
Chronically mentally ill	High low 2	High low 1.5	High low 1.5	High low 1.7	Low low 1
Mean	Low medium 2.7	High low 2.0	High low 2.0	High low 2.2	Low low 1

Notes:
*d = (a + b + c)/3.
Scoring: high high = 6, low high = 5, high medium = 4, low medium = 3, high low = 2, low low = 1. Some ratings are between numbers. When scoring is between numbers and the score is below 0.5, the word labels correspond to the next lower whole number. When ratings are between numbers and the score is 0.5 or higher, the word labels correspond to the next higher whole number.

Coordination among agencies and personnel receives a much lower score in the United States than in Britain—not only for the frail elderly but for the homebound and the chronically mentally ill as well. Historically, Britain has delivered medical and social services through public authorities, both the central and local governments. But in the United States, medical and social services have historically been considered to be more the responsibility of local governmental and voluntary organizations. And while the federal government finances many medical services for the elderly, the services are delivered—for the most part—by providers in the private sector. In the contemporary United States, most social and medical services for these three disability groups are delivered by a complex mix of private nonprofit service organizations and for-profit agencies and clinics (hospitals, doctors offices, nursing homes, home nursing, vocational service organizations, etc.). Moreover, responsibility for the funding of services is divided among federal, state, county, municipal, and private sector authorities. With so much fragmentation in the delivery of services, programs are poorly defined, organizations are frequently forced into narrow niches, organizations tend to be undercapitalized and underfunded, and agencies provide narrowly defined services to narrowly defined target populations (Alter and Hage 1993:74–75). As a result, coordination is much more difficult to achieve than in Britain where there is less complexity in the funding and delivery of services.

In both countries, programs are better developed than resources. Hence, for each client group, program development receives higher scores than both the provision of funding and personnel and access to services.

Moreover, in both countries, the programs, resources, and access to services are best developed for the frail elderly, are next best developed for those who are homebound and under age 65, and are least well developed for the chronically mentally ill. Also in both countries, the comprehensiveness of services relative to needs is better developed than coordination of agencies and personnel delivering services.

For both comprehensiveness and coordination, the British score better than the Americans. For each of the three disability groups in Britain, programs are better developed, there are more resources relative to need, there is better access to services relative to need, and there is more coordination among central and local governments, among different agencies of government, and among various types of professional staff.

IV. POLICY IMPLICATIONS

The previous papers and the discussion in this chapter suggest that the problems of access, funding, and quality of services for those who are frail elderly, chronically mentally ill, or homebound with chronic health problems are enormous. Given the demographics of these disabled groups, during the next decade these problems are likely to become, if anything, more critical in these and other advanced industrial societies.

This is indeed a pessimistic message at this critical moment in the history of medical care in the United States. The Americans are having one of their few serious debates about how to provide better access to medical care and to contain its costs. So far, the debate has focused relatively little attention on the health needs of the three populations under review in this volume. But there are many indications that these populations will increase in number and their needs will expand. Hence, the problems faced by these populations need to be part of the national discourse on how the health needs of all the American people will be met over the next decade.

Neither country has yet developed adequate programs for pooling the risks of long-term care or for spreading the costs for caring for the severely disabled over long periods of time. As a result, much of the burden falls on those who need long-term care and their families. Families may be destroyed by the stress, anxiety, and costs associated with the provision of care for those with severe chronic illness. Previous studies report that home care either prevents or postpones further deterioration in the functional abilities of those with severe chronic illness. Moreover, it tends to improve their morale and life satisfaction (Rivlin and Wiener 1988:198–99). Because a greater percentage of citizens in advanced industrial societies are going to suffer from severe chronic illness, it is important that these societies begin to plan for the long-term financing and delivery of such services. Hopefully, this volume will contribute to giving these issues more prominence in policy discourse.

Any discussion involving policy proposals should be sensitive to specifying the performance and outcomes that one wants to maximize in a system of care. The performance and outcome criteria that have been discussed in the previous papers and that we believe these two countries should try to achieve are access to care relative to needs, high coordination among the various agencies and personnel providing care, and high quality care at low cost (often termed *social efficiency*).[3]

The structure of the care systems in the two countries has evolved from a complex history and probably will not be substantially altered in the foreseeable future. Hence, the problem is how to achieve the desired outcomes and performance criteria without requiring a total restructuring of the system. Within Britain, the NHS provides relatively accessible medical care to these three disability client groups, though the system is seriously underfunded, with the result that these groups do not always receive the level of medical care which they need. At present, the Clinton administration and the Congress seem to be on the verge of proposing that a minimum level of medical care be provided to all Americans. Whatever the final program enacted, over the long term it will probably suffer from the same serious deficiency as the British NHS: It will be underfunded relative to the needs of many citizens. In other words, in both countries, all citizens in principle will be guaranteed a minimum level of medical care, but low-income citizens in both societies will receive somewhat less medical care than upper-income groups who purchase private insurance and long-term care will not be thought through.

But the serious problem in both countries will still be how to guarantee that citizens who need *both* social and medical services as the result of serious chronic illness receive the care essential to their having a decent level of well-being. At the moment, the British system performs better than the American system in providing services for the groups discussed in this volume, but in both countries all three groups are badly underserved. How might one approach rectifying this situation?

One considerable problem in both countries is to keep one disabled group from consuming most of the resources. Because the frail elderly are the most numerous of the three groups, have higher status, and have powerful lobbying representatives, they are in a position to shape public policy in such a way that resources for the severely chronically ill are directed to them. As a result of the influence of the elderly, the homebound under 65 and the chronically mentally ill are likely to receive few new resources. The often-stigmatized chronically mentally ill, especially, find it difficult to contest with the frail elderly for resources. The question then becomes how to enhance the possibility of providing equal care for people with similar levels of disability, regardless of the reason for their disability.

Bleddyn Davies's paper in this volume briefly discusses a body of literature (Martin, Meltzer, and Elliot 1988; Martin, White, and Meltzer 1989) that is very relevant to the problem of how policymakers might develop a socially efficient and fair system for providing services to the severely impaired. Drawing on this and other literature (also see Manton and Stallard 1991), we suggest having an index of disability, ranging on a scale from 0 (disabled in no activity) to 10 (disabled in all activities). Among the various dimensions that might make up a disability index would be the following: locomotion, reaching and stretching, dexterity, seeing and hearing, personal care, continence, intellectual functioning, communication, and behavior. We do not wish to minimize the difficulty of developing such an index. Nor do we contend that we have identified all the dimensions of such an index. The construction of such an index will be complicated and will require a good bit of trial and error. The attractiveness of using such a disability index is that the index provides a tool for scoring or ranking the degree of disability of individuals suffering from a variety of problems.

The central government could, beyond assisting in developing the index and applying it to determine disability, establish the threshold above which clients might receive public medical and social services, on the basis of the extent of the limitations on their functioning. With such a procedure, each community would have an identified number of people entitled to public medical and social services as the result of disability.

Obviously, all people with the same level of disability would not require or receive the same services or resources. Two clients with the same disability score might have very different types of illness, requiring different therapies and costs. At the field level, there would have to be evaluation to decide what technology and services were required by people above the disability threshold. But it would be understood that individuals above the disability threshold would be entitled to public medical and social services. At the level of the community, the mix of services to be made available to the disabled would be determined. Updating of disability status information would be necessary, as conditions for established clients changed and new clients entered the system.

There are various choices as to how these services might be financed in the United States. There are current proposals—as suggested above—to provide policies that will assure a minimum level of medical care for all citizens. However, there have not yet been serious proposals for long-term care policies or for home medical and social services. Obviously, there are several strategies that could be employed to finance services for those with serious disabilities. We will mention three possibilities.

1. Because the United States finances many social services from local taxes, much of the funding for services could be raised at the state, county, and local levels. For administrative purposes, the services would be designed and operated at the county level. Obviously, under this plan, governments would differ in their ability to provide resources for care for the identified disabled; some states, counties, and local government would have neither the financial resources nor the political will to finance care. To address these problems of lack of resources or lack of will, we suggest that each state, county, and local government be evaluated in terms of what might be called tax effort. Governments would be expected to contribute to meet the needs of the identified disabled, according to the abundance of their resources. Thus, tax effort would be calibrated according to such resources as per capita assets and/or income at the local, county, and/or state level. If a governmental unit's tax effort could not yield sufficient funds to provide services for the disabled,

central government funds could supplement the local effort. In this way, political units below the central government with inadequate resources to care for the disabled would receive central government subsidies. Sanctions would have to be established for political units not meeting their tax effort quota—ranging from unfavorable publicity to more severe penalties.

Beneficiaries of the program would be the disabled above the threshold on the disability index. Because many people with disabilities would not qualify for various services, it would be important that governments publish data frequently, indicating how many people were being served and how many with specific levels of disability were not being served. This type of data, unlike our present meager fund of information, would permit intelligent public policy revision and fine tuning.

Those receiving services based on the disability index would do so based on a means test, administered in a standardized, nonpunitive manner. Thus, well-to-do disabled citizens who could pay easily for their own care would not use public resources for home care, while those who could not pay would be served. Ideally, both means tests and sliding scales of charges might be used.

2. Under the second plan, the federal government could finance the program for services for the disabled from a payroll tax. Each citizen and employer would be required to contribute 1 or 2% of the employee's wages to finance the program. However, this would not be a social insurance plan, for our recommendation would be that eligibility for benefits under this plan also be means tested. Only those who did not have private-pay resources would be entitled to receive governmentally financed services, with federal guidelines and eligibility criteria used for means testing. With this approach, too, the number of people falling above the disability index and lacking home services because of the means test would be constantly monitored. The federal government could adjust the means test criteria if needy disabled people above the disability index threshold were unable to receive home care due to financial reasons.

3. The third method is for the federal government to enact a mandatory long-term care insurance program. Special provision would have to be made for payment and enrollment of citizens outside the work force. With this method of financing, means tests would not apply to receipt of benefits. At present, there are many problems with the insurance available for long-term care, including the tendency of private insurance companies to screen out disabled applicants. A more equitable and fair system would come into existence as a result of a mandatory national insurance plan for long-term care. Moreover, it would be more efficient than a private system, for the high costs of private marketing would be

eliminated. Such a plan might cover long-term institutional care, home care, or both. Because there are as many disabled people under age 65 as there are over age 65 (U.S. Bureau of the Census 1986:11; U.S. National Center for Health Statistics 1987:iii; Rivlin and Wiener 1988), the demands for long-term care could be quite high.

With a mandatory social insurance approach to the provision of long-term care, it would be desirable that there be a disability index. All those who are in real need, above the disability index threshold, would receive services.

Whichever of these programs is used to finance long-term care, the overall quality of care for the severely disabled should be improved. Moreover, the emotional and financial burden on patients and their families should be relieved.

In several ways, the proposal to construct a policy involving long-term care in the context of a disability index addresses the issue of social efficiency and equality. Funds would be targeted on those who most need care, while those with less than a threshold amount of disability would not receive publicly financed services. Certain disability groups could not crowd out others. Publicly financed care would be dependent on the individual's disability status, and not on group identification or regional residence.

Such proposals only partially address the problems of coordination in caring for the severely disabled. Because of the active role of the central government, there should be rules and norms establishing a variety of the basic procedures used to serve clients. Nevertheless, as knowledge becomes more specialized and as client needs require services of many different organizations, there will still be serious coordination problems. The common patterns of resource dependence of organizations should, however, assist in promoting coordination. This kind of power of the purse has the potential to enforce compliance and cooperation among multiple agencies, while preserving local community responsibility for care giving.

One of the most serious problems in coordinating social and medical services for the severely disabled is the difference in training and perspective of providers. Separate types of schools for training health providers result in poor communication, even conflict, among caregivers. We have reached the point, in the late twentieth century, at which the increases in specialization and fragmentation need to be countered by provision of more common training for those who serve the disabled. One suggestion is that training programs—for social workers, physicians, psychologists, etc.—receive an increasingly interdisciplinary emphasis. Having several types of professionals work together, side by side, is often not enough to overcome poor communication. If, at the very minimum, the various types of students went through some common training and were socialized as part of their professional training to work together, the prospects for coordination of client care would be improved. Moreover, this kind of common training is necessary if the type of disability index discussed above is to be viable. Some aspects of the index require evaluation by physicians, others by psychologists, and others by social workers. Because team evaluation will be necessary, common training centers for different professions must be established.

We are not under any illusion that these proposals are a panacea to the problems of caring for the severely disabled. However, their consideration and adoption would do much to improve the plight of these rapidly expanding populations, at present receiving such inadequate care. Such proposals would enhance the equity (fairness) and social efficiency of use of resources, and should facilitate greater coordination.

NOTES

1. *Coordinating Human Services* by Michael Aiken, Robert Dewar, Nancy DiTomasco, Jerald Hage, and Gerald Zeitz (1975) has been very helpful in its conceptualization of coordination.
2. Medicare is a federal health insurance program covering those over 65, all people with end-stage renal failure, and those who have received Social Security Disability Income benefits for 24 months. Medicaid is a federal/state medical program under which all recipients of Supplemental Security Income (the indigent aged, blind, and disabled, as well as the poor) are covered. States may include other specified groups in Medicaid and have some options about the types of services provided (Hollingsworth 1986).
3. For an extended discussion of social efficiency, see Hollingsworth et al. 1990.

REFERENCES

Aiken, Linda H. 1987. "Extended Care: The Hospital's Perspective." Pp. 15–24 in *Medicare and Extended Care: Issues, Problems, and Prospects,* editd by Bruce C. Vladeck and Genrose J. Alfano. Owings Mills, MD: National Health Publishing.
Aiken, Michael, Robert Dewar, Nancy DiTomasco, Jerald Hage, and Gerald Zeitz. 1975. *Coordinating Human Services.* San Francisco: Jossey-Bass.
Alter, Catherine and Jerald Hage. 1993. *Organizations Working Together.* Newbury Park, CA: Sage.
Barker, P. R., R. W. Manderscheid, G. E. Hendershot, S. S. Jack, C. A. Schoenborn, and I. Goldstrom. 1992. "Serious Mental Illness and Disability in the

Adult Household Population: United States, 1989." *Advance Data* (Centers for Disease Control, National Center for Health Statistics, No. 218).

Barker, William H. 1984. "An Annotated List of Readings and Related Resources on Geriatric Health Services in Great Britain." *Journal of American Geriatrics Society* 32:623–27.

———. 1987. *Adding Life to Years*. Baltimore, MD: Johns Hopkins University Press.

Brickner, P. W. 1978. *Home Health Care for the Aged*. New York: Appleton-Century-Crofts.

Brickner, Philip W., A. J. Lechich, Roberta Lipsman, and Linda Sharer. 1987. *Long Term Health Care: Providing a Spectrum of Services to the Aged*. New York: Basic Books.

Brocklehurst, J. C. 1984. "Conference on Vocational Training in Geriatric Medicine." *Age and Ageing* 13:179–80.

Brocklehurst, J. C. and K. Andrews. 1985. "Geriatric Medicine: The Style of Practice." *Age and Ageing* 14:1–7.

Burton, J. R. 1985. "The House Call: An Important Service for the Frail Elderly." *Journal of the American Geriatrics Society* 33:291–93.

Carboni, D. K. 1982. *Geriatric Medicine in the United States and Great Britain*. Westport, CT: Greenwood Press.

Caro, F. G. and A. Blank. 1985. *Home Care in New York City*. New York: Community Service Society.

Carrier, John. 1990. "Sociopolitical Influence on Mental Health Care Policy in the United Kingdom." Pp. 118–36 in *Mental Health Care Delivery: Innovations, Impediments and Implementation*, edited by Issac M. Marks and Robert A. Scott. Cambridge: Cambridge University Press.

Cherkasky, Martin. 1987. "Epilogue." Pp. 167–72 in *Medicare and Extended Care: Issues, Problems and Prospects*, edited by Bruce C. Vladeck and Genrose J. Alfano. Owings Mills, MD: National Health Publishing.

Connolly, M. P. 1980. "Health Visiting, 1850–1900: A Review." *Midwife, Health Visitor, and Community Nurse* 16:282–85.

Davies, B. P., A. C. Bebbington, H. Charley, in collaboration with B. Baines, E. Ferlie, M. Hughes, and J. Twigg. 1990. *Resources, Needs and Outcomes in Community-Based Care: A Comparative Study of the Production of Welfare for Elderly People in Ten Local Authorities in England and Wales*. Avebury: Gower.

Dunn, A. M. and K. P. Patel. 1983. "Integration of Geriatric with General Medical Services." *Lancet* 2:1139.

Evans, J. G. 1983. "Integration of Geriatric with General Medical Services in Newcastle." *Lancet* 1:1430–33.

Griffiths, Sir Roy. 1988. *Community Care: An Agenda for Action*. London: HMSO.

Hedley, R. and A. Norman. 1982. *Key Issues in the Home Help Service*. London: Centre for Policy on Ageing.

Hollingsworth, Ellen Jane. 1992. "Falling through the Cracks: Care of the Chronically Mentally Ill in the United States, Great Britain, and Germany." *Journal of Health Politics, Policy and Law* 17:899–928

Hollingsworth, J. Rogers. 1986. *A Political Economy of Medicine: Great Britain and the United States*. Baltimore, MD: Johns Hopkins Press.

Hollingsworth, J. Rogers, Jerald Hage, and Robert Hanneman. 1990. *State Intervention in Medical Care: Britain, France, Sweden and the United States*. Ithaca, NY: Cornell University Press.

Hollingsworth, J. Rogers, Robert Hanneman, and Jerald Hage. Forthcoming. "The Effect of Human Capital and State Intervention on the Performance of Medical Delivery Systems."

Hollingsworth, J. Rogers and Ellen Jane Hollingsworth. 1992. "Challenges in the Provision of Care for the Chronically Ill." *Journal of Health Politics, Policy and Law* 17:867–78.

Jamieson, Anne (ed.). 1991. *Home Care for Older People in Europe*. Oxford: Oxford University Press.

Johnson, C. L. and L. A. Grant. 1985. *The Nursing Home in American Society*. Baltimore, MD: Johns Hopkins University Press.

Jones, Kathleen. 1987. "Trends in the Organization of Mental Health Services in Great Britain in the Past 25 Years." *International Journal of Mental Health* 16:94–107.

Kayser-Jones, J. S. 1981. *Old, Alone, and Neglected: Care of the Aged in Scotland and the United States*. Berkeley and Los Angeles: University of California Press.

———. 1982. "Institutional Structures: Catalysts of or Barriers to Quality Care for the Institutionalized Aged in Scotland and the United States." *Social Science Medicine* 16:935–44.

Knapp, Martin. 1990. "Economic Barriers to Innovation in Mental Health Care: Community Care in the United Kingdom." Pp. 204–19 in *Mental Health Care Delivery*, edited by Issac Marks and Robert Scott. Cambridge: Cambridge University Press.

Langley, Ann. 1987. "The Federal Perspective on Extended Care." Pp. 137–44 in *Medicare and Extended Care: Issues, Problems and Prospects*, edited by Bruce C. Vladeck and Genrose J. Alfano. Owings Mills, MD: National Health Publishing.

Lawrence, Diane Bolay and Clifton R. Gaus. 1983. "Long-Term Care: Financing and Policy Issues." Pp. 365–78 in *Handbook of Health, Health Care, and the Health Professions*, edited by David Mechanic. New York: Free Press.

Lawson, Robin and Bleddyn Davies, with Andrew Bebbington. 1991. "The Home-Help Service in England and Wales." Pp. 63–98 in *Home Care for Older People in Europe*, edited by Anne Jamieson. Oxford: Oxford University Press.

Koren, M. J. 1986. "Home Care—Who Cares?" *New England Journal of Medicine* 314:917–20.

Mangen, Steen P. and Bridget Rao. 1985. "United Kingdom: Socialised System— Better Services?" Pp. 228–63 in *Mental Health Care in the European Community*, edited by Steen Mangen. London: Croom Helm.

Manton, Kenneth G. and Eric Stallard. 1991. "Cross-sectional Estimates of Active Life Expectancy for the U.S. Elderly and Oldest-Old Populations." *Journal of Gerontology, Social Sciences* 46:S170–S182.

Martin, J., H. Meltzer, and D. Elliot. 1988. *The Prevalence of Disability Among Adults*. London: HMSO.

Martin, J., A. White, and H. Meltzer. 1989. *Disabled Adults: Services Transport and Employment*. London: HMSO.

Mather, J. H. and R. W. Abel. 1986. "Medical Care of Veterans: A Brief History." *Journal of American Geriatrics Society* 34:757–60.

Mechanic, David. 1983. *Handbook of Health, Health Care, and the Health Professions*. New York: Free Press.

———. 1989a. "Community Care of the Chronically Mentally Ill. III: Summary Comments." Pp. 73–80 in *Community Care of the Chronically Mentally Ill*, edited by C. M. Bojean, M. T. Coleman and I. Iscoe. Austin, TX: Hogg Foundation for Mental Health.

———. 1989b. "Toward the Year 2000 in U.S. Mental Health Policy Making and Administration." Pp. 477–503 in *Handbook on Mental Health Policy in the United States*, edited by David Rochefort. New York and Westport, CT: Greenwood Press.

Mechanic, David and Linda Aiken. 1987. "Improving the Care of Patients with Chronic Mental Illness." *New England Journal of Medicine* 317:1634–38.

Mechanic, David and David A. Rochefort. 1990. "Deinstitutionalization: An Appraisal of Reform." Pp. 301–27 in *Annual Review of Sociology*, edited by W. R. Scott and J. Blake. Palo Alto, CA: Annual Reviews.

Mundinger, M. D. 1983. *Home Care Controversy: Too Little, Too Late, Too Costly*. Rockville, MD: Aspen Systems.

Nepean-Gubbins, L. 1972. "The Home Help Service: Past, Present, and Future." *Community Health* 4:77–82.

Pegels, C. C. 1980. *Health Care of the Elderly*. Rockville, MD: Aspen Systems.

Rivlin, Alice M. and J. M. Wiener, with R. J. Hanley and D. A. Spence. 1988. *Caring for the Disabled Elderly*. Washington, DC: Brookings Institute.

Rochefort, David A. 1989. "Mental Illness and Mental Health As Public Policy Concerns." Pp. 3–20 in *Handbook on Mental Health Policy in the United States*, edited by David A. Rochefort. New York and Westport, CT: Greenwood Press.

Shaddish, William R., Arthur J. Lurigio, and Dan A. Lewis. 1989. "After Deinstitutionalization: The Present and Future of Mental Health Long-Term Care Policy." *Journal of Social Issues* 45:1–15.

Smith, R. G. and B. O. Williams. 1983. "A Survey of Undergraduate Teaching of Geriatric Medicine in the British Medical Schools." *Age and Ageing* 12 (supp.):2–16.

Somers, Anne R. 1976. "Geriatric Care in the United Kingdom: An American Perspective." *Annals of Internal Medicine* 84:466–76.

———. 1982. "Long-Term Care for the Elderly and Disabled." *New England Journal of Medicine* 307:221–26.

Thornicroft, Graham and Bebbington, Paul. 1989. "Deinstitutionalisation—From Hospital Closure to Service Development." *British Journal of Psychiatry* 155:739–53.

U.S. Bureau of the Census. 1986. "Disability, Functional Limitation, and Health

Insurance Coverage: 1984/85." *Current Population Reports: Household Economics Studies*, Series P-70, No. 8. Washington, DC: U.S. Department of Commerce.

U.S. National Center for Health Statistics. 1987. "Current Estimates from the National Health Interview Survey: United States, 1986." *Vital and Health Statistics*, Series 10, no. 164. Hyattsville, MD: DHHS.

Vladeck, Bruce C. 1980. *Unloving Care: The Nursing Home Tragedy*. New York: Basic Books.

———. 1987. "History of the Medicare Extended Care Benefit." Pp. 5–14 in *Medicare and Extended Care: Issues, Problems and Prospects*, edited by Bruce C. Vladeck and Genrose J. Alfano. Owings Mills, MD: National Publishing.

Wegner, Eldon L. 1990. "Deinstitutionalization and Community-Based Care for the Chronic Mentally Ill." Pp. 295–324 in *Research in Community and Mental Health: Mental Disorder in Social Context, Volume VI*, edited by James R. Greenley. Greenwich, CT: JAI Press.

Wing, J. K. 1991. "Vision and Reality." Pp. 10–19 in *The Closure of Mental Hospitals*, edited by Peter Hall and Ian F. Brockington. London: Gaskell.

Yellowlees, Henry. 1990. "Administrative Barriers to Implementation and Diffusion of Innovative Approaches to Mental Health Care in the United Kingdom." Pp. 167–78 in *Mental Health Care Delivery: Innovations, Impediments and Implementation* edited by Issac M. Marks and Robert A. Scott. Cambridge: Cambridge University Press.

Zawadski, R. T. (ed.). 1983. *Community-Based Systems of Long Term Care*. New York: Haworth Press.

Zawadski, R. T. and M. L. Ansak. 1983. "Consolidating Community-Based Long-Term Care: Early Returns from the On Lok Demonstration." *Gerontologist* 23:364–69.

Biographical Sketches of the Contributors

Bleddyn Davies of the Personal Social Services Research Unit at the University of Kent at Canterbury, England has a first degree and doctorate in economics. He has increasingly specialized in the analysis of equity and efficiency in the British welfare state. The focus of the PSSRU, which he founded in 1974, is equity and efficiency in community- and long-term care. He is author of about 20 books and more than 100 papers. His work and that of the PSSRU have been closely associated with the ideas on which the recent radical reforms of community care in the United Kingdom have been based.

Allen I. Goldberg, M.D., M.M., is Professor of Pediatrics, Loyola Stritch School of Medicine, and Director, Pediatric Home Health, Loyola University Medical Center, Chicago. He is the President-Elect, American Academy of Home Care Physicians and Chair, Society of Home Care Management, American College of Physician Executives. As a Fellow of the World Rehabilitation Fund (1983) and World Health Organization (1986), he has published studies on international models of home care. He has also conducted studies for the U.S. Congress, the Office of Technology Assessment (1985), and the U.S. Public Health Service Division of Maternal and Child Health (1983–1987).

Ellen Jane Hollingsworth, the Research Director of the Mental Health Research Center of the University of Wisconsin-Madison, is the author of several books and numerous articles on organizations providing social services to the underrepresented (e.g., welfare clients, those needing legal asistance, the severely mentally ill, etc.).

J. Rogers Hollingsworth is Professor of Sociology and History and Chairperson of the Program in Comparative History at the University of Wisconsin-Madison. He is the author of several books on comparative medical systems. His most recent books on medical care are *The Political Economy of Medicine* and *State Intervention in Medical Care: the Consequences for France, Great Britain, Sweden, and the United States* (co-author).

Anne Jamieson is a Lecturer in Gerontology at Birkbeck College, University of London. Her main research is in the area of health and social policies. She was formerly a Research Fellow at Bath University, where she worked on an European Community-sponsored research program on care delivery systems for older people in the European Community. One of the publications from this project is Jamieson, A. (ed.), *Home Care for Older People in Europe: A Comparison of Policies and Practices* (1991).

Robert L. Kane, M.D., holds an endowed chair in Long-term Care and Aging at the University of Minnesota School of Public Health. He has a long record of research in health services, especially as they affect older persons. Much of his work has addressed ways to improve the outcomes of care and the linkages between acute and long-term care. With his wife Rosalie, he has conducted several international comparisons of long-term care and has analyzed the American long-term care situation. He has been a long-standing champion of linking regulation and payment for care more closely to the outcomes achieved and encouraging more accountable creativity in the way long-term care is provided.

Theodore R. Marmor is Professor of Public Policy and Management at the Yale School of Organization and Management. Professor Marmor's specialty is the modern welfare state, with particular emphasis recently on medical care and health issues. A fellow of the Canadian Institute of Advanced Research, Marmor is also a member of the Institute of Medicine of the National Academy of Sciences. Professor Marmor's most recent book (co-authored with Jerry L. Mashaw and Philip L. Harvey) is *America's Misunderstood Welfare State: Persistent Myths, Continuing Realities* (1990). A prolific author, Professor Marmor has published in a wide range of scholarly journals and has written essays for a number of newspapers and magazines.

Shulamit Ramon is course director of the post-qualifying interdisciplinary Diploma/MSC Innovation in Mental Health Work at the London School of Economics. A clinical psychologist and social worker by training, she has published extensively on the development of community mental health on a cross-national basis. Her most recent book is *Psychiatric Hospital Closure: Myths and Realities* (1992).

Index

Activities of daily living, 36
Advocacy, 12, 94–95, 166–167, 186–187, 199–200, 217–220
Analytical framework, xi–xvi, 3, 9–14, 212–220
Antipsychotic drugs, 156, 189
Array of programs
  aspect of comprehensiveness, 199
Assertive Community Treatment, 193
  characteristics, 157
  continuing services, 158
Availability of resources
  aspect of comprehensiveness, 199

Balance of care, 51–53, 121–122, 131–135
Barriers, xv–xvi, 2–3, 7–8, 10–14, 18–19, 41–43, 60–61, 66–67, 71–72, 75–76, 96–100, 107–109, 135–136, 141–143, 166–168, 194–195, 220, 225–226
Burnout
  caregiver, 155

Capitation
  mental health, 166
Care system
  access of mentally ill, 162
  access to equal, 222
  burdens, 162
  characteristics, 162
  informal provision, 118
  lack of access, 164
  models, 129
  private sector role, 9

Case management
  Community Care Act, 182
  Local Authorities, 127–128, 157–161
  providers, 184
Centralization, 5, 49–51, 58, 64, 146–148
  advantages of, 7
  consequences, 13
Chronic mental illness, 141–198
  access to services, 184
  care paradigm, 141
  characteristics, 176–177
  community-based care, 141, 179
  defined, 173
  historical treatment, 147
  inpatients, 176
  numbers, 173–174
  public system, 146
  types, 175
  vocational experience, 177
  younger clients, 179
Communal establishments
  residents in Britain, 118–119
Community Care Act, 65
  contents, 182
  goals, 67
  independent sector, 65
  joint planning, 64
  provisions, 64
  services for mentally ill in Britain, 180
Community psychiatric nurse (CPN)
  number of, 188
  services, 186
Community-based care, 1–14, 17, 20, 53, 67, 69–72, 85–95, 113–